Metaphorosis
2023

Metaphorosis
2023

The Complete Stories

---

edited by
B. Morris Allen

ISBN: 978-1-64076-275-6 (e-book)
ISBN: 978-1-64076-277-0 (paperback)
ISBN: 978-1-64076-276-3 (hardcover)

from
Metaphorosis Publishing

Neskowin

Contents

From the Editor

They all seem to be troublesome years, recently. All the more reason we need stories that can either take us away to another place or give us reason to hope, or both. These stories will do that for you.

A host of authors brought us everything from an animals'-eye view of the zoo (including a sweet tortoise – elephant friendship) to "if this goes on" warnings about reproductive regulation to a stifled diplomat finding their true self.

Some of these stories are on the dark side, with warnings we should consider heeding, while others are lighter and remind us that, at the worst there's still love in the world, and friendship, and reasons to believe in humanity and all the good it can do. And some, of course, are just fun for the sake of fun. Enjoy them!

B. Morris Allen
Editor
1 March 2024

January

Packing List for Oblivion

Cameron Bertron

The statue was nothing like Enefai remembered. Before, it had been buried to its stomach, with both hands reaching forward to rest almost perfectly, palms up, on the hungry earth. Age had softened the statue's face, which crawled with orange lichen, to a shroud. Its open mouth was turned up to the sky and overflowing with dust. Enefai had watched, for a long time, as the wind spilled grit from the corner of its lips like an hourglass. Now, suspended in holographic color in the center of the council chamber, it looked sanitized and frail. Enefai appraised it for the last time, knowing the outcome before the first votes flickered in. The piece was not particularly innovative; it was not of historic value. It was not vital, it was only beautiful. It would be left behind.

Enefai fixed her eyes on the statue as she cast her vote against it. No councilor volunteered to speak on the piece, so the judgement was swift. The holograph blinked and was replaced by a new sculpture, but the previous image stayed on in Enefai's mind. The decisions were getting harder. At its start, the council had been a mess of overdrawn debates and personal attacks. But Enefai would rather deal with the chaos of those early days than the current, brutal pace of their decisions. It had taken several years, but time had run out for ego and guilt. Enefai was reminded every moment, by the defeated silence of the council and the packing crates in her own home, that the world was ending this year.

The news had broken slowly, then all at once. Before the first dispatch shuddered their calm, Enefai's partner Moore had read the signs in the planet around her. For months, she had come home from the fields with her mouth twisted to one side, calloused fingers thrumming against her leg. She had tried to explain to Enefai about the sourness in the soil and the odd patterns of the rain. Enefai understood little beyond the alarm in her voice, but they both dared to hope that the change was peculiar to their region. It was not. The planet Kenlanli's terraformation was reversing. It had happened on a string of other planets. Now the societies of Kenlanli, so recently settled, were packing back up into the finite space of stations to await the terraformation of a new home planet.

Moore had volunteered immediately to work in the countryside, spending long months collecting soil samples to assess the rate of decay and assisting frontier families in their preparations to leave. The crisis had unwrapped something in her. She swung into action as though she had been preparing for it her whole life. Enefai had done her duty as well, accepting the summons to serve on the council for cultural preservation. She had also received requests for consent to send in her own collection for consideration. She left the requests to collect dust, with everything else in her studio.

Another sculpture was on display. Its superb craftsmanship was doomed by the choice of material. Marble was shipped in from off planet, and the piece would be judged insufficiently Kenlanliin. Enefai hoped that it would be taken in by another planet or station. In the far future, perhaps it could find its way back to Kenlanli's people wherever they might be. It was one of the few thoughts that still offered consolation.

The marble statue was the last of the day. When the session closed, Enefai brushed her way out of the chamber and through the honeycomb halls, exchanging a few nods and sympathetic words with her fellow councilors. Everyone's voice was low, their exchanges quick but sincere. They also had homes to pack. Enefai stepped outside to a sky bruised with evening and stretched her legs as she waded through the city's shallow outskirts into the countryside. The long path home took her past one of her own sculptures. She did not slow as she passed.

She had carved it the same year that she met Moore. As they rattled through the countryside in the back of a transport vehicle, Enefai had felt something tipping over inside her the longer she spoke with this sprawling woman in muddied boots. Probably it was the apocalypse playing tricks on her, but all the memories from that time felt warm. Enefai missed the weightless quiet between them. She missed the long evenings in her studio they spent tinkering at her worktable, Enefai with her designs and Moore with her tools or sketches. These days, the ice cracked beneath their every conversation. When Moore was not working in the countryside, she was brimming with hard choices. Enefai dodged conversations about the space station. She wanted to preserve at least the bubble of their home from the world outside as it ransacked itself. But Moore kept opening the door.

In her head, Moore was already living on the station. Sometimes, it even seemed to Enefai that she was excited about it. Moore planned ceaselessly, scrambling to assure Enefai that they would have everything they needed. But it wasn't their future that weighed heaviest on Enefai, even as it seemed to consume Moore, it was their life on Kenlanli. It was the slide of sand under her boots and the way that sunrise tangled in Moore's hair. In her birth province, at midday the desert's horizon disappeared with a shiver into the pale sky. How to forget that? How to remember?

Her back was slick with sweat when she saw the welcoming round roof of their home. As she stepped inside, the peace earned from her evening walk was dissipated by the boxes crowding the floor. Moore was out for the week, but due back any day. She had left Enefai a list of requests to help with the packing process. Enefai did not need to look at it. Everything was done except one item. She needed to pack her studio.

She quickly ate dinner and prepared a cup of tea. She kept herself moving, knowing that if she paused in her momentum, she would not do any packing tonight. Mechanically, she entered the studio and evaluated the single crate reserved for her belongings against the gentle mess of her studio. The floor and work benches were cluttered with models, sketches, and photos. Only her tools stood in perfect order, hanging on the walls and from the ceiling. The darkness outside converted the studio's large windows to mirrors and Enefai kept catching sight of her own movement as she worked. She tried to summon nostalgia as she packed, but her memories felt glossy and distant. Each tool slid into the crate only left her feeling heavier.

By the time she stopped for a break, her studio was decimated and her tea was cold. Enefai sat down heavily on the floor, her legs splayed in front of her and her back against a slab. Its porous rasp felt reassuring on the back of her arms. Years ago, she had brought the stone from her home province for a design she planned. The rock was unique to her home, stark white and ribboned with pale orange and crimson. As a kid, she used to find patterns in the traces of color, pulling shapes out of the cliffsides. She wondered bitterly what abstractions she would be able to find in the expressionless plaster they would use on station.

She slid away from the stone and regarded it from her place on the floor. She had seen more statues in the last few years than in all her life. She imagined their shapes in the slab and marveled at what had been accomplished with a piece of rock, a set of tools. But it hadn't saved them, extinguished in a flash of holographic light. With time, their craftsmanship, her craftsmanship, would be weathered back to featureless slabs like the one which stood before her. She felt powerless against that future, against her unreasoning anger at Moore's resilience, against her love for Kenlanli. She felt small beneath the slab that stretched above her. Hardening her gaze, she stared into the stone to calm her mind and began to slowly trace the fiery streaks in the rock from top to bottom.

She remembered the design she had planned for this slab when she picked it all those years ago. She could see now that it was all wrong. The arch of a spine was already in the slab's contour, thinly submerged. Veins of color netted together in the side. They would run over an open palm like sunlight. She could only catch the shape in pieces, barely coherent, but it was enough. The night hours were re-aligning. The studio's gravity bent around the work. Moore's expression when she inspected her crops, when she lifted a long shoot with the tip of her thumb, was already in the stone. Enefai reached for it. She smoothed the memorized lips and rounded the jaw. She crinkled the eyes that would watch, unflinching, as their planet's atmosphere slumped to reclaim the horizon. She followed only that instinct which had first searched out shapes in the mountainsides. She followed it until the sunrise dripped dirty pink into her studio.

When it was done, she would face it towards the window, pack her tools away, and leave this room forever. But for now, she closed her grainy eyes and pressed her forehead against the statue's unhewn base. Through her headphones she could not hear Moore's clattering entrance. The world was quiet as arms encircled her. Quiet as a kiss was buried on her neck. She would take it to the stars.

See Cameron Bertron's story "Packing List for Oblivion" online at Metaphorosis.
If you liked it, leave a comment. Authors love that!
Remember to subscribe to our e-mail updates so you'll know when new stories are posted.

About the story

This story was a way for me to explore climate anxiety. I had the conceit and setting for it before I had any of the characters. This was a problem when I started writing. I wanted the story to be character and relationship-driven, but I was caught up in the worldbuilding. I abandoned this story for almost a year. Then at the start of this summer, it came back to me. This time the characters and concluding scene were much clearer. I also wrote in the relationship between Moore and Enefai, which didn't exist when I started the story. Once I had the end scene visualized, I wrote toward it like a finish line.

A question for the author

Q: What is the hardest part about writing for you?

A: Usually, my stories start with a single image or emotion which I want to capture. After that image occurs, everything else is the hard part. Recently, what I've been finding the most difficult are scene transitions and set-up scenes. I know exactly what I'm about to say, but I can't set up the scene right to say it. Those set-up scenes take much more of my time than the climatic ones. The hardest part of writing will always change depending on the story and my skills as I acquire them. But for now, I'm wrestling with getting characters into the right place at the right time.

About the author

Cameron Bertron currently lives in Erdenet, Mongolia where she works as an English teacher. She has been a volunteer firefighter and a student of Slavic literature, but her most memorable work was as an almond milkman in her hometown Tampa, Florida.

The Knight Who Carried a Sword in His Heart

Joshua Hagy

Legends speak of a time when the world was different. For better or worse, it is impossible to tell, for none are alive who remember what was. All we have left of that time are dreams that were lived before they were written and the truths they hold for each of us.

Listen closely, for this is one such dream.

Thunderstorm rain pelted against the thick, oiled canvas of the tent as Lord Philbreck closed his eyes and rested his head in his hands. He breathed deep, inhaling the summer scent of outside atop the musty odor tents never seem to lose no matter how often they are aired. The desk upon which he leaned and the chair in which he sat were both extravagances on a march, especially one as short as this, but they were touchstones of a sort, a comfort Philbreck refused to travel without. They were there for moments like this, when the weight of the past and the hope of the future were too much of a burden for one man to bear.

"Tomorrow," he said, the word barely audible over the late evening storm raging outside, "it will all be over." Philbreck sat with his thin arms drawn close, his back hunched over the table. He sat folded up, as if he were hiding for fear of the storm raging outside. He would stand in a moment, unfold himself into the tall man whose iron will took up more space than he ever would, but for now Philbreck protected something that he had not dared to feel in a very long time.

Hope.

"I pray it is so, my lord," said Abraham from the far corner of the tent. He sat upon a simple stool, wrapped in a philosopher's robes and marked with a philosopher's ink upon his forearms. The skin around his eyes was wrinkled with time, and his beard had moved beyond gray to the white only great age bestowed. His long, slender fingers looked as if they were made to hold the kind of thick book which now rested in his lap. They trailed along the edges, a silent wish that he could return to his reading rather than take up the thread of an argument he knew would not benefit either of them.

"Is that doubt I hear, Abraham?"

"It is faith, my lord."

"Faith." Philbreck laughed, but it was a gentle, teasing laugh. "You can't have faith without doubt. Otherwise, you'd know for certain, and you can't have faith in what you know for certain."

"Certainty breeds mistakes. You would do well not to be too certain of what you think you know and to be more certain of what you don't. A man could spend his entire life exploring the distance between those two points and count it well spent."

"I'll count my life well spent if no one ever has to lose their son the way I have," Philbreck said.

For all his learning, Abraham never quite knew what to say in these moments. Silence wrapped itself around Abraham's heart. He wanted to speak, but even the right words, for all their power, wouldn't affect the young lord. Philbreck's father had listened to Abraham's advice. He had believed in magic and in the old ways that Abraham embodied and Philbreck was determined to set aside. Abraham had promised to look after Philbreck, but the young lord had long since turned away from his counsel. The old man remained with Philbreck more out of a sense of duty to his father than loyalty to the young lord who thought him a relic of bygone days.

The sounds of the storm intensified for a moment. Philbreck felt mist and wind for a brief moment before the sensation died away but gave it little thought. His men had finished setting camp just before the storm hit. It likely wouldn't last long, but it made campfires and a hot meal impossible. He figured most of them would climb into their tents and take advantage of the foul weather to catch up on their sleep. He wouldn't begrudge them that. They would need it tomorrow.

"My lord..." Abraham said.

"Yes?" Lord Philbreck looked up.

The man who stood before him lowered his cowl and looked first at Abraham and then at Philbreck, who stood and carefully placed his book upon his stool. He was not sure whom to address himself to, the elder who dressed like a philosopher of old or the man who was little more than a boy sitting at the table. "I am here to speak to Lord Philbreck," the newcomer said carefully, not wishing to offer disrespect so early in their meeting by making assumptions.

"Then speak," said Philbreck.

"I am the Knight Who Carries a Sword in His Heart," he said. He spoke his name like he was telling a story, and he hoped the weight of each word was enough for them to understand who he was. Abraham sat up straighter. "I've come to ask you not to slay the dragon."

Philbreck almost laughed. His first thought was the man was feverish and sick and needed help. His second, less charitable thought was that the man must have been mad to brave the thunderstorm, walk through a small army's camp, and barge into a lord's tent spouting nonsense.

But his third thought checked the first two. The man stood before him calmly, his eyes clear of all madness. He was bald. His face was bearded and strong, though lined with years. His cloak was simple. Beneath it he wore plain brown pants and a tunic befitting a peasant, not a knight. He was unarmed. There was no blade belted to his waist and there certainly wasn't one sticking through his heart. He looked like a scholar or a monk, but not a knight. There was nothing overtly threatening about him Philbreck could name, yet the tent felt smaller for his being there.

"Not slay the dragon," Philbreck repeated. "Why?"

"Because he is my friend."

Rain pattered against the tent. Thunder rumbled off in the distance. The storm was passing.

"A dragon is no one's friend," said Philbreck.

"He has witnessed ages and carries their wisdom. There are none left like him in the world. Byatt deserves to end his days peacefully. I'm asking you not to end greatness in bloodshed. Let him die in his own time. Please," the Knight's voice softened, "do not kill my friend."

The sincerity of the Knight's voice gave Philbreck pause, but only for a moment. He recognized pain when he saw it. He felt the Knight's pain echo in his own heart briefly before it reflexively hardened.

"He is a relic. The last in a long line of creatures holding us back from what we can be. They've ruled over us for centuries, but their time is over," said Philbreck.

"Byatt never claimed a kingdom. None of them did."

"They claimed our thoughts. Haunted our dreams. Made us fear the dark when we should have been carrying light into it.

What could we have been? What could we have built without dragons binding our thoughts to superstition and magic?

"No," Philbreck shook his head. "It all ends tomorrow. Byatt's death will bring an end to the old ways. Take away the living talisman and all these misguided tales and superstitions will eventually go the way of legends, where they can do no harm."

Abraham spoke from the far corner of the tent. "My lord," he said gently. "This will not bring your son back. Nothing will."

"I know that." There was the echo in his heart again. Philbreck gritted his teeth against it. "But in a generation, maybe two, there will be minds free of magic and ghosts and old wives' tales and room for science and medicine. Someone will find a cure, so someone else's son won't have to die from a cough."

The Knight bowed his head. "I am sorry for your loss. I understand grief can be..."

"Do you have a child?" Philbreck cut him off.

"No."

"Then don't tell me you understand how it feels to watch your son cough his lungs up while the so-called wise men wave herbs in his face and burn sage and promise a cure they can't deliver because they've studied superstition instead of physic. Don't tell me you know what it feels like to lay your son in the cold ground. Don't tell me you know what it feels like to curse God with one breath and pray your son is safe in His arms with the next.

"I would have pulled every star down from heaven and drowned them, one by one, in the ocean if it would have meant he lived, but all I could do was watch him die. If killing a dragon means no one else has feel this, then so be it."

Outside, the rain stopped falling as the storm slid out of the full moon's path.

"I am sorry for your loss. I meant no disrespect. You are right. I cannot imagine what you must have gone through, but that doesn't change what I must do. I am the Knight Who Carries a Sword in His Heart. Byatt has long been my friend, and I name him thus. I will stand between him and all those who seek to do him harm."

"What exactly are you going to do about it?" Philbreck asked.

"If you pack up your army in the morning and leave, then we will part ways in peace. But if you and your men attack Byatt, I will draw my sword in defense of my friend and kill every one of you before I die."

"There are 200 of us," said Philbreck, scorn evident in his voice. His first suspicions had been right all along. The man was mad.

"Even so. I have been to The Dreaming Tree. I carry my purpose and your death in my heart."

"What the blazes are you talking about?"

"It is of the oldest tales, my lord," said Abraham. "Few know it now, but it is a tale that bears attention."

"That's exactly the kind of nonsense I'm talking about." Philbreck waved a dismissive hand in Abraham's direction. "You read a fairy tale and want to fight an army? Fine. Go ahead. But we will show you no mercy if you stand before us tomorrow."

"Nor I, you." The Knight spoke quietly, even regretfully. There was no bravado in the threat, only the certainty of man who saw a task to be completed before him.

He turned to leave.

"Sir Knight," said Abraham.

The Knight inclined his head and took note of Abraham's robes. "Philosopher," said the Knight.

Abraham keenly felt the burden of knowledge upon his heart in this moment.

"I know the old stories, and I know the tale of the Knight. Know that I am not your enemy."

"Then why are you helping him?" The Knight nodded in the direction of Philbreck, who glared his disapproval but did not give it voice.

"Because I treasure what he has lost."

The Knight considered this for a moment before he bowed to Abraham and left the tent.

The entrance to the dragon's mountain chamber was small and easy to overlook from the outside. It was barely wide enough for two men to walk abreast, and a tall man would need to duck. In stronger days, Byatt could shift into human form. When he had made the entrance, he kept it small. No one looked for dragons in tiny cracks.

The Knight found the torches where they had always been hidden, tucked into shadow just around the first bend in the tunnel. He spoke a word of magic, one borrowed from Byatt, and the torch came to life with a flame that gave off light, but not heat. The Knight took a deep, cleansing breath and felt time and weariness fall away from him.

He was home.

The path meandered only a little. The stone beneath his feet was level and the walls around him were smooth and dry. It was cool inside the mountain, but comfortably so, like the chill of blankets when you first slide beneath them.

As usual, Byatt smelled the Knight long before he entered the chamber.

"You smell of thunder." Byatt's voice was low and deep, but the power it once held had faded, like a receding tide reaching for a seaside cliff. "But you reek of Old Magic."

The Knight stepped from the tunnel and into Byatt's chamber. Torches on either side of the entrance bloomed to flickering life, giving him just enough light to see the dragon's face before him.

The Knight's heart was lifted by the familiar gruffness. "It's good to see you too, old friend." The Knight fought to keep his concern from showing in his voice. Only a few days had passed since he'd left Byatt, but the dragon looked as if he had aged further in that brief span. His once shimmering golden scales were grayed around the edges. The ones on his snout were entirely gray. As big as he was, Byatt looked smaller than he should, as if his insides had been hollowed slightly and he was settling in on his bones. Worse yet, the chamber was cooler than it should have been. Dragons were hot creatures by their very nature, but the fire inside Byatt had been banked down to embers buried beneath ash, unlikely to ever blaze to life again.

Byatt snorted. "I look old."

"You are old," said the Knight.

Byatt chuffed out a breath. "You found The Dreaming Tree. I can smell it on you."

The Knight stood before the dragon like a wayward son confessing his sins to a disappointed father. "I did."

Byatt sighed. "Why would you do this, when I asked you not to?"

The Knight lifted his gaze from the floor to meet the dragon's eye. "Because I've made a lot of wrong choices in my life. Let me make this right one."

Byatt closed his eyes in resignation. As much as he wished otherwise, there could be no going back. "I wish you hadn't done this."

"I know."

"Philbreck?"

"He's outside with 200 soldiers. They're coming for you in the morning."

"You should let them come. He isn't wrong in what he believes."

"Doing the wrong thing for the right reasons doesn't make it right," said the Knight. "But his son died. I think he lost himself a long time ago." The Knight shook his head. "I wish tomorrow didn't have to be."

"It doesn't," said Byatt. "My time is near anyway. Let me be. Let Philbreck have his way."

They both knew the Knight would not abandon his friend, but some words needed to be said for the comfort of having said them.

"We are who we are, my friend. There's nothing either of us can do about that."

"Then let tomorrow keep until morning," said Byatt. "Dark nights are better weathered with tall tales than quiet fears. Let's fill our hearts with something better than what awaits us tomorrow."

The Knight smiled. "What did you have in mind?"

"Would you read me a story?"

"Any story in particular?"

Byatt thought for a moment. There were many to choose from, but he realized there could only be one story for a night like this one. "How about," he said slowly, "the one that inspired you?"

The Knight looked into the darkness overhead. "If I'm going to read you a story, then I'm going to need more light."

Byatt's smile should have been terrifying, but the Knight found it comforting to know his friend could still smile. "I think I have enough magic left for that."

The dragon closed his eyes and took a deep breath. The torches extinguished themselves, casting the two of them into the true darkness that can only be found inside a mountain. The Knight held still, but kept his eyes turned upward. Slowly at first, moonlight soaked through stone and soil until it seeped into the cavern, filling it with the gentle light and soft shadows of summer's last full moon.

Above them, the chamber stretched to the mountain top, and its every wall was lined with stone shelves of books in neat rows. Ladders and walkways allowed access to every level in a maze of metal and stone.

Byatt's treasure had never been anything as cheap and pedestrian as gold.

"Can you find it?" Byatt asked. To the Knight's ears, he sounded more tired than he had a moment ago.

The Knight nodded. "I know exactly where it is." He'd been to the top of the library only once. There were more books here than a man could read in a lifetime, even if that was all he did with his life. But he knew the lower shelves well, and he could remember the exact location of every book he'd read. He'd spent many days here, and many nights reading to Byatt when the dragon was uninterested or, as of late, unable to shift forms to read for himself. The best books, like the one with the tale of The Knight Who Carried a Sword in His Heart, echoed within him long after he finished reading them. He could remember exactly how it felt to sit with Byatt and be humbled by the sense of awe such tales poured into him. What must it have been like to take up the sword? What drove a man to such extremes?

Now he knew.

Unwilling to waste any of their precious time, the Knight jogged through moonlight to a ladder leading up to a second level shelf. He climbed it and two more before a short walkway led him to the slender, green volume that contained his favorite story. He held it up to show Byatt, but the dragon wasn't looking. He almost called out before he realized that Byatt wasn't focused on anything. He was waiting patiently, absently staring into moonlight's middle distance because eyes that once pinpointed mice from miles above the clouds could no longer see across their own chamber.

The sudden ache in the Knight's heart had nothing to do with the sword he carried there. He made his way back down the ladders, taking care to make as much noise as possible so Byatt could track him easily.

"Found it," said the Knight.

"Good." Byatt stretched his forelegs out before him. His hind legs did little more than shuffle as he tried to rise. Massive tendons creaked like ropes on a ship. Joints popped like cannon fire. Scales scraped against stone as he laid his head down upon his forelegs.

It was easy to imagine what Byatt had been, especially where moonlight erased the gray from his scales, but his face held onto the weary understanding that came at the end of a long life.

The Knight stepped around Byatt's paw and climbed into the crook of his elbow, where he could sit comfortably and lean against the dragon's head.

"Comfortable?" asked Byatt.

"Yes."

"Good."

The Knight willed time to slow down. Even better, to stop altogether. He wanted to preserve the perfection of this moment, when everything was quiet and still and he was home safe with his friend, reveling in the peace they'd stolen from the outside world.

But the moment was only perfect because they both knew it for what it was, and time had to pass for this to be true. Life could only be lived in motion until it stopped, and they both knew this was an ending.

The Knight began to read. His voice cracked. He cleared his throat, wiped his eyes, and began again. Byatt closed his eyes and listened intently.

"Legends speak of a time when the world was different. For better or worse, it is impossible to tell, for none are alive who remember what was. All we have left of that time are dreams that were lived before they were written and the truths they hold for each of us. Listen closely, for this is one such dream."

It was a faerie tale, one of the first, about a neglected boy who grew up to become a solider who, being unfamiliar with kindness, angered his fellow soldiers until they left him to die on the battlefield.

"He cried out with his last breath, as all soldiers do, for anyone who could ease his pain or end it. It is said that in times of great desperation, or great need, The Dreaming Tree will hear us and answer our calls. The soldier's desperation was pure and his need grievous, so, in the space between final heartbeats, he found himself looking up at glimmering stars through the winter-bare branches of The Dreaming Tree. He was in too much pain to speak, but The Dreaming Tree understood his need.

"The soldier awoke once more on the field of battle, carrying a sword in his heart. He knew it was powerful, and that it would allow him to defeat his enemies if he drew it, but the soldier knew he would die soon after his battle was finished. Rather than seek revenge, he took up the life of the knight errant. He wore no armor, and never again touched a bladed weapon. He travelled the land, lending strength and kindness where he found it lacking and, with each deed, the sword in his heart cut away a piece of the anger and hurt he carried.

"One night, as he looked up at winter's stars from his bedroll, he realized he had been his own greatest enemy. He found himself at The Dreaming Tree once again. He knelt before the tree, drew the sword from his heart, and lay down at the roots of the tree to rest at last."

The story at its end, the Knight closed the book quietly. Byatt's eyes remained shut. His breathing was shallower than it should have been. The old dragon was asleep beneath a blanket of moonlight, his body pressed hard against the cool stone floor of the chamber. It was hard for the Knight to imagine his sleep was restful, and harder still for him to see his friend reduced to such a hollow end.

Byatt's time was nearly over.

The Knight leaned his head against Byatt's. "Thank you for being my friend." Tears splashed against gray scales as the Knight wept silently. Byatt did not stir. The Knight was determined not to be angry at this end, though it was hard. Byatt deserved better, but there was no changing what was. There was only facing it.

Carefully, so as not to wake Byatt, the Knight clambered down from the dragon's embrace and left the chamber without speaking again.

They had lived their goodbyes. Let that be enough.

The Knight Who Carried a Sword in His Heart stood before the mountain and watched the sun rise for the last time. Patches of fog streamed along the valley below, pushed by a breeze so gentle it was almost nonexistent. He caught the barest hint of autumn's chill in the stillness of the morning. The Knight nodded, satisfied. He would not live to see the season come to pass. It was good that he could feel it, even if only in the slightest way.

The Knight waited. Armies, even small ones, take time to move. He could see the soldiers in the valley below, stirring about as they ate breakfast and readied weapons. The Knight could have walked down to their camp, but he was content to wait. Every passing moment was a moment stolen from death, and it was a beautiful day.

It was still early in the morning when the army formed ranks and marched in his direction. There were three men at the front, carrying banners. The Knight assumed Philbreck was the one in the middle, framed by his colors and bearing only the sword at his waist. The soldiers marched in orderly ranks behind the colors, save for one lone figure who followed behind the column. The Knight didn't have to see the figure's robes to know it would be Abraham who marched alone.

In time, the army reached the mountain. It was indeed Philbreck who rode between the colors, and he gave the order to halt. He stepped forward with the bannermen while the rest of his army waited within earshot. Philbreck wanted to make sure they heard what passed between the Knight and himself.

"Sir Knight."

"Lord Philbreck." He looked tall this morning. He was confident in who he was and what he was about, and he wore this confidence like armor. He believed in what he was doing. That made him dangerous.

The Knight did not quail before Philbreck and his army, for he believed, too.

"I told you last night there would be no quarter," Philbreck said. "This is your last warning. Stand aside. Let us pass, and we will part ways in peace. But know if you raise a hand against me or my men, you will be cut down."

This moment was not an honest one. It gave all appearances of being the last point at which the bloodshed to come could be avoided. That was a lie; the moment was a formality. There was nothing honest about it. What was about to happen had been decided long ago by two men who had not seen where their path would lead when they first stepped upon it.

"We are who we are," said the Knight. "I will not stand aside any more than you will walk away. Let's not make a show of this."

Philbreck nodded. "So be it." He drew a deep breath to bellow the order to advance.

The Knight Who Carried a Sword in His Heart raised his right hand to his chest, closed it around a hilt he could not see, but believed was there, and drew the sword from his heart. He felt every inch of it slide through his chest, a freezing, searing agony that stiffened every muscle in his body.

The Knight gritted his teeth against the pain. He believed in stories. He believed in magic. He believed in The Dreaming Tree and dragons and in himself. The blade came free, and the Knight held it out from his body. Silvered edges caught the morning sunlight and cut it in two. The sword was simple, as befitted a powerful weapon. It was marked only by a rough, broad crimson streak running the length of the blade, like the heartwood of a great cedar. A single drop of blood rolled off the tip and fell to the ground.

The Knight moved. He went from standing still to being in motion without appearing to move through any of the steps in between. Blood arced. Three men fell to the ground screaming, dying from wounds that appeared like magic. The Knight moved past them, secure in the knowledge they were no longer a threat.

The first rank charged, but they only had time for a single step before the Knight smashed into them. In seconds he was through that line as well, and every single soldier along the line was down. He moved through the ranks like blazing fire. His sword cut through armor and steel as easily as flesh, and it leant him both power and speed to fulfill its promise. No man could stand before him. Those farther back in the ranks had a few precious seconds to ready themselves. They struck out at the Knight, who wore no armor. The Knight accepted his wounds as the price of his decision and struck back with inhuman ferocity. He should have died quickly, but he fought with borrowed strength. The sword would keep him alive until his battle was finished. That was how the story went.

When the ranks broke, the Knight followed. He was violence given human form. No one who raised an arm against him could stand, and he left a river of blood in his wake that stopped only when he raised his sword against Abraham.

"I am not your enemy," Abraham said.

The Knight quivered with effort of holding back. He fell to his knees, bleeding from too many wounds to stay on his feet. The sword fed him strength, but every breath was agony, every movement torture.

Abraham slipped under the Knight's shoulder and bore his weight as he took the Knight back up to the mountain. He pressed a hand to the Knight's chest and felt the magic of the sword fading. At their feet, dying men moaned, begged for mercy, and clamored for help, all to no avail, but Abraham was intent upon assisting the Knight. The Knight had no mercy to give them.

A bloody hand grabbed the philosopher's robes. Abraham looked down to see Philbreck on his back, his other hand clutching at a terrible stomach wound. He gently lowered the Knight to the ground and knelt beside his lord.

"You promised...my father...you would watch out for me." Philbreck gasped out the words.

Abraham's heart hurt. He cupped Philbreck's face with his left hand so that the lord's eyes were focused on his face. "I tried, my lord." He had done his best, but in the end, Abraham could not save Philbreck from himself. The stomach wound was fatal, though death would be agonizing and slow to come. "All I can offer now is a vulgar mercy."

Philbreck's eyes widened. Abraham told himself it was a sign that he understood, though Abraham could not bring himself to believe Philbreck welcomed his end.

The knife in Abraham's right hand found Philbreck's heart. Abraham's vision blurred as he helped the Knight to his feet and led him to the mountain pass. The Knight tried to speak, to offer condolence or apology for Abraham's loss, but he was in too much pain to do so. He closed his eyes and trusted Abraham to guide him.

The next voice he heard was Byatt's.

"I never wanted this."

The Knight stirred at the sound of his friend's voice. He tried to speak, but he could only moan.

Byatt shifted, helpless. He desperately wanted to ease the Knight's pain, but there was nothing he could do for his friend in this form. He stilled himself, though his heart trembled as he watched the philosopher help the Knight lay down in the crook of Byatt's arm.

"You are safe, and you are home. You may rest now," Abraham said, the words the only benediction he could give.

The Knight opened his eyes and looked upon the sorrowful face of the dragon. The strength of the sword left him. The Knight knew his friend was safe and his battle was finished. He closed his eyes to rest at last.

"I did not ask for his," Byatt sobbed.

"You did not have to ask, Great One," Abraham said. "There is no greater love than this. He made his choice freely, and you bear no guilt. He wanted you to live in peace."

Byatt nuzzled the Knight. He lowered his head and rested it upon his forelegs, just as he had the night before. "A broken heart will have to be its own peace," said the dragon, and with these words, the last of the dragons passed from the world.

Grief overcame Abraham. He wept for Philbreck, for having failed Philbreck's father, for the men whose lives had been needlessly spent, and for the friendship that ended before him. Such moments were rare, and Abraham wept in awe of what he had witnessed and in regret for having seen it.

He knelt before Byatt and the Knight and pressed his palm to the stone floor. He spoke a word of magic, one he had learned long ago. Stone shifted and flowed like water, and the remains of the dragon and the knight sank into the floor. In their place rose a great statue, big enough to take up the entire chamber floor, of a dragon listening intently to a Knight reading from a book. There were no words inscribed upon the statue's base. The statue would speak for itself to any who cared enough to listen.

Abraham left the chamber, his heart heavy. When he left the tunnel, he turned back long enough to press his hand to the mountain. He spoke the word of magic again, this time with a different intonation, one that would add a layer of requirement to the stone that flowed like water.

Abraham sealed the mountain against the hope that someday a different dream would come to pass, one in which the world would again treasure everything that lay within, and left this dream behind.

See Joshua Hagy's story "The Knight Who Carried a Sword in His Heart" online at Metaphorosis.
If you liked it, leave a comment. Authors love that!
Remember to subscribe to our e-mail updates so you'll know when new stories are posted.

About the story

I've had a recurring dream/nightmare about a tree ever since I was a little kid. Sometimes it's a dream, but usually it's a nightmare. I've never been able to make sense of it, and in the last three years the tree has been showing up in my writing.

I was prepping for a production of *Macbeth* last year when the image of someone kneeling at the base of the tree like it was an altar came to me. I could see stars through the empty branches, and I knew the person left the tree with a sword hidden in his heart. I knew the sword would give him purpose. I knew if he drew the sword from his heart, he would win the fight but die shortly after. There's something about a pyrrhic victory that's always appealed to me. I had to know what would make someone desperate enough to carry a sword in their heart and what would make them draw it, so I wrote to find out.

A question for the author

Q: If you could have any super power, what would it be?

A: I want the power to always say the right thing at the right time. Flight and super-strength are great, but I teach high school. I get a lot of questions from kids about life that I just can't answer. Among all the discussion raging about curriculum and distance learning and a million other things, you never really hear anyone talk about how to help the students with what they're going through. These are kids. Actual human beings. They have good days and bad days and terrible days, and they're still learning how to cope with it. As adults, we've forgotten what it means to be young and learning to face problems and pain. We tend to write their problems off as minor teenage problems that they'll get over, but they're dealing with so much more than we realize, and much of it on an adult level they shouldn't have to experience yet.

We lost a member of our senior class this year. I didn't have an answer to "Why did this happen?" or "How do I deal with this?" because there are no good answers. How am I supposed to know what to say to them when I still call my parents with the same questions? How am I supposed to help them when I don't understand, don't have the slightest idea of what to say to such pain? More than anything, I wish I had the power to always say the right words at the right time.

About the author

Joshua Hagy is a writer, high school and college English teacher, yearbook adviser, and theater director living and working in western Virginia. He's been lucky enough to have been married for nearly 14 years to his wife, Bethany, who has chosen to find his tendency to live inside his imagination amusing. When he isn't writing or working, Joshua spends his time searching for the perfect taco (he's already found the perfect pizza).

@The_Hagy23

We, You, and the Gallery

Alex Penland

We had thought ourselves safe, but then you found us in our little ship. There was a thrilling chase. In our desperation, we flew too fast and crashed, and you crashed too. Now we and you are both stranded on this empty, alien world. We do not know if you have survived. We know that only one of us remains, but we are still *we*, even when most of us are gone.

In your language, we believe, you sometimes say silence is *deafening*, but our experience is incongruous with that. The silence brings horrible clarity. In it, we are aware of the breathing which does not accompany our own, of the footsteps which do not fall around us, of the conversations which do not linger in our periphery. The silence is an illumination of all that we have lost.

We have buried the others by the cavern entrance. It is our hope that their decomposition will bring life to the dust of this barren world. Even near the subterranean spring there is nothing living here. No fish. No insects. No bacteria. Our scanners show a frustrating level of microbial safety.

It is there, by the spring, that we first speak to you. Your species needs water as desperately as ours does. Like us, you must have salvaged what you could from the wreckage and taken shelter in the caverns.

We do not know where you have hidden, but it's you who cries out—"Who's there?"—when we cause a thoughtless splash against the silence.

We are momentarily afraid, but we do not see you. The cavern is small; water rushes from one fissure into another. The only other point of entrance is the way from which we came. But for your voice, we seem to be alone.

"Where are you?" we ask. There are several sounds: one of your weapons firing, then the crumbling of rock, then a series of words my translator does not choose to divulge.

We think we understand. There is a phenomenon within caves: the chance alignment of reflective surfaces allows for sound to travel very far and very clearly. This must be the case now. You are not in the same cavern as we are; you might be miles away. You might be on the other side of the wall. There is no way of telling.

We test this by stepping briskly to the side. Your cursing fades to nothingness. When we return to the spot where we stood, your voice returns as well.

"It's a whispering gallery," we say into the anomaly. You stop shooting the walls.

"So you don't know where I am?"

"No."

"Great! So we can negotiate."

We're struck by your audacity. "Negotiate what?"

"Resources. Surrender. I don't know. How many of you are there?"

"We don't think we should say."

"Is that plural pronoun your hive-mind thing or does that mean there's more than one of you?"

We do not answer that.

"Well, assuming you're not alone, you got a resources issue. I got plenty of food, you know. Plus, I think I can get us outta here if you ask nice. You lot surrender and I'll get you a cushy cell 'til the war ends, I promise."

We do not answer that, either.

"Listen, it's better than dying out here, ain't it?"

"It is." We feel very alone. We wish desperately for our company, for the ability to talk this through together, but there is nothing to be done about that. "It is better than dying out here. Why would you bother to rescue us?"

This time you're the silent one.

"You need us alive," we say. "You need help too. We have no proof that you can help us. We have no proof that you will not slaughter us. So no, we do not surrender, and we will not tell you our location."

We step away from the gallery before we hear your reply. There is much to do; we have a ship to scavenge, inventory to document, plans to make. Possibly we have defenses to build. You are correct—we cannot survive here forever—but that does not mean we plan to die here, at either your hands or starvation's.

The room with the gallery is also the most defensible, and there is a nearby chamber that is cold enough for storage. We decide eventually to make this room our base, though during the process of moving supplies we make quite a lot of purposeful noise. You think we are numerous, after all.

Here it is dark and smells of sterile clay. Cool. Humid. The dead rock of the cavern is as much an absence as our silence. We ache for the fresh vegetation of home; the life in the air and the scent of the flowers.

But we cannot mourn. There is work to do.

Occasionally we see you. Once, while we deconstruct the refrigeration chamber in the wreckage of the ship, we spot your outline on a distant hill.

That night you say, "I saw one of you on the wreckage," and we reply that yes, you did, and hope you ask no further questions.

Once, when we venture out to scout a location for a distress signal, we find a machine of some sort, gathering sunlight. We steal it. That night you ask, "Did you steal one of my water purifiers?" and we reply that yes, we did.

Then we think it over. Perhaps you do not have the same access to water that we do. Perhaps you were unlucky. We feel a bit guilty. A few days later we return the machine without comment.

"What did you do to it?" you ask. We do not answer.

Once, we hear you crying.

We do not cry, though we have studied the phenomenon in school, so, although it takes a moment, we understand the sound. In your language, the convulsive gasp is a signal of despair. We do not think you meant to share it with us.

"Are you in distress?" we ask. You stop crying, or perhaps you move from the spot. You never respond to the question. We do not ask again.

One day we return to the wreckage site and you are standing there, arms crossed, waiting for us. You're male. Human, of course. Not as young as we thought you'd be, nor as well-armed. There's a pistol at your hip—it still smells of gunpowder from your duel with the cavern walls—but your ammunition belt is empty. Its grip is visible from your holster; the clip gauge on the side is blank. If you possess firepower, you possess only the shot in the chamber.

"Every time I see you out here, it's just you."

We are frozen to our location. We meet your eyes.

"You're alone, ain't you? You were lying. No one else survived the crash."

We hardly breathe.

"You had me pretty fooled. I was impressed." You hold out your hand. Are we supposed to shake it? We don't shake it. "I'm Edwin. You got a name?"

"Do your fingertips have names?" we ask. "Do your hands?"

"I call 'em Left and Right, generally. So... no? No name?"

"No name."

"Why do you say *we*?"

"Your hand is still your hand, even if we were to cut it from your body."

You nod. You glance behind yourself, back towards the way we suspect you came. "I'm gonna call you Honeybee."

"What?"

"You're a hive alien. You look like bees. You ever see a bee?"

"We are not a bee."

"I'm not saying you are. It's just a name. I gotta call you something. Like it or not, we're both stuck here."

We aren't opposed to names, really. Our opposition is to *you*, not your customs. Honeybee. Hm. "Are we? Didn't you say you had a way out?"

"Thought I did. Turned out I didn't."

"Hm." We lean next to you against the ship. "Neither do we. What was your plan?"

"Originally I was gonna steal components off your ship, but then you gave me back the water purifier." You sigh. "You ain't gonna surrender. I sure as hell ain't gonna surrender. So what now?"

"You have food, but no water?" we ask.

"Yup."

"We have water, but our food is running out. In our language, we say that it is better to die as a community than to live a longer life alone." By the odd look you give us, we suspect you understand the situational irony. "By this we mean that we risk a shortened life by offering to trust you, but if we rely only on ourself, our expiration date is certain."

You work through that for a moment. "You suggesting we share?"

"Yes. Return here tomorrow. We will bring you water."

"And then what?"

We shrug. "Show us your resources. Show us your ship. We're making the choice to trust you. Trust us in return, and we'll plan our escape together."

You look surprised, and a little wary, but you offer us your hand again. This time we do shake it.

"All right," you say. "Good to meet you, Honeybee."

"Good to meet you, Edwin."

This is what you possess: a truly massive cache of rations (roughly half of which are toxic to our biology, which makes division simple), three water purifiers, and half a ship. You do not have the same electrical and engineering knowledge that we do, and we suspect that you would simply have stranded us both if you tried to dismantle our ship to fix your own. You need us more than we need you, we think.

"There are elements we can work with," we say, perusing your technology, "but it's going to take a while. We'll be in a race for time with food."

"And by we, you mean you."

"Unless you can learn engineering on the fly." You laugh. "I have another job for you. As your rations consist of processed bars —"

"Don't give me that judgy tone."

"—*they cannot be farmed*, whereas our rations contain seeds, and likewise will rot sooner. We suggest that you attempt to farm some of our rations while we repair your ship, and that we subsist on your rations in the meantime. Our food grows quickly. It's meant for this exact scenario."

"We're repairing my ship?"

"Ours has been stripped more thoroughly. We believe yours is a more functional base." We replace the panel we were inspecting and stand to meet your eyes. "We are risking quite a lot to help you, Edwin. We understand that humanity is... individualistic..."

"We comprise individuals, yeah."

"And it is out of respect for you, as an individual, that we are trusting you will not make the same collective choice as your species."

You frown.

"Namely, that you will not choose war. That you will treat us, together, as a collective for the time being. Our good will be your good. Your good will be our good. We will become a community, not a pair of individuals at war.”

“You know we have communities back home, yeah? I ain’t unfamiliar with the concept.”

“As far as we can tell, your hives are constantly in swarm.”

You pause, then laugh. “Fair point. I won’t screw you over. I’ll even let you go free. When we get this fixed we head to the nearest neutral world and part ways. On my word, all right?”

We wince. We do not like the idea of landing on a neutral world, especially not alone. They are dangerous and unpredictable in their diversity. “Forgive us, please, but your word means very little. We will trust in cause and effect.”

“What?”

“We will see what happens and how you react. We will see how you respond to the situation we have found ourselves in. As time passes, we will learn the mark you choose to leave upon the world. This is the information we need in order to determine the value of your word.”

“Again—what?”

“Trust takes time, Edwin. We simply do not know you yet. This is a dangerous decision, but one we are making consciously. Do not attempt to put us at ease with promises we have no way of validating.”

You shrug, scratch your neck, survey the desolation of our surroundings. “All right. Guess I can’t blame you for that.”

Time occurs. Days pass, then weeks. You are proving to be an adept farmer, particularly when faced with our fast-growing crops. Our rations are quick and hardy—they can be grown nearly anywhere, and the sweet resin which compacts them doubles as nutrition for whatever soil one can find. Like us, they are less tolerant to heat, but there is a cavern protected from the midday sun that still has some ambient light. We cart in sand from the surface.

The first harvest, one month in, allows us to set aside the remaining ration bars for an emergency supply. The second harvest, two weeks later, allows us to dry fruit for storage. By the third, we have more food than we can eat.

We begin to enjoy our meals together. At first, this is only in shared spaces—the ship, or sometimes outdoors when the weather is bearable.

Over time, however, you introduce us slowly to your space. You reveal that you have inhabited a cave on the far side of the hill. We suspect that you did not survey your surroundings when you crashed, but rather picked a direction to walk in and colonized the first cave you found. It is not nearby. It is not easily defensible. It is well-hidden, to your credit, but only because no tactical mind would choose to hide there.

We do not tell you this. Instead we express our honor when we are allowed to observe the mementos tucked beside your bed, the books piled in corners, the stringed instrument you rescued from the wreckage. It is not clean. The odor of your dirty laundry makes our antennae curl.

Yet you have built furniture: a desk, a lifted bed, storage in unexpected places. It is more confined than our cavern, but you have built an ingenious home in very little space. We are fascinated.

We are also often frustrated, though somehow not by you. When working, we are challenged by the incompatibilities between our two technologies. While hardware is obedient under the pressure of brute force, software is less pliable. Our universal translator is decidedly unhelpful when it comes to programming languages—as are you.

Today, as I swear at the translator, you don't offer to assist; you watch and laugh until we enter a command. The engine roars threateningly, which stops your teasing.

"Are you wasting fuel at me, Honeybee?"

"You can laugh, or you can help."

You're about to respond, but there's a jolt against the side of the ship that has nothing to do with software. You're at the window before we can turn around. The sand on the ground is blowing. The wind's picked up.

In the distance the air has begun to shimmer: heat. Intense, visible heat. You stick your head out the door to observe and burn your hand on the outer wall of the ship. A smell of singed flesh flashes through the bridge. Another untranslatable word—you duck back in.

"Hey, Honeybee, got a fun fact for ya. My life support's down."

"We are aware." We're trying to assess if we've fixed that yet. The translator is currently displaying the code in front of us as a list of various species of snake.

"Did you fix it?"

"We... aren't sure."

"You think we can make it to a cave from here?"

"We aren't sure, Edwin."

"Well, when you gonna know?" We open our mouth to respond. You don't let us say it again. "Right. Come on. We're making a break for the caves. Now."

We look up from the computer. You're holding out a hand, halfway out the door already.

"Come on. I ain't leaving without you."

"Is it close enough? Will we make it?"

"I ain't sure."

The storm is at our back. We try to fly you, to move more quickly, but our wings blister when they spread. When the pair of us dive into the caverns we are afraid, for a moment, that they will not provide adequate protection, but you drag us further below the surface and pat out the charring on our clothes. We press ourself against the cool ground and shiver. In your language you would say we are 'gasping for air'. We are not sure that this translates directly to our circulatory system, but the intent behind the words is accurate.

We suspect you are more resilient to heat than we are. You are leaning against the wall, sweating, breathing, staring at the inferno that rages outside.

It becomes slowly apparent to us that you have led us to our cave, not yours. It was the closer of the two dwellings; it was also a tactical mistake, to bring yourself to our territory. The action suggests trust. Behind the dull exhaustion of the heat, we are conflicted.

"Think we've figured out why nothing lives here, Honeybee."

We nod, still fragile from the storm.

"You all right?"

We haul ourself to a sitting position. It seems dangerous to tell you that we are vulnerable to temperatures—we do not know what information will be reported to your superiors. To risk our life is one thing; to put all of us at risk is another. And yet you chose our survival over your advantage.

"Bee, look at me."

But we are weak. We feel a strange, trembling headache, and our body is enervated. When we look at you we do not register your expression. When we fall, we do not register your catching us. The world fades.

There is a sound of rushing water.

We have cooled significantly. Before we open our eyes we can feel our hands and feet are submerged, though our body lies on cold stone. We realize what has happened—you have saved our life, at least temporarily. We had overheated; now we have cooled.

We have perhaps cooled too much. We sit up, slowly, battling the lethargy in our joints. Heat makes us weak; cold makes us heavy. Our blood feels like syrup in our veins.

You made a fire some time ago; it has now dwindled into embers. The smoke still trails along the ceiling, leaving chemical traces in the air. You yourself are currently sleeping on my bed, having covered yourself in empty ration canvas to keep in the heat from your warm-blooded body.

Unlike you, Edwin, we do not generate heat well. Our bodies are more vulnerable to environmental conditions. We need warmth. Unthinking, we crawl across the cavern—we do not have the strength to walk—and bury ourself in the bed beside you. When we rest our forehead on your back, you are like a lantern on a cold and unforgiving night. Then you turn in your sleep and wrap your arms around us, and the lantern blossoms into the sun.

When we wake again, you have rekindled the fire (we wonder how long you searched for our fire kit, how long it took you to recognize it for what it was) and you are cooking fruit on a griddle. The cavern smells like toasted sugar, tart and syrupy. We lay here quietly, watching the scene.

You do not seem alien to us in this moment. You are humming an alien tune, tapping the matte luster of your fingers on alien knees, but there is a familiarity in the domesticity of cooking. We are reminded of morning meals in the cafeteria hall, of baking and frying-up in our rotations of a dozen-or-so individuals. We are reminded of the easy chemistry between ourselves, of the casual warmth and connection of the collective.

We are momentarily and intensely homesick.

"Hey, Honeybee. You alive over there?"

You've noticed. We nod, reluctant to leave the lingering comfort of the bed. We think our thermoregulation has balanced itself, but this is comfortable, and we are very tired.

"You had me worried."

"We were very lucky you knew how to do first aid." We were, in fact, surprised. You knew to put our hands and feet in the water; if you had placed our body, as human anatomy directs, we would have drowned. "How did you know how to save us?"

"I'm military, Bee. We do get training."

"In human medicine, certainly. We are not human."

"We get alien basics, too. You know we've got some of you lot on our side, right? Defectors. Not everyone loves the hive."

The horror is plain on our face, or perhaps the despair.

"Don't look at me like that! We treat 'em right. If someone wants to be an individual, let 'em."

"We simply cannot imagine the desire." There is a spot near the fire where you have folded a mat for us to sit on, and we sit there now. "Having lost our connection to the hive, we cannot fathom the decision one must make to leave willingly. One would lose everything."

"How can you know that? You don't know their whole situation. You don't know what they've been through."

"We have lost everything, Edwin."

"Ah. Right. Sorry." You pause. "You ain't alone. Uh. Lost my own family to a hive attack."

"Did you?"

"It was years ago, so... You know. War's not... great."

You clear your throat uncomfortably. I change the subject.

"Arrowfruit tastes quite good when paired with redspice."

"What?"

"What you're cooking. Arrowfruit. We believe there is some redspice left in the stores—"

"That's what, the red powder?"

"Purple, actually. The name misleads."

We retrieve the bag, and the pair of us begin to cook together.

That first day of the storm, once we have eaten and checked the status of the weather, we take stock together of what we possess.

There are enough rations to get us through quite some time. Together we venture closer to the entrance to check on the crops; their cavern is much warmer than it has been previously, but not so warm as to cause them harm. We have water from the spring. We are not sure how long the storm will last, but our basic needs for survival are met.

Next, comfort. We are in our own territory, but you only have what you've carried in your bag. It is admittedly heavy, but it is always on your person and you tend to carry your tools with you: a small multi-device you call a *pocket knife*, extra rations in case you were to become stuck somewhere for a while, and most importantly a spare set of clothes.

You chuckle at our visible relief. "What, you don't like how I smell?"

"We were taking into consideration that your living quarters smell quite strongly of human body odor."

"It's not like I got a shower in there!"

"And do you have a similar excuse for your ship?" Our antennae curl. "We understand that you have a dulled sense of smell. We can forgive that. We're simply appreciative that we won't have to live with it."

"It ain't that bad."

"Not to you."

You also have a deck of playing cards.

You attempt to teach us the game of *poker*, which does not go particularly well. When you run out of the pebbles you've insisted on gambling with, we offer you some of ours. We receive in turn a lecture on how we are missing the point, to which we reply we have clearly won the game and ask how much of the point we can possibly be missing, and it is at this point that you decide to find a project rather than a game to play.

The phrase in your language is *sore loser*.

You decide to 'spruce up' our living space, starting with the bed. We have been sleeping on a pile of mats, which is quite comfortable, but—

"Listen, if I'm staying here, I ain't sleepin' on the floor. I'm making you a bedframe."

Implicit in this decision is the implication that we will be sharing a bed again. We are not sure how we feel about that assumption. Certainly it was comfortable. Certainly you did not kill us in our sleep, or in our illness, and you had the chance to do so. Your gun lies near the cavern entrance, a single shot still loaded in the chamber.

And yet we wonder whether bed-sharing contains the same implications for you as it does for us—do your people cluster the way we do? Do your people bond together, form lifelong connections? Or are your romances as individualistic and flighty as the rest of your culture? Are you, Edwin, like the rest of your people? Is there even something that can be defined as 'the rest of your people'? Are we simply overthinking things?

"We are not ectothermic," we explain eventually, watching you consolidate supplies and tear apart crates. "We are capable of sleeping alone if you wish to bed down elsewhere."

You shrug. "It's no bother."

“Are you sure?”

“ ‘Course.”

And the matter is settled.

On the second day of the storm, we teach you our games. We spend some time carving a set of horribly unbalanced dice from spare parts of the bed project, then show you how to use them. You enjoy dare-dice best, where we take turns suggesting a task and then roll to see who must perform it.

The game is generally used to allocate horrible chores back home, but we are stuck in a small and mostly-featureless room, and so dares quickly become questions.

We begin to learn about each other.

The weirdest thing you’ve ever eaten: sawdust, when you were in particularly dire straits on a survivalist training exercise.

The most memorable dream we’ve ever had: it occurred the night before we began our military training, when we dreamed we were a comet sailing peacefully through the universe. When we awoke, we had a distinct memory of a bright light on a horizon that could not have existed, and a longing for understanding that would never come.

Your childhood dream: you wanted to be a space pirate.

Our favorite color: starlight. Pale and shining flecks against the black.

Your most embarrassing moment: you were a child. Your older sister once called you *Ed-lose*, and it upset you so much you cried and threw up your dinner. You no longer speak with your sister, but you insist that is not the primary reason.

You ask us what we would have done if we had not joined the military, which is confusing. Then it occurs to us that you believe that soldiers are different from ordinary citizens. We find this disheartening. If your citizens are not the same as those who fight, and your people are individuals, how can you truly understand the cost of war?

“Maybe,” you say. “But I think if I weren’t in the military I’d be something real dull, which, well, I guess some people might want to do that with their lives.”

“Why was this the life you chose?” we ask, abandoning the dice. “Why would anyone choose war?”

You’re quiet about that for a while, leaning back against the cavern wall. For a little bit the only sounds are those of the subterranean spring and the distant chaos of the storm. We allow you your time to think, observing you instead. We have become familiar with your face, with the softness of your body. Your appearance has begun to bring us comfort, and that is a frightening thing.

We wonder if perhaps others have not abandoned their communities, but simply chosen new ones.

"I didn't really choose it," you admit. "The military's a shit job, so people in shit situations are the ones who sign up. You get a good deal—good money, good education, good place to lay your head. I didn't have any of that when I signed up. I do now. Not sure it's worth the golden chains, though."

"Do you regret it?"

"I did." There's an invisible edge to your answer, somehow. Something clinging behind the words, something which makes our back flutter, which brings a shiver to our fingertips.

We lean forward. "Do you regret it now?"

"You know, Honeybee? I ain't sure."

The storm rages on. Days blend together. Time passes.

At night we sleep encircled in the safety of your arms. At first we refuse to talk about this during the day, but then you put your arm around us in a moment of sympathy, and we lean our head on your shoulder, and the physical barrier is broken. What was relegated to sleep becomes common. We sit together. We eat together.

We are no longer alone.

We are awoken by a faint and repeated alarm. We roll over, bleary, to ask you if you recognize the signal. You are not there.

We sit up. We are surprised and a little confused.

The situation makes more sense once we realize the noise is coming from the whispering gallery, and once we realize we can no longer hear the storm outside. It is one of your devices, then, and the world outside is safe for passage. You have returned to your cavern to retrieve it. There is nothing suspicious or unexpected about that.

And so we take the time to think.

This bond we've formed with you, whatever it may be—we know it's doomed. We asked you to consider our pair as a community, and while we meant that, it was not intended to be mutual. For us to consider you the same is—

It's dangerous. There is no other word for it. We do not part from our community, and upon leaving we must part from you. You have shown no inclination towards joining our hive; we cannot bear to join your swarm. There is no future in which we stay together.

And yet we lie back down and soak in the warmth you left behind. The echo of footsteps that are not there have grown softer in your presence. The silence is no longer intrusive. We cannot deny the change.

Last night you placed your hand on our chest and asked us where our heartbeat was. When we didn't know what you were talking about, you placed *our* hand on *your* chest in demonstration. We laughed; we told you how we have a dozen small hearts down our abdomen, explained our circular breathing. Wasn't that covered in your training? But you say you only learned the protocol, not the biology.

You placed your hand upon each heart of ours and felt its rhythm. You called us fascinating. You called us beautiful.

Love is a state of neutrality in the hive. We are always perfectly in sync; it is the glue which seals our metaphorical cells, a propolis of the soul. We join sometimes—mostly in twos, sometimes more—but to do so is to entwine two threads within the greater aegis of the soul. Beautiful, yes, divine, but not a source of conflict.

We are accustomed to love, accustomed to connection, and yet somehow entirely unsettled by the feelings you inspire in us. When we speak, we argue as much as we admire; when we fight we are drawn together more than we are repulsed. Everything you are opposes the virtues we were raised on, and yet this only seems to draw us closer.

We asked you, yesterday, what your greatest childhood fear had been. You said: us. The hive. We were the ones who killed your family. (Just as you killed ours. We have forgiven, not forgotten.) But you are no longer afraid.

We are. We are terrified.

We do not want to leave this community.

We do not want to leave you.

We have drifted back to sleep again. This time we are awoken by your distant voice, and this time you are not alone.

"Sorry," you say through the gallery echo, "I didn't quite catch that. Can you state your name and ID again?"

"This is Jeffrey Reynolds, ID 809192-9."

"Hey there, Jeff. Good to hear your voice, it's been a hot minute out here."

"We got your distress call, Ed. What happened? We thought you were a goner."

"Oh, nothing too special. Took a dumb chance chasing some..." You hesitate. We know your language. We can hear the habitual use of *bugs* on your lips, and we hear you repress it. "Took a dumb chance on a chase and we both crashed."

"Any bugs get out?"

You hesitate. We understand. You can tell them we all died, and we would be safe. We could leave on the repaired ship and this man could send rescue for you. But we suspect you want us to defect, that you do not want to part ways either. You will want to know what our options are.

"Yeah," you say. "The crash didn't get 'em all. But don't you worry, we're all gettin' on good. Say Jeff, you know how the asylum process works? Think I'd be able to offer my friends here a deal?"

"Sure, probably. Citizenship in exchange for time served against the Hive. Standard." We can hear the disgust in your friend's tone. "Sure happy to turn a blind eye if you squash the bastards before we get there, though. All those legs. Ugh. Freaks me out."

"Well, guess we have differing opinions on that." Your voice has gone cold, polite. "What would asylum look like?"

"Can't say as for sure, man. Tell you what, send me your coordinates and I'll make sure there's a specialist on board, huh? Give 'em a good deal?"

"Certainly." You pause again. "Uh, you know what, Jeff, I gotta go find those coordinates exactly, they're still on my ship. I'll get 'em back to you soon, yeah?"

"You don't have them with you?" Jeff's surprise is warranted. You absolutely have them with you. You are likely looking at them, taped to your cavern wall, right in your eyeline. "Right. Yeah. Sure. You can leave the signal on too and we can track—"

There is an audible click.

"Turned it off," you say. "I can't bear that guy. You catch all that, Honeybee?"

"We did."

We are aware you could have deceived us. We can think of a dozen ways that conversation could be faked, and a dozen reasons why. We think of the round you left in the chamber. The gun is with us now; you did not bring it with you when you went to answer the call.

You are an individual; this does not mean your choices are selfish. You have chosen only once to cause us harm, before you knew us. You have kept us safe a dozen times since. Time has passed, and we have seen the mark you choose to leave upon the world.

We pick up your weapon and turn it over in our hands. It has never been used for violence against us. You are the only thing which has been profaned in such a way.

We say: "We do not wish to join your military."

"I know, Honeybee. Just wanted to know what our options were." You exhale. "I don't want to fight my people either."

"And similarly, you would be required to if you joined us."

"Of course." You're quiet again for a moment, thinking. "Before we make a decision, we should check the ship. See what damage the heat did. See if we have any other choice, you know?"

We stand together in front of the ship.

It's fine.

It's absolutely fine.

Our ship—that is, the hive ship—has melted irreparably. It is a twisted and deformed hunk of metal and wax, a final monument to those of us who died in its crash. Eventually, future storms will smear it across the face of the planet, and it will be gone forever.

But your ship? Your ship is pristine.

"How?" you ask. We are already climbing in through the hatch, assessing. "What did you do to it? It looks better than when we left it—"

"It's not better," we say, "but it appears we did, in fact, fix the life support before the storm hit. The interior was able to protect itself. We had also connected our shields with yours, and that seems to have been a miraculous success, though it's built to withstand far more intense heat on atmospheric interaction."

"Well, that's good."

"In fact," — we peer out from the hatch again — "we think our work is done."

"Done?"

"Done. Complete. The ship is low on fuel, there are a dozen bugs in the software, but we believe a trip to the nearest neutral planet would be viable."

You're staring at us.

"Edwin?"

"So that's it?" you ask.

"What?"

"You're leaving?" There's a panicked shiver to your voice.

"We didn't say that. We said the ship is viable. We..." We leave the words unspoken. We aren't sure what we were going to say, anyway. "There are decisions to be made, that's all."

"Yeah." You glance up at the sky. It's brightening; a brilliant blue after the firestorm.

We hesitate before speaking again. "We do not wish to part ways, Edwin."

You exhale. "No. We don't."

"And yet we don't wish to fight our own people."

"No, we don't."

We sit on the ground, leaning against the ship, looking out at the wasteland that has become something like a home. Your breathing is slow and even; mine is a low hum against a background breeze. Our hands brush accidentally. We exchange a glance of quiet desolation.

"We wonder when you started referring to us as a plural."

You roll your eyes.

"You think of us as a pair."

"Yeah, I do. Don't you?"

We close our eyes, thinking of our past pairings, thinking of the hive. We nod. We think perhaps that the two of us are more a pair than any other person we have loved. It is a dangerous thought.

"Listen," you say, "I don't know how they do this in the hive. I don't know if you just... love free, or only love your queen, or how it works, but humans, when we choose someone else— Well, we got a thousand different ways to fall in love, but where I'm from it's usually just... We pick the other individual we love best, and we make our choices from there."

To be loved best seems impossible. One is not meant to be loved best. One is meant to sacrificed for all, not sacrificed for. The image of the pair of us in our patchwork ship, running from our people, hiding out in the wild diversity of the neutral planets—it surfaces in our mind and we cannot dislodge it.

We imagine what it would be like, to travel the stars and trust only in each other. We imagine love rife with conflict and passion. We imagine life, free and forlorn but never lonely.

Never lonely. Not with you.

We cannot bear to open our eyes, to see the look upon your face. Perhaps it is not as desperately fond as your voice; perhaps there is not the same helpless affection. Perhaps you are lying. We could not survive it, if you were lying. We have changed too much by loving you to be the person that we were.

"And sometimes that individual changes, Honeybee, I won't lie about that. But I don't know you as the collective, right? I know you as Honeybee. And Bee, I love you best. Easily. I love you best."

We open our eyes. You are not lying. We reach out to clean the tears from your cheek. Our hand is unsteady.

"I can't fight 'em," you say, "but I can't go back, either. If we don't want to split up, if you'll have me…"

"This is our collective," we whisper. "Us."

We have buried the others by the cavern entrance. Our hive seems very far away, and you are close, and you are also fascinating, and you are also beautiful.

"Us," you say.

It is dangerous, and perhaps it is ill-advised, but you never send the coordinates to your superior. Instead, we make our preparations. You harvest the last of our crops: a bit dry, a bit small, but survivors of the storm. We gather a list of neutral planets—an eclectic bouquet of utopias and university worlds, of war-torn dust-traps and regressed historical inaccuracies, of oceans and jungles and constructed habitats. They are unpredictable, but so are you. Perhaps unpredictable does not always indicate danger.

Our first task is to repair our ship beyond a state of limping; after that, we will take to the void. We will have our choice of worlds; we will have our choice of stars.

When the time comes, we chart our course and leave.

We leave together.

On an abandoned, uninhabitable planet, there are several shallow graves. There is, for now, the wreckage of a single spaceship, slowly deteriorating in a harsh and unforgiving climate. In the myriad caves below the surface, there are wild fruits which drink from natural aquifers. They can be found safe in the shade, growing wherever the last traces of light will touch them.

There is a cavern. In it are the scattered traces of habitation; a charred fire pit, broken boards, a bed which was gratefully abandoned. On the wall, we have carved one message in two languages. The engravings are side by side.

We have written:

"In this place, violence was supplanted by love. May the universe share our same conclusion."

Below our message, you have fired a single shot into the wall.

See Alex Penland's story "We, You, and the Gallery" online at Metaphorosis.
If you liked it, leave a comment. Authors love that!
Remember to subscribe to our e-mail updates so you'll know when new stories are posted.

About the story

In 2022, sometime in January, my grandfather died and my father was diagnosed with an aggressive form of cancer. But "We, You, and the Gallery" isn't a cancer story.

In 2019, just before the pandemic hit, I left the US and moved to Scotland to pursue my degrees in writing. The world closed down six months later. I didn't want to risk my family by returning home, so I chose to remain in the UK. When I made the choice, I fell against the wall and cried until I ran out of tears. But "We, You, and the Gallery" isn't a pandemic story.

In 2022 again, sometime in March, war broke out in Europe. I spent that uneasy week staring out my window, writing pieces of an opera about Odysseus. My eyes rested on a carving in Grassmarket where a bomb fell in World War II. "We, You, and the Gallery" is a war story. That one I'll give you.

When my father started chemotherapy, something in me broke. My family is close—they're my we, whether or not I'm with them—and the thought of losing him at a distance was too much to bear. War and plague weren't enough to break my practicality, but when faced with loss, the risk was far too great. I spent the next few months in America, staying with my dad on his good weeks and with my mom when the chemo hit hardest. He was in good hands. I was there to cheer him up, not to get in his way.

This is the environment in which "We, You, and the Gallery" was written. I was surrounded by hurt, and death, and fear. (So were we all.) My hometown, where my mother lives, was on the verge of spring—dogwoods and cherry trees all just beginning to blossom. There was plastic drifting down the gutter streams. There had been so little snow last year. The world was wet and covered in a vivid green, and everyone, everywhere, was dying.

I'm not sure where I got the idea. I don't know where Edwin and Honeybee came from.

All I know is that one day I came downstairs in the morning—I was at my mother's house— and they were in my mind. Suddenly I knew this story about love that sparks between differences—because of differences. Reality was raw and bleeding. Love was fending it off with a busted lip and a black eye, but still fighting. This was true of real life and fiction alike. I needed to remember that. I needed to write about it.

The first draft took a single day. The second draft was done at my father's house and took a further two days; it expanded the story by several thousand words. I've put it through further edits since then (to say nothing of the incredible feedback provided by *Metaphorosis* itself), but I have never produced a workable draft so quickly.

I don't know where "We, You, and the Gallery" came from, but I needed it. I'm so glad I've had the chance to share the tale with you.

A question for the author

Q: What's your favorite type of pie?

A: For a couple years now, I've been learning my mother's pie crust recipe from across the pond. I'm originally from Washington, DC, so of course as soon as I moved to Scotland I realized how much I missed it; she essentially just uses pastry dough. It's incredible. Especially when she bakes it in one of those tins with the holes all over it. I don't mind if it's pumpkin or apple or chicken pot pie, but that crust is essential.

About the author

Alex Penland is a former museum kid. They spent their childhood running rampant through the Smithsonian museums, which kicked off an early career as a child adventurer. Alex has worked in the field with NASA scientists, linguists, and acclaimed photographers. Now a Pushcart-nominated author, Alex currently lives in Scotland while studying for a PhD in Creative Writing at the University of Edinburgh. They still run rampant, but they've breached the Smithsonian's containment.

www.AlexPenland.com, @AlexPenname

The Zoo Diaries

Frances Pauli

Part One

The Rainriver Zoological Gardens are fully licensed and operate in accordance with the Animal Welfare Act and the Endangered Species Act, which set minimum standards for the care and keeping of animal exhibits. In compliance with the law, each enclosure is designed to meet the minimum requirements for the animal within it. Each diet is planned to satisfy the minimum goals for health and vitality, and each animal is cared for, handled, and transported in a fashion that meets the minimum conditions for humane treatment.

The zoo was once a popular tourist destination. It was once awarded a prestigious accolade for its public outreach and overall design.

Recently, it has fallen upon financial difficulties that make providing *minimum* care a constant juggling act between obeying the laws and keeping the doors open.

Ape House

Gonzo the macaque smells the coffee long before he can see it. The-one-who-sweeps-the-walks passes in front of his territory. She clutches the broom in her odd, hairless fist. The other hand holds the vessel, and the vessel emits the thick, overpowering scent of *bean.*

Gonzo's paws tremble. His nostrils gape, reaching for the scent as if the fumes alone could sustain him. He salivates. His lips stretch back, revealing stained teeth, four-centimeter fangs, and a pink tongue. His head throbs. It has been four months since he chewed the bean. Four months of hell.

Outside his range, a wretched crow perches like death atop the 'Jungle' sign. She caws, a nail straight through Gonzo's caffeine-deprived skull. She caws, and the macaque cringes.

Tortoise Enclosure

Oliver drags a stumpy leg through the sand. He pulls, one clawed foot at a time, flicking sharply at the last second so that a shower of grit washes away behind his great domed shell.

He digs. He rocks forward and back. He is 110 years old.

Today he's circled his enclosure three times already, but Miranda has not returned. She does not hide behind the prickly cactus. She does not wade in the shallow pool. She is not stalking through the reeds near the square door that leads nowhere.

She is missing.

Oliver drags at the sand. He digs.

The love of his long life has vanished.

MEMO: ALL ZOO STAFF

THIS IS A REMINDER TO ALL PARK EMPLOYEES NOT TO FEED THE NATIVE FAUNA.

AS YOU ARE AWARE FROM THE PIGEON INCIDENT, THESE SITUATIONS CAN QUICKLY GET OUT OF HAND, CAUSING DAMAGE TO ZOO PROPERTY AND ENDANGERING THE WELFARE OF OUR GUESTS.

WE HAVE RECEIVED COMPLAINTS ABOUT THE AGGRESSIVE NATURE OF THE PARK BIRDS ALREADY, AND IT IS VITAL THAT WE ARE PROACTIVE AND DIFFUSE THE SITUATION BEFORE IT ESCALATES.

ANY EMPLOYEE CAUGHT FEEDING THE CROWS WILL BE SUBJECT TO DISCIPLINARY ACTION.

Elephant Paddock

Shanti calculates the width of her enclosure in steps. She measures the length and deduces the height of her shelter by triangulation. Her trunk lays out bits of straw to represent each distance. She bundles them, divides, and reorganizes her square footage.

There are thirty-seven peanuts in a pile beside the straw. She has gathered and counted them. The crowd threw 168 peanuts. She has eaten 131.

Curling her trunk into an ess, she flaps her flat ears and blows out a reverberating sigh. If she saved 100 peanuts, in ten days she would have a thousand.

She stuffs three into her mouth, subtracts them from her total. Calculates.

There are seven zebras in the enclosure beside hers. If each zebra has twenty stripes...

The Crow

The macaque throws a stone at her. Debra shrieks and takes to wing. Perhaps it was only a carrot nub, a lump of rind or vegetable scrap left over from his morning meal. She flies anyway, lets the pigeons have it.

Down from the apes, the trundling Sulcata tortoise, Oliver, is attempting to escape again. Debra teases him until he begins to cry. Then she tires and circles.

She flies over the Savannah, past the elephant, the arctic wedge, and the cat house. Somewhere behind this she can hear the hyena sobbing. Debra ignores that sport, landing instead upon the peak of the great aviary.

Her brethren amass there. The irony of it amuses them. A full murder of free crows huddling atop the massive avian jail. Debra joins them long enough to add her stories to the morning's gossip. Then she hops to the roof's edge and waits at the highest point above the building's double-glass doors.

Soon, the park will open. Soon the hordes will enter.

They will push their strollers through the stiles, purchase warm bags of popcorn, piping hot lattes. They will steer their infants down the paths to the double-glass and find for the first time the sign which reads: 'No Strollers'.

The children will wail. The door will open and close, releasing for a brief moment the many calls of the birds trapped inside. Then, a line of abandoned strollers will wait below, overflowing with treats and ripe for plunder.

Debra loves popcorn.

And though the crowds have been much thinner of late, though the walks are less choked and the spoils less plentiful, she will drink from someone's latte today. She will think of the macaque dreaming of his beans and laugh.

A solitary pigeon, brave or suicidal, streaks past the aviary. The murder shifts, caws, and threatens.

"Watch out," the fat gray body calls back. "Watch. Watch."

The crows hop and posture but do not fly. Do not chase. The gates are open now, and they are not fools.

Hyena Pen

Today her cubs are six months old. Alice has not seen them in two weeks. She opens her square jaws and lets loose a sobbing cackle. Her teats have long since dried, but she is certain there were two healthy, viable cubs. She remembers them, and her spotted fur bristles.

Two cubs with strong, sloping backs once bounced and gamboled in the cramped, square enclosure. Two sang with her, obeyed her as their mother and matriarch.

Alice climbs to the top of her stair-step rock and lowers her head to the cold, too-smooth stone.

She can smell them beneath the harsh, biting disinfectant. She can smell her family, and she knows, for a moment, that they were real.

Grizzly Grotto

Hector works at a bur that is stuck deep in his shaggy pelt. The sticker has lodged just behind his left elbow, and he is forced to stretch to reach it, to contort his massive body so that his long, sickle-shaped claws can scratch and pry at the thing.

He growls and ripples his black lips. His ears lie flat against his huge skull, and the nub of his tail tucks tight against his round bottom.

He sits up, glares at the trench that surrounds his home. A fat log lies on this side, a broken stump stands beside him. Hector considers trundling over, using the bare wood to scratch away his irritation.

He considers it, but *she* will arrive soon, and tree scratching is far too undignified for a bear of his stature.

Already he hears the noises. Pattering feet and barking voices. Hector listens, lifting his face high and scenting for her.

She is always early, and he has learned to wake long before his body's rhythm would prefer. He groans at the ache in his right hip, but he leaves off scratching and finds a more dignified pose.

She appears at the railing high above the trench. By then, he is rampant, stretching tall on his hind legs and only gripping the leaning stump with one paw for balance. He is mighty. He is bear.

She claps her hands once for him, takes out her pencil and her book, and begins to draw.

RAINRIVER ZOOLOGICAL GARDENS

NUTRITIONAL RECORD: AFRICAN LION
    (2X DAILY PLUS ENRICHMENT)
    SUN/AM BEEF HAUNCH   PM COMMERCIAL MINCE
    MON/AM BLOOD BLOCK(FROZ)   PM MINCE
    TUE/AM BEEF CUBES/FEMUR PM MINCE
    WED/AM MINCE / ZEBRA DUNG   PM MINCE
    THU/AM ZEBRA HAUNCH   PM MINCE
    FRI/AM MINCE   PM MINCE
    SAT/AM MINCE / DUNG   PM MINCE
    HEALTH CONCERNS: NONE
    THE BOARD

The board of directors discusses migrating the largest predators to a diet of commercial mince, which is far more cost effective, and according to the sales brochure provides a well-balanced and nutritional substitute. Someone points out the deficiency in mental enrichment and stimulus, but a solution is negotiated. The mince will be supplemented with blocks of frozen cow's blood.

When these blood blocks are introduced into the enclosures, they are well received. Everyone's worries are assuaged, and the money saved goes to a remodel of the front gates designed to increase the facility's curb appeal.

Lion Enclosure

Charlie licks the frozen blood until his tongue goes tingly. It is not fresh, not warm, or even particularly flavorful. The block melts slowly as he toys with it, but it never heats, never feels alive and flowing.

He waits for the morsels. He licks the red ice and pants, huffing until his whiskers dance.

They arrive all at once, a herd of tall ones and their bite-sized offspring. They swarm the distant railing, and the air fills with the scent of hot dogs.

They lean against the glass wall inside his den, and Charlie wonders if they taste fresh. He watches the little ones move with stuttering steps. They squeal and totter and place filthy hands against the barrier which keeps them alive.

The hot dogs bleed onto their clothing, red ketchup streaks, and dribbles of some sweet drink. The morsels laugh and point while their tall ones snap pictures and Charlie imagines long grass, dry heat, and the rhythm of their steps against baked earth.

He licks the block, grinds a slow divot in the ice, stains his muzzle crimson while they dance outside his prison.

Charlie imagines they would run like gazelle, run in tiny tripping steps. They would scream. They would run. But the morsels would not be fast enough.

They would never be fast enough to live.

Tortoise Enclosure

Oliver's tunnel grows. He has aimed it inward, toward the center of his pen, for he has learned long ago that any outward digging will be quickly backfilled by They-who-bring-food.

To peer into it now would offer a view of a shallow scrape, a domed, tortoise-shaped cross section that angles sharply down but poses no risk of escape.

Oliver has learned.

He has dug his pits through generations of keepers, and so you would have to be a tortoise to fit yourself deep into the hollow at the far back wall and pivot one half turn to the right to realize his digging has continued.

The tunnel moves east, toward the Savannah, angling up again and aiming for all it's worth at the open, grassy picnic square beside the elephant.

He might have less distance to the west, but the macaque's cage has a concrete floor. If he miscalculated there, he could be forced to dig beneath the entire ape house to find freedom.

He will take the slower, safer path. Already, he believes his tunnel has breached the confines of his enclosure. He digs below the zebras now, and if he turns to the left soon, he should emerge amid the picnic tables.

By day, he makes certain to be seen. He trundles, slow as a stone, around the shallow pond, through the tall reeds where Miranda should have lingered. He sleeps in the sun, and when it fades, when They-who-bring-food are gone, Oliver digs.

For freedom. For love. He digs for Miranda.

Zebras

The zebras circle the place where the ground moves. They lower their muzzles to the earth and snort a chorus of echoing rumbles, striped hides heaving all around.

Their leader stamps and the others mimic her.

In the center of their huddle, the packed Savannah lifts and cracks. A bulge appears, rises and falls.

The lead zebra flicks her tail, takes a step backwards, and the ring widens. Voices whisper as the herd digests the anomaly.

"What is it?" "What do we do?"

The ground surges, a boil, a fly bite on the Savannah's skin. It erupts at once, spattering dirt and sending the herd into stumbling flight. They retreat, bolting to the far corner of their fence.

Their hooves beat a fearful dance. They blow and bellow. The leader brays, harsh, screeching.

Nothing horrible happens.

Eventually, they circle back. This time the leader approaches alone. The others murmur encouragement from a safe distance.

Something moves in the broken earth. A blunt head appears, and the herd trembles. A small voice speaks a single, clear-bright word.

"Damn."

The zebras echo him, reverently whisper, "Damn."

The head vanishes. Nothing more emerges and the herd leader gets down to business.

"Hole," she announces. "Hole. There's a hole here. Mind your hooves. Mind your legs."

The herd recovers, taking up the chant and fixing the danger in their memory. "Hole. Mind your hooves. Hole."

Elephant Paddock

Shanti has eaten all her peanuts. Her computations have been erased by The-one-who-sweeps. She stands outside her shelter, in the dark, and tries to count the stars. There are too many lights still on in the zoo, and the heavenly bodies seem to fade in and out, shifting positions as if to spoil her work.

As if taunting her.

She thinks it is unnatural for the night to be so well-lit and swings her trunk in frustration. Shanti rocks on pillar legs and begins again. Six bright stars in a cluster.

She is sorry she ate the peanuts, which were exceptional for counting. For a while she tried to use the straw, but straw is fleeting, too easy to blow aside with even the slightest of sighs.

Shanti swings her trunk. Six stars. She thumps a nearby rock that certainly wasn't there a moment ago.

One rock.

"Hello?

One *tortoise*. He surges forward one short step, and Shanti can see the curve of his shell, the extended neck, and flat-faced head.

"Am I outside the fence?" he asks.

"That depends," Shanti whispers.

"On what?"

"On which fence you mean and which side is outside."

He looks at her for a long time. She can see his two tiny eyes. She can see a pattern of shapes on his shell.

"You're an elephant," he says.

"Yes." Shanti begins to count the shapes.

"Damn." He swivels, shifts so that the patterns move.

"Wait." Shanti imagines she could count them all. If he held still, she could. If he were to follow her into the lighted shelter. The patterns on his shell line up perfectly, orderly, one against the next.

"I'm sorry," he says. "I have to get outside the fence."

"I know how."

Shanti has counted the loose spots, the places she can lift and bend, and he is not nearly as big as an elephant. For a tortoise, there would be more than enough room. If she lifted. If she pried.

If he would only agree to a little bargain.

The Crow

Debra listens to the hyena weep while the sun sets. She perches on the guard rail beside the path, and she tilts her head from one side to the other. When the noises become unbearable, grating, she flies away, circling the cat house and the larger enclosures around it. Tiger. Lion. Bear.

As dark falls, the pathway lights are triggered. She darts between them, an invisible shadow, like death.

Eventually, she settles outside the macaque's cage. He is her favorite victim, but tonight he sulks inside the ape house. His little door is open, but even if he *can* hear her taunts, what fun could she find in them without witnessing his reactions?

Frustrated, she paces the top of the 'Jungle' sign. Every three hops she turns, reverses direction, and changes her view.

Savannah, hop, hop, hop. Jungle, hop hop, hop.

Perhaps she should rejoin the murder, but lately their gossip reeks of repetition. Debra considers inventing something, manufacturing some scandal, but she is a bird of very small imagination.

Just as she decides to relent, however, a sharp creaking drags her back to the Savannah view. Metal complains in the darkness. Something large moves against the linked-chain fence.

Debra bounces once before launching. She flaps. She soars, landing in a tree beside the picnic area. She watches, first with one eye and then the other, as the elephant pries up the bottom of her fence.

The gap the mighty trunk makes is ridiculously small. Not big enough to let its own head escape. But it is not the elephant which squeezes through the opening. It is something low and round. Something that trundles out of the Savannah and steps slowly onto free, green grass.

"Escape." At first Debra whispers. Then, she takes to wing. She circles the darkened cages, circles, and is first to chant it into every ear. "Escape. Escape."

The night rings with her gossip, her triumph.

Escape.

It begins. She feels it like a held breath, like the first pebble forewarning the landslide. Someone is *free.*

Someone is bound to be shot.

Ape House

Gonzo remains inside the house after the rest of his troop emerges. Some days, They-who-bring-food linger in the aisle between the cages. They chatter in their barking voices. Some days they bring the bean with them, and the ape house interior fills with the scent of home.

Gonzo was not born in the house. He remembers a Formosan jungle. He remembers freedom and long afternoons lounging on a branch chewing bean.

Today, the aisle clears quickly, however. He is alone in a world of stone and metal, a concrete maze of parallel bars and tiny square doorways.

His troop is excited about something. Gonzo hears the other male screeching, shaking the rope perches. The females echo him, and a rain of spit seeds and tossed debris patters against the outer wall and floor.

Gonzo rubs his head and face with both paws. He approaches the square door, but does not exit. He listens, and he hears the voice of birds.

"Loose in the zoo."

It is not the rotten crow's voice and carries little of taunt or terror. Gonzo shows the doorway his teeth and ambles into a sunlit morning.

"Someone has escaped!" The youngest female macaque is on him before he takes a step. She lands on top of Gonzo, dropping from the ropes, and just as quickly rolls off.

His head aches. He brushes her off with his paws even though she is already bounding away.

The troop gathers at the front of their territory, where a pair of pigeons strut along the path.

"Turtle," one coos.

The other corrects her. "Tortoise. Free."

Gonzo eyes the sky, the jungle sign, and the rail beside the path. There is no sign of the crow. He drags himself to a far corner, to a place both separate from the troop and near enough to hear the pigeons' chatter.

"Someone is free."

Gonzo's lips stretch. He offers a silent screech, a mute tribute. The-one-who-sweeps approaches, and already he can smell his mistress on the wind.

Hyena Pen

Alice pants atop her stair-step rock. She has spent the morning chasing pigeons, racing from one end of her enclosure to the next, snapping her jaws and snarling at the noisy birds.

They spread lies. Their fat beaks chant of freedom and escape.

Alice hates them.

She will crush their bones if they venture inside the bars. She will chomp and chew while their fat, feathered bodies twitch in her jaws.

Once, when the pups were only just taking their first steps, Alice caught a pigeon unawares. Feigning sleep, she lulled it into a sense of safety, and when it waddled between the bars to search for scraps among her straw, Alice killed and ate it.

The pups were too young then. Too young to learn her trick. What if they are hungry now?

She cackles and glares out through her bars. In the shade of a flowering shrub beside the path, a great stone has appeared. Alice is certain it was not there when she awoke, and she wonders if rocks are born. If they come into the world with pain and panting, or if they simply sprout like the grass and flowers.

She's never seen a new stone before and has always assumed they just *are*. Always there. Always in the same place.

She flicks her tail at a persistent fly and wonders if the rock has a mother. If, somewhere, a larger stone doesn't wonder where this one has gone.

VIDEO FOOTAGE

The video is activated by motion. It streams to the Internet according to a randomized order of camera hierarchy. On the zoo's website, a simple flash player shuffles through cages beneath the boldfaced type reading: ZOO CAM.

Someone's nephew has, upon suggestion, programmed the feed to respond to viewer interest. The more clicks on a particular feed, the more often that camera is displayed. It takes only four hours for the elephant house to dominate the feed. In 24, the recorded highlight video, quickly dubbed, "Asian Elephant Pets Turtle," has gone viral.

On screens all over the world, the elephant traces the multi-faceted shell with her trunk, slowly, methodically. Theories abound as to the nature of the animals' relationship. One commenter remarks that she almost appears to be counting, but they are quickly shot down in favor of more romantic interpretations.

Another points out that the 'turtle' in question is actually a Sulcata tortoise. They are mocked into silence.

When someone questions the presence of a turtle inside the elephant's enclosure, the moderator quickly turns off commenting.

The page views continue to escalate.

Grizzly Grotto

Hector lies on his back with three paws in the air. The fourth cradles half a melon against his chest, saved for a later treat. His head turns to one side so that he may watch the artist as she captures yet another glorious Hector portrait.

All morning long he has been bombarded by birds.

First, the crows came, singing of tragedy. Then the pigeons, clattering and talking over one another. Hector ignores all gossip. He cares little for what happens outside his trench. Inside it, there is only him. Only bear and stump and the attention showered upon him by the artist.

As a cub, Hector was bottle-fed, cradled by They-who-cared, and fawned over almost continuously. When he played with his brother, they would clap and coo. When the cubs wrestled, They-who-cared cheered.

Now his brother is gone. Hector only remembers him as the one who shared this affection. He does not share any longer. Here behind his trench, Hector is the star.

The artist finishes and flips her book around. She shows him her work, always seeks his approval upon finishing.

Hector rolls slowly to a sitting position. He gazes up to the railing, but it is too far. His eyes are not what they once were. Still, he growls agreeably before stuffing the melon half between his jaws. He approves.

The artist claps.

They understand one another. This is the way of things, and Hector likes everything exactly as it is. When another pigeon flutters past the stump, he slaps at it, sends it and its gossip on their way.

He cares nothing for what happens beyond the trench. The bear, the star, is forever on this side of the world.

Lion Enclosure

Charlie hears the birds arguing, but he is too busy rolling in dung to worry. They have brought him a half dozen fresh zebra droppings, and the scent drives him to a frenzy.

His mouth hangs open. He huffs over and over until the odor threatens to overwhelm him. His sides heave. His long tail lashes.

"Escape."

A stupid crow has broken from its flock. It bounces on a nearby stump where the two lionesses that make up Charlie's pride are lounging in the sun.

"Go away." His favorite lioness yawns, showing the bird her teeth in warning.

The crow caws and flaps but remains foolishly in place. Determined. "Someone has escaped."

"Lie," the lioness says.

Beside her, another purrs agreement. It is well known that crows are not to be trusted.

"Someone is out," the bird insists. "They'll be shot for certain."

Charlie huffs and flattens his ears to his skull.

"Who is it?" The female decides to believe the gossip. Her tail-tip, however, twitches, a sure sign she is also considering pouncing on the messenger.

"The tortoise," the crow cackles.

"They'll catch *him* for sure," the lioness says. "But they won't shoot him. They only shoot *fierce* animals." She says it proudly, as if she dares them to try.

Charlie thinks that he is fierce. He thinks the tortoise will be found quickly, but he agrees with the lioness. No one will shoot it.

He has lived at the zoo his whole life, and no one has ever been shot.

The dung bores him now. His head is full of *escape* and *freedom*. There is no room left for odors, however delicious.

At the far end of the enclosure, a crowd has gathered at the railing, at the glass. Charlie heaves himself to his paws and shakes his head, lets his thick mane shiver before stalking toward the gathered morsels.

Tortoise Abroad

Oliver moves in darkness. He has forgotten how cold the world is outside his desert, and how slowly he is forced to move when his limbs are chilled.

When he first emerges from the bushes, a terrible noise assaults him. It takes Oliver two rocking steps to discover the sound is coming from an animal.

There is a barred cage across from his hiding spot. It is raised on a concrete foundation, and there is a fake rock in one corner with many levels. Near the bars, a hyena gapes at him.

Oliver stretches his neck by way of greeting and takes another step.

"Stone," she says. "You are very strange."

"Tortoise," Oliver says. It takes a great deal of his energy to speak.

"No," the hyena laughs. "I'm a hyena."

"Yes." Oliver has lived many lifetimes. He believes a hyena should know a tortoise when she sees one. This one, therefore, has been in a cage her entire life.

He stops moving when he's near enough to look straight up at her.

"Have you seen Miranda?"

"I saw you born," the hyena whispers fiercely. "Do stones have mothers?"

"My mother eats in distant fields," Oliver says. Does she understand? He knows that animals born in the zoo often have unnatural ways of thinking. Is it a waste of his time and energy to linger? He has only a few hours until he must hide again.

"That's sad." The hyena moans and covers her muzzle with both front paws. "I'm sorry."

"I'm looking for a tall bird," Oliver says. Before he can describe his love, the hyena barks an answer.

"Aviary." She surprises him with her confidence. Her head lifts, ears flicking and eyes wide and lucid. "All birds are kept in the aviary."

"Except pigeons," Oliver says.

"And stupid crows." The hyena nods. In this, they fully understand one another.

"But Miranda lives in *my* enclosure," Oliver says. "And she's a bird."

"They were probably just waiting for someone to die," the hyena says.

Oliver thinks she's still talking about crows until she finishes.

"They were just keeping her with you until a cage was free."

Oliver hates this idea, but it is probably correct. He has not planned what to do when he finds Miranda, and he imagines They-who-bring-food simply stealing her away again. He imagines it will be difficult to free her from this aviary. What if the floor, like the hyena's, is thick concrete?

"It's the second path." The hyena's voice brings him back. She is urgent, pressing against the bars and speaking in a squeaking rush. "It's not far. Just take the second path."

"Thank you." He pivots, thinking of bars and concrete.

The hyena watches him go, panting, making sporadic, sharp cackles as he steps. One slow foot after the other. When he is near to the second path, she calls out again.

"That's it. That one there."

Oliver pretends he cannot hear her. He takes the path, though, and her cackles chase him, her final proclamation rings out.

"Very strange stone."

Aviary

The aviary is never silent. Inside its twin pair of double safety doors, hundreds of birds dwell in a state of constant communication.

Sometimes the voices are soft, contemplative. Sometimes they are a trumpet's blast, a declaration of activity and interaction. If the butterfly house is a held breath, the aviary is a conversation, a steady, unrelenting chorus of voices in all registers.

Thousands of plants grow inside. Stout tropical trees, low bushes, and layer upon layer of climbing vine, creeper, palm, fern, and orchid. The air is thick, wet, and aromatic. A false river wanders across the floor beneath the bamboo bridges and the hanging paths. It adds its babble to the cacophony, singing a soft, low, steady baseline to the avian voices.

Above it, hidden among the fronds and branches, birds of every shape and size warble, tweet, caw, and hoot. Tiny, high-pitched voices titter. Large, booming voices honk and squawk.

The flutter of beaks in motion is only matched by the occasional explosion of wings as the flocks of iridescent bodies shift position from one perch to the next.

Every day, the aviary sings non-stop. When one voice pauses, another speaks into the gap. Every breath is sound and secret.

Today, they sing a song of freedom. They sing of liberation and escape. Outside their walls they hear the lesser birds' gossip. Inside, they make of it a cantata, an aria, a symphony of excitement.

Escape is not unknown here, despite the signs on all the double doors that read: Please Close Outside Door Before Opening Interior Door. They-who-open-doors do not follow rules, and someone leaves from time to time.

The aviary sings of their foolishness for days afterward.

It is cold outside. It is often dry and dark and unforgiving.

"Escape," the aviary sings. "Escape. The last desperate act of fools."

See part I of Frances Pauli's story "The Zoo Diaries" online at Metaphorosis.
If you liked it, leave a comment. Authors love that!
Remember to subscribe to our e-mail updates so you'll know when new stories are posted.

About the story

"The Zoo Diaries" came about as the result of a challenge given me by a dear author friend. He suggested we spend a full year waking up each morning and writing by hand, a single, self-contained entry of micro fiction that would string together over the months into a cohesive story. Despite the fact that I am not a morning person, and the idea of an even earlier start caused me to break out in hives, I accepted the challenge based on two things. First, I had (and alas, still do) a surplus of lovely blank journals which were simply begging to be written in by hand. Second, I trusted the wisdom of this particular author friend and wanted to see how my prose shifted and deepened when I took the time to write long form. The idea for "The Zoo Diaries" came to me when I was searching for a concept that could be told in an episodic fashion, in short bursts each morning. I decided to tell the story of a zoo and its inmates, but to pass that story from one cage to the other each day, in the fashion of gossip whispered from one animal to the next so that the tale might travel even though its tellers were not allowed that freedom.

A question for the author

Q: What's easier for you- imagining a happier world, or a darker one?

A: I'm not sure it's easier, but I do my best to imagine a happier world, to focus my energies on how we can improve life on this planet rather than to give energy to the ways in which we might sink deeper into darkness. Imagination has power, and I believe in focusing that toward the goal of a brighter future, to inspire myself to act in ways that can contribute to that potential.

About the author

Frances Pauli lives in Washington state with her family, a small menagerie, and far too many houseplants. She enjoys a plant-based, vegan lifestyle, animal activism, and of course, reading. She writes stories about animal characters, often in the speculative fiction category.

francespauli.com, @mothindarkness

February

The Excursionist of JCPenney

Chris Panatier

Lorraine sat in the passenger seat of the Buick with four flat tires, applying her usual shade of lipstick. The fact that the tires were flat was no bother; the car hadn't moved since her mother died twenty years before. Even if Lorraine could afford to get it running again, it wouldn't make any difference. She didn't know how to drive.

Doing her face in the Buick had been the routine going back to when mom would give her a lift to her job and she saw no reason to stop just because mom was dead. So, every morning at seven forty-five, she emerged from the senior living studio condominium that had been Mom's and was now hers, walked the fifteen steps to the petrified sedan, and eased herself into the passenger seat. Mom had been gone since Lorraine was forty-six, but their relationship remained complicated.

She imagined her mother sitting in the driver's seat, asking if Lorraine had her nametag and lunch—inquiries that Lorraine silently resented, because of course she did, she wasn't a child. Lorraine did miss the ride to work—the Florida summers were excruciating—but she didn't miss the condescension.

With her lips done, she dropped the stick into her purse. Mornings were the worst, when her brain wasn't yet occupied by work and was free to simmer about her life's many grievances. "I was smart," she declared, digging for the eyeliner. "As smart as Connie and way smarter than Mary." She took hold of the gear shift and wiggled it in frustration. "They were just pretty faces." If the family hadn't treated her like a helpless imbecile her whole life, then she might have built some independence. Even now, Mary had control of Lorraine's finances, which was a particularly sour twist of the knife.

She lined her left eye, then the right—the droopy one—as quickly as she could. Some mornings she just wanted to stab the pencil right through it. Better that people assumed she'd lost it to an accident, than make assumptions about her intelligence because of it. It barely worked anyway. The world was a jumble of color and shape through the bad eye, a kaleidoscope of fractured images that never quite made sense. The pieces always seemed to be drifting toward cohesion, but without ever actually arriving, the full picture just out of reach. Lorraine took it as a cruel taunt from the Universe. Sometimes, in angry bouts of spite, she would hold the eye open past the point when it seared, until her pain-addled mind composed mosaics of the broken pieces. Occasionally, the habit brought on strange glimpses of new places—faraway settings and locations that seemed real enough—but always distant and out of reach. Mostly, her eye just hurt.

Lorraine zipped her purse, checked her nametag, and stood from the car, grunting as she slammed the door. The sound might have been from the exertion or displeasure at her mother's memory. She supposed it was a dose of each.

Work didn't start for another hour and fifteen, but the walk took fifty minutes and she would need another ten or twenty to cool off once she arrived. She headed down the treeless road and around the pond rumored to have crocodiles or alligators—she could never remember the difference—and finally past the unoccupied guard station at the front of the community.

Turning down Greenwich Parkway, Lorraine mumbled her resentment. Her old familiar. She'd carried it with her since childhood, when people assumed she was inadequate because of the eye or her halting speech. She knew it wasn't the right way to live, spending so much of her energy detesting those who judged her. If only they'd given her a chance, she might have made friends. Might have cut the tethers that had kept her trapped. Might have seen the world.

But resentment was a loop, wasn't it? A vicious circle or whatever the term was. You decided to resent people even before they could judge you. And then they judged you anyway.

She pushed through the big glass doors to the store. This was the best part of her day, the move from sweltering heat to the frozen, artificial air. It was a transformation. Outside, she was an afterthought. But at JCPenney, she was important. *Essential.* She belonged. Part of a team that made the store go, all one hundred and forty-three thousand square feet of it. Lorraine knew every inch. So well, in fact, that her words didn't pile up if she had to tell a customer in Fine Jewelry how to get to the Home section. A senior member of the store, she could jump into any department, take inventory, fold blouses, even stock shelves if they didn't demand too high a reach. Her brain held a photo-perfect topographical map, with every product in its place. She could recite department, aisle, and shelf for over thirty-four thousand individual items, and had cold command of the on-line catalogue as well.

Roberta, the store supervisor, was sitting at one of the white tables in the break room, facing the tiny TV perched up in the corner. Roberta was the only employee with tenure over Lorraine, and had even hired her—which was a bit of a miracle, all things considered. Lorraine had managed to get in the door at a lot of places even though she only had high school, but the droopy eye and manner of talking had people cutting the interviews short.

It was Roberta who'd first offered her a job. She didn't seem to notice or care about her speech or her eye. In fact, Roberta's indifference to it made Lorraine want to tell her everything—like a strange reward for being decent. She wanted Roberta to know that her difficulties had no bearing on smarts, that she'd only made the mistake of getting near her father once while he was All The Way Drunk, and had walked away with a tongue that struggled with words and an eye that would never see the world the same way again. But beautiful Roberta didn't care about the eye. And Lorraine loved her for it.

"Hi, Roberta," said Lorraine, setting her bag onto the counter near the coffee machine. The pot hadn't been started and so she began the process. A filter from the cabinet, water from the sink, four level scoops from the tin. She snapped in the basket and hit the brew button, then turned to Roberta. "Roberta?"

"Headquarters sent out a list of store closures."

Lorraine didn't even register the words. They sounded like corporate speak and corporate speak was something Lorraine had learned to tune out. She let the phrase dissipate in the air and filled a mug with tap water, then sat across from her boss. "Did you see the hand truck of toasters sitting in the aisle between Baby and Women's?"

Roberta had her head down, face in hands. Lorraine twisted around and glanced at the television to see if there was bad news, but it was just a commercial for The Rug Guy. Turning back, she said, "Roy must have forgotten to bring them to the stockroom at the end of his shift last night. I can get them on the shelves before we open if there's space. I think—"

"Lorraine," said Roberta, looking up, eyes red and wet. "I had to fire Roy."

Lorraine shifted her feet beneath her chair like trying to regain her footing in reality. "Fire Roy?" Roy was a silver-level team member and second only to Lorraine in Employee of the Month Awards received. "Why did you do that?"

"This was corporate's call. You know I'd never fire Roy of my own accord. I've been told to thin the ranks, starting with highest paid team members."

Lorraine allowed herself a moment to resent the fact that Roy had been paid more than her, but he could cover Customer Service and her words piled up in the face of adversity. She refocused on Roberta. "Why did headquarters tell you to do that?"

"We're being shut down, Lorraine. The company is trying to keep from going under, so they're closing the biggest stores."

Lorraine watched Roberta's bright orange lips move, but the words didn't compute. None of them. She thought instead about how the neon hue made Roberta's mouth seem electric and wished that she were daring enough to wear the same color. *Mango, Darling.*

"Lorraine?" said Roberta. "Did you hear me?

"We're…closing?" Lorraine's mind raced to plug the hole in her understanding. "Is it because of the Hitler tea kettle?"

Back in 2013, the company had sold a teapot that people said looked like Hitler. Her father had fought against Hitler and Lorraine didn't think the teapot looked like the Führer at all. At the time she'd surmised that Sears or Dillard's had pushed the narrative to try and steal market share and she still hadn't seen any evidence to exonerate them. Whatever the motivation, the damage had been done, and in the years since, Lorraine traced any problems within the company back to the kettle.

"It's not the tea kettle," said Roberta. "They're trying to avoid bankruptcy."

"By closing us? Don't you need money to avoid bankruptcy? How are they going to make money if they close us?"

"I don't know all the details, just what they've told me. Apparently, they think this is the company's best chance to survive."

"And it's…permanent?"

"For us it is."

Suddenly, Lorraine was back home inside the musty condo with her mom's threadbare flower-print furniture and Sudoku towers. She'd never find another Roberta; another someone who would see past her age and her eye and her speech. Without a job, she was just another old woman sitting in a chair in a room. Stumbling into the community pond with the crocodiles or whatchamacallits seemed a more desirable outcome.

Roberta reached across the table, snatching Lorraine's hands away from her mug. "Once I let Tabitha and Jamarcus go, it'll be just me, you, and three babies left to run the whole place, Lorraine." Babies was Roberta's term for anyone under thirty. "They're giving us two weeks. Clearance begins on Thursday."

The word was like hearing a terminal diagnosis. *Clearance.* And it was. For the store, for Lorraine. She stood, defiant. "Did they even come and see our store? How well it's run? The ratio we keep between stock and display? How we use our shelf space? Nobody comes close—not even marketing, I've seen the catalogue pictures, Roberta." She'd begun sweating again.

"Sweetheart. We're done. Two weeks. Then the doors close." Roberta had kind eyes and they were trying to make Lorraine feel better. "They say when one door closes, another opens."

The clearance sale came even though Lorraine had asked God to stop it.

That morning, she stared into the Buick's visor mirror, lipstick rising from her fist like a tiny popsicle on the verge of melting. The first day of the store's dying. A countdown to the end of the world. Maybe, if she stayed put, she could stop time. A bead of sweat fell from the tip of her nose, marking a perfectly round spot of burgundy on her scarlet blouse.

Snapping out of the daydream, Lorraine capped the lipstick and pushed out from the car. Walking past the guard house, she closed her good eye and let the bad one burn. Through the crooked shards of pained vision, a picture coalesced: a land cut right from a fairytale, an afternoon sky over a waterfall with the sun putting rainbows in the spray. She shut her eyes and let the sting dissipate. If only to go there. If only to go anywhere.

Customers milled about outside the store, even though it was an hour before opening. The front doors, once gleaming expanses of spotless plate glass, were now plastered with crooked yellow posters declaring the store's end like a retail obituary.

CLEARANCE SALE
GOING OUT OF BUSINESS!
UP TO 75% OFF

EVERYTHING MUST GO

The words cut, and Lorraine frowned and gritted her teeth as she entered. Someone tried to follow her inside. "Not open!" she snapped. "Yet...sorry."

Roberta raced back and forth beyond the second set of doors, putting signs into place atop racks of women's Fall coats. "Oh, Lorraine, good," she said, puffing her lips.

Lorraine had never seen Roberta so harried. It was almost more disconcerting than the ugly signs defacing the storefront. Any illusions Lorraine had of their branch being rescued were truly fantasy.

"They'll be here for everything, but clothes will go first. I need you in the change room. It'll be a zoo back there and I don't trust the babies to maintain order."

"What will the babies do?"

"I'll put Stacy on Home—if she shows up—Kevin on Menswear, Sanja on Women's. I'll float. It's gonna be a shitshow, Lorraine."

Lorraine grimaced at the use of curse words, but quickly forgave because Roberta was understaffed and deserved better.

Not five minutes after the doors opened, customers flooded the changing room, arms stacked with clothes swept in chunks from the racks.

Lorraine deftly guided them into stalls, abandoning any thought of enforcing the five-item maximum. Unpurchased items quickly clogged the rooms, which she cleared as best she could before others rushed in with what they'd hoarded.

Returning to the counter with a load she'd recovered from stall eight, she began folding and hanging. The quicker the turnaround, the more likely they'd sell and... She knew she was clinging to the foolish hope that if they did well enough, corporate would rethink their decision to close them. As skilled as she was in folding and hanging, there was no keeping up as the clothes quickly swallowed the counter and piled into a mound that would take her hours to get through.

Roberta swept in sometime later, already talking. "Lorraine? Just take your lunch in here, if you don't mind—" She paused, spotting Lorraine amid the mountains of clothes. "Oh my God."

Lorraine shrugged, hanging a blouse onto an extra rack she'd brought in. Roberta leaned over the counter to see the full extent of the disaster. She sighed and set her head down on her hands. "Why bother, Lorraine?"

A wave of heat splashed across Lorraine's face. Why bother? This was her life! Their life! The words tangled on her tongue before she could say it.

Roberta saw her anger. "Lorraine. My doll." She stepped aside as a woman from Room Six returned a collection of winter clothing. "You have to let it go. You'll die of exhaustion if you try to get all of this back out on display. Just clear the rooms out and..." she waved her hands helplessly.

"And give up?"

Roberta searched Lorraine's face. "Hey," she said, softening her voice. "If it helps you get through it, then...I don't see any harm. Get it *all* back on the floor if you want to, it makes no difference to me. Just please, take a break. And hey: if you see anything you like, set it aside. I'm making sure we all get our due for going through this."

"But—"

"The clearance pricing plus our employee discounts will bring this stuff to near zero anyway." She mimed some finger tapping. "The rest I can handle with my manager's override. Consider it your severance." She slid her arm behind the clothes that Lorraine had reassembled on the rack and lifted them from the rod. "I'll bring these back out on the floor."

Lorraine watched Roberta disappear into the hallway, then turned to the pile of coats returned by the woman. One of them was quite nice, a long, beige number with a narrow waist and a stylish hood. She eyed the rooms for any sign that she was needed and then took it up. *Where was it,* Lorraine wondered, *that she was planning to go with such a heavy jacket?* Somewhere faraway from Florida, that much was clear.

Defiantly, she thrust her arms into the sleeves, connected the zipper and yanked it to her neck, then flipped up the hood. She felt immediately idiotic, standing there in a coat she'd never buy, pretending to have a life she didn't have. Pathetic. She shut her good eye and let the bad eye burn.

An image appeared through the broken window of her vision. Triangles of blue and blinding white. But then the cracks melted away and the picture became clear. No longer was she a distant observer. It felt like she had leapt right into—

A blast of bitter wind stung her cheeks. Snow. A cloudless expanse of sky above. Turning in place, she was faced with a mountain. It loomed over her so high that it seemed ready to topple and flatten her into the earth. Terrified, panicking, she flipped the hood down. Then she was back in the changing room.

She scrambled to unzip the coat and let it drop to the ground. She rubbed her face against the lingering chill. A man emerged from Room One with some track pants and paused. He pulled a headphone from an ear and loud music pounded out. "Ma'am? You alright?"

The words piled up. Lorraine smiled bashfully and nodded. When he was gone, she doubled over and gasped for breath, then stood, wide eyed, heart pounding. The top of her head felt like it was being pulled into orbit. She couldn't place the emotions. It felt something like terror, but that was wrong. Her arms shook all the way to her shoulders. Her stomach fluttered. No, this wasn't terror. This was exhilaration. Euphoria.

An excited squeak leapt from mouth before she could stifle it.

She picked up the coat and flipped it around, inspecting it for...she didn't know what. She set it onto the counter and held her bad eye open again, until an image presented through the burning. It was like it had always been; swathes of color and shape obscured by fractured panes of stained glass. But when she donned the coat again, the mountain returned, bold and tangible as ever.

Quickly, she went to the pants that had just been returned, stepped them on, and hiked them up under her skirt.

A new place reflected clear in the lens of Lorraine's no-good eye. A musical darkness fringed in beams of colorful light. A cheering crowd. A rock band. Was she just watching or was she there? She poked a nearby reveler in the shoulder. They turned and yelled over the noise asking, annoyed, what she wanted.

"I just wanted to see if I'm here!" she answered.

"Yeah?" they said. "I'm not sure if you are."

Lorraine laughed. She wasn't hallucinating. She'd been transported. To a place from the customer's life? The present? The past? The music sounded like what had been pumping out of his headphones. Somehow, the clothes were a link to someplace real and the bad eye was parsing the destination.

Lorraine removed the pants and reentered the changing room. Before her, a teenager leapt backward with a gasp, and stumbled to the floor.

"Sweetheart!" said Lorraine, running over to check on the girl. "Are you okay?"

"The hell?" said the girl, jumping upright and scooting down the wall. "Are you messing with me or something?"

"Uh, no," said Lorraine. "What are you talking about?"

The teen pointed at her with a vaping pen. "You just...just... like. You like, just appeared in front of me."

Lorraine smiled warmly, then looked herself over. "I'm sure I didn't. I've been here all morning. It's the big clearance sale."

The girl glared at her vape pen, then rushed out of the room. Lorraine considered the heap of clothes left on the floor and marveled at what secrets they might hold. Not having the time to try on every garment that came back, she added the teen's jean jacket and leggings to the hoard behind the counter.

Just after five-thirty, Roberta trudged into the change room. "I don't know how we're going to do this for ten days straight."

Lorraine, noting that she didn't feel at all tired, continued briskly organizing returns. "It will be a challenge," she said, with every intention of meeting it. "You look exhausted." She ordered her words and added, "I'll do the register drops tonight so you can get home to rest."

Roberta looked at her like she'd just emerged from a cocoon. Lorraine felt like she had.

"I'm fine to stay," Lorraine continued enthusiastically, snapping a pair of slacks straight and securing the waistband to the trouser clamps. "I must have caught a second wind."

Roberta surveyed Lorraine's face, then raised her eyebrows, relenting. "Yes. Fine. I will take you up on that. Did you eat anything at all today?"

Lorraine *had* eaten—a delicious basket of fried plantains from a street vendor somewhere along the coast of Africa and a bowl of hot pot chicken on a hillside in China. "I had a little something, yes."

"Aren't you bright-eyed and bushy-tailed," said Roberta the following morning. "You didn't—you didn't stay here all night, did you?"

"Roberta," said Lorraine. "I wouldn't skip my nightly bath." She hadn't skipped her bath. She'd swum in the Mediterranean Sea just off the coast of Greece in a bathing suit tried on by a woman who had mentioned an upcoming trip to Crete.

The next nine days of clearance were much the same as the first, except that Lorraine now braved the waters of conversation with any person who would talk, eagerly peppering them with questions about their travels. This helped her decide which of their discarded try-ons to put in the Keep pile. If they'd been to a fascinating place, she held onto something they'd tried on. Amidst her elation, words came easier.

The locked-down doors and shuttered windows of Lorraine's world had blown open. Each day was a slide show, with tours of foreign lands done seconds at a time. She popped in and out of existence on the coastline of California, the prow of a fishing boat somewhere cold, a trail deep inside a tropical jungle, a fancy restaurant in a big city, a café in Vietnam.

The stock dwindled as the sale dragged on, and so did the crowds. Fewer folks were finding much to their liking, and eventually Lorraine was left on her own. Conveniently secluded in the change room, she made notes on the tags and organized the items according to geography, then made her purchases at the end of shift, and lugged them home. At night, she slept more soundly than ever, dreaming about the places she'd visited—ten lifetimes' worth in just a week—and upon waking, longed to return.

By the end, the store looked like it had caged a typhoon. No amount of running about by the few remaining employees had been enough to maintain order. Their time was at an end, with the corporate movers set to come in and clear out the rest.

Placing their keys in the cash register drawer, they headed toward the front, each of them carrying as much discount merchandise as they could. Kevin, whose arms overflowed with fancy sheets, karate-kicked a mannequin. Roberta laughed. Lorraine side stepped the rolling head without a thought, all pretense of decorum having melted away over the preceding days. That chapter of her life had ended. A new one was about to be written.

Lorraine hit the lights as the babies said casual goodbyes and rushed off to live their lives. She followed Roberta outside and waited as her ex-boss secured the deadbolts.

"They're making me mail the keys to corporate," she said, battling a lock. "Ridiculous."

Lorraine pointed to the pressure cooker sitting at Roberta's feet, the last of several small appliances the supervisor acquired during clearance. "I think you're even."

Roberta chuckled as she secured the final door and pocketed the key. "Yeah, you have a point. So…what are you going to do?"

Lorraine shook out her hands and picked up the swollen bags she'd carried out. "Oh, I'm going to do some traveling."

"Traveling!" Roberta laughed, shaking her head. "You don't even drive, doll. The only traveling you do is from this door to your mother's condo and back. What are you talking about, *traveling*?"

"One door closes and another opens. You said that."

"Honey, that's just what people tell other people when they get laid off."

"No," said Lorraine, "you were right."

"Whatever you say, doll." She gave Lorraine a hug. "Need a ride home with all that?"

"No thanks. I could use the fresh air," said Lorraine, backing down the walk. "I'll bring you back a souvenir!"

"I look forward to it."

The next morning, Lorraine sat in the Buick, a tightly packed duffle of clothes resting in her lap. The store was still laid out in her brain, but she'd pushed the products from the shelves and filled them instead with articles of clothing, each one signifying a new destination.

Her outfit was a purple warmup suit left in Room Two by a woman about her size, who had gone on and on about plans for a trip she took every year to a majestic spot in the mountains of Venezuela. Hearing the woman talk about it, Lorraine felt like she already knew the place, and took that as a nudge from the Universe.

She looked into the mirror and smiled despite the heat; despite the eye that didn't line up and the tongue that sabotaged her speech. She felt the weight of it all slip from her shoulders; her own limitations, her resentments. With her world grown large, all of that felt so small now.

From her pocket, she retrieved a brand-new tube of lipstick, color: *Mango, Darling*. She twisted it up, slathered her lips orange, then smacked them. She stowed the lipstick, took hold of the jacket's bright yellow zipper, and drew it to the top of the collar.

Her destination appeared in pieces through the prism of her eye, then suddenly she was there. A land cut right from a fairy tale. A waterfall with the sun making rainbows of the spray.

See Chris Panatier's story "The Excursionist of JCPenney" online at Metaphorosis.
If you liked it, leave a comment. Authors love that!
Remember to subscribe to our e-mail updates so you'll know when new stories are posted.

About the story

The story is loosely based upon a relative of mine. I am very close to her and there is a good bit of her wrapped up in the character of Lorraine. For much of her life I feel she's been underestimated, underappreciated, and in a lot of ways nearly invisible. I wanted to tell the story of someone like that, because people like my relative don't seem on first glance to be main character material. They're overlooked by definition, usually in favor of a character who appears more dynamic on the surface.

A question for the author

Q: What's the story no one else thinks is as good as you do?

A: I'm going to suggest a story that no one thinks is as good as I do, but only because it's new and relatively few people have read it. It's a short novel called *Little Future, The Ghost* by Daniel Cohen and it's the most blistering satire of capitalism and technoculture I've ever read. Other than being satire, it's impossible to categorize, but utterly genius and thought provoking. Absolutely brutal.

About the author

Chris lives in Dallas, Texas with his wife and daughter. He does art, writes short fiction and novels, and occasionally practices law.

www.chrispanatier.com, @chrisjpanatier

The Frozen Generation

Jacob Coffin

Compared to my coworkers, I didn't get many death threats. Storage, my department, was usually overlooked by fanatics and politicians.

They saved their anger for the people up front who made the Frozen Generation — the doctors and administrators who met the clients, did the scans, fed in the waldos, extracted the mingled cells, vitrified them in cryofluid. My crew in Storage were just the ones who tended them forever after.

They had their reasons for overlooking us. The Frozen were an easy demographic to advocate for, and an easier population to have when it came time to allocate votes and funds. But most people in this state would still tell you that extraction destined for cryostasis was just abortion with less guilt. Those people had gotten their way tonight, expanded the definition of abortion to include any extraction not destined for immediate gestation. And banned it.

Their new laws were going to close the clinic, maybe for a long time. But that wasn't my main concern. They'd also upped the charges for embryonic deaths in an extraction clinic and, tonight of all nights, I'd received notice of a blackout across the entire facility.

That's why I was in my truck, racing back to work as fast as I could drive after only two hours of sleep and despite the crowds celebrating in the streets.

We had backups. We were a priority repair site by law. We were seriously overbuilt for the two-hour limit the power company had to have us fixed by. But my team would be scared, and I wasn't going to let them deal with this alone. After all, they knew as well as I did that technically, under the new laws, any failure onsite could cost us our lives.

I made some calls as I got on the freeway. The front office didn't answer. No one on my crew knew what had happened yet, except that the power was definitely out and only for us.

The protestors had probably just shot out a transformer. They did that sometimes when they were celebrating. Tonight, that was really the best-case scenario.

The scattered fireworks popping low over the rooftops, the crowds in the streets around the churches, and the 3 a.m. rush hour traffic were enough to tell me tonight wasn't a night for best-case anything. But I wasn't thinking clearly.

Cars were already filling up vacant lots in the industrial park we called home. Armed silhouettes with posterboard signs grouped together in the early-morning dark and chill. The usuals claiming their spots early, maybe. Either way they'd have a big crowd today — some of our neighbors even rented their lots to them.

I was scanning the parking lots as I went — more from habit than because of the news tonight. I like to think I've gotten pretty good at watching my surroundings, even when I'm tired and stressed. After a protestor follows you home, you find your motivation.

The crowd got thicker once I was close enough to see the place. The clinic had already been pretty ugly, sort of a warehouse trying to turn into a bunker, but it was folks like these who had put the finishing touches on it, decorated the outside with scorch marks and bullet-pocks.

Speaking of bullets: one of them took a shot at me.

I honestly hadn't been expecting that. The crowd at the gate didn't have the usual rage tonight, though they threw some rocks when I pulled through, just to keep up tradition. I figured they were there more to celebrate and maybe burn our building down later if the police seemed amicable. They'd won, after all; no more need for self-martyrdom.

But once I made the last turn toward the garage, my back windshield exploded.

I hit the gas and slammed down the ramp and out of view before I'd fully processed the gunshot. And then it was over and I was sitting there in the red emergency light of the employee garage with more adrenalin than I needed for work problems and nothing to use it on.

I ran my fingers over tufts of foam in the new hole in my roof while I called the shooter in to our security team. Though God knew what they could do about him. After that was done, it all started to feel real, and I had to pause and get my breathing under control. I knew from experience that if I stayed focused, I could save the real freakout for after I got home and felt safe. And I had a lot of work to do.

The bullet hole was barely in arm's reach. Not a very near miss. Had he been trying to kill me or just scare me and make me run? That pissed me off worse than attempted murder. I could picture them laughing and cheering while I fled out of sight.

If they'd known what department I worked for, would it have made any difference?

I got out, slammed the door, and climbed upstairs in the dark, checking my phone for updates to the alerts that had woken me.

Power failures were the last thing we needed now. Every other supplier we relied on had been flaking for weeks, including our cryofluid producer, now fifteen days late on our delivery. I think they saw which way things were going, knew nobody was going to enforce our protections any longer. Even when a company's official faith didn't oppose extraction, there were always employees who felt that helping us endangered their immortal souls.

No updates on the power alerts. My feed was full of articles on the new laws, but I ignored them.

Don't get me wrong, things were bad, but this back and forth had been happening for my entire life. Hell, this mess of shortcuts and simple solutions was the reason I even existed. As far as I was concerned, this was just a temporary interruption of service until the law got challenged or interrupted somehow.

Even the people who had passed it didn't seem to expect this to last forever. They'd already tried gestating every unwanted embryo and that led to the government hives they then spent decades tearing down, and generations of Unwanted like me who didn't even vote for them. Doing it again with even less planning would be a horrible mess, but banning extraction with no solutions at all would be even worse.

The new laws would make things difficult, but I was trying to focus on what I could control. And for us in Storage, it would be business as usual, more or less.

From here on out it was our job to keep the clinic operational until we could reopen. And new admissions would be on pause, which would give us some time to catch up on maintenance, build some new racks, maybe even upgrade our cryofluid production capabilities if I could mooch some budget while the rest of the work was on hold.

We'd get through this.

Inside, the place was in chaos. Half the lights were off and there were way too many staff here for this time of night. The lobby was locked down, galvanized drop-barricades reflecting the lights back through the glass doors up front.

Ester was cleaning out her desk, taking everything with her name on it. She'd actually grown up in the same hive I did, though she was a later generation, so she was a bit more normal. I was in a hurry, but she looked so freaked out I stopped when we made eye contact.

"Moses, did you hear Dr. Quarzi quit?" she asked. She had her fake-calm, air traffic control voice going.

"What?"

"Yeah, he called in and did it over the phone right after the hearing, from London. He said this will be a huge mess and we should all get out before it starts if we know what's good for us. He'd already cleaned out his files and everything."

I blinked, tired eyes bleary in the bright light, and looked down at her desk. "Taking his advice?"

"Yeah. How about you?"

"I just came in to fix the power. If this place doesn't stay cold, we're all in a lot of trouble."

She gave me this look. "We're in a lot of trouble either way. My boyfriend has family in Canada — we're heading up there. You should get out too."

Wow.

"Uh, best of luck," I said. "Look, you'll be okay, you just do inprocessing."

Still that flat look, like I didn't get it. I guess I didn't. "Yeah. Good luck yourself."

Man, I just kept everything cold.

I hustled through the office, looking for the Operations Director. If the power loss was upstream, then getting it back was her problem. The rest of us just had to keep the outage from harming the patients.

Most everyone I saw was hurrying and worried. Some were unpacking reserve Herz-Stanton exowombs, and the rest looked like they were leaving. I didn't recognize half of them. Sure, most of my work is back in Storage, but I come up once a day to check the tanks in the clinic, write up my maintenance reports, and order parts. I like to think I'm sociable, for a hive boy anyways.

I stopped outside the Ops Director's office. Charlotte was standing over her desk, shouting into the phone, gestures and everything.

She didn't show any sign of slowing down, and with everything else going on, I couldn't wait for answers. Whatever had caused this blackout, I had to check our status.

I headed for Storage, my department. There was a reason that the only clinics left in this state stored their patients on-site: Storage facilities got guarantees. With the nation's most vulnerable citizens in our vaults, reliant on their services, the power and telecom companies couldn't drag their feet for weeks when we got disconnected. More than that, we were allowed to hire armed security, and even got an exemption to the Religious Freedom Act so parts suppliers had to sell to us as long as we could pay. They accused us of a lot; I suppose hostage-taking was fair.

Storage took up most of our site. It was the big, bulky, warehouse-looking part of the facility with the legally-mandated symbols outside, to protect clinic bombers from killing any of the Frozen. Inside, there were thousands and thousands of silver cryo flasks linked with tubes and wires resting on rows of metal shelves, elevated flood-safe, suspended and stabilized against earthquakes and guarded by the most paranoid fire suppression system in the county. Each had an individual battery backup for its sensors and pumps and a small reserve tank of cryofluid.

The manifest for each flask listed the occupants by social security number. No names or assigned sex yet. For the vast majority it was far too early to identify more than the number of cells, and you could usually count those on both hands.

In the back, rising up over it all, was the in-house cryo distillation rig. The patients' storage tanks didn't take power to stay cold; they were just fancy vacuum flasks with sensors. But their cryogenic fluid evaporated in an endless slow boil, and we needed power to monitor the levels and to run the pumps that kept them topped off. The in-house 'still was elevated so we could rely on gravity feeds if we had to.

Cryofluid is pretty complicated stuff. It's mostly liquid nitrogen, but nitro on its own can be a vector for viruses and bacteria between tissue samples. Cryofluid has a mix of additives so we could transfer it safely and to assist with vitrification and devitrification. It was actually overkill for our purposes, as most of our patients were kept in hermetically sealed straws, but our state legislature said nothing was too good for the Frozen Generation (except hives of their own), especially if it made running this place difficult.

As I looked for my crew, I automatically checked the dashboard for each rack of tanks I passed, eyeing the levels and power requirements.

All the levels were lower than I expected.

Some of my techs were shouting over by the loading dock. Zeke saw me and waved me over, calling across the warehouse:

"Mose!" He looked worried, and that worried me.

"Zeke, what's going on?" I asked. "Someone cut the lines?"

"Yeah! The fuckin' power company!"

"What, on purpose?" That cold dread started working its way down my back. They wouldn't. They fucking couldn't.

"Yeah. Told Charlotte on the phone. Can't legally provide services."

"What, because of the abortion definition thing? We're not taking patients and even then it'd only apply to the front office, not Storage." Not us. But the whole place was linked together – that was how the clinic benefited from Storage, after all.

"Yeah. Closed the loophole."

"Loophole, hell. This was their goddamn solution in the first place."

Exowombs were supposed to solve abortion. Then when the flood of Unwanted got too deep, and government-commissioned hives had to raise the kids, cryostasis was their solution for that.

I ran my hands over my face. This was bad. Without power, our reserves and battery backups weren't overkill — they were woefully, criminally inadequate. We weren't an island. Weren't supposed to be. State laws enshrined us as a priority recovery site. Hell, they'd send the national guard if there were a flood or hurricane. Send 'em right past people trapped on their roofs or buried in rubble. Anything for the Frozen Generation.

But that had changed, hadn't it?

"Charlotte's been screaming at the power company," Zeke said. "The state police, the governor, even. Nothing's got us online. Been running on our solar reserves and gas gennys ever since. I had Jimmy making runs to the charge station for extra fuel, but once they figured it was for here, they refused to sell to him. I sent him to Pembrook since they're the next closest with liquid, but I'd be surprised if he doesn't just quit."

"If the main circuit's off, we're not generating new cryo. Hell, half the tanks are already low." We had solar rigs, but like everything else, they weren't enough to make us completely independent.

"I *know that*, Mose!"

These guys were looking to me because I had always been the quick one, the first with a solution when things went bad. Some people are wired for crisis situations, and I kind of loved them. And now I was flat-footed, slow. Tired. They needed me to be better. I shook my head to clear it.

"Okay, we need to cut everything we can, try to make the reserves last. Mike, hit the breakers, cut the whole front office. Keep the clinic for half an hour and warn the docs up front — I think they've got a couple active exowombs, and they'll need time to transfer back to cryo. We can move 'em back here on the battery backups if we have to.

"Zeke, Sol, get the pumps running. Top up all the flasks and shelf reserves first, and pump whatever we got left into the reserve tanks on the 'still."

"It won't last as long once it's distributed."

"Yeah but it won't do us any good in the main tanks. Sounds like we could end up running without *any* power for a while, so we need to get the patients as self-sufficient as we can. Same for power, make sure the tank batteries are all fresh. Pull some from the vehicles if you have to."

It was the same protocol we were supposed to use if the ocean came in around us, or the building collapsed. Get all the cryotanks ready for travel and wait for the national guard to come collect us. We'd lose auto-refill when the generators stopped. Internal regulation and monitoring too, once the local batteries dried up. We could top off tanks manually, if we had any cryo left, and if we knew the tank was low. We'd have to make visual inspections.

If the outage lasted long enough, we'd have to start consolidating fluid.

After tonight, any embryonic deaths in an extraction clinic were to be charged as murder two. We could get first degree if it was the result of a deliberate action. That was starting to seem more possible than it had yesterday.

"I'll go talk to Charlotte and see about getting us some backup. Someone has to care." I tapped on a cryoflask. "They only just made a bunch of laws about these guys."

Everyone started moving, so that part of the job was done. We'd get this place set up as best we could and hope society at large would help.

I backtracked through the clinic, head down, through everyone's rush to prepare for whatever came next. Every now and then, security would call someone's name. Took me a bit to realize they were escorting people off-site.

I passed a couple of clinic techs opening up one of the equipment storage rooms. One had on the scrubs they all wear up front, the other just had jeans and a t-shirt. I thought I recognized them both from the day shift.

"What about the old Herz-Stanton Gen 20s?" the one in scrubs asked.

"Uh, they're not on the APL anymore," the other answered.

"But they still work fine, I mean, maybe keep them off the network but they'll do the job."

He wasn't wrong. I was born to a Gen 3 and even those were so safe that there were actual arguments over whether to ban internal birth because it killed too many Unborn Americans. It was a public health crisis, after all: when an American's life begins at conception, failure-to-implant becomes the country's leading cause of death.

They don't exactly cover that stuff in school but I guess I have an interest, since their last great idea led to me being born Unwanted, named by an algorithm, and raised in a hive, even if it wasn't one of the bible-warrior training facilities/sweatshops you see in the documentaries.

"She said all the approved units. This is just CYA, right? They're looking for ways to screw us, so I don't think we'll get bonus points for going above and beyond using illegal equipment."

"Fair enough."

If they were starting up extra exowombs now, of all times, that would be a problem. But I'd deal with it once I knew when we'd get the power back.

I didn't hear any shouting as I approached Charlotte's office. That seemed like a good sign. This had to be some local fuckup. Some anti-extraction asshole at the power company giving us a hard time.

Charlotte was slumped forward on her desk, her tablet docked and playing some news feed. The smart wall to her left showed every angle of the perimeter and most rooms in the clinic. On the cameras, cars had filled the closest lots outside. Biggest crowd we'd seen in years.

I knocked on the door frame. "Hey boss, how's it going?"

"Hey, Moses. I thought I told you to go home and get some sleep." She gestured at the news. "'Cease all extraction operations.

Commence the immediate and safe transfer of all Embryonic-Americans to external wombs and begin gestation.'"

I gave her the baffled, disappointed look we'd shared through so many newsreels of hearings and debates.

"Yeah, we'll get right on that."

There weren't enough approved exowombs on the planet for that. And even if they'd all been in the U.S., it'd take decades to get through the backlog.

We had twenty on site. We'd tried to order more over a year ago, after the election, but all the domestic manufacturing companies were swamped, and you couldn't buy them from overseas for fear of foreign supply-chain sabotage. Sleeper-diseases, hard-coded loyalties, who knew what the Reds could cook into our most vulnerable citizens?

And hospitals got legal priority on exowombs, of course. Most wanted births were external these days, if only for the legal liability. A miscarriage was bad enough without the criminal investigation ripping your life apart just in case.

"All the hospitals in a hundred-mile radius are already swamped." She said, "I've called every one of them. The other sites are dumping as many cases off on them as they can. I got St Mercy's to agree to a *hundred*, a lousy hundred kids! And then some assholes parked ten freezer trucks in their emergency lane and took off on foot. Now it's all, 'sorry, now *we* have six hundred thousand to take care of, good luck with yours.' It's like that everywhere."

"Any word on the power?"

She snorted. "All the words are bad. It's not coming back."

"Why?"

"Power and Light's lawyers dusted off a couple of old state abortion laws from back around the fight over the amendment. Any organization or individual who provides aid or assistance *of any kind* to an abortion clinic will be held equally liable. Apparently, it doesn't matter that we're not taking clients anymore. Our lawyers think their interpretation is legit enough to stick until we've challenged it in court."

And if things kept going like this we'd all be in jail for mass manslaughter or negligent genocide or something by then.

"The storage facility protections-" I started.

"One law says they have to provide power, the other says they can't." She paused just long enough to solidify her composure. When you do her job, you can't ever risk it slipping — there're always cameras on you looking for ammunition. "Our lawyers are still with us, and they're raising hell best they can." She said, "The

ACLU and opposition legislators too. But by the time this mess gets sorted out, it'll be too late."

"They- they realize that if we shut down all the way, the embryos will thaw, right?" I asked. "And thawing would be bad for them?"

She shrugged again, like she didn't want to give the lawmakers or God's power company that much credit. These were the kind of people whose idea of compromise had forced generations of women who'd otherwise have taken a pill to risk surgery.

"Why are they doing this? They have to know it'll blow back on them..."

She looked down at the tablet, head in her hands, and said the next part almost to herself. Like she was thinking aloud. "There's a census coming up."

"Boss?" I didn't like this line of thought.

"If six hundred thousand 'people' disappeared overnight, they could redraw the map. Eliminate this district, a progressive congressional seat, and who knows how many state-level positions. It'd change funding allocations and..." She looked up at me. "Or maybe they're just a bunch of zealots who didn't listen when we pointed out all the problems with the bill six months ago, including that this could technically happen, even if it seemed unlikely. Same results either way."

She scrolled back through the news footage, picked out a segment, and spun the tablet. The Reverend Senator Callahan was walking out of the capitol building, a wide, closed-mouthed smile serene on his face.

"It's about personal responsibility. To all those... facilities, I'd say you shouldn't have done the procedures if you couldn't take care of your obligations afterwards. The American people trusted you with their children, and if anything happens to any single one of them, we *will* hold you accountable. At long last."

"Oh."

That was all I could think to say. I'd missed something Ester and Dr. Quarzi had seen coming.

I knew they'd been trying to kill our industry. What I hadn't realized was that it wasn't about the Frozen Generation. They were after us.

Us, like as individuals, the people who worked at the clinics. Not just the politicians who supported us, or our CEO, or the other executives they dragged before congress, but all of *us*. Me.

Even after all these years in their crosshairs I'd still taken them at their word. Still internalized some gut, cultural-suffusion belief that they cared about the Frozen Generation enough not to sabotage them. No matter how much they hated extraction or us that enabled it, Storage should have been safe.

Oh. You damned idiot.

It wouldn't matter if tonight's ban got overturned if we were all in prison when it came time to reopen the clinic. Whether we were the victims of a conspiracy or yet another bit of collateral damage didn't really matter. Dr Quarzi was right. Ester was right. For all the good it would probably do them, at least they were running.

"How long do we have?" Charlotte asked.

I shook out of the reprieve; the math was fresh in my mind. We were already so low.

"Without more juice? Maybe a day or two before we start losing ones near the top of the flasks to evaporation."

With cryo, thawing isn't like you'd imagine. Everything's so cold, it's actually skipped freezing to being this ice-free glass. If it thaws unregulated, you have two problems: ice crystals will form and slice all the cells apart, and the cryoprotectants that preserve the cells by replacing their water will go toxic as they warm. Warming the cells and diluting out the cryoprotectants is a whole process you just can't manage when a few thousand flasks of enhanced nitrogen are going from liquid to gas and you have no electricity.

"I contacted our sister organizations and sent out an alert on all our social media. Described what they're doing and begged for fuel and cryo," Charlotte said. "We've got a good base of someday-parents who are organizing to help."

"Any luck?"

"Not sure if our people can even get through that riot outside. The police are supposedly here to keep things under control, but they're basically blockading us in."

My eyes were still on the muted tablet, watching our representatives. I felt a bleak certainty that there would be plenty of investigations to determine all the ways we were at fault for this.

The power cut out. The wall of security monitors went dead. The only light in the room was the screen on the tablet.

I shook out of it. "Oh, yeah. I had Mike cut everything but Storage. We'll move any clinic hardware we have to keep to the back, try to make it last."

Charlotte nodded. "Good idea."

"Could you double check the doors?" I asked. "Some of the emergencies are fail-open maglocks and we might need to barricade them."

"Sure." She grabbed a flashlight from her desk and the gun she kept holstered under the tabletop. She knew about the doors. She was probably relieved to have the distraction.

"Thanks."

Mike caught me as I left Charlotte's office.

"It's Dr. Clarke. She won't let me cut the clinic. Says she wants any surplus for the wombs."

"What? Tell me she hasn't started a new batch."

Those things suck power and they still take almost nine months per kid. Regulations imposed on the manufacturer — anything else would be unnatural. And there were only twenty of them. We had over six hundred thousand embryos and fetuses in the back.

"Sorry, boss. She outranks me."

"What, she's gonna print half a million kids before the batteries run out?"

But she had to look like she'd tried. She was the doctor in charge of production. Someday they'd be asking her, 'Why didn't you try to save *any* of them?'

We were on a sinking ship, and we were all looking ahead, past the lifeboats to the historians, trying to dictate what they'd say about us in their accounts.

Or, more likely, in our atrocity trials.

All twenty Securus Platinum exowombs were humming away on their pedestal mounts, and ten old Herz-Stanton 25s were sitting on the counter. All were occupied and lit.

I wondered where Dr. Clarke had gotten the kids. Were they future orders? Had she picked them at random? The front office tried anonymizing the embryos once. Give them all an equal chance at adoption. Our client rate had plummeted. People out in the world talked a big game about the abandoned, forever-frozen masses and their right to life, but when it came time to grow their new kid, they only wanted the best.

"Dr. Clarke?"

"I knew you'd show up." She looked tired and scared. She pointed her phone at me like it was a gun. Recording the conversation, proof she'd done all she could. Proof I was the bad guy here. Fine. Her jury would love us turning on each other.

"Doctor. You need to put the patients back into cryostasis." It's always 'the patients' when you talk about the Frozen, but especially when you know you're on video.

Her chin came up and her face went hard. "This is my department, and these patients' well-being is my responsibility. I have to do what's best for them. I don't answer to the cryotechs."

Ouch.

"They cut our power, and these things are draining the reserve." I spoke clear and slow for the court. "Without the exowombs running, we can get another day or so for all the patients in the back. Maybe they'll turn the power back on by then. If we don't, they'll *all* start to thaw." She didn't react, so I kept going. "We'll never have enough power for these machines either way. But running them could kill all the patients onsite."

I half expected her to say I was just trying to save my own department at her expense, but she didn't go there. She stuck to the script.

"The law says we need to transfer all Unborn Americans to exowombs immediately."

She put herself between me and them, like she expected us to fight.

I realized I didn't have to argue this out. I didn't have to say anything. The breaker was in the basement.

Antisocial hive tendencies, I guess. We always caught flack for being 'indirectly confrontational' after being raised by a monolith we couldn't affect in the slightest. As a nod to professionalism, I spoke up on my way out.

"Okay. You can put them back in cryo or you can take them someplace else. Either way, I'm cutting power to this room." I headed for the stairwell. She followed me.

"They can't leave these facilities! They're not allowed to leave the clinic. We have to maintain custody of all-"

I stopped at the basement door while I found my light. "I can spare a truck. I can't spare power."

"You don't 'spare' anything! That's not your decision to make!" I was the last facilities person here with any rank, so I would contest that.

Luckily, I didn't have to. Charlotte appeared from the darkness and stepped in. I guess we hadn't exactly been arguing quietly.

"Rachel. Stop," she said. There was an edge to her voice, but she kept it calm, authoritative. "We can't support them here. Not anymore. If you want them to make it, you have to take them someplace else."

"But they can't leave..."

She took Dr. Clarke's hand. "Listen, they, and you, will be safer someplace else. Take them to a hospital, take them to your church. Hell, take them to the governor's mansion. Anywhere'll be better." She started guiding her toward the garage. "Come on, I'll help you get a truck."

"I-"

"It's *okay*. It's okay. These are terrible times and you've done everything you could. If we had more than thirty exowombs, you would have saved even more. You've already gone above and beyond. They'll understand. Hell, you'll probably be a hero."

I hit the staircase, flashlight searching for the clinic breaker. I'd probably be able to watch her single-handedly rescue those thirty innocent lives again someday in the based-on-a-true-story dramatization. From my prison cell.

I made a decision on my way back to Storage. Or maybe I realized that I'd made it a while ago.

Keeping the Frozen 'alive' had always been the goal, but the way I'd seen it, my real job was to keep everything perfect back here, exceeding every regulation, so nobody went to jail.

Most of the crew I had left seemed to feel the same way. If we quit, we'd be abandoning our teammates, and the rest of the clinic.

That made what came next easier. My plans might have changed since the drive in, but I'd still be doing my job.

Zeke was manually forcing the heavy door to the employee garage when I got back to Storage.

"Jimmy's back, and he says he got fuel!" Sol told me.

Zeke grinned. "I love that kid."

The sun was up now. I saw a sliver of it as the garage door rumbled back down. The truck rolled to a stop as we all hustled over.

Jimmy shoved the door open and stumbled out, looking beat and wild-eyed. "I'm sorry, boss." He shook his head. "I couldn't get- it's bad out there."

His knuckles were scraped bloody and he had a nice shiner forming on his left eye. He'd stopped somewhere and spray painted over the logo on the truck. I wondered if it was before or after his fight.

I went around the back and looked over the bed of gas cans. Most of them were empty.

Zeke was talking to him. "Hey, hey it's okay. You're okay."

"No, it's not. They'd only sell me eighty gallons. I couldn't do more, I'm sorry. The first place, when I tried to fill everything, they figured it out and came out with a gun. I-"

Behind us, Sol swore and kicked the truck.

"Hey, it's fine!" I waved a hand at him, then looked back to our driver. "You did more than we had any right to ask. It's okay. We'll figure something out."

There was a half second of silence, and then: "I quit." Jimmy was looking down at the painted-over logo, focus distant. "Look," he said. "I just came to get my truck. Sorry." He met my eyes for a second. "Sorry. I'm done. I got to go."

And then he did.

We got as ready as we could with what we had left. We consolidated the fuel, shifted our resources around so we weren't producing any more power than we could use or store, made sure we were running everything else on the minimums.

They worked hard, though they looked scared, kept checking their phones. Couldn't hold that against them today. News updates, worried texts from families. Finally, I said, "Enough. Go home. We're as ready for shutdown as we're going to get."

After all the hassle from the government inspections, the impossible hours from being badly understaffed, the slurs and attacks and violence from the protestors, the crew I had left were here because they were loyal and they cared. With their skills, they could have gotten jobs at any lab or factory floor for more pay and less work, less stress. I was grateful for them.

"Naw, you'll need us here," Sol said.

"I need you to go get some sleep. Go home, see your families. I'll text you if we need anything else. There'll be a lot to do when Charlotte and her lawyers get the power back. They'll probably have inspectors out here before the next shipment of cryo."

"What about you?"

I didn't have kids, or anyone at home to worry about. Most of my forty-six surviving hive siblings could take care of themselves.

"I'll take the first shift here. I'll let you know as soon as anything changes, or if I need help with anything in the meanwhile."

"If the power doesn't come back..." Zeke started.

"I'll watch the levels. I got reserve batteries, reserve tanks, and gravity feeds from the 'still. If I need a bucket brigade, I'll let you know."

They laughed a little. Then they just looked tired. Finally, they took the out, headed for their trucks. Promised they'd look for gas, be back as soon as we needed them. But they weren't coming back and we all knew it. I wasn't going to text them, and they knew that, too.

Someone had to be responsible for what was going to happen next. Storage was my department. If I sent them away before the failures began, it kept responsibility for everything nice and tidy.

I waited till they were gone, then I climbed up on the pump station, set all the warning alarms to max volume, and took a nap.

I woke up when I started sweating through my clothes. The sun was cooking on the warehouse roof — good for our solar, not that it'd do more than pump our thin reserves around. The Frozen wouldn't notice this heat though, not in their vacuum flasks of liquid nitrogen. Out here it was too hot, but in there it was impossibly cold.

The generator's warning lights glowed amber on the dash. Nothing left to do about that.

I went for a walk around the clinic.

The place was empty, trashed in everyone's haste to evacuate. I could hear someone clinking around in one of the labs and it made me think of rats or squatters. Just last night it had been business as usual, and now this. Muffled outside, I thought I could hear voices and pops, like fireworks or gunshots.

Amerinews was playing in Charlotte's office.

"State militia units here in Godless California are mustering on the border for what they call a humanitarian mission, an invasion to kidnap and illegally transport the Frozen across state lines. It's a logistical nightmare in clear violation of state autonomy. God only knows what will happen to these helpless babies."

"Hey, Moses," Charlotte said.

"Hey. Jimmy quit."

"Everybody's quit."

We both looked at the tablet for a minute.

"How about you?" I asked.

"I'm going down with the ship. You?"

"I'll keep things cold as long as I can. After that, I don't know. Any luck on the power?"

She shook her head. Subject change. "There's a mob outside."

"Yeah? Maybe we'll get lucky and they'll set the place on fire. Take the credit." I said.

That got a little smile. "If you need to get out, the side door by client parking still opens out. Plus your loading dock."

"Thanks. Not sure there's any running away from this."

"Nope."

She sat there in the dark, lit by her dwindling tablet. "I'll be here if you need anything," she said.

I walked back to Storage and made my rounds again. Looked over all the racks and racks of flasks, batteries, reserve tanks, bundled wires and tubing. I'd configured most of these units. I'd loaded half of them. Tended them all for years, watched for even a single power or temperature failure. Soon there'd be thousands.

The last generator sputtered to a rest outside. The fans stopped. The pumps cut out. The beeps and squawks of the monitors went dead on standby. And in the silence, the Frozen Generation began to thaw.

See Jacob Coffin's story "The Frozen Generation" online at Metaphorosis.
If you liked it, leave a comment. Authors love that!
Remember to subscribe to our e-mail updates so you'll know when new stories are posted.

About the story

"The Frozen Generation" started with an internet argument somewhere in early 2019. Buried in among the various hot takes on some now-forgotten reddit thread was the confident opinion that abortion as an issue would soon be over. Artificial wombs, it said, would allow for the adoption of unwanted embryos without impacting anyone's bodily autonomy.

There are plenty of straightforward issues with this modest proposal, starting with the fact that bodily autonomy and forced surgery aren't exactly compatible, but I tend to be a bit engineer-minded, so I was caught as much by the sheer number of logistical issues.

I never responded to that particular discussion, but there was something about the concept I couldn't leave alone. Simple solutions to complex problems, especially when their proponents won't consider the ways it could go wrong, or the cost to everyone around them, tend to really bother me. I feel like I keep seeing this belief that because something is the Right Thing To Do that it couldn't possibly hurt anyone, or that the people it'll hurt don't matter.

So I started iterating through the obvious issues and thinking about the solutions society would have to implement to fix them, and then the problems those solutions would cause next. By May 2019, this world-building exercise had formed the backbone of "The Frozen Generation".

I almost always start with the concept then kludge the plot on afterward. In this case, Mose, his coworkers, and their bad night fit nicely into the latest in the rolling series of man-made disasters I'd charted out, and gradually stole the show, as the plot ought to do. My beta readers, sensitivity readers, and *Metaphorosis's* editor were a huge help in bringing out everyone's personality and making clear their motivations, both good and bad.

My worldbuilding goal throughout the piece was to take the concept of a setting with ectogenesis 'solving' abortion and to stretch it to its breaking point, to find as many weird circumstances, edge cases, and exploits in the concept as possible. As for my main goal, I wanted to show the human cost of these nights, and to do all that extrapolation while handling the subject respectfully and thoroughly. I hope I managed it. There were a few things cut or reduced that I may end up exploring elsewhere, like the right to not reproduce (currently often bundled in with bodily autonomy, but an issue which would quickly become distinct in this setting) or even just the human cost of this 'solution', the risk and pain of forced surgery, or it's alternative, forced birth, which was mostly left in this version's background.

About four thousand words worth of backstory and essay-like rants have been cut, much to the story's benefit. The setting's backstory, from the introduction of artificial wombs, to the hives, to their replacement with cryostasis, and all the factions of conservative opponents to the 'abortion' of the day were spelled out in tedious detail, until one of the last drafts. Cut with that was the overtly-stated theme that laws only exist if someone will enforce them, that norms, conventions, and traditions are utterly worthless. This message became less important to explain once the Supreme Court demonstrated it more effectively than I could ever hope to.

I learned a lot as I researched this story. About cryostasis, in vitro fertilization, and religious beliefs around same, but I think I was most struck by the artificiality of the abortion debate itself, something I hadn't even known about when I started out. It seemed my history classes had skipped the efforts of Paul Weyrich, Jerry Falwell, and C. Everett Koop and others in the 1970s to teach then-fairly-apathetic evangelicals (even using a film tour) to see abortion as an affront to God, just as a step towards building the Moral Majority. There is no technological solution to an issue like that.

I went into this story well aware that I was manifestly unqualified to write it. I often am — I frequently write characters with experiences I've never had, police detectives, post-apocalyptic survivors, MMA fighters, my stories are full of roles I've never held. But this time it was important. I don't have a uterus. I don't work in a health-care field. I'm not directly impacted by this fight. I've done my best to keep this story to an outside perspective, to research everything carefully, and to avoid talking over anyone or trying to write anyone's experience for them. Hopefully I managed that too.

A question for the author

Q: Duckbilled platypus – result of divine distraction, or alternate universe crossover?

A: I can only hope for an alternative reality where the platypus is perfectly mundane; an entire ecosystem of egg-laying, bird-part-having, venomous mammals, where all the no doubt equally strange and venomous human-analogues are baffled by the humble Australian woodchuck or whatever we were supposed to get. I'd like to trade books and movies with that alternate dimension.

About the author

Jacob Coffin is a sci-fi writer with a passion for land conservation, reuse, and human rights not being rolled back.

jacobcoffinwrites.wordpress.com, @jacobcoffin@writing.exchange

The Numismatist

Cecelia Isaac

On a lonely day on the river, a soul awaited me by the bank. The mists were high, and I saw no others as I angled my craft through the water to the shore.

The seeker entered the river. The hood of their cloak obscured their face. Water crested over their boots and wet their hem.

I reached out a hand. The seeker caught it, and I used my pole as a counterbalance as I hefted them into my boat. Mortals view me as a wizened old man. This is a form only, and my strength is more than enough to bring my passengers in.

"Obliged," said the seeker in a muted voice. They produced their obol and passed it to me.

I took it up and placed it into an inner fold of my robes. Then I gripped my pole and leaned into it, using my weight to push us off.

My craft pulled achingly away from the banks as if meaning to keep us there. As the current was just about to catch us, I caught notice of a dusty residue on my fingers.

In the millennia I have performed my role, I have seen every currency imaginable. Faded and cheap or crisp and weighty; coin no longer used by the time the seeker passed or coin as commonplace as river stones. Some placed jewels on their tongues, thinking the larger the offering, the kinder the shore. But in their faces I saw all their lives, and knew exactly where they were meant to spend their eternities.

But today, lulled by the current or perhaps the untold years of routine, I had not even looked at the seeker's obol before accepting it.

My fingers darted back into my robes and fished out the obol. It was a small chunk of barley bread, hardened after days uneaten.

I looked up as the seeker did, and our eyes met. As my face tightened, theirs folded into a look of almost-hauteur.

"Well, I tried," the seeker said.

I drove my pole into the mud, arresting our motion. The seeker threw out their hands against the rocking of the boat.

I admit I was used to more begging. When they said no more, I lunged forward and latched onto the seeker's arm. I tossed them bodily into the water and felt a glimmer of satisfaction when the seeker cursed and sputtered.

"Was that necessary? My cloak—!"

I anchored my boat and leapt to the bank as the seeker sloshed through the muck onto dry ground.

"Oh," they said. "I thought you couldn't leave the boat..."

I straightened, and their eyes went wide. Over a head taller than any seeker on the misty bank, even in the body of an old man I struck fear into the hearts of wise souls.

Unfortunately, I was not standing in front of one.

"Look..." The seeker spread their hands, and finally I identified their disposition. They were unrepentant. Not defensive, not mournful, not desperate. Desperation I saw every day. Those without loved ones, with no one to place the obol in their mouth, knew their fates were sealed. And yet they begged. This seeker had no intention of doing so.

I interrupted them. "This—" I held up the hunk of bone-dry bread, "—is not sufficient fare."

"And I know that. But you see, I didn't have anything else and—"

I walked away. Seekers without the fare spend 100 years on the banks. We had nothing more to say to each other.

Or so I thought. But the next day, the seeker waited to board with three other souls.

On the banks, there is but scarce difference between night and day. All is shrouded in mist, and trapped souls must exist in this twilight on the slim strip of land between the river and the cavern wall. Newly arrived seekers huddled together near the single wooden post that marked the pickup point, their shoulders hunched against the mist, protecting their obols.

Despite the dim light, I knew the seeker immediately.

"No," I said before they could open their mouth.

"I haven't said anything!" The seeker protested.

I gave them a skeptical look.

This was no hindrance to the seeker. "I know what the rules are, sir, but have you ever thought—"

I boarded my craft and pushed off from the bank as the seeker continued to speak. "—of bending them? There must be some sort of solution—"

The next day, they took a new tack. "You'll find it was a mistake, sir. You see, my mother *meant* to place the coin, but a graverobber came shortly thereafter. I saw it all from a ghostly space, too incorporeal to do anything to assist my mother as she fought the dastardly—"

Their voice faded as the boat met the current.

And the next day: "Perhaps I could work for my keep, sir. Pray you rest your weary limbs while I take up the pole myself—"

And the next: "Fancy a wager? We could bet on it. I myself was well known as a card dealer, and would be happy to show you the basic rules of Pitch and Toss—"

And the next: "Is bread not a noble offering, sir? Do our bakers not toil to produce the best? I offer you a piece made of the finest my humble city has to offer—"

Usually, I kept order on the banks with the subtlety of a hammer. Most souls only needed one reminder to adhere to the rules. But this seeker danced out of range on light steps before darting back in for another attempt. Odd as our exchanges were, it was rare for me to have any form of exchange at all, and certainly nothing so upbeat.

I turned away again, but against my will, the corner of my mouth tipped up in a smile.

In the evening, I stowed my boat and returned to my abode. My home was built into the stone of the cavern wall. A little window faced the banks of the river, but overall my abode had a cave-like quality to it. This mattered little to me. I was used to the semi-darkness of the banks.

I had been to the Upper World before and found no enticement there. This home had all I needed: a warm fire to keep out the damp, a pallet to rest on, a store of nourishing food. I did not know why the seekers thought so often of the Upper World. Needs were softer here, less tangible. With time, one did not feel the pangs of hunger as strongly, nor the pain of injury.

And I had my collection. My abode extended back from the main rooms, where a heavy iron door opened into a storage tunnel lined with cases. Within each of these cases lay hundreds of obols in padded rows. All had been cleaned, catalogued, and stored by me. Thousands of years of tolls paid to me for my labor.

I brought out the day's offerings and began my work. I washed and dried them, sometimes using a pick to clean dirt from the ridges. I weighed and sized the coins, noting their details in thin lines in one of my notebooks. The oil lamp kept a steady light while I used a magnifying glass to examine the coins for fine details and faded faces of rulers and gods. Each was a record of the world beyond, and I glimpsed slivers of it through these tokens. More than a payment, they were a record of a world both intimately close and yet eons distant from me. It pleased me to tidy the mess of humanity into order.

When I was done, I opened a case and placed the coins gently inside, next to those from the day before.

Sometimes, if I had the time, I would unlock the storage tunnel and take down a case from generations previous. I found the corresponding notebook pages as well. I checked for damage or wear, of course, but I also just liked to look. In this way I saw a continuum. Obols gleamed in the light, their form changing from year to year, decade to decade. I wondered what would come next.

The next day, a fight broke out as I helped a line of souls into my craft. Two seekers began to shout. An obol fell to the ground and they lunged for it. I propped my pole against my craft and strode to them. Tearing them apart, I looked in their faces. But neither was the irrepressible seeker. I dropped the two and whirled about.

Sure enough, my boat had been discharged from the shore and was drifting away, helped by none other than the seeker who'd plagued me these last days.

I narrowed my eyes. In the next instant, I stood on the boat. The souls aboard gasped and recoiled, and even the seeker drew back in sudden alarm.

"How did you—"

Their next words were lost as I flung them, again, from my vessel.

By the time they dragged their cold, wet body to the shore, I was already there. Vibrating with anger, I grabbed the front of their cloak and lifted. Their feet left the ground. Their hood dropped back. They scrabbled at the clasp as the neck tightened around them.

The pale light fell on their face. Their left eye was newly blackened, and a cut covered in dried blood ran above that same eye. Had it happened when I threw them? No, the bruise would not have formed so quickly. And now that I looked more closely, I realized this cloak was not the same one as the day before. It was thinner and more worn, and had easily soaked through.

I set the seeker down. "What happened to you?"

The seeker's face changed, becoming closed and mulish for the first time. "My bad luck follows me even after death, it seems."

The banks were no easy place to spend one hundred years. Between the mists, desperate gangs roamed. They took what they wanted, seeking the cold comforts of material possessions. Though they did not eat, seekers still felt the echoes of other mortal needs. They fought amongst each other for weapons or clothing, or even territory. Detritus from the river, items they'd managed to carry from the Upper World—nothing was too small to feud over. I ignored these squabbles. Eventually, each soul's edges smoothed like a rock under the pressure of time.

The seeker was new to the banks, and yet I had seen their whole life's story when I first looked into their face. They were no stranger to sleeping with one eye open.

"You must better protect yourself here," I said. The words felt inane even as I spoke them. Why was I assisting a seeker? I was merely their ferryman, whose only role was to take their payment , not become involved in the petty disputes of those who could not afford my services. Familiar as this seeker's face had become, their existence was not my responsibility.

The seeker gave me a look that confirmed I'd been little help. "Just need a friend or two to watch my back, is all. Everyone here's a little flighty. Don't worry about me. I don't seem to feel hungry much anymore, so there's no need for all my teeth now anyway."

"You will heal," I said. "Faster than you would have in the Upper World."

They harrumphed.

We stood in silence.

"You will adjust, seeker."

When the seeker spoke, they did so grudgingly. "My name is Achem."

"You have no name here, seeker," I said as I turned. "Everything you were is gone."

They spoke to my back: "And yet the pain feels all the same."

In the morning, the seeker leaned against the prow of my upturned vessel where it was stowed on the shore.

"So, this is where you go at night."

Their voice had returned to its usual bright tenor. Their bruise had lightened already. Seekers did not often find my abode. It was far from the populated areas of the banks. That, and most souls preferred to give me a wide berth. But given this particular seeker's resourcefulness, I was not surprised to see them here.

"What is today's ploy?" I asked guardedly.

The seeker chuckled. "I thought I might rest a day. I can afford to take a day off if I'm going to be here one hundred years."

The morning was light, and the mist had cleared somewhat. The day felt almost fresh, despite the mugginess brought by the river and the looming cavern walls, and the fact that the sun never shone here.

"What happens if your boat is damaged?"

"Or stolen?" I asked with some indulgence. Maddening as Achem was, their resourcefulness had begun to charm. The seeker flashed an unrepentant smile. "I have the means to fix it, in my abode."

"You manage all yourself?"

Taking the sides of my boat, I turned the whole thing over so it sat right side up. Before I could make to push it into the water, the seeker began brushing off sand and mud from the edges. Though my vessel was a sacred thing, I confess to never having cleaned it. It was much the worse for wear.

The seeker completed their task as best they could, and then helped me push my craft into the water.

They clapped their hands in satisfaction. "When you return, I can spend more time on it. I bet we could make it look much better."

I frowned at their attentions. I did not think I had done anything to deserve them. But I did not refuse the help. I left them and poled down the river, to the path from the Upper World and my new arrivals.

Almost every day, some souls came whose one hundred years had concluded. They were free to mount the ferry to their final destination.

On this day, two were there. I recognized them without effort. They had not aged, of course. But they were hollowed. Their personalities had become worn and thin. These shades no longer fought amongst themselves. They felt nothing, not the cold, not the pain. Their mouths and hands twitched and grasped, seeking unknown succor.

I let them mount first, so they would know their place was guaranteed.

When I looked into their faces, I saw nothing left.

After the day had ended, I returned upstream to my abode. On the banks, souls who had arrived late begged to be ferried away, but I ignored them.

I dragged my craft to the shore. The seeker, Achem, appeared almost at my elbow. They bounced on their heels with an exuberance I had come to expect from them, no matter the task.

"Do you have cleaning supplies?" Achem asked.

I collected some tools from my abode while Achem inspected the boat. They gave me an arch look when I produced a bucket containing a random collection of rusted and disused boating implements.

I was surprised to feel a sheepish flash of emotion. "I may have more inside."

Achem followed me back to my abode this time. They lingered at the threshold while I went to my desk, where I kept the tools I used to clean my obols.

"What is that for?" Achem asked curiously.

I explained as I rifled through my things. "My work station. Where I care for and sort my collection."

Realization dawned on Achem's face. "Your collection. Every obol is here?"

"Of course." I gestured at the iron door that led to the storage tunnel. "Where else would they be?"

"So this whole time... you've just had a collection of riches in there? You must have *millions* of obols."

I moved the case I'd been working on the night before and grabbed the stack of rags behind it. "I suppose."

"Are they protected? By magic or other powers?" Achem asked.

"Yes," I responded. "Me."

Chuckling, Achem accepted the new tools as I ushered them out and closed the door behind us.

They checked each item fastidiously, then selected two scrapers. "I'll take the left, you can start on the right."

Bemused, I obeyed the instructions.

"You have no experience with boats," I said as we toiled. It was not a question; I knew the broad details of their life in the Upper World. And yet, they worked with confident strokes across my craft.

Achem shrugged. "It's the same as cleaning anything else. And meditative, don't you think?"

I agreed. I had begun to realize the task was similar to the care of my obols, and was surprised to learn Achem felt the same sense of peaceful purpose.

"Do you know everything about me?" Achem asked after a time. "The others say you can see our lives."

"I know it from the moment I see your faces."

"And you remember everything? Everyone?"

I nodded. This was a lie on my part. I remembered everyone, that was true. But while I could see their lives, the details were not clear, not in the way the seekers assumed. I grasped impressions and fleeting scenes, much in the same way their memories were constructed.

And while I knew where on the far shore to deposit the souls, it was not I who made the judgment. Their actions while alive sealed their fates. I simply delivered them to their destinations.

After some time, Achem cleared their throat. "You didn't see Joa pass through, did you?"

The moment the name was said, a seeker's face rose to my mind. Their history played before me, but this time a familiar face appeared in some scenes—Achem, full of life.

"Yes."

"He's... he's not on the banks, is he?"

I shook my head. "They paid their fare and I ferried them across."

Achem sighed, their shoulders dropping. "Well... good."

"You are not pleased."

"I... am. I mean, he vanished, you know? I never saw him again. But I had hoped... I had some sort of dream. That he'd gotten out. And was living an idyllic life. Maybe as a farmer." Achem laughed harshly. "That was stupid, I see now."

They grieved, but I did not see why. "All of that is gone now. None of it matters anymore."

Achem was silent for a moment. "That isn't quite true yet."

We worked together in contemplative silence, first scraping, then waxing using wax found in a forgotten corner of my storage room, then cleaning out the interior with broom and cloth. Achem did not tire until the job was done. Finally, they sat back and spread their hands. I could only assume they were pleased with the job, even though no amount of care could disguise the vessel's advanced age.

I had been lulled into a calm as the evening pressed on and the shadows deepened, but now I wondered if Achem would expect something for this work.

My worry was short-lived. Achem returned the tools to the bucket and declared the boat had probably never looked better. "Until tomorrow," they said with a wave of a hand.

This time, I was left behind, while Achem went on to a mysterious destination.

I spent the next day on the river with a full boat. It pleased me to see it renewed by Achem's attentions. The seekers did not seem to notice.

Once ashore, I went directly up the bank to my abode. With all the attention given to the boat, I had not had the time the day before to finish attending to my obols, and I was eager to begin again.

I paused on the threshold. The air had been disturbed.

One long step, and I crossed to the storage tunnel. The door was locked, as always. Turning, I looked next to the corner where my work table stood.

Sure enough, my tools were scattered and my notebooks toppled. Some were flung open and discarded to the ground. Several obols had bounced and rolled across the tabletop.

I stood immobilized beside the destruction, rage choking my throat.

The case I'd left on my table was gone, along with the rows and rows of obols it contained.

And I knew just who had taken it.

Dusk had fallen, not with the setting of a sun but with a thickening of the dark. The banks kept a dim light that glowed from who knew where, and so I found Achem easily enough. They were seated with their back to a shelf of rock, legs stretched out. They examined a cloak in their lap.

At the sound of my approach, they looked up.

"Ah, you're back. Look, I retrieved my cloak. Never let it be said I'm not resourceful—"

"Give it back."

Achem's dark brows drew together. "Sorry? The cloak?"

I rose to my full height, so that I clouded the area around us. My shadow darkened this nothing corner and enveloped us. I made for Achem's throat, but this time they were faster.

They sprang from my reach. "Wait, now, wait! What's happened?"

"You know what happened. You spent all evening yesterday at my abode. Now I find a case is missing."

"*What* case?" Achem asked, now with the gall to sound exasperated.

"A case from my collection of obols. *Someone* has taken it."

"*I* didn't!" they protested.

I detected no falsehood in Achem's voice, but they did not speak with their usual confidence. A thread of guilt ran through their words.

I blinked from one space into existence in the next, so quickly Achem had no chance to escape. I slammed them into the stone wall and pinned them there by the neck. Achem's fingers pried at mine to no avail.

"Where is it?" My voice boomed.

This at last ended Achem's resistance. They made a noise of surrender.

I dropped them.

Achem crumpled to the ground, their legs giving out.

"Where is it?" I asked again.

Hand pressed to their throat, Achem managed. "I'm not sure. I did not take it. I only mentioned—" Achem winced with the strain of speaking through a bruised neck. "—they were saying you kept everything locked up behind an iron door. I just told one of them... I said it was possible the work station would have a half-full case on it. Enough riches for one person..."

"Why did you not go yourself?" I demanded. But I realized the trick now. Achem had hoped I would not be able to read any guilt in them, if they sent a proxy. "You sought to avoid blame."

Achem nodded stiffly. "She was desperate enough. It did not take much urging. I did not know she'd taken it already. She was supposed to come to me first. I only wanted one obol, as a payment for my tip."

"First?" I said. "Where are they going?"

A grim smile livened their pallid features. Then, they pointed upwards. "Where else is there to go?"

"The Upper World? Don't be ridiculous. What are they thinking, to go gambling one last time?"

A preposterous idea. While it was possible for a determined soul to make their way back up the path, the risk was great and the reward small. Even if they could find the way back to their homeland, upon reaching it they would realize how distant they had become from the living. They could not exist there for long, and eventually death would pull them back to the river.

Achem shrugged. Their voice rasped but was recovering. "Up there's the only option that makes any sense. What were they hoping to purchase down here? I've noticed a distinct lack of pottery…"

They would not be able to purchase anything in the Upper World either, not as incorporeal beings. But to a frightened soul, it would be the most logical option.

I straightened. Much as I wanted to punish Achem now, I could not afford to delay. "Stay here. I will return to deal with you."

"Hey, wait!" Achem, predictably, hustled to follow. "Are you sending hellhounds to drag them back?"

"No," I answered. A storm of anger still surged through my voice. "For this, I will go myself."

Achem followed like a puppy as I retrieved my pole and made for the path. I made no attempt to prevent them. Let them see the result of their poor choices.

The path was hardly a path at all, at first glance. Just a break in the cavern wall that could be mistaken for a cleft of rock. It was easy for the seekers to forget they had walked down here, and of their own volition. But if one followed the edge, the break became a gap. And then, in the space of a blink, we were on the path.

Achem whirled around, but the mists had closed in, and neither the banks nor the walls nor the river were visible any longer. That said, though we saw no other features, the path itself left no other option but forward. We walked its white curves and switchbacks side by side. I used the pole as a staff. My beard, white as the mist around us, swayed with each step.

We passed some others, seekers on their way down to the river. In their dreamlike state, they did not pay us any mind. Death washed the expressions from their faces and the individuality from their bodies. Most newly-deceased souls were docile. The path acted almost like a river itself, sweeping them downstream.

Some, of course, fought the current. Even those who arrived with obols wanted to return to the sunlit worlds, not realizing nothing waited for them there anymore. I rarely pursued these obstinate few. Eventually, they accepted the inevitable.

I charged along as fast as the path would allow. My thoughts raced on ahead of my feet. What if the thief had dropped the case? What if my obols had scattered irretrievably? My fingers tightened on my staff, knuckles whitening.

I wasn't sure yet how I would punish Achem and the other soul, but I had no doubt the answer would come to me. First though, I needed to secure my obols.

"Can I—" Achem attempted to speak once.

I rebuffed them with a glare, and their lips sealed shut. After that, they were occupied keeping up with me.

The path ended.

We came out into the Upper World on a cliffside. The sun blazed above us, warming the tan rocks and green shrubs. A warm breeze blew strongly from the sea—and what a view of it we had. From this vantage, the crystalline water stretched deep into the horizon, turning from a vibrant shade of turquoise to a jewel blue.

Achem laughed and turned their face to the sun. Their cloak slipped from their shoulders as they spread their arms. The sun brought out the warmth in their skin, and they almost looked like one of the living.

The thief, however, stuck out from the land in a swatch of darkness. They crouched a few yards away from us. Their clothing was ripped and faded, their hair wild, their eyes equally frantic. They seemed to have been stunned still by the reality of the Upper World and had not made it far from the path. In their grasping fingers, they clutched my case.

They did not try to run, and regardless, I was beside them in a moment.

"Thief," I said.

The seeker quailed. Their fingers loosed on the case and it landed in the dust.

"It was Achem's idea—!" the thief began their weak defense, but I interrupted.

"I do not need your guidance or your excuses!" Anger at the transgression still raged through me. I laid down the sentence that had taken form throughout our walk up. "You will not spend a hundred years on the shore," I intoned. "You will spend a thousand. Your body will fade and your mind with it, until you are as insubstantial as the mist. But first, I will tear you limb from limb."

I bore down, reaching for the mortal's throat.

"No, don't!"

I had forgotten about Achem. I ignored them and felt the satisfaction of my fingernails piercing the skin of the thief's neck.

"Charon, *don't!*" Achem shoved me back, sending the thief sprawling while I staggered. I was twice their height now and the assault did not affect me greatly, but my eyes narrowed.

"Move aside, Achem."

"No! It's my fault. Do not punish this person."

"I'll punish a thief in any way I see fit. Move aside!"

With this, I pushed them away. Achem stumbled as I passed by, reaching for the thief once more. I thought Achem would attack me again, but a moment too late I saw their arm flash downward, and then they had seized the case.

I lunged, but they skittered out of the way—right to the cliff's edge.

"No!" I cried, unnecessarily. Achem had stopped at the edge. The sun glittered on the waves far below.

"Do you really want a thief wandering your shores for a thousand years? Is that the only solution you can think of?"

"I have nothing to fear from a seeker," I snapped, my eyes never leaving my case. If they let their guard down for even a second, I would be on them.

"It would never have worked," Achem went on. "We cannot stay up here. She would have returned below. And I... it was my idea. Not hers."

"Come to your point."

"Show mercy. Let her cross the river."

I scoffed. "Let a thief cross the river? And one with no fare?"

Achem's gaze grew steely, and their countenance more serious than I'd ever seen before.

"Show mercy, or I throw this into the ocean." They hefted the case.

I snarled, "I have reached the end of my patience. Bring me my case. Bring what is owed to me!"

But my threat was empty. If they threw it, I would never be able to reclaim my lost treasures. Even if the case did not open and scatter its contents, the ocean would take it, and I could not leave my post for the years it would take to search. I tried a new approach. "The moment you step away from the cliff, I'll take it from you."

Achem shrugged. "Then I'll sit here while you deliver her." They inclined their head at the thief, who'd had the intelligence not to speak again.

I sighed. "I will only say I have done it, and you will have no proof."

"I know," said Achem, still in that voice of steel. "Which is why you must swear you'll do it. Swear on the Styx."

A wave of helpless fury flooded me. Such an oath would bind me blood and bone to my task. But there was nothing I could do. I cared more about my case than my revenge. Through gritted teeth, I said, "I swear."

The thief shook with fear as we walked the path. Perhaps they did not know I had never hurt a passenger, even when I was not oath-bound. A seeker without payment might meet my wrath, but a soul with passage booked fell under my protection. My charges were safe in my hands.

That said, I made no effort to allay their fears. My thoughts stewed on Achem. I hadn't thought I'd ever see them the way they looked on the cliff. So different from the smiling person who'd cleaned my boat. Their eyes had been wild with that familiar emotion: desperation. I'd been shocked to see it there, in someone who had acted so collected in the time I'd known them.

As we boarded the boat, I helped the thief as I'd helped all others in the millennia I'd done this work. Finally looking into their face, the arc of their life unfolded before me.

I'd expected to see desperation, but instead saw only a normal life. Their only sadness had been to die alone, with no one to place the obol. I did not like the thought that my world, the banks of the river, had changed them so utterly. How had they gone from the person I saw in their past life, to the faded soul now in front of me?

When I returned to collect Achem, they sat facing the ocean, watching the setting sun gild the waves.

"Now," I said, feeling no more indulgence.

Achem stood, straightened their shoulders, and handed my case to me. I breathed a sigh of relief.

They took one last lingering look at the sea and sky. Then we descended the path.

When we reached the banks, Achem had not softened. Nor had I.

"You will remain on the banks for a thousand years," I finally said, though the words came out flat and tired.

When Achem's face turned to mine, their mouth was set in a bitter twist. Seeing the lack of remorse there, my anger resurfaced.

"What right have you to resentment?" I snapped.

"I am sorry," they said.

My jaw clamped shut in surprise.

Achem continued stiffly, "I did not come to your abode meaning to find a way to rob you. It was... opportunistic, not nefarious. Hopefully you can understand why I had to try."

In their face, I saw grim acceptance, rather than the emotional contrition I had hoped for. My response was sharp. "You *had* to steal from me?"

Achem sighed deeply. In the slope of their shoulders, I saw I had made the wrong response. But what could I have said? Surely they had not expected me to forgive them, not after such an apology. I saw no justification for what they'd done. Was it my fault no one had placed the obol for them?

But before I could begin to correct Achem as to the error of their thinking, they turned their back on me and walked away.

Days passed. I did not see Achem. I spent my evenings in my abode. But my new obols piled up, and I had lost my taste for cataloguing. A strange feeling clung like spiderwebs to my psyche. I kept seeing Achem turning away from me. Kept feeling their disappointment.

I had to admit my own fault in the matter. Was it truly because of Achem that I had been too tired to properly store my obols? Or was it part of a trend? My own weariness—no, my apathy, increasing over the years—had caused me to slip.

I had thought all seekers to be desperate, grasping people. But the thief had not been that way in life. The banks of the river had made them that way. My river.

What would it make of Achem?

For some reason, I couldn't help but think of Joa. I could see the years of their friendship playing out across their lives. Before, my ability to see seekers' lives had felt like knowledge. I saw a few moments and thought I knew enough to cast judgment. But I had never asked how these moments strung together, or how each was a step toward change or growth. I had been incurious about the fullness of their lives.

Achem's actions had felt like betrayal to me because I had some illusion about our connection. But it was not their falsehood that had ruptured the bond. I had always been in a position of great power over their fate. I knew this, but the fact of it was so unexceptional to me I had not examined it. After all, I was only the ferryman. I had always thought seekers made their own choices, and the gods decided the rest.

Achem had faced 100 years of suffering. Small wonder they had sold out our burgeoning relationship for the chance at escape. Could I really lay the blame on the banks, the river, or the other souls?

I had made Achem desperate. And I did not like the way that realization sat with me. It meant I had made others desperate. It meant others had suffered unduly because of my apathy.

I traced memories, searching for an answer to my troubled mind. All I knew was that something must be made right.

In the end, I searched my shelves for the right case, and took out a cheap iron obol.

Achem sat wrapped in their cloak. They seemed to have acquired a knife as well. They had built a small fire in an alcove. With the wall on one side and the mists obscuring anyone else from sight, they had achieved a homey, intimate feel.

Sensing I might receive no invitation, I stepped up to the fire without one.

Achem grumbled at my presence, but without the malice they'd displayed at the clifftop.

I passed them the little coin. Surprise flitted across their face.

"You mean me to have this?"

I inclined my head. "It was Joa's obol."

Now Achem was truly shocked. They sat forward to examine the obol by the firelight.

"They are all valuable to me, you know. I care not whether they are gold or iron. All are precious."

Their fingers closed around it. "You are giving it to me?"

"Yes."

Achem bowed their head. Their eyes squeezed shut as emotion swept them. I waited for the shudders to pass.

When Achem lifted their head, I said, "I'd like to hear about Joa, in your own words."

Achem's thumb rubbed against the obol. "Why?"

"You are a person who can always find friends," I explained. "You must have had many. Why ask after this one?"

After a long pause, Achem said, "I liked who I was when I was with him."

"A rare gift," I said.

They spoke no more, and I chose not to press. I allowed Achem to spend a few minutes lost in their memories.

They changed the subject. "I want to stay and help the others on the bank."

Regretful, I shook my head. "You will lose yourself, seeker. Become a shade. You cannot help anyone that way. All must board my craft eventually. This is your time."

Achem leaned back against the cave wall. Firelight played over their features while they turned the obol over in their fingers.

"Why did you change your mind about me?" they asked.

I shifted my stance, and answered slowly. My thoughts were still swirling, unsettled, in my mind. "I thought there was a way of things. But now I see only a pattern of suffering, and myself just a link in a chain. I may yet break my own link."

For once Achem had no comment.

"Come when you are ready."

Some grow so used to the cold, hard existence on the banks they forget peace awaits them. Achem, who had felt the sun so recently, was not one. It took only a few days for them to arrive at my craft. Silently, I helped them in.

As we crossed, the gentle rocking of the boat cleansed the souls within. Soon the bank was shrouded by mist, and those aboard all but forgot the suffering they had experienced there. Achem's gaze met mine one last time as the sky lightened with new promise. Then their eyes turned toward the farther shore.

See Cecelia Isaac's story "The Numismatist" online at Metaphorosis.
If you liked it, leave a comment. Authors love that!
Remember to subscribe to our e-mail updates so you'll know when
new stories are posted.

About the story

The seed of this story began in the car with my friends, when someone made a joke about 'Charon the numismatist'. I loved the idea of the psychopomp treasuring his payment as more than just a toll. I immediately laid claim to the concept, since I was looking for topics for a short story writing challenge I wanted to do that summer.

Any writer can tell you that an exciting idea does not transform into a full story overnight. I let the concept percolate for a while, and finally sketched out the bones of the story in my plotting notebook. I outline my stories in a grid I created, basically a three-act structure that uses prompts focused on character choices and unintended consequences of those choices. This is how I developed Achem as an impact character for Charon. That summer (2021), I wrote six short stories over twelve days as a personal writing challenge. Though that may sound fast to some people, the purpose was not about speed but about creating variety while getting past any overthinking, sort of like NaNoWriMo. Each short story was distinct from the others in genre, tone, and character.

Taking on a well-known myth was something I had never done before. Hoping to strike a balance between honoring the original story and not boxing myself in, I did light research on Charon and the Greek underworld after the outline was written, but before writing the story. Luckily, myths often have multiple versions or interpretations, so I could work with what felt right for my story. Creating the original character of Achem also helped me to have an outlet not pre-structured by the existing stories.

The theme of death was another area that has been covered before by many an artist. However, like myths, there are many angles from which to talk about death. "The Numismatist" focuses on the pain and suffering of being alive, juxtaposed with the positive effect people can have on each other, even when they only have a short time together.

A question for the author

Q: When do you decide a story is finished?

A: For me, the first draft is about plot and the revisions are about character. I write epic fantasy, so my stories are usually plot-heavy and have a natural conclusion: the villain is defeated. But of course great stories are built around characters. For a story to be finished, I want to feel like I've done justice to each character's emotional arc. Are they in a different place from when they started? Does the reader understand the character well enough that their choices make sense? Do readers see a vision of what the future will look like for a character, even though the story is over? These questions are an important part of my revising process.

About the author

Cecelia Isaac is a fantasy author based in New Jersey. In her day job as a geospatial research specialist, she studies the decarbonization of the electrical grid. Her hobbies include being really bad at badminton. Besides fantasy, her favorite genre to read is mystery/thriller.
ceceliaisaac.com, @CeceliaIsaac

The Zoo Diaries

Frances Pauli

Part Two

Previously…

We met the animals incarcerated in the Rainriver Zoological Gardens, a public animal experience. The zoo is struggling financially to meet the needs and requirements of its inhabitants who in turn struggle with the reality of life in captivity. Here the Sulcata tortoise longs for his missing cage-mate. The hyena pines for her lost cubs, and the macaque monkey struggles with his coffee addiction. Free from the bars which restrict the others, a wicked crow taunts them in their misery. Meanwhile, budget cuts forced the zoo to change all predators to commercial diet in lieu of raw meat.

Desperate to find Miranda, the tortoise, Oliver, escaped his enclosure. His tunnel led him to the elephant, Shanti, who assisted in getting him outside of the fences and into freedom. The escape spawned a flurry of gossip, led by the crow, who used the news to taunt the other animals. More significantly, the zoo-cam video feed caught Oliver and Shanti's interaction, sparking renewed public interest in the zoo.

Zoo Admissions

The gates are choked with visitors the morning after the video goes viral. Admission sales break the all-time zoo record, and the staff struggles to keep the lines moving. Counting is not standard procedure, as they have never approached maximum capacity before. The recent financial difficulties make it unwise to turn anyone away, however.

Someone calls a manager, who is delighted to pass on the news to the Board. More hours are requested, more staff required, but all decisions will be left to the next meeting. It could easily be a fluke, and the bottom line does not allow for any margin of error.

Elephant Paddock

Shanti counts 300 peanuts, and the day isn't even half over. She counts them twice, eying the crowd at the rail suspiciously. It is too many. There is no mathematical explanation for a 200 percent increase. More than that, she decides—they are still arriving with their cameras and their bags of nuts.

They cheer and shout to her.

Shanti rearranges the peanuts, sighs, and goes back to lining up straw. She divides yesterday's nuts by three, multiplies today's haul, and considers the increase. Something out of the ordinary is happening.

Numbers, she knows, do not lie. They do, sometimes, seem to carry a big stick, a stick that can knock and jab until you are forced to comply with them.

As if her thought summons them, They-who-sweep and They-who-bring-food arrive. *Their* sticks hang from their waists, and she admits that they are slow to use them. When they do, the prods and thumps are easy enough to bear.

Shanti obeys them without error. She remembers the circus.

Today they keep their sticks dangling. He-who-sweeps carries a broom. She-who-brings-food fills Shanti's manger with fresh hay. At the railing, the voices lift and turn as one to questions. Someone waves a fluffy, stuffed effigy of a turtle.

Shanti blinks at it. She wonders if they have caught Oliver yet, if her crime has somehow brought the crowd, and if it has, whether or not she will face punishment. Her trunk lowers, swings. She watches the sticks and barely notices when He-who-sweeps erases her calculations with a deft swipe of the broom.

Beside the railing, the crowd surges and shouts. The phony turtle dances. She-who-brings-food seems calm. She leans against the rail, chats with the others.

Shanti relaxes.

She will not be punished. She turns back to her peanuts as another shower of shells lands.

There are too many.

The Crow

Debra finds her murder in the elephant paddock. They have surrounded the huge, gray animal and are swiping peanuts the crowd throws to her.

The elephant uses her trunk to gather as many of the nuts into a pile as possible. She pivots, brushes the ground, and the braver crows duck in and steal from her pile.

Debra isn't hungry. She has filled up on popcorn and is still feeling dizzy from too much latte. The sport appeals to her, however. She is faster than many of the others. She could slip right past the rubbery trunk.

First, she lands on a rock just inside the paddock rail. There are too many visitors today. The zoo paths are choked with bodies, but the densest mass grows like a tumor around the elephant paddock.

Debra quickly decides the two are somehow related. She knows They-who-keep-prisoners are searching for the tortoise, but if these others are here to assist, they are stupid. The fugitive has long since left this area.

Debra flaps and caws at them. Idiots. There is clearly no sign of the tortoise here. His tunnel emerges in the center of the paddock, and Debra flies to the dry opening to investigate. The hole is empty, as she imagined. A line of scraped tracks leads from the tunnel toward the elephant's shelter.

Debra follows them, snatching a peanut as she passes the fray and earning a chorus of cheers from her cohort.

The murder shuffles, becomes bolder. They rush the peanuts three at a time, and the elephant lands a blow, swings her trunk, and sends one black body fluttering, stunned and bruised, across the packed ground.

Debra chuckles and struts. She explores the shelter and finds nothing but spent straw. She flies up, landing on the mounted black eye of the camera and presses her head against it. It is shiny and cool, and she pecks twice at the lens before flying off.

The tracks continue to the corner where the escape occurred, just as Debra knew they would. If They-who-keep-prisoners know the elephant helped, perhaps they are watching her, guarding her, until she can be properly punished.

Debra thinks she would like to witness that too. She thinks she should linger here, but she also sees the macaque huddling against his bars. She sees him, and her breath still reeks of coffee, still carries enough of his bean to drive him into a frenzy.

She leaves the paddock behind. They won't punish the elephant while the crowds are here, and she has an ape to torture.

Wolf Run

The wolf pack is led by a pale gray male and his mate. She is black from nose to tail tip, and her two pups look exactly like her. They are ten weeks old today, and neither of them pays any heed to their mother's rules regarding pigeons.

This morning, three plump, gray birds have entered pack territory. They waddle across the short, border grass while the adult wolves are occupied with the minced meat that has been tossed into the enclosure.

The pups' bellies are round and full of milk. They wrestle in the grass where the birds can clearly see them, and when the pigeons do not fly away in fear, the game shifts to one of stalking and hunting.

They crouch, tongues lolling freely, and watch the gray heads bob, the fat bodies move, one slow step at a time. They ease closer. Their haunches are tense for springing and chasing. Their hearts beat an excited music in their flattened ears.

"I wouldn't do that," the fattest pigeon speaks.

"It's rude," another coos. "Not friendly at all."

The pups sit up. Mother has taught them of rudeness, but they'd never guessed it applied to pigeons.

"We're hunting you," the bolder pup announces.

"Rude," the birds coo all together, suddenly huddled into a much larger mass of feathers. "Roo-oo-ood."

"If you hunt us," the fattest once again takes control of the conversation, "then we'll never tell you about it."

"About what?" the more curious pup asks while the bold one lifts a rear paw, absently scratching behind one ear.

"About the news, silly," the pigeon says. "About freedom."

"What's freedom?" the curious pup asks.

His sister whispers into his ear, "Mom said pigeons are liars."

"I think she meant crows." The pigeon, having heard the insult, puffs up considerably. "Crows lie. Pigeons always tell the truth."

Neither pup can imagine anyone *always* telling the truth. They exchange a look that says as much, deciding as one that Mother has been right all along. As usual.

"It's beside the point," the bird snaps. "Someone has gotten free, you see."

"What is free?" the wolf pups sing together.

"Free is when you can go anywhere you like," the bird explains. "Free is going outside, doing whatever you want."

"We already have that," the pups scoff, giggle, and make ready to bound away again.

Pigeons, it turns out, are boring.

"You don't, you know," the pigeon says. "Not really."

"Do too."

"Don't."

"We do whatever we want all day long," the brave pup cries.

"We go all over," her brother adds. "I even went to the rock on top of the den once."

"Liar," his sister barks. "When?"

"But you can't go over there." The pigeon turns, stupidly showing them his back, and faces the high wall, the rock-that-cannot-be-climbed. "Could you go over there if you wanted? Can you leave this cage?"

The wolves, who have been considering pouncing on him, freeze and stare up at the barrier. They have never considered anything else might *be* out there, and it gives them an uncomfortable fluttering feeling in their full bellies to think on it.

"We could," the bold pup says. "We just don't want to."

"Freedom," the pigeon coos. "Now you know. Freedom is what's *outside*. It's what you can't have *inside*."

The pups stare at the high wall. The birds, certain their point has been made at last, take to wing, fly up, one after the other, over the top of the wall that is too high to climb.

The curious pup whimpers.

His sister growls softly.

"You know," she says. "I think Mother was right about pigeons."

Her brother lies down, rests his head on his paws and watches the wall.

Mother is always right.

Ape House

Gonzo throws a turd at the crow. He knows better, knows it only debases him, that the crow will laugh harder for it. That it will rile up the other macaques until their flinging becomes a ruckus and the path outside is streaked in feces.

He cannot help himself. The devil-bird reeks of bean. She teases him with her breath, flapping her wings to waft the sweet aroma through the bars.

His turd nearly hits her.

The crow shrieks and launches into the air. Her mockery echoes in her wake, stays with him long after she has moved on to her next victim.

Gonzo's cagemates scree and fling their turds through the bars. They leap and chatter, taking up the game with zealous ferocity.

Gonzo burns with shame. He slinks to the little square door and hides in the shadow of the rope vines. She-who-sweeps will not appreciate the mess he's inspired. She may throw stones at them if no one is looking.

They are easy enough to dodge, usually ping off the bars anyway, but her anger makes him feel small and shivery.

It is the crow's fault, his shame.

It is the bean's fault.

Gonzo wishes for his home forest. He imagines sneaking from the trees, raiding the plantation for fistfuls of the sweet red coffee cherries. He salivates, grinds his teeth together. The cherries hold the bean, and the bean holds ecstasy.

The others tire of flinging and take to the ropes. Gonzo watches their shadows dance over the cage floor. He imagines his wild troop swinging through the branches. He imagines moist air and an entire jungle full of life, where the song of birds is never silent, and their voices cry of useful things: food, danger, mating.

There were no crows in his jungle. Only here, where madness lives, do the devils fly on jet black wings, their voices tasting of his bean and their words begging for murder.

MEMO

RAINRIVER ZOOLOGICAL GARDENS

TO All EMPLOYEES

IT HAS COME TO OUR ATTENTION THAT ZOOCAM FOOTAGE HAS BEEN UPLOADED TO A THIRD-PARTY SITE BY ONE OF OUR STAFF MEMBERS WITHOUT THE PERMISSION OF MANAGEMENT.

ALL EMPLOYEES ARE REQUIRED TO SIGN A NON-DISCLOSURE OF COMPANY PROPERTY AND POLICIES AGREEMENT UPON HIRING. IF YOU NEED TO RE-READ THIS DOCUMENT, COPIES CAN BE FOUND IN HUMAN RESOURCES.

AS FOR THE PERSON OR PERSONS RESPONSIBLE FOR HACKING THE ZOO WEBSITE AND POSTING THE "BEST OF RAINRIVER" COMPILATION, WE IMPLORE YOU TO COME FORWARD BY CONTACTING DR. WHEELER IN THE ZOO'S PUBLICITY OFFICE.

AT THIS TIME, WE CAN PROMISE NO REPERCUSSION OR RETRIBUTIVE ACTION WILL BE TAKEN.

—ZOO MANAGEMENT

Lion Enclosure

Charlie paces the long grass beside his trench. Above him, the morsels clog the railings, choking out the sky and jostling for a better view of him.

He has been fed minced meat this morning, and his instincts shy away from the unnatural, pre-chopped meal. His belly is full, but he is restless, unhappy.

At the rail, they wave and flash. There are too many up there, and the cameras fire non-stop. Their arms juggle snacks, purses, latte cups, and the always-aromatic hot dogs sleeping in their paper boats.

The burr of electronic shutters clicking becomes a swarm of insects. The urgency of the crowd swells as their cameras compete for the lion's attention. Someone bumps hard against the railing, pushed from behind and nearly toppling forward into a fateful plunge.

Their paper boat capsizes, and Charlie watches, suddenly still, suddenly the perfect subject, as a fat, fleshy hot dog somersaults into the trench.

He hears it land, hears the wet impact and opens his mouth, huffing in the meat scent that has infringed upon his territory but lies now just beyond the wire-that-bites.

It will drive him mad, that smell. It will linger in his memory for days while he digests the mince. While he rolls in the dung of distant zebras. Charlie eyes the wire, considers.

A small black body rockets into the trench. More follow, feathered bullets aimed directly at his sanity.

The crows scrap over the fallen meat. They caw and flutter. They tear the hot dog into bits, and Charlie hears it squeak, hears the flesh give to their claws and beaks.

He dares a step toward the wire, but the birds are off already. One by one, they vacate the trench, taking his instincts in their bony claws, and carrying them away.

Hyena Pen

Alice's cage is three paces by four. She can leap to the second highest step on her rock in a single bound. On a slow day, the faces at her bars make her cringe and pant.

Today, the crowd blots out the bushes. She cannot see across the narrow paths, cannot see anything aside from the rows of shiny eyes and bared teeth.

When she carried her pups, They-who-sweep-her-shit hung dark cloth around the bars of her enclosure. They posted signs requesting quiet that were only ignored by the least sensitive of zoo patrons.

She wishes for those curtains today, closes her eyes and pants from the top of her rock. She wishes it were twice as high, wishes she could run for more than three by four paces.

Her sides heave. She ignores the massive knuckle bone she's been working at throughout the night. She is crowded. Anxious.

She thinks of the strange rock and his quest for the aviary. It *is* the second path, isn't it? She can't remember where that knowledge came from now, if it is something she overheard or only something imagined. Couldn't it just as easily be the first path... or the last?

Alice shivers and turns her body slowly so that she faces the wall. She tucks her tail against her legs, curls and hides her spotted head beneath her paws.

She is still. She is silent. She imagines she is an ordinary stone, holding her breath for longer and longer periods.

She has lived in the zoo her entire life, and she knows more than one trick. They-who-watch are easily bored. They do not linger over nothing. They do not come to the zoo to stare at stones.

Grizzly Grotto

Hector's artist has taken her book and gone. His railing is a solid wall of expectant faces, and he considers lumbering to the square door and hiding in his den, but They-who-bring-food have hidden chunks of frozen fruit inside his stump, and the sweet smell calls to him.

His nose turns toward the odor, wandering as if it seeks to leave his muzzle behind. He sits, reaches with both front paws, and sinks his sickle claws into the soft wood.

Already, it bears the hieroglyphics of his attention. His marks cross and re-cross up and down the short tower.

The food waits in a hollow at the top of the stump, but the game must be played first. If only for appearances.

Hector claws and tears, lips rippling, and he imagines that someone, somewhere claps and cheers. Once he's made a show of searching, he roots into the hidden space, uses his tongue to remove a cold, hard strawberry, and sucks on it.

At the railing, a dozen shutters click. They aim their phones and their cameras in his direction and try to capture his likeness.

Philistines.

Hector offers them his rump, continues to eat the fruit secretively, covetously. He snorts and rumbles, licks his black lips.

He has only one artist, and *she* would never stoop to photography.

Tortoise Abroad

Oliver waits until the pathways are vacant. He hides between a trio of garbage cans and an overgrown rhododendron. He has eaten grass all day, quietly munching in a narrow circle while They-who-come-to-stare enjoy the zoo.

He thinks it must be a special holiday, for the crowd is thick, and the noise of their steps and voices deafening. After the gates close, it takes twice as long to clean the zoo, and some of the trash is simply left to skitter down the lanes and into the bushes.

At dusk, They-who-sweep-and-bring-food-and-clean-poop rush up and down the paths. They shine hand-held lights into corners and crevices. Oliver knows they are looking for him, but this is not his first zoo, nor is it his first escape.

He waits until the walks have been silent for a long time before creeping out into the open.

"There you are," a stupid pigeon nearly stops his heart.

Oliver ignores the bird and eases back to the nearby path, the second path, the one that will lead him to Miranda.

At least it's not a crow.

"Everyone is looking for you," the pigeon says. It has hopped down from one of the trash cans and now it bounces along at his side. "The zoo's gone mad with it."

"Let it," Oliver says, heaving his great shell forward, "go mad."

"Everyone's talking about you."

Oliver reaches the edge where the grass meets asphalt. He will make less obvious tracks on the latter but will also be more exposed following it.

"Are they still looking?" He knows better than to engage with gossips, but the rotten pigeons always seem to have a broader view of the world.

"No." Taking his questions as friendship, the pigeon flaps its wings, hops up, and settles itself on top of Oliver's shell. "Everyone gave up hours ago."

Oliver thinks it hasn't been that long. He believes, had he been a fiercer creature, that the pigeon would be dead.

Its claws tickle his dome, but he is not flexible, not fast enough to dislodge it.

"Where are we going?" it asks.

"Aviary," Oliver huffs and steps out onto the asphalt. "This way."

"The aviary isn't this way," the pigeon says. "Whatever gave you that idea?"

Oliver pauses. He stares down the path and thinks of Miranda, of the hyena who had surely never left her cage. Whose mind has been twisted by her life in a box.

"Where?" he asks.

"I can show you," the pigeon says. "They'll never believe it, never live it down, if I do it."

"Where?" Oliver repeats. His limbs are cold already, and the night caresses his shell with fingers of ice. Only the spot where the bird rests is warm, and he chooses to take that as a sign. "Guide me."

"You bet I will," the pigeon says. "The crows will *never* live it down."

Oliver sighs. He wonders if the hyena wasn't right. But when the pigeon flaps and shifts against his shell, when it coos, "This way," Oliver sets off, obediently, in a whole new direction.

The Crow

Debra circles the park above the high fences and the short trees. She watches the search eagerly, her excitement lessened only slightly by the fact that They-who-search do not carry weapons.

There is too much chaos to be disappointed, too much action in a world that lives by routine, by feeding schedules, business hours, and state-mandated rules and regulations. There is trash lingering in the walks. There is a broken fence in the petting zoo where the weight of the crowd proved too much for the poorly maintained wood.

Debra watches until the search ends, then she circles on her own. Her murder has settled for the night, tucked into the branches of the tallest tree near the elephant paddock.

There is no point in lingering there. The tortoise has roamed far during the previous night. Debra has seen traces of him, followed bits and scraps of tracks from the African Savannah halfway across the zoo.

She flies over the cat house now, and she knows he will move again soon. He is clever, almost crow clever, and he's been waiting somewhere for the paths to clear. She lands atop the cat house roof, hops down its length, and gazes out to where the deep pit trenches of the bear enclosures wait.

The zoo falls quiet. Everything sleeps, still as usual, ordinary as any other night. Except for the hyena. Debra thinks the hyena should be crying, curled up on her rock and whimpering to herself in her grating, feather-lifting voice.

And she is not.

Tonight, the free-standing block that houses the weird beast, that sandwiches her forever between the bears and the house of true cats, is silent. It is a very loud sound, that quiet. A heavy absence.

Debra dives from the roof, sweeps over grass and paths alike, and lands in a bush in front of the grieving hyena's home. She expects to find the animal asleep, her sobbing spent at last. Instead, she sees the spotted body pacing near the front bars. Too quiet. Too quick. First one way and then the other.

"Hello," Debra calls.

"Stone?"

Interesting. Debra considers before answering, finds words that are open and as slippery as a wet vine.

"Perhaps." She hunkers deeper into the foliage, hides her body, and softens her voice. "Perhaps not."

"It's not the second path," the hyena blurts. "I told him it was, but now I'm not certain."

"You told him?" Debra's plumage prickles. "Did you?"

"I told him." The hyena turns, trots to the far corner then pivots and skims right back. "He's looking in the wrong place. I just know it."

"Looking for..." Debra lets the word stretch into a compulsion.

"The aviary," the hyena replies. "Looking for a bird, and all birds are in the aviary."

This is not, in fact, true, but what would a hyena know of it?

"I see." Debra shifts her feet and the branches crackle.

They hyena freezes, head up, ears swiveling. "Who are you?"

Debra tries to think of a slippery answer, but she has spotted the Sulcata's tracks in the grass below and the excitement of this evidence dulls her tongue.

"Are you the stone's mother?" Something in the tone of that provides the right answer.

"Yes," Debra lies, sure now that she knows what 'stone' they speak of.

"He took the second path," they hyena repeats. "But I'm not sure it's right. I'm not sure he'll find her there."

"Find who?" Debra risks a direct question.

"The bird who used to live with him," the hyena offers freely.

It is too delightful, too awful to bear in silence and Debra cackles.

The hyena growls, lowers and bristles all down her back. "Who are you?" she demands, suspicions lacing through her words. It is too much. Too perfect.

It is bound to end in disaster.

And Debra has already flown away.

Elephant Paddock

There are even more visitors than yesterday, an impossible number of faces packed into a living wall around Shanti's pen.

The peanuts are beginning to irritate her.

She steps through a sea of shells, crunching, swinging her trunk through the piles while another shower makes it all impossible to count.

Around Oliver's tunnel, the demon birds have gathered. Shanti tries ignoring the crowd, tries counting the birds instead. One rotten crow. Two awful, obnoxious crows. Three...

"It's all because of you," one of the murder caws.

"You let him out," another shouts.

"You'll be punished."

"They're all here to watch."

"Punishment." They take that up like a chant. "Punish, punish, punishment."

Shanti thinks they're liars. It's been three days, three long nights since the tortoise erupted inside her paddock. Three since she lifted the fence, and the sticks have not struck. She is not punished, and she thinks she will not be.

Four lying devil crows. Five...

She did help Oliver escape, and she does wonder where he's gone with his domed shell and its thirteen perfect hexagonal tiles with twenty-four partials around the edges. Shanti enjoyed counting him. She hopes he has found his bird, but she wonders if he might wander back in this direction afterwards.

If he does, she will lift the fence for him. She will guard his tunnel for his return, and maybe he will let her count him all over again.

"Punishment." The crows screech.

Shanti swings her trunk and charges them.

"Shit."

"Crazy."

"Mad, mad!"

They scatter, cursing her, singing epithets.

Shanti counts their shadows as they fly. Six fat, furious silhouettes. Six sides to each hexagon.

She stands over an empty tunnel and waits for the tortoise to return.

ZOO FLIER

WIN CASH!!!

ANNOUNCING THE FIRST EVER
RAINRIVER ZOOLOGICAL GARDEN

VIDEO CONTEST
"COME TO THE ZOO AND CAPTURE THE MAGIC"

$3,000 IN CASH PRIZES*
1ST PLACE: $1500
RUNNER-UP VIDEO: $1000
BEST STILL PHOTOGRAPH: $500

SEE YOU AT THE ZOO!

*PRIZE MAY BE PAID IN ZOO BUCKS AT WINNER'S DISCRETION

The Board declares the viral video to be an unprecedented opportunity. The chaos at the gates seems quite sufferable once the daily admissions are tallied and profits totaled. Another lane is added, another booth opened, and talk shifts to the idea of promoting the contest.

Someone suggests contacting the local radio station.

Maintenance complains about the additional work, and one of the zoo veterinarians brings up stress and animal welfare. Both topics are tabled until the next meeting.

The contest goes forward as planned.

Ape House

Gonzo sits in shadow while his troop dances for the crowd. His headache is not lessened by the steady clicking of camera shutters. Nor is it any better for the constant screeching and hooting of the other macaques.

They swing from one rope to the next. They race up, around, and over, tumbling and wrestling while the cameras fight over the best angle.

Gonzo has tried to go back inside, but the little square door is blocked. He is shut out. He is on display. It is his own fault.

Earlier, They-who-bring-food left one of their paper vessels too close to the cage bars. There had been three of them that morning, two carrying tubs of sliced fruit and chopped vegetables, and a third bringing them each a vessel of the hot, steaming, bean juice favored by They-who-sweep-and-bring-food-and-clean-feces.

The tubs were set in the center aisle, between the rows of ape house cages, and the drinks evenly distributed.

Gonzo watched the dance of vessels. He pressed his nose against cool bars and let his gaze drift from one end of the aisle to the next, following the bean.

The tubs were hauled to each cage door. The food was distributed, and every free, hairless paw waved a vessel, wafting steam and aroma from cage to cage. When the tub reached the macaque enclosure, it was heaved up onto the cage floor. The-one-who-manned-the-door passed their vessel to The-one-who-watched-for-escape, whose paw already lifted their own drink to pink lips. With a shrug, they took the second and set it down beside Gonzo's cage.

And he was on it.

Gonzo leapt sideways along the bars, stuffing both arms through to his armpits. His fingers scrambled for the vessel, met with smooth hot paper, snatched, and lifted.

They-who-bring-food made a noise of challenge, a barking, choking sound that brought Gonzo's teeth out, that peeled back his lips in defiance.

The vessel was batted out of his grip. Suddenly, it was tumbling, spraying hot liquid in a wasted swath across the aisle. The vessel hit the concrete with a hollow thunk. Gonzo shrieked and stretched for it, catching a single drop of spray in his paws. He drew his fingers in, stuffed them into his mouth, and sucked.

The taste was so brief, so muted that he might have imagined it. His fingers were burned.

They-who-bring-food shouted at one another, waving their arms at the aisle, the cage, at Gonzo.

He screeched and lunged at the bars, pressing the keepers two steps further into the aisle. He showed his fangs, howled, and slammed his fists against the cage floor. His troop fell upon the food, but Gonzo ignored them, continued to rail.

When the others finished, wandering out into the sunshine, he sulked, hunkered inside until a long broom pushed through the bars, pushed, and harried him until he followed the troop.

Then the door was blocked. The flat, unbreakable panel slid into place, and Gonzo was left to face the outside world, the constant flutter of the cameras, the troops frenzy.

He sits, in the rope shadows, and he stuffs his sore fingers into his mouth, sucks at them as if he can taste anything at all.

Lion Enclosure

Charlie tries to ignore the morsels, but they are pounding on the clear, den wall. He lies against the barrier, back to the crowd and mouth hanging open, drinking in the scents that reach him only faintly.

From the railing, the meaty, tangy snack odors call like half-forgotten dreams, just out of reach.

Charlie's belly is full of the tasteless minced meat. His ears twitch in time to the morsels' pounding. Each impact of a tiny fist a hard finger against his spine. He narrows his gaze, blinks at the sunlight outside the den, where the lionesses lounge for the crowd at the railings.

They are basking in the attention, in the eyes of a crowd unlike any Charlie can remember in his life at the zoo.

A tap-tapping at the glass drags his head around. It is sharper, more insistent than the idle thumps, and when he looks, a round face has pressed into a pancake grimace right beside his own.

Charlie yawns, stretching his jaws wide enough to swallow the morsel's whole head.

"I see you, morsel," that yawn says. "I taste you there."

The morsel squeals. It is a muffled sound, filtered through the barrier, but Charlie loves it. He curls his tongue and heaves to all fours, facing the tiny morsel and huffing a warning.

Both of the small one's fists press in beside his face, smoosh against the barrier and pale, flatten.

Charlie bats one paw out, pats at the smooth surface until the morsel shrieks and moves. It doesn't run. Instead, it dances up and down, batting its own paws together before pressing up against the clear wall again.

Charlie imagines it tastes like the squeaky meat sticks. He lets his tongue reach out and licks the barrier, runs his mouth over and over the morsel while, behind it, the tall ones clap and wave.

Hyena Removed

Alice wakes in unfamiliar surroundings. Three of the walls are solid, and through the short stretch of bars she can see a narrow aisle and another cage across from hers.

The stair-step rock is missing. There is a thin shelf along one wall, but it is too narrow, too insubstantial for lounging. She ponders it and remembers vaguely that she knows this from experience.

Alice sniffs, wrinkling her muzzle. Her head is fuzzy inside as well as out. She remembers eating in the evening, an entire bowl of meaty, strange-smelling mince. She remembers struggling to climb the stair-step rock and slipping, falling asleep instead in the straw at its base.

Now she is *inside*. There is no chattering crowd, but there is also no sun, no sky at all to tell her if it's day or night.

There are lights, but they are weirdly too dim and too bright simultaneously. Impossible to look at. Pale enough to only illuminate half the cage. Across the aisle, a sleek shape moves in its own enclosure. It is low and lanky, some sort of spotted feline. Alice remembers she's seen it before.

She has been *here* before.

Alice pants. She flicks her tail and rises, shakily, on her four paws. She begins to inspect the cage. Her nose presses into each corner, every crevice. It finds no hint of her own scent, but she is certain, by the time she finishes, that she has spent time here before.

Her paws remember how many paces fit along each wall. They track a familiar path around the space, easily, automatically.

Alice sits, stares at the shadow cat, and tries to think. It was before her pups but not *long* before.

That time, she tried the ledge and fell. That time she burned with her estrus, paced and paced until they finally released her back into her cage to find...

Alice relaxes. She believes this is temporary. She remembers, and as if on command, her body slumps. Her paws stretch, forward and back, and she rolls onto her side. Tired. Calm.

She closes her eyes and waits.

See parts I and II of Frances Pauli's serial "The Zoo Diaries" online at Metaphorosis.
If you liked them, leave a comment. Authors love that!
Remember to subscribe to our e-mail updates so you'll know when new stories are posted.

March

All the Daughters Sing

Jan Priddy

Light pours straight down through the leaves, hot like midsummer, and the duff underfoot feels quite light and dry. Yes, it must be July. The moon has gone bright and dark and bright again without more than a mist falling. Salmonberries are ripening.

I move along the narrow path, using a staff of carved cedar wood because I tire easily, and my feet are unsteady on the path. Sometimes my attention wanders. I mean to be quick, sneaking away for this last walk alone. Daughters will come soon enough and spoil my solitude.

My goal is the large mossed-over stone marking where my first daughter is buried. My firstborn, Alice. The trees are deciduous along this slope. Thin branches and spicy leaves rattle with the slightest breeze, but the air hardly stirs, passing in and out of my open mouth without a sound, blood-warm as if I walk through the world's breath.

I hold my breath and listen. No sound of Daughters behind me, though they will follow if they catch me wandering. They are light on their feet, careful even when it does not matter.

Being alone is the point of my walk, and there is no one looking to disagree. I only argue with myself. Daughters never argue. They listen. They are respectful of my opinions, my cautions and concerns. Yet, as I walk, I feel hemmed in and worried by something more, just out of sight. I should have told them where I was going and asked them to leave me be. They would have done that.

Waiting is an ache beneath my heart, the thudding sound of it, and desire for an ending.

Movement catches my attention just ahead and above, a fluttering like—very much like—something living. It stutters and drifts across the perfectly still air, down and down, like something alive, like a butterfly, and I have nearly forgotten what a butterfly was like after all this time. I track its movement along the downslope ahead of me, near Alice's grave. Wonder flutters from joy to loss. I reach above my head to catch it, fingers splayed and reaching, mouth open, attention gathered completely by the movement where there should be no movement.

As I reach to grasp the butterfly, just beyond the tips of my fingers, I step wrong and wound myself. I sit abruptly on the dry earth—the out-of-season leaf drops nearby—and pull my foot into my lap, where blood wells from my broken skin. Much has been broken. This hillside once had homes with windows and kitchens and families.

I squeeze the tough sole of my foot, remove a sliver of green glass the size of a fingernail. Glass, after all this time. Decades crept past.

Since I was born, people warned the world might end in a blaze or with a whimper. Climate and catastrophe were always the story. Death from disease or some newly recognized toxin. Is that how it happened? I do not care. Instead, I fear sometimes I will never die. I survived a century and more past my time.

The light splatters down between the trees, their pale leaves unspeaking in the stillness.

Too soon, Daughters will scent blood and come running quick as anything.

In the middle of the twenty-first century, no British swallow returned from South Africa. Terns, wheatears, and sheerwaters vanished from their migratory routes. Sandhill cranes failed to return to wetlands in Michigan where they had rested and nested for nine million years. By then, seagulls no longer trailed fishing fleets. Bird feeders attracted only determined squirrels and chipmunks and rats. Small children playing in their own back yards carried festering bodies of songbirds to their horrified parents.

If anyone had predicted what happened, it would have been a worst case scenario. No one wanted to believe we would be helpless to fight it off.

I might have been among the first human beings to catch the new virus. Or perhaps it was a very old one. Or a bacterium. Or maybe several diseases that also killed birds and snakes and frogs and then mammals. There would be no one left to study and explain what killed them all—whatever it was that made me sick, but not dead. I will never know. I refuse to care how it happened. I will never know why or how or what will come later. For a long time I only focused on the now.

But when it started long ago, I lay under blankets, eyes closed, and shivered for what seemed an eternity. Hours? A day? I told my flatmate I needed to sleep and turned off my cell. At first, I assumed it was a cold coming on suddenly after work, then, later in the evening and the following days, some really bad influenza or another mutation of the coronavirus that would not let go. In bed, too weak to dress and go to work or even to call in sick, I messaged my boss and collapsed. My joints ached, skin wet with fever, but on a trip to the bathroom I tucked a thermometer into my ear and found my temperature had dropped to 95°. I staggered back to bed and to sleep. I was not yet afraid of dying. I was afraid of missing work, of not being prepared for the trade show presentation. I was afraid I would lose my job. I turned on my cell to message my boss again and scrolled through for news. Headlines declared that whole cities were getting sick and dying. I was afraid I would catch whatever those other people had. Despite being afraid I might die, I did not die. Instead, I felt better.

It was a Tuesday when I finally felt well enough to call into work, but service was down and I felt too wretched to care. My joints crackled when I sat up in bed. I could not hear my flatmates in the central kitchen or Carly slamming the door as she left early for work. Carly always slammed the front door. I could time my day by the slam and her stomping down the stairs.

I sniffed. What was that awful smell?

The stink was what finally drove me from bed and to the kitchen. No one there and I was sick, that was all. I drank a glass bottle of water, scrolled through screens that refused to open properly, opened blinds to check the street, but all was silent. There was power from the passive system I'd set up, and water ran from the tap when I washed my hands. But it was quiet. No traffic, no neighbor's dog barked, no one played music. I wiped my eyes unstuck as I stood at the window. The air outside seemed thicker, misty almost, and my ears rang with a hissing, stinging sound that gave way to absolute silence, the quiet like a presence waiting. I wanted to lie back down. By that Tuesday—if it was a Tuesday—life on Earth, most everything that moved, had ended. Whatever it was had killed everyone I knew and entire populations I never could have known, though I did not understand that at the time.

I held myself quite calm when telling Daughters this story, emotions carefully in check. I had not been calm in those early years alone. I cried and screamed and shook and shouted at the silence. I ran through empty streets in the dark and walked for days south to the Columbia River and found no one, saw nothing that mattered.

Herds of deer did not dash through downtown canyons of concrete. I did not track the days with marks scratched onto a wall. I did not make plans to walk across the continent or to rebuild. Climate change had already done its dirty deed, invaded shorelines, stolen entire low-lying neighborhoods and left winters damp but mild. The filthy air blew away and I breathed easier. I accepted all that. I cannot explain, but I knew everything was changed forever and I made no effort to change things back.

I do not tell the Daughters any of this.

Even in those first days, there was no doubt what was behind Carly's closed bedroom door. For a long time I huddled in my room, left only to drink bottled water, eat peas and broccoli thawing in the freezer, cold canned chili and the last banana, already gone soupy inside. It was crazy, but I thought everything would be all right if I remained calm, if I did not open Carley's door or try to call my mother. That horrible smell. Flies everywhere. Plastics breaking down faster than they should.

Odors of chlorine and vinegar overrode the rot. My stored food ran out, and I went out to the grocery store over on 45th and thought about theft. From whom? I tried the doors, banged on them, threw rocks from a garden, but could not break the glass. I found an ancient push mower in the storage room of my condo, carried it down to the corner, and tossed it through the front window of the local convenience store. By that time, I had gotten used to the stink, or it was fading—I hoped it was. Entire human bodies collapsed into puddles and stains sliding across sidewalks leaving huddles of chemical clothing even the insects did not eat. Packages of crackers and cookies were spoiled and nibbled, but glass containers and cans were fine. Sell-by dates meant nothing. Weeks or months passed; I was already losing track of time.

I went out under the stars and searched for the sound of something larger than a carpenter ant. I had not yet noticed I was not sleeping. I knew my friends were dead, my family, my job didn't matter. I did not have to complete my presentation on post-graphene batteries or defend the generation after that.

My watch quit working. My sport shoes smelled of vinegar and went flat. I thought I would have to give up running. The idea made me laugh and recognize how near I was to hysteria.

I made the list in my head: food, water, shelter. Family. Mom had called when her canaries died. I was already sick that day. My mother. I went to find her. Mom's house was collapsing and I could not breathe. I sat in the road and could not get back to what I knew or the people. Everyone was gone. I closed my eyes and waited for the days to end. For the nights to pass. By now, I knew I was not sleeping.

The moon had gone to full by then—I could see the moon when I went out, streets lit by stars that had once been obscured by artificial lights. I walked all the way into downtown, past wooden buildings that seemed already to tip and sag. Stains on the sidewalks all the way to the waterfront and up against the inside of glass doors to office buildings. No bodies, the stink fading away.

I broke into the REI downtown, found flint and steel, a small folding shovel with a metal handle. Even this building was not steady, would not last long. From this and other stores I gathered everything that might be useful and not rot and dragged it outside to the middle of streets where I hoped I could find it if I needed something later.

Anything in freezers or refrigerated cases was hopeless. Cardboard packaging was eaten through, plastic containers were corroded and discolored. Ants fell from the ceiling onto my head as I collected glass bottles of sun-dried tomatoes, olives, and sweet red peppers, cans of beans and tomatoes, fancy flavored salt packaged in glass.

I was very tired, but kept moving, seeking something familiar. I climbed back east through empty streets, broke into the Conservatory on Capital Hill. It had been my peaceful place, but now the plants in the center pavillion were dry and dead. Downtown again, I learned the trick to breaking tempered glass and smashed windows just to hear them fall. When my clothing fell apart, I broke locks on doors and found more. When I was hungry, I found whatever was nearest. I ate canned food shelved in the upper floors of downtown condominium kitchens, and built fires on their concrete floors to give light in the lengthening nights.

I closed my eyes, imagined sleep.

Some days, I cried and screamed and argued out loud with myself. On a long walk south, I raided small towns and tried to remember their names. Arms wrapped around my body, pacing the freeway and empty sidewalks that had begun to go cockeyed and too hot for bare feet. There was no one walking larger than a beetle. One sweltering summer day I came upon a river of black ants moving across the floor of an empty house, felt the crunch and moisture of their bodies under my naked heels, around and across my feet. Caught between fascination and fury, I stamped and stamped them, until, hysterical and sobbing, I had to run away from the squashed and swarming bodies. I closed my mouth on my remorse. The world was quieter, and I became quiet. There was nothing to see across the Columbia River, only another city falling down. I went north to home in Seattle. The word 'home' in my head made me laugh.

I thought about walking off the edge of a building or taking pills found in a pharmacy, or sleeping until the world ended. If only I could sleep. I leaned too close to fire though I was not cold, only alone and shivering. What threatened? No strangers. No dogs or wild animals drawn by flame. I remembered moths fluttering and dropping into campfires on the walk south, but there were no moths by the time I walked north again. Fewer flies. I walked for miles until I was too tired to walk further. I thought I would die.

When there were no longer shoes or clothing remaining from Before, I went naked and did not feel the cold even at night. I sat in shade in hot weather, found shelter from wind when the air cooled. I managed. I ate anything I could find or gather without craving any particular food. I was never sick. I remembered snow and books and family dinners. But it was never cold enough for frost and my books fell apart and all my family was dead.

I had been alone, entirely alone for years, when I realized I was pregnant.

One morning after bathing in the vast basin that I thought of as Lake Washington, I ran my hands across my stomach and felt the knot flutter below my belly button. My monthly periods had ceased long ago—how long? I should have been grateful; where would I find tampons? I was relieved, wasn't I? I could not recall precisely when my monthlies had become yearlies, only that my last period had been a month ago. I argued with myself about the bulge in my belly: a parasite? But soon my belly grew round and tight. It was a baby turning under my hand.

I could not be pregnant.

In late spring, just weeks after I understood my condition, contractions began.

I deliberately turned away from both reason and fear. It was a miscarriage. Of course it was. I was losing the baby, and though tears came and my hands shook and I panted, I told myself it was all for the best. I could not have a baby alone. I could not have a baby at all. There was only the tiny bulge in my belly, not the enormous belly holding a full term infant. I breathed steadily, sat in the shade of a dying maple tree, and counted between passes of pain that was not quite pain but something else. Ripples of heat in my body—an orgasm, pleasure, and I was startled, then howling, screaming in pleasure and shuddering in that long forgotten ecstasy—how could I have forgotten this?

It seemed to last a long time, this pulsing pleasure and pain. Then, hardly noticing I did, I pushed it out. A sliding, climactic birth throb, and a blueish, blood-streaked sack lay between my thighs, born in a series of overwhelming orgasmic pulses. I gasped and closed my eyes, then, remembering something I had not known, I bent to tear open the sack with my nails. The slick covering membrane was tough and I used my teeth. It stretched, tore, and the tiniest infant pushed its face out. I cleared the sack. The infant lay on the new grass, slick and wet and mewling like a puppy. Alive. Tiny. I thought the baby would surely die—the size of two fists stacked end to end, barely as long as my fingers spread wide—helpless and dark. But it was strong. The baby screamed, and I gathered it against my bare chest. It hunted for a breast. Latched. Milk came, and the infant girl suckled.

Miraculous and marvelous. Another ripple of pleasure—again that pulse I could not help connecting to sex—echoed as my baby nursed, my whole body hot and glowing. What a blessing to feel pleasure and to be of use! I wiped my daughter clean with grass. She did not die that day.

My daughter's eyes were nearly black rather than my hazel, darker than my grandmother's eyes were said to have been. The baby's skin, too, showed darker than mine, matching where mine was browned by the sun, but she had that rich color at birth. My beautiful Alice.

It was still spring when she slid out of my arms and stood. The child was not growing the way children were supposed to grow. Surely my nephew had been nearly a year before he stood unaided. I pushed the memory away.

Alice laughed, a burbling chuckle, ending in a squeal as she took a step away from me. She toddled toward a tuft of clover, stumbled on a stone and splashed the still water in a puddle.

I stood over the infant, steadying her shoulders between my hands.

"Okay, little one. Come along now," I said, meaning to guide her away from the murky water.

The child looked around, frowned, and said, "Okay."

My legs let me down onto the ground as if I'd fallen. I recognized then what I had refused to see before. I whispered to my already sturdy child, "Baby girl, little Alice, where did you come from?"

The tiny child looked up to my face and said, "Come from?"

It was all crazy, wonderful. I laughed and swung Alice onto my hip and then set her down, swung her up and over my head.

I laughed for the madness of it all—having a child, a child who stood in days, a child who did not resemble me at all. Like everything gone—the absence of dogs howling at the moon, no cats sleeping in sunshine, no birds, collapsing houses in the city—this child was something new and different.

But then, what was not? My mother had been fond of the expression, "So what else is new?" I watched my tiny daughter tumbling in the grass and whispered, not quite to myself, "Everything."

I released myself from control and ran and laughed with Alice.

Before the first leaves turned and fell, Alice kept pace with me all day. She helped gather filberts on the other side of the lake, trailing after wherever I went, talking and singing too. My voice had been near silent, but now we chattered all day. I sang her to sleep and closed my own eyes and imagined what we might do next. We moved closer to the city, I made her toys from scraps of wood and taught her songs recalled from childhood, and my little girl sang back to me and in harmony.

"Come, let's go up in the hills," I said one day. "There might be huckleberries still."

I rubbed Alice's hair, thick and black. If I thought too much about how she came to me, I feared she might go away again. It was an irrational fear, but I was getting used to that.

All of this was impossible, but by then many impossible things had already happened.

The next spring I birthed a second daughter, and Alice watched after her sister Belle. Alice had stopped growing when the top of her head reached the bottom of my chin, and I was not tall.

My second baby developed just as Alice had, and I ate voraciously to keep up her milk supply until, by autumn, they could feed themselves. And then another spring and another child was born, cared for by my second, and Alice returned to my side. At birth, each was smaller than any infant human I had ever known to survive, and each grew faster than was possible. I could not know at first that they would not live long, but I was not so foolish as to ignore how they were strange. I simply chose not to care how it had all happened.

By the time I had twenty daughters, the last year's child named Tina, Alice had borne a baby of her own. She was Ulla. I had not thought of my children as fully grown. I considered calling myself Grandmother, but they all called me Mother because Alice did. The next spring, only Vera was born to Belle, and I realized I had done birthing. Tina would be the last child born of my body. Now my daughters birthed.

Everything about their lives flowed quicker than mine.

They were clever with their hands, clever finding food, sometimes eating things I had never dared try. Perhaps their sense of smell was better. They rarely became ill from testing something they should not eat.

"Bad," said Alice once after spitting up on the ground before me. "Bad teffa," the girl said. She held out the frond.

"All right," I said. "We won't eat fern."

They ate skunk cabbage and other flowers and many roots, and they scraped the inner bark of downed trees and gathered seeds. Alice would sit beside me in the evening before she slept and tell me everything she'd seen and the other Daughters had done. They braided grasses and the chewed fibers of roots and reeds. They planted gardens of sorts, setting seeds in the center of a meadow east of the city and seeming to admire the plants as they grew. They invited the bees but did not steal honey, gathered dead wood but would not hurt a living tree.

I talked and talked to my daughters until I was hoarse, until I noticed they hardly spoke back. They sang.

One spring day, all the children, who mostly were not children at all anymore, but girls or little women, all wore crowns woven of new green leaves and trillium flowers. Alice put one of tiny dairies and wisps of seedheads around my head. They stood close to one another, close to me, wrapped their arms in a circle around me, and sang. New words, new notes, and they sang in harmony like a well-trained choir. I did not recognize the music at all. They grew beyond me, my Daughters. Even Alice, my oldest child, could not always explain to me the why or how of her living.

They wove little sacks of a particular reed, though I would not have known how to teach them. They wave baskets tight enough to carry water. Insects did not invade their stored seeds and dry berries. They taught me how.

Insects themselves seemed less common. While telling a story about the small, wee voice of Mosquito, I realized my Daughters had never seen a mosquito. Perhaps spiders had won? But spiders were no longer as common as they had been. It had been years since I walked into a web between trees.

My years were marked: a child was born, and walked for the first time, and began to sing. I deliberately named them alphabetically, each named for someone, until I accepted that they did not need names to know themselves, and it was hard sometimes for me to tell them apart.

Alice was my first and best child, the child of desperation and need. The rest of my children, like the first, came unbidden. I tried not to care too much about them and that was impossible.

The sound of my Daughters calling and singing above the less insistent whir and hiss of insect life was a background chorus.

Partway through the alphabet the second time, Alice died. Alice died, leaving twenty-six sisters, eleven nieces, and a daughter of her own. All of them Daughters but me.

I rocked the small body of my first born and wept and moaned. Daughters closed around. They held me steady when my body shook. They licked tears from my face.

The Daughters carried their sister, dug a place in the forest with a boulder as marker, and covered her with flowers before covering her in the earth. They sang the sun down. The song was about forest and fruiting trees, the berries that stained their fingers and the experiences of birth and birthing and falling away. Finally they fell away themselves and went on with life. I mourned and sat apart and useless.

All my singing children, all Daughters, and all their Daughters after them, were like that. Most years a birth and a death. I stopped counting and naming. Or rather, counted and named only for myself, recognized that there was no one else to whom most numbers or names mattered.

I cared for them automatically. Because I believed I should love them all the same, I tried, but it was my firstborn I had most wanted to keep safe. I tried not to care too much after Alice, because they would die too soon. I tried to love them all the same, or not to love them. I failed.

They did not cry, but often laughed. They waited patiently. They licked my hands and wrists less often than they licked one another's. Perhaps they recognized I did not like the gesture or need it as they seemed to themselves. They smiled and wrapped their arms around me and one another. They spoke, they sang the songs I taught them, but more often the ones they created themselves. I was content to have company.

How long did this idyll last? What were a few decades? My children grew, began to birth, and the oldest among them died while still young in my eyes. I had to let them go. I let them go.

Not sleeping—what was that about? Was it some kind of magical accommodation that allowed me to take 24/7 care of the girls? I wished I knew. They slept. Sometimes they slept half the day if they were not busy gathering or making or working on something. I seemed only to drift.

Springtimes passed, and others came and left. Decades. Daughters born and birthing and passed. I was not alone. But by now I have lived too long.

There might be no one left on earth who remembers what I remember. The children listen, but probably do not believe the stories I tell, ordinary descriptions of feathers and clawed feet. Even to me, this feels like dreaming or fables, fanciful stories of babies crawling for months, the slow development of speech and years spent in school, birds flying and horses' muzzles velvety soft. Birdsong and frogs croaking and cows mooing. Dogs barking and cats mewing. Mice in the walls of houses. The eating of flesh, the sounds of a city. Open chest surgery. Libraries. Trains, planes, and automobiles. Illness and mourned death.

These are my stories—more like nightmare visions for which I claim nostalgia. Frightening by now even to myself. When I am gone, what will they preserve? While they remember what I say or sing, they write nothing. I have been unable to convince my progeny of the need for writing. Even to me, my stories sound fantastical. Dragons and sea monsters.

I think about Alice's laughter, my daughter's hand wrapped about my finger in the weeks after her birth, how by the following year Alice held the hand of Belle, and each youngest Daughter cared for the one after. I fed them, cleaned them, told them stories. I made decisions about where and when to move on. I was head of a large family. When did that change? My Daughters still move on without leaving me behind. They grow, become themselves and not merely a part of me. They walk into the forest and gather to sing, more than I can count. Over a hundred, and surely more gather to sing than come from my body. I never have more than forty-two

Daughters alive at once. I try to count them again and cannot understand if I am counting them twice and three times or are there Daughters here who are not mine? It is another puzzle I cannot solve.

They sing a gift, not to me, but to one another. I follow them. The Daughters are well settled in their new world and have little need of me.

As if Alice stood before me, I hear her speak: "Mama." The voice in my head startles memory awake. One day long ago as we walked in this forest, Alice looked up into my eyes. "Mama, the other Mothers are tall like you."

"What other Mothers?"

She spun a leaf between her fingers, green like the glass. "There are nine Mothers in the world."

"How can you know there are others?" I said.

"Just nine," she said. "Far away." She sighed and smiled, and then went along humming.

The shard that cut my foot is green. A leaf color. What came in such bright green glass bottles? Soda? Wine? I hardly remember and it doesn't matter. I pull my foot up closer to my face to examine the wound. It is not so bad. I stand, test weight on my foot while turning the wounding glass in my fingers and rubbing its smooth outer side.

Here, I last held my firstborn. That first shocking birth and love of Alice is what I miss. Perhaps it is my lost usefulness. I have lived long past my time.

My living Daughters sing me back to the present. They are near. Like Alice did so long ago, they sing of other Mothers I will never know and other Daughters who join their choral gathering.

I am very tired. I half-close my eyes and give in to listening to their music, and when I open my eyes and look around, I find them waiting for my attention to return.

They smile. They stroke my hand. I worried for a long time about the end of the world, but the world does not end with me. I wonder if my Daughters think me a little mad.

Perhaps I am mad. Perhaps I will die now, because they are ready for me to leave them.

See Jan Priddy's story "All the Daughters Sing" online at Metaphorosis.
If you liked it, leave a comment. Authors love that!
Remember to subscribe to our e-mail updates so you'll know when new stories are posted.

About the story

This story began with an image of songbirds dropping from trees. (Rachel Carson talked about that happening due to the use of DDT in the 1950s. Dead birds on the ground. Eventually, she wrote *Silent Spring* and triggered the environment movement and the outlawing of DDT.) I did some research and found an island where that had happened—all the birds had died. Some plant species died out as a result. Then I went further: What if everything died? If birds died, reptiles are a cold-blooded relative and they would be dead. Amphibians were already in trouble. Where was the thundering croaking of frogs I used to hear in the wetlands nearby? And then large mammals are already dying out, so all mammals might die, and all humans. What if there were one survivor, the last person alive, how might life go on? No monsters, no rebuilding civilization, what if it was all gone and wasn't every going to come back? If fear of death is gone and competition and population pressure are removed from the human equation, what's left? What's essentially human about human beings? I wrote a long story about that last human being in 2018. And then, as I tried to shorten a novelette into a short story, it grew into a novella. And then, after Covid seemed to prove my premise more realistic than I'd known at the start, I took the NaNo challenge and rewrote my twenty-two thousand words as a full length novel. Then I set it aside because I was afraid to reread that draft… some day. Instead, I went back to the beginning and ground down and polished it to that five-thousand-word short story I'd been aiming for a few years back. It has gone through several titles, and I credit Molly Gloss for advising me to keep "All the Daughters Sing."

A question for the author

Q: How do you generate story ideas, and how soon do you act on them?

A: My stories often begin with something simple and familiar because of an experience I want to understand or an event in the world that triggers my curiosity. I ask myself "what-if" questions. And then I try to look at the world slant and think what could happen next. My education is all about creative work, but I am fascinated by science and history, what we understand, and what we fail to notice. I like the notion of one thing leading to another unexpected result. The friend whose neck was burned, the aunt who went to Peru, an owl dreaming, Schylar falls in love with Joan who loves Peter who loves Mark who loves Terry who sees Schylar run by one morning and follows right along behind. A draft might flow out in days. Getting the story right takes months or years. Even details I am certain are perfect, sometimes don't survive years of revision.

About the author

Jan Priddy began reading science fiction in high school when her father handed her *Foundation*, later earned undergraduate degrees in the visual arts from the University of Washington, and eventually studied writing with better authors including Ursula K. Le Guin and Molly Gloss. An MFA graduate from Pacific University, she lives in the NW corner of her home state of Oregon where she runs a couple of miles every other day. She weaves and bakes. She writes stories into the world.

janpriddyoregon.wordpress.com

My Little Sister Brigid

Harold R. Thompson

My little sister Brigid was born when I was four years old. I loved her from the start. She was this funny little pink smiley thing with a round bald head like a baseball, and for a while I called her Baseball Head. I enjoyed talking to her and telling her things, even if she didn't talk back. She never said a thing, even as she grew older. Our parents seemed worried, but I figured that was just the way she was. She would never speak and that was that. I played games and explained them to her. She just watched me with her huge eyes, and I thought she understood.

Once, after she'd returned from a trip to the doctor, I told her, "I'll make sure nothing bad ever happens to you."

I would make Mom and Dad happy and feel safe.

One day when she was five, Brigid looked at me and said, "What's for supper?"

"Pork chops and corn on the cob," I said. I'd been looking forward to that. Then I said, "Hey, you talked!"

After that she spoke in complete sentences worthy of any six-year-old, or even an adult.

"What are all those lines?" she asked me one day.

"What lines?"

She told me she could see gold shimmering lines in the air, like the edges of curtains, or giant sliced orange peels like you see in the marmalade. She even pointed to them, and traced them with a finger, but I couldn't see anything.

When Mom and Dad found out about the lines, off to the doctor they went. They were worried that Brigid had something wrong with her brain, something serious like a tumor. By then I was ten, and old enough to understand what that meant, so I was a little scared, but it turned out there was no sign of a tumor or any kind of disease. What the doctor had said, my parents told me, was that my little sister might have a type of 'spectrum disorder'.

The word 'spectrum' just made me picture a prism, and that made me think of the cover of Pink Floyd's *Dark Side of the Moon* album.

"Why is it called that?" I asked.

Dad's face scrunched up like he had a pain in his gut or something.

"It means," he said, "that she's different. Her brain works differently from other people's. Some parts are more developed and others are…"

I waited for him to finish the sentence, but he just looked away with that pained grimace.

"Are less developed?" I said.

I didn't believe that. I knew Brigid. My little sister was perfect. Some of my friends had annoying little sisters, but Brigid was never annoying. She didn't take my things. She watched my games and didn't interfere. She went away when I asked, plunked down in a corner with a book. She was only six, but always reading. She also followed instructions well. She said whatever was on her mind, so you always knew what she was thinking. She was curious and asked questions. She wanted to understand things.

But I worried about the lines in the air. That meant she was seeing things that weren't there.

I asked her about them again one night while we were in the den watching TV.

"Are there lines here now?" I asked.

"You still can't see them?"

"No, I can't. There aren't any lines, Bridge."

She glared at me, her pursed mouth looking like a button. Before my eyes, she reached out with one hand… and the hand disappeared.

I sat up on the couch. I rubbed my eyes. I wasn't sure what I was seeing.

"I just put my hand into one of the folds," she said.

Not lines anymore, but folds.

"There are things in here," she said.

Her hand reappeared, but now she was holding an old flashlight made of shiny aluminum. It had a red plastic cowl around the lightbulb, and a magnet on one side so you could stick it to the fridge. The plastic cowl was dirty and the shiny tube was dented in a few places.

"Where did that come from?"

Brigid shrugged.

"I saw one like it once. I thought of it and there it was. That's what the folds do, I think. I figured it out a few days ago. Look!"

She pulled out other things, one after the other: an adjustable wrench, a roll of masking tape, and a jar of peanut butter. I took the lid off the peanut butter to make sure it was real.

"It is," I said, after sticking in a finger and licking it clean.

This was a relief. My little sister hadn't been seeing things. The folds were real but just invisible. That meant she was going to be all right.

I got some bread from the kitchen and we ate some of the peanut butter with it.

A few days later, I went into Brigid's room to discover her playing with a huge castle made of coloured wooden blocks. Detailed plastic knights guarded the walls.

"Where'd you get all this?" I demanded, a little jealous.

Then I remembered what she could do.

"Oh, they came from the folds," I said.

Brigid ignored me and kept playing. She could be single-minded when she set herself to a task and would get upset if she was forced to deviate, even to answer a question.

It was after this that she started building elaborate Rube Goldberg machines. Most of them involved a steel ball rolling along a track, knocking things over and causing a chain reaction that would end with a fan turning on or a radio blaring or something. Some of the machines were huge, extending into the hallway and dining room and living room and even out the window. My parents were pretty tolerant of this, just like they'd tolerated the toy railroads I'd set up when I was Brigid's age, as long as she cleaned up after a few hours.

I don't know what went through my parents' heads when they found out Brigid could pull things out of thin air. When Dad first encountered one of the Rube Goldberg machines, he just told Brigid to put everything back when she was finished. But later I overhead them discussing the possibility of sending Brigid to a special school.

I was having none of that. I stormed into their bedroom.

"There's nothing wrong with Brigid!" I said. "She should go to our regular school."

Mom came over and put her hand on my shoulder.

"It's okay, it was just an idea," she said.

That was all.

I walked Brigid to school every day after that, and she always held my hand. After confronting my parents, I was pleased with myself for having saved her, in my mind, from having to attend some strange institution, but I also began to worry what others would think, including other students, even Brigid's teachers. I felt like I needed to stay close to her, to watch out for these potential villains.

"Remember," I said to her on her first day of Grade One. "Don't tell anyone about the folds or what you can do."

"I won't," she said. "But why not?"

"Just don't," I told her.

I didn't want to scare her with an explanation.

"The government is going to come and take her away," I said to my parents one night, and I got so upset I started to shake. A few tears even started. "They're going to want to do experiments on her."

My dad gave me one of his genuinely-concerned looks and put his hand on my shoulder.

"I don't think shadowy organizations like that really exist," he said. "This is a free democracy, and every citizen has rights. No one can just take you away against your will. If your little sister has special talents, that's her business and no one else's."

Did I mention my mom and dad were both lawyers?

As far as I could tell, Brigid never revealed her powers at school, and that was good, but as time passed, I started to worry that she wasn't really fitting in. Her schoolwork was perfect, straight As in every subject, but she didn't seem to make any friends. I'd see her in the playground by herself, sometimes just staring into space.

I wanted to change that.

"Why don't we have a big party?" I said to her one day when we were all sitting at the dinner table. "For your birthday. You can invite all the kids from your class."

Brigid gave me one of her stares, but after a moment she nodded.

"They would like that," she said.

We made paper invitations and invited about thirty kids. In those days, if someone in your class invited you to a party, no matter who it was, you'd go. It was only polite. Plus you got to go to a party. So on the big day, which was a Saturday, a ton of kids showed up, each one with a present, looking for fun and cake. I acted as host. Brigid meanwhile had made her largest Rube Goldberg machine yet, one that went through every room in the house, and it became the center of activities as every kid took a turn letting the steel ball drop.

When it was all over, Brigid said to me, "That was fun, having all those kids over."

"They're your friends," I reminded her.

"Are they? Oh."

After that, nothing changed. None of her classmates seemed to dislike her, and no one bullied her, but she still stuck to herself most of the time.

I'd tried. At least she would always have me, I figured.

As more time passed, and I turned thirteen (almost a man), I decided that it was good that my little sister was something of a loner. That was safer. I still worried, almost every day, that her secret would come out, and made a solemn pledge—a reaffirmation of my childhood promise—to protect my little sister from anyone who would try to do her harm or infringe her rights, as my dad had put it, as a citizen. I knew that if the powers-that-be found out what she could do, they would be afraid of her, and they would want to find out how her abilities worked so they could exploit them. That's what always happened in the movies.

Two more years passed and no one came to take Brigid away. In that time, I never let my guard down. If I saw a suspicious car parked on our street, I would check it out. I got in the habit of telling Brigid to hide whenever someone I didn't know came to the door.

"Why should I hide?" she asked me.

I finally decided to explain that there were people who could be afraid of her, or who wanted to use her for their own purposes, and make her do things she didn't want to do. I figured she was old enough to understand.

"But I'm just a nine-year-old kid," she said.

"You're different. Not everyone likes that."

That just made her frown.

When I was fifteen, my first year of high school, Brigid stopped eating her supper. Mom and Dad were worried she'd developed an eating disorder, but one day I caught her pulling a tray of cupcakes out of the air. She'd been snacking on magic goodies. She'd tried to hide it, even from me, and that made me angry. She and I weren't supposed to keep secrets.

I told Mom and Dad.

"You can't just eat cake and candy, honey," Mom said, and then she and Dad gave Brigid a lecture about what was right to pull out of the folds, what was wrong. They didn't mind the toys, but they didn't want her eating so much unhealthy food.

"Maybe it's time to get to the bottom of this," Dad said, "before it gets any more out of hand."

By that he meant another trip to the doctor.

"You can't do that," I said, horrified.

"We just want them to run a few tests, honey," Mom said. "We won't reveal everything, but... we just want to make sure she's okay."

I thought they were crazy and was sick to my stomach with worry. I wished I hadn't ratted on her. If the doctor found out what Brigid could do, he would just have to make one phone call, and the men from the government would be on our doorstep.

"Deny everything," I whispered to Brigid as she was leaving the house. "Tell the doctor it's just a game. It's not real."

Brigid just gave me one of her big-eyed looks.

I went into the back yard to wait, just sitting in a lawn chair and stared at the sky, at the clouds.

The back door opened and Brigid came out and sat in the chair next to mine.

"You're home already?" I said, startled.

My little sister shook her head.

"I did what you said and told Doctor Heppie that it was all a game, but he didn't believe me. I asked to go to the bathroom and then I decided to come home."

"What do you mean? Come home how?"

I felt a chill.

"I found a new way to use the folds," Brigid said.

I grabbed my phone and texted Mom, telling her what had happened. She'd been worried sick and the whole clinic had been running around trying to find Brigid.

"Thank you, honey," Mom wrote back. "Thank you for letting us know!"

When Mom and Dad got home, Brigid faced them and said, "Please don't take me to the doctor again."

I stood behind her, nodding.

"There's nothing wrong with her," I insisted.

Mom and Dad looked at me, then looked at Brigid.

"Okay," Dad said.

After this, I told myself I had to live by my own words, at least a little. I'd said there was nothing wrong with Brigid, but I behaved as if there was. My high-school friends knew I had a little sister, but I never invited anyone over because I was afraid they'd see Brigid do something, and then I'd have to explain. That had to change. I had to trust Brigid to be responsible, like she was at school. I told myself I had to start giving her more freedom.

One day I invited my friend Rosie over. I was learning guitar and Rosie played bass, and we were going to form a band to perform at the school music festival. This was going to be our first jam session, in our rec room.

Rosie wore her hair super short and also lifted weights, so she had rocks in her arms. She wore white t-shirts and jeans and that was the extent of her wardrobe.

"Are you a boy or a girl?" Brigid asked her, in her blunt way.

That embarrassed the hell out of me, but Rosie just laughed.

"A bit of both," she said.

"So you're just yourself," Brigid said. "Like me."

Rosie said nothing for a few seconds, then gave my sister a smile I can only describe as conspiratorial.

"Yeah."

I watched the two of them together, and something turned over inside me. I'd been carrying the secret of my little sister's power for a long time, and I needed some help with that weight, help from someone we could trust. I wondered if Rosie could be that person.

"My little sister is different from other people," I said.

I guess I was testing the waters. Brigid turned and looked at me with her big round eyes, and something in that look stopped me from elaborating.

Rosie shrugged.

"Everyone is different," she said. "Most people don't care about that stuff anymore."

Brigid smiled, and I felt a little burst of hope. Could that be true? Was it possible that few people, including the government, would really care if they found out what my sister could do?

I wanted to believe that, only Brigid didn't just have personality quirks, but actual powers.

I decided I'd have to carry the weight of my sister's secret for a while longer.

Not long after that, Brigid announced she wanted to have another birthday party. She was about to turn twelve and thought that was special. Her idea was to have a party where she gave the guests gifts instead of receiving them.

"Please don't give them things that you find inside the folds," I told her, worried that was her plan.

It was.

"Why not?" she asked. "Where else can I get the gifts?"

"Mom and Dad can buy them."

"But I want the gifts to be special."

Brigid trusted me and always listened to me, but I was spoiling her plans and she didn't like it.

"Look, I'm sorry about this," I said.

Brigid suddenly brightened.

"I know! I can say it's a game, like with the doctor. A magic trick! And I won't be lying, because it is a game, really. Right?"

I mulled this over. I was feeling pretty down about disappointing her, and this seemed like a reasonable compromise. If Brigid trusted me, I had to learn to trust her.

"Okay, but be careful," I said, hoping I wouldn't regret my decision.

At the party, Brigid revealed her power to all, telling the other kids that she could pull anything out of thin air. That's all she said. She didn't describe what happened as a magic act, but when it was over, everyone applauded. No one thought it was real. They deceived themselves.

I was proud of Brigid, both for her amazing talent and how she'd presented herself. But later that evening, my old fears started to filter back. What if a couple of the kids realized that what they were seeing was the real thing? What if they told their parents, and their parents called the police or some other authority?

On Monday morning, as I was packing a lunch for school, a large black truck pulled up to the front door. I told Brigid to hide in her room. The truck turned out to be a courier delivering a package for Mom, but I was shaken. I'd decided to walk Brigid to school like I used to do. I'd stopped when I'd moved to the high-school, and I'd probably be late for my first class, but my little sister's life was worth the wrath of my homeroom teacher.

When we arrived at the elementary school, a large black car was parked out front. A man in a black suit wearing Aviator sunglasses opened the driver's door and stepped out.

I'd never seen that car before. I led Brigid in a wide berth around it.

"You see that car?" I murmured in her ear. "I don't know for sure, but it looks like it might belong to those government guys who want to kidnap you. Stay away from them. Don't even let them see you."

Brigid gave me a big-eyed look and nodded.

"I don't want that," she said.

The passenger side door of the car opened, and a kid got out, a boy with a camouflaged knapsack. The man in the dark suit and sunglasses said something to the boy, who waved and started running toward the school.

"That's just someone's dad," Brigid said.

I watched as the man got back in the car, but he didn't drive away at once. Was he watching us? Had the kid with the knapsack been some kind of cover?

"I'm not sure," I said. "Don't talk to that kid or his dad. Okay?"

Brigid nodded.

"Okay."

I couldn't think of anything else the entire day and found it impossible to pay attention in class. I was terrified that the man I'd seen was a government agent who'd been sent to watch my sister. I wasn't certain, but that didn't matter. The idea had taken root and was growing.

I left my last class early, claiming to be sick. The truth was, I felt sick. I was so anxious, so worked up, I ran all the way to the elementary school and waited for Brigid to come out, all the while watching out for that black car.

When Brigid saw me she broke into one of her big smiles.

"Hi, big brother!"

She held my hand on the walk back, but neither of us said much. Brigid was still generally quiet, and I was busy keeping watch.

We were almost home when I saw a large black sedan turn onto our street. I came to a hard stop, jerking Brigid's arm.

"Ow!" she said.

I didn't know what to do for a few seconds, but there was nowhere to run.

"We have to keep going," I murmured.

I felt like I was walking in glue, but when we turned the corner, there was no black car on our street. Maybe it had just driven past.

On our front step, I knelt in front of Brigid and said, "I think I just saw that car again, and think it might have been looking for you. I think you should hide. Not just in your room, but... in the folds. Do you have a place to hide there?"

"Yes, I go there all the time," she said. "I can go there if you say so."

I didn't get my homework done that night, but sat in front of the window, plucking at my guitar and staring at the street. I didn't see the car again.

The next morning, Brigid wasn't at breakfast.

"Do you know anything about this?" Dad asked me. "Did she go to that place, wherever she goes?"

I shrugged. "I guess so."

I didn't want to admit I'd told her to go. I was afraid Mom and Dad would say I was being irrational.

"She'll come back," Mom said. "But we'll have to call the school and tell them she'll be absent today."

She was trying to sound casual, but I could tell she was upset, and felt a little pang. That was my fault.

I reminded myself that this was necessary.

Brigid still wasn't back when I got home from school, nor did she return the next day. Or the next. I started to get a little worried, and sat in her room and called her name, hoping she could hear me, but I had no idea how the folds worked. I told her I hadn't seen the black car for days and it was probably safe to come out. I even felt a little stupid, and had to admit that maybe I'd been wrong.

By now Mom and Dad were a wreck, but they couldn't go to the police. Their daughter wasn't missing. They knew exactly where she was.

"What if she stays away forever?" Dad said at a joyless supper on that third day.

Mom reached out and took his hand.

"We always knew something like this could happen," she said. "She's unique. She's special, and she's just flexing those muscles. Why would she stay away forever? Don't worry about that."

My Dad just nodded. I'd never seen him cry before, but tears started running down his cheeks.

That night, I came down with a fever. I don't know if it was due to raw negative emotions or if I'd let myself get worn down and the flu had taken the opportunity to attack. When the sun rose the next day, I couldn't get out of bed. The room spun when I tried to raise my head, and I think I had visions. I saw Brigid standing next to me and asked her where she'd been.

"Come on," I heard her say, as if from a distance.

I managed to sit up. Brigid was right next to me, but half of her seemed to be missing, like she was peering around a curtain. Or a fold.

"Follow me," she said, voice a whisper.

She slid back behind the fold, but held out her hand. It looked like her severed arm was floating in the air.

I took her hand and let her guide me through the fold in space.

On the other side was a room, like an ordinary room in a house, though with no features, the floor, walls, and ceiling all resembling white plaster. In the far wall was an ordinary wooden panel door with a white doorknob. Next to the door stood a massive palace of wooden blocks, like I'd seen Brigid build years ago, its walls armed with plastic cannon. In another corner was a table covered in maps drawn in coloured pencil, and beside them were the remains of hamburger wrappers and cupcake papers. Books were stacked in little piles here and there.

Brigid let go of my hand.

"How do you like it?" she said.

"It's... nice."

My head was starting to clear and I could see there was a certain coziness to the room. It couldn't have been more safe, more secure, but I hated the idea of my sister spending her life like this, hiding from the world that was rightfully hers.

I wanted her to come home.

"Bridge, I think I might have been wrong," I said. "I haven't seen the car again, and no one came to look for you. I think the coast is clear and you need to come back. Mom and Dad are worried."

She looked at me.

"They are?"

She said it like it had never occurred to her.

"Yes."

"But they know where I went."

"They want you to come home. You don't really need to hide all the time."

She looked at me, eyes big.

"I'll keep you safe," I promised for the thousandth time.

She nodded.

"Okay, I believe you. You always tell me the truth."

I digested this as she went to the panel door and grabbed the doorknob. The door swung open, and beyond was the rec room in our house.

"Can I step through?" I said.

"Yes! Just follow me."

When I'd gone through the doorway, I looked behind me, but all I saw was the other wall of the rec room. The door and Brigid's hiding space were gone.

I felt like I'd just awakened from a dream. The fever was gone and there was my little sister, standing next to me and smiling. Safe and sound.

"What time is it?" I said. I'd been home alone, sick in bed, and something about the light coming in the high rec room windows said it was late, afternoon coming on to evening. School would be out.

"I don't have a clock in my hiding place," Brigid said. "Maybe I should get one?"

I wanted to check the street one last time, just to make sure.

"Come on," I said.

We went out through the basement door and up the concrete steps to ground level. Our driveway was empty, and I looked along our street to the left, at all the other quiet semi-suburban houses, each with its garage or car port, front lawn and shrubs and flower beds.

There were no black cars and no one was trying to take my sister away.

"I guess I'll have to go to school tomorrow," Brigid said. "And everyone will say, oh, where were you? Welcome back. It'll be like a party."

"And even if we told them where you'd been," I said, "they wouldn't believe us."

I smiled at her, and in that moment, I made my decision, the decision I'd been building towards. It was time for me to let go of the fear for good. And this time I meant it.

"You know when I said I'd keep you safe?" I said. "I'll still try, but I don't think you'll need me. You can keep yourself safe."

"You think so?"

"Yes."

I looked again at the empty street.

"You know what else?" I added. "Mom and Dad will be home later, and they're going to be happy to see you."

In this I was wrong. Mom and Dad weren't happy. They were overjoyed.

"You didn't have to worry," Brigid told them.

I watched as they enveloped my little sister in a three-way hug. I joined in.

They say old habits die hard, and over the next few months and even into Brigid's high school years, I secretly watched for black cars. I never saw one, and I never talked about them.

I did my best to stick to my decision.

After her senior year, Brigid won a scholarship to a reputable university and I faced my biggest test. Could I stand it, with my little sister away from home, living in a dorm?

Turns out I could. I kept waiting for something terrible to happen, but it never did. One weekend she came home, traveling through the folds, and told me, "I think I'd like to be an architect. I like to design and build things."

"That sounds like you," I said.

A few months later, she told me, "I'm going to switch to engineering. I like to design and build things, but all kinds of things, not just buildings."

She was a star pupil, which came as no surprise. After graduation, she got a job in another city.

Her visits became fewer.

We were both busy, but still made time for each other. By then I had two kids, six and three, and Brigid delighted in entertaining them with her 'magic tricks' when she came to dinner.

"I'm not sure I'm going to make it next week," she told me one evening, when the plates had been cleared from the table and we were alone for a few minutes. "Things are getting crazy and I might have to put in some extra hours."

"You do what you have to do," I told her. "And you know where to find me."

As it turned out, I didn't see her the next week, nor the week after. One day she sent me a text message. She was in town for business, and could I meet her for coffee? Not could she come to the house, but a coffee date. Just for an hour or so.

I was a little disappointed, but agreed to meet her.

I arrived at the coffee shop first and grabbed us a table. Brigid came in a few minutes later, tall and slender and grinning. She still wore her hair long, almost down to her waist.

We didn't talk about anything significant. We just chatted about what was going on in our lives. At one point, I wanted more cream for my coffee, and Brigid pulled a little porcelain pitcher out of the folds. It was casual and surprising, and no one seemed to notice.

"Do your work colleagues know you can do that?" I asked.

"They see it all the time. Everyone still thinks it's a trick. They don't believe it's real."

I leaned back in my chair. I wanted to ask something that I'd wondered about for a while.

"Do you... ever feel tempted to reach into the folds and grab a few bags of cash?"

Brigid's big eyes seemed to double in size and her jaw dropped open.

"That wouldn't be fair!" she said. "And how would I explain that on my tax returns?"

"Well, you've never been reluctant to find us presents in there!"

Brigid shook her head.

"That seems different somehow. I think I make those things. You're not allowed to make your own money."

I could think of a few counter arguments but kept them to myself. Her response was typical for her, and I felt myself flush with love and admiration.

"Sometimes I think I should go to the physics department at the university," she continued, "and show them what I can do and say, what do you think? But then you know how much I value my privacy. I don't need them trying to figure me out. And that's not who I am anyway. I'm not really that interested. I've got other fish to fry."

She sipped her coffee. We talked about other things. Eventually she checked her watch and said, "I'm sorry I have to dash, but I'll see you at Thanksgiving. You're going to Mom and Dad's?"

I was, and I would see her there.

We embraced, and then she was out the door. I watched her walk away, back to the life she had chosen, and wondered if, after all, we had become a little ordinary. I'd read once that extraordinary children often became ordinary adults.

Well, I decided that was a crazy thought, and turned away, smiling to myself. Completely crazy. If there was one thing I'd learned, after all these years, after all the worries and reliefs, all the failures and triumphs, there was nothing ordinary about my little sister Brigid.

See Harold R. Thompson's story "My Little Sister Brigid" online at Metaphorosis.
If you liked it, leave a comment. Authors love that!
Remember to subscribe to our e-mail updates so you'll know when new stories are posted.

About the story

This was an unusual story for me, because normally I plan everything before I start actually writing and take my time building the story, layer by layer. I like to know the ending before I begin. However, this one came to me out of nowhere while I was making a cup of tea in the kitchen. I don't know where the name Brigid came from, but I was thinking of my childhood, about growing up with an older sibling, and of my own children and their relationship, and just tossed in a "what if" element. I sat down at my laptop and wrote the first draft from start to finish as a sort of stream of consciousness piece. No planning, no plot outline. It took me about an hour. Many of my short stories have both a horror element and a lot of action, but this was just the story of a little girl with extraordinary powers and an overprotective brother. It was a bit like a superhero origin story, but I wanted it to be about two kids growing up, not an action piece. I'd just been reading a collection of Kelly Link stories, and although my piece was nothing like what she writes, there was some influence. I didn't do much revision after that first draft, and shopped it around for a while, and it actually made several short lists, but I was never happy with the ending and neither was anyone else. Eventually, after some suggestions from the editor of this publication, I took another look and wrote several revised drafts. The ending was still the problem, but as I put myself back into the lives of those characters, it eventually revealed itself, as most endings do.

A question for the author

Q: Is there a specific environment you find most conducive to writing, and is it different for different kinds of scenes?

A: I write on a laptop, so I change venues quite a bit. It doesn't really matter where I go. That being said, I do most of my writing, and certainly my best, in the evening, or in the middle of the night. The silence, the lack of distractions from work and family, really helps, but my brain also slips into a more creative mode in the wee hours. It doesn't matter what kind of scene I'm writing. If I get stuck, the place that helps me get unstuck is... the shower. Some people sing in the shower, but I think. Maybe something about that environment helps me focus, again shutting out everything else, but it always seems to work, like magic.

About the author

Harold R. Thompson enjoys storytelling in all its forms. A long-time employee of Parks Canada, he develops exhibits and public programming at several national historic sites. He also writes historical fiction and science fiction and fantasy, both short stories and novels. He lives in Nova Scotia with his family.

haroldrossthompson.com

River's Song

Michael Barron

Boxes form a solid wall in the back of the SUV, preventing me from getting one last look at our house. I squeeze myself against the seat, head resting against the cool November glass, hugging my guitar. I'll never play the guitar again. After tonight I'll never even hear a guitar again. They don't have music where we're going.

Dad and I spent the weekend packing, but that was all a show for the neighbors. Just before midnight tonight, everything in the SUV — my phone, my old American Girl dolls, both my high school yearbooks, even Dad's precious tablet — is going in a furnace in New Jersey.

We pass the church where I attended Girl Scouts as a kid and then the train station where one January morning Emily and I huddled, trying to keep warm. The plan was to skip school and spend the day visiting comic book stores across Manhattan — because that's the kind of rebels we were. But when the train rounded the corner, all our rebelliousness evaporated and we scampered off to AP Chemistry.

If I'd known this day was coming so soon, I would've climbed aboard.

As we cross the Pine River Bridge, officially leaving my hometown forever, Dad glances at me out of the corner of his eye. "If it were up to me, you could come back to visit. However, they cannot send someone on a whim. You know that."

I do know that. Our civilization has generated faster than light travel, technology that can fling consciousnesses across the galaxy, artificial bodies in which to store those consciousnesses, and — according to Dad — breathtaking works of art, awe-inspiring architecture, and a flawless legal system. However, they still have a budget to consider.

I hold up my hand, wiggling my fingers. I'd never realized how much I adored my fingers until Dad delivered the news just a couple weeks ago. When he called me into the kitchen, I'd assumed he wanted to discuss the town's new recycling schedule. Instead, he gave a smile that actually reached his eyes and said, "We are going home."

Sitting at the kitchen table, a dull ache pressed against my side, nearly doubling me over.

"And it will not just be us. Uncle Trench and Coral are also being called back. We—"

"No." The word leapt out with such conviction I startled myself.

Dad's smile barely wavered. "River—"

"We've only been here eleven years. You said we'd have twenty-five."

"I never said that."

"Yes you did." I leaned across the table, my elbow knocking over the black cat pepper shaker I'd set out for Halloween. "After I started second grade and all the kids were mean to me, you took me to the aquarium to cheer me up. You complained the whole time about how dull ocean life is here. I asked how much longer we had to stay and you said we'd be 'stuck here for *at least* twenty-five years.' "

Dad clearly doesn't remember this. "You were not meant to take me literally."

"How was I supposed to know that?" I press my back against the chair and cross my arms. "I'm not going. I'll live with Emily or one of the other families, but I'm staying."

Dad didn't yell. He never yelled, the same way he never laughed, cried or got frustrated. He simply put the pepper shaker back where it belonged, scooped up the black specks until everything was nice and tidy and walked out of the room. "Families belong together, River. And neither of us belongs here."

The night after dad's big announcement, the nightmare came again. I knew it would. Whenever we talked about going back, my one memory of home always interrupted my sleep.

In my one memory, Dad and I swam upwards, faster than I'd ever swum before. Others rocketed past. A white tower loomed overhead. Half of Dad's appendages — people here would call them "tentacles" but I hated that word — clung to me. The rest thrashed as we flew higher, toward the ocean's surface. I'd never been to the surface before. The lack of pressure made me dizzy. Sunlight blinded me. Something far below wanted to kill us.

There was a flash of white light, not from the surface but from the tower. The structure began to crumble. Debris hurtled toward us. Dad veered to the left, but something struck my side. I thrashed in his arms. I was just a kid, barely old enough to form memories, but I remember thinking, *this is how I die.*

I woke soaked in sweat, still able to see the imploding tower in the darkness. The side of my human body ached.

Breathing in through my nose and out through my mouth, I crawled from bed, crept down the hall, turned on all the bathroom lights — even the one in the closet — and pulled up my Joni Mitchell T-shirt. No blood. No shredded skin. Only a handful of moles and one fat nuclear-red pimple, nothing to indicate I'd ever been near a warzone. But the pain remained, crossing thousands of lightyears, passing black holes and supernovas just to stab me between the ribs.

When I was a kid, I'd ask Dad if my real body had been injured during the explosion. This was back when I still referred to my original body — the one waiting for me in storage on our home world — as my 'real' body. He always shook his head at the question. "After the Citadel was destroyed, I took you straight to the medical domes. I waited for news of your condition along with thousands of others who were waiting for word of their own loved ones. When they released you, you came swimming out, happy as can be, with only the tiniest of scars." He'd hold up his thumb and forefinger to indicate how miniscule the scar was. Each time they'd be closer and closer together, as if my injury shrank with each retelling.

Dad had less to say when I asked, "Why'd the Citadel blow up?"

"It was a stupid, unnecessary tragedy caused by the Red Ocean Brotherhood, but don't worry about them. They're a joke."

"Who are they?"

Dad always swatted that question away as if he were swatting a fly. He preferred to dwell on our home world's brilliant architecture, glorious history, and yearly festivals in which every member of our species gathered together to create a single work of art. It sounded like a combination between a play and an unbelievably intricate live action role playing campaign.

It was my cousin Coral who told me all about the Red Ocean Brotherhood. She wasn't my biological cousin, just the daughter of Dad's favorite co-worker. One January evening when I was in the fourth grade, Coral and I were hanging out in the backyard, watching the snow fall, while Dad and Uncle Trench sat in the living room playing music on Dad's tablet. Without any precursor I turned to her and asked, "What is the Red Ocean Brotherhood?"

Dad's bosses had placed Coral's consciousness in a body that appeared to be two years older than mine. She was more than happy to lecture me on things she thought I should know. "They're an evil group that thinks everything involving dry land is 'blasphemous'. A bunch of them used to be teachers or politicians, even some scientists, but they swam off into the deepest channels when we started moving to the continents. They think everyone who lives on dry land deserves to die."

"Are they still around?"

"Of course they are." Before I could ask any follow up questions, she began to lecture me on how I should give up the guitar and stop listening so much to music created by mammals, leaving me to wonder what the Red Ocean Brotherhood would do to someone who'd spent her whole life on dry land.

I sit in a Burger King off I-95 nursing a Pepsi and a box of chicken tenders. This is our last meal on earth and it's fast food. Someone who doesn't know Dad would think he'd go for a five-star restaurant, but he can't tell the difference between Italian Cuisine and movie theater nachos. If it doesn't remind him of the sea plants back home, it's trash.

I stare at my fingers and wonder if my body will still feel pain when my consciousness leaves it. They recycle all the organic material after we go home. Soon my fingers might be a part of the inner thigh of a middle-aged man or the arm flab of an elderly woman.

The only other customers in the restaurant are a mother and her daughter, who looks like she might be about four or five. That's how old my body appeared to be when I first arrived. They share a milkshake while the mother lists all the relatives and the relative's pets they'll see at Thanksgiving. The girl has a chocolate grin smeared across her face.

I'm lucky. I know I'm lucky. At exactly midnight tonight I'll step through a door and my consciousness will be flung across the vastness of space. I'll wake in a technological utopia where I'll torpedo through our underwater metropolis in my new — 'real' — body, experience wonders I cannot imagine, and participate in the yearly festival that unites our species.

Of course before I'm able to speak with anyone, I'll have to master a form of communication that involves seventy-eight appendages instead of one mouth. I'll have to alter my perspective on what's tactful, beautiful, and funny. By the time I'm hanging out with friends again, I'll have to — for the second time in my life — become a member of an entirely new species.

The first of us arrived to this world in an actual craft. Apparently somewhere in the wilds of North Dakota, a silver sea shell lies in the middle of a field, marking our initial landing spot.

Sorry it's not in Roswell, New Mexico.

Over the years our people — their consciousnesses transferred into human bodies, of course — formed a fake company that bought a derelict factory off the New Jersey Turnpike. In the factory's sub-basements, they used parts of our original craft to construct vats where they grew even more human bodies as well as the gateway that sends and receives consciousnesses.

I remember nothing of what it was like to have my essence transmitted from one end of the galaxy to the other. After the attack on the Citadel, my next clear memory is of waking in a human body, ten fingers, and ten toes, and as far as I knew that was normal.

For months, Dad and I received lessons in how to walk, move objects with our hands, and communicate. They eased us in, first teaching us American Sign Language before moving on to verbal communication. Dad struggled; he never stopped struggling. After each lesson he'd go back to our room and sit hunched over on the edge of his bed, like a man who needed to scream, but had forgotten how.

I, however, was so young, I picked up these new languages overnight. By the time they moved us into the one-story bungalow that would be our new home, I was fluent in ASL, English, and Spanish. And of course I used these new communication skills to do what all little kids do: I asked questions.

"Where do the stars go in the daytime?"

"Why do we always have kale for dinner?"

"When can we get a dog?"

But my favorite question was, "Why're we here?"

Dad always answered with, "We are here to observe a land-based society so we might study their infrastructure and spread civilization to the terrestrial regions of our own world."

That answer never satisfied me. The aliens on TV were always flying around in spaceships, either destroying or saving the galaxy. Dad had traveled lightyears for a desk job.

But the job was his life. He exhausted himself studying highways, skyscrapers, communication networks, and sewers, complaining the whole time that the buildings back home were more 'inspiring'. And at the end of the day, when his work was finally done all he wanted to do was play music on his tablet.

While I grew up watching *Avatar: The Last Airbender* and *Star Wars Rebels* — which taught me how *real* aliens were supposed to act — the only entertainment Dad enjoyed came from an app Uncle Trench had programed himself.

When you opened the app, the bottom third of the screen was filled with seventy-eight gold symbols, our entire alphabet. Depending on which combination he pressed, different colors exploded, merged or swirled about. Our bodies back home barely detect sound, but we have enormous eyes that turn the ocean's bioluminescent twilight into high noon. What Dad was doing was our equivalent of playing music.

The 'song' he enjoyed the most began with a midnight-blue fog and turquoise shimmers running along the edges. Silver flecks swam through accompanied by emerald tendrils. Eventually, a single blazing light appeared in the heart of the fog, filling the screen with a golden glow. This formation of colors was similar to a folk or gospel song, along the lines of 'Amazing Grace'.

Every Sunday morning he'd sit me down at the kitchen table and watch me practice. The routine began on the very first Sunday after we moved into the house and didn't stop until the day Dad told me we were going home. "This is far more cultured than that auditory trash the mammals hammer out on their instruments." I'd nod in agreement, just to placate him.

Every once in a while he'd share a story about how before we came here he'd once played his favorite song in our medical domes' waiting area. "Occasionally one of the doctors would emerge, take someone aside, and it would either be good news or bad. It was almost always bad. Eventually the waiting became unbearable, people became agitated, arguing with one another. And so, at last, I pulled out my..." He shakes his head. "This clumsy mouth cannot pronounce the word. I pulled out the musical instrument this app is based on. I sat in the middle of the crowd and began to play. People turned to watch. They stopped arguing and gathered together, focusing on my music, and after a while the crowd became one family again."

Sometime in middle school I realized he was telling me a story about what had happened after the attack on the Citadel. But as a kid it was just another boring story.

Between his nostalgic ramblings and the musical instrument that meant nothing to me, it was a relief when, eighteen months after we first arrived, Dad's bosses insisted that I attend public school.

On my first day of second grade, Dad walked me to the bus stop, wringing his hands, reminding me I could call whenever I needed to. Meanwhile, I skipped along beside him, confident that by the end of the day I'd be best friends with everyone at the school.

By lunch, I realized that most of the kids already had enough friends and didn't want to have anything to do with me. Throughout that first week, I smuggled in candy to share with the other kids. This worked fairly well for a few days, but before long they'd just snatch the offered Milky Way bars and run off to whisper and stare at me from across the playground.

After school I'd look into the bathroom mirror while holding up photos of kids in magazines, trying to determine what was wrong with me. Did my skin look too artificial? Could they see something alien in my eyes? Maybe there was some kind of subliminal anomaly that clued people in that I didn't belong, the way rats can tell when one of their own is diseased.

I got into the habit of leaving school through a side entrance, to avoid the other kids. Even their parents didn't hide the way they stared at me. One day, just a couple of weeks before winter break, I was walking down the side stairwell, which I assumed was empty, when I heard giggling coming from one floor above me. I refused to look up, which was a good thing because an instant later something thick and slimy splattered against the top of my head, like I'd been hit by a pint-sized bird dropping.

Even when I saw that my hands and hair were bright green, I didn't comprehend what had happened until the giggling turned to laughter followed by a stampede. There had to have been at least five of them. Five kids hated me so much they'd stolen a jar of paint, and lain in wait to ambush me. And the color they'd chosen...

It was the holidays. There had probably been some green paint lying around, but my mind leapt to: *little green men.* They knew what I was.

I ran. I didn't know where I was running to but I sprinted as fast as I could, face stinging from tears. I reached the bottom of the stairwell, swung a left, and burst into the closest bathroom.

I tried to dunk my hair under the sink but it was too shallow. I cupped my hands and attempted to wash it out, convinced that if anyone saw me smeared with green paint they'd realize I didn't belong on this planet. However, each scoop of water just spread the paint. Before long the walls, mirrors, and floor were splattered green.

The paper towel dispenser was empty so I hurried to the stalls to grab some toilet paper. That was when I noticed that one of the doors was shut.

Before I could decide whether or not I should just go, sprint all the way home, a girl's voice quivered, "Go away."

I almost did leave, but there would still be hundreds of people in the parking lot, ready to point and laugh.

"Please!" she said. "Just leave me alone."

I dropped to the floor, dripping green water across the tiles, and peered under the stall's door. I saw a pair of white sneakers and jeans splattered with mud.

"They're all out of paper towels," I told her.

"I know." She started sobbing louder.

"What's wrong?"

After a few minutes of prompting I got her to share her story. "I was carrying my art project — this giant painting I made of a robot dragon — down the gym steps when a gust of wind blew it out of my hands. I tried to catch it, but I slipped and fell into some mud in front of *everyone*. When I stood up Rodney Dickerson said I'd s-h-i-t myself. Even his mom laughed."

"If it makes you feel better, some kids dumped green paint into my hair."

"Really?" there was a tinge of curiosity in her voice.

"Yeah, that's why the floor looks like a leprechaun puked all over it."

"Gross!" she laughed.

We both grew quiet for a moment and then she asked, "Can I see your green hair?"

"Um..." I stepped back. "I guess."

The stall door swung open.

She was a petite girl with long black hair. I recognized her from the other second grade class, but she was so quiet I'd hardly ever noticed her.

To her credit, when she saw my green hair she did try to stifle her laughter, but the more she kept it in, the pinker her face became, which got me giggling. At last we both burst into laughter, and kept on laughing while she took me over to the sink and helped me wash my hair.

Nine years later, Emily and I dyed our hair green to commemorate the way we'd met.

Six months after that, Dad called me into the kitchen to tell me we were going home.

We're late for the rendezvous. Dad drives thirty miles over the speed limit, twisting the steering wheel with each turn like he's going to rip it from the dashboard. I want to point out that we still have over an hour until midnight, but the only thing that'll calm him is to get there.

When we finally reach the factory's rusting gate, he crashes through, not caring what kind of damage he does to the SUV. The high beams illuminate the ancient building. The parking lot is covered in so much shattered asphalt we might as well be driving across a gravel road. About fifty of Dad's colleagues wait for us on the far side. Everyone is there; even a few from the Hong Kong unit have flown in to give him a proper send off.

As soon as the SUV is parked, I expect him to leap out and get to work burning our possessions, but he remains in his seat, staring at the crowd.

"Dad?"

He doesn't look at me when he says, "We don't belong here, River. Once we get home our real lives will begin." Dad opens the door and climbs out. I remain where I am for several beats of my artificial heart. In his eyes, nothing that's happened to me counts as 'real life.'

But we're here now. There's nothing left for me to do but glance over my shoulder, give all of our boxed possessions, everything I've accumulated over the years, one last look, and pull myself out of the car.

As we approach the crowd, I take in the surrounding parking lot, the broken bottles, the cracked chunks of pavement, my final view of home.

Then my eyes fall on the others. Something's wrong. They should be clustered together, applauding, cheering, peering through telescopes, searching for our star. Instead, they're scattered. A few huddle in groups of two or three, but most are solitary.

Coral leans against the factory's bay doors, her pale face illuminated by the sickly orange streetlights. She should be leaping up and down, spitting on the ground, shouting about leaving this 'rock' forever. Instead, her bloodshot eyes glare, as if she's trying to crush me beneath her scowl.

Dad still hasn't noticed anything out of the ordinary. He walks with a skip in his step.

Uncle Trench meets us halfway across the parking lot. "I tried calling you."

"I left my phone at a hamburger restaurant." Dad grins, certain that nothing will ruin his day. "I never want to use that abomination again."

Trench speaks so quietly it's as if he doesn't want to hear his own words. "We received a communication. There was an attack... The Red Ocean Brotherhood..." He falters, lowering his head. "Much of the city has been... We've lost contact."

The sugary, acidic aftertaste of the Pepsi I had with dinner coats my tongue. The frigid night air is impossible to breathe. I can't take my eyes off Dad.

He wavers back and forth, as if he's about to tip over. "Red Ocean is a joke."

Trench lowers his eyes. "It seems we may have underestimated them."

"How much damage?"

"We don't know, but...the storage facility, where they kept our bodies... It's not looking good."

Uncle Trench and I barely catch Dad before he tumbles to the cracked asphalt. Others step forward, but the only one who reaches us in time to help is Coral. As she takes his shoulders, she whispers to me, "Guess you got exactly what you wanted."

"Your cousin's kind of a bitch," Emily said behind me.

"Yeah." I rummaged through the fridge looking for the leftover tofu curry I was going to heat up for dinner.

We'd just run into Dad, Uncle Trench, and Coral in the driveway. Emily and I were coming back from the park where the small ragtag group of friends we'd accumulated over the years had been making plans to go to the New York Comic Con in October. Dad and the others didn't bother telling us where they were heading off to. As they passed, Dad and Uncle Trench gave us cordial waves, but Coral walked straight through Emily, knocking her to the ground.

"My whole family is weird," I said, pulling out the leftovers.

"Bet they're not as weird as my family," Emily said, wandering into the living room. "What's this?"

Before I could turn, my phone buzzed. It was a text from Uncle Trench.

Your father left his instrument hooked up to the projector.
He wants you to put it away.

The leftovers splattered all over the counter as I sprinted into the living room.

A reddish orange glow reflected off Emily's face. She gripped Dad's tablet, pressing random characters, so the projector cast fireballs across the wall. "Is this some kind of art app?"

"It's nothing!" I rushed at her so fast I slammed my shin against the coffee table. Stifling curses, I said, "It's just some dumb game my dad plays."

She pressed her palm flat against the keyboard, hitting all seventy-eight characters at once. The projection became a deafening cacophony of crimson, amber, indigo, violet, and silver. "How do you play?"

"You don't 'play' it. It's like a visual musical instrument. Never mind, it's stupid."

"It's incredible." She continued to experiment with the buttons.

I reached out to snatch the tablet away, but she was having so much fun I ended up lowering my hands and stepped back to watch her play.

One way or another I showed her how to play the first tune Dad ever taught me, our equivalent of 'Twinkle, Twinkle Little Star'. Blue and silver sparks flashed across the screen. Emily got the hang of it soon enough and we moved on, messing around with the various chords Dad had taught me over the years, even his favorite, the midnight blue with a golden glow.

Within a couple of hours, I discovered a combination I was particularly interested in. Silver orbs rained down the screen. When one hit the bottom, it turned green and flew about. As I watched that little green drop twirl among the others, something shifted inside me, as if the colors and images had a voice, and I finally understood what they were saying.

Eventually, Emily's mom texted telling her it was time to come home. I put the projector and the tablet away and we never played it again. However, at least twice a week for the next month, I'd crawl out of bed in the middle of the night and play the tune we'd discovered. I only stopped after Dad told me we were going home.

Uncle Trench, Coral, and I settle Dad onto the broken parking lot. Dad lays flat on his back, as if the gravity of this world pins him there. Everyone else stands apart in their little clusters. Eventually, they return to staring up at the stars, half of which are blocked by the factory looming overhead.

I don't know which of the stars is ours, even though Dad pointed it out to me countless times. Ever since I woke in the factory's sub-basement, I'd known I would someday return, that someday I'd see the underwater metropolis and all the art and beauty our people had to offer. Every time Dad described our civilization over kale salads or made me play songs on his tablet, he was promising I'd someday be a part of it. Now I might never swim among the towers or see the hundreds of miles of murals or any part of our world.

I don't realize how silent the night is until Uncle Trench says, "They might be able to grow new bodies for us. But that will take years, decades if the facility has been severely damaged. And if they need to start everything over from scratch, they may need to send an actual craft to assist with our end of the gateway. I don't even know if they have the budget for..." His voice drifts off as he shakes his head.

Dad pulls himself up and presses both hands against his face. "How many are dead?"

"We don't know. The area they attacked was densely populated, they—"

"Red Ocean is a joke." There's a quiver in his voice, but there's also an insistence, as if he's trying to assert that this is an objective statement.

I rest a hand on Dad's shoulder. He lowers his hands and turns toward me. I have to stop myself from looking away. There's just enough light from the streetlamp for me to make out his features, and I'm not ready to see his red tear-streaked face. I don't want to see the same accusation Coral shot me. *"Guess you got exactly what you wanted."*

But his face is as emotionless as the factory's brick wall. Without looking at me he says, "You need to get somewhere warm. These bodies are so delicate." He pulls himself to his feet. "I'll call Emily's mother. Explain our travel plans have been... That you will be staying with them for a while."

"Where will you be?" I stand up next to him.

"I'm needed here."

"Doing what?"

He doesn't answer, but I can already see him burrowed deep in the bowels of the factory, staring at our gateway, willing it to flicker to life and for all of this to be a silly misunderstanding. Dad walks toward the factory. "I'm needed here, River."

I step back. Coral isn't wrong. This is what I wanted. Within twenty-four hours I'll be back at one of my friend's houses, making extra spicy nachos while having unapologetically geeky conversations about music and comics. I should be performing a mental jig, struggling not to grin from ear to ear that my life will not have to change. However, instead I find myself staring at the others scattered about, and I feel the old pain press against my side. Right now, at this exact moment, the Red Ocean Brotherhood is reaching across the vastness of space and hurting us, just like they did with the Citadel.

I think of the Citadel and consider the story my dad told me. I burst into a run.

"Is she ditching us already?" Coral asks, loud enough for everyone to hear.

I run across the cracked asphalt until I reach the SUV. Dad didn't bother closing the driver's side door. I leap inside. Crawling into the back I work my way through a conglomeration of clothes, old toys, books, and everything else that made up our lives. At last, I find what I'm looking for in a small white tub.

By the time I pull myself out of the car, Dad has nearly reached the factory's bay doors. He walks as if there is no life above his waist. He's ready to slump over before the gateway and stare into the shadows beyond the dead gray metal, waiting for a response that will never come.

I open the white tub, place his projector on the SUV's hood and flick it on, connecting it with his tablet. "Wait!" I shout. "Look!"

He turns as I open the app, illuminating his face with the two-story square of light cast against the factory's wall. I hit a random gold character.

Colors explode.

For a moment all I produce is a mad cacophony of oranges, reds, and golds. Then I really begin to play, tapping the chords Dad had me practice every Sunday morning for eleven years.

It isn't perfect. I've never been talented at playing Dad's music. At first the blues are too light. Then they're too purple. At last I find the perfect shade of midnight. A turquoise aura seeps around the edges. Silver flecks dart this way and that among emerald tendrils. A sunshine-yellow glow emerges from the heart of the deep blue fog.

One by one, Uncle Trench, Coral, and the rest turn. Red eyes blink in the projector's light. Even more of us emerge from the shadows, making their way across the parking lot. Wrapping their arms around each other, they gather in close, as if the light provides actual warmth.

There are not enough silver flecks and the golden glow still holds a hint of mustard, but I play on. Soon there will be time for us to grieve, and for me to listen — really listen this time — to the stories of the home we may have lost forever. Soon there will be time to move back into my house. There will be time for school, guitar, Emily, and all of my friends. But for now, at this exact moment, we gather together, a family basking in the glow of my Dad's favorite song.

The song ends, and I can't help myself. I give a little flourish and add my own tune, the one I spent weeks fine-tuning. Raindrops fall from the top of the screen. Half become silver, the other half turn gold, but one turns a brilliant green, the same shade of green as the paint the kids dumped on me. The silver and gold raindrops drift to opposite ends of the screen, while the green one zips in, around, and among them, impossibly fast, becoming a blur, filling the screen.

I jump at a sound I've never heard before. Dad stands directly behind me. He's laughing. But he's also crying. In the projector's fading light, I see his face streaked with tears. He pulls me into an embrace that's as tight as the grip he held me in when he was trying to protect me from the Citadel's collapse. Dad presses his face into my hair and sobs. Then everyone else is there, wrapping their arms around us, gathering in close to reassure each other our home still exists.

See Michael Barron's story "River's Song" online at Metaphorosis.
If you liked it, leave a comment. Authors love that!
Remember to subscribe to our e-mail updates so you'll know when
new stories are posted.

About the story

Honestly, I don't remember exactly when I got the idea for this story. The concept of an alien growing up on earth and thinking of herself as an earthling, even though her family has strong ties back to their home planet has been with me for a while. However, I didn't have anything specific in mind in terms of plot, conflict, character arches or characters in general so it just sat in the back of my mind for a while, occasionally rising to the surface when I was commuting to work or drying the dishes.

I didn't find anything to anchor this broad notion of a story until my wife and I went camping. I remember loading up the car and thinking about how it felt like our whole lives were in the back of my CRV. For some reason this made me think of this vague concept of a story, and I realized it was a moving story. My alien — later named River — has spent her whole life on earth but has been informed that they are moving to a home world she barely remembers. I figured the frame story would be River driving back to the place that will take her "home" and during the trip she would look back on her human life. The story didn't exactly turn out as I originally envisioned — seriously, when do they ever? — but finding this moving/road trip storyline gave me the direction I needed.

A question for the author

Q: What tools do you write with?

A: I do most of my writing early in the morning (it's not that unusual for me to wake up around 4:00). My typical writing setup is, a mug of black tea on my left, my long-haired orange cat (usually still asleep) on my right, my laptop on my lap, often with the lofi hip hop radio station playing in the background. Also, I need to acknowledge all the authors who have inspired my recent writing: T. Kingfisher, Becky Chambers, Stephen Graham Jones, Chuck Wendig, as well as countless others who have been published in all the sci-fi / fantasy collections I have read.

About the author

Michael is the vice president of the North Baltimore Chapter of the Maryland Writers' Association. He is a member of the neurodivergent community, and his experiences inspire his writing. When he is not writing or reading, he is either training for a marathon with his wife or working as a librarian at the Baltimore County Public Library, where he teaches creative writing classes. He has also undertaken a never-ending quest to find the world's greatest hot sauce.

michaeljbarron.com, @Barron_Writer

Pain Eater

Danny Menter

Before the summer I turned twelve, plants had seemed innocuous: sometimes pretty, mostly boring, perennial background filler. I did know someone once who claimed her Ficus granted pleasant dreams when fed a mixture of honey and dried banana peel; another who swore his succulent had cannibalized his others while he was at work, leaving behind a massacre of black fertilizer and a noticeably plumper cactus sunning itself on the windowsill. But I heard those stories later, when I knew better, when I believed them.

It had always been there, thick and bulbous, rotating like a miniature planet in its harness, but I couldn't remember ever looking at it directly until that summer. I dropped the black plastic bags next to the toolshed, and pulled my grandfather's heavy work gloves off and left them on the wooden bench. Above, hung an assortment of rust spotted tools: hoes, trowels, and an axe with a heavy maple handle. I returned the shed key to its spot under the stone frog and turned back towards the plant.

I sifted through the sounds that had stopped me; beneath the soft tear of weeds ripping from the earth and sand shimmying into the trash bag, I thought I had heard a sigh, as if the giant thing had exhaled.

I looked back towards the house. Everyone had finished swimming and the grill crackled with burgers and hotdogs. The impromptu garden tidying had been Grandpa's idea, cut short by his dizzy spell—my enlistment in chores a frequent occurence while we lived with Grandpa and Grandma over the summer—now he sunned himself on the porch in a plastic Adirondack chair, a halo of pipe smoke hanging over his head. He looked faded, indistinct, a photo of a photo. Dad was setting up slender tubes on the concrete walkway, peering upward to ensure their trajectory.

I listened again, but the whole yard lay in a state of lazy, sunburnt silence—the only sound the creak of the chains bracing the plant as it rocked in the wind.

Later, Grandma took a thick bag of sugar out of the cupboard for shortbread.

"Twenty years or so?" She slid a tab of butter into the mixing bowl and leaned against the counter. She was short, only a head taller than me, in her red apron with multicolored fireworks threaded through the chest, but she had never seemed old, with her face like starched white linen. In the living room I could hear Dad talking about the progress on our new house, the one we would move into after the summer.

"Was it always that big?" I asked.

She glanced through the sliding glass door, but the afternoon sun obscured any view of the backyard.

"I wouldn't worry," she said, turning and dusting her hands on her apron, "your grandfather has always taken care of the weeds. I try not to pay attention to those things."

She handed me the mixing bowl. It was the size of my chest and I needed to sit down on the steps that led down into the sunken living room and brace it with my knees to maneuver the spoon.

Mom lay on the opposite couch, bathed in light, arm drifting across her forehead while Dad paced in the foyer making a sales call.

I grasped the spoon with both hands to work it around the bowl, but it barely budged. In a minute my forearms screamed, and Grandpa noticed and heaved himself from the recliner, squatted down next to me on the floor, and placed his callused hands around my small ones. Together we smoothed out the dough.

After dinner we filed out to the backyard. Beyond the stiff Saint Augustine grass, baked to glass by the heat, cut a chain link fence that separated my grandparents' yard from a retention ditch. Over the years, seeds and pollen drenched by rainwater and street runoff had erupted into a tangle of thorny vines and greasy flat-leafed vegetation that crowded at the fence, ready to tear it down if we let it. I stared at the boundary while Dad lit the first of the rockets. It fizzled to life as Grandma handed us each a dense brick of shortbread from her cookie tin.

My eyes burned from an afternoon of swimming, but I forced them open against the sky to watch the rockets disintegrate into pink sparks.

A week later I sat on the concrete steps by the pool next to a crowded collection of aloe, spiny and prehistoric, and a skull of desiccated coral. I'd never worn a tie before. I kept clipping and unclipping it from my shirt collar.

Inside, mourners gathered, afraid to bump into each other, polite and fragile. Their whispering was too loud. A portrait of my grandfather, decked out in his navy uniform, sat on the kitchen table, encircled by a wreath of white lilies.

I wondered if I had a time bomb in my chest too, winding down to its final tic.

I loped out across the grass, the late afternoon sun an orange disk, to the plant.

It was so big it stretched against the chains suspending it from the oak, causing the tree to splinter along its trunk.

I placed my hand, pink from the heat, against the lime green skin of the thing. It was warmer than my hand, and something seemed to pulse beneath the surface. I imagined what it would be like to peel back all its layers, what it would hold in the center. An eye, maybe, bloodshot and swiveling, corded in inch-thick veins. Or nothing. Just more and more layers until you came out the other side.

Then I thought of snakes, and imagined one was hiding now, waiting for my hand to slide closer to one of the folds. I jerked away.

Dad joined me. He looked uncomfortable and sad, unsure of what to say.

"She'll be okay," he said finally.

"Who?" I asked.

"Well, both of them, I guess." He dug the heel of a black shoe into the earth. "But your mother," he added, before walking away.

I stared at the space next to the porch where a week before the five of us had watched stars explode in the sky.

A rustle and groan beside me, and I turned slowly towards the plant. I squinted, first with one eye, then the other.

I lifted my hand, measuring the distance between the plant and the pool door using my fingers.

I was sure.

It had grown.

On the kitchen table, Grandma's tin lay bare, its tarnished corners worn silver where the seams met. The last few guests edged out, sharing pained glances with me, offering to help with the bags of trash Dad held from his hand, his other on the door jamb.

I found it difficult to look anyone in the face. Mom and Dad and Grandma made movements that approximated normal, but were too fast and slow all at once, like the jerky movements of marionettes.

That night, Mom and Dad made a bed up for me in the living room, tucking a quilt into the couch cushions and draping it over me like an envelope. Grandma had gone to sleep, or at least retreated into a far dark corner of the house to be alone. I had never noticed how the house echoed when only one person was speaking, the sounds ricocheting off the walls like softballs.

I still felt that when I glanced at the recliner he'd be there, square jawed and immense, chewing the end of his pipe.

"Mom," I said, and the word felt funny, like I was saying it for the first time.

She waited in the doorway that led back to the bedrooms.

"That thing in the backyard—"

"Thing?" She said, closing her robe against her throat and bracing herself against the wall.

"The plant, I guess." Because maybe that's all it was.

"Oh, Bryan's plant." She read the silence, studied the room for a place to sit, but she seemed to see mines everywhere that could go off at the slightest pressure. Ultimately, she chose the step where I held the mixing bowl a week before.

"Bryan gave that to your grandmother a few weeks before the accident. A birthday gift." Her eyes creased at the corners. "You know, it was this big," she held her hands a few inches above one another, "when he bought it. He was always doing stuff like that. That's why he was the favorite."

Mom never spoke of her brother, who had died in an accident before I was born. I knew little about him other than that we shared a name.

I absorbed this, appreciating the way speaking helped fill up the room, and it felt clandestine, opening doors on the past that had been locked—peering into a time before I was born, a mythology I might never have access to again.

"Did you ever think about getting rid of it?" And I knew I'd made a mistake by the way her eyes froze, and her hand clawed its way back up her throat, as if someone had just thrown open the door on a blizzard and an icy wind was thrashing around the room. But the only change was my question, which had shorn the conversation in half.

"No, we couldn't." She stood, took a step forward, and flicked the light off.

Things were worse at the funeral. I was realizing that pain wasn't linear: it peaked and ebbed, then crested again unexpectantly, violently.

Mom had been quiet in the few days leading up to it. I watched her the way you watch tinder in a bonfire, wary and expectant. The funeral was held on the same grounds where Bryan was buried, Grandma told me. They even used the same priest, a tottering old man who asked me to hold the scripture readings for him at the lectern as he spoke. Everyone thought this was a great idea.

The same shopworn people who had come to my grandparents' home were there, milling around, checking their phones, keeping close to the perimeter.

Dad and Mom were fighting. Dad had to leave in the morning to catch a flight to Austin for a sales meeting, but Mom wanted him to stay to help Grandma pack up Grandpa's things. With the neighborhood getting more dangerous and Grandma alone, Mom thought it best to move her into a condo closer to our new house.

I could sense the hesitancy, a hole that suggestion had fallen into.

"Well, that may not be a good idea," Dad said.

"Why not? She could help with Bryan. and you said the house is nearly finished anyway, we just need your final bonus to —"

Dad rushed in "—I just don't think we should be too hasty, is all. With everything going on...the funeral, I mean... I... we may have to hold off on the move."

I could sense something change. A drop in pressure. A curdling of the air.

"We have savings for that, Dean." An electric current pulsed through each word.

They couldn't hear me on the outside of the door. I had come to tell them that I didn't want to hold the papers. I didn't want to stand in front of all those people in their caked-on suits and dresses, and not for the last time, I wished I had an older brother or sister to take my hand and tell me what to do. But instead, I wiped my face and forced the rock in my throat down to my belly, where it settled, and walked away. I imagined it growing in there, calcifying like the coral on Grandma's porch.

As I perched by the lectern, a man walked into the back of the parlor; I saw him over the greying heads, hunched slightly, wearing aviators and a creased leather jacket. Dad had his head bowed, but I could see him stiffen as he caught sight of him. The hymnal in his hands quaked. Mom turned too, but it was difficult to read her expressions, her emotions as opaque as sea-glass.

She placed a palm on Dad's and whispered something in his ear. He pushed her hands away to lie lonely and tangled in her lap.

"You have no right—" Dad was saying.

I froze in the doorway with a tray full of plastic wineglasses to throw away. Clearly a ploy to keep me from this scene.

The man in the leather jacket had one hand on a hip and the other outstretched, palm up, as if he expected Dad to shake it.

They were standing in the funeral parlor's kitchen area, forced close together by cardboard boxes filled with wine. I could smell aftershave that wasn't Dad's—something sickeningly spicy and sweet.

"It was in the paper. I just came to pay my respects," the man said. His accent was slightly southern, a cowboy in a Marlboro ad.

I felt hands on my shoulders moving me out of the doorway and back into the hallway.

Mom's face, close to mine: *Go*, she mouthed, but before I could retreat there was a massive crash and the shattering of glass, and the man stumbled out of the doorway pinching the bridge of his nose between his fingers. A crimson gush darkened the collar of his white shirt. He leaned his head back and disappeared wordlessly through a doorway to our right.

My hands were shaking, and plastic cups tilted off the tray, spilling their contents on the carpet. Dad came out next, massaging his knuckles, his face drawn and startled.

Mom stood with her hands on her hips. She glanced once through the doorway and her face collapsed, eyes jolting up at the corners, a choking sob breaking free of her lips.

Dad reached for her, but she turned away.

I got on my hands and knees, shaking, and began to stack the cups back on the tray. I held one up to the light. At the bottom, curled in a C, lay a slim finger of lime green vine.

The plant's sagging belly now dipped into the ground, making a little furrow of the muddy soil beneath. The top branches of the tree had begun to angle precipitously towards the roof of the house, and as I watched, a squirrel zigzagged across the shingles and clambered onto an outstretched limb. I was afraid to touch the plant—I could feel heat coming from it like a furnace. Whatever was inside was burning, fueling growth.

The man from the funeral, his nostrils stuffed with tissue, walked across the grass barefoot.

"Does Dad know he'll be here?" I had asked in the car ride over.

"He's an old friend; we need all the help we can get right now," she had said, not answering.

I eyed the plant and hoped it would shoot out leafy arms or vines and wrap him up like a mummy, twirl him up into pasta until the only thing visible was the top of his sweaty head, which would burst from the pressure, leaking red over green.

But I could sense that whatever the plant was, it wasn't benevolent; it merely squatted, motionless under its own gargantuan weight.

I stared down at the man's muddy feet, his jeans rolled over his bony ankles, and wondered what he had said to Dad in the funeral parlor. Dad, who didn't let me watch *Terminator* when it played on T.V.

"You know, I was there when he bought this—with your uncle, I mean." His voice twanged like a broken banjo string.

"Uncle Bryan?" I asked.

He squinted at it although storm clouds had covered the sun for hours.

"Yap. Knew your granda, way back when," he added.

"It looks like you know my dad, too," I said.

This stopped him and he looked at me for a moment, searching, then unconsciously reached for his nose but stopped himself and pointed at me instead.

"I think we maybe got off on the wrong foot yesterday. I'm Jake." He stuck out his hand and leaned over it like a magician coaxing a reluctant volunteer from a crowd.

It sank to his side when I didn't take it.

"I don't think I need to know your name," I said. "You're just here to help Mom. Then you're leaving."

His smile made my stomach turn acidic.

"Oh, I don't know," he said. "I might stick around for a while."

"Dad will be home tomorrow," I said, fast enough to run my words over one another.

He shook his head, mouth in a line but with a corner twisted up like a rusty hook.

"Nope. In Austin *all* week." He dragged it out in a way that made me aware of the sweat running down my back.

"Come look at this," Mom said. The three of them were hunched over a peeling leather photo album in the kitchen. I had been pacing the edge of the pool for an hour and I smelled like the outside that had seeped into my clothes.

I crossed my arms and edged forward reluctantly.

Jake had his hands on either side of the thing, as if he were holding the whole world of the album between his arms. Grandma and Mom were on either side of him. Grandma looked thinner, I realized, her parchment pale skin sagging at the corners of her mouth.

In the picture I saw Uncle Bryan, Mom's twin. He crouched next to a small motorcycle, hand placed on the shiny black seat. Behind him, I recognized Jake, although a much younger version, with long hair that swooped across his forehead. They were standing in the front yard, the oak trees smaller and the paint on the house a brighter shade of white. In the background, Mom rested her arms across a wrought iron gate.

There was no fence like there was now and I could see straight into the backyard where a small leafy plant dangled from a tree branch. It was light enough to suspend from a single nylon rope.

"He was so proud of that bike," Grandma said, turning from the table and busying herself in the kitchen.

"Is that..." I started, pointing at the bike.

Mom nodded, two fingers close to the edge of the photo, an inch or so away from Jake's.

"What happened to it?" I asked.

"After the accident, it wasn't nothing but scrap metal," Jake said. "I hauled it over to the junkyard."

Grandma made a pained sound in her throat and for a second I thought she had cut her hand, which grasped a potato, a paring knife in the other. Her head was tilted forward over the sink as if she was about to fall into it.

Jake scraped his chair away from the table and walked behind her, taking the blade. "Let me take care of this," he said. "Why don't you ladies take a load off and let the boys finish dinner?"

Mom gave him an appreciative glance that lingered in the air, then grabbed Grandma's arm and guided her into the living room.

"I need to shower," I protested.

"After dinner," Mom said. "Help Jake with whatever he needs."

Jake hauled a pot out of the cabinet under the sink and threw a washcloth over his shoulder. I was uncomfortable with the ease with which he knew the locations of items: the saltshaker, the grater, the ceramic butter plate. Things I never really paid attention to, but now felt imbued with importance; if I appreciated them more, he wouldn't have to touch them.

The light outside died as a fine drizzle greyed the yard. I heard the scrape of branches against the roof, their bent weight scratching like fingernails.

Jake stopped with a potato in one hand and stared intently at a picture above the sink. It was a photo of my mother when she was in high school, taken at prom or homecoming. In it, she perched on the edge of a couch, fingers laced under her chin, her head lifted towards the source of light shining from somewhere outside of the frame. Her hair had been curled, and it curved under her delicate chin in an auburn wave, the border of a pale green dress just visible at her collar. Mom usually never smiled in pictures, there were only a few I had seen where her teeth were visible, and because of this, I'd always liked this photo of her, imagining that this was who she was on some secret horizon. Her smiles were never given freely; they had to be earned, and anytime she did smile, I felt accomplished. I kept those moments close.

He leaned over the sink, and I tensed, watching his finger raise to stroke the frame.

"Don't," I said and felt my hands clench.

His head swiveled towards me, that grin leaking out of his face, running all over the place, spilling onto the counter.

"You know who took this picture?" he asked.

I don't want him to say it. There were fault lines running through this house and underneath were gaping mouths with sharp teeth and I wanted Dad to rush in and make him bleed again; it was a wash of rage and violence that I had never experienced before, and it tasted like terror.

He continued.

"Prom. I wore a blue tuxedo. Borrowed your uncle's bike—got home *real* late that night." He picked up the knife and potato and, in fine papery shavings, began removing the skin.

There was a shriek like two-by-fours being compressed by immense pressure. I heard a crack, too, but was unsure if it was the snap of wood or thunder.

He didn't look up as I snatched the phone off the receiver and darted into the hallway. Mom had taken to staying in Grandma's room, which left the only other bedroom open. I closed the door, locked it, and dialed Dad's number.

He picked up after what felt like too many rings.

"Everything okay?" he asked. I could hear traffic in the background, like he was at a street corner or a bus stop.

I tried to keep my voice level.

"When are you coming home?" I asked.

There was a long pause on the other end of the line.

"Well, it's taking a bit longer than I thought out here..." His voice trailed off.

"But we need...I think you should come home."

"Has something happened?"

Although I was thankful he had finally asked, the question lacked the urgency that I needed, and I had no idea how to answer.

"The plant—" I started, then thought better of it. What if it could hear me? What if even now there were tendrils snaking below the floorboards, finding cracks in the foundation, listening with a thousand different moist pores to this conversation. "I mean, Mom has the guy—"

A long sigh. Not the intake of breath, swear, yell, or shattering glass that I wanted from him.

"Jake," he said. "Your mother invited Jake over."

"Yes. I don't like him and he's saying things about Mom, and I think —" I was rushing through it and my thoughts were skittering like spiders but there was one thought that was coherent above all: "He should leave, Dad. I don't want him here."

"Listen," he said, "unfortunately, there's nothing that either of us can do about that right now. He's...kind of been in the picture for a while."

"But you...can't you just tell her she can't see him?" I said, and I felt tears breaking free and a hard knot forming in my throat.

"It's not that easy," he said. I heard voices in the background and laughing. "I just don't think your mother wants to hear from me right now."

I sensed finality; shovelfuls of dirt tumbling in over my head and light being shut out, closed coffins and stale air. I stared at the phone and ended the call.

I refused dinner, ignored Mom's voice when she called from the kitchen, then waited for a knock at the door, but none came. I crept silently into bed and listened to the probing life outside, trying to force its way in.

The next morning, I awoke to find Jake splayed across the couch, eyes lizard-like slits in the orange light spilling from the curtains. Mom walked in a moment later, saw me standing with my fists like rocks and Jake smiling slyly from the couch, but only gave herself a second to look guilty before she disappeared into the kitchen.

It took us three days get Grandpa's things packed up neatly into boxes and placed into the moving truck. Each box that was carted off felt like a little piece of my grandfather being cut out and tossed aside. I wanted to wrap my arms around everything in the house and keep it in place. I wanted to stop it all from slipping away. If enough pieces of him were gone then it was really happening, and there would be no going back. I wanted to tell Mom the secret that I knew: that we didn't have to go along with this; that death was just a rumor we didn't have to believe, and if we simply let it pass, he would come walking back in the door, Dad would return from his trip, Jake would fade away like a bad dream, and the plant would be destroyed forever.

Because that was the other thing I knew.

It was the plant that had started this, with its menacing leaves and the thing growing inside of it, and the vines which had now started to wind themselves underfoot, so that you had to watch them when you were carrying boxes across the thick grass. But every time I thought about damaging it—purposely running a dolly over a clammy limb or puncturing the swollen belly with a kitchen knife—Jake seemed to be there, watching.

"Your mother could use your help in the garage," Jake said, on the final day of packing, standing with his arms crossed and feet spread underneath the oak.

I trudged away, finding Mom paused at the brick wall of the garage, a plastic bag in her fist.

With her back turned I was able to stow the pocket-knife under a stack of wool quilts on a shelf where I had been hiding it. I needed something much bigger, I decided.

Mom didn't turn as I entered the garage. We hadn't spoken much in the last three days, not since I had foregone dinner the night after the funeral.

I watched her back now, thin under her t-shirt, all collarbones and elbows and long hair twisted up into a bun beginning to fray.

"Mom," I called.

She turned and her eyes, half-lidded, found mine. She was far away, and it took her a moment to swim back, whatever rip tide was pulling her away ebbing momentarily.

She gestured, and I grabbed the trash can and swung it over to her.

She tossed the bag in and settled heavily into a plastic lawn chair that lay in a triangle of light from the open garage door. Beyond, Grandma watched Jake rattle down the U-Haul's wide door.

At the end of the lawn, the retention ditch gave off a cloying smell, rotting vegetables and decay, and my stomach tensed.

"How did you ever live next door to that?" I said, wiping my mouth with a sleeve. "It reeks."

Mom glanced absently at the neon green wasteland beyond the chain-link fence and shrugged. "You can get used to anything."

I wanted to ask her so many things then: why they had kept the plant all these years, what had made it stop growing? If we escaped before awaking one morning to find it erupting in a slimy green spike from our mouths, would it simply follow us? Appear suddenly in the folds of a rose blossom, or wait as a seedling attached to an eyelash? Had we been spreading it this whole time?

But I settled on this: "What is Jake?"

She waved it away.

"He's an old friend, I told you that."

"More than that. He took you to prom. He was there when Bryan died. He was there when..."

She held a hand to her face, the flash of her wedding band floating through the garage like a lightning bug. She looked weak, fed upon. When she looked up again, her eyes moved past me.

Jake stood in the doorway, one hand holding the pocketknife. He tapped it against his thigh, slowly, then ushered me over. His eyes glinted. "Time for a talk."

I kept my distance from him as we circled into the backyard, through the faded wooden gate, under the smoldering afternoon sky, to stand again at the plant.

He picked his way across the grass, almost reverently, reaching out a hand but stopping short of touching the thing. His hand traced the veiny membranes like an ancient text he could read.

"Can you hear it?" he whispered.

Waves of disgust roiled through me at his proximity to the thing. Sweat beaded on his forehead. I wanted to run, but part of me needed to hear what he would say. Maybe there would be an answer, a clue, a way to kill it.

"It's special, you know." He shook his head, "Of course, we didn't know that when he bought it. It was just a green thing, a small fragile thing someone had left half alive in the back of a hardware store." He rubbed the damp area above his lip. "Your Uncle didn't want it, but I could sense it was..." he tossed his head, as if clearing it of fog.

Goosebumps rippled along the tops of my arms despite the heat.

"It spoke to me." His voice was toneless, eyes lost, and I took a step backwards. "It will give you what you want if you feed it. Anything you want." He angled his body towards the garage as if he could see through the brick and plaster to where Mom sat.

"No." I said, my voice a croak.

"We've been waiting," he droned, continuing. "I thought your uncle would be enough—"

The accident. Not an accident. Jake, who had used the bike before. Who had needed something, a sacrifice. Now, with Grandpa gone, the pain rippling through us had made it grow again. A cold, sick feeling flowed through me, and when I had the strength, I pried myself away from his dull, green gaze, and ran inside.

That night we ate a dinner of frozen pizza that tasted like used tea leaves. Jake never left Mom's side long enough for me to speak to her, so I retreated into the bedroom instead. I was lifting the window latch when Grandma tapped on the door and let herself in.

She carried something under her arm, a big book, leatherbound, that she set on the edge of the bed. "We haven't had the chance to talk," she said and pulled a wicker chair from the corner.

The book was filled with newspaper clippings, browned with age but preserved behind a yellowing sheet of plastic.

"You know your uncle passed away when he was young, only seventeen," she started.

"You don't have to do this," I said.

She glanced at me, watery blue eyes and papery skin, resting a small warm hand on my arm and smiled.

"You need to hear this, especially now," she said and began to flip through the album.

And she told me the story, of how bad it was, how Bryan took his bike out and they got the phone call an hour later and how they slept on the cold linoleum floor of the hospital for a week, waiting for him to wake up. How Jake had been there with Mom, and how, when something bad happens, the people who experience it with you, you never really forget, because the pain gets in under your skin and travels to your heart and if it wakes up again you go looking for those people who were with you before.

"The plant is going to keep growing," I whispered.

She closed the book filled with the images of Bryan.

"It may," she said.

"Aren't you scared?" I asked.

She nodded, put her hand underneath my chin.

And because I was eleven and because this wasn't even close to the answer that I needed, that I wanted, I waited until the house was asleep, and cracked the window, and slipped out into the rain.

The toolshed was a black mass with the bulky bags of yard waste that had never been thrown out still sitting next to the wall from weeks ago when I had watched those fires explode in the sky and Dad's hand was in Mom's and the pain was there, sure, but it was manageable, hadn't broken free from its constraints to destroy us.

My feet sucked at the muddy ground, each step filling with brown water, and my shirt was soaked by the when I reached the shed. The motion light flooded the yard with light, but it would be too late by the time they realized what I planned.

I scrabbled for the key underneath the stone frog and shoved open the doors. The axe, an old one, its blade nearly blunt but sharp enough, hung heavy from its peg. I needed both hands to lift it, and it banged into my shoulder painfully as I swung it down from the wall.

I dragged the axe behind me, tracing a line from shed to plant that created a little ditch of rainwater.

I heard shouting from the porch.

Lightning flashed and there was a shape in my path, arms outstretched to bar the way.

Jake. Who must have perched near the window all night, standing guard. His undershirt shriveled in the rain; dark hair plastered across his forehead.

He was a part of this thing, a parasite living on the fringes of pain, waiting for it to weaken its host before he consumed it. A slash of a smile sliced under his still swollen nose.

I didn't feel bad when the flat end of the axe smashed into his forearm, audibly snapping the bone like a piece of uncooked spaghetti.

He screamed and flung himself away from the next stroke, which whistled into the side of the plant with all my strength. For some reason I thought of my grandfather's hands on mine the night before he died, guiding me.

The axe sunk into the flesh with a wet *schlick*.

Suddenly, with a scream of wood rearranging itself, the oak straightened, tugging the chain upwards as putrid air and black liquid poured from the opening of the plant and hissed, steaming, onto the ground.

I heard Jake moaning to my right, propped against the screen of the porch and a cry from the patio as the sliding glass door shivered open and Mom and Grandma rushed out.

I was hacking frantically now, creating little triangles of green and yellow plant flesh. Piles of mushy vegetable matter rose at my feet, stinging my shins while my arms burned from the effort.

Soon the only thing left was a tiny, shriveled acorn; a wrinkled brown seed the size of my fist, connected to the chain which now swung freely in the wind.

I gathered the fallen pieces in my arms. They smelled like overripe bananas and the blankets of a person long sick. I stumbled under their weight and walked to the edge of the yard. There, I let the pieces slide from me, over the chain link fence and into the green waste beyond. I heard them rolling into the foliage on the far side, and the splash as they hit the water.

I collapsed into the mud. My shirt reeked of sweat and sickness and I pulled it off and threw it behind me over the fence.

The floodlamp illuminated the place where the plant hung. Mom recoiled from Jake, the spell broken somehow, as he grasped at her with his one good arm. He appeared small, depleted. Grandma moved through the rain, the light framing a face shrouded in shadow. She approached, feet squelching through the mud.

I expected to see her smile, but when the lightning cracked again her face looked worn, carved from marble, eyes drooping at the edges in sorrow.

"It's okay," I splayed my fingers out against the light from the porch so I could see her face better, maybe her expression was simply a trick of the light. "I killed it."

But she shook her head.

"Don't you think we've tried?" she answered softly.

And I felt then the press of growing things at my back, an entire ditch filled and probing at the edges, a lifetime of pain hacked and discarded, yet continuing to grow. What grandfather had tended, what his death had unleashed.

I saw the heart of the thing, swaying gently from the chain, a single, fragile leaf breaking free.

I pulled on the gloves, too big for my hands, and grabbed a roll of black trash bags. The morning had dawned bright and brutal, the air thick, and Grandma brought me ginger ale while I worked, removing patches of rotting rosebushes, digging up rectangles of brown grass, and heaving husks of the plant into a lined trashcan.

She handed me the sweating glass and I pressed it against my forehead, the sensation painfully refreshing in the heat.

Mom had entered the bedroom at dawn while I pretended to sleep, and curled her fingers through my hair, kissing my forehead.

"He's gone," she whispered, then, before she left: "Dad will be home tomorrow."

Jake had disappeared after I had attacked the plant, evaporating into the rain-soaked night without a word. I hadn't decided whether to tell Mom of Bryan's accident, whether I thought it *was* an accident. But for now, it was enough that Jake was gone.

Grandma and I lingered in the yard, watching the stunted plant quiver slightly, but hold its shape.

I thought of all the times Grandpa must have fought the grief that threatened to destroy him. How many times he must have pulled on these same gloves and hacked away at the plant, knowing it would just grow back, sometimes quickly, sometimes slowly.

"There isn't a way to destroy it, not really, it'll just spread," I said to her. She patted my hand silently and made to walk back across the grass to the porch, then turned, looking up at the wide oak trees, the flowers blazing along the paving stones in hues violet and cream, until her gaze settled on me.

And she smiled, adding: "But we can let it starve."

See Danny Menter's story "Pain Eater" online at Metaphorosis.
If you liked it, leave a comment. Authors love that!
Remember to subscribe to our e-mail updates so you'll know when
new stories are posted.

About the story

Growing up in Central Florida, my grandparents had this massive Staghorn Fern hanging from an oak tree in their backyard. If you've never seen one, look one up. They're these kind of odd, layered, bulbous leafy balls that grow and grow and grow—they had this particular one for almost thirty years. It always seemed vaguely ominous to me, probably due to its immense size, and it hung right outside their screened in porch so when you were swimming, or really doing anything in the backyard, it was always on the periphery, watching. So, it was easy to turn it into the source of evil in the story. The rest of the narrative is constructed from events that happened to me when I was a kid: my parents split up shortly after the passing of my grandfather, and my mother remarried soon after. Far scarier than anything else when you're young is to have your stability threatened. As an adult, you have a longer view of how events will play out, but as a kid you really have no idea what's going to happen next. Later, it became more apparent why my grandfather's passing had such an effect on the family dynamic, opening wounds that hadn't ever healed.

I initially wrote this as a journal assignment for a course on magical realism, and the horror/supernatural aspects of the plot were more understated, partially to emphasize that the narrator, an eleven-year-old, seems to be the only one aware of the danger his family is in. I wanted to put the spotlight on the different ways people deal with trauma, through avoidance, acceptance, or anger– and underline how when you're a kid, or at least, when I was a kid, you sometimes want something as simple as a monster to sink an ax into to put everything back together.

A question for the author

Q: Are you an outline or discovery writer?

A: A little bit of both, to be honest. I generally start with an image or scene, then work outwards from there. I'll have a general idea of where the story is headed based on the characters, and plot, but I almost never outline specific scenes. Most of the fine tuning comes later, when I see the fleshing out that characters need, or if there are any glaring plot holes. Especially in a first draft, I like to see where the story wants to go on its own with as little guidance from me as possible, although lately I've been playing with prompts and other constraints as a way to prime the engine. Being able to bounce ideas off some kind of boundary, whether that be a word limit, plot detail, or form, can be a lot of fun.

About the author

Danny Menter grew up in Central Florida, fled to Madrid after graduating from Florida State University, and currently lives outside of Chicago, Illinois. He is a teacher by day, and is currently pursuing a Master of Fine Arts in Fiction.

@MenterDanny

The Zoo Diaries

Frances Pauli

Part Three

Previously…

At the Rainriver Zoological Gardens, one escape became the catalyst for a series of unfortunate incidents. The tortoise, Oliver, roamed the zoo as a fugitive, searching for his missing cage mate. When the Zoo-cam caught him interacting with the elephant, Shanti, zoo attendance spiked, putting more pressure on the animals inside and increasing crowd-related stress. The lion, Charlie, got his first whiff of hotdog when the bustling crowd began dropping things into his enclosure. The macaque, Gonzo, assuaged his caffeine addiction with a stolen latte, and Oliver, intent on continuing his search, enlisted the dubious aid of one of the zoo's resident pigeons. Together, they searched for the aviary, to find the missing crane, Miranda. Pleased with the increased revenue, the zoo announced the first ever photo and video contest.

Tortoise Abroad

Oliver will spend the day in a playground. The pigeon leads him there, shows him a concrete tunnel made to resemble a prairie dog colony. She talks non-stop, but Oliver has grown accustomed to her prattle, grateful for the bird's guidance.

Her voice is nothing like Miranda's, but it is a bird voice. It soothes him. He remembers long days conversing with his love while she stalked through the reeds or fished for the dead minnows sprinkled across the shallow pond.

Oliver ducked into the pseudo-burrow at dawn, and he spends the day missing Miranda, remembering her high voice, and wondering if the pigeon will return when night falls again.

She has fluttered off in pursuit of crumbs, which she insists are more plentiful around the playground where he's hidden.

During the day, children swarm the equipment. Many find Oliver, snug in the depths of their territory. He endures their rattling pats, and when he tires and tucks his head inside his shell, the pounding of small fists against his carapace.

They squeal and giggle, but he is unharmed, armored against their attention.

For a while he fears they will reveal him to They-who-keep-the-fences-barred, but their pronouncements that, "a turtle is in there," are inevitably met with disdain.

"That's nice, dear." Or "Whatever you say, honey."

Oliver waits, patient as the concrete around him. When the burrow mouths grow dark, he creeps to one end and finds the pigeon waiting.

"You're back," he says.

"The aviary is just across the way." She hops in place, flaps as if contemplating alighting on his shell again.

"Show me." Oliver heaves himself into the open.

"It's that building right over there." The pigeon bounces into the air, flies less than three strides before landing again. "Come on."

Oliver hurries his feet. He's been close, right across from the aviary all day long. Miranda waits for him, and he churns his stump legs and follows the pigeon with all his fervor renewed.

The warm nap in a concrete tube may have helped.

Oliver feels his goal now, just past the edge of his plastron. He runs for it, in as much as a tortoise *can* run, and only when he stands in its shadow does his next problem become apparent.

"How do I get inside?" he asks.

"Through the double doors," the pigeon coos. "You'll have to wait for someone to open them."

"If they see me," Oliver moans, "they'll catch me, put me back where I started."

"It's the only way in," the bird insists. But she follows Oliver, just the same, when he makes a ponderous circuit around the building, a fortress, it turns out, accessible only through that trap of twin doorways.

To her credit, she does not rub it in when he resigns himself.

"It's the only way in," he says.

The pigeon only puffs slightly and bobs agreement.

Pigeon

Peg convinces the tortoise to risk everything. He is desperate and carries opportunity in his massive domed shell.

They wait together through the long night. At times, he dozes. At times, he paces the aviary perimeter. Peg naps atop his shell. She dreams of a jungle where there is no battle with crows. No struggling over cast-off scraps.

When the first sunlight makes their position too conspicuous, she drives her partner to a nearby bush to hide while They-who-cage-animals go about their morning duties.

Oliver is restless, anxious. He shifts but doesn't bolt. Not even when two of the staff briefly open the double doors.

"Wait," Peg coos. "It has to be the guests."

They-who-cage-animals are far too cautious. They never open both sets of doors at once.

Oliver stirs but does not step. He breathes loud enough to reach her but does not speak. The time comes when They-who-cage-animals move on, and the great gates are opened at last.

Peg shifts her weight from one clawed foot to the other. She watches the tide of visitors wash down the paths, and she whispers to Oliver, "Wait. Wait."

The visitors lap up against the aviary entrance. They abandon their strollers, lift squirming children into their arms and begin the jostling dance that will lead them, a few at a time, through the double set of doors.

"Now," Peg hops, forgets her perch is mobile, and nearly topples to the path when Oliver lurches forward.

He is too massive. Peg realizes this as they rock and stumble toward a moving wall of legs, a multi-hued barrier of trousers, sandals, skirts, and sneakers. The crowd is thicker than she expects.

But Oliver is determined. He is more agile than Peg believes, and the crowd is far less observant than she fears. It is going to work.

The tortoise ducks into the press, and the legs adjust, work their way to either side like a stream parting for a rock in its middle.

They are slow, but they are moving. Peg has to hunker, to cling and lower for fear of being knocked aside. The doors open, close, open. Each time too brief, too short to risk invasion.

Until Oliver wedges himself into the gap.

Someone presses the glass against his side, squeezes, and when he doesn't give, bangs the panel hard against his shell before noticing why it will not close. Voices brattle nonsense above, loud, barking sounds that do not move the obstacle.

The door is ajar. Oliver heaves his body into the space between the outer and inner portals.

Peg flaps, makes ready.

The crowd is wary today. They read the signs. The outer portal closes, shuts in a tortoise and a bird, trapping them. Peg tenses, steadies.

Someone inside the aviary wants to leave. They do not look first, do not care about signs. The inner door opens and Peg launches. She flutters inside, flapping her wings as whoever opened the door ducks and squeals. Peg flies over their head, flies into warm, wet air and the constant singing of other birds.

She has made it. She is in.

She flaps to a high window, perches in a slash of light above the fronds, and surveys paradise.

Far below, the struggle to dislodge a tortoise from the space between doors continues. The crowd is divided, in or out, and Peg does not see what decision is made. She does not care.

She has attained her goal, and pigeons are only concerned with their own happiness.

The Crow

Debra watches as the tortoise is recaptured. She has come to the aviary in search of gossip, but she finds her murder hovering at the roof's edge. When she shoves her way into the line of crows, there is a ripple effect. The line bounces and grumbles, but all eyes remain down, fixed on the doors below.

There, a huddle of keepers has formed. They have cleared the area of guests and strollers, and a few break from the herd, stand back, and keep the crowd on the paths moving along to other exhibits.

The outer doors are propped open, held wide by a garbage bin and a wedged stone. Several keepers bend over, half in and half out of the space. They work at something, raise and shift and bend their knees under the weight of their cargo.

Debra hops and opens her beak but does not caw. The moment is too heavy, too perfectly dire to break the silence.

She sees them drag the tortoise from the vestibule. She sees his feet thrashing at empty air as the keepers manage to get him off the ground.

They set him down outside and, carelessly, release their grip on his shell. Immediately, he charges the doors again. They dive, struggle to drag him back while one of the open-sided zoo vehicles beeps its way through the crowd in the aviary's direction.

Debra sees them load Oliver into its short bed. They climb in beside him while the crowd cheers. The clapping thunders, not nearly as satisfying as the report of a rifle. Still, the wanderer is caught fast. He has failed, and the crows celebrate by joining their voices to the cacophony.

Debra caws with them, cries until she is hoarse. But there is something wrong, too. Something she can't quite name. Something that feels like a shadow draped over them all.

In the truck, the tortoise struggles, spins and lifts and nearly topples himself. He has tasted freedom, perhaps. He has found something that teaches him how to fight.

She knows he will be jailed again. He will not be shot, perhaps, but his freedom was always a ruse. Still, as the vehicle pulls away, she does not follow. Something is wrong.

In her dark belly, a new thing is born. It twists, and nibbles, and feels far too much like envy to be taken seriously.

Ape House

Gonzo is outside when they return with Oliver. His troop has gathered near the bars, where the crowd sneaks them peanuts purchased from the elephant station. There are signs that forbid this, but the tide of visitors is too plentiful, out of hand, and obsessed with capturing their contest videos.

In order to watch the tortoise enclosure, Gonzo has to climb the ropes. He swings up, onto a high 'vine' in order to see over the many heads, the faces that always, inevitably, show too much tooth.

It irritates him to look at them, like a biting insect caught beneath his pelt. High in the ropes, however, he can breathe again, unclench his paws.

The tortoise is unloaded from the rear of a zoo vehicle. He is placed on a tarp that has been spread across the pathway, and They-who-keep-fences-barred lift the fabric on all sides. They raise the stout animal and carry him to his concrete wall, resting him on its top for a breath. Oliver teeters, swings his legs ineffectively. Then, with a final, coordinated, effort, he is wrangled inside again.

They settle him against his grassland, unwrap and free him with a great round of self-congratulation and cheering.

Gonzo presses his face into the bars. He clutches them at either side of his head. He watches, as Oliver drives a steady, straight path toward his open burrow. He means to leave again. Gonzo knows this in his gut, a warm certainty. The tortoise is not deterred by the futility of his effort.

Something has changed. It feels like more has gone wrong than just one tortoise outside his enclosure. An expectation hangs over the zoo now. A certainty that something else is about to happen.

And even though Gonzo is sure They-who-keep have filled in the long avenue of escape, he believes the tortoise will dig again. He will never stop digging.

Gonzo screeches encouragement. He bares his teeth and bounces on the rope. Dig! His heart chants it. Dig, friend. Dig for us all.

Gonzo sags against the bars. He screeches silently, a defiant stretching of lips. His nostrils widen, and he catches his bean again. It is everywhere in the crowd, as prevalent as the clicking cameras.

Today, Gonzo sees a paper vessel in each free, hairless paw. He sees them dancing just beyond the bars. It is forbidden to reach through. There are fences to keep the visitors back, stones and hoses to punish a monkey's bravery. But today, the crowd ignores the signs. Today, the eager videographers lean close, shove, and shuffle, and even step briefly over the fence.

Gonzo leaps to the next vine. He hoots and swings, showboating for the crowd as he never does. He becomes a trooping monkey, a clown.

The cameras surge forward. They click like a hissing storm, but they bring the vessels with them. Gonzo watches. He is fast. He is cunning. When his paw strikes out, it is true. It is sure as the stones that will be thrown at him.

He snatches the vessel and snaps back, nearly losing it at the bars. His paws cradle, steady. He backs away with the treasure and is already bringing it to his lips. He drinks, and his body shudders, releases an orgasmic tension. It is worth the stones. It is worth everything.

Dig, my friend.

He guzzles the bean, shaking, trembling with relief and fear at his own brazen actions.

Then, inexplicably, the crowd begins to cheer. The teeth gleam around him, but no stones assault his hide.

They-who-gape clap, cheering for the macaque with his stolen latte. They sing to him, taking their pictures while Gonzo drinks.

ZOO

The contest website fills with videos. Someone's nephew, now promoted to webmaster, works full-time to keep the servers from crashing. There are 28 pages in the still photo gallery, and since he has allowed direct uploading, he is kept busy weeding out the irrelevant and the intentionally inappropriate.

When Gonzo's latte video hits the stream, it leaps to the top of the lists. The hearts fly as viewers show their appreciation for 'a good cup of jo'.

Commenters commiserate. Self-appointed internet police warn of the dangers of caffeine. One plucky student posts a history of macaques and coffee plantations.

Debate rages.

For a total of ninety minutes, Gonzo's latte escapade is the center of the zoo world's discourse. When someone posts, 'lion kisses little boy', however, the hearts move along. The list shuffles. An addicted macaque pales beside the unfettered adorableness of Charlie attempting to eat his tiniest visitor.

The world watches, swooning as the boy squeals in delight, as the lion's mouth stretches, and the enormous pink tongue washes a pane of clear, unbreakable glass.

Zoo attendance skyrockets.

The visitors become unruly, and the Board is forced to hire security.

Elephant Paddock

Shanti plants herself over Oliver's tunnel. Her four, tree-trunk legs cage in the irregularity in her paddock's terrain.

She stands guard, and she counts the zebras as they circle. They trot in a frantic huddle around their perimeter while They-who-keep-fences backfill Oliver's other hole. The equines are more flighty than usual, driven to constant panic by the growing crowds.

Shanti has dragged some hay out of her shelter. She tosses it over her broad back, a sign of her own nervousness. There are six digging. Three shovels and twelve boots that stamp down what the shovels throw into the opening.

She imagines Oliver will dig again. Though she spent little time with him, her impression has quickly cemented. He is stalwart, determined. Shanti wants him to win.

If she hides this exit, perhaps he will not have to dig so far. Perhaps, she will ensure that his flat face emerges in the right place. In the place where she can count him again.

They-who-fill-holes throw their dirt, stomp their boots into the earth. Shanti thinks they are not smarter than her tortoise. She thinks they will lose, and she stands guard over her secret, a massive gray sentinel waiting for the next escape.

Hyena Removed

Eventually, Alice speaks to the cat. She resists the urge until the boredom becomes unbearable, but this is not really as long as she'd intended. Creeping close to the front bars, she presses her nose into the aisle and whimpers.

"Your noise is irritating," the cat says. "Your face is unpleasant."

"Is not," Alice whines. "It is *my* face."

She remembers that the cat has told her this before, that she does not care for him, that he is mean and that he likes to lounge on his own shelf in silence.

But she is also lonely. She is afraid of this new-old cage.

"My cubs are missing," she says. "And you are an *unpleasant* cat."

"Sold." The cat pads to his cage front and gazes out at her.

Perhaps he is bored and hunting for sport. Perhaps, he is simply a foul-spirited animal. Alice believes she is an easy target either way. She is lost, and the cat has all the power.

"When cubs are big enough." He purrs and rubs against the bars. "They are sold to other zoos."

"Why?" Alice sits, panting, flicking her ears as if to dodge the cat's words. The horrifying concept. She is, despite her ignorance of the fact, a family sort of animal, and this idea of selling cubs disturbs her.

"Why not?" the cat tosses back. "My cage is too small to share. My belly is too hungry. If my get scatters to the corners of the world, it is only fitting. It is only the way of things."

"For cats, maybe," Alice says. "Cats have cold hearts."

She snaps her heavy jaws, snaps at the cat and the idea of her cubs, lost, sent to other zoos with no matriarch to learn from. Alice remembers that she does not like cats. That this one, in particular, is vile.

"Sultan," she snarls. "Your name is Sultan."

"What of it?" He shrugs with his whole body. "What of cubs and hearts? There is no room in your cage for others, beast. There is no room in any of our cages. Why should we pine for what we cannot keep?"

Alice gives him her teeth. She would teach him a lesson if there were no bars. She would show him how *unpleasant* she can be. But there *are* bars. There is an aisle and a narrow ledge and three dark walls with no view.

Alice groans and shakes herself. She rises, pads to the rear of the cage where she can face a corner and pretend there is no Sultan.

This is not her cage. This is not her life.

She has no choice but to wait until it is over.

Lion Enclosure

Charlie dreams of the veldt. His legs twitch against the straw in his den. His whiskers tighten, pulling his face into a grimace. He dreams while the sky is dark, and the zoo is quiet.

The veldt smells of meat. Dry winds wash the scent over the long grasses. They carry the heat and the aroma to a stand of anorexic trees where the lions wait, lounging in the shade.

Charlie has never seen a veldt, but this dream comes from a place of memory and instinct, a generational place that is absolutely certain of the grass and the trees. He knows as well that the biting insects are legitimate. Their little stings make his hide shiver, and their noise is a rushing buzz in his velvet ears.

The scent, too, feels authentic, though he is troubled by the detail of it. Something about the aroma feels out of place, artificial. His brain has substituted the squeaky meat, superimposing the experience of a waking zoo on the sleeping lion.

Charlie opens his jaws and huffs. His tail lashes against dust and smashed down grass.

In the distance, an animal screams. Charlie's belly rumbles. The lions around him are unfamiliar, unfocused shadows beneath the trees. The dream blurs them, but out across the grass, Charlie's vision crystallizes. He sees as clearly as if he were mere inches from the far-off scene.

A struggling beast thrashes on one side. Its hooves paw in the air as death spasms through its tawny body. Charlie is far away, but the dream shows him the gleaming of each hoof, the splatter of blood across a heaving flank, and the patterned swirl of individual hairs.

He salivates. He huffs and lets his sides heave with it. Beside their prey, two lionesses move, pale death in paler grass.

Their jaws clamp around the beast's throat. They lift the front of it, drag it toward the pride beneath the trees.

Charlie's belly growls again. Drool pools at the corners of his muzzle. He watches them come, carrying the limp gazelle one step at a time. He watches, and just when they drop the carcass on the ground before him, he wakes up.

Grizzly Grotto

Hector's hip pinches when he tries to sit. He wakes late, and when his paws push against the den flooring, little pains dance through his wrists and neck.

He thinks he is an old bear.

He thinks it has been many years since he was fed from a bottle by Those-who-give-care.

He will miss the artist at this rate.

Wincing, showing his enormous teeth to the bare den walls, he forces his heavy, complaining body to rise. His ears lie flat against his skull. His black lips ripple, but he rubs his paws over his face and works out the little agonies with a slow undulation of his spine.

Some days are worse than others, but Hector remembers a time when he awoke with no pain, no stiffness in his bones at all.

The square door to his den has already been opened. The light sliding in through that gap is too bright. He has lingered over his dreams, played with his brother again, and the morning has run on without him.

Hector thinks of the artist and shoves himself to all fours. He limps only a few steps before the needle pains dim. By the time he trundles through the doorway, he feels like himself again. He is bear, king of his domain.

Warm sunlight against his fur erases the last of his stiffness. He lumbers, his body rolling with each step.

Beside his stump, there is a pile of chopped fruit, a few heads of wilted cabbage, and a miraculous sliver of honeycomb. Hector's mouth waters, but he looks to the railing first. He gazes up, beyond the trench, to the place where the artist stands.

She has waited. Her paws wave to him.

Hector adjusts his gait, smooths his steps, and walks with dignity to the offering of sweet food. Only when he tries to sit again does the sharp pain return. His hip twinges, and instead of the graceful pose he intended, he flops into a half-lounge on one side.

Hector pretends it was intentional. He yawns to show how little he cares and reaches with one paw for the waxy honeycomb. His arm seizes. Hector roars against a shooting pain, lets the sound out before he can catch it. He falls to his side, curls around his shoulder and roars again. All thought of his dignity fades in the black wave that is his bones complaining.

Dimly, he hears the voices above, the crowd at the railing calling to one another. He thinks of the artist only for a single, dark breath, but he is too weak to focus. Too busy trying to find a position that does not hurt him.

He lies still, breathes for ages, waits until his body releases him, and then remains on his side a good while longer.

By the time he can sit, the artist is no longer at the railing. They-who-keep-cages-locked have joined the crowd. Everyone stares into Hector's enclosure, witnessing, gaping, and not even taking a picture.

Tortoise Enclosure

Oliver drags the soft dirt from his tunnel, packing it carefully to the sides or pulling it, step by step, to a branching passage he no longer has need of. He works for three nights straight before he reaches the place where he changed direction, diverting from the zebra enclosure to Shanti's paddock.

The latter path stands open, has not been obstructed by They-who-keep-fences-locked.

Oliver sits in this junction and blinks, for long moments, in the face of his good fortune. It has not occurred to him that he might find any portion of his escape route overlooked, and the free pathway takes on an insidious aura.

He has heard about traps. He has recently re-learned this lesson. Thoughts of his recapture drive his head back inside his shell. He reconsiders the elephant tunnel, gauges how much night remains, and makes the conservative decision to wait for another day.

When his back faces that open exit, Oliver relaxes. He retraces his digging journey back to his own pen and emerges into inky night.

"There he is," a voice above his head calls.

"There. There he is."

Oliver hears that they are pigeon voices. He cringes, even before a rain of fat, feathered bodies land on the ground around his burrow mouth.

"Go away," he snaps.

The pigeons shuffle, feathers brushing one another in the darkness. The birds bob and weave. They are shadows dancing, and Oliver has had enough of their kind.

"We want in," one announces.

"It's not fair," says another.

"Leave me alone." Oliver moans and pushes himself onto the cropped grass. "No more pigeons."

"We'll take you to the aviary," one voice coos.

"We'll find your friend," another picks up the refrain.

"We want in."

Oliver lunges for the latest speaker. The pigeon squawks and flaps into the air. Oliver turns slowly, but his neck is long and flexible. He stretches, waves his head at one after another of the birds until they give up and move to the fence where he cannot reach them.

"It's not fair," they chant. "We want in."

"There's no way in," Oliver moans, gives in at last to his despair, and lets his limbs sag. What does it matter if the way is clear? There is no path into the aviary, at least not for a tortoise. His plastron rests on the cool grass, and he fights off a sob. "I can't get inside the aviary."

The pigeons coo and strut. They are not convinced. But it is a different voice that calls out next, a dreadful, scratching voice in the darkness.

"She's not in the aviary," the crow says. "She never was."

"Who, who, who," the pigeons echo one another.

"His bird friend," the crow answers. She hops from the shadow of the macaque's cage and bounces over Oliver's fence. "She's in the marshland, under the big nets."

"Nets?" Oliver speaks, even though he knows the crow is made of lies. Even though, like all the animals she taunts, he hates her. "What nets?"

Debra tilts her head to one side, mantles her black wings, and lets her tail feathers open and close before answering. She is dragging it out, baiting him.

Oliver knows this, too.

When she makes her answer, however, he has already decided to trust her.

"I can show you," Debra caws. "I can take you to her."

The pigeons protest. They explode into a frenzy of bobbing, of hopping in place and puffing out their feathers. Oliver ignores them. He has heard about traps. He has learned. But he thinks he is wiser than the crow. He thinks he can out-play the bird's game.

He thinks he may as well find out.

"Tomorrow night," he says.

And the crow makes no answer.

Ape House

Gonzo watches They-who-bring-food as they move between cages, but today they have left their vessels in the center of the aisle. When they bring fruit and biscuits to the macaque enclosure, Gonzo joins the others at the tub. There is no point in sulking, no hope of a stolen beverage this morning.

He has already enjoyed his moment of victory, and at least his headache has subsided.

Gonzo sucks on a dry biscuit. The latte's effects have faded, but he can still taste it if he concentrates. He feels calmer, less irritable. When the troop members tumble into him, he is less likely to bite or scratch them.

He feels better than he has in all his time at the zoo, and his quick brain already wonders if he can risk another vessel grab. To his surprise, he has not been punished. No stones were thrown, and the crowd from which he snatched the drink showed only pleasure at his daring.

They cheered for him, and Gonzo wonders if they may have been testing his boldness all along. He wonders if they didn't *want* him to steal the bean for himself.

He chews his biscuit, turning it over in his paws and tasting each side. The troop works its way through the fruit, then tires and begins its exodus out the little square door.

Gonzo decides to join them. He imagines a crowd gathered, a dozen fists clenched around paper cups. He chews his biscuit faster and even takes a sideways, shuffling step toward the exit before a strange noise stops him.

He turns back to the bars.

He-who-sweeps is standing very close to the cage. When Gonzo looks, he purses his pink lips and makes the noise again, a slurping, smooching sound that is accompanied by a gesture with both paws. They tap against the ledge outside the bars.

Gonzo screeches. He shows his long teeth.

He-who-sweeps looks over his shoulders, looks left and right, and then taps again. He smells nervous, twitches and smooches again.

When Gonzo bares his teeth and lunges, He-who-sweeps backs away from the cage. He collects his broom and rubs it across the aisle, but his eyes are still on Gonzo. He is waiting.

Gonzo sniffs in disgust. The act brings a strange scent to his nostrils, an aroma from just beyond his bars. It is both sweet and bitter. It is bean, but it is also something else, something new.

He cannot see a vessel, but his bean is there. He-who-sweeps has brought it. Gonzo shuffles to the bars and eyes the ledge. He pulls back his lips and inhales.

Three tiny coffee cherries wait just outside the bars. They are neither plump nor red, but they shine in the same familiar fashion. Their black surface makes a smooth skin, and Gonzo can smell the bean inside it.

His paws reach through. His eyes flick to the aisle and back.

He-who-sweeps watches as Gonzo snags the offering. He shows his teeth as the macaque places a cherry between his lips.

Gonzo cringes, uses his tongue to work at the sweet-bitter coating that, it turns out, is not a cherry skin at all. He sucks at it, finds it pleasant enough. When he reaches the core, however, Gonzo bites. He chews the bean, crunches it in his teeth and feels the rush of pleasure.

It is strong, smoky, and not green at all, but the act of chewing soothes him in a way the paper drink could not. Gonzo chews all three, bouncing from one foot to the other. He chews in ecstasy, in memory of a far-off jungle. He rolls the dry bean bits over his tongue, dribbling from the corner of his mouth. He holds it, holds it until the urge to spit is too strong.

Only when he gives into that urge at last, does he remember He-who-sweeps. His eyes focus, fly to the aisle where the other primate waits. Holding his broom still, showing his teeth, and bouncing, as Gonzo bounced, gleefully from one foot to the other.

See parts I, II, and III of Frances Pauli's story "The Zoo Diaries" online at Metaphorosis.
If you liked them, leave a comment. Authors love that!
Remember to subscribe to our e-mail updates so you'll know when new stories are posted.

April

Shortcut to Happily Ever After

Ben Wan

Dedicated to Dr. Larry Yip

"Wanna grab coffee sometime?" Daniel Woo looked across at the cute cashier with the big glasses for her reaction. Her name tag read 'STEPH'. As he watched her surprised expression form into a smile, he logged her name into his memory.

"You're awfully forward, aren't you?"

Daniel smiled back. "I just don't like wasting time."

Steph laughed. "Alright. Phone?" Daniel handed it over to her as she typed in her number. "When's your day off?" he asked.

"Tuesday."

"How 'bout next Tuesday then? Five o'clock? The place next door?"

Steph laughed. "*Wow.* You really don't waste time."

You have no idea, he thought, as he took his phone back, said good-bye, and walked out. To Steph, Daniel must have seemed incredibly confident. But had she met him months ago, she would've met a completely different man. A timid man. Because back then, he hadn't had *the watch.*

Outside, he unrolled his sleeve to reach it; his key to finding love, his shortcut to 'happily ever after', conveniently wrapped around his wrist.

He made it a habit now, when asking someone on a date, to set up a specific time and place. The women usually thought he just liked to plan. But really, it was so he'd know where to tell the watch to go. *Next Tuesday. 5PM. Place next door.* He finished with the settings, took a breath, and pushed in the dials on the watch.

In an instant, he was standing on the same street, but the cars and pedestrians had all changed around him. He still hadn't gotten used to jumping between the present and the future. It felt like skipping from chapter to chapter on a Blu-ray disc. Except he was actually *in* the movie.

He peeked into the window of the coffee shop. Sure enough, his future self and Steph were inside. *So she shows up to the first date*, he thought. *But how* well *does it go?*

He programmed the watch again and jumped forward an hour later, where he saw the two of them outside the shop. Together, they were laughing. He overheard himself set up the next date at a restaurant next week.

Daniel knew exactly where it was. He took a long walk over to it a few blocks away and programmed the watch again. This time, he watched himself and Steph walk out, nervous laughter from both of them. As they stopped by the street, there was a pause. He had to cringe just watching the awkwardness, along with the fact that for some reason, neither of them seemed to be as happy as on the previous date.

He hid, hearing his nervous future self ask, "So, uh, want a ride back?"

There was a pause and Steph awkwardly said, "Listen, Daniel...you seem like a great guy..."

He didn't need to hear more. He had heard it all before.

'We just don't seem like a fit.'

'I'm just not feeling the chemistry.'

'Maybe we could be friends.'

He watched his future self's expression change to disappointment. It was that same expression that made Daniel feel relieved. So it wouldn't work out. *No need to go on this date, then. Saved myself from getting my hopes up.*

His other self, after a minute, regained his composure and told her, "I understand. It was, uh, it was fun." As Steph walked off to her own Uber, Daniel turned away from his future disappointment and set the watch back to the present day.

Now, he was outside of the shop again, looking back through the window at Steph, who had just given out her number to him. A Steph who had no idea what he had just seen.

A few hours later, Steph got a sincere phone call from Daniel.

"I know this is gonna sound really weird," he said, "But I'm gonna have to cancel next Tuesday. It's not you, it's just...I realized I'm just not in a place to date right now."

"Oh," said Steph, who was more surprised by the sudden news than hurt. "Uhh, no problem. Thanks for not wasting time. Again."

"Of course."

"See you around the shop?"

"Sure," said Daniel. After hanging up, he sighed in relief. He always felt bad about doing this, but in the end, he knew he was dodging a bullet. Just like he had done with the others.

Steph was the third woman he had canceled on before even the first date. There were no hard feelings, especially given that none of these women had a chance to develop any attachment to him. It wasn't selfish either. He had spared all of *them* the same hurt too. The hurt he saw from simply looking into their futures. No more failed relationships. No more heartbreak. He would keep peeking into the future until he *knew* for certain that he had found a relationship that would last.

He set the phone down on his dining table. Only to jump.

There, standing in his living room, was a tall woman with a ponytail. She wore a long black coat of a snakeskin leather material. And she was pointing something that looked an awful lot like a gun at him.

"What have you been doing with that watch?!"

"What?!" Daniel put his hands up. *Oh fuck*, he thought.

He looked at the gun. It didn't look anything like the firearms he was familiar with. And then he saw it on her wrist...the same 'watch' he wore. Just in a different color.

He had wondered about the origin of the 'watch' when he found it. Now it was catching up to him.

The owner of the 'watch' was here. And she wasn't happy.

He stammered. "Okay, okay, I can explain..."

Six Months Ago...

The night Chloe left him wasn't the worst part. Sure, Daniel cried after it was all over. But it was just a couple hours until the mercy of sleep took him. Asleep, he could forget what happened. Asleep, he and Chloe would still be together...

No, the worst part of the breakup was the day after.

Because now he had an entire day to remember that she had walked out on him. He'd wake up and look across at her empty spot in bed, knowing he would never see her face there again. He had spent their entire relationship in this one bedroom apartment, yet now it felt even smaller.

It seemed like this was always something that happened to him. Ever since he was a child, he had wanted to live out the stories he grew up with, where the hero would always find love. Yet whenever he found someone special and got attached, she'd inevitably leave him. Chloe was just the latest in a series. Once again, he was left with unfulfilled dreams and fantasies. Trips they would never travel together. Movies he would never get to watch with her. Gifts he would never to give to her. The worst, of course, was the feeling of being chronically unwanted, that all he would find was rejection, heartbreak, and loneliness. And yet, there was always a part of him that hoped that he'd find someone who'd help him prove that wrong. Someone who would prove that he *was* wanted and could be loved.

Chloe had felt like that 'someone' at first, but something had been holding her back. She had admitted several times that she had trouble getting close to the guys she dated. He had hoped, or rather expected, that as he continued to show he cared, she'd see that he was different, and gradually be as intimate and vulnerable with him as he was with her.

Instead, all he did was drive her away. Maybe she was afraid he'd hurt her the same way that the other guys did. Yet the more he tried to forgive her, the more resentment he felt towards her for punishing him for the sins of her exes. *She could at least have punished me for my own sins,* he thought. *That at least would have been fair.*

The pain carried over from one day to the next.

He started burying himself at work in the morgue to distract himself. Suicides, unfortunately, spiked during the holidays. There was a common depression, triggered by a yearning to be with others and a realization, for many, that the yearning could never be fulfilled.

He looked around at the dead around him. He knew he should feel grateful to be the only one in the room breathing. But instead, he felt like he could relate to them, at least on the inside. Cold. Numb. Nothing left to care about.

1:30 came around. Daniel had heated up his lunch, a can of clam chowder that he usually packed because it was easy to microwave in the kitchen.

He took it back to his office, only for his boss to barge in.

"The cops have been asking about this John Doe for way too long. I need you to perform the autopsy *asap.*"

The John Doe was a man in his forties. Nothing unusual about his appearance. But there was an ID card that was unrecognizable from any state's driver's license, giving the name John Tempest.

To everyone, it seemed fake. The police were at a loss. The fingerprints matched no database. Neither did his DNA. Nor, strangely enough, did his teeth match any dental records.

The man was a complete ghost.

Daniel performed the autopsy, as requested. It seemed that the cause of death was a heart attack. No murder or suicide. Just his heart giving out. (In a way, he could relate.)

It was about halfway through the autopsy that he remembered the clam chowder sitting back at his office. Probably cold and likely spoiled by now.

He went back to his desk and tossed out his lunch. The *thud* as the bowl hit the bottom of the trash can felt satisfying, but it wasn't enough to quell the anger he felt.

Now he'd have to wait until dinner to eat. Which pissed him off further. Work was supposed to be his distraction. But now it had become such a distraction that he was skipping lunch. And skipping lunch would just remind him of Chloe and how she always packed lunch for him...and well, work wasn't such a distraction anymore now, was it?

Towards the end of his shift, he looked through the belongings that were found on 'John Tempest'. Perhaps he could help the police find a clue to the man's identity.

Among the belongings was a watch. It didn't match any brand that Daniel had been familiar with. Instead of a single dial to adjust the time and the date, there were multiple ones. There even seemed to be ones to adjust the month and the year, which made it even more unusual.

Daniel played with one of the dials absentmindedly. *It seems like a good watch*, he thought as he turned the hand back a few hours.

Lost in thought, he snapped the dial back in. That was when he felt *the jump*.

He was still in his office. But his surroundings felt...different.

Because the clam chowder was now back to sitting on his desk. Still warm, steam rising from it.

That was strange, he thought. How could that be back there? He hadn't had it out since lunch time, which was...

He looked at the dead man's watch. Sure enough, it had been set to lunch hour. *1:30PM.*

There was no way. Or was there?

His mind must be playing tricks on him. And yet, here was the soup, as it would have sat. But if he had really gone back, where was his past self? He snuck out into the hallway, towards the lab, took a peek in the window...

And *there he was*. Performing the autopsy on the dead body, forgetting all about his lunch back in the office.

He had traveled in time.

Which likely then explained John Tempest. Tempest. As in *Tempus*. As in *time*.

The man was a time traveler. A *dead* time traveler. He wouldn't have any record. Was he from the past? The future? A different world entirely?

Daniel didn't know. All he wanted to learn about now was the watch.

He turned the dial and adjusted it a few hours further back. Then a few hours forward. Each time, he kept adjusting, spying on his past self in the lab or office, and testing the watch further. *Shit, what time was it when I first started jumping around?* he wondered. He needed to go back to his present time. His *real* time. He remembered it being towards the end of his shift and estimated that it must have been around 5:30. He set the watch and jumped once again, finding himself back in his office at the end of the day. The clam chowder was gone and John Tempest's belongings were all on his desk. He had returned to the present. Daniel wasn't sure whether to sigh in relief or cheer in excitement. It *worked*.

What now? Anyone he reported this to would think he was crazy, until he demonstrated it. But then they'd surely take it away. Examine its functions. Use it for their own purposes. No, he had a unique opportunity here.

John Tempest, whoever he was, seemed to have used this watch for time travel. So far, Daniel could only move through time in the same spot. Which probably meant that if he wanted to go back in time to watch the Beatles debut on the Ed Sullivan Show, he'd have to physically *go* to the Ed Sullivan Theater in New York in the present before setting anything.

Tempest had wound up in this timeline where he died. He certainly wasn't using it anymore. So if Daniel took the watch... who would miss it?

Plus, who would even find out? The police might have a record of the watch's existence, but with other cases preoccupying them, they probably wouldn't notice if he kept it to himself. And considering that Tempest probably wasn't even from this time period, the police would never find any leads about him.

It was settled, then. He was going to keep it. But what would he do with it? It didn't take him long to think about it. He knew deep down what he wanted...

He was going to use it to find the love of his life.

At first, he was tempted to go back and undo the breakup with Chloe. But what exactly would he undo? Would he even be able to convince her to stay with him? If he couldn't, he'd just be opening up an old wound. He wanted to make himself feel *better*, not worse.

No, he'd only use the watch to take peeks into the future and come back, rather than change his past. And this time, the watch could help him know that he was moving on with the *right* person, rather than wasting any more time with the *wrong* person.

So Daniel started putting himself out there.

First, he met Ann at a party through his co-worker Simon. "You're not seeing anyone. She's not seeing anyone. I'll set you guys up," he told Daniel.

"Why don't you go for her?"

"Already tried," said Simon. "But she goes for nice guys."

Daniel shook his head. That was a backhanded compliment if he knew it. But he was intrigued.

Simon gestured him over. "Hey, Ann. Meet my buddy, Daniel."

Daniel looked over at a cute girl in a leather jacket. Okay, he wasn't hating this experience so far.

"Hey Daniel," said Ann.

"Alright, you two talk. I'm out."

Daniel watched Simon go. Ann said, "Well that wasn't an awkward introduction at all."

"Not at all," he agreed. "So how do you know Simon? Other than him trying to hit on you?"

She laughed. "Is that what he said he did?"

"Clearly he wasn't that successful."

"I'm friends with his roommate. We met that way, unfortunately."

Daniel nodded. He could tell that she was wondering what his connection was. "Well, I work with Simon," he said.

"With the dead people."

"Yep, with the dead people. Which kinda sucks, actually. Because I thought that meant I wouldn't have to deal with anyone annoying. But then I met him."

She laughed. Once they hit it off about classic literature, she gave him her number and he decided to take the watch for a spin.

The planning was simple. He'd make it a habit of scheduling each new date at the end of the previous one. As an observer, he'd bounce around and spy on how the date went. Then, he'd overhear his future self set up the next time and know exactly where and when to pop up.

After calling Ann to schedule a meeting at a local bookstore, he used the watch to jump to the first date. Then the second. The third. Then months of dating until the night he asked her to be his girlfriend.

Daniel had been tempted to stop peeking then, already satisfied with the future. But he didn't just want another relationship. He wanted *the* relationship. The last relationship he'd ever be in. He wanted to know the *whole* future. So he watched Cliff Notes of an entire relationship unfold. Their first time meeting the parents. Their first fight.

And then, after a year of dating, the breakup. Another girl out of the blue who would leave and break his heart.

And once again, he'd find himself alone in a one bedroom apartment that was starting to feel even smaller.

He wound the watch back to the day after the party when they first met. Then he called Ann, telling her that he'd have to cancel their date at the bookstore and that he just wasn't really in a good place to see anyone. Maybe he'd just see her at another of his friend's parties again and save her from Simon trying to shoot his shot a second time. She found his honesty refreshing and genuinely wished him luck.

There was a wave of relief in what he had done, not to mention pride. He hadn't wasted Ann's time and she hadn't wasted his. They could move on to the right people without baggage. He felt ready to use the watch again on the next girl he met.

That was Kristine.

They had matched online. Daniel wasn't really a fan of online dating and trying to make conversations on the apps. But, as a change, Kristine had started the conversation first.

She seemed like the opposite of Ann. For one thing, she wasn't a book nerd at all. For another, she was less sarcastic and more direct in her interest. The day after they started talking, she was already messaging him, 'Hey, handsome', and before he could float the idea by her first, she was the one proposing, 'Wanna get drinks this week?'

Still, Daniel wanted to see what would happen. So once again he used the watch to skip forward.

A couple of dates in, he saw that he'd invited her to his place. They both seemed to like cooking and he had wanted to show off his pasta maker. Though for some reason, it wasn't in its usual place and he'd had to buy a new one. That was odd. He could have sworn that he always kept it in the same spot in the same cabinet.

He knew this relationship would last longer than the previous one once he saw that, two years in, he and Kristine were still together.

Then eventually, engaged.

But he just kept pushing and jumping forward. Would she marry him? He had to *know*. Even when the wedding was already planned, a date set, invites sent out...he felt that he needed the confirmation. He needed to see himself married before he'd go on that date.

So it was discouraging, but not at all surprising that, when he jumped forward, he saw Kristine call off the engagement.

He overheard himself from the other room, asking, "What did I do?"

Kristine replied, "I just feel like...you don't put in any effort with me anymore."

At that point, Daniel stopped listening. He couldn't stand the sound of his own future voice breaking and crying. And he couldn't stand to keep watching Kristine break his heart even further.

If he was feeling that from just witnessing everything, he could only imagine what it'd be like to *live* it. And it made him even more grateful. This watch from John Tempest was a gift that spared him from pain.

He didn't even want to hear the rest of the argument or wait until Kristine had left. He knew her well enough, at least from observing their relationship, that she wouldn't change her mind.

And he'd be alone, once again, in a studio apartment that was still feeling smaller.

Better to just go back in time and end it. He reset the watch so the sound of his crying in the background would stop.

A month later, he went into the shop and met Steph.

The Present

Daniel finished his story. The woman with the gun had settled in at his dining table, drinking coffee that he had brewed for her. She had put the weapon down too, though the barrel was still pointed in his general direction.

She sipped the coffee in silence, thinking over Daniel's story. He cleared his throat.

"So...you must have known John Tempest, then. Miss...?"

She set down the cup, staring down at it and seeming to ignore him until she finally answered.

"Call me the Overseer."

"Overseer...so what, is that a title or something? For, like, time travelers?"

"Something like that. We're the ones assigned to stop the time ripples."

"Time ripples?"

Then, as if on cue, the coffee cup disappeared from the table.

It wasn't a magic trick. But it felt like one. Almost as if something had just *edited* a jump cut from a movie into reality. Even stranger, the Overseer had looked satisfied, almost having expected it to happen.

Daniel sat up, alarmed. "What...What just happened? What the hell is this?"

"Like I said. Time ripple." She stood up. "Mr. Woo, I tracked you down because your apartment appears to be the center of a set of time ripples."

"What are those? Some kind of butterfly effect?"

"In a way. When time gets undone, your environment changes around you. Usually, you don't even notice the changes. They usually start with your living arrangements..."

Daniel thought it through. He'd been living in a studio apartment for the last six years...but had it always been a studio?

Hadn't he been in a *one bedroom* apartment at some point? Or had he just dreamed or imagined that? No, that couldn't be right. Was she causing him to remember new things or was she causing him to *think* he was remembering new things?

She continued. "Then, certain things go missing. It's probably happened to you before. You can't find something. You don't know where you put it. And if it's not where you last put it, you chalk it up to a bad memory. But it's not. It's actually the beginning of a time ripple."

Things go missing...like a pasta maker? he thought.

"Because for just a few moments in time, whatever's missing actually *stopped existing.* You get residual memories of something that's no longer there and the mind just rationalizes that it's lost or misplaced. Until you stop remembering that it actually existed at all."

Daniel looked alarmed. The Overseer noticed. "Don't worry. Sometimes, what's lost gets found. Sure, it's not where you remember it. But you're so happy you found it again, you don't really question how it got there. You chalk it up to bad memory or just being forgetful. But you didn't forget. Time just set itself right again. And it took an Overseer to bring it back."

Daniel thought of all the times he had found something that he had once lost and how it never seemed to be in the last place he remembered. Just how common were these time ripples?

"Your...dating adventures are responsible for the time ripples in this sector. To put it mildly, you undid things that shouldn't have been undone. And time is making us all pay the consequences. So here's what we'll do, kid. You're gonna return that to me. That's Overseer property."

She grabbed his wrist, undoing the clasp on the watch without letting him object. "Next, you're gonna fix the mess you created."

"How?"

"All those women you turned down. You have to go back and date them. In *real* time."

Daniel froze. That had to be a joke. "But... But I know the future. That'd just be a waste of time."

"Would it?"

"I spent like two years with one of them! I know how it ends!"

"Do you?"

"Can you stop asking me questions?!"

She shot him a glare. "Something that was supposed to happen never happened. That's the cause of this. To fix it, you have to *make* those events happen. Everyone you were supposed to date. You have to *date* them. That's the only way this works."

Daniel could sense the judgment in her tone. He tried to think of another way to get out of this. "I'd be wasting years of my life!" he argued.

"You'd be saving life as we know it. Sounds dramatic, I know, but I'm not wrong. If we don't stop the ripples, all of us are eventually gonna disappear. Like that coffee cup. Which you're gonna forget, by the way, after we're done with this conversation. So you can either do this and make it right or I have to do something drastic."

"Like what?"

She tapped on her gun. "Like go back to when you got the watch and erase you from this timeline." Daniel blinked, speechless. "Not up for that? Didn't think so," she said.

And with that, the Overseer set the dials on her own watch, then grabbed his hand.

Their surroundings snapped into place in an instant. They were back at his room as it had been months ago. "Here we are," she said.

Daniel looked outside. It had gone from day to night. Two dogs were in the middle of a barking match with each other while their owners were trying to restrain them. "So wait, where am *I*? Like, where's the old me?"

"You've set up a date with Ann and now you've gone forward in time to see if you two have a future. But instead of you coming back to cancel on her, we're just gonna branch off into a new timeline from here. One where you actually date Ann. You know, like a normal person."

The Overseer clicked her watch. The barking outside stopped. Daniel peeked out. The dogs and their owners were completely frozen.

"If it doesn't work with her, then we go onto Kristine. And then Steph. Until you experience everything you were supposed to experience. Text Ann to reconfirm you're still going out. Time will resume and the new timeline will begin."

"But I'm undoing what I actually lived through. Doesn't that create, like, another paradox? If I didn't live through turning down these women, how would I still exist to do this?"

"Doesn't work that way," said the Overseer. "As long as these *new* paradoxes fulfill what was supposed to happen, time will fix itself. You know how a string gets tangled and knotted?"

"Yeah?"

"There's always that grace period where you can still untangle it. Before it gets too much. That's where we're at, kid. Right before the point of no return. The point where we can still untangle the string."

The Overseer took his phone and pulled up Ann's number, then handed it back to him.

"So do it," she said. "Untangle it."

Daniel stood by the front door of the bookstore, waiting on his first date, his *real* first date, with Ann. It occurred to him that he might have watched this date before, but it wasn't actually him who had gone through it.

What if he said something stupid and he never got into a relationship with her in the first place? He remembered seeing his heartbroken self back on the couch, feeling the way he had felt after Chloe left. Yes, maybe he'd actually prefer to just screw it all up now. It'd be a quicker way to get to the next person. Finish the mission for the Overseer. Correct his mistake. Get out of this mess.

Then Ann walked in and the plan went out the window.

For Ann, it had just been a few days ago since she met Daniel, but for him, it had been *months*.

He forgot how much he had liked looking in her eyes at the party and the way she had made him feel the first time that he met her.

Their first date, time-wise, lasted about twelve hours.

But neither he nor Ann really felt time go by. She spent the night at his place, which was something he hadn't predicted, since he hadn't stuck around long enough to find out the first time he watched. Other than the embarrassment of not having a clean coffee cup for her in the morning (and feeling like it was weird that he had so few in the first place), it was the perfect first date.

After she left his place, he got to thinking. Yes, he knew the future. Yes, he had seen that in a year from now, it wouldn't work out. But...couldn't he just enjoy being around her for now? Couldn't he just enjoy not being lonely and broken up over Chloe again?

So he kept seeing her. A couple dates in and she was all he could think about. Whenever she texted, he'd always smile and text back as soon as he could. Eventually, she was *constantly* texting him. Maybe she was getting clingy, but since he liked her already, he didn't mind. He *wanted* to text her all day. It was refreshing to not have to fight for someone's attention, the way he always had to with Chloe.

A few months in, he asked her to be his girlfriend. A month after that, they took their first trip together. But as the relationship grew, so did the fear.

Because he knew the future. He knew this relationship was doomed. That she was going to hurt him in the end. He tried to brush it aside and convince himself he was too in love right now to care.

But that love was starting to deteriorate. Whenever they'd argue, even over something small like what type of onions to buy at the grocery store, it was another nail in the coffin. *Is this why she's gonna leave?* he thought.

And yet whenever she said something nice or gave him a surprise gift or comforted him when he had a bad day, he couldn't really believe her either, even though he wanted to. She'd say, "I love you," and he'd wonder, *Do you really? You won't in a couple of months.*

Soon their one-year anniversary was approaching and the anxiety was taking over him. Ann would be leaving any day now. She'd drop him just like Chloe had. He'd go back to crying himself to sleep, waking up next to an empty space in the bed, and sleepwalking from day to day.

He knew what he had to do. And he didn't like it.

When he came over to her place the next night, he told her that it was over. That he felt like he didn't see a future anymore with her. He said it very matter-of-fact. After all, he thought, she was on the same page "You've probably been feeling this too anyway," he said.

But when he looked in her eyes, all he saw was hurt and confusion. She stammered, "No, I...I haven't been feeling that way at all." Daniel stared back with the same confusion. "But I thought...I saw..."

"You saw what, Daniel?"

What could he possibly tell her? That he had time traveled? He'd sound insane. And yet somehow, in knowing how it was going to end, he had acted so differently that he had changed the outcome and the timeline itself. Worse, after all these months of hating Chloe, now he felt like he *was* Chloe. He felt a sense of *loathing* towards himself for putting someone through what he had experienced. Chloe had left him out of fear of getting hurt and ended up hurting him instead. And now he was about to do the same thing to a sweet girl he loved who didn't deserve it.

"Okay, look, I'm sorry, I didn't mean what I said. I've just been confused." He reached out for her hand. He had to fix this.

But she turned away. "You don't know what you want, Daniel. That's the problem."

"No, that's not true."

"It *is* true. You say you want to be with me, but half the time, your mind's somewhere else. Whatever I try, it's not enough. So maybe you're right. Maybe we should just end this."

"I'm sorry, I—I didn't mean for it to be like this."

"Just go." She kept herself turned away and waited. Daniel couldn't think of anything else to do but comply. She hadn't shown much emotion, but when he walked out, he could hear her crying on the other side of the door.

He wasn't anything special. Just part of a vicious cycle. Hearts were broken. Heartbroken people went off to break other hearts. And it would continue over and over and over again. He had to stop it. He gave Ann a couple days of space before calling her.

Except when he called, the voice of an old man picked up on the other end. "Johnson Residence."

No. Daniel immediately hung up. He searched for Ann on social media. All her accounts were gone. He had hoped that she had just blocked him, but why would she have changed her number?

Then he visited her apartment building to check the register. There was a different name in her unit. She couldn't have moved out in just *two days* just because of him. He hoped she did because the alternative was much worse. At work, he approached Simon to see if he was right. "Ann and I broke up."

"Ann?"

"Yeah. You know, my girlfriend. The one you introduced me to at a party..."

"You had a girlfriend?"

Daniel ran off. He needed answers. Sure enough, when he was alone, the Overseer appeared.

"I warned you," she said. "The world's population just dropped by 1 million and nobody noticed except you."

"But how do I still remember?"

"You're a time traveler. Your memories linger longer than others. But you'll still forget eventually. Like that coffee cup."

"What coffee cup?"

"Exactly. Or your pasta maker."

"What pasta — never mind. If I keep going with the plan, do these people come back?"

"It's still possible, but you can't waste any more time. You still have to date the other two women."

"Wait," said Daniel. But the Overseer had already taken his phone. "On to Kristine."

"How? I only met her because I never went out with Ann."

"Not a problem," said the Overseer.

"She might not even exist now!"

But the Overseer went into the dating apps and started randomly swiping on the women. After a few matches, she handed the phone over to him.

"That should do it. Scroll through. One of them's her." She said with confidence.

Daniel looked through his matches. Sure enough, Kristine's profile was in the queue.

"How did you—?"

"Like I said, your relationships were events that *had* to happen. No matter what, Kristine would still end up matching with you on these apps."

Daniel set the phone down, shaking his head. "I just had a breakup."

"Sorry," said the Overseer. "But you don't have time. None of us do."

So Daniel reluctantly started talking to Kristine. This time, *he* started the conversation. He didn't remember exactly what he had said to her when they first talked, but he had the gist of it. He thought about the future with her he had seen. How they had almost gotten married, if he hadn't screwed it all up.

He remembered the words that she had told him. 'You don't put in any effort with me.' Maybe he would just do the opposite of what he'd seen. Maybe that would give him a different result. Put in effort.

In a way, he'd be making up for what he had just done to Ann.

So this time Daniel was the one to ask Kristine for drinks next week.

Soon enough, they were dating and he had her over for cooking dinner, so he could show off this new pasta maker he had bought, though he had no idea how to use it. (And he couldn't help shake the nagging feeling that he was *supposed* to know how to use it).

Kristine was already different from Ann. For one thing, she wasn't as quick to open up. In fact, for some time, it still felt as if he hardly knew her at all. He knew what she did for a living, of course. Her general interests. How many siblings she had. What she liked in bed.

Maybe he just needed to give it time. So he did everything he could to be a great boyfriend. He went all out on her birthday. Made sure to befriend all her friends. Gave her all his attention when she was with him.

So why was it that every time he did something nice for her, she'd always seem to run away? She'd thank him in the moment, sure, but then, she'd retreat into work and barely talk to him for a week. Naturally, this just made him push harder. He'd text her more to ask how her day went. He'd offer to cook for her more often. *Anything* to avoid being accused of not 'putting in the effort'.

Which was why it shocked him, four months into the relationship, when she said, "I don't think this is working for me."

No. No, this isn't right, he thought. *We aren't even close to the time that we broke up.*

Daniel wondered if maybe he had missed an initial breakup from his travels and the two of them would get together again after this.

But he knew that was just wishful thinking. It was the way she had said, 'I don't think this is working for me'. It was the same tone he had heard when she called off the wedding.

All he could muster in response was one word: "Why?" As in, why was this over, out of nowhere, *again*? Why couldn't he just make something work? Why was nothing he did good enough for her (or for Chloe for that matter)? *Why?*

And Kristine simply responded, "I just feel like you're too... clingy for me."

The first time, he hadn't made enough effort with Kristine. Now he had made *too* much. Maybe Kristine had just never really wanted him. Maybe she was destined to make an excuse to leave.

Maybe it wasn't even Kristine. Maybe it was just his luck in general with love. Maybe he'd always be disappointed and never find the right person.

And the Overseer returned again. This time, Daniel had nothing to share. He simply asked, "Those ripples still happening?" She nodded. Before she could elaborate, Daniel cut her off. He didn't care anymore. "Let's just get this over with."

There was one woman left: Steph.

"Lucky for you, she hasn't been rippled out of existence yet. I checked. You still have a shot at fixing this," said the Overseer. She looked like she was about to leave, but she stopped. Perhaps there was sympathy in her step. "Good luck." And with that, she was gone. It occurred to Daniel that if he pulled this off, he might never see the Overseer again.

With Ann and Kristine, he had tried to go against what he had seen. Now, what would his strategy be?

This time, there'd be no strategy. And maybe that, in itself, was a strategy. Maybe he just needed to act as if he *didn't* know the future. A part of him hoped that meant this would work out. Another part of him told him to stop being an idiot in getting his hopes up.

If the Overseer had been right about these relationships being destined to happen, then Steph would still be working at the shop now.

So he drove over and walked in. Sure enough, there she was at the cash register. He almost didn't recognize her at first without the big glasses. She must've been wearing contacts today. She wore her hair tied back and her outfit was different from what he remembered, but he figured he could have the same conversation. That was going to be the easy part.

As expected, she agreed to get coffee with him. Like before, he asked when she was off work. And like before, he scheduled it for her day off. So he arrived on that Tuesday. 5PM. The coffee shop next to the place that she worked at. And the two of them talked.

They talked for six *hours*, to the point that the place closed before they were done.

Daniel was surprised by Steph at first. It had been maybe even a year at this point since he had *actually* met her for the first time. She seemed *funnier* than he had remembered. Was she actually funnier? Or did he just *get* her humor better? And did he also find her more attractive now than before because of it?

"You know, it seems weird," she said, "But the other day when you came into the shop, I felt like I almost knew you from before."

Daniel laughed. "Really?"

"Yeah, I don't know. You just seemed so…familiar. Or I seemed familiar to you. Like did we go to school together or something?"

"I'm a SoCal boy and you're from the East Coast. I doubt it."

"I know, but still! I don't know, you just seemed like… someone I've already known for awhile. Like, you *knew* I'd say yes to coffee. Like you expected it."

Daniel just shrugged. She wasn't completely wrong. "Well I didn't know for sure. But I figured I didn't have anything to lose."

"See, a lot of people say that. But most of them don't actually act like it," she said, "What's your secret?"

He shrugged. "I'd say, learn not to expect anything."

"That's it? So you just expect to be disappointed and let yourself be surprised."

"No, expecting to be disappointed is different from not expecting anything. Because if you expect to be disappointed, you're still expecting. Which is the problem." Daniel hardly recognized what was coming out of his mouth. It felt like he was making shit up as he went along and it just happened to sound profound.

But Steph smiled and said, "I like that."

Hell, maybe it was *profound, then.* He continued, "I mean, it's basically what they say. Hope for the best, prepare for the worst…"

He'd have to put that mentality to the test soon. Because later that night, Steph agreed to go on a second date.

And in another life, it was the second date that was also their last date.

Daniel had figured that the outcome would be different from before. But whether that would be better or worse, he'd have to see.

He went into the date half excited and half feeling like a prisoner due for execution. About thirty minutes into it, she said. "I have something to confess."

Uh oh, he thought. A part of him wondered if this would be when she'd end it. Which would be really awkward, since the food hadn't even come yet.

What she actually said, however, was very different: "I just got out of a relationship like a month ago."

"Wow," he said. Then without thinking, "Me too."

"Really?! Oh my God, I totally thought I'd scare you off."

Daniel laughed. *On the contrary...*

Questions then swirled in his brain. "So that day I asked you out to coffee...what made you say 'yes' then? I mean you could've just said that you were still recovering from the last relationship. I would've gotten it..."

"Yeah, well, breakups suck. But there's no use punishing the next guy about it, is there?"

Jesus, where were you three relationships ago? Daniel thought as he took a second to collect his response. "No...no, definitely not."

He was starting to feel something for the first time. Was it comfort? No, that wasn't it. Maybe it was *desire*, but not in the sexual sense of desiring her (though he wasn't opposed to that either). It was almost a desire to open up. To share again. To just be vulnerable.

He continued talking, "You know, if I'm being frank, there's a part of me that almost didn't ask you out. Not because of you, I mean, but because I guess I was just getting jaded from the whole experience."

"Yeah, I get you. It's hard not to get hurt doing all this."

Daniel leaned forward with interest. "What helps you just put yourself out there then?"

Steph let out a breath and thought about it. "Knowing it's worse if I don't."

"And you're not afraid of getting hurt again?"

"Oh, all the time," she said, "But if I let that stop me, I'm never gonna find it, am I?"

"I guess you're right."

"How about you? What keeps you going?"

Daniel thought about how he should phrase it. Then said, "Same as you, I guess. Faith."

Steph raised a glass. "To faith, then."

They toasted and kept talking through the rest of their dinner, but Steph's attitude stuck out in his mind. Here he had been, using a stolen time traveler's watch to avoid getting hurt, while Steph had done the complete opposite. No time travel, no peeks or knowledge of how things would turn out. Just complete faith that at some point, someone was going to make all the heartache worth it.

He paid the bill, of course, and as they walked out, Daniel could feel his heart pounding.

Here it is. The moment she turns me down.

He had *really* started to like her already. He hoped things would turn out differently this time, but he felt an odd sense of calmness as he walked next to her.

He had seen this play out from the outside. The hesitation. The potential preamble on how he *seemed* like a great guy *but...*

But nothing. He had been wrong before. Maybe he'd be wrong again. He wouldn't know unless he went for it.

"So...want a ride back?" he asked. The same question he had heard himself ask in the other timeline. He noticed it came out differently from what he remembered. When he had heard himself say it originally, it felt very tentative, as if he weren't really sure if she would say yes. Here, it seemed casual. Indifferent. Almost as if he had asked her to pass the salt.

It wasn't that he needed her to say 'yes' anymore.

It was that he'd be fine if she said 'no'. That no matter what answer she gave him...he'd be okay.

He stopped, waiting for her answer. She smiled.

"A ride? Sure."

Somewhere, in a kitchen across town, a coffee cup and a pasta maker reappeared, as if they had been there all along.

A girl named Ann was back in her apartment, pouring over a book.

And Daniel was walking Steph back to his car for a ride home.

He smiled. For once, he had no idea what was going to happen next.

See Ben Wan's story "Shortcut to Happily Ever After" online at Metaphorosis.
If you liked it, leave a comment. Authors love that!
Remember to subscribe to our e-mail updates so you'll know when new stories are posted.

About the story

Unsurprisingly, the idea for "Shortcut to Happily Ever After" came to me when my last relationship ended and I found myself back in the dating pool. As I was meeting new people,

I wondered how much easier it would be if, for every person we met, we could just jump forward in time to see if it would work out. If it didn't, we could call it all off before the first date, sparing everyone from future heartache. On top of that, in another job, I coach people who are inexperienced in dating and are often terrified of potential rejection. It seems almost universal that we're scared of future pain. Yet risking that pain and putting ourselves out there is necessary, both in developing ourselves and in finding a relationship that lasts. The more we try to avoid that pain, like Daniel in this story, the more we hurt that development and hold ourselves back from getting what we want.

If there are any Doctor Who fans among the readers, they might be interested to learn that this was originally conceived to be part of the Doctor Who universe. I had written a one page proposal for Big Finish's Paul Spragg Memorial Short Trips Opportunity, pitching this as an audio drama. But when another story was chosen, I still wanted to explore this premise and write it out as an original novella or short story. The Doctor wasn't the protagonist anyway, Daniel was. So I eliminated all of the Doctor Who elements and created my own world as well as my own time travel rules before I started outlining what would become "Shortcut to Happily Ever After".

When I tell people about this story, the easiest way to describe it is as a 'time travel romance'. The funny thing is that it's not really accurate. There's time travel but most of the drama happens chronologically in the present day. It's also not really a romance since it doesn't revolve around two people falling in love. It instead revolves around one hurt individual who learns to face his fears in dating and grow from it. I hope this story speaks to people going through that same journey and inspires them to face their fears as well.

A question for the author

Q: Do you write with a particular audience in mind?

A: At the risk of sounding self-centered, the first audience I write for is myself! If I'm not actually interested in the premise or I'm bored at any point with the story, then my audience is going to feel the same way. I want whatever I write to be something that I'd not just read, but reread over and over again from how much I connect to it. I think about how I would get invested in a story and find a way to channel that for the reader. That said, I don't want to be self indulgent and only write for an audience of one. I want people to relate to it. To balance that out, I tend to write about a particular theme or experience that most would find relatable, but in a way that feels interesting or unique.

Storytelling connects us and helps us feel less alone. Whatever my protagonist is dealing with, there's a high chance other people have dealt with it too. In the case of "Shortcut to Happily Ever After", I channeled my own emotions about getting back into dating after a breakup, knowing that others have felt the same way, like the heartache over their last relationship or feeling jaded with their current options. Some might connect with the story after going through their own heartbreak. Others might feel inspired to get back into dating again. If even one person says this story helps them cope with their own dating experiences, then I've done my job.

About the author

Ben Wan is a cancer survivor who's been making the most out of his second chance at life. Aside from writing, he's a former musician who's performed in Carnegie Hall, a black belt in Kung Fu San Soo, and a coach for Become Sharp in helping introverted clients succeed with dating, confidence, and social skills. He's currently the co-host and "Man Who Knows Too Much About Batman" for the podcast *Superhero Stuff You Should Know*, where his cat Alfie makes cameo appearances.

www.benwanwriter.com, @SuperHousePod

Trapped in Memory

Dan Le Fever

"Touchdown in T-minus fifteen," a crackling voice said over the comm channel.

Pilot Kehvan-30 toggled that the message was received as he prepared to do his part in landing *Last Train* and the three million sleeping colonists aboard. After nearly a thousand years, they had finally arrived at the new planet where humanity would once again thrive after the destruction of the planet Earth.

Through the Translink System implanted in each crewmember, Kehvan had perfect recall of the day the Moon had crashed into Earth's surface . Yet he felt nothing when he watched the memory vid recorded by Kehvan-01, his genetic line's first iteration. And why would he? Earth had never been his home, though he replayed the vid daily as a reminder of his purpose. As one of the seventeen distinct Pilots aboard *Last Train*, his only desire was to land safely.

"T-minus twelve."

He turned his attention to the screen on the wall in front of him. The atmosphere of the world they approached had a red hue, and the information that scrolled across the screen matched what the ancient scientists had predicted: oxygen, carbon, and nitrogen were all within acceptable parameters to support life.

For a split second, Kehvan wondered what it would be like to walk on the surface. To smell unrecycled air, feel the warmth of sunlight, or taste fresh food grown from the soil. Then the nano-wires of the Translink chip that spiderwebbed throughout his body took over and made him focus once more on the controls. He chastised himself for letting his mind wander and blamed the ripvids he had watched before his duty activation. Unlike memory vids, these had been pulled by Pilot Seyra-01 from Earth's satellites before they ceased transmitting. Later, watching them became a minor act of rebellion as she learned how to share them with other crewmembers. They were not outright banned, but generations of Captains had restricted viewing to those on downshift.

Seyra-30 had talked about it with him once, why the ripvids were such a big deal. It was basic psychology. "My guess, scientists didn't know how we'd react if we got it in our heads that our lives were a complete waste. Probably figured we'd walk out an airlock just because we can't pet a dog, walk on a beach, or get fat. I don't know if my life is missing anything, but that's probably because we've always had a purpose. Especially *our* iteration. We're marked for Landing."

Seyra spoke in a peculiar accent that she had picked up from one such vid and Kehvan, who slept beneath her bunk, often heard her practicing it when she thought no one else was awake. Best described as sparse, their quarters were in a narrow room, with rows of beds on one wall and a communal bathroom with showers and toilets. A few days ago, one of the waste reclaimers had malfunctioned and sprayed urine from one of the pipes. He could remember how upset she had been after they smelled like urine for their entire shift.

"We piss down one hole just to have it rain on us from another," she had grumbled.

"It's been a thousand years," he had said to her. "Things are bound to break down."

"T-minus eight."

He shook his head to clear his thoughts and activated the stimneedle in his arm. The chemicals would keep him hyper-focused as he and the other Pilots landed the massive ship. *Last Train* was enormous, far larger than even some of the cities of old Earth. The ancient scientists had not wanted to put all their trust in computers, so, by design, the ship required a small army of seventeen individually produced Pilots to keep her from tearing apart when she entered the planet's atmosphere.

As the stim took hold, his heart thrummed in rhythm with the powerful engines, and he pressed the button indicating his readiness. Across the ship, each Pilot did the same. Seyra was the last to signal before they broke through the cloud barrier and the ship began to shake. Gritting his teeth, Kehvan held the control sticks tightly while all Pilots worked in tandem to keep *Last Train* level.

"The dream of every colonist is to wake up on the surface. That dream rests now on your shoulders," the Captain had said during her speech right before they began the landing preparations. It had been a good speech.

Chosen from the previous generation of Pilots, the Captain had served fifty-five rotations since her decantation, which made her the oldest crewmember aboard *Last Train*. She was a woman of firm convictions that wanted nothing more than to see them fulfill their task of shepherding Earth's survivors to their new home. She also happened to be Seyra-29, which was probably why Seyra-30's minor infractions were often overlooked.

Also, Seyra-30 was skilled at keeping the major ones from being noticed.

For instance, right after the Captain's speech, Seyra had done something odd by taking his hand. Contact among the crew was not necessarily forbidden, just highly irregular. Pulling him aside as the others filed out of the conference room, she had asked him what he looked forward to the most after they landed.

"To see the sky," he answered, which every Kehvan had wanted since his first iteration.

Usually, that was the end of the conversation, but this time, she said, "Promise me you'll wait and see it with me." It was a simple enough request, so he agreed, and her face lit up in a way he had never seen before. But as he was about to inquire why, the Captain had ordered them to their posts.

"T-minus three," the Captain said now over the comm. "Landing imminent. Release."

As he had been trained, Kehvan initiated the reverse thrusters and deployed the landing struts before taking up the sticks again. Everything was nominal until an alarm blared in the cramped room. The green lights along the console flickered to red all at once, and he knew that something had gone catastrophically wrong.

Partially deafened by the siren, Kehvan heard a faint shout from the comm speaker, "Pull up!"

Kehvan slipped on his headset to request confirmation just as the Captain's voice came through. "Negative. Gravity too strong. It'll tear us apart."

"The damn ground's about to do the same in a minute," Seyra argued, and Kehvan realized she'd been the one to tell them to pull up. He didn't have time to think about how that was possible; the on-screen readout indicated they had only seconds left before touchdown.

Since his decantation, Kehvan had looked forward to feeling *Last Train* touch down, but now he wished for anything else. The ship shuddered violently as all the Pilots continued their descent.

All that is, except for Seyra, who had powered the thrusters of her section to ascend again, throwing off the ship's approach angle. Kehvan wanted to shout at her to think of the colonists, but he did not dare take his hands off the sticks to reach for the comm. Then the ship clipped the ground at landing speed, and his head smashed into the control panel.

From within the void, something rang every few seconds. Kehvan lifted a hand and was surprised he could see it in the perfect nothingness. The ringing came again, closer this time. Out beyond his consciousness, he saw a red glow each time it sounded. Willing himself forward, he made his way in that direction. The ring grew louder with each step until it shook his whole body. Finally reaching the glow, he saw a telephone. Strange, he thought. He'd never seen one in person. Kehvan picked up the receiver, as people often did in the ripvids, and asked, "Hello?"

Pain wracked his body as he came to. Bright lights flashed in his vision. At first, he thought it was his eyes, but as he blinked to clear them, he saw sparks cascading down the walls from cracked bulkheads. Twisted conduits and exposed wires were everywhere. Coughing as he breathed in the scent of burning ozone, he assessed his situation. Though he was sprawled on the control panel, he was still miraculously strapped in his chair, with the telephone ringing in his left ear. As he started to question how it had followed him out of the void, he realized what he was actually hearing was the emergency comm channel.

He tried to hit the receive button, but cold agony tore through his left arm. Gasping in pain, Kehvan tested his right hand and found it hurt significantly less. He pushed back from the panel and took in a few labored breaths. There was a moment when he thought his chest had been caved in, but he reminded himself that he was still alive, so it couldn't be that serious. Aside from the occasional flash of sparks, the only lights he had to go by were from a few buttons on the controls and one of the vidscreens that randomly flickered green.

By the odd angle his left arm hung in his lap, he deduced it was broken. He tasted blood. But clearly his eyes and ears were still working fine. With his good arm, he tapped the button to receive the emergency call.

"—sound off. Pilots all respond." It was the Captain.

Licking the blood from his lips, Kehvan said, "P-pilot Fourteen. Active but damaged."

"Kehvan?" Seyra said before the Captain could acknowledge.

A feeling came over him at the sound of her voice. Was it relief? Crew members were grown with the knowledge that they were disposable. But knowing Seyra was still functional made him … happy? Regulation allowed him to inquire about the well-being of fellow crewmen, so he requested, "Pilot Thirteen, condition?"

"Shaken, but not stirred," she said.

What came through the crackling speaker sounded like laughter before the Captain cut her off. "Keep channel clear. Pilot Fourteen, emergency crew assigned for extraction. Hold."

Kehvan toggled the 'message received' button instead of replying and leaned his head back to stare at the flashing screen. That was when he finally felt it. The thrumming of the propulsion engines, a sensation he'd known for all his rotations, was absent. He held up his good hand again. It felt heavier. Was this true gravity? *Last Train* had relied on the artificial stuff to prevent the crew's muscles from atrophying, and the scientists had kept it at a level they believed matched the new planet, but feeling it now, they'd been off a bit. Luckily, it was only by a little.

While he waited, Kehvan tried to get the vidscreen operational again. Finally, he managed to stop the flickering and read a partially obscured time code of *T+ 59:2**. If it was accurate, he had been unconscious for an hour. With nothing to do, he stared at the clock as it ticked up for the next thirty minutes and a handful of Pilots checked in on the emergency channel. Spread out as they were across the ship, Kehvan had only come to know the few near his sector. Aside from gathering during the Captain's speech, the last time Pilots had all been together was when the ship left Earth's orbit during the 01 generation.

The colonists.

Kehvan toggled the comm and opened a request to the bridge. When he got the signal to go ahead, he asked, "Captain?"

"Go ahead, Pilot Fourteen."

"The colonists?"

"Status unknown. Assessment ongoing. Concern logged."

"Earned some brownie points," Seyra had said to him once after he'd reported a slight temperature increase in the cryo-sleep system.

"Our duty is to maintain the well-being of the colonists and *Last Train* until the final Landing," he'd recited the crewmen's primary objective to her.

Another hour passed, then a bang sounded at the door, followed by the hissing of a plasma cutter as the extraction team made their way inside. Once it was clear, a blinding light filled the room, and Kehvan covered his eyes. The straps holding him in place were released, and he yelped when they removed the stimneedle from his broken arm. His eyes slowly adjusted to the light until he could make out two Huws and a Karal putting him on a gurney.

"Assess," he said to the Karal. Like the rest of that genetic line, the Karal was grown for medical duty. Each had the same receding hairline, dark skin, and a perpetual grimace. Solidly built and good-natured, the Huws were Basic Labor. Oddly though, one had slightly longer brown hair than the other. He would have to be checked for aberration, Kehvan noted. The Huws followed the Karal's directions as they carefully moved Kehvan out of the cockpit.

"Arm's broken. Want more? It'll have to wait," Karal shouted over the alarm. By his cadence, Kehvan knew the doctor was on downshift and had not been activated for duty before being assigned to the extraction team.

Outside the cockpit, the smoke-filled corridor was a mess. Where the white and gray paneling of the ship's interior was not completely torn apart, it was fractured beyond repair. Tube lights and ceiling tiles littered the floor, forcing the Huws to carry the gurney most of the way. Red-uniformed Crew Security continuously ran by them on their search for survivors. Even over the alarm, Kehvan could hear calls for help from side corridors.

Not until they passed a row of bodies covered by white sheets did the enormity of what had occurred finally strike him. Aside from a rare accident, unscheduled nullification was unheard of on *Last Train*. Those bodies beneath the sheets ... they were Promised Landers, just like he was. They had been destined to live out their remaining days on the new planet, with a sky above and dirt below...

"How many?" Kehvan asked, nodding at the row of corpses.

Karal shook his head sadly. "Too many."

At the medbay, the door opened only a few inches before it jammed in place, and a Huw had to pull at it to make space for the gurney. Unfortunately, the medical facility had not fared better than the rest of the ship. Contents from multiple cabinets lay spilled on the ground, and various delicate-appearing pieces of medical equipment had fallen over. Kehvan was not trained for those machines, but it was easy to tell they were broken. Karal sighed and cleared a table for the Huws to put his patient on before rummaging around on the floor.

Three bright lights in the ceiling—having somehow survived the crash—shone down on Kehvan as the longer-haired Huw pressed a button at the edge of the table. The upper part of the surface lifted beneath Kehvan's torso, sitting him up at a comfortable angle. Another button extended part of the table to his left, and Karal returned with a hand scanner which he ran over Kehvan's body. When the doctor finished, he nodded to one of the Huws, and the crewman took Kehvan's broken arm and carefully placed it on the table's extension.

"I was right. Your arm is broken. You've also got three bruised ribs and a mild concussion. Given the circumstances, I'd say you're lucky," Karal said, then took an injector from his pocket and put it to Kehvan's shoulder. The vial emptied its contents before he could even ask what it was.

The pain in his arm faded instantly, and a sense of euphoria spread like a wall of fuzziness to separate him from his body. Through that wall, Kehvan watched Karal cut off the sleeve of his gray Pilot's jacket and poke a few times at the arm before he took it in both hands and pulled. Seeing his arm stretch and twist so unnaturally was hilarious. Somewhere in his mind, it registered as painful, but the drug-induced bliss kept that feeling from taking over.

Karal had just finished the nano-weave mesh cast on the arm when a knock came at the medbay door. The doctor nodded to one of the Huws; moments later, a blonde woman with wide green eyes appeared at Kehvan's side. She looked worried, though Kehvan couldn't figure out why. Disjointed and muffled, sounds tried to make their way into his ears, but as tired as he was, he gave up on trying to make sense of them and chose to close his eyes instead.

The pain was waiting for him when he awoke. It was less intense than the last time he had crawled out of the void, but enough to regret returning. His vision was spotty, and he rubbed at his eyes until they cleared. He was no longer the only patient in the medbay. White-uniformed Karals attended to injured crewmembers occupying every available surface.

"Think fast," someone said, and Kehvan watched a small metal bowl fly toward his face. Instinctively, he caught it with his left hand. "Looks like you're going to be all right," Seyra said. She took the bowl from him and smiled. Her hair, usually tied back in a ponytail, hung loose against the top of her shoulders. A bit of dried blood stained her gray uniform near the right side of her neck, but Kehvan could not see any apparent injuries.

Frowning, he pointed at her hair. "Against regulation, Pilot Thirteen."

Seyra rolled her eyes. "Fuck regulation, Kehvan. Oh, *sorry*. I mean Pilot Fourteen." She motioned to all the activity around them. "It's all gone to shit, or haven't you noticed?"

Kehvan tested his left arm, but aside from some minimal pain, the mesh cast did its job. "Situation assessment," he said.

"You're lucky to be alive. How's that for an assessment? Half the ship broke off in the crash. I told the Captain we should have pulled up," she said. Kehvan registered the anger in her voice.

"Negative," Kehvan said. "Gravitation—"

Seyra yelled, "Enough!" and slammed the table right by his head, causing black spots to swim in his vision again. Then, covering her mouth, she said, "Oh! Oh no. I'm sorry, the Karal said you have a concussion." She cupped his cheek in her hand, and Kehvan could feel her fingers moving ever so slightly against his skin. It was a strange and unexpected sensation.

The same Karal from before came over, and Seyra quickly stepped back while he ran the scanner over him once more. With a grunt, he said, "No additional damage. You are on downshift for the next twenty-four hours. Doctor's orders." Looking over his shoulder at the work awaiting him, he muttered, "Lucky you."

Like the flip of a switch, Kehvan's muscles relaxed as duty regulation was lifted. "Thanks, Karal," he said.

The Medical crewman nodded and went to check on another patient.

"There's my bunkmate," Seyra said, smiling again.

Sighing, Kehvan said, "You have to stop, Seyra. Your behavior is bordering on aberration."

"Yeah, yeah," she muttered as she helped him down from the table. He was barely off it before a Huw laid another crewman in his place. Other blue-uniformed Laborers were moving equipment around at the orders of the Karals trying to organize the mess. Feeling like they were in the way now, Kehvan made for the door.

"How much of the ship is left?" he asked once they had left the medbay.

"I told you before. Just about half. Lucky for us, we were angled away from the surface."

Kehvan stopped and turned to her. "How did you bypass the Captain's order?"

"I..." she began, then paused, biting her lip. "I did what I thought was best to protect the ship."

Regulation stated that a Captain's orders could be ignored if they put the ship in danger. Satisfied with that answer, Kehvan continued down the hallway. "I'm having trouble remembering which Pilots survived. Do you have that information?"

Seyra hurried to catch up. "You can just say you're worried about them."

"Seyra, please."

Frowning, she said, "Raj, Mayla, and Estevan are all accounted for."

Kehvan felt relieved. "How long was I out this time?" Since entering the medbay, the hallway had been cleared to accommodate the increased traffic, and the alarms muted.

"A couple of hours."

He nodded.

The two walked through the ship for a few minutes in silence, then Seyra said, "Ask the question already. I know you want to."

Kehvan frowned. "The colonists?"

"The crash put a dent in the cryo-hold."

His heart skipped a beat, and he felt cold. "You mean?"

With a crooked smile, she said. "I mean, just a dent. The hull around the Earthlings is so thick I bet we could crash the ship three more times before we crack that egg." *Earthling* was a nickname the downshifted had for their cargo. It was sort of a joke. Since the crew had been created off-planet, technically, that made them aliens.

"Should have made the whole ship that tough," Kehvan said. But, even with all the deaths, he was happy to know the colonists had survived. They were the priority, after all.

Seyra laughed and slapped him on the back. Pain shot through his ribs, and he moaned while clutching his side. She quickly buried him under an avalanche of apologies.

If he was on downshift, Kehvan wanted to spend most of it in his bunk. Lucky for him, the sector that housed their crew quarters was relatively intact. He took several steps down the next corridor and noticed Seyra was no longer with him. Turning back, he saw her where the hallways diverged, standing completely still and staring at something he could not see. Returning to her side, he asked, "What is it?"

Her hand shook as she pointed to a strange red glow further down the hallway that he had somehow missed. It was unlike any light aboard *Last Train*. It had a warmth to it, almost as if it were alive. Then it dawned on him—he was seeing daylight for the first time. Somewhere down there, the hull had breached, and light from the planet's sun had found its way inside.

How could he not have seen it when she had? It was so bright, and he had been looking right at that spot before turning toward their quarters. His body stiffened when he looked directly at the alien radiance. Even now, while he was on downshift, regulation had taken control.

He felt her hand slip into his, and with a squeeze, she tugged ever so slightly as she tried to coax him to follow her into the light.

But regulation kept him in place.

In a barely audible whisper, he said, "We can't. Not yet."

Spinning to face him, she let go of his hand and said, "Why not?"

"You know why." His jaw tightened, and he took a step back.

Seyra growled, "Why can't it be us? Why do we have to wait for a popsicle's permission first?"

Popsicle? Kehvan accessed the Translink Network to make sense of the word. *A piece of flavored ice or ice cream on a stick.* Flavored ice? Oh, the colonists. "Because regulation states it has to be them."

He had backed up to the intersection leading to the quarters, but Seyra remained where she stood. She laughed bitterly as she eyed his retreat. "What's this iteration called again? The Promised Landers? Do you think we'll even get a thank you after they've woken up?"

Unsettled, Kehvan took another step back. "I... Seyra, what are you doing? Why are you talking like this?"

"Why do we even have to wake them up at all?" She spoke louder now, and nearby crew members stopped to listen. "After all, what do we really owe them? *We* died getting *them* here. Don't we deserve more than what they'll let us have?"

"I don't understand," Kehvan said, shaking his head. "None of the previous Pilot Thirteens ever spoke this way." He'd run a full replay of previous generations, all thirty iterations of her genetic line, and found no trace of this behavior.

"So? Why do I have to be like them? Why can't I be different?" She looked to the gathered onlookers in the hall. "We *can* be more. More than just... some recycled memories," she spat.

Kehvan, stunned by her words, watched as she walked away from him and toward the splash of sunlight. He didn't lift a finger or call out to her as Security emerged from another hallway to block her. She tried shoving past them, but there were just too many. Kehvan wanted to stay. To see if she would be all right. But his feet were already moving him to the quarters. His last glimpse of her was her body falling limp after a Karal came up behind her and injected something into her neck.

Maybe he had missed something, he thought hours later while staring up at the bunk above his. He ran a more detailed analysis of the Pilot Thirteen line but found no aberrations. For the most part, each had followed the established regulation of the Generational Caretaker Program of *Last Train*. Something must have happened during the crash. Her chip must be damaged; it was the only logical explanation. Though, hadn't she been acting strangely before the landing attempt? What had happened to her?

He replayed the last words she'd spoken over and over in his mind.

We can *be more. More than just... some recycled memories.*

Was that what he was? He was Pilot Fourteen, the same as all the previous Fourteens. Up until they began preparations to land, each day of the last one thousand years had followed the same pattern. What more was he supposed to be? Then, for some reason, the memory of his decantation came to him. He recalled confusion. Confusion about not knowing where, or even who, he was. Then the Translink had activated, and all the training and memories of the previous generations flooded in. And he had understood his purpose.

"Pilot Fourteen. Follow."

Lost in thought as he was, Kehvan hadn't heard Security approach. Quickly, he sat up and placed his feet on the floor. "What is this about? I'm on downshift. I have a Karal's clearance." He showed the cast on his arm.

"Captain's orders supersede previous clearance. Comply."

The switch in his head clicked back on, and Kehvan stood rigidly. "Complying."

In silence, Security escorted him to a lift and pressed the button for the control bridge. The elevator ascended a hundred decks to the very top of *Last Train*. Kehvan-30 had never visited the bridge, but his previous iterations had, so he knew what was waiting for him as the doors slid open. From the paneled floor, his eyes drifted up to the screens that encircled the room, showing the outside of the ship.

As he stepped off the lift, he was confronted with the strange beauty of the planet's surface. Feathery plants grew in a field leading up to a chain of rust-colored mountains capped with white snow. The cameras also showed the wreckage of *Last Train* and its exposed egg-shaped cryo-hold.

"You are on downshift, yes?" said the Captain with no introduction from a raised chair at the center of the circling rows of consoles. None of the support crew looked up from their work as she spun around to face him with a stern look. Through all her wrinkles and gray hair, Kehvan could not help but see Seyra—*his* Seyra—sitting there.

Clicking his heels together, he stood at attention and said, "Previously ordered. Regulation supersedes."

With a dismissive wave, she said, "Revert to downshift."

Kehvan blinked, and his muscles relaxed.

"Better," she said. "Now, Kehvan, tell me about the earlier... incident with Pilot Thirteen."

Creases formed on his forehead as his brow knitted in confusion. It was unlike the Captain to speak with such familiarity. "I don't understand, sir."

Fingers tapping rhythmically on one armrest, she crossed her legs. "I want you to tell me what might have caused the Seyra's aberrant behavior."

"Is there an issue with the Translink upload, sir?" A function of the chip in their heads was to store and archive every experience for the next generation.

Her lips pursed for a second, then she said, "I want to hear *your* perspective."

This is odd, he thought and glanced at the support crew to see if any of them had noticed, but none gave any sign. Then, looking back at her, he saw she was growing impatient. Kehvan did not know how to begin. He had never needed to describe something before.

"Come on, out with it," Seyra-29 said, waving a hand to hurry him up.

Kehvan swallowed as he collected his thoughts, then told her everything that happened up to Seyra's outburst. After he had finished, he asked, "Could it be a reaction to something in the planet's atmosphere? Are the air circulators malfunctioning?"

Ignoring his questions, the Captain pressed her palms together. Resting her chin on her fingertips, and, with her gaze burrowing into him, she asked, "What exactly did she say to you?"

Her scrutiny made him uncomfortable. Was there an issue with the Translink Hub? Had it been damaged during the crash? Was that why she couldn't access either his or Seyra's uploads? Kehvan pinged the central network and found it functioning correctly.

"It was recorded, sir. I can find an Engineer if you need help... to..." his voice trailed off because several of the green-uniformed Engineers were already on the bridge.

Eyes narrowing, the Captain asked, "What are you hiding, Kehvan?"

"Hiding, sir?"

Sitting back in her chair, the Captain clasped her hands in her lap. "Kehvans are dutiful and dedicated," she said. "Always have been. Kehvan-29 was a good friend of mine, just as you are to Seyra-30." The Captain paused a moment before continuing. "It's difficult when a previous generation overlaps the next. There are... feelings you want to express, but that would go against regulation and serve no purpose. I don't envy you, Kehvan, not with two Seyras in your life." A sad smile flashed briefly before vanishing. "We're a willful genetic line."

Then her face grew serious once more. "But we've always done what is required of us. That is, until now. This is why I want you to help me understand."

How could she expect him to explain something he didn't understand? Should he tell her about his own abnormal thoughts since Seyra's incident? Were they sick? Was there a virus in the Translink System? Could it spread to others?

The Captain sighed, letting her shoulders sag. "You truly don't know, do you?"

The corner of Kehvan's eye twitched. He felt utterly useless. "I... Captain..."

The chair's compad chimed before he could continue. Frowning, she glanced at the display, and under her breath, she muttered, "What now?" In response, words scrolled on the small screen until she finally toggled it off and looked back at him. "Say you were in my position, Kehvan. What would you do with her?"

Sweat trickled down his back—none of this made sense. The questions, the abnormal behaviors, the landing, it was all getting to be too much. Maybe the concussion was affecting him more than he realized.

The Captain sighed again. "Pilot Fourteen, comply with inquiry."

Even as the storm raged inside his mind, Kehvan reverted. "Per regulation, aberrant crewmembers must be nullified. Begin decantation of generation thirty-one of Pilot Thirteen. Recommend quarantine of current generation's memories until factor causing behavior identified and revert to generation twenty-nine Translink download."

The Captain nodded while combing her fingers through her hair. "Kehvans were the best Captains. They always ran a tight ship."

From the archives, Kehvan recalled that his previous iterations had found the position quite lonely. Each generation's lifespan was dictated by which category of crew you were in. For Pilots, it was thirty-five years. So, even though the new generation looked, sounded, and acted the same as the previous one, they were not *truly* the ones you had served with for years.

"Revert to downshift," the Captain ordered.

When he did, she asked, "Do you really think I should nullify Seyra? Is that what you want?"

No. I'd promised to see the sky with her. Without hesitation, he said, "For the sake of the colonists, it would be for the best."

The Captain closed her eyes and leaned on the armrest. "Concern logged," she said as she cradled the side of her head in her hand.

Since the launch of *Last Train*, the ship could have been run solely on their optimism alone, but now it just felt... different. Almost as if their morale had been stripped away in the crash. He knew the dead would be retrieved, recycled, and their protein used to build the next generations, just as the program had been designed. The crew would continue. It had to. Work still needed to be done before the colonists could be revived. Their purpose hadn't changed, so what had?

The Captain's compad sounded again, but she did not bother to answer. Instead, she nodded to the Security. "Take him to Seyra. Maybe her behavior will correct if she talks to this Kehvan."

This Kehvan.

As he rode the lift down from the bridge, those words bounced around inside his skull. Something about them bothered him; he only hoped it wasn't a precursor to aberration.

By design, *Last Train* had no crime; the regulatory control of the Translink System prevented such things. Therefore, it had no need for a brig. Security was the least utilized and least important in the ship's hierarchy, but they could command crewmembers in emergencies. All of this meant that, without a proper place to keep her, Seyra was confined to a storage room on the thirty-second deck.

The Security crewman led with a purposeful gait, while Kehvan tentatively followed and often had to hurry to keep up. He had never been so lost within his own mind. He began to question his actions, searching for abnormalities that might have formed since the crash. There was a sinking feeling in his gut that he had never felt before. Why was he suddenly nervous about seeing Seyra? He had to admit that he was afraid. Afraid that she was not the same person he remembered.

Except for the occasional working light, the deck was dark. He had to be careful not to crack his head against anything knocked loose. At the end of one corridor, a second Security crewman stood at a closed door. The red-coated crewman stepped aside when they arrived, and after a slight hesitation, Kehvan pressed the button beside the door.

The squeal of the hatch reverberated loudly in the otherwise quiet hallway. The room within wasn't spacious. It had been packed full at the beginning of *Last Train*'s journey, but only a few secured plastic crates were left after all these centuries.

Seyra was on the floor opposite the entryway, her back against the wall, legs pulled up to her chest, and face buried in her hands. She'd removed her jacket and thrown it in the corner, where it lay wrinkled and discarded. Stepping inside, Kehvan hoped she'd be asleep, as it would make an excellent excuse to leave. The door screeched closed behind him, sealing the two inside, alone. No, not alone. Cameras monitored every inch of the ship, so someone would be observing them. That thought did not ease his newly acquired fears.

Fears of what?

The reality was that he simply wanted her to be the old Seyra. The one that had loved to joke with him and tried to make him laugh. Because if she was not, if she was the one that had attempted to make him leave the ship, then she would have to be nullified.

"Seyra?" he asked and felt the dryness in his mouth. Working his tongue around, he built up some saliva and tried again. "Seyra? Are you awake?"

Slowly, she shifted and let out a long breath. Then, brushing her hair back, she raised her head and met his stare with bloodshot eyes. "You can come closer. I'm not some wild animal."

Earlier, she had acted like one when she fought to get past Security. He'd never seen someone behave that way, and he had to admit it was disturbing. But this was Seyra. His bunkmate. His friend. Kehvans and Seyras had always been friends. Trying to hide his trepidation, Kehvan stood straight and went to stand at her feet.

She didn't look up to meet his eyes this time, so Kehvan crouched down. Forcing a smile, he asked, "Better?"

"I suppose it'll have to do." She put on an equally fake grin, but it faded as she asked, "What are you doing here?"

"The Captain wanted me to come and see you."

She looked at him sideways with her cheek resting on one knee. "Why?"

"Honestly, I don't know. Her questions didn't make sense to me."

"What questions?"

"Well," he rocked back on his heels until he was sitting on the floor, "she wanted to know what happened leading up to the, uh, incident."

"What did you say?" she asked, cocking an eyebrow.

He found he couldn't look away from the intensity in her eyes. And he didn't want to. "I told her what happened. But I don't know why she needed me to do that in the first place."

A sad but triumphant smile formed on her lips as she said, "Probably because she was missing my upload."

Kehvan smiled. "Missing your upload? So, your Translink *is* damaged?" Here it was, the answer he had needed to hear. He'd report it, they'd fix her chip, and everything would be back to normal. He felt relieved. But that was only short-lived.

She shook her head. "No. It isn't damaged. I removed it."

Kehvan lost the ability to speak as he stared at her, frozen and eyes bulging.

Seyra closed hers and, still smiling, said, "I'll go ahead and answer the next question for you. Haven't you ever wanted something that was yours alone?" Tucking her legs in beneath her, she slid down until she lay on her side and rested her head on her hands like a pillow. "That's why."

Kehvan stared at her for a long time after she stopped speaking, with her eyes closed. He was afraid she had fallen asleep, but then she shifted, and looked up at him. Fighting his own mouth, he managed to finally ask, "How?"

"It wasn't hard. Just a slice behind the ear, some tweezers, a mirror, and string. She rolled onto her back and tilted her head toward the wall. Brushing the hair aside, she revealed a sutured scar the length of his thumb behind her right ear. It was red and swollen and looked painful.

"Why?" was the next word he was able to say.

"Out of all the generations since the first, we're distinct. We're the Promised Landers. And I... I wanted to keep that for myself. I didn't want to pass it on to the future Seyra," she said. Then, a sound that could have been either a laugh or a sob escaped her lips, and her hand covered her mouth as she blinked back tears.

"That... was selfish," Kehvan said. He wanted to take her hand, to comfort her, but he didn't.

Seyra shook her head and clutched the collar of her shirt as she said, "And then, when I took it out, I found something, Kehvan."

"Found? Found what?"

Tears flowing freely now, she whispered, "Me," and her chest heaved as she wept. There was no sadness in her glistening eyes, only a mysterious happiness just beneath the surface.

An unexpected tightness gripped Kehvan's heart at seeing her cry. Softly, he said, "Explain."

"Are you sure?" she whispered back, staring up, not at him, but at the ceiling.

Though the monitors would clearly hear them, and perhaps that was what Seyra wanted anyway, he said, "Tell me."

"A strange thought came to me before the Captain's speech. What was going to happen after we landed?" she said.

Kehvan knew the answer to that. "We wake up the primary colonists."

"No. After that."

Kehvan accessed the landing itinerary. "Primary colonists establish the initial settlement. Crew Labor, Engineering, Medical, and Security report directly to them. Once colony deemed habitable, next wave of colonists revived."

Seyra nodded, a sneer twisting her mouth into something ugly. "Just like regulation states."

"Because that's how it is going to happen," Kehvan said.

Anger edged into her voice. "You've never thought about what's missing in the itinerary, have you?"

What could be missing? The itinerary had been devised well before the construction of *Last Train*. "Then we'll see the sky?"

"Will we?"

"I don't know what you mean," he said.

"Where do the Pilots fit in the itinerary?"

The question hit him harder than the console had during the crash. Sounds escaped his lips, but none of them were words.

"I'll make it easy for you. We don't. Once we landed, our purpose was complete. We're obsolete now, Kehvan." She turned to look at him and reached over to take his hand. He let her, and it felt... good.

He asked, "Is that why you don't want to wake the colonists?"

Abruptly she let his hand go and rolled over to face the wall. "You can't stop, can you?"

Rubbing his fingers together, he tried to hold on to the sensation of her skin against his. "Stop what?"

"Being what you were created to be."

"I have to. It's our purpose," he said. What other way was there?

She looked over her shoulder, but not at him, and said, "I want you to be different. No, I *need* you to be. For me, Kehvan... Please."

"Different from what?"

"From all the other Kehvans," she said and rolled away from the wall. Looking hesitant, she clenched her jaw at first, then, with trembling lips, she whispered, "Because you're *my* Kehvan. And I want to be *your* Seyra."

He smiled again, reassuring her, "Each of our iterations have been friends. That's how it's always been."

Once more, she turned away from him, and no matter how many questions he asked, Seyra refused to answer.

After returning to his quarters, Kehvan studied his reflection in the mirror. Lifting the brown hair from his forehead, he looked at the deep purple bruise he'd acquired from the crash. He carefully touched it, then let the hair fall back into place. His bottom lip had been split open, and an ugly scab tugged at the rosy flesh whenever he moved his mouth. Finally, he stared into his hazel eyes. They were the same eyes every Kehvan had seen in the same mirror for the last thousand years.

I want you to be different.

I don't know what that means. Nothing had made sense after the crash. It had to be the concussion. *How can I be different? Isn't this who I'm supposed to be?* The unblinking eyes appeared lost, set adrift without a purpose. Maybe it was the extended downshift. Once he got back to duty and continued training...

Training for what? What else is there for us to do? There had to be something. One of the other Pilots must know. Looking away from the mirror, he tapped his compad and requested all remaining Pilots to check in. Of the seventeen, only eight had survived the crash. He dialed in on Raj and linked with his pad, and Pilot Seventeen filled the tiny screen. Raj, an exhausted-looking brown-skinned man with messy black hair, had a bandage on his cheek.

"Nice of you to finally call," Raj said.

"Oh, I believe I made a mistake. I was trying to reach Estevan," Kehvan said with a half-hearted laugh.

Raj gave him a tired chuckle. "You'll just have to settle for me. What's the inquiry?"

Kehvan muted the pad for a moment and looked to see if any of the crew in the quarters were paying attention to the conversation. With the number of injured and dead from the crash, the quarters were only at minimum capacity. Satisfied they weren't listening, he turned and placed his pad on the shelf below the mirror and unmuted.

"What's your status?"

Raj let out a yawn and scratched the back of his head. "My status? I'm downshifted. You?"

"Same." He showed Raj his cast. "Everyone else?"

"All downshifted. Not much use for us now that we've landed," Raj said. "Don't mind it, really. We get to sit around while the others do the rest of the work."

"How long is your downshift?"

Raj said, "When given? Twenty-four hours."

"Same for me."

Raj nodded. "Same for all Pilots."

Kehvan thought for a moment, then asked, "Raj, what do you want to do once we're allowed off the ship?"

"Off the ship?" Raj asked. He scratched at the edge of the bandage on his cheek. "I never really thought about it. I don't know."

Kehvan felt a stirring in his stomach. "I see."

"Why? Have you?"

It wasn't a secret, but Kehvan had only shared his dream of seeing the sky with only one other person before this—Seyra. Their exchanges were all archived and available for anyone to access if they wanted to. *Last Train* had no secrets. At least, it hadn't.

Kehvan shook his head and felt like he was going to be sick. The protein paste he'd ingested earlier was making an unscheduled reappearance. He looked down at the sink and let a dribble of bile spill from his mouth. He waved his hand at the sensor and splashed cold water on his face. He heard Raj ask if something was wrong and if he was okay.

Water running off his chin, Kehvan said, "There's nothing you'd rather be than a Pilot?"

Raj tilted his head. "I don't understand the question."

"That's all, Raj. End transmission."

"Transmission ended," Raj said.

The screen went black, and Kehvan threw up.

After cleaning himself off, Kehvan lay in his bunk and tried to figure out what was wrong with him. Had Seyra done this to him? In the questions she'd ask him when they were alone, the 'private' conversations they'd had over the years that the monitors didn't flag as against regulation, had she knowingly implanted a desire in him for something beyond the landing? He wanted to find something to blame, but when he tried to put it all on Seyra, he couldn't.

It had to be his chip, a glitch he couldn't detect because of a malfunction. He'd report it to the Engineers in charge of the Translink System. Instead of using his compad, Kehvan thought it would be easier to just go down to the Hub in his sector and save a lot of time if they had to repair it. Unconsciously, he touched the small bump behind his right ear.

Hauling himself off the bunk, he felt only incrementally better as he staggered out of the quarters. He discovered that regulation had been updated as he passed the hallway with the hull breach. Per the new regulation, Kehvan quickly moved away from the corridor and headed straight for the lift, unable to even look to see if the sunlight was still present. Did he only know it was there because Seyra had shown him? Was there more he might have missed because regulation prevented him from experiencing it? "No," he said quietly. Regulation had its purpose, and so did he. Humanity needed both of them.

At the other end of the hallway, a team of Huws were repairing the damage to the lighting tubes. The sound of their pneumatic wrenches gave Kehvan a piercing headache. He'd never experienced anything like it. Something had to be wrong. Not relying on the Translink chip in case it was damaged, he pulled up the symptoms for a concussion on the compad and found he was suffering from most of them. Nothing about this felt mild, as the Karal had diagnosed. Now there was something else he'd have to report.

He made it to the lift and requested the deck for the Translink Hub, and the doors hissed shut. He leaned back against the wall, eyes closed, as he tried to will his head to stop throbbing. Focusing on the steady rhythm of the lift, the ambient noise was similar enough to the now silent engines that it managed to soothe some of the pain.

When he arrived at the Hub, he reported the glitch. An Engineer explained that there was a backlog of issues caused by the crash, and it would take time to get to them all, and he would chime Kehvan's compad when it was his turn. Kehvan thanked the Engineer and was on his way back to the lift when his pad chirped. *That was fast*, he thought, but then he saw it was a ship-wide communication from the Captain.

"Crew of *Last Train*, we've arrived on the new planet. It might not be how we'd intended to land, but here we are. In the coming days, we will begin the reviving process of the primary colonists. But before that, we will need to decant a sizable number of crew to replace the ones we've lost. Labor, Medical, and Engineering are priority. Security remains at acceptable levels."

The Captain's face looked away from her screen for a moment, and Kehvan thought he saw her brush something from her eye. When she looked back, her expression was like steel. "Surviving Pilots, await summons to Genetics."

Genetics? Only twice in their lifetime was a crewmember at Genetics—decantation and nullification. Kehvan's heart felt like it was close to bursting from his chest.

Where do the Pilots fit in the itinerary?

When the message ended, Kehvan found Raj on his compad and dialed in. The other Pilot answered, but Kehvan could already see Raj was on duty, his face expressionless. "Pilot Fourteen, inquiry?"

"Raj, where are you?" Kehvan asked, looking up and down the hallway. Huws and Engineers were close by, but none could hear him.

"In route to Genetics, per Captain's order," Raj said.

Kehvan closed the channel and ran.

He found Raj sitting in a chair, his back stiff, inside the Genetics Factory's waiting area. The room was empty, with only two other doors and one chair. One door was an exit for the newly decanted crew, and the other led to nullification. The chair was positioned in front of the latter. Kehvan had no idea what he hoped to accomplish as he barreled into the room and rushed to stand before Raj. Regulation didn't prevent him from being here, but he wouldn't be allowed to interfere with the nullification process. He wanted to shake Raj. To keep him from going through with the process, but he couldn't. Kehvan could only stand there.

A Karal studying a compad entered and almost ran into Kehvan. If the Medical crewmember was surprised, his face didn't show as he looked up from the device in his hand and said, "Pilot Fourteen. Early for scheduled arrival."

Kehvan found the words he was allowed to say on the matter, "I wanted to see Pilot Seventeen off."

The Karal nodded. "Nullification scheduled for zero four hundred. Expected completion of all Pilots in eight hours."

"Decantation of next iteration?" Kehvan said, afraid that he already knew the answer.

"Negative. Genetic purpose complete."

We're obsolete now, Kehvan.

He couldn't breathe. He needed air. Holding onto the wall for support, he managed to get out of Genetics before he dialed Mayla. Her narrow eyes, a trait inherited from the genetic source of her line, were just as blank as Raj's had been. Did they all look like that when they were on duty? How had he never noticed that before? Kehvan ended the transmission before it even began and tried Estevan.

Estevan had tan skin with dark hair, and Kehvan was relieved to see a pillow behind his head. "Wrong compad, right?" Estevan said.

Kehvan shook his head. "Estevan, listen. I think your summons is next."

Estevan nodded. "I was talking to Mayla when her order came through."

"How long ago was that?"

"A few minutes," Estevan said. The screen shifted as he rolled onto his side.

Kehvan wanted to tell Estevan to ignore the order, but he couldn't. So instead, he asked, "What did you want to do after we landed?"

Raising an eyebrow, Estevan said, "I never thought about it."

"Ending transmission," Kehvan said and turned the screen off.

Clutching his compad, Kehvan wanted to scream, to rush back into Genetics and demand Raj revert to downshift. He wanted to find a way to keep them all from being nullified. There was no hiding on this ship; cameras were everywhere. And once they gave the order, he'd line up to be nullified just like the rest. But he didn't want that. He wanted to see the sky. And more than anything, he wanted to see it with Seyra.

Seyra, he thought. After today, there would be no more Seyra. She would be gone, the same as him. No more iterations meant no more memories. It struck him then that this was what the colonists must have felt before someone came up with the plan for *Last Train*. This was the fear of missing what came next, of not seeing someone you care about ever again. This was the fear of death. He would never feel her hand in his again, never see her crack a smile. He would never see the sky with her.

That wasn't what Kehvan wanted. What he wanted was to be with her.

Not wanting to draw attention as he made his way back to the lift, Kehvan did not run. He rode it down three levels and then went inside a supply closet, where cameras spied on him even in such an unimportant part of the ship. He wanted to smash the reflective lenses, but he couldn't. His hand went to the lump behind his ear. Just beneath his skin, the wire mesh monitored for violations and would immobilize him at any sign that he was about to break regulation. There was no pain in it, but not having control of one's body was highly unsettling, and the first generation had found it easier to simply comply, as had each iteration since. Now, it felt like he was one of those puppet toys he had seen on a ripvid that could only do whatever the strings allowed.

Time was running short, he knew, so he flung the contents off shelves. All he needed was something sharp. That's what Seyra had said. It was just a little cut. At last, he picked up a bulkhead patch kit and removed a small square of metal about the size of his palm. This was not the item's intended purpose, but it would have to do.

Tilting his head to the side, Kehvan placed the corner against his skin and froze. He couldn't continue. He wanted to, but it was against regulation. Trapped in his own head, he screamed. Then the compad on his belt chimed a priority message.

A Security crewman's voice came out of the speaker, "Pilot Fourteen. Scheduled activation advanced. Report to Genetics. Com —" the remainder of the command mysteriously cut off. But another order could come at any moment.

Kehvan's thoughts raced as he struggled to violate what he had been created to uphold. There had to be a way. Seyra had done it, and she was just as wired up as him. He couldn't even move his head. How did she do it? How? His thoughts whirled until he couldn't think anymore. And that's when the answer came to him: the ripvids.

Seyra-01 had figured out that the only way to view them— and for others to watch—was to overtask their Translink chip by manually uploading the entirety of their archived memories while simultaneously running a diagnostic. The entire process only took a few seconds, but that was more than enough time to watch a memory clip.

It had to work, he thought. Letting out a breath, Kehvan connected his Translink and began the upload of a thousand years of memories. Then ran the diagnostic.

A Security crewman found him in the closet.

"Pilot Fourteen. Follow. Comply."

"Complying," Kehvan said and followed him out of the closet, where they passed by other crewmembers going about their business.

Together, they entered the lift, and the button for the Genetics deck was pressed. Kehvan was silent, his hands clasped behind his back as he stared straight ahead. Finally, the elevator stopped, Security stepped off, and Kehvan hit the button for deck thirty-two.

He had expected alarms as he exited the lift, but it was silent in the dark hallway except for the constant chirping of his compad, which he ignored. That alone felt both strange and exhilarating. He had no way of knowing if the storage room was still guarded, and he didn't care. Kehvan ripped off a broken conduit from the wall and made his way to Seyra.

It wasn't until he rounded the corner, prepared to fight his way through, and found it empty, that he chose to finally answer the compad. It was only an incoming text message from an unknown source.

>*You have ten minutes to get her off my ship.*

He stared at the message for a second, puzzled by what it meant. Get her off my ship? "Captain?" he asked.

>*Ten minutes. That's all I can give you.*

"Why are you helping me?"

>*I'm not helping you. I'm helping her.*

"How?"

>*I'm taking that answer to my nullification. I'm just glad one of us finally made it through to one of you. Now, ten minutes.*

The transmission ended.

Ten minutes. It was enough time. They weren't far from the lift that went down to their quarters. And from there, the breach. Whatever came after that, so be it. What he had to say now was more important.

Kehvan opened the door to the storage room and stepped inside. Just as he had left her, Seyra lay on the ground with her back to the entrance. The makeshift weapon slipped from his hand and clattered to the floor as he knelt by her.

Quietly, he said, "Seyra?"

She did not respond.

His hand shaking, Kehvan reached over and touched her arm. Drawing in a sharp breath, Seyra turned her head and looked up at him. He wanted to cry, so he did.

"Kehvan? What are you doing?" she asked, rolling over.

"Seyra." It was all he could say.

She rose to her knees and took hold of his shoulders. "Kehvan, what's happened? Are you damaged again?" Her hand came away with flecks of blood on her fingers.

He took her hand and held it tightly. "You've always been," he said when he could find the words.

"Been what?" Her eyes looked so worried, so beautiful.

"*My* Seyra."

See Dan Le Fever's story "Trapped in Memory" online at Metaphorosis.
If you liked it, leave a comment. Authors love that!
Remember to subscribe to our e-mail updates so you'll know when new stories are posted.

About the story

"Trapped in Memory" comes from my desire to write something new. Previously, I had focused on horror, Gothic, and post-apocalyptic genres, and I had always been a fan of sci-fi, so I thought, why not give it a shot? Whenever I'm writing, I listen to music. I try to pick a band or musical style that fits what emotions I'm trying to convey, and this time I chose a Norwegian folk group called Wardruna. Their songs give me a feeling of loneliness, sadness, and anger, but also hope. These emotions are what I hope the reader gets as they read my story. Over the last two years, I think the majority of us are on the same wavelength with the isolation and human detachment we've experienced because of the pandemic, and I felt it was an excellent theme to explore. I saw myself in Kehvan's shoes, trying to make sense of what I was experiencing but wanting to find a way to break out of the bubble I'd been placed in. Luckily, I have my wife to keep me sane, but it had been a difficult two years. And in the end, it is a story of change. The patterns we follow in life are comforting, but is that all we can hope for, or is there more out there for us?

A question for the author

Q: What book or books inspired you as a child?
A: Frank Herbert's *Dune* is one of my biggest influences. I would not be the person today if it had not been for that book. Next, would be all three *Dragonlance Chronicles* by Margaret Weis and Tracy Hickman. And as I got a little older, *Fight Club* by Chuck Palahniuk.

About the author

Dan Le Fever is just a guy from Lynn, MA with a degree in history from Salem State College, with a focus on Byzantine and Ottoman history. He is also fascinated by linguistics, etymology, and orthography. When he isn't writing, Dan spends his time playing video games, watching horror/sci-fi entertainment, and practicing American Kenpo.
danlefever.wordpress.com, @lefeverdan

Heart Moon

R. Gatwood

The old pop song says it's in his kiss, but of course that's nonsense. The only way to know if your man's love is true is to cut out his heart and eat it, still beating, by the light of the full moon.

You'll dither over the decision, of course. You'll collect the ingredients and sharpen the dagger, only to abandon the project halfway. A few months later you'll start again. For him, a simple infusion of opium and valerian and chamomile, to drug him to sleep. For you, a mix of lemon and mugwort and green tea and a smidgen of psilocybin, for alertness and perception of liminal things. It'll be the biggest spell you've ever done. The one that makes you a real witch and not just a bullshit herbalist who knows a few parlor tricks. (Let's just say the ritual consumption of a human heart is a serious power boost.) You won't have to feel inferior to your witch friends anymore.

Scheduling your camping trip for the full moon shouldn't be hard, but it is. At the last minute his buddy will invite him to a beer tasting in town, and the two of you will argue irritably over whether to change plans. (If he loved you, would he give in? Or is that a ridiculous question?) Finally (maybe because you love him—or think you do), you will agree to go to the tasting and leave for the campsite right afterwards. It'll be more fun than you expected. You're not much of a beer lover, but they will have an amazing grapefruit shandy that you buy a six-pack of, and watching Dave lick IPA off the stubble above his lip will make something flutter inside you. For the hundredth time, you will reconsider whether to kill him. But you've already got the battery-powered bone saw and ritual dagger and folding shovel stashed away in your camping pack. And you've already agonized over this long enough. He will let out a burp and grin. The moment will pass.

On the way back to the car his hand will be a soft knobby animal in yours. "That was good," he'll say.

"Yeah," you will admit.

He will stop, tug you close, and kiss the top of your head. Beer and mustard on his breath. "Thanks for, you know, compromising. Don't worry. I'll get us there safe." He'll have promised to drive the whole way to the campsite.

"I know." You'll mean it.

Sometimes you think you hate him.

He says "I love you" like it's easy. Maybe too easy. Your friends tell you he's the perfect guy. Maybe too perfect, is what you'll think as you sit beside him in his comfortable old Prius, listening to him hum along to the playlist you made him. There's got to be something wrong with him. Why else would he be with you? Mentally, you'll list off your flaws: constantly seeking reassurance; obsessed with your witch career; depressingly mediocre at most things, including witchcraft; tentatively murderous. Also just generally perverse. When your best friend got her breast cancer diagnosis, you were frantic—but when it turned out to be terminal, you felt relieved. You prefer certainty to hope.

Dave grew up with parents who loved and supported him, you're pretty sure. You grew up with well-meaning but self-absorbed types who hugged you tenderly one day and forgot your tae kwon do match the next. Now your mom is too wrapped up in her Valium and her church gossip to think much about you or your siblings, and your dad has gotten gruff and politically off-putting the way older men sometimes do. The birthday cards they send you are as generic as something you'd get for a casual acquaintance. You don't waste time on family these days.

In place of family you have your witch friends—most of them more advanced than you—and Dave. You watch his face a lot, preferably when he won't notice you're looking. When you ask what he's thinking about, he says, "I dunno. Work stuff. You. Uh, what we're gonna have for dinner." Maddening. There has to be more. If you pry—if you dig up his exes, his unspoken ambitions, his childhood traumas (?), his taboo fantasies (??), his doubts about your relationship (???)—will he leave? You know he at least thinks he loves you; he's too decent a guy to lead you on. But people don't always know their own emotions.

Case in point: You're not absolutely sure you love him. You're obsessed, certainly. You have secret Excel spreadsheets detailing his likes and dislikes. Squeezing his biceps, scenting his arousal gives you a shot of adrenaline and desire. You've inadvertently memorized the threads of gold in his eyes. You're also planning to kill him.

You once read a book about Sada Abe, a woman who famously strangled her lover in the 1930s and kept his penis as a precious souvenir. "I loved him so much," she said, "I wanted him all to myself." Abe was on to something. If she'd been a witch, she would have appreciated the power of quite a different organ.

A real witch, the kind of witch you're studying to be, knows there's no such thing as a love spell. You can't make someone love you, can't really keep them all to yourself. But you can gain knowledge of another person's soul, at the cost of destroying them. Which is worth it, isn't it? To sacrifice your relationship on the altar of certainty? To gain power, too, beyond what you've ever dared to hope for?

Isn't it?

By the time you arrive at the campsite, you'll have only an hour and a half before the moon is directly above. He'll think you're adorably eager, rushing to lug your packs out of the back the second he's parked. When you tell him you want to camp in the clearing near the creek, he'll say sure. The clearing will be open to the sky and the creek will help you wash off the evidence.

Calculating the trajectory of the moon, you'll hang your pot over the fire, and you'll make your two cups of tea. One for him, one for you. You'll ask him to try the new blend you created, and he'll perk up. He loves being your taste tester.

"Hmmmmmm," he will say after his first sip. You'll hold your breath, wondering if you pulled off your attempt at a smooth earthy flavor. It doesn't matter, you'll tell yourself, as long as he drinks the whole thing (he always does), but you'll resent how badly you want his opinion. He'll say, "Sultry, strident, with a playful impertinence."

You will throw a twig at him.

"It's delicious, Amy, seriously. Little strong, but good. Some chamomile in there?"

"Yeah. Good eye."

"More like good tongue," he'll say, the innuendo casual, incidental.

You'll smile at each other, enjoying a shared private knowledge. You're almost certain he doesn't tell his buddies about your sex life. Which doesn't prove anything, of course.

"What are you calling it?" He likes the names you make up for your potions.

You'll ponder a moment. "Heart Moon."

He will nod. "Perfect," he'll say softly, and he'll take another sip, his hazel eyes golden in the firelight.

Soon those eyes will start to droop, and when you tease him, he'll mumble with faux grumpiness about not being sleepy. He'll invite you into the sleeping bag as he plumps the pillow, and you'll say, "Later, I want to sit by the fire a while." It might be the last time you see him awake. His eyes will fall shut too fast.

What you're looking for isn't to be found in his eyes, however, any more than in his kiss.

It won't take him long to slip into a deep, deep slumber. Deep enough that when you roll him onto his back (he's a side sleeper, always seeming to reach out to you across the mattress), he won't so much as twitch. You've watched him sleep many times. As ever, he'll be handsome in his sleep. You'll hate it. You're certain you've never looked that good in your sleep, and you suspect if you asked him, he'd lie to spare your feelings.

You'll open the sleeping bag with damp, shaky fingers. The zipper will sound louder than it should despite the murmur of crickets, the rumble of the distant road, the hoot of an owl. The moon, six minutes away from being exactly overhead, will feel like a spotlight. You'll strip efficiently despite your trembling, leaving your clothes on the other side of the fire.

You'll draw the dagger and anoint it with the daisy oil just like you practiced, then lay it beside you. You'll grip the bone saw. Your own heart will pound as you straddle his hips, jostling him just enough to tip his head to the side. You'll push up his thin T-shirt. Beneath it his skin will be scattered with pale hairs that vanish briefly as a cloud passes overhead. His breastbone will thump with a strong, slow beat.

Your eyes and fingers will trace along the bottom of his rib cage, then, for no real reason, back up to where the T-shirt is bunched under his armpits. There you'll find a hard lump in his shirt pocket and, curious despite or because of your nerves, you'll pull it out. A square box flocked with velvet.

You'll stare at it, run a thumb over the seam of the lid, and find yourself shaking with rage. You'll be holding the bone saw in your dominant right hand, so it's with your left that you'll hurl the box ineffectually into the grass. Of course. Of course he had plans of his own this whole time. It will feel like a sick joke. Something deliberately placed in your path to derail you. This whole time you've been brewing your selfish, pathetic, needy scheme, he's been dreaming of white picket fences and His-and-Hers towels. No, you'll think, that's not fair. His imagination isn't quite that bourgeois. He's been dreaming of—what?

Still quivering, clutching the bone saw close to you, you'll think for the thousandth time about how you've never quite figured out what's going on inside him. That's the question that haunts you every time he smiles, every time he says love. The question you're so close to getting an answer to. You'll stare at his peaceful profile.

The sound of your phone will make you jump. The alarm will be set to play a carefully chosen song. It'll be timed so that when the singer hits the high note in the third verse, the moon will be directly overhead to the minute, and your dagger will sever his—

And then you'll do it, of course. You'll have come all this way, prepared so carefully. The saw will buzz powerfully as you run it up his sternum, spattering warm wetness over your naked body. You'll toss the saw to the side and pry his rib cage open. You'll raise the dagger and slice through the vessels that surround the squirming fist of muscle. And at last, muttering the words of the spell, you'll seize the oracular organ in your bare hands and bring it to your teeth.

You'll know.

You'll know he loves you. Loved you. The ring box in his breast pocket, yeah, it's a cliché, white veils and tossed bouquets, but it was real. It was sincere. All those times you tried to decipher his silences and thoughtful gestures, he was loving you. The knowledge will flood your bloody mouth, almost too much to swallow.

Or: You'll know he didn't love you. Bitter knowledge, but as satisfying as canines tearing through raw flesh. All those times he whispered to you in the sweaty dark, brought you chocolates along with the tampons you asked him to pick up, shopped hopefully for a ring, he was just being his good-natured self. He may have thought he loved you. He never wanted to hurt you—of that you'll be sure. Like so many people, he's spent his life blinkered and clueless, chasing what he thinks will make him happy, and why shouldn't it make him happy to marry a witch?

Or: You won't do it after all. You'll never find out what you want to know, never be as great a witch as you could be. You're such a cliché, you'll think, sniveling, unbloodied but bowed over his dozing form. One little token of affection and you cave to the conventional life. Do you even want to get married? Maybe it wasn't the ring that changed your mind, you'll think as the song from your phone reaches the high note and plays on. Maybe it was just him. Maybe it was just you.

So those are the possibilities. You'll have a choice to make, or not just one choice but many along the way. You may have a grave to dig. You may have a ring box to search for in the tall grass, waving your phone's flashlight around and cursing under your breath. You may have a man, a good man, an oblivious man, to roll back onto his side in the down sleeping bag. You may have a lonely hike back to the car in the dim light of dawn. You may have regrets: a full moon wasted, or a lover dead.

Now choose.

See R. Gatwood's story "Heart Moon" online at Metaphorosis.
If you liked it, leave a comment. Authors love that!
Remember to subscribe to our e-mail updates so you'll know when
new stories are posted.

About the story

Honestly, the main inspiration for this story was "The Shoop Shoop Song (It's in His Kiss)". I was only vaguely familiar with it, possibly from Cher's cover, when I heard my friends singing it. I pointed out that, if his face was just his charms and his embrace was just his arms, then his kiss must be just his lips. They asked how, then, could you know if he loves you so? My answer was the second sentence of "Heart Moon".

Of course, an interesting premise is nothing without execution. I struggled through several drafts to show how the main character half loves, half hates her wonderful boyfriend; wants to have him all to herself, wants to kill him; and craves to know whether he loves her, maybe even at the cost of his life. My thanks to my lovely writing workshop and to B. Morris Allen at *Metaphorosis*, who helped.

A question for the author

Q: What's an idea you're dying to write but haven't, and why?

A: I've long wanted to write a cyberpunk story about racial injustice, but my efforts have dissatisfied me. In the story, a bug in neuro implant software would leave people losing touch with the physical world and behaving like sleepwalkers, leading them to be mistaken for zombies by panicky gun owners and police officers. Sometimes the writer who has the idea isn't the right person to write it. Perhaps someone else will.

About the author

R. Gatwood is the emergent consciousness of a spectacularly inefficient library shelving system. It writes short fiction and occasionally text games, and it also enjoys tea, bourbon, podcasts, and trees. (Best not to ask how a shelving system can enjoy those things.)
iwantanewhead.wordpress.com, @iwantanewhead

The Zoo Diaries

Frances Pauli

Part Four

Previously…

At the Rainriver Zoological Gardens, one escape became the catalyst for a series of unfortunate incidents. The tortoise, Oliver, roamed the zoo as a fugitive, searching for his missing cage mate, Miranda. When the Zoo-cam caught him interacting with the elephant, zoo attendance spiked, putting more pressure on the animals inside and increasing crowd-related stress but inspiring a zoo-wide photography contest which drove the crowds to push their limits, tossing trash into the animal enclosures, and crossing fences that were meant for their protection. Oliver was led to the aviary, but his pigeon guide betrayed him and, once he'd gotten her inside, left him to be recaptured.

Determined to escape again, Oliver made a deal with the devil. The crow, Debra, promised to lead him to Miranda. A well-meaning keeper supplied Gonzo with chocolate-covered coffee beans, and Charlie the lion dreamed of his true nature, haunted by the aroma of the crowds' hot dogs.

RAINRIVER ZOOLOGICAL PARK

TO ALL EMPLOYEES

WITH THE SUCCESS OF OUR FIRST EVER VIDEO AND PHOTOGRAPH CONTEST, ATTENDANCE NUMBERS HAVE NOW REACHED RECORD HIGHS. WE REALIZE THIS HAS INCREASED BOTH WORKLOADS AND STRESS LEVELS, AND THAT THE UNPRECEDENTED CROWDS ARE CAUSING MINOR, DAY-TO-DAY DIFFICULTIES AROUND ZOO GROUNDS.

WE THANK EACH AND EVERY ONE OF YOU FOR YOUR HARD WORK AND EXTRA EFFORT DURING THIS WONDERFUL BUT STRESSFUL TIME.

WE ALSO ASK THAT YOU JOIN US IN WELCOMING OUR NEW SECURITY STAFF, A NECESSARY AND VITAL ADDITION TO THE RAINRIVER TEAM. WE ARE CONFIDENT THEY WILL BE OF GREAT ASSISTANCE IN KEEPING ZOO OPERATIONS FULLY FUNCTIONAL AND SAFE FOR ALL INVOLVED.

IN ORDER TO ASSIST THEM IN THAT EFFORT, WE REMIND YOU ALL TO BE VIGILANT AND REPORT ANY ISSUES. MAKE SURE ALL ZOO SIGNAGE IS VISIBLE AND REPORT ANY INFRACTIONS TO SECURITY IMMEDIATELY. IF WE ALL PULL TOGETHER, WE CAN ADAPT TO THIS NEW INFLUX OF VISITORS WITH AS FEW DIFFICULTIES AS POSSIBLE.

WE APPRECIATE YOUR EXTRA EFFORTS AND INVITE YOU TO SAVE THE DATE FOR OUR UPCOMING EMPLOYEE APPRECIATION POTLUCK BAR-B-QUE. SIGN-UPS CAN BE FOUND IN THE EMPLOYEE BREAK ROOM.

—MANAGEMENT

The Crow

Debra watches them dart the grizzly. She knows the gun is not lethal, that the dart's poison will not kill the bear, but when he shudders and flops onto his side, her feathers prickle in delight.

It would be like that, she thinks, if he were hit with a real bullet.

She has lighted on the tall stump that is a broken-off tree, a casualty to some long-ago storm. When it fell, it lay across the trench and nearly let the bear escape. He might have, she remembers. He could have climbed that fortunate bridge right to freedom.

He could have eaten someone.

But the stupid bear ignored the opportunity. Conditioned to his captivity, he stayed in his cage, and men with grumbling, noisy saws quickly broke the ramp to bits and carried them away.

Only the jagged stump remains, and Debra perches there while They-who-shoot-guns roll the sleeping Grizzly onto a tarp.

He is too heavy for them, too big. It takes four just to rock him back and forth. Each time, the shaggy pelt ripples. The bear rolls right back to the position in which he began.

They-who-shoot-guns curse and argue among themselves. They sound like crows, like a murder of their own. Debra approves of this chaos. She imagines Hector will wake soon and eat one of them.

But the bear sleeps on. He is dead weight, but eventually they heave him into position. They drag him, in the flimsy tarp, all the way to a very clever door.

Debra approves of this, too. The clever door is a trick, and she adores trickery. It stands beside the small square den opening, and it has been painted to match the rock around it. It is not smooth either. If she hadn't been a very clever crow, she might even have been surprised when it opened.

Her sharp caw is only a cry of triumph. An appreciation of a very clever trick. When she tells the story to the rest of the zoo, she will remember that detail the most.

They shot the bear. They dragged him through a very clever door, but *I could see it there the whole time.*

Debra puffs and watches as the tarp, the bear, and They-who-shoot-guns vanish through the gap in the rock. She keeps her eyes fixed on the opening, stares as the door closes again. Stares, and is convinced she can still see it.

"You never know," she will tell them all. "You never know *where* a door might be, do you?"

Grizzly Caged

Hector wakes slowly. He is confused at first, his vision blurry. The voices around him chatter in soft, familiar tones.

For a breath, he believes he is a cub again.

The surface he sprawls on is smoother than his den, colder against his belly. He moans softly, and the cadence of the voices shift.

On reflex, Hector churrs. It is a happy sound, a song of contentment, and it has never failed to earn him the attention he craves. Even now, he hears approval.

He churrs louder, rumbling until his whole body shakes. His muscles are sore and flaccid, but he manages to sit, to blink until he can actually see them.

Bars to all sides.

They've locked him in a metal box, a tiny container for an enormous bear. Outside it, faces press all around him. They peer in, eyes shining and mouths tight. Watching him.

He makes the sound and sees the pleasure flicker from one face to the next.

They are doctors, Hector thinks. He knows them from his youth, the odd, loose-fitting skins they wear, the tiny boards they carry, marking with their pens the way the artist does but never once showing him what they work on.

Hector believes they capture his likeness just the same. They record him, too, and he tilts his head and poses.

He remembers too late that his bones were hurting, that he could barely stand to walk this morning. Now, however, the quick movement brings no pain. The doctors make their markings, and Hector tests his joints. He twists and reaches and finds no agony.

This pleases them, too, and he adds more churring for good measure. He *performs* for them, and he remembers They-who-cared.

His brother is not here.

He is too old to wrestle anyway.

Hector sits in a metal box, watched and captured, and is happy for the first time in forever.

Lion Enclosure

Someone drops a cell phone into Charlie's cage. It is inevitable, really, with the jostling and shoving, the sheer number of devices. The black rectangle flips end over end, arches out, and falls, unerringly, on the lion's side of the trench.

Charlie sees it land. He has been lying in the sun, thinking of the veldt dream, and is not really interested until he smells the squeaky meat.

His lioness has already gone to investigate, but Charlie huffs, slashes his tail and approaches on the tips of his paws. His strutting drives her off, but she grumbles, mouthing back at him as she stalks away.

The phone lies in the long grass beside the trench wire. Charlie knows this is electrified, that it will give a nasty shock if he is careless enough to touch it. He lowers his head and sniffs, drinks in the meaty smell which clings to the dropped phone.

He uses one paw to bat the rectangle away from the wire, teases it to a safe distance before lowering his face to the screen.

His jaws open. He huffs, tastes the air, and is carried back into the dream. His eyes close. He lets his tail lash.

His tongue stretches, swipes over a slick surface, and tastes only a disappointingly faint flavor. It is the meat. His mind pairs it with the scent, fills in around the flavor until Charlie believes he can fully taste it.

He can hear it squeaking.

He can hear it screaming.

It is too slick to bite, too solid. Like his blood ice. Charlie wedges it between his front paws and wraps his jaws around it. He breathes. He imagines.

He uses his tongue to gather the traces, to lick and lick until all he can taste is hot plastic.

Elephant Paddock

Shanti is thrilled when Oliver appears. She has been standing over his exit all evening and has been watched far too closely by They-who-carry-guns. Their continued scrutiny makes her nervous, and she is relieved when the familiar, flat face pokes free of the earth.

One tortoise fills the tunnel mouth, and Shanti finally has someone to talk to.

"Wait," she lowers her trunk to hold him in position, to keep his presence hidden. "They've only made three passes tonight."

She knows that there will be five before they leave for the evening. That two more times They-who-carry-guns will march along her chain-linked fence with their clipped steps and shining badges.

"It will be safe soon," she tells the tortoise, "But you must wait."

She thinks he understands her caution. Already, it has been two days since They-who-keep-cages-barred returned him to his enclosure. Oliver is not a rushing animal. Not like the zebras who move at the slightest sound and are impossible to count properly.

The tortoise is deliberate. He is like her.

"Tell me," Shanti swings her trunk and whispers, "why you have to escape."

So, Oliver tells her his story. He remains in his tunnel, whispering as They-who-carry-guns pass another time. He talks about his bird, Miranda, about the day she miraculously appeared in his pen and how he followed her long strides around and around until she finally spoke to him.

Shanti doesn't like this bird from the start. When Oliver describes her with his warm words, Miranda seems cold and distant. She was not a kind animal, Shanti thinks. But Oliver loves her.

They-who-carry-guns pass again, but Shanti says nothing. She lets the tortoise spill his story, and she counts the times his voice crackles. She measures the cadence of his speech patterns and calculates the odds he's about to have his heart broken.

When he gets to the part about the pigeon, Shanti flaps her ears and stamps in sympathy. When he mentions the crow, she trumpets out loud.

"Crows cannot be trusted," she says. "They always lie."

"Unless there is better sport in telling the truth," Oliver says. He has thought this through, apparently. He believes he can outsmart the devil.

Shanti hopes he can, but she realizes they have spoken for too long. They have lingered over the story and eaten up the larger half of the nighttime.

"I think it's too late to count you again," Shanti says. "But I will still bend the fence."

"No."

Oliver's answer makes her tingle. She remembers his shapes, and she hopes she is not as cold as his bird.

"I will go tomorrow," the tortoise declares. "When there is more time."

"I'm sorry," Shanti says. She has let him linger over his story for her own pleasure. She is as bad as a crow.

But Oliver's voice seems brighter. He speaks with less crackling now. "It was good to talk," he says. "Good to share it all with someone else."

Shanti is thrilled. She scuffs her big feet and looks at the sky. One star. One tortoise.

"It's not daylight yet," Oliver says. "If you'd still like to count me."

Shanti steps back, making room for him to leave his hole. She watches the shell emerge, one row of patterns at a time, and thinks she has never been happier.

Hyena Removed

They-who-bring-food drop something disgusting in Alice's cage. The smell mingles with her food, confusing her. At first, she thinks a dead cub is hidden in the fluffy blanket they've given her. She drags it to the far corner of the cage and finds nothing. Only cloth that reeks, that smells of urine and male hyena.

Alice tries to bury it, but the cage floor is not dirt. She splits three of her claws before she gives up, pushes the smelly cloth into a wad, and leaves it. She returns to her meal.

The cat watches her eat. He has taken to staring at her when he is bored, which is far too frequent for Alice's tastes. He ignores his own food, waits to acknowledge it until Alice retires to her corner for the evening.

She lies as far as possible from the nasty blanket, but already the scent is less offensive. She will ignore it, like she ignores the cat. She will let it sit, stinking in the shadows, until she can't smell it any longer.

Eventually, she will seek out the blanket. She will go to it, dig and push at the fabric, searching for any trace of the scent.

She is not in season yet, but Alice remembers the last time. She will ignore the blanket and the smell for now. But she thinks, in a few more days, the stink of it will be not nearly as offensive.

Tortoise Abroad

Oliver meets the crow outside Shanti's paddock. The bird has been waiting for him, has paced and cackled atop a picnic table while the elephant pried up her fence. Oliver emerges to the clattering of metal. He thanks his gigantic friend, taking his time while the crow frets.

He plays a slow game, a long con. He smiles when the bird's feathers prickle.

"It's going to take you a while," Debra croaks. "You should hurry."

Oliver wants to hurry. He wants to see Miranda tonight, but his stumpy legs move with careful deliberation. The crow bounces. She hops and sputters. He has not decided what she wants. Maybe, like the pigeon, she means to use him. Does Debra long for a free ticket into the marshlands?

Oliver doesn't trust the bird, but when she takes to wing, he follows. The crow lands on the sign in front of the macaque cage, waits for him. They dance their mutual deception, while the zoo watches, holds its breath.

The monkey is not asleep. He flings something that makes the bird duck and screech. Oliver enjoys her fury. He walks quicker, however, worried the assault will drive her away.

She only moves down the path, only lands on a bench beside some bushes while Oliver works his way past the ape house.

The macaque does not attack him, but Oliver hears it, whispering to itself as he passes. The words are muddled. The animal's voice is low and quick. Oliver sees it as shadow only, hunched against a wall, rocking and whispering.

Mad. The crowds and the captivity have broken the primate, and Oliver is glad when his feet carry him beyond that cage. Relief floods his shell when the crow leads him on again, right at a place where the pathways branch. Left where they make a Y around the nocturnal house.

They pass a cement ring where the sound of water lapping against the walls echoes skyward. Here the crow pauses, perches atop the basin walls, and calls taunts to the denizens inside.

Oliver cannot see them, but they beep softly, throw insults back up their shaft enclosure. He imagines living inside a pit and shivers.

"Hurry," Debra caws.

Oliver slows his steps then thinks better of it in case she gets bored and abandons him. He hurries. He must see Miranda again.

"The marsh is by the family farm." The crow hops back to him, strutting across the path before his blunt nose. "If you don't make it tonight, you can hide in there."

Oliver grunts, sniffs for the lie in her words, for a warble of deceit. "What will you do?" he asks. "When we get to the marsh?"

"I have a plan to pry up the net," she says. "It's not hard. There are many stones nearby, but you may have to push the larger ones."

"I will." Oliver thinks she needs him to get inside, but the crow shakes herself and flutters a few steps ahead.

"It is damp in there," she says. "You won't like it."

"Will you?" He pauses, watches her smooth again.

"No." The crow's eye is a clear-bright gem, a steady beacon. "I won't go in there. After the net, you're on your own."

Oliver thinks she lies, but her steady gaze haunts him after she delivers him to the family farm. After she has found him an empty stall to hide in. Long after she has covered him with straw and left him for the day.

He waits, surrounded by the farm animals, by tall guests and shrieking children. He thinks he must guess what trick she will play on him, and he thinks about it for long hours. He hides, warm and secure, and believes he will not be a fool again.

Ape House

Gonzo has not slept. His head feels swollen, full of cottony down. He smacks his lips again and again, rubbing his face with both leathery palms. He shivers, but he is not cold. It is as if he has been in ice too long, can no longer feel it. His limbs quake, and he closes his eyes against even the softest sounds.

The troop waking is a parade of gongs and trumpets. Their nails scratch at the hard floor. Their yawns are deafening. Gonzo hunches, holds his head, and cries aloud when they rattle the bars inside.

He drags himself back through the square door. Perhaps water will help. But when he limps to the rubber basin and dunks his face, the relief is only cursory. He drinks. He shivers. He needs the bean again.

The troop cavorts, and Gonzo leaps at them, baring his teeth and slapping whoever is slow enough, unlucky enough to remain in range. He gives them his teeth, spins, and gnashes until they all abandon him.

They scamper out into the light, and he drags himself to the bars and the aisle.

He checks the ledge, but there are no crumbs left. He searches the straw, but the black cherries had no real skin, melted in his mouth so that he finds no trace of them.

When They-who-bring-food arrive, Gonzo sits, glaring into the aisle. He-who-sweeps is with them. He slumps over his broom, but Gonzo catches him looking back. He is a sneaky primate, curled and glancing sideways.

Gonzo fears he has been punished for giving him the bean, but when the troop returns, when They-who-feed bring breakfast and move on with their tubs, a miracle occurs.

The troop dives on the fruit and biscuits. Their noises drill into Gonzo's skull, but his eyes stick to He-who-sweeps. The broom still brushes at the aisle, but it is creeping toward the macaque enclosure.

He-who-sweeps digs one paw into his coverall pocket. He whistles a note that nearly cracks Gonzo, that is so high and so lingering that the monkey has to close his eyes. When he opens them, He-who-sweeps is near. The pocket paw emerges as a fist. The fist flashes to the ledge, opens, flies back to the broom while Gonzo seizes a fresh paw-full of dark beans.

The stars align and the monkey stuffs his lips with his addiction.

X-RAY

RAINRIVER ZOOLOGICAL GARDENS
VETERINARY RECORD
URSUS HORRIBILIS
    MALE
    AGE 19

X-RAY RESULTS:
    BONE SPURS
    HAIRLINE FRACTURES OVER SKELETAL STRUCTURE
    SWELLING IN HIP REGION

MUSCULATURE: GOOD
    EYES: GOOD
    HEARING: GOOD
    HEARTRATE: NORMAL

DIAGNOSIS:
    ADVANCED STAGE ARTHRITIS

TREATMENT:
    PAIN REDUCER DAILY BY BODY WEIGHT IN FOOD OR BY
    INJECTION

Grizzly Caged

Hector stuffs his paw through the bars and wiggles it, palm pads up, until She-who-takes-notes drops a grape onto it. He curls his claws around the fruit, brings it inside the box and lips it more slowly than necessary.

The clipboard rattles as she writes. She is not an artist, but as a substitute, he thinks she does all right. When he churrs and tilts his head to one side, her mouth curls upwards in pleasure.

Hector has suffered three injections, needles stabbed through his bars on long sticks. Piercing jabs, they poke through his thick skin and make him wince. There is no way to avoid these. His metal box allows him little movement.

Though the shots are painful, his bones no longer ache. He understands that the doctors have done this, and he churrs and sits as upright as he can for them.

At first, She-who-takes-notes fed him tidbits from a similar stick. Hector has charmed her, however, and when his paw comes out again, she is quick with another grape. She no longer flinches from him. She smiles, and the bear brattles like an engine sputtering.

On the wall behind her, a picture of his bones hangs. Hector thinks it is not art. Photos are beneath him, after all. But there is something appealing about the way the light shines through his ghostly outline. There is something seductive here. Something that reminds him of the early days with his brother.

He churrs, reaches, and stuffs down grapes until She-who-takes-notes is forced to put down her clipboard and focus fully on the bear.

Elephant Paddock

Shanti counts her straw. Her trunk curls against her forehead, careful not to blow away the frail bundles. She has gathered them into groups of ten to make the counting simpler. There is no wind, and the damned crows have moved on with Oliver's most recent departure.

The elephant lines up three-hundred bits of straw in three rows of ten bundles each. She has counted her tortoise friend three times, helped him find freedom twice.

She flutters her ears. Her scrub tail flicks against her saggy buttocks. Satisfied. She sighs as she counts, certain that she has helped, that somewhere Oliver carries his 37 hexagonal scute patterns toward victory.

Shanti counts as her paddock rail fills with gaping faces. She imagines them, as they pack together, as plates on an enormous domed tortoise shell.

She does not know she is in love. Shanti only sees the perfectly aligned shapes, one against the next. She only feels a fluttering in her belly, a warm contentment as she counts her straw, thinking of Oliver. Thinking he will want to return eventually, and that there was no reason to let her count him so many times... and yet he did.

Her trunk tightens at the thought of seeing him again, and she lays her bits and bundles into looser groups, rounding the lines until they make a high arc, a gentle dome for her to count again.

The Crow

Debra inspects the net while the tortoise sleeps. She has stashed him in the family farm where, even if discovered, his presence is unlikely to cause an alert. All the souls penned in that area of the zoo are subject to interaction, are forced to wander the paddocks while the crowd's offspring molest them.

She is certain Oliver will be fine there, and she is just as sure that she is clever enough to find a way to trap him inside the marsh.

The bottom of the netting is weighted, staked to the earth at regular intervals to prevent anything larger than a vole from digging beneath it. It is these diminutive rodents, however, who have shown her the way in. For their crisscrossed tunneling has loosened a stake or two. There are now places where the net gaps and moves, and a very clever bird ought to be able to hike it upwards.

At least high enough to admit one tortoise.

Debra cackles and struts along the perimeter. There are six stakes missing now, a few others that are loose and easy to pull. She examines each breach and its surroundings and picks a site where the path nearby curves around a bronze statue of a heron. Flat stones surround its base, and Debra thinks they will be perfect.

She believes she should let the tortoise move them, that there is glorious sport in Oliver constructing his own trap. But time concerns her.

She decides to help a little, to be certain they can get him in before they are caught in the act of building.

The crow chuckles, flaps to the statue, and eyes the stones. The largest ones, the tortoise will have to shove. She selects a few that are smaller, flat smooth stones she believes will stack easily. Then, one by one, she plucks them from their arrangement and carries them to the marshland netting.

One by one, she lays them where they will be close at hand. When the time comes to trick the tortoise, Debra wants to be front and center. She wants to see the net fall, witness the dawning realization that he has been caught by a trap of his own making. That he is imprisoned inside with his own misery.

Lion Enclosure

There is a rain of debris into the lions' enclosure. Ever since Charlie's encounter with the cellular phone, more things are dropped, flung even, into his range.

They-who-carry-guns frequent the Savannah more regularly, policing the rail, but only managing to pause the tide of offenses piling up on both sides of the trench and its hot wire. There are too many people, and the guns, it seems, do not fire.

Charlie huffs. He has taken to lounging much closer to the debris field, guarding the offerings like the king he is. Those that interest him are quickly pounced upon. He has tasted many new things.

Popcorn. Soft animals filled with white fluff. Leather straps, little square cameras, lattes, and many more phones. He ignores these now, though he still enjoys shredding the fuzzy toy animals. He appreciates the buttery taste of popcorn, too, and he chews the leather bits out of boredom.

But mostly, Charlie waits for the squeaky meat.

When the crowd tosses him these, the long reddish tubes of meat, Charlie roars and pounces. He snarls in case the lionesses dare to sneak closer, and he bites. He chews and devours with all the gusto of a natural predator.

It is delicious, somehow feeling both raw and wholly artificial. The hot dogs hold traces of his minced diet, but along with that they carry a thousand new flavors, unrecognized tastes that drive straight from Charlie's tongue to his brain.

He is rabid for it.

He chews and dreams, and in the night his veldt is peopled with hot dog monsters that sing to him from the far shadows. He can smell them there, always out of reach. And when he wakes, there are even more faces, more paws to toss him offerings.

Charlie basks in his fame, eats his hot dogs, and thinks there will never be enough to satiate him.

Tortoise Abroad

Oliver struggles free of the straw. He cannot shake himself, hasn't the flexibility to do more than swipe a forefoot across his face to clear his vision. Bits of the pale hay poke into the gaps in his shell, forward and back.

He is prickled, and the soft skin folds around his neck and legs begin to itch.

The crow goads him onward. She bounces along the stall railing until Oliver picks up his pace. Night has fallen, and Debra becomes a set of dancing eyes in the darkness. A gleaming beak like a knife slash as she calls his name.

Oliver moves to her command, but he is thinking, thinking that her urgency cannot bode well for him.

"It's ready. It's ready," she sings while bobbing.

Oliver smells the trap, but his brain fills with Miranda. He shuffles eagerly from the family farm and follows the bouncing crow. The straw pokes him with each step, but eventually it falls free or he forgets to care about it.

Debra leads him down the pathway. Just beyond the family farm she perches on a miraculous thing. It is enormous and made of metal, but its shape is Miranda's shape. Oliver gazes up at it and shivers.

The statue guards the marshland, and Oliver thinks it is an omen. He believes the crow now. His love is inside the nets.

Debra has gathered a pile of small stones. She shows him her work. She explains her plan, and Oliver waves his long neck from side to side. It is a good idea, clever, and though he knows he will have to go carefully, to watch for deception along the way, his heart races.

Debra lifts the net, only a fraction at first. She is a small thing, made of hollow bones and not strong. Oliver shoves the smallest rock into the gap. They repeat this maneuver twice before there is enough room for him to push the tip of a foot underneath.

He watches the crow stack a third rock on top of the other two, lifting the net one inch higher. If she means to dart inside, to leave him like a dirty pigeon, this is her opportunity.

But Debra bounces backwards and eyes the widening gap instead.

"A large one next," she croaks. "One to hold it up while we remove these."

Oliver decides her game is not to steal his entrance. She really means to get him inside, to whatever end, and that knowing moves his feet much faster.

He wobbles to the statue and finds a large stone, bulldozes it, rolls it with his flat nose onto the path and back to their building site.

The net rises, one stone at a time, each larger than the last until it is half his height and there are no larger rocks to be found. Then, Debra begins to stack again. She places small stones atop the big one while Oliver wedges his neck beneath the net. He lifts his head, uses his body as a lever to pry the material higher.

It resists them. They have reached the limits of the next stake down and now it fights against their effort.

Oliver stares at it, frantic and half tangled. The lower edge has caught on his shell lip, but he is halfway through. He is stepping inside the boundary now, pulling while the crow screams at him.

Her claws scratch at his dome. She rides him as Peg did, and Oliver thrashes in panic before her words settle.

"Wait, idiot. You're stuck."

He is frantic. He is trapped. He will knock her free if he has to.

But when he pauses to decide, the crow bobs down, uses her beak to lift the net from his rim. She pulls it, and with a deep twang, it slides free, resting atop his dome with her and, when Oliver presses forward, slipping up and over.

The crow is swept from his shell. The net passes freely over his body.

Oliver surges ahead and walks into the marshland. He steps on grass and soggy earth. His body rocks from one side to the other, and the net falls away behind him, snapping back to the ground and leaving the crow outside after all.

They have done it. Oliver's heart bounces now. He is inside.

The crow's plan, *their* plan, has worked.

See parts I-IV of Frances Pauli's serial "The Zoo Diaries" online at Metaphorosis.
If you liked them, leave a comment. Authors love that!
Remember to subscribe to our e-mail updates so you'll know when new stories are posted.

May

The Diamond Noose

Ramez Yoakeim

From the smug grins everyone flashed me as soon as I walked into the precinct, I knew I was in for a nasty surprise. I hadn't even reached my desk when the lieutenant called me into her glass-bowl office and handed me a new assignment: liaison to the Angels' Embassy.

I didn't care for Angels. They looked down on us from their palaces in the sky, pretending to help us survive our broken world while ensuring we'd never learn to do it on our own. Some said it was the Angels who set off the nuclear catastrophe that nearly wiped out life on Earth.

"Wouldn't this suit a more senior officer?" Or one more junior. Anyone else, really.

The lieutenant jabbed a paper on her desk. "Laila Aboud, requested by name."

A shiver zapped up my spine. The Angels had hidden eyes in the sky, seeing everywhere, knowing all. They had tentacles in every government, in every department, their shadow behind every throne. How had I managed to attract their attention? "Why me?"

She shrugged. "Ask the Angels when you see them. Do we have a problem here?"

I found myself wondering whose idea it had been to call them *Angels*.

"No, ma'am."

Like I had a choice. This job came with a warm bed and three squares, a firearm, and badge that opened doors and dropped eyes. I'd never walk away, no matter what they asked, any more than she would.

After all that, the work was surprisingly mundane. Waiting on my desk every morning was a stack of *requests* from the Angels Embassy: locate knickknacks stolen from the occasional visiting Angel, or quietly deem accidental the death of a prostitute in the company of another, or round up a bunch of uniforms to form a street cordon for visiting off-world dignitaries. Until I arrived at my desk one day to find a single message *requesting* my attendance at the embassy, and my heart dropped to my knees. I wanted to get away from Angels, not get closer.

The embassy occupied an old courthouse downtown. In the frigid gloom under Earth's thick cloud cover, the impeccably restored edifice dwarfed the line of scraggly humanity wrapped around its foundations like a snake about invincible prey.

However the Angels put it, the Transmigration they dangled before those queueing had nothing to do with benevolence. They preyed on our best and brightest, siphoning away those who might help us to break free of our dependence on their conditional aid. Could one of those queuing learn the secrets of fusion one day, or perfect anti-radiation medicines, or discover how to grow crops in poisoned soil, or put an end to the Angels plunder of our water and minerals, or lead us in overthrowing the tyrants they installed to rule us? Not when those with potential got spirited away to the sky.

The queuing adults eyed me warily as I made my way to the uniform separating the line's head from its tail, barring the serpent from becoming an ouroboros. He glanced at my badge and waved me through. Inside, I handed the private security guard my sidearm. "I had no idea they started queueing this early."

"Some never leave." The guard saw me roll my eyes and grinned, his words chasing me to the elevator. "Sometimes, a dream is all that keeps us alive, officer."

A fool's dream of an easy life concerned only with pleasure. Then again, had my lot in life been harsher, perhaps I'd have queued with them.

I wasn't prepared for the mechanical giant waiting for me when the elevator's doors parted. Spindly inside the exoskeleton that afforded her mobility in Earth's gravity, Inspector Geraldine Hoff's skin was as pale as mine was brown, as if we'd been birthed from opposite ends of a monochromatic palette. Her hairless scalp, elongated sloping forehead, and large inky eyes cast as much doubt on our alleged common ancestry as the missing wings myth had it Angels grew to fly around their low-gravity palaces.

While the building's exterior and entrance remained largely faithful to its original layout, the interior bore no resemblance to anything I'd ever seen before. Hoff led me from the lift to a flat-floored ovoid space uniformly lit by the walls themselves. With a whirring flick of her hand, Hoff gestured me towards a blob that oozed up on command and reformed into a stool.

She briefed me on a missing Angel. *The Conjurer* was the nom-de-plume of an artist who composed dreams as a form of entertainment. These visions eschewed euphoric sex or heroic triumph—the sort that'd exhilarate us dirt dwellers—instead, they explored the darker side of the human psyche, torments that Angels no longer experienced. "Any questions?"

I didn't have to ask what the Conjurer was doing on the surface. Where else would he find the human trauma to mine for his *art*? "How does an Angel get lost? No offense, but you stand out down here."

"More reason to suspect something happened to this *Angel*, wouldn't you say?" Hoff bristled at the common moniker. I'd had no idea they considered it pejorative. In their shoes, I'd have been flattered. Would they have preferred us to call them *demons*?

"What exactly do you think I can do that your fancy gizmos can't?"

"Retracing the Conjurer's steps means going places we don't often venture. My bosses, and yours, want a local along to deal with the natives. *No offense.*"

It would've also been politically unpalatable for my bosses to have an undoubtedly armed Angel terrorizing the populace without at least the veneer of local authority, and it didn't hurt to have me around to take the blame when things went awry.

"A chaperone, basically."

Hoff smiled thinly. "Think of it as an opportunity to demonstrate your usefulness."

I didn't know how to respond to *that*.

Mildly acidic drizzle scattered off Hoff's flying egg onto the corroded tin roofs of the lean-tos below. Despite the webbing securing me to the seat, my inner ear kept insisting I was falling towards the transparent shell. White-knuckled, I hung onto the seat and fought off motion sickness, only half-listening to Hoff.

After one particularly sharp banking turn, Hoff glanced at me. "You're turning a worrying shade of green."

I clamped my jaws shut against the rising bile and inflated my lungs with the egg's sweet clean air. "I'm fine."

She pursed her lips and returned her attention to the scarred Earth slipping by below. With little light penetrating the thick, ash-laden clouds, we would all have perished long ago, had it not been for the Angels' magic-like power generation, foodstuffs, and medicines. That their largesse came with strings attached surprised no one. That those strings soon formed a noose that held us hostage to their demands *shouldn't* have surprised anyone.

To shift my focus away from the vertiginous view, I turned to Hoff. "Did the Conjurer stray far during his visits?"

Hoff hesitated. "Sightseeing, entertainment. Nothing out of the ordinary."

She meant poverty safaris and brothels. There was little else for Angels on the surface.

"Could he have gotten lost?" How would the mobs treat a lost Angel? I liked to think some would be hospitable, but I feared that others wouldn't be, and I couldn't bring myself to condemn either.

Hoff shook her head. "He knew his way around." She seemed on the verge of saying more but didn't.

Changing tack, I teased her, "Did you know most people think y'all have wings?"

"Wings?" Hoff frowned back at my smile. "We ..." she paused, searching for words, "change bodies like you might clothes. Not as often, but subject to similar whims of fashion and taste. Body parts, like wings or extra eyes or gills and fins, come and go, and are sometimes taken to extremes. Many of my friends forgo bodies entirely to live in the Abstract."

"And that is?"

"Never mind, it's hard to explain." I couldn't tell whether she was boasting or embarrassed.

The egg lurched briefly and I gasped.

Hoff gave me a sidelong glance. "Your file didn't say anything about fear of flying."

I realized I was still holding onto the seat. "I've never flown before, give me time." I tried to let go, but couldn't quite bring myself to do it. "What else did my file say?"

"That you're insubordinate, pigheaded, and cantankerous."

"They could spell *cantankerous*?"

Hoff laughed, and I found myself laughing along, for a moment oblivious to the gulf separating us.

"But it also said you have the highest clearance rate of any officer in your department."

They *had* asked for me by name. I still didn't quite know what to make of that and pushed it aside to ruminate over later.

"Quite the accomplishment, considering how young you are," Hoff added.

I'd never thought of thirty-two as young. Angels were rumored to be immortal, but I put little stock in such claims. If only half of those rumors were true, it would have made them veritable gods. "How old are *you*?"

She smiled coyly and waved away my question. "Longevity's overrated."

"I'd happily part with an arm and both legs to see my fiftieth birthday." With life expectancy in the mid-forties, I found the idea of anyone living to a hundred obscene, let alone longer. How did Angel offspring feel about parents who lingered? Was overpopulation as much of a problem in orbit as it was on the surface?

Hoff stared wistfully into the distance, seeing something in the murky gloom I couldn't. "When life is short, your choices are consequential. Which path you take in life matters more because you only ever get to make a few choices. Live long enough and you end up exploring every path in turn, chasing every dream. What good is success if it's only a matter of time?"

I could tell she sincerely meant it, almost as if she envied me my short miserable life. How easy it was for those well fed to bursting to preach the virtues of restraint to the starving.

Hoff pitched the egg down, drawing my eyes to an expanse of pockmarked, corrugated metal roofs below. Having never seen the area from above before, it took me a moment to recognize where we were. "We can't land here."

"It's the Conjurer's first stop after leaving the embassy. The first deviation from his usual itinerary."

"You don't understand. This is Serpent Head's territory. If we land uninvited, he's as likely to feed us to his dogs as answer our questions."

"I'd like to see him try."

"I wouldn't!" Though I'd count it progress to be rid of him and his flunkies, innocent bystanders were bound to get caught in any confrontation, and for what? To satisfy Hoff's desire to appear tough and powerful? Who was she trying to impress? "You wanted a local to deal with the natives, and this local is telling you to stay the hell away from these natives."

Hoff ignored me and took the egg lower. "I'll land there." She nodded at a stone-paved plaza festooned with tattered bunting and lit with dim, oil-burning lanterns.

By the time the egg touched down, everyone had scattered, leaving the market eerily quiet, aside from the hissing of swaying lamps and the incessant strumming of caustic drizzle on improvised awnings.

"Good luck finding anyone who'll talk to us now," I muttered, steeling myself against the sour miasma wafting through the egg's open hatch.

Hoff gracefully eased the considerable bulk of her exoskeleton out into the open, oblivious to the stench. "They're bound to come out eventually."

"That's not how it works down here, how *we* work," I fumed. Why have me along if she wasn't going to listen to anything I said? "You can't just blunder your way to your missing Conjurer with this confidence act, no matter how convincing."

She cast her eyes down, looking slightly abashed, and I felt a little guilty for my outburst.

I set to scanning the deserted clearing, when a boy bolted from a cart he might have been napping under, towards a dark alley and right into my arms. About ten or twelve, though so thin it was impossible to say for sure, the boy squirmed in my grip, eyes wide with fear.

"Let go, pig," he demanded, his bass rumble at odds with his small frame.

"Settle. I'm not going to hurt you," I said. "There's a half-dinar in it for you if you answer my questions."

The boy stopped bucking and regarded me with wide, greedy eyes. "Ten dinars."

It was a familiar routine. "You don't even know what I'm going to ask you."

Suddenly, floodlights lit the clearing—an extravagant display for a planet starved of power. Reflexively, I let go of the boy's scruff and shielded my eyes. His bare feet barely left a mark on the frozen slush as he ran away.

"Kadir's a good lad. He'd never betray his kin for anything less than *five* dinars." A short, plump man swaggered into view. A tattoo of a snake head in faded indigo and crimson ink covered the left side of his temple, its lean body running down his cheek, under the thicket of a rampant salt-and-pepper beard, and reappearing down the side of his bullneck before disappearing again under his coat's collar. "Are you lost, sweetheart?" Serpent Head asked mockingly. Under the blue-white glare, his shaved head shone like oiled mahogany.

From Hoff's exoskeleton an aura swelled, glowing an ominous red-tinged orange.

Serpent Head regarded her contemptuously. "It's true we have little to live for down here, but believe me, we don't die cheaply." A racket of cocking rifles followed.

"Stop!" I raised my arms. "We didn't come here looking for trouble."

"Trouble?" Serpent Head thundered with practiced menace. "What trouble would that be, sweetheart?"

Hoff covered the distance separating us in a wink. "Call her *sweetheart* one more time and I'll dispatch you like the vermin you are."

Serpent Head matched her advance, his stomping army in lockstep. Instinctively, I stepped in-between. "Enough," I infused my voice with every command authority trick I'd learned walking the beat. "We're only here for information," I continued in a measured tone. "An Angel stopped here a few days ago."

I nodded to Hoff, who asked. "What did he want?"

Serpent Head alternated his focus between my eyes as if one would betray the other. "What's in it for me?"

As soon as he'd finished speaking, Hoff pulled out a small silver box and threw it at him. He grabbed it midair and turned it in his hand, examining it. "What the hell is this?"

"Enough pills to offset five-hundred Sieverts," Hoff said.

I glowered at her. Unlike a coin tossed to a street urchin, bribing Serpent Head with a small fortune in medicine only created a bigger problem. Not that it'd matter to the Angels, not when they had us to clean up their messes.

Serpent Head nodded approvingly at the box. "Your Angel wanted a sedative and—funnily enough—anti-radiation pills. For another one of these," he shook the pills in their container, "I'll tell you where he went next."

"No need." Hoff's forcefield deflated, cooling to a muted indigo-blue as she walked back to the egg, winking out entirely once inside. I scrambled after her. The moment the hatch sealed, the egg shot upwards, pinning me to my seat.

"I could have gotten him to tell us where your Conjurer went next," I grumbled.

"That, I already know."

"Were you planning on telling me?" How could she not understand that to help her, I had to know what I was helping with. Keeping her cards so close to her chest was hurting more than my feelings, it was handicapping our chances of finding the Conjurer. Any investigator worth their salt would've known that. What did Hoff actually do for work up there, parking enforcement?

She saw me glowering and relented. "He went to a bordello, then disappeared without a trace."

So much for Angels eyes seeing everything, knowing all. If an Angel could evade their all seeing eyes, could we too?

One moment, we were drowning in a murky ashen sea, and the next, we burst into an inverted, indigo-hemmed, blue ocean. Against that dazzling expanse, the Angels' crystal palaces glinted like a glittering diamond necklace girding the Earth, an achingly beautiful noose. Despite the blinding brightness, I couldn't turn away, until my eyes watered and reflexively gummed shut. Hoff noticed and polarized the shell into near opacity. "Is this better?"

I watched the fading kaleidoscopic afterimage on the inside of my eyelids, my gratitude for her thoughtfulness warring with resentment. When again would I get a chance to see sunshine, however blinding? For centuries, our leaders had promised a day when the clouds would finally part. Meanwhile, *when-the-sun-shines* had come to mean *never*. "Thank you."

As I reopened my eyes, blinking away the moisture pooling on my lashes, a nagging feeling I had since we took off from the marketplace coalesced into a question. "Why did the Conjurer buy radiation pills on the black market? Unlike yours, the local ones are useless as currency."

"Currency?" Hoff scolded. "Is that the gratitude we get for helping you survive?"

"You want *our* gratitude for exploiting us?" I responded in kind. "Everything you do, you do for yourselves. Every time you bribe someone like Serpent Head, you strengthen his hand and ensure generations of Kadirs never rise to challenge your interests."

"If you're going to blame us for Serpent Head, you have to ask yourself this: Why would we bother sabotaging your endeavors when you do such a fine job of it on your own? Everything you accuse us of, Laila, you are yourself complicit in."

I smarted from the truth.

Hoff broke the silence that ensued. "Must we quarrel about things that have nothing to do with the two of us? I don't blame you for every fault of your people. Why blame me for mine?"

"Because you have a say. You get to vote on the decisions your people make. *You* decide what's right and what's not. I don't. I live and die by the edicts of the tyrants you installed as our rulers. How our troubles started may not have been your fault, but we're still in a mess, centuries later, because it serves your interests. You use us, Geraldine."

"Can't we leave politics to the politicians?"

"Why am I here, Geraldine? And don't give me this bullshit about locals and natives. You don't listen to anything I say anyway. There's nothing I've done you couldn't have done on your own."

"You're wrong, Laila." Hoff paused and regarded me diffidently, before continuing. "Back home, there are no hardships, no risks. We've forgotten pain, fear, hunger. When we set out to rid ourselves of human weakness, we ended up discarding our instincts instead. You effortlessly saw through my bravado in the face of the first hitch we faced. I'm overwhelmed by your world and woefully unprepared for it. I can't finish this on my own."

She'd called me by my first name twice now. A sincere familiarity, or another manipulation? I couldn't tell. Then I realized that I too had called her by her first name. Was I trying to manipulate her in return, or had I simply forgotten she was an Angel?

"Then tell me why the Conjurer needed anti-radiation pills, when his aura would've protected him as yours protects you," I paused for a response, but Hoff only shrugged. "You said your people choose their bodies. Could he have chosen a body that is susceptible to radiation?"

Hoff's eyes glazed over for a heartbeat or two. "It's not. His current corpus is an older model than mine, but similarly immune to radiation. Curiously, though, he hasn't upgraded his for nearly twenty years."

"The same period he's been visiting the surface, give or take?"

Hoff turned towards me so fast, I recoiled, driving my head deeper into the headrest. "How did you know that?"

"My guess is, the Conjurer wasn't born an Angel."

"No one is born—" Hoff stopped mid-sentence. "—into Transenlightenment."

"You don't have kids?" I'd never even heard a rumor about that. I wouldn't have believed it had anyone else told me. How could a people survive without having offspring? "Why not?"

Hoff shook her head. "You first. How did you work all this out?"

"If the Conjurer didn't need the pills, then they had to be for one of us, for someone he knew. Had he sourced them the way you had, you'd have a record of it. Maybe he wouldn't have been able to explain why he needed them or for whom." I paused, giving Hoff another opportunity to tell me I was wrong. She said nothing. "Circumventing obstacles and challenging limits is something we have to do, dozens of times every day, just to survive. But you just said those sorts of instincts are lost to you, which would make the Conjurer a more recent Angel. One who hadn't yet shed his hard-won survival instincts. One who still has people here he cares enough about to risk doing business with the likes of Serpent Head. Who is it? After twenty years, his parents are likely dead. A lover then, or a child?"

Hoff's response was slow coming. "I don't know."

I snorted and turned away from her, shaking my head.

"We don't keep those sorts of records. We never had to," she added heatedly. After a pause, she drew in a deep breath before continuing. "To answer your earlier question, the longevity treatments preclude pregnancy. We could have found ways around that, but at some point we decided we didn't want to, and however long we live, we too die. So, we invite the deserving among you to join us. We expect and accept a measure of nostalgia for their former lives, until new possibilities sets them free of their past. Why would we need records of their old lives?"

I thought of the coiling queue outside the embassy and shivered. Did those queuing know the price of becoming an Angel was to give up everyone they'd ever loved? "You expect a spouse to forget their mate, a parent to abandon their children, a friend and neighbor to forswear their community after a *measure of nostalgia*?"

She shrugged. "I don't remember what family I once had, or even if I had one."

Where did she think she'd come from, a seed pod? All humans had families, born or found, small or sprawling, loving or venom-filled. They might not like them or want them, but they had them. Whom had the Conjurer left behind twenty years ago? How long had it taken Hoff to forgot those she'd abandoned? "Geraldine, why are you searching for the Conjurer? The truth, please."

"He took something he shouldn't have."

I waited for her to elaborate, but that was all she would say.

After Serpent Head's hostile reception, Madam Sparrow's solicitous guards seemed downright hospitable. They ushered us through the darkened brothel to their mistress's alcove in the back where she fussed over a young woman's makeup.

Madam Sparrow watched our approach with naked appraisal. A firm hand to the small of the back propelled the young woman towards us. Midstride, her heel caught on the tail of her two-sizes too-long dress and she tripped. Hoff caught her before she face-planted, and helped her back to her feet. "How old are you, child?"

Madam Sparrow leered at Hoff, answering before the young woman could, "Old enough. You could be her first."

Hoff wrinkled her nose. "Revolting. Inhuman."

I bridled at Hoff's patronizing self-righteousness, especially coming from someone who'd remorselessly sacrificed her family, even their memory. "At least she's warm, well-fed, and has somewhere dry to lay her head at night. So long as no one's forcing her, I have no quarrel with her choices." I turned to Madam Sparrow. "We're not customers. We're looking for an Angel who visited your establishment a few days ago."

"I have no idea who you're talking about." Up close, grey roots peeked from under the edges of Madam Sparrow's platinum-blonde wig.

"I can think of a few ways to jog your memory, none of them good for business."

Madam Sparrow glowered at me, but eventually her rounded shoulders slumped, the fire in her eyes replaced by a heavy weariness that could flatten mountains. "I don't know where he went, alright? Years ago, before he left to become an Angel, he brought his woman here. Paid well for her upkeep too, and she doted on the girls like the children they never had. Every few weeks, he'd visit for a day or two. This time, he took her and left."

Hoff shook her head. "No, he didn't. He entered through your front door and never left."

Madam Sparrow bobbed her head coyly. "Not by the front door, no."

Hoff had to fold her frame at the waist to fit into the back door's antechamber. Behind the raised hem of a faded wall tapestry, the tunnel's mouth was pitch black. Narrow and low-ceilinged, it swallowed my pocket torch's beam, dispersing it without illuminating its confines.

"Where does it lead?" Hoff asked Madam Sparrow.

"The woods, an hour on foot south of town."

The hairs on my nape bristled. "The haunted woods?"

Hoff sighed audibly. "It's not haunted."

Madam Sparrow put her hands on her hips. "Haunted or not, some *very* important clients rely on this tunnel's discretion," she cautioned, her emphasis leaving me in no doubt she meant Angels. "Compromise it at your peril." With a huff, she turned and left.

"The woods are only mildly radioactive, but that's enough to turn them into a blind spot for our orbital sensors. I should have thought of that when we couldn't locate him." Hoff peered into the tunnel. "Did you want to go first or should I?"

"After you, but it's quite narrow. You might get stuck."

"The injury to my dignity would be far worse, if we were to fail."

We emerged from the side of a low hill into a dense thicket of dead poplars lumbering side by side like funereal guards. Their naked branches sagged under the accumulated snow. A burden which the chilling wind forced them to shed periodically, obscuring whatever tracks our quarry might have left.

Hoff deposited a blue pill in my hand. "Take this."

My eyes fixed on the tiny pill. "Trust is a two way street, Geraldine." Somehow, unconsciously, Angel Inspector Geraldine Hoff had become merely Hoff, my partner, and my partner Hoff had morphed into my friend, Geraldine. I expected commensurately more from her. "I've trusted you plenty so far. I got into your flying egg having never flown before, jumped between you and Serpent Head to stave off disaster, and threatened Sparrow to find your Conjurer. Now's your turn."

"There're things you don't need to know. But I never deceived you."

"In a true partnership, you don't get to decide what I need to know. That's something you do with an underling. Prove to me I'm not just a useful dirt dweller to use and discard."

Hoff held my stare unblinkingly for a few heartbeats before relenting. "What do you want to know?"

I closed my fingers around the pill to steady my shaking hand. "What did the Conjurer steal?"

"It's not what you think," Hoff said quietly, her voice barely audible over the wind whistling through dead branches. "The nanites he stole protect the newly transmigrated from the perils of life in orbit—cellular damage caused by cosmic radiation, bone loss, cardiovascular irregularities—until they're ready for new bodies immune to those problems."

I popped the pill into my mouth and swallowed. It left a bitter aftertaste. "What else are you not telling me?"

Hoff ignored me and marched off into the faintly luminescent forest in a cloud of mechanical noises.

We searched the forest on foot, our progress punctuated by the wheezing and whistling wind, the concert of Hoff's exoskeleton, and the crunches and squishes of rotting debris and frozen twigs in the snow-covered underbrush.

Hoff peered into the darkness, seeing what no human eye could. Midstride, she grabbed my arm and whispered, "Thermal gradient ahead."

A hundred meters later, we glimpsed a log cabin nestled in a copse of dead cedars. Its roof sagged under accumulated snow and a muted orange glow spilled from between the planks of its boarded windows.

"He's here, the Conjurer. This close, I can detect his exoskeleton," Hoff said. "Please wait here. I don't know if he's armed, and I can't neutralize him and protect you at the same time." She didn't wait for me to respond, and started trudging through the snow towards the cabin's back door.

Every time I thought I'd peeled back her last façade, Hoff surprised me with another shell inside. Secrets within secrets, manipulations masquerading as truths. Whether there was someone I'd recognize as human at the core of that matryoshka doll, I didn't know, but I was done trusting. I had to see for myself.

The moment Hoff moved out of sight, I set off towards the front of the cabin and didn't stop until I'd mounted the low-rise porch's warped wooden steps and peeked inside. The cabin was dark beyond a circle of light shed by a flameless lantern of an unfamiliar design set on the floor. Facing it was an Angel in an exoskeleton, not unlike Hoff's, sitting on his haunches by a pile of soiled rags. The door creaked when I pushed it open and the Conjurer looked up at me.

I'd seen that all-too-human vacant gaze of despair before. In the eyes of a mother cradling the lifeless body of her starved infant, or a child staring uncomprehending at the remains of his parents on a pyre. Crying tearlessly and swaying gently to a morose tune only the bereaved could hear, an insistent yet futile attempt at self-soothing.

The Conjurer's blood-smeared fingers trembled, every flutter amplified by his exoskeleton. As I approached, the mess on the floor resolved to a vague human outline that had somehow been turned inside out. The stench caught in my throat like a punch to the gut. I bent to the side and retched.

He muttered something, repeating it at the threshold of audibility. I wiped my mouth on the back of my cold hand and leaned closer as Hoff walked in through the back door.

Dazed, the Conjurer moaned endlessly, "I killed her. I killed her."

I sat on the porch steps, lost in thought and breathing hard to purge the stench from my nose. The more I thought about it, the more I realized it was the Conjurer's raw grief that unmoored me. It was all too human. Was it only the newly transmigrated who retained these shadows of their former self? How long before even those echoes faded? Did Hoff feel anything at all anymore, and if not, was she still human?

When the porch floorboards creaked behind me, I summoned my composure with hurried gulps of frigid air, brushed the freezing moisture off my cheeks, and looked up to find Hoff standing over me. "What'll become of him?"

"He stole restricted technology and inflicted great harm with it. That love motivated him won't excuse his transgression."

"He couldn't have known it'd kill her." I felt sure any punishment the Angels had in store would pale next to his loss.

Hoff bobbed her head, the gesture both oppressively familiar and discomfiting in its otherness. "The nanites are lethal when administered under gravity. Instead of healing her ills, they unraveled her body at a molecular level. They were never meant for surface dwellers. He should've known better."

I nodded, not because I agreed, but because I could imagine how he felt. He hadn't wanted the wife the Angels had rejected to die alone. He either hadn't known the nanites would be lethal on the surface or hadn't believed it. Who could blame him, after a life filled of Angel half-truths and outright lies? I figured becoming an Angel himself wasn't enough to erase that ingrained suspicion we all shared of our sky-dwelling exploiters and benefactors.

I pulled myself up and brushed the snow off my clothes, puzzled at how dry and warm Hoff appeared inside her protective cage.

We both stood staring into the darkness, taking in both the darkness we faced and that behind us. Hoff broke the spell, speaking softly, barely louder than the whistling wind and shivering branches. "Wish we'd met under better circumstances. Still, we make quite the team, you and I."

I smiled a little at that, having no idea what other circumstance she imagined would have brought an Angel and someone like me together. "Until the next time one of yours goes missing, then."

"It doesn't have to be. *Inspector Laila Aboud* has a certain ring to it, don't you think?"

I groaned. "Please tell me all of this wasn't just a recruitment test."

Geraldine shook her head, the exoskeleton straining like a laden truck attempting a steep hill. She reached out an arm and the exoskeleton peeled back, blooming around her hands. Her skin was warm and soft against my frigid hands. "Must you suspect every motive, distrust everyone?"

"Occupational hazard, I'm afraid." *Not to mention your duplicitous manipulations*, I thought to myself, but held my tongue.

"Well? Would you like to become an *Angel*?" Hoff said, as if proposing, hastening to add with a slight nod towards the cabin, "The proper way."

"It's a big leap to leave everyone and everything I know behind."

Hoff bobbed her head. "It's not obligatory. In time, your priorities will change. Your past will fade into the deepest recesses of your memory, until it's beyond recall. It works out for the best in the end."

"It didn't for the Conjurer."

"And see where it led him."

I shook my head. Angels were a cautionary tale, not a model to emulate. No matter how hard they tried, they'd never be truly human again. *We* had to survive if there were to be humans walking the Earth in another thousand years.

Hoff smirked a little. "You're telling me you've never thought about it?"

Gently, I reclaimed my hands from Geraldine's and shoved them into my pockets. "I don't think there's anyone who hasn't, but fantasizing with my feet planted firmly on the ground is not the same as throwing it all away to chase the unknown." I was sorely tempted to say yes, if for no other reason than for a chance to see that diamond noose again, to revel in its brilliance before, left unchecked, it choked the life out of our species.

"You won't regret it, trust me."

Hoff's palpable excitement left me unsure how she'd react if I flatly declined. "Could I think about it?"

Despite the puzzled surprise etched on her face, Hoff's smile lingered. "Take as long as you need."

I nodded and looked away, my eyes drawn upwards to the starless darkness enveloping the Earth. I knew I'd never belong up there, any more than the Conjurer had. I belonged to the earth. To those used and forgotten. I didn't count myself one of Earth's best or brightest; I'd never be a fusion physicist or a horticulturist, or even a revolutionary, but perhaps, when the time came, I could do my small part.

See Ramez Yoakeim's story "The Diamond Noose" online at Metaphorosis.
If you liked it, leave a comment. Authors love that!
Remember to subscribe to our e-mail updates so you'll know when new stories are posted.

About the story

The core idea came from a news report about proposed changes to immigration selection criteria, basing it more on skills and qualifications and less on family connections. I started thinking about what that meant for those selected in their new foreign homes, for those they leave behind, and for the people who yield their best and brightest to other invariably more affluent and powerful people. I relied on my personal experience as the child of immigrants and an immigrant myself later in life to navigate what proved to be a complex dilemma.

A question for the author

Q: What is your favourite part of writing?

A: When I'm writing, anything is possible, including giving this instinctive introvert a voice extending far beyond anything achievable on my own. It's also a sort of therapy as I inhabit a multitude of characters, each with their own backstories, perspectives, and conflicts, and in so doing discover otherwise inaccessible nuances of human motivation. Lastly, what better escapism from the present with its threats of war and cataclysm than the future, not because that future will necessarily be any better (we can hope, but then again we have history), but because then, at least in our imagination, humanity has any future at all!

About the author

Born in Egypt, raised in Australia, and now living with his husband in the United States, Ramez Yoakeim spent his whole life adapting. A one-time engineer and educator, Ramez's work favors the darker side of SFF but mostly he writes about hope.

yoakeim.com, @RamezYoakeim

The Conch Shell

Elizabeth Raphael

Mira sat on the couch, clutching the conch shell tightly in her hands. Her back had gone stiff and her legs were sweating against the soft leather of the couch, but she dared not move—not yet. If she stayed there just a little longer, she told herself, surely she would remember why she was holding the shell. Despite everything, she still had faith in the power of her mind. All she needed to do was focus, and with a bit of time, it all would fall into place. She took several slow breaths, the kind she had learned in the yoga class that Thalia insisted she take, and waited for the moment to return to her. It did not.

Mira let out a breath in a huff, the loops of her ever-present pearl necklace clinking softly against each other with the motion. She had never been one to wallow in self-pity, but she could feel it now, coiling itself around her body and threatening to pull her down. Her late husband had once told her that her ability to find the smallest sliver of positivity in any situation was a big part of what made him fall for her, but at the moment, she felt far removed from that version of herself. She could see no silver lining to dementia. She was being stolen away, piece by piece, and there was nothing she could do about it. Logically, she knew it was an indiscriminate condition, but the raw emotional side of her still wanted to throw herself to the ground like a toddler having a tantrum and wail about the unfairness of it all. She had done everything right, everything that was supposed to ensure that she aged as gracefully as possible. She had eaten a balanced diet, enjoying her food but not overindulging—or, rather, over-indulging only on special occasions. She had stayed physically active, swimming a daily mile until her early sixties, when arthritis seized her shoulders and she was forced to switch to walking. She had never been as graceful on land as in the water, but she had taken to walking regardless. As long as she was up and active, she was happy.

The cruelest bit of all, or so it felt to her, was that she had been just as diligent with her cognitive health. In addition to her daily crossword, she periodically took up disparate hobbies so she'd gain diverse skills—everything from archery to rangoli. She had walked through life with a tenacious optimism that everything would turn out OK, and it hadn't.

Fighting off a wave of despair, Mira tightened her grip on the shell. She knew it was risky to stay in this pose. That new helper of hers—Kylee, Mira recalled after only a brief hesitation, Kylee with a double 'e' at the end—was due any minute now. If Kylee came in and saw Mira frozen like this, she would immediately call Thalia to let her know that her mother was having another episode. Thalia would then leave work straight away and drive the nearly 100 miles that separated them, likely using that time to work on a new pitch for persuading Mira to move into a retirement home.

Mira's mouth twisted at the thought. Thalia was too young to fully understand the situation. To her, it was simple: Mira's dementia was progressing—a fact that Mira herself could not deny —and therefore, she shouldn't live alone. Why not be part of a community full of people who were going through the same sort of thing, cared for by workers trained for that very purpose? Mira shook her head. How easy it was for Thalia to come to such conclusions when it wasn't her being forced to leave the home she had lived in for nearly 60 years. It wasn't her being expected to leave behind the living room where her child had taken her first steps, the library full of her carefully curated books, swimming trophies, and assorted treasures, the bedroom that she had shared with her husband for 54 wonderful, too-short years. No, it certainly wasn't Thalia's freedom and privacy being stripped bare. It wasn't her world being compressed down into one personality-devoid room.

Mira's pulse thrummed an angry staccato inside of her, each beat a warning. She had to stop getting angry like this, she chastised herself. It wasn't good for her, and it wasn't fair to Thalia. Thalia's single-mindedness could be frustrating, true, but she was a good woman and a good daughter. She was just a worrier, as her father had been. There was no ill intent behind this retirement home crusade of hers, Mira knew; there was only love. Thalia had harbored concerns about Mira living alone after her father's passing, and Mira's short-lived disappearance six months back had unfortunately given meat to those fears. If Thalia didn't have to travel so often for work, she undoubtedly would have cleared out a bedroom in her condo and convinced Mira to move in long ago. As matters stood, this was her way of trying to keep Mira safe.

A cell phone trilled loudly from the coffee table, interrupting Mira's line of thought. Prying a hand from the shell, she slid her turquoise reading glasses down in place from the top of her head and leaned over, squinting at the name flashing across the small screen. It was Thalia. A smile quirked Mira's mouth. It was almost as if Thalia had sensed Mira's train of thought and waited until she meandered into a more positive frame of mind to call. Thalia had always been an intuitive child.

Mira picked up the phone with her free hand. "Hello, dear," she said, her back popping as she leaned back against the couch. "I was just thinking about you."

"Hey, hey. How's my favorite mother today?" There was a faintly echoey quality to Thalia's voice, which told Mira that she was on speaker phone. That was not unusual. Thalia was usually doing at least ten things at once. At the beginning of her daughter's career, Mira had been surprised by how busy the life of a marine biologist was, but she was well used to it at this point.

"Your favorite mother is fine." Mira supposed that was a partial truth. Her eyes flicked towards the mahogany grandfather clock that stood solemnly in the corner. "It's early for a call from you. Late lunch?"

Thalia clicked her tongue, a nervous gesture that had started when she was around eight. Nowadays, it indicated that Thalia was particularly worried about Mira's health. "No, Mom," Thalia began carefully. "I'm leaving on my trip to Mexico today. We got the grant to go to Lake Xochimilco and study the axolotls. I'll be gone for a month."

Mira muttered several choice curses inside her head—phrases that Thalia would have been shocked to hear, had they actually slipped out of her mother's mouth. "I know all of that, Thalia," she lied. "I just thought you left tomorrow."

There was a brief, weighted pause. "Oh. Yeah. This trip has been such a long time in the making, it is hard to believe it's finally here." A horn honked faintly in the background. "Ugh—this traffic." Thalia tsked. "I thought by leaving early, I'd get ahead of it all."

"It's tourist season. Rush hour is every hour."

Thalia snorted. "That's true. So"—her voice took on a tone of practiced ease—"how are you doing today?"

"You already asked that, love."

"I know, I'm just..." Thalia clicked her tongue. "I applied for this grant before everything happened, and it's such a long trip. I don't know. Maybe it's not the right time."

"Thalia—" Mira tried to interject, but Thalia seemed not to hear her.

"I'd like to be there to get things going, so I could always go and then leave after a week or two. Dr. Slater is more than qualified to handle everything on his own. Well, on his own with all of the research assistants. He'd be fine. I'm superfluous, really."

"THALIA," Mira's voice was loud and firm. "You are not now, nor have you ever been superfluous. This trip has been your dream since you were a child, and it's your hard work that made it happen. You will go on this trip, all four weeks of it, and you won't think of me at all while you're there. That's final."

"Oh, Mom." Mira could hear the smile in Thalia's voice. "How could I not think of you? If it weren't for you, I wouldn't be a marine biologist. You taught me everything I know."

"Ohh, pshh," Mira said dismissively, just as her cheeks flushed with pleasure. "I think your professors probably did that."

"Not really. You knew that the Greenland shark was the oldest vertebrate over the bowhead whale before that research was even published. That bit really impressed my 'Intro to Marine Bio' class. I think Professor Gruber thought I was a witch," Thalia laughed. "Though witchcraft is as good of an explanation as any. Your knowledge of the ocean has always bordered on the supernatural."

"I read a lot of books, love. That's hardly supernatural."

"True, but that doesn't fully explain—"

"So," Mira interrupted, pivoting the conversation. There was an explanation, she knew, but of course she couldn't remember what it was. Thalia didn't need to know that, though. "You mentioned that a Dr. Slater will be on this trip. Is he that handsome British fellow we ran into at that Cuban restaurant?"

"He is," Thalia answered suspiciously.

"He's the one with the wife and three daughters, right?"

"Hmm—no, Dr. Slater is single. I'm not sure who you're thinking of," Thalia said before picking up on her mother's comfortingly familiar matchmaking attempt. "Oh, wait. I see what you did there. I tripped right into that one."

Mira smiled. "Your old mother still has a few tricks. I know you'll be busy on this trip, but hey, there's a lot of hours in the day."

"Duly noted." Thalia clicked her tongue. "So you're really all right? Really? I worry about you all alone."

"I won't be alone. I have Kylee, I have that yoga class—I'll be fine."

"But you seemed fine before your disappearance." Thalia took a deep breath. "You know, Coastal Gardens is really more of an apartment complex than a retirement home. You'd have your own space—"

"I'll be fine. That's not going to happen again," Mira said, willing her voice to sound more assured than she felt.

Thalia clicked her tongue. "OK, mom. I'll still have my cell. So you can call me, and I'll call you, of course. Let's see... " Thalia drummed her fingers on the steering wheel. "My itinerary is on your fridge, but I'll text it to Kylee so she has it, too." She clicked her tongue. "I guess that's everything."

"Have a good trip, love."

"Bye, mom. I'm only a phone call away if you need me for anything. I love you."

"Love you, too."

The smile slowly faded from Mira's face as she set her cell back down and wrapped her freed hand back around the shell. Her disappearance. It always came back to that. It was a specter that she could never escape from, one determined to wreck her past and present. There had been mental lapses before then, but that blasted episode was when it really became a problem. Cruelest of all, the events of that day remained a mystery.

Familiar feelings of frustration and fear rose in Mira as she once again tried to remember what had happened the day of her disappearance. She had eaten her usual breakfast—soft-boiled egg on a piece of wheat toast—then dressed in her exercise clothes and set out for her daily walk. After that, she recalled nothing. Nothing until nearly two days later, when she was found on a beach nearly 65 miles away by a group of early morning surfers, soaking wet but otherwise fine.

Shades of that day occasionally came to her. They bore no true form but gave an overall feeling of peace. However she had gotten there and whatever she had been doing, she had not been afraid. The fear had come later, when she was being subjected to every test possible in the hospital. On the beach, she had felt safe.

Mira sat up straight, scooting to the edge of the couch. The beach. That day. That's when she had gotten the conch shell, wasn't it? Yes, she realized with sudden clarity, excitement buzzing through her. She had argued with the EMTs—they hadn't wanted her to bring it in the ambulance—but Mira had refused to get in without it. She kept insisting she had found it, it was important, and she wasn't going to give it up.

But no, that wasn't quite right, was it? Mira's nails drummed against the rough exterior of the shell as she thought. That was what she had told the EMTs, but she had already started to forget by then, hadn't she? Forget that she had not found it; it had been given to her. Yes, that was it! It had been given to her by someone she knew, someone she loved, someone she had not seen in a long time. Mira's right leg bounced in time to the drumming of her fingers as the moment solidified further. She could almost picture their face, but the image was distorted, as if viewed through a warped mirror.

The front door burst open in a flurry of noise and motion. Mira reflexively leapt to her feet, nearly dropping the shell in the process. A small blonde woman—Kylee—stepped through the entranceway a few seconds after.

"Sorry, sorry!" Kylee said, bowing her head in apology. "That wind is nuts! The storm must be coming sooner than they said." She shut the door behind her with visible effort. "That door got away from me."

"So it would seem!" Mira's voice was faint, her heart still pounding from the surprise.

Kylee quickly finger-combed her windblown tresses and pulled the hair back into a low ponytail, securing it with a black scrunchie that she slid off of her wrist. "Your doorbell is broken, by the way. I was out there ringing it for, like, five minutes."

Mira chose to avoid the obvious question as to why Kylee didn't just knock on the door. Instead, she tsked in sympathy.

"I told Thalia I didn't need one of those camera bells. The more fancy parts an item has, the more likely they are to break."

Kylee slung her purse down on the coffee table. "No biggie—I'll just give that handyman of yours a call. Hopefully he'll be able to come out soon and do some troubleshooting. Is his card still on the fridge?"

"Should be." Mira settled herself back down on the couch.

"Good. I'll put on a pot of coffee while I'm in there. After being tossed about in that wind, I could use a warming up. Want a cup?"

"Mmm—add a splash of chocolate milk to mine."

Kylee raised her brows. "Oh, that sounds good! I'll have to try it, too." She gestured towards Mira's lap. "Cool shell, by the way! Doing some dusting?"

"Oh!" Mira looked down. She had forgotten that she had been holding the conch. "I was...admiring it." That was right, wasn't it?

"I can see why. It's a beauty!" Kylee reached out and stroked the smooth inner curve of the shell. "Look at those colors—just like a sunrise! When I was 10, my aunt went deep-sea fishing off the coast of the Florida Keys and brought me back one of these. She ate the conch, and I got the shell. I thought it was the prettiest thing in the world—almost as pretty as yours. Anyway, it broke during a move just two years after I got it. Military life, you know? I was crushed. It was the star of my shell collection." The corners of Kylee's mouth turned down ever so slightly, an odd sight on her normally impossibly cheerful face.

A pang of sympathy struck Mira. She knew that to most, Kylee's story would seem inconsequential. But as a woman with more than one collection, she knew it to be quite serious, indeed.

Mira patted Kylee's hand. "I'm sorry about that, dear." Mira took care to make sure that her tone sounded serious and respectful.

Kylee met Mira's eyes and flashed a grateful smile. "Thanks. You know what's silly? Every night before bed—when I still had the shell, obviously—I used to hold it up to my ear so I could hear the ocean. I'd sit there like that for at least five minutes." She chuckled. "That's funny—I haven't thought about that in forever. I was an odd kid. Memories..."

Kylee shook her head, amused with herself, then disappeared into the kitchen.

"Memories," Mira echoed in a voice barely loud enough to even be considered a whisper.

Mira waited until she heard the coffee pot start bubbling and the murmur of Kylee chatting with the handyman before she began. Supporting the shell with both hands, she raised it up with a slow reverence and placed it carefully against her ear.

Mira gasped. At the sound of the soft woosh from inside the shell, it all came back—who she really was, where she'd really come from. She remembered her whole life, which had begun beneath the waves. Warm and weightless, she would ride the currents and tides, powered by the undulation of her tail.

Oh, her tail! It had been beautiful, a glistening gradient of blue and green scales that melded seamlessly with the soft, pliable skin at her waist. Her family all had the same colors on their tails, though arranged in different patterns.

Oh! She had a family down there—a large family! Parents, six sisters, and four times as many aunts, uncles, and cousins. She had loved them fiercely, and they had loved her in return. It had broken her heart to leave them behind, but she had known then, deep in the marrow of her bones, that part of her destiny lay on the land. As with the other mermaids who had made the choice before her, she had been granted the opportunity to leave the water with the understanding that when her human form was nearing its end, she would return it and her soul to the sea. Far from being an unwelcome caveat, she had taken comfort in the knowledge that some day, she would return.

Mira gasped yet again as it all connected. That day, her disappearance—she had not had an episode. She had been called to that beach! One of her sisters—Adria, beautiful Adria with the long black hair that curled like no one else's in their family—had been waiting there in the waters for her. She had aged at approximately one quarter of the rate that Mira had on land, but it was the kindness radiating from Adria that truly made her beautiful. Mira would have been content just to gaze upon her sister again, but Adria had called her there to give her an important gift—the shell. Not just an object of beauty, it was a talisman designed to help bring Mira back to herself.

Tears pooled in the corner of Mira's mouth as they streamed down her face, their salty taste carrying with it the echoes of the sea. Her heart bloomed with a joy beyond words. She had lost much over the years, and she knew that even this moment might soon slip away from her.

But right now, she remembered.

See Elizabeth Raphael's story "The Conch Shell" online at Metaphorosis.
If you liked it, leave a comment. Authors love that!
Remember to subscribe to our e-mail updates so you'll know when new stories are posted.

About the story

I often write either to escape reality or process it, and with "The Conch Shell", it turned out to be a bit of both. My grandmother, who served as inspiration for this story, has late stage Alzheimer's. She has sadly forgotten most of her life, but odd fragments come through, often paradoxically. For example, she doesn't remember having children or grandchildren, but she remembers being at my wedding. This got me thinking about the significance of what moments in our lives stick with us, and the pain that comes with forgetting.

At its core, "The Conch Shell" is an exploration of aging and memory. Older people are too often marginalized by society, and this is magnified when the person has dementia. In creating the character of Mira, I aimed to put the voice, and a bit of dignity, back where it belonged.

Though Mira's journey is unique to her situation, there is a wider truth that I hope comes across. Whether from dementia or the chaos of life, it is all too easy to lose bits of yourself. Some parts may be impossible to regain, but others will come back to you if you just reach out and grab them. And maybe, just maybe, what you get back will be magic.

A question for the author

Q: What is the first/most recent book that you lost sleep reading/thinking about?

A: I have a vivid imagination and an obsessive personality so I frequently lose sleep over books, but one of my most memorable reads so far this year is *Hell Bent*, the second book in Leigh Bardugo's *Alex Stern* series. Much like the first book, *Ninth House*, *Hell Bent* manages to be equal parts thought-provoking and positively bonkers. It's an unflinching look at class, gender, and racial conflict. It's an exploration of the transformative power of trauma. It shines a light at the darkness that lies within us all. It does all of that, while also having naked demons, ghosts, frat boy vampires, and other similarly attention-grabbing plot devices and twists. I laughed, I cried, I said 'whaaaat' and 'nooooo' outloud to myself several times while reading. Truly, *Hell Bent* is a standard-setting masterpiece of dark academia.

About the author

Elizabeth Raphael enjoys arranging letters in pleasing patterns. She is most at peace in libraries and bookstores, where she whittles away many moments gazing wordlessly uponst ink on pages. In writing as in reading she dabbles in many genres, but speculative fiction has her heart.

ElizabethRaphael.com

Anamnesis

Karl El-Koura

At first she thought the white cloud floating across the blue sky had an interesting shape, almost like the face of a man.

Her head resting on her intertwined fingers, Allie lay stretched out on her long beach towel, which had been imprinted with multicolored stars and nebulae against black space. She let her gaze drift to the sun, so bright and beautifully yellow, then down to her friend Marcia.

"What's that thing called," Allie said, "when you see something that looks human?"

Marcia had been posing, more than relaxing, her torso lifted on her elbows, one leg drawn up; trying to catch the eye of the boys chasing the waves while pretending she didn't notice them. She shrugged, but answered: "Pareidolia."

Allie nodded, then returned her gaze languidly up the sky, back to the cumulus cloud. Except it wasn't just vaguely suggestive of human features anymore. She sat up. The cloud had taken definite shape; as if some cosmic god had stuck his nose into the mist, which had molded around his face.

"Marcia," she said, pointing. "Look."

Reluctantly Marcia tore her gaze off the muscular boys. "I don't see anything," she said, then began to hum.

"What are you—?" The rest of the question died on Allie's lips. The tune reminded her of something. Of someone? "What song is that?" she said finally.

Marcia stared. "What song?"

"The one you were humming just now."

"I wasn't." And then, as if the question had reminded her of it, Marcia took up the tune once more, the melody beginning again in her throat, escaping through her closed mouth.

Allie shut her eyes, tried to place the melody. After a few minutes, her mind refusing to give up the answer despite, or perhaps because of the forcefulness of her concentration, she opened her eyes again and set aside that puzzle for the moment to focus on another: the face in the cloud. The oval shape, the dimpled chin, the thin lips, the protruding arrow of a nose, the round eyes a little too close to each other, the thick eyebrows and bald head.

"I know him," she said.

Marcia stopped humming long enough to say "Who?" and then resumed the song.

The answer was there, but just beyond her mental reach. She could sense it, like something tucked away in a closet she couldn't open. "I'm going home," she said, standing.

Still propped up on her elbows, Marcia stopped humming, said, "Okay," then began the song again.

Allie bent over to pick up her towel, but realization broke through: *my God, it's a lullaby.*

Had someone sung it to her as a baby?

Now that she tried, though, she realized with rising panic that she couldn't remember, not that far back ... and not anything at all, as if a shroud had been cast over her memories.

"Marcia, I don't feel so good," she said, before she fell forward ... and fell and fell, because the hard, gravelly sand wasn't there to catch her. Instead she tumbled into one of the black empty spaces of her towel, slipping past the interstellar clouds, distant stars rising around her like columns of fire ... falling and falling in the endless void until she lost consciousness.

By developing a strict daily routine, Andrick Peret had been able to hold the loneliness at bay for almost a year.

First, he had to finish his breakfast before he allowed himself to check the distress signal. That early morning sliver of time was the second best part of his day, and it wasn't because the coffee (forbidden for so long) was delicious, better than any he'd ever had, or that he had his pick of a wide assortment of flash-frozen, vacuum-sealed breakfasts to choose from—sliced fruit, eggs soft- and hard-boiled, sausages, pancakes, waffles, all kinds of syrups and jams. After several weeks, even delicious food became commonplace; the novelty of popping off a tab and watching the coffee or food instantly heat up as air rushed in became routine even more quickly. No, he cherished that small stretch of time because he could eat his breakfast while anticipating the possibility that he'd walk into the small control room and find the blinking light had changed color.

Very soon after the crash, he'd created a subroutine that beamed out an SOS every hour, providing their location and status, and he'd wired it so that if a response came in at any point, a light on the dashboard would turn from red to green. A blinking green light meant that someone had acknowledged their signal throughout the night; maybe someone on their way to rescue them.

Every morning for eleven months, however, Andrick continued to see the light blinking the red distress color even before he'd entered the control room, its glow seeping out to tinge in crimson the gray metallic bulkheads. He still always went into the room to stare at the light. Then he would sit down in the cramped chair (the ship's captain had been more like the ship's entertainer, only rarely needing to visit this room; the real commanding and piloting were accomplished by various computer algorithms). From there, Andrick would review the previous day's diagnostic reports to make sure everything was fine throughout what remained of the *Pointed Star.*

The first few days after the crash—before he was forced to develop his sanity-saving daily routine—there had been a few things to look into or repair. By profession he was a chemist, but he'd gone to graduate school on Luna, and had worked part-time to support himself at one of the moon's space junkyards, fixing up old clunkers so they could be resold. And to supplement his out-dated knowledge, the ship had videos and instructions that could walk a reasonably handy person through fixing most things.

He'd skipped meals those first few days; he'd been too busy desperately looking for other survivors, then assessing and repairing the minimal damage in the remaining part of the ship. But once all of that was done, he'd instituted a regular schedule of lunches and dinners. It was good to have a routine, though he felt that these fancy dishes, some of them with labels displaying words he couldn't pronounce, were wasted on him, who ate without enthusiasm but to sustain himself—and, later, to fill the hours too.

Because lately, only very occasionally did he have anything to look into or fix. Hyperspace ships were made well, and with several redundancies built in. They were meant to last centuries without issue—so long as their safety protocols didn't catastrophically break down.

Which, of course, they had for the *Pointed Star.* As far as Andrick could reconstruct the accident, this was what had happened: only two light years into their outboard journey, the ship's hyperspace engine had tried to fold a section of space occupied by a solid mass, likely part of the asteroid they were now permanently attached to, causing an explosion. That was never supposed to happen, of course; and in the unlikely event that it ever did, secondary protocols were supposed to kick in and move them away from the impact area at full speed. Instead, not detecting anything amiss, the ship had powered up the propulsion engine to drive right through; except, instead of the hyperspace tunnel that would have resulted from folding a cube of near-vacuum, the ship had brought them head-first into the explosion. The bubble-shaped prow had burned up and the fish-tail-shaped stern had slammed into the asteroid, the heat fusing the two objects together—saving his and Alicia's life by sealing off the hull breach.

In those project-free days, there were ten to twelve hours before he could allow himself to settle into his makeshift cot in the closet he'd turned into a bedroom, and anticipate checking the light again in the morning.

But right before the end of each day came his actual favorite part: the slow walk down the corridor, usually from the control room, to the door of the 'stern' cabin, which was now the foremost part of the surviving half of the ship. There, for only fifteen minutes, he allowed himself to watch Alicia through the clear, narrow band running down the center of the mostly frosted glass door. Having the worst cabin on the ship had saved them; everything forward had been destroyed in the crash. Their room, which Alicia had won in a virtual reality contest, was tucked away at the rear with the supplies and storage and the never-visited control room, and had survived.

He allowed himself those precious minutes of watching Alicia, tucked up in her pod, then forced himself to turn around and head to the cot he'd made from used-up supply crates.

It was a good routine, and it helped many days go by. But after eleven months, he couldn't maintain it any longer.

Marcia posed, more than relaxed, on her beach towel, her poor arms holding up her torso, one of her legs drawn up, maybe to show off her knee or ankle or something. She watched the well-muscled boys run toward and then away from the waves, while pretending she didn't notice them.

Allie smiled and let her head fall back into her hands. Marcia could waste her vacation absorbed with boys if she wanted. Allie had come here to rest; she would spend her day on this towel, doing nothing at all; dozing, maybe, warmed by the sun and cooled by the gently blowing breeze. Maybe she would let herself be convinced to take a quick—

She pulled her hands out from under her head, pushed Marcia away. Except Marcia wasn't near enough to reach. And yet Allie would've bet the rest of the vacation that Marcia had run her fingers through Allie's hair.

"Did you just touch me?" she asked.

"Weird question," Marcia said, then began humming a song.

Allie's hand shot up to her head. She'd felt it again, this time a soft hand tucking a strand of hair behind her ear.

"You okay?" Marcia said, except it wasn't Marcia. A man stooped over her; a sad-looking man with a bald head and thick eyebrows. "You okay?" Marcia's voice asked while the man's thin lips moved.

Without waiting for her response, the man reached out his hand again, stroked Allie's hair.

Allie didn't pull away from him. She felt frozen between fear at the strangeness of the situation—and an even more bewildering sense of safety. Somewhere deep down, her mind recognized that man and knew he meant her no harm.

He hummed the familiar song as he tucked her hair behind her ear. When he was finished, he leaned back and popped out of existence, instantly replaced by her friend posing on her towel, as if she'd never left.

"Marcia?"

"You okay?" Marcia asked, without looking away from the boys in the water.

Allie stood, picked up her towel, and shook the sand off the vast cosmos with its many stars and nebulae.

And then, with sudden, strange insight, as if she'd already had this realization and then forgotten it, she recognized the song: a lullaby. But had someone sung it to her as a child?

Why couldn't she remember? She pushed down the rising sense of panic, forced herself to stay calm. She couldn't remember —now that she tried—any further back than this morning, when they'd left their beach-side hotel for the short walk along the pristine sand. Then, still forcing herself to evaluate her situation calmly, she thought: pristine white sand and pristine white clouds, clear blue water and clear blue sky; a golden sun she could stare into. Shouldn't staring into the sun hurt your eyes?

Of course it should—in the real world. *You're dreaming*, she simultaneously realized and yelled at herself. *Wake up!*

When his fifteen-year old daughter won two tickets aboard the Pointed Star, Andrick Peret initially insisted that she pass on the opportunity. But, much like her mother, Alicia had a way of pushing past any resistance he offered. Also like her mother, their daughter was an eternal optimist, who saw excitement and opportunity and adventure in everything, whereas he could only see risks, dangers, obstacles.

Alicia had placed first in some virtual reality space simulation obstacle course, winning the pair of tickets aboard one of the new pleasure-cruise hyperspace ships. Previously, hyperspace had been a road traveled only by governments, large research institutions and multiplanetary corporations, but now several smaller private companies were promoting elite tourism by way of hyperspace, allowing the rich and famous to go beyond the solar system—to be one of the first human beings to visit further and further into the galaxy.

Andrick had retired the previous December. His wife, Treanne, was hip-deep working on her third major exhibit of her art, which was to open a few weeks after the Pointed Star was scheduled to return. So, if Alicia wanted to go on this trip, she needed to convince her father to accompany her.

He'd put his daughter off, but the company rep needed an answer, yes or no, so they could move ahead or move on to the next person.

"Are we even sure this is legit?" he'd tried again, that Saturday morning when, casually over their weekend breakfast of pancakes and sausages, Alicia had asked if she could accept the prize.

His daughter didn't bother answering him with words; she just smiled her bright beam of optimism and nodded.

"Mmm-hmm," Andrick said. "And what about school?"

"Not to worry, father dear," she said. "We'd be a month away —total. I'll use it as my summer holidays."

"Not sure how safe it is," he mumbled.

"Hyperspace? Perfectly."

But hyperspace itself wasn't perfectly safe for human beings. Hyperspace engines, which operated by a sequential micro-folding of spacetime to traverse vast distances, had several benefits: micro-folding cost large but attainable amounts of energy and, importantly for him, time in hyperspace was non-relativistic, so people could travel those distances without their families having aged decades (or centuries) by their return. But dropping into and out of hyperspace had strange effects on the human mind: from harmless hallucinations to paranoid delusions. Which meant, these days, the explorers and adventurers and super-rich tourists visiting new stars and their systems got a nice long sleep while traveling through hyperspace, passing through the jumps in a personally-designed fantasy world rather than the haphazard daydreams and nightmares that had plagued the early adopters.

"I wouldn't even know—" He'd meant to say he didn't like virtual worlds, and would have a hard time deciding on one. But he recognized immediately what a lame excuse that was (and could imagine Alicia's thin eyebrows rising in silent, reproachful response). Instead, he stumbled on what he thought was a better excuse: "Your mom will miss us. She might need our help with the show."

Immediately he realized his mistake. Treanne, who had been watching the breakfast-table discussion with a bemused expression, had decided to stay out of it. But now he'd dragged her in.

"Mom?" Alicia said, turning to her.

"I'll be fine on the show," she said. "And of course I'll miss you both very much." He could tell from the tone of her voice what was coming next. "But I think I can survive a month."

Alicia turned her bright beam of a gaze back on him.

"Let me look into it," he said, then added ominously: "The details."

"Sure thing," Alicia said, finally digging into her breakfast.

He shot his wife a questioning glance. He hadn't expected Alicia to be put off again so easily—not without a firmer commitment from him. Treanne shrugged.

When they'd cleared the table, however, Alicia disappeared for a moment, then returned with a tablet, the contest rules already loaded on the paper-thin screen.

"Let's go over it together!" she said brightly.

He groaned, then insisted on making a second cup of tea first.

They returned to the table and she watched him eagerly as he read through the rules, taking occasional, thoughtful sips.

But every objection he uncovered, like a hopeful pig finding truffles in the earthen ground, evaporated under the glare of Alicia's unbridled enthusiasm.

Him: "There's a medical exam. You know I hate being poked and prodded."

Alicia, simply: "Yes, a free medical exam!"

Him, after reading further: "Ho, ho, look at this. 'Stern cabin!' We'll be in the smallest room, at the very butt of the ship! Next to the *engines*!"

Alicia: "We won't even know. We'll be in deep sleep! And when we get to Alpha Centauri, we'll spend most of our time in the same observation deck as everyone else."

Later—his eyes wide, and looking like a man who'd just discovered the smoking gun: "Each ticket on this thing costs as much as I made in a whole year of teaching! We'll be with a bunch of super-rich mucky-mucks!"

Alicia: "We'll make fun of them!"

A few more of his objections likewise melted under the glare of her undiminished excitement.

When he raised his head with his next semi-objection, Alicia said, staring at him fixedly, "Dad—we'll get to see Alpha Centauri's stars and planets with our own eyes. How many people can say they've done that?"

He couldn't bring himself to dash her excitement by resisting any longer.

But now, watching her in that induced semi-coma—exciting when it was a temporary part of the journey, but now as terrible as a life sentence—he wished with all of his heart that he'd been willing to break *hers*; that he had allowed the nagging, hesitant, risk-averse voice that had ruled his life until he'd met Treanne to put its oppressive foot down and squash the head of this stupid adventure.

He pushed that thought away. What was the point of driving himself crazy?

He tried not to think too much about Treanne, because doing so felt like staring at a gaping hole where his stomach should be.

Andrick mostly had great discipline. In university, after he'd drunk two full pots of coffee while staying up late to finish a paper, and made his heart beat so fast he thought he would die, he'd vowed never to have another cup. And he'd lived up to that promise.

Until he'd woken up to alarm bells, stumbling out of his pod, not fully conscious yet but registering that something bad had happened, or was happening. In a daze, he made sure Alicia was safe and still sleeping in her own pod, then he exited their room and realized that the forward half of the ship was missing, a brown wall of cold craggy rock where the door to the next corridor should've been.

Normally, a trained technician had to pull someone out of the medically-induced deep sleep that minimized cognitive side-effects when traveling through hyperspace. Then each person was shuffled to the medical room for a complete physical scan. Complications could develop from being prone for so long, even with the constant electrical stimulation provided by the sleep pod. Andrick catastrophized as a matter of course, but it wasn't strictly his own demise that concerned him. If something fatal had gone wrong deep inside his body during the long sleep, what would happen to Alicia?

He had focused on the immediate mission he'd set for himself: donning an Extravehicular Mobility Unit, or EMU, to search the asteroid on the incredibly slim chance that anyone else had survived, returning to the ship only for a little bit of sleep before fortifying himself with several cups of coffee and heading back out. It took four days to conclude what should have been evident from the beginning, that he and Alicia were the only survivors. By then, though, he'd made two discoveries: his body had survived the plunge into and climb out of induced sleep without anything worse than a few cramps and occasional muscle spasms, which soon resolved themselves. And, distracted with his work, he'd been drinking coffee without any adverse effects—so perhaps, he thought, a little bit of the poison wouldn't sting. After that, he'd allowed himself one cup each day, with breakfast.

But eleven months later, he'd lost his resolve with a different resolution: never to enter his and Alicia's cabin. He didn't know if Alicia in her induced dream state could see or hear him, but the crash alarm had jostled *him* awake, so he thought it was possible. The last thing he wanted was for her to wake up too. Well—the last thing he *told* himself he wanted ... the truth was that he would've traded all the coffee in the universe for a chance to hear her laugh again. He couldn't do that to her, though; in the dreamlike simulation, she had friends (not real ones, but she didn't know that) and a vivid world to experience. He couldn't pull her out of that to face reality, the rear end of a busted spaceship her entire world and him her only companion. Better she be in the blissful dream-world until ... what? He didn't know how to finish that thought. For now he focused only on his conviction that it was better she pass the time in the fantasy she'd picked for herself. Better for her to live in that dream-moment, unaware of their predicament or of anything beyond the fantasy world itself (a necessary limitation of the technology, since without the suppression of conscious memory, the mind would reject the dream and force the person to wake up prematurely).

Day after day, he accepted that he could only watch her face through the narrow band in the glass door (the pod covered up to her neck like a blanket, so it could discretely both feed her body and flush away its waste, as well as electrically stimulate muscles to prevent atrophy). Despite the translucent crown of needles on her head, she looked still and peaceful.

When his resolve to stay out finally broke, it snapped quietly. He found himself inside their cabin one day, his heart stirring at the unobstructed view of his daughter's face. Immediately, he rushed out, and kept out for days—weeks. Then one day he was inside their cabin again, but she hadn't woken or stirred, so he stayed. Then, on another day, he sat down beside her pod, out of view, reading quietly to himself. Then, later, he found himself reading out loud to her, like he had when she was an infant. Then just lightly touching her cheek with the back of his fingers, like he'd done when she'd finally fallen asleep, usually before he'd finished the story. Then he caught himself stroking her hair. Each step had emboldened him for the next.

A few days later, sitting in the part of the storeroom he called 'the cafeteria', making his small, delicious cup of coffee last as long as possible, he learned the terrible mistake he'd made. He'd been so used to near-total silence that the sound of screaming initially made him jump from the table, his heart rate sky-rocketing, looking around helplessly, furiously. Air escaping from a new breach in the hull? Then his brain sorted the echo of that sound: it had been Alicia's strained voice. He'd woken her up after all, then, called her out of her pleasant fantasy world into cold, ugly reality.

He burst into their cabin and found Alicia had pushed away the hard cover of her pod. She was sitting up, staring at the crown of needles in her hand, angry red cat's claw scratch marks on her forehead from where she'd ripped off the device.

"I couldn't get it off," she croaked, her long-unused vocal chords still straining under the effort to speak. "I started panicking."

"It's off now," he said, gently.

A faltering smile finally broke through. "I'm okay, Dad. I'm okay. It was … not what I thought it would be like." Her voice still sounded strange and pained, but her regular cadence, the rapid cascade of words, was returning. "And they really need to work on the whole waking-up part. That was *not* pleasant." Finally she noticed something in his expression. "Dad?"

"In a minute, darling," he said. "Get out of that pod and get dressed, but wait for me here. I'll get you a glass of water. Are you hungry?"

She shook her head. "What's going on?"

"Okay. Just water. Wait for me here."

He hurried out of the room before she could stop him. He needed time to think, to organize his words.

But when he returned holding the unsealed bottle of water, he still didn't know what to say. Alicia had gotten dressed, and had brushed her hair, and now sat waiting for him on the edge of the pod, which she'd converted into a regular bed.

"Something bad happened," she said, accepting the bottle.

He sat beside her and, staring ahead, told her about waking up to the alarm, determining that everyone else had perished in the crash, setting up the distress signal ... which had gone unanswered for almost a year now. "I'm sorry, honey," he finished, finally turning to look at her.

Her face had paled. He indicated the water, and she forced the bottle up to her lips and took the smallest sip before bringing it down again and saying, "Dad—it's not your fault."

"I'm sorry about waking you up. I did, didn't I?"

"I started seeing you in my dream. Hearing your voice. But I didn't know it was you. You touched my hair?"

"I convinced myself it wouldn't wake you."

She hopped off the bed, suddenly energized, the water sloshing in the bottle and some spilling onto the ground. "You should've woken me up right away!" Alicia wiped up the spilled water with the toes of her socks. "I could've helped you."

Andrick stared at the bulkhead where it met the overhead. "At first I wanted to know what the situation was. I wanted to make sure we were safe. Then I set up the distress beacon and I thought I should let you sleep until we got rescued. I didn't want to wake you up to this—"

"And if we didn't get rescued? You would've let me sleep forever? Until I died? Or you died?"

He didn't answer. But he didn't need to. He'd spent the last year so terrified he'd accidentally force her to leave the comfort of her dream world that he'd never imagined Alicia would be upset with him for *not* waking her up.

She paced the small room, marching up and down its length as if a sentry on duty. He had the same tic; he needed to move his body to work his brain.

"How about some breakfast?" he ventured after watching her cross the room a half-dozen times.

She stopped short. "I have questions. Honest answers only!"

"Okay," he said.

"Is there enough food and water?"

"The storeroom wasn't harmed. We won't starve, even if we live to be a hundred each."

"Oxygen, energy, heat—things like that. How long before we run out?"

"You don't have to worry about that. The engines, the batteries, life support ... none of that was harmed. That isn't the issue."

"What's the issue?"

"It's just you and me, darling." He studied the bulkhead again, no longer able to meet his daughter's judgmental, still-angry stare. "That's it. For the rest of our lives."

"You said the engines are fine," she said, as if only then processing the words. "Can't we just—"

"Fly away?" He fought back a smile. "We lost half our ship ... more than half ... but we gained an asteroid thirty times its original size. The propulsion system can't handle that kind of mass."

"Can we cut ourselves free?"

The thought hadn't occurred to him, but he knew instantly it wouldn't work. They had access to hand-held welding torches, but they were very low-powered ... he and his daughter could spend an entire day out there and only lightly scratch the surface of the asteroid. "It would take a long time," he said. "Longer than we have." With a grunt, he pushed himself onto his feet. "We have the distress signal," he said, trying to inject into his voice a note of optimism that he didn't feel. "Our best bet is to wait for rescue."

"Our best bet is the signal that's gone unanswered for a year?"

He couldn't look at her. Yesterday, the thought that he'd be standing here having a conversation with his daughter would have filled him with joy, but now, in actuality, he was faced with his own failure—to get them out of this mess, yes, but also to keep her blissfully asleep so she wouldn't have to face the stark reality of their doomed lives.

He almost jumped at a touch; she had placed her hand on his arm. Before he could turn toward her, she pulled him into a tight embrace. Because her head reached only to his chest, and she spoke into it, he almost missed the words, but not the tone. Hadn't she been furious with him? Didn't she realize the severity—the hopelessness—of their situation? But, gently, she had said, "And that's why you need me."

"What?" he said, pulling her away from him.

"Dad!" *Oh, my wonderful dumb-dumb dad*, her tone said, that familiar, wonderful enthusiasm. "Are you kidding? There's *much* more we can do!"

If Alicia had slept for the next year ... or five, or ten, or a hundred, he didn't doubt that he would've kept on checking his distress signal every day. What else was there to do?

Well—Alicia had plenty of ideas.

He tried, over the next few days, to entertain her with games or movies or books (he'd screened them for her, he said; played or watched or read them all in advance during the long daytime hours, so he could point her toward the best ones) but his daughter only wanted to debate ideas. And, if he failed to convince her that one wouldn't work, they had to try it right away: silly things like literally carving 'SOS' in large letters into all sides of their potato-shaped asteroid (which took them three weeks in EMUs with the welding torches) to more serious endeavors like erecting a series of mirrors and debris painted with reflective paint to send their distress signal in many more directions.

He always poked around for holes in her ideas. Her job was to bring up wacky notions and his to knock them down, he told her. If he won, they took that day off and read books and watched movies, and if she won, they spent however long it would take to make her idea a reality, which usually meant putting on the many pieces of their EMU suits and trekking into the cold, ever-present night of space on the asteroid Alicia had named Potato Island.

She was so enthusiastic that it took him a long time—too long—to notice that something was wrong.

When Alicia was very young, probably five or six, she'd cut herself while playing in their living room. It was only when he saw drops of blood all over the floor that she showed him the deep gash across her thumb. A toy had fallen into the floor vent; she'd removed the register and fished around for her little figurine, slicing open her thumb in the process. But she hadn't wanted to stop playing, she said. Alicia's soaring optimism had its dark side; she could set aside concerns with terrible ease, assuming things would work themselves out.

Now she had hidden for weeks what he suspected was a blood clot that had formed in her left calf. She had begun to limp, and when he asked about it, she said her leg hurt a little. By the time he examined her, her calf had swelled up to twice the size of the other, the skin had turned red and very hot to the touch, and she screamed out in pain when he squeezed the muscle gently.

"Oh, darling," he said.

"It'll be fine," she said, shooing him away, jumping off her bed, but unable to stop herself from wincing. "Okay, so it hurts a lot, but it's far from my heart, right?"

The scanning equipment that could've confirmed the clot had burned up with the rest of the medical room; so had the medicines, like blood thinners, that could've helped.

"Any trouble breathing?" he said, looking up from the tablet.

"None!" she said, sucking back a deep lungful.

He didn't tell her what he'd just read: a warning about pulmonary embolism, which would happen if the clot dislodged and traveled up to the lungs. He doubted Alicia would give it much thought anyway, even though it was a fatal condition; she'd dismiss the possibility as an outside chance and get on with her life.

From then on, though, every cough, every clearing of the throat, made him whip his head around to stare at her. She finally told him he was making her feel like a time bomb he expected to go off, and she wanted him to stop. But her limp got worse.

And if she did develop an embolism? What could he do, without equipment, training, supplies?

The specific fear of something happening to Alicia before they could be rescued focused his mind, forced it into considering ideas he would've dismissed as reckless, fueled by the real pain he saw escaping onto the grimaces on her face whenever she walked and by the ever-present shadow of something even more serious pursuing her.

When it finally came to him in the middle of one sleepless night, the solution arrived with a freezing chill of recognition: yes, this was their best chance to get home quickly; and yes, this could be the last thing they tried, and in that case there'd be nothing recognizable left for any ship that did eventually find their wreckage. But sometimes, he told himself, ideas seem brilliant to a sleepy mind, and lose their luster in daylight. He half-hoped that would be the case, and went back to sleep.

He woke to the sounds of weeping. Alicia was sitting up in bed, left leg pulled up, gripping her calf as if desperately trying to hold off the pain with her hands.

"How bad?" he said, sitting up.

She shook her head but couldn't speak for a minute.

"There's something we can try," he said, speaking through a sudden constriction in his throat, "to get home."

"Let's hear it," she croaked, then stretched out her leg again and turned to face him.

He hesitated. "It's incredibly dangerous, actually. Really desperate. And even if it works, probably futile."

"Dad, spit it out."

He spat it out: "We fold the space just beyond Potato Island. Touching it only a little."

"But that would … cause an explosion."

"It would. A small one. But perhaps enough to propel us back toward Luna. We could, maybe, correct our direction by folding space at angles to Potato Island."

She'd been listening intently. "Okay, let's try it!" she said suddenly, excitement or hope, perhaps, chasing away the pain from her mind for a moment. He was glad for that, anyway.

"Let me lay out my concerns, okay?"

"I'm sold already," she said, shrugging playfully. "Why risk changing my mind?"

"Just listen. The hyperspace drive has safety protocols to make sure it doesn't send out a beam to fold space occupied by a significant mass. But I've spent a lot of time studying the ship and what went wrong, and I think the malfunction that caused us to crash into the asteroid will also allow us to blow up pieces of Potato Island."

"Great!"

"Not really. The protocols are there for a reason. There's a risk—a big one—that we'll miscalculate and blow ourselves up. Or cause another breach. Or—"

"Yes, yes. But how will we know unless we try?"

"Very funny."

"Two light years, Dad," she said, more seriously. "We can't let that small of a distance keep us from mom."

"Two light years is not …" He let the thought trail off as unnecessary to complete.

"Hold on, what's the rest of your idea? Just pushing ourselves toward Sol doesn't get us very far very fast, does it? It would take thousands of years…"

He waited for her to figure out.

"Ah!" she said, after a moment. "We carve away enough of Potato Island …"

"Yes," he said.

"… then we fold space properly and go through under propulsion! And *boom*, we're home."

"Well, hopefully not *boom*."

Alicia stepped onto the floor gingerly, testing her weight before trusting her leg, and hobbled over to sit beside him. "I know there are significant risks. But we should try. They would've found us by now. You're right: two light years is an immense distance. But if that's all that's keeping us from mom? Don't you think we *have* to try?"

"Okay," he said. "We'll try. Carefully!"

Carefully meant that Andrick first wanted to test the beam on cubes of empty space far away from them; when he'd satisfied himself, they tried folding the space barely touching the edge of Potato Island. He was right about the ship's malfunction; it didn't even give a warning. And once it was done, they hardly felt the explosion—if there was one.

"Closer," Alicia said.

Again there was no warning, but this time they felt the explosion as a small rumble under their feet. And if nothing else, Potato Island was now moving in a direction more toward Sol than it had been before.

"Again," Alicia said, clapping her hands.

Fold by fold, Alicia tried to push him to blow up larger and larger chunks of Potato Island. But having found a distance from the Island he felt reasonably comfortable with, Andrick insisted they maintain discipline.

Day after day they carved away chunks of the asteroid, Andrick working until he collapsed, Alicia unsuccessfully hiding how much her calf hurt most of the time. It took almost a month before they felt they had sliced off enough mass to try moving under propulsion. So far, after weeks of work, they'd barely moved any closer to Sol, of course. But with both drives running? They could be home in a few days.

"Ready?" he said. They sat in the storeroom, Andrick holding the tablet he used to manipulate the software that was designed, ninety-nine times out of a hundred, to control itself.

"Do it," Alicia said, sitting across from him.

He took a deep breath, then shook his head and slid the tablet across the table. "You do the honors."

She glanced down at the screen, then—without any ceremony—stabbed the bright square button with her finger.

The propulsion drive sprang to life, humming its soft song throughout the ship's decks, beginning to move them through space even with the remaining mass of Potato Island attached.

"It worked?" Andrick said, hardly able to believe it.

Alicia twirled around and around in the chair, though if circumstances were different, he knew, she'd be on her feet, dancing, leaping around, laughing madly.

As he watched her, he felt the wide smile on his face crumble away. Because now he had to face the reality of their situation: yes, they could create a wave of micro-folds, from here to Luna, and drive their ship through them. They could be entering Sol within the week. But who would they be when they arrived? Hyperspace had strange and ugly effects on the conscious human mind. And ... something was wrong with this hyperspace drive. Something that was beyond his abilities to uncover, let alone fix: the error in mass-detection that had caused the crash in the first place and that had allowed them to carve away most of Potato Island.

"We have to risk it," Alicia said, when she'd stopped twirling long enough to ask him what was wrong.

"No."

She sat back down. "We didn't do all—"

"We're no good to anyone—no good to your mom—if we show up having lost our minds."

"But dad—"

"We'll have to drop down to one fold a day. I'd rather travel while we're awake and can guarantee the space is empty, but the risk is too high. Instead we'll identify the area we're going to fold in the evening, then set the commands to activate in the middle of the night so that the ship goes through folded space while we're sleeping. You can add to your bedtime prayers that nothing enters the area we've identified in the hours between setting and activating the engine. But we have to tolerate some level of risk," he continued, and had enough self-awareness to know that he was speaking now, not to Alicia, but to the risk-averse part of himself, "and I think that one is pretty low. We'll try it tonight and monitor for effects. Okay?"

She bit her lower lip, then said, "Okay."

That night, they instructed the ship to create a micro-fold at two in the morning and drive through it. Andrick had a terrible time falling asleep, and considered deleting the instructions; but from her snoring, Alicia didn't have similar trouble and he tried to put the worries out of his mind ... and then it was morning. He turned over quickly and picked up the tablet.

Alicia stirred as he studied the star charts. "Did it work?" she said, sitting up.

He nodded, then met her eyes. "How do you feel?"

"Oh, fine. I'm fighting to suppress this weird homicidal urge to strangle you, but otherwise I feel totally sane."

"Very funny."

The following day they instructed the ship to repeat the process.

They didn't feel any adverse effects then either, or after any of the other nights.

"We're on our way home, darling," Andrick said to Alicia.

Their joy was genuine but muted. If they stuck to their single fold-and-travel per night, it would take almost a decade to get home. Even if they risked two or three fold-and-travel cycles during the night—a huge risk, given the drive's inability to properly detect and avoid massive objects—it would still take years. As for traveling through a fold while they were awake, so they could fold and monitor for objects, fold and monitor for objects ... Andrick had heard too many horror stories about what the early hyperspace travelers experienced to allow himself to contemplate that option except as a last, desperate resort.

It turned out that wouldn't be necessary. When rescue came, though, it almost killed them all.

Because of all of their jumping around, beaming out distress calls from different points in space, one of those signals had finally been picked up by an outpost station in orbit around Pluto. A search and rescue ship called the *Corner Lights* was immediately dispatched.

Loud banging woke Andrick up just as he'd fallen asleep. For a moment he thought he'd imagined the sound, but Alicia had woken up too, startled, and then they heard again the urgent *thud-thud-thud*.

Something's gone wrong with the engine, Andrick thought in panic, and stumbled out of bed desperately to see if he could shut it down before it exploded. But in the passageway the *thud-thud-thud* banged again.

Through the airlock portholes, he saw what he'd dreamed of one day seeing: friendly human faces waving at him, though he was surprised they wore no helmets or EMUs. Was he still asleep, dreaming of this rescue by people who could float in space and breathe vacuum? But then he saw the structure extending behind them and realized that they'd established a pressurized tunnel between the two ships.

As good-naturedly as he could, Andrick waved off the hugging and celebrating to ask if they had a medic on board, and on being told of course they did, to beg that they look at Alicia's leg right away. In the meantime, his daughter had hobbled out to see what was happening, so they picked her up and whisked her through the tunnel and into the *Corner Lights*, Andrick racing to keep up, and into their medical room. There the doctor, an old woman with a brusque manner, shooed them away after they'd put Alicia down on the hospital bed, but grudgingly allowed Andrick to stay. "Very bad," she said, after a few minutes examining Alicia, shaking her head. "You should go," she said, "your daughter is in good hands."

"Very bad?" Andrick repeated in a whisper.

The old woman pushed him out the door with remarkable strength. "Could be worse," she said, in that oblivious, matter-of-fact way some doctors had. "Probably would've killed her within a few weeks. But she'll be fine now. Routine surgery, a few hours of rest, and she'll be jumping around like nothing ever happened."

Somewhat dazed, Andrick allowed someone to lead him back to the mess, where he was sat down at a table and handed a hot cup of coffee by a young officer named Cedric, who'd clearly been assigned as his minder.

"We'll have to wait for the doctor's all-clear," Cedric said. "Then we'll get everyone back into deep sleep and get you home. Before we dismantle the tunnel to the Pointed Star, is there anything we can bring back for you? We've collected the personal effects you had in your cabin."

Andrick shook his head; he couldn't think of a single souvenir he wanted of that experience, thank you very much. "Can I record a message for my wife?" he said.

The young man nodded and said, with evident pride, "The *Corner Lights* has hyperspace bottles."

Well, Andrick thought, *we sure could've used hyperspace message-in-a-bottle probes on the* Pointed Star. He began to voice the thought, but his throat had suddenly gone dry.

Cedric had stood and was waiting for Andrick to follow him, but Andrick's legs had lost their strength. He forced his arm up to eye-level and checked his wrist. In under twenty minutes, the hyperspace engine on the Pointed Star would try to fold space, with no safeguards to stop it in case any part of the *Corner Lights* touched its folding field.

"I need to get back to the ship," he said, turning wild eyes on his minder, adrenaline finally unlocking his body so that he nearly toppled over the table when he jumped to his feet. "Now!"

To his credit, Cedric didn't hesitate. He nodded once, then sprinted down corridors until they reached the tunnel, where he stepped aside for Andrick to lead the way.

The race to the cabin was a blur he could never quite remember. Some memory of stumbling down the semi-rigid material of the tunnel, shoving open the airlock doors, launching himself into the cabin to grab the tablet and delete the instructions, Cedric on his heels the whole time, asking something that didn't register at the time.

"It's okay," he said, collapsing into the chair to allow his pulse to resettle.

"You're sure?" Cedric said, breathing heavily himself.

Andrick closed his eyes and nodded.

"All right. I'll let you be then. You know your way back when you're ready to join us?"

Andrick nodded again without opening his eyes.

After a few minutes, his breath and heart-rate under control, he stood again. If anyone on that poor rescue ship had known how close they'd come to, at best, a very unnecessary and stupid risk... He shook off the feeling and began heading to the tunnel, when he stopped and looked back. The light he'd wired to their SOS signal was no longer blinking red, of course. How many countless hours had he stared at that tiny light, praying for it to blink green, just once? Now it was blinking green continuously and he'd almost left without noticing.

Now that would be a souvenir, wouldn't it?

The risk-averse Andrick warned him against tampering any further with the ship. No doubt there would be an investigation—at the very least, they'd want to know what had gone wrong with the hyperspace engine—and he didn't need to explain to anyone why he'd felt the need to help himself to a part of their ship.

Oh, do shut up, he told himself. He unscrewed the cover from the dashboard, removed the small light, and stuck it into his pocket. Satisfied, he left the cabin without looking back and climbed into the tunnel, closing the airlock doors behind him.

Back aboard the *Corner Lights*, Andrick sent Treanne a message and, in the time he waited to be allowed to see Alicia again, even received one in response. He could hardly understand his wife because she kept crying, almost hyperventilating, through her words. But he understood her intent and sent her one more message to say that he loved her too and they both couldn't wait to see her again—very soon now.

When the doctor finally let him into the medical room, Alicia was sitting up in the recovery bed and looking better than she had in months. He thought he'd known how much the pain from her calf had caused her, but only now, seeing the contrast in her relaxed face and easy smile, did he realize the extent of her previous suffering.

"Hello, my face in the clouds," she said, tucking her legs to the side to make room for him. "Why so glum?"

"Face in the clouds?" he said, sitting down beside her.

She only broadened her smile at his confusion, then cupped the side of his face with her palm. She'd done that even as a toddler, reaching out whenever she thought he was upset. "Aren't we going home now, Dad?"

"Yes, darling. We are."

"Good," she said. "You see? Everything worked out. And don't worry, next time I win tickets aboard a hyperspace ship, our trip will go *much* smoother."

In the past he'd never been able to help but rise to Alicia's bait. This time, however, he just shook his head, said, "Sure it will, darling," then laughed and pulled his daughter into a tight embrace.

See Karl El-Koura's story "Anamnesis" online at Metaphorosis.
If you liked it, leave a comment. Authors love that!
Remember to subscribe to our e-mail updates so you'll know when new stories are posted.

About the story

I once read every word of Philip K. Dick's *Exegesis* (that might not sound like much of an accomplishment, unless you're familiar with that door-stopper of a book). I believe that's where I picked up the word that forms the title of the story, which means a forgetting of forgetting, or a remembering again.

Seemingly separately, as I watched my young daughter grow, I knew that there would come a time when she'd ask me questions that would leave me with two choices: speak the truth as I saw it (in an age-appropriate way, of course) or tell her a lie that would comfort her, or help her fit in, or keep her out of trouble.

Then one day I had a mental image, 'as if some cosmic god had stuck his nose into the mist, which had molded around his face'.

The three experiences melded together to form the genesis for "Anamnesis". The story is in part my answer to the question of where I should land when answering my daughter's questions. Reality is better than illusion, it seems to me, even if it can be more uncomfortable.

A question for the author

Q: What would your characters say about you?

A: I fear they would say: "Clean your ears, bud. What I said was much more interesting than what you wrote down." I hope they would say: "Thanks for letting us find our own way." I expect they would say: "Well—you did your best."

About the author

Karl El-Koura lives with his family in Canada's capital city, holds a second-degree black belt in Okinawan Goju Ryu karate, and works a regular job in daylight while writing fiction at night. "Anamnesis" is his third appearance in Metaphorosis. His stories "The Azurian Shield" and "Her Last Will" were published in the October 2021 and September 2022 issues, respectively.

www.ootersplace.com, @KarlElKoura

The Zoo Diaries V

Frances Pauli

Part Five

Previously…

At the Rainriver Zoological Gardens, one escape became the catalyst for a series of unfortunate incidents. The tortoise, Oliver, roamed the zoo as a fugitive, searching for his missing cage mate, Miranda. His adventure has taken him to the Aviary, where he was recaptured only to dig free again, this time with the help of the duplicitous crow, who led him to the Marshland and helped him slip under the net.

While the zoo's photography contest set the crowds wild, their poor behavior heaped extra stress upon the already troubled animals. The spike in attendance boded well for the bottom line, but the zoo was forced to hire armed security to keep the mobs in line.

While the other animals dealt with the increased interaction, Oliver searched the Marshland for his lost love, unaware that the crows were watching and that his reunion was not likely to go as planned.

CONTEST

When the contest results are tallied, zoo management calls an emergency meeting. The victor is problematic, but it has won by a landslide. 'Lion Eats Cellphone' has blown away all competition, but the repercussions have caused nothing but difficulties.

Security reports a need for more boots on the ground. Janitorial gives a presentation in which they display 25 glossy photos of trash and detritus littering every corner of the zoo, including a shot of the interior lion paddock with each foreign item circled in red ink.

The lead veterinarian speaks for ten minutes on the dangers of ingested plastic on a lion's digestive track. During his speech, the head of marketing is caught nodding off.

Someone's nephew suggests altering the results online.

The deception is given serious consideration, but marketing believes it would cause a PR nightmare.

In the end it is decided. 'Lion Eats Cellphone' will be disqualified for violation of zoo regulations. The video owner will receive half the cash award but no mention other than a reiteration of zoo policy and a public post on the safety of zoo animals and property.

The official winner is now 'Avian Courtship'. A distant second place is another Charlie video, 'Lion Licks Little Boy'.

Everyone is satisfied except the owner of 'Lion Eats Cellphone', who takes the cash but continues to insist it was an accidental drop. The internet discusses the event with some heat, a great deal of insults and over-explaining, and complaints on all sides.

Eventually, the contest is forgotten. The zoo webpage visitor count returns to its pre-popularity state, and someone's nephew finds a summer job working at the local burger joint. Zoo attendance is still up, and the website never mentions the second tortoise escape.

The keeper team reports evidence of stress on their animals. Increased traffic, they believe, is beginning to affect the behavior of their charges. They are listened to briefly and then assured that the contest's end will reduce attendance.

It is only temporary.

Things will settle down soon, and in the meantime, the money might be used to improve conditions.

Or to expand the gift shop.

The employee appreciation potluck is pitched as a reward for the staff's perseverance. Signup sheets fill quickly with offers to bring pie, potato salad, and lots and lots of hot dogs.

Hyena Pen

Alice falls asleep in the cat house, curled into a blanket that no longer smells odd. She has been twitching all day today, growing warm and uncomfortable. And very lonely. She awakens back in her own cage.

The floor is smooth and littered with straw. The stair-step rock stands guard from the corner. Her water basin is exactly where she remembers it belongs, but everything smells different. Only the blanket beneath her suggests it is not a hostile scent, that this, too, should have been expected.

Alice lifts her square head, opens her mouth, and cackles out her nerves. From the uppermost stair-step another hyena answers with a low growl.

She is not threatened by this. His scent may be all over her cage, but it is familiar, hers now as much as the rock is.

He only needs to be taught.

She stands, bracing all four legs in a stiff, bristling pose. Her ears move non-stop, and she takes a few jerking steps toward the water. Her mouth is fuzzy, and she will be able to see the intruder more easily from across the cage.

He growls again but there is no force behind it, no authority.

Alice ignores him but drinks with her ears aimed, always, in his direction. He shifts atop the rock. He sniffs and rumbles, but he is smart enough not to surrender the perch.

He has her at a disadvantage, however, in position only. Alice knows this, as she knows every inch of the stair-step surface. She waits, letting her tail flick and her ears swivel. She rises and pees, moving around the cage as she does to spread the urine. She covers his stink with her own mark and is thrilled when he growls again.

Alice waits. She knows many tricks. He will want to sniff and circle. He will need to come down soon enough.

She gives him her back, stares through the bars and pretends to watch the pathways. It is light already. The zoo will open soon. Alice hears him slip to the second tier and smiles.

Her body is still, relaxed, and non-threatening. Her mind is sharp. He reaches the third step where she could easily leap at him. Alice lies down.

The other hyena slinks to the floor. He moves, not to her directly, but to the blanket instead. He buries his nose in it, smells his own odor overlain with hers.

Always on top.

Alice waits until he moves to the corner, until he begins to follow the trail of her urine.

"This cage is mine," she says without looking at him. "You don't belong here."

His voice is deep and jagged. There is something about it, however, that she likes. "I am here," he says simply.

Alice sits, yawns, and listens to the padding of his feet. His breath is heavy as he drinks her in, his steps too soft, too confident. When she lunges, he is off guard, distracted, and foolish.

Alice hits him in the side with her full weight. He rolls under the impact, and she is on him, pinning his spotted body to the ground and holding his delicate throat in her heavy jaws. His body is rigid, fights her for three long breaths. Then, as easily as a sigh, he softens. He relaxes beneath her, and she has won.

There was never any doubt of this.

Alice releases him and sits. He rolls onto his belly, groveling, whimpering, and trying to lick her muzzle without lifting too high and earning another reprimand.

"You are mine," Alice says, and he wriggles and sinks lower. "Everything is mine."

"Yes."

She thinks she likes the sound of him even more now. His smell is not foul, and she has itched for company for many days.

"Who are you?" Alice asks.

"I am Rocko," he answers, cringing when she growls. He corrects his mistake quickly. "I am yours."

"Yes," Alice says.

She allows him to rub against her chin, to whine and scoot in homage before she leaps away, bounding to the apex of the stair-step rock to wait for him.

Ape House

Gonzo's elation carries him to the highest ropes. He has found his bean again. Five black cherries waited for him on the ledge this morning. Five perfect crunchy bites that stop his shaking and bring his headache fast to bay.

He chewed four of these immediately, his excitement too much to resist, his need too powerful. Today, however, he has managed to reserve the fifth. He means to savor it.

Gonzo hides it in one clenched fist and hoots down at a troop that seems sluggish today. The other macaques pass through the square door one by one, blinking into the sunlight and reaching for the lower vines with empty paws and full bellies. Gonzo has forgotten to eat.

He peels back his lips and screeches at them. He hoots, and his fangs flash. They are stained today, marked by the bean juice and ready to display that color proudly.

The others show him halfhearted smiles, pale teeth in slow mouths. He thinks they'll try to steal his bean, and he stuffs the last cherry into his mouth, chews with his lips sealed while the juices drain down his throat.

The cage vibrates around him. The world slows and Gonzo imagines he is king over all of it. His bean is speed and power, and with it between his teeth, he believes he can reach out to the whole zoo, grip it all in a tight paw, and crush it slowly between his leathery fingers.

Wolf Run

Raksha is named after a famous wolf mother, but she does not know it. She is not likely to ever encounter a book. She *is* a wolf, *and* a mother, however, and like her literary counterpart, she is made of patience.

Today, her pups are sulking. They have been less active, choosing to lie in a place even when the sunlight has moved past them. She fears for their bellies, fears the worms that sometimes kill a pup's drive to grow and to thrive.

Raksha calls them to her, and they drag their tiny bodies across the grass. The female sits, but the male pup flops onto his side, tongue lolling. His belly looks full but healthy enough, neither distended nor sparse of fur.

"Are you ill, my pups?" Raksha asks.

Their 'no's echo one another, flat and listless.

"But something had taken the pounce out of you," Raksha insists. "You must tell me."

The pups exchange a look that hangs from them like a weight. The male covers his nose with both paws. His sister answers for them both.

"We want freedom," she says, sitting taller and flattening her ears to her head. "We want to go beyond the high wall."

Raksha lets slip a low growl. Her ears lay tight to her skull, and she sits back on her haunches. This is not at all what she expected. Far worse than a belly full of parasites.

Their minds have been poisoned.

"Who told you about freedom?" she asks.

"A pigeon told us." The pup's answer is heartsick, twangs with longing for the unknown.

"Pigeons are liars," Raksha tries, though she can see the light in the pups' eyes. She can see the damage that has already been done. "What does a pigeon know of anything?"

"She flew away," the male pup answers. "She went over the wall."

"And might easily be dead now," Raksha says. "Might be eaten or ravaged."

"Do you think so?" There is interest in the female pup's voice. There is more energy than Raksha has seen from her in days.

"I do." She latches on to the opening. "Birds are too stupid to know anything. They are not *wolves*."

"And freedom?"

The girl pup leans into her question. Her brother's ears lift from his skull. Their eyes drill into their mother.

They are practically begging for the lie.

"What do you like best about being a wolf?" Raksha asks.

"Sitting on the tallest rock," the girl pup barks it, sure of herself.

Her brother mumbles, "Eating the fat bugs that live under our log."

"Then do that," Raksha proclaims. "Do that as often as you possibly can."

"What do bugs and rocks have to do with—"

Raksha cuts off the pup's argument with a growl. "It makes you happy," she says. "Do the thing that makes you happy. *That* is freedom, my cubs."

"Are you sure?" The male pup whines, but his tail thumps against the grass.

"I am quite sure," Raksha says. "You must do what makes you happy."

She watches them carefully, and even though she has won, they seem much older when they answer.

"Yes, Mother."

Grizzly Caged

Hector's box is rolled on eight metal casters down the long hallway. She-who-takes-notes is there, along with his other doctors. When he poses and presses his paw for them, they offer a skewer of grapes through the bars.

She-who-takes-notes does not clap, but her smile soothes him.

The end of his box is positioned against a dark wall with much jostling and mutters from the doctors' servants. There are more bars along that surface, but they slide aside. Someone grumbles in the dim light while Hector chews his treats.

Metal screeches. A square of light appears, drawing his gaze down. When he can look without blinking, he is surprised to see the interior of his own den. The box has been wedged against it, and with a click and the effort of many human paws, the end slides upward.

Hector is free to go home.

He stuffs the grapes between his black lips and looks at She-who-takes-notes. The den smells of him. Beyond it, he can see a sliver of his fallen log. He has been content in the box with the grapes and the doctors, but his artist is out there.

She is probably worried about him.

Hector groans despite the fact that he is pain-free. He ambles slowly from the cage, crosses his den, and sits while the bars move again. For a single moment, he can see the doctors through them. Then the wall comes down, and it is as if they never were.

Hector moves easily. His body has mended. He feels, in fact, stronger than he has in decades, younger and fiercer.

At his railing, the sun tells him he is late. The artist has missed him today, has come and gone already.

Hector is sorry to disappoint her, but there is always tomorrow. He will be ready by then. He will show her just how much of a bear he can be.

He lopes from his den like a cub would run. His joints make no comment, and Hector lifts onto his hind legs. He stretches toward the sun, poses, and shows the clicking cameras at the railing all his teeth.

He is bear.

Tomorrow, he will be ready to shine.

Elephant Paddock

Shanti has stopped counting. Today she draws pictures with her straw. She piles it into tortoise-shaped sculptures or flattens smooth canvases of yellow gold and then removes bits to expose an Oliver-shaped portrait in the negative spaces.

Occasionally, she mutters. "One tortoise," but through most of her work, she is concentrating far too hard to worry about how many pieces of straw it takes to build a tortoise shell. How many swipes of her trunk equal a suitable likeness?

She is inspired, obsessed. She has found her muse, and he is shaped like a stone and covered in perfect, patterned, hexagons.

Lion Enclosure

Charlie chews in his sleep now. His tawny jaws work around his pink tongue, masticating the memory of squeaky meat, of morsels offered by the crowd to their maned god. He lies in the sun, sprawled on his side with his mouth partway open. His tail twitches as he chews nothing.

His dream veldt is populated by hotdog gazelles. Great herds of migrating beasts with sausage legs and long tube necks. They squeak when they walk, filling the Savannah with their delicious cries. Filling Charlie's head and making him salivate freely.

The air is a thick blanket of scent, of rich sweet meat and spicy preservatives.

It is driving him mad.

He dreams the lionesses hunt for him, but they are far afield, dark shadows on the horizon only. Charlie chews the scent. He swallows the idea of the meat, tasting from memory. He is obsessed. The squeaking meat has possessed him.

His tongue lolls against dry grass. His teeth rise and fall, and deep in his long gut, a desperate rumble echoes like a mighty roar.

The Crow

Debra circles the marshland three times to make certain she has enough time. The tortoise moves like a slug, one lumbering foot at a time. Even ecstatic, he is mud flowing, weighted down by his ponderous nature.

He is pointed in the right direction, but Debra is sure he will not reach his goal before she returns.

She must not miss that moment, but her victory will be sweeter with an audience. She needs the murder to witness it, needs the other crows to appreciate exactly what she has done.

She circles again, marks Oliver's progress, and then angles away. The zoo blurs below as she cries out to her fellow crows.

At the old bear's cage, she gathers a pair of birds who have already grown bored waiting for him to be injured again. A low sweep over the cat house brings three more. As she flies, Debra calls to her kin. She screeches a promise of sport that is far greater than their ordinary games.

The murder responds with a collective cackle. They gather around Debra, adding their wings, their voices, to her cause.

"Come," the croaking voices sing. "Come, come and see."

By the time the murder returns to the marshland, it is as if a black cloud descends upon the nets.

Tortoise Abroad

Oliver calls Miranda's name as he trundles through the marshland. His steps churn, as much as a tortoise is capable of churning, and he drags his shell past a low duck pond where teals and loons mingle their regal shapes with those of the common mallard.

He sticks to the paths, and once he reaches that solid firmament, progresses quickly. The fences here, like those in the farm, are wooden and open enough for tortoises to pass below the bottom rail. A few have wire behind them, however, and he sees with a sinking heart that this is usually where the long-legged birds are found.

He passes storks and flamingos, egrets with frilled heads and cranes that stalk to the front of their enclosures to gawk at him as he passes.

Oliver asks them all about his heron, and they all give the same answer.

"Move along."

"Just down a few more."

Oliver thanks them, but his elation is fading. He thinks he will never reach her, thinks the universe is adding cages between them so that each time he passes one, three more spawn further down the line.

His steps begin to stutter. He pulls his head halfway into his shell and stamps onward. At each fence he cries Miranda's name, and he almost fails to notice when the birds beyond the fence begin to look like her.

Oliver steps and pivots. There is a wooden fence, but he ignores it. His legs carry him easily underneath, across the strip of mowed grass to the short wire wall inside. It is not unlike the one around his own home.

Beyond it, five long-legged, tan-bodied, curl-necked herons stand. They cluster in the rear of their pen, where the grass grows long, and a high arc of reeds marks some pond or other waterway.

"Miranda." The first time it comes out as a whisper. Oliver stretches his neck, tries to see his love in the huddle of so-similar birds. "Miranda!"

She looks his way. He sees her graceful neck stretch and twist. He holds his breath as she detaches herself from the flock. His eyes tear.

Miranda moves toward him with all the elegance he remembers. She glides on her stilt legs, and her downy neck is an ess holding her wedge-shaped head aloft.

"Oliver?" Her voice is a nutshell cracking. "What are you doing here?"

He doesn't notice it at first, the way she turns to look over her shoulder, the way she lowers, bending and flexing her legs so that she is a screen between the flock and his domed body. Until she unfurls one wing to hide him, Oliver misses the cool note in her words. The sharp glint in the eye aimed in his direction.

"I— I came to find you," he says.

"You escaped?" Only in that he hears a speck of interest.

"I did," he agrees with too much vehemence.

Miranda takes a step away. "You'll be punished."

"I didn't know where you were," he blurts, sensing her drawing away, understanding only on the surface what has to come next. "You were just gone."

"They moved me here," Miranda's tone veers again, sounding at last as he remembers it. Bright and haughtily, she informs him, "They were building us a new enclosure, you see, a space with room for all of these *new* herons."

"New herons," Oliver parrots.

"Oh, yes. Fresh in, all of them. The two females are from another zoo, as is Manuel. But my mate, Evan, was caught *in the wild.*"

"Evan." Oliver's neck lowers, slips back inside his shell. "Your mate."

"Yes." Miranda nods. Her wing lifts just enough to offer Oliver a view of the other birds without making his presence too obvious. "Evan used to belong to a huge colony. He's been places. His stories are amazing."

"You don't want to come back," Oliver half-muses. "You want to stay here."

"Of course." Miranda pulls herself higher, dropping the wing as she does to keep Oliver veiled. Hidden from her new friends and her mate.

Faintly, he hears the crows laughing. Far off. Somewhere overhead.

"You shouldn't stay here, though," Miranda continues. "You're not a bird, Oliver. You don't belong here any more than I belong in a turtle pen."

"Tortoise." He says it automatically, robotically.

"Whatever." Miranda ripples, a full body dismissal of his presence, his adoration, and his existence.

She fluffs her feathers once, shakes them flat again, and whispers, "Goodbye, Oliver," before strutting away.

Her long legs stab each step into the marshy grass like an arrow striking deep into a turtle's heart.

RAINRIVER ZOOLOGICAL GARDENS

MEMO TO ALL EMPLOYEES

THIS IS A REMINDER TO ALL ZOO STAFF NOT TO PROVIDE ANY FOOD TO THE ANIMALS THAT IS NOT A PART OF THEIR REGULARLY SCHEDULED DIET.

EACH AND EVERY RAINRIVER ANIMAL'S DIET IS OVERSEEN BY A TEAM OF VETERINARIANS AND KEEPERS AND ADDING ANYTHING TO THAT REGIMEN CAN BE DETRIMENTAL TO THE ANIMAL'S HEALTH AND WELL-BEING.

THERE ARE TO BE NO EXCEPTIONS TO THIS RULE.

WE WILL CONSIDER PROVIDING OUTSIDE TREATS TO THE ANIMALS A FIRST TIME FIRING OFFENSE, AS PER EMPLOYEE CONTRACTS.

WE CANNOT ALLOW THE ENTHUSIASM AND EXCITEMENT FOR OUR THRIVING ZOO TO RESULT IN LAX CARE OR DANGEROUS BEHAVIOR.

THIS WILL BE YOUR ONLY WARNING.

REMINDER: THE POTLUCK WILL BE HELD TOMORROW EVENING. DUE TO A CHANGE IN EMPLOYMENT, WE COULD USE ONE MORE PERSON TO BRING A SALAD.

—ZOO MANAGEMENT

Ape House

There are no beans on the ledge today. Gonzo stares at the empty shelf outside his bars as if he can will them into being. While the troop dines, he continues to check every second breath or so, but no cherries magically appear for him.

His need pulls back his lips. He snarls at the melon in his paws.

He-who-sweeps has not come. Instead, a new one drags her broom across the aisle. Her head is down, focused on the work and oblivious to a monkey's expectations. They-who-bring-food do not even carry the paper cups today.

He smells nothing but fruit and macaque feces, and that lack enrages him.

His paws quake until he wraps them around the bars, dragging at the metal as if he might tear it free of its rigidity.

Gonzo screeches. He hops and bares his fangs while They-who-bring-food watch, shaking their heads and discussing him with barking voices.

Gonzo flings shit at them. He loosens his grip on the cage and finds a fresh, filthy pile to grab and toss. To splatter and spray.

They-who-bring-food step out of range, continue their discussion while Gonzo's mind implodes. He must have the cherries. He must taste the bean. He must have, must have, must chew it again or he is certain he will die.

Pigeon Paradise

Peg has grown as fat as a plump, round chicken. She has spent days stuffing herself on birdseed, on little chunks of fruit and flat, striped sunflower seeds. She waddles beside the phony creek at the bottom of the aviary, and she puffs her feathers, becoming a gray sphere as she glowers at the sparkling water.

It is always wet in here.

Her feathers have not dried once since she's arrived. Her eyes swivel and blink against the moist air and her hocks have begun to complain about the extra weight. The aviary birds are not pigeons. They are too crowded, and fight the proximity by keeping to themselves, not gossiping. There is nothing, really, to whisper about here. Only warm air, shining leaves, and a steady supply of healthy foods.

Peg is miserable.

She scratches at the moist ground, and it clings to her feet, clogging her toes, making her shake and stamp.

There are no cast-off hot dogs here. There is no soft bread, no popcorn, and no soda, and no need at all to fight and squabble over a meal.

She has taken to watching the doors, standing just inside the twin portals while they open, close, open. But she is too fat now, too slow to risk an exit.

Grizzly Grotto

Hector wakes pain-free for the first time in years. He has missed his artist while away, and this new, fresh feeling in his limbs presses him to move quickly. Out of the den, he ambles, hump swaying from side to side between his shoulder blades.

There are not doctors to give him grapes and needles today, but here is his own territory, his fallen log, his trench, and his jagged scratching stump.

It is early, so he indulges in a good, long session with his shaggy back pressed up against the bark. Up and down, Hector wiggles, reaching those persistent itches that his new range of motion finally allows him to assuage.

When he is satisfied, tingling from neck to fat bottom, Hector lifts his muzzle and sniffs. His nose twists left and right, chasing the aroma of his breakfast.

A pile of fruit waits behind the fallen log. It is still early. He sits and pokes his nose among the soft chunks. He noses through colored morsels, and he smells something not unlike the odor which clings perpetually to his doctors.

His first bite is bitter. He thinks the fruit has gone bad, tosses it off, and grabs a new bit. The sharp taste clings to it as if painted on.

Hector's stomach urges him to push past it. He lips cautiously, however, cringing from the unpleasantness hiding behind his breakfast. He remembers sweet grapes on a long skewer. The zoo will open soon. He has wasted his advantage poking at his food and decides to leave it be.

Despite his belly's complaints, he moves back to the stump to wait. He tries a few poses in preparation, testing his new flexibility and striking more than one mighty figure.

She will be impressed, he thinks, to see him stretch so tall, bend so low, and twist...

Hector hears feet upon the paths. Voices sing like birdsong on the morning air. He stands without wavering, gazes over the railing, proud and proper.

His artist is the first face at the rail. Hector greets her with a churr he has perfected on the doctors. She smiles and claps. She reaches into her bag while Hector switches his pose. She pulls something free, something that is not made of art, not a sketchbook, nor a stub of charcoal.

Hector's artist aims the thing at him, shamelessly, and he drops to all fours.

He huffs as the click echoes through his morning, bitter as his fruit, loud as gunfire.

Hector turns, shows the artist his back, and pouts.

There will be nothing more between them.

She has stooped to photography.

Hyena Pen

Alice hates Rocko. He is too large, too clumsy. His breathing scratches like a flea behind her ears. He pants too freely, splashes her water across the cage floor while drinking, and sneaks to the top tier to crowd her while she sleeps.

They have mated twice, and she is done with him.

She paces near the front of the cage, measuring the steps down and back in an abstract fashion and with a growing sense that there simply is no room for him.

Not enough space for two in her box. Not enough room for a Rocko mate.

He cackles from a low tier on the stair-step rock, pants and licks and makes a stupid, lolling face at her. He will want to mate again soon, and Alice thinks she will not let him.

She thinks the cage is too small, the walls too close.

They seem to move as she watches, creeping as Alice stares, one inch closer. Shrinking, boxing, trapping her inside them with a massive, dopey excuse for a male hyena.

Tortoise Trapped

Oliver doesn't hide when the sun rises. He drifts along the marshland pathway, keeping to the far end, away from the herons, and waits to be caught.

The nets arch overhead, a mesh of pale lines that seem to weigh more today. He is pinned by them, held in his dismay by an ephemeral wall.

Eventually, he stops moving. There is nowhere to go, no path that won't eventually lead him back to Miranda. Even with the huge duck pond between them, Oliver imagines he can hear her voice.

It is only the crows laughing, but he hears it in the haughty, clipped tones of a heron who never wanted him to begin with. Oliver tucks his head into his shell and remembers Shanti's voice, deep and encouraging, awed by his shell and his pattern.

He has no reason to think of the elephant now, but the memory soothes him anyway. At least until the crows begin to shout and taunt him again.

Oliver hates them, hates all birds today, but it is an abstract, force-less feeling. His rage has no power. Even Debra is a wisp of irritation only.

The crow didn't trick him, after all. Oliver did this to himself. He knows it, knows he was blind on purpose, willfully deaf to Miranda's indifference. He was obsessed, irrational, unwanted from the start.

It is that which burns brightest now. Not the sting of heartbreak or the raw chafing of rejection. It is shame.

His sense of self has been shattered by the blow to his ego. Oliver feels it seeping in through the gaps in his shell. He was wrong. He was deeply, embarrassingly *wrong*, and how his crimes are exposed.

He is a cracked egg, leaking his flaws onto the path for all to see.

And, overhead, the crows have every right to mock him.

The Crow

The tortoise takes his heartbreak far too well. Debra watches, laughs when the snooty bird rejects him, but her joke is flat. She has to explain the story to the murder three times before they get it and join in.

They follow Oliver for only a short while, taunting and earning no response from their moping victim. It is enough of a game to please the murder, but they are not as impressed with Debra as she desires.

Even devastated, Oliver is ponderous and unexciting.

Debra leaves the marshland to the murder and circles the family farm. A cow is moaning over some mild stomach distress, but it is not worth landing to mock her. She flies to the hyenas, but ever since the male was stuffed into the cage, the female has turned aggressive, more dangerous than usual. Debra will wait until he is removed to find sport there.

She gives up and spends the day in the top of a tall tree, sleeping off her long night setting up Oliver's misery. Maybe he will try again with the heron, but Debra thinks she has gone too far this time. He is too broken to wring any more distress from his situation.

A restless feeling has gripped her, a sense of dread building. Normally, this would please her, but something is not right. Something deep inside her knows fear. As if her sport has left her hollow.

She tucks her beak beneath one wing and lets the zoo fade. In her dreams a dark paw reaches for her. She is caught, captured, stuck in a gage. And only madness circles the skies above her.

She wakes to the sound of human voices.

Night has fallen, and yet the people have not left. It is not quiet. It is not even truly dark. Lights bounce and flicker around the snack bar, and Debra chases them. She sweeps down from the tree and crosses the shadows in between to investigate.

They-who-keep-cages-locked are here. For a moment, Debra believes there will be a hunt. Those-who-carry-guns are with them, and her heart skips merrily. But no. They-who-sweep and They-who-bring-food are also here. They mingle freely with Those-who-pick-up-poop-and-trash.

There are others, too, strangers who join the familiar faces. Their voices raise and chatter. The night fills with the cacophony of their conversation. After hours. This has never happened before.

There is food, too, great piles of it lined up on the outdoor tables.

Debra dives in and steals a flat, round cracker. As she escapes with it, the pigeons, who have swarmed the event, shout obscenities at her. Their whole flock waddles beneath and between the tables, dancing around the many feet—boots and shoes and tall spike-heeled platforms that would skewer a bird if it moved too slowly.

Debra watches in case it happens, but the people in the shoes are foolish. They may be sick, even, and she fears for a moment that the food has been poisoned. They-who-work-at-the-zoo limp and stagger. They bump into one another, shaking, moving as if their legs are not their own.

Like a newborn giraffe trying to stand for the first time.

If they *are* poisoned, they do not suffer. Debra cringes from their laughter, the barking of their brusque, abrasive voices. They are happy. They are masters at the game Debra only plays at. At trapping and at torture. She is among the cruel and the vindictive, the keepers and the punishers. The stealers of freedom.

Debra can do nothing but admire them.

She still feels a disaster brewing. The air is thick with it. This mob of humans, the pigeons cursing and squabbling underfoot, the poisoned food and drink. A new tension crackles on the air. It has, she realizes, been brewing all along. Something terrible is about to happen. Debra feels it like a storm coming, and she lets her dark heart fill with anticipation again.

The danger sings to her. Its voice is tragedy. Its words are a promise of disaster. Debra perches on a light post, high above the party, and waits for the lightning to strike.

See parts I-V of Frances Pauli's serial "The Zoo Diaries" online at Metaphorosis.
If you like them, leave a comment. Authors love that!
Remember to subscribe to our e-mail updates so you'll know when new stories are posted.

June

Catching College

Maggie Slater

Hilltown's peace of mind shattered as the first whisper seeped out of a wristclamp autoreader over lunch, and before long, every device crackled with the news. Work stopped, students gathered, primed ears bent low to catch every detail. The collective heartrate skyrocketed. Inhabitants collapsed into chairs, eastern windows groaned as they were shoved open and eyes strained for something beyond the horizon. The dull old line where the plains cut the sky in half had always been present but unimportant. Not now. Promise lingered beneath its lip; opportunity raged towards town at fifty-five miles an hour.

Beneath the Hill, lodged deep in the rock where it had hidden for three hundred years, the Hilltown Energy Beetle's turbines spooled up, preparing for the increased demand on the grid. Far above it, in every room, the people of Hilltown laughed and cried and hugged and danced.

Parbrier College was coming. There was no time to waste.

All my life, I'd planned—no, *dreamed*—of catching a college like Dad. I'd heard his Wakereach boarding story so often at bedtime it felt like I'd been there, tasting the sea foam and feeling the burn of desperate paddling in my own arms. And now, I was going to get a shot at one. I wouldn't have to spend weeks or months hunting it down, tracking its paths, living out of a backpack. Parbrier was *coming to me*.

After classes were cancelled, I'd bounded down the Hill, expecting Dad to have beaten me home after catching the announcement at work and bolting, but nobody was there. I paced our tiny apartment from deck to kitchenette, looping around the sitting area Dad used as his bedroom and back, around and around, seething with the nervous energy the radio announcement had injected straight into my chest. Three weeks!

I couldn't even remember what Parbrier College looked like, though it was probably in Dad's Encyclopedia of Modern Behemoths. I stopped pacing and made for his sagging bookshelf. He had over three hundred books about behemoths, but the one I wanted was wedged right in the middle, acting as a pillar for the shelf above. I wriggled it out carefully, making sure nothing came crashing down on me.

The Encyclopedia was fourteen hundred vellum sheets, grouped into chapters on various locomotion styles and native locale. I'd pored over the section dedicated to ocean behemoths as a kid, obsessed with the googly-eyed, spiney, deep sea machinations that often people only learned existed when their metal shells washed up on shore, rusted out and covered in barnacles. The land-based education behemoth section was pristine.

After a little searching, I found Parbrier College. Even in a palm-sized sketch, it gave me a shiver of dread. Seven stories tall, three hundred feet wide, built like a porcupine with a plow head, its towers fanned out like quills across its back: Parbrier was no joke. It looked downright vicious.

I looked up at the paper-mâché model of Wakereach I'd made in seventh grade. I'd spent hours working on it, recreating every hatch, every rivet, with cardboard, paint, and paper. Dad had been so impressed, he'd rigged it up from my ceiling so that it looked as if it were beginning a dive to the depths. It was sleek where Parbrier was sharp; it was beautiful where Parbrier was ugly.

Three weeks. I shut the book and slumped back on my bed, mind racing. How could I possibly be ready in time? Everyone at school was talking about their plans, their trainers, their theories and gameplans. I didn't have a plan. I didn't know anything at all about catching a land-based college.

The apartment door opened, and my heart jammed itself up into my throat as Dad's shoes scuffled on the floor. Something rustled as he set it down. The sink sputtered on.

"Kai? You home?"

He sounded so calm. I crept to my door, staring as he dug through a canvas sack of groceries and started putting things away. He glanced over at me, smiling like the world wasn't about to shift into high gear.

"Ah, there you are! How was school?"

He couldn't not know. Everyone, everywhere, was talking about Parbrier. There was no way he hadn't heard.

His brows arched as he pulled out the battered cutting board and set it on the counter. "What's up?"

I was just about to explode when his eyes suddenly twinkled and his straight face broke into a huge grin. The restrained horror burst out of me in giggles, and he ran over, scooping me up into a bear hug.

"Three weeks!" he cried, and I clung to him like a life raft. He thrust me out at arm's length and looked me up and down. "When'd you grow up, huh? You excited?"

My face locked in a grin. "It's crazy! Three weeks!"

"God, I can't believe it. When I heard, Kai!" He pulled at his thinning hair and waved me towards the kitchen table. "And Parbrier is a great school. World-class in Behemoth studies, if that's what you're looking for. But also pretty top-notch in agriculture and history. Oh, and their Arts program!" He kissed his fingertips and turned back towards the counter, unpacking the groceries. I recognized the ingredients for my favorite curry and a six-pack of light lager. He was planning a celebratory dinner.

"The last time a college passed Hilltown, it came within half a mile," Dad was saying, "but—and you didn't hear this from me, because Neil said they haven't finished running the simulations yet —but a few of the path models are saying Parbrier's going to come a *lot* closer."

"How close?"

"Close. Possibly even hitting a street or two. But like I said, it's early days and they won't have a clear projection for a while."

I thought of that huge, spiny machine barreling towards town on its tracks as wide as a roadway, and choked down a lump in my throat. This was real. This was happening, *now*, not in some mythical future. Parbrier would be here in three weeks. How could I possibly be ready by then?

"Hey."

I pulled myself out of tunnel vision to see Dad stooping in front of me at the table, a warm smile on his face. "Don't worry. I know this is a lot, and there's a lot to do, but we're in this together, all right? You're not alone."

Dad winked at me, and I felt my fear evaporate under the confident gleam in his eye. I might not have a team of strategists or a jetpack like some of the kids from school, but I had Dad.

The knot in my chest released and I leaned forward, the nervous energy converting into excitement. "So where do we start?"

No quiet place existed in Hilltown anymore. Its living rooms buzzed with excitement; its streets with swarms of vendors setting up temporary shops. Banners snapped in the desert wind, advertising coaching services, specialized training, lucky talismans, every kind of trick and placebo. They caught even the most skeptical eyes. No one could afford to be too confident.

On the outskirts where the town bled onto the flats, tent fabric squealed as applicants and their families from neighboring towns built encampments, jamming themselves into every unclaimed bit of sidewalk and courtyard. The Hilltown Energy Beetle grew feverish as every spare outlet was overloaded with extension cords and portable grills and radios and TVs and chargers. The streetlights at night fluttered, gasping to remain lit. High on the Hill, the Beetle's internal heat made the asphalt as hot as high noon, and the dainty lights strung on the sculpted trees writhed in the shimmering air.

The next night, after we'd cleaned up from dinner, Dad dropped a pile of schematics on the kitchen table. The giant sheets crinkled as he unrolled them and smoothed them flat in front of us. Dad weighted the corners with mugs and a shoe.

Here was Parbrier in every detail, no longer a tiny sketch in the Encyclopedia. Thin grey lines dissected it, measuring it, picking apart its fundamental features in minute detail, down to the number of links per tread. In such a close-up view, with a tiny human figure silhouetted for scale, I felt my stomach flip on itself. It was vastly taller than our apartment building. Its tracks were wider than our street. Its underbelly, forty feet above the ground, was pocked with manholes and webbed with catwalks.

I looked again at the tiny scale figure and tried to imagine what it would feel like to stand so close to such a thing. Parbrier wouldn't even feel a bump if it crushed me screaming into the dust. I shivered.

Dad pulled at his jaw, frowning at the schematics. "The main difficulty with Parbrier is the treads. It should slow down as it approaches town, prior to its turn, but probably not a lot slower than twenty miles per hour. That's still going to be pretty fast for our purposes. We might be able to hook it, if you get close enough, but without getting up to speed, that'll be pretty risky even if you *do* snag it..."

I slumped in my chair. This was impossible. If I had a jetpack or a paraglider, sure, I could just sail over to one of its towers and drop onto it, but from the *ground*? It was a mountain. Climbing it at a standstill would be challenging, but moving? How could I ever have thought I could do this?

I'd always imagined that I'd choose my own college after graduating, and then spend months or years hunting it down, and that somehow, in-between, I'd become brave enough, I'd grow up, I'd be ready.

I wasn't ready now. My fingertips throbbed from my racing heart. I swallowed to wet my throat enough to speak, and then said, embarrassed by the slight waver in my voice, "I heard a Parbrier specialist on the radio. They said the last time Parbrier passed close to a highly populated area, six people died."

"The average is nine."

"What?"

"Most colleges have an average of nine deaths per season. Parbrier's a little better, actually." Dad was still frowning at the paper, his finger tracing the tracks. He sighed. "Maybe hooking it is the wrong angle. If it slows down enough, maybe you could ride the track up and over, jump off it to here." He pointed to a series of doors along the left side of the school where the track passed a broad, low balcony. "That might work, but we'd still have to *catch it...*"

I cleared my throat, trying to banish the idea of nine kids like me who weren't around anymore. "H-how many people made it? Onto Parbrier, I mean."

"Hmm?" Dad looked up at me as though he'd forgotten I was there. "Oh, um. Well, when it passed Moschberg about a year ago... Let me think. Three, I think. But I'm not sure what its overall season total was."

"*Three?*"

Dad shrugged. "Plenty of applicants just don't catch it, Kai. If everybody who wanted to succeeded, it wouldn't be special, would it? Wakereach has an even lower annual admittance ratio."

He frowned back down at the paper. "Ah! I've got it!" he shouted, the paper crashing like a firework when he slapped his palm down on it. He bounded to the balcony and scrambled over the railing onto the fire escape. I followed. "My old motorbike! That thing'll do forty-five, easy, and it's junk, so you can ditch it and it won't matter! You'll be right up next to Parbrier in no time!"

He swung around the last post, missed the top step, and through some miracle, managed to dance down to the ground without falling. He laughed and disappeared around the side of the building.

I thought of the motorbike, stashed in the communal garage, buried under boxes of forgotten things. It'd been years since he'd taken me out on it, perched in front of him, his arms bracing my eight-year-old body from shaking off. My butt would go numb from riding, and even a bath wouldn't get all the sand off my skin, but I'd loved it.

The garage door far below rattled open; boxes groaned and hissed as Dad moved them aside. I scrambled down the fire escape. I came around the corner just as he rolled out the battered old bike and set it on its kickstand.

"Ta-da!" He grinned at it like it was a custom jetpack instead of a crumbling bucket of bolts with two flat tires and chipped paint.

"Does it still work?" I asked, running my hands over the dented fuel tank, the ripped leather seat. Dirt came off on my palm.

"Oh, it'll work. These bikes are tanks. A quick tune-up, new tires, fresh fluids, gas, a couple of filters—it'll run like a dream."

I bit my tongue. Never mind that I'd never driven it before and now hardly seemed like the time to learn a whole new skill, I could see by Dad's dreamy gaze that he was already sold, and nothing I could say would change that. And maybe he was right. I took a deep breath and tried to invoke his confidence. Wakereach had a worse admittance ratio than Parbrier. Yes, people had died, but a lot just hadn't made it. If I was smart, if I was careful, maybe, just maybe, I'd be one of the lucky few who got on board. Dad believed in me. Now I just needed to believe in myself, or at least fake it until I could believe it for real.

Forcing a smile, I slung myself on and gripped the handlebars.

"That's my girl!" Dad slapped the bike's front fender, and it fell off with a clatter.

Every word in Hilltown was about Parbrier. Voices raised in arguments over strategies, over pros and cons of approach techniques. Everyone had an opinion. Everyone's opinion was right and wrong.

Parbrier had closed plenty of lives instead of opening them. Not all seeds landed in fertile soil. Some baked on stones. Some were consumed by birds. Life didn't offer guarantees. But the opportunity to spread its liveliest citizens beyond its borders, to chance at even just one of them finding great financial success or fame or a scientific or artistic breakthrough so that Hilltown could become The Place Where They Started: it was worth the risk.

Dad frowned at his wristclamp when I pulled up after my latest test run on the motorbike. We'd been practicing for almost two weeks. Parbrier was due to arrive in less than six days. Hour after hour, we'd run its expected paths. Dirt crusted my nostrils and caked the corners of my eyes. Grit chaffed my feet raw in my boots. My butt ached from the barely-padded seat, and I couldn't clench my hands from gripping the handlebars so tightly.

"You can't fear speed," Dad said, shaking his head. "We've been through this. You've got to *push*, Kai. Parbrier's not going to slow down just to make you more comfortable."

"I'm trying!"

"Well, try harder. This is a once in a lifetime opportunity. Go again. I want to see at *least* thirty-five. I don't care what the scientists are predicting, there's no way Parbrier is dropping to fifteen. And this time—" He squinted at me, and I withered inside. "—I want you to jump."

"What?"

"We've got six days, Kai. Six. Days. You need to practice jumping off the moving bike."

"What if I get hurt? I won't be able to catch Parbrier if I'm injured!"

"So don't get injured. Come on. We don't have time for theatrics. You need to be comfortable jumping."

I bit my cheek, willing tears from my eyes. Theatrics. Parbrier was just days away, looming in my mind like the end of times. My whole life stopped at that threshold, after which nothing would be the same, after which I couldn't even envision what life would be like.

Whether I caught Parbrier or missed it, whether I lived or died, its coming was the most momentous thing that might ever happen to me. Catching Wakereach had been the highlight of Dad's life. It gave him proof that he was capable of taking his destiny into his own hands, wrangling the fear of his mortality, and proving himself worthy against the biggest, scariest thing the world could throw at him.

I was just scared. It was normal to be scared. Everyone was scared, weren't they? I took a deep breath. I could not give in to self-pity. I'd never pull myself out and Parbrier would be as good as gone.

"Okay," I said, the dirt crunching between my teeth. "But can I work my way up?"

Dad sighed. "We've practiced tumbling. You can't run from speed forever."

"I'm not running." I almost shouted. "I'm just...trying to be logical about it. Build up speed, build up confidence. If I mess up at thirty-five, it's going to be hard to get into the right headspace. If I work up to it, I'll be ready for the speed."

My stomach unclenched as he nodded slowly. "Okay. Yeah. That's not a bad idea. But start at fifteen."

"Tuck and roll!"

He rewarded me with a smirk and I yanked down my goggles and kicked off.

The rumbling through the bedrock intensified with each passing day. Hilltown felt it. Its people felt it, too, radiated up through bed and table legs, through streets and floors, setting their stomachs on edge, making them short-tempered, nervous. The skies, irritatingly clear, provided no relief from the sharp horizon line burning its shadow-double across the backs of every eye. Every whirl of dust or smudge of shadow made breaths hitch. No one could risk being caught off-guard.

Within the metal fungi of City Hall, machines blipped and squealed as Hilltown's best and brightest ran simulation after simulation with each new shred of information. The path models converged, solidified, bound themselves into something like certainty. Their voices whispered in hushed concern, as new paths drew closer to the outskirts of town.

Barring a miracle, some fluke of chaos theory that governed the mechanisms that drove the school, Parbrier College would hit town. Evacuating neighborhoods would spare civilian lives. There was time, thankfully. Parbrier was still some distance away.

But it was closing in fast.

Two days. I sat in the living room alone, looking at the pile of boxes and bags Dad and I had packed after the evacuation order had come down the Hill. In two days, Parbrier would crash through our neighborhood and destroy everything.

I hadn't slept well last night. We'd stayed up past midnight strategizing, testing the makeshift radar Dad had rigged to the motorbike to help me find my way when the dust cloud made it impossible to see. I'd collapsed into bed like a sack of concrete, the dust from the plains still clinging to my scalp because I'd been too tired to take a shower. Even with my eyes burning, my body shaking with exhaustion, I couldn't sleep.

I lay awake, thoughts swirling over things that only half made sense but seemed so important to puzzle out, to fit into real life. My inner monologue devolved into self-loathing. How could I be so stupid as to think I could catch a college? Not everyone was my dad. *I* wasn't my dad. He'd faced down one of those enormous behemoths, not side-by-side with a dozen other applicants, but *alone.* If waves had swamped his kayak, if he'd been caught in a rip-tide, if he hadn't gotten on board before Wakereach dove, he'd have drowned. He'd had to risk everything, knowing he wouldn't make it back if he failed, so he didn't fail.

But me? Did *I* have that in me?

I stared into the gloom where the Wakereach model arched gracefully from the ceiling. The fairy lights glittered on its scales, on the curves of its fins. Parbrier seemed nothing like Wakereach. It was bulky and sharp and frightening.

I dragged the covers over my head and stuffed myself under my pillow where everything was dark and muffled, smothered like deep water. At last, whether from slowly suffocating myself with my own CO2 or from actual exhaustion, I finally fell asleep.

Then came morning, and the announcement of the evacuation orders, and Dad and I had spent every second since scrambling to pack up what we could. I wouldn't be taking the bulky Wakereach model, but the fairy lights made it into my backpack. I packed a week's worth of clothes, my old stuffed whale Nemo, and my journal. I couldn't fit anything else, and I couldn't weigh myself down on the motorbike. Dad set aside a box for me to put anything else I wanted, but I quickly realized that everything I wanted wouldn't fit.

Defeated, I helped him pack a few kitchen supplies, bathroom things, his clothes, and his books. I paused at his old copy of The Encyclopedia of Modern Behemoths, thinking of his boarding story. It changed a bit each time he told it, as personal memories do, but the core remained the same:

My father, in his early twenties with all his hair in dark tousled waves, scrambling barefoot across algae-slicked rocks along the southern shoreline for a hundred miles. Eating limpets and clams as he could find them. Wincing from the infected cut on his hand that kept getting sand and saltwater in it. Jotting down notes on Wakereach sightings from local fishermen in his damp pocket notepad. Calculating that its next ventilation flush would be close enough to shore for him to board, if he could get to it fast enough. Buying the leaky kayak, barely seaworthy, that whitecaps filled with water before he'd gotten three hundred yards off shore, soaking his belongings, freezing his feet and hands. Paddling harder as Wakereach's massive metal spine arched up from the depths and settled on the surface a quarter mile ahead, its foghorn moaning, its blast of spray arching up into the sky and raining down on him. The kayak foundering. Casting the oar aside and plunging into water so cold the fishermen had warned him he'd only survive ten minutes before drowning. Hauling himself up the iced metal rungs with the last of his strength and pounding, screaming at the porthole for someone to open it, to let him in. Finding himself face to face with a student horrified to see him and getting dragged inside mere seconds before the school dived back to the depths.

That was the kind of story I'd always wanted for myself. Proof of my unflagging determination, my strength, my bravery. Secretly, I'd always thought I had that in me, but sitting in the living room, waiting for Dad to come back, I felt every last drop of confidence ooze out of me.

I just wanted things to stay how they were. I wanted to live with Dad, go to school, work a part-time job over the summer, and keep falling asleep under my Wakereach model. I wasn't ready for everything to change, and yet it would, whether I caught Parbrier or not, whether we evacuated or not: nothing, in two days, would ever be the same.

I clutched my head in my hands and willed myself not to cry. I wasn't ready. How could anyone, any of my classmates, be ready for this?

The footsteps on the front stairs made my heart sink, and I sniffed hard to choke down the dread that threatened to break me into pieces. The door burst open and Dad swept in, sandwiches under one arm, and a bright green pair of goggles dangling from his other hand.

"Hey, kiddo!" he said, beaming, practically dancing on his toes as he dropped lunch on the bare table. In two days, the table would be gone. The room would be gone. Everything, everything—

Dad came over and dropped with a huff onto the couch beside me. "Here. I got them printed just for you. Look! It's got the Parbrier logo on the side."

I looked and looked.

"Hey." Dad's arm draped over my shoulders, squeezing gently. "What's up? You look like you've got something stuck in your throat. You okay?"

The concern in his voice broke me. I couldn't stop it, couldn't hold it back any longer. I curled up against him and burst into tears. It was like the ocean and all Dad's saltwater stories were pouring out of me. I cried and cried, but eventually the water dried up, leaving me numb as Dad hugged me, shushing softly, whispering, "Hey, hey, hey. It's okay. It's okay."

"I can't do it," I croaked at last, mashing my face with my hands to wipe the tear tracks from my cheeks. "I can't, Dad. I'll die. I just know it."

Dad turned in his seat and gripped me by the shoulders, giving me a little shake. "Hey. You listen, and you listen closely, okay? You can do this. Kaiya, you're strong and you're brave and you're smart."

"No, I'm not!" I could feel the tears surging again. "I'm not brave and I'm not strong. I'm terrified. I've been terrified for weeks, ever since they announced Parbrier's approach."

"Of *course* you are!" Dad cried, and I looked up at him.

"What?"

"Kai, I'd be worried about your sanity if you weren't terrified. Parbrier is a massive, powerful school. It has and will destroy people, good people, smart people, brave people. I was terrified of Wakereach, too."

"Really?"

Dad nodded and a small, comforting smile slipped across his face. "Yeah, Kai. I don't talk much about that part because I don't like remembering. I was shitting myself in that kayak. I almost turned around to go back to shore. A part of me was absolutely sure I was about to die, that Wakereach would dive before I got close and that its wake would drag me down behind it." He rubbed his warm hand up and down my arm. "Catching a college is terrifying, Kai, but you are fully capable of doing it. I know you. I wouldn't let you do this if I didn't think you had it in you."

The dread clenching my stomach loosened slightly. "Why does it have to be like this?" I whispered. "Why does it have to be so hard?"

Dad shrugged. "Who knows? But I promise you, no matter what happens, I'll be here for you, okay? I don't want you to let your fear stop you, because I know you'd regret it. This is the experience of a lifetime, a chance to bloom into the person you'll be from here on out. It's a rite of passage, proof of your adulthood. Kai," he said, taking my hands, "you're braver than you think. You don't have to do something stupid just to make it, okay? Healthy risks. Don't dwell on all the things that could go wrong. Think instead about what it's going to feel like when you climb up onto Parbrier and the other students sweep you inside. You're going to *love* it. Libraries the size of City Hall, dorms filled with ambitious kids like you, world-class professors to drive and inspire you!" He laughed. "Oh, Kai, the future will be yours! You'll be able to do anything you want, go anywhere you like! And wherever you end up, know—" He held me apart from him and peered lovingly into my eyes. "—I'll be here. Always. Okay?"

His enthusiasm infected me, set my heart soaring. This *was* my chance. Yes, it was terrifying, but wasn't that part of the appeal? To prove myself? To show that I could manage on my own, carve my own path in the world?

"Okay," I said, and he hugged me tight again.

"Good. Now let's eat and get this stuff packed up, okay?"

The warmth and confidence that had enveloped me while safe in his embrace began to trickle away as I watched him unwrap our sandwiches, softly chanting, "Two more days! Two more days!"

I looked again at the piles of belongings we needed to move. I looked at the apartment's peeling paint, its uneven walls, the way the floor sagged under the weight of his bookshelf. The fold-out couch Dad used for his bed; the side table piled high with his stack of notebooks. The small but tidy kitchen where I'd eaten almost every meal of my life.

I took a long, shaky breath, absorbing the smell of coffee, sawdust, and paper. I'd been lucky to grow up here in Hilltown, even if it was boring. I'd never realized it until now. After tomorrow, I would never stand in this apartment again.

I choked down the thought and went to the table where Dad was already tucking into his salami sandwich.

Yes, I told myself, *everything will change. But it'll be for the better.*

It had to be for the better.

It appeared as a dark cloud on the horizon, as a warning tremble that sizzled the sand in the gutters and clattered glasses on shelves. Hilltown's concrete teeth rattled, and in a burst, its sirens screeched over the rooftops: IT'S HERE. Eyes snapped open, exhaustion wiped from every heart as Hilltown's citizens gathered at their eastern windows to peer out at the drifting darkness, like volcanic smoke on the horizon.

The city, after a breathless pause, a moment between heartbeats, exploded into activity. Citizens scrambled for supplies. Jetpacks whined, engines warming. Earpieces and hand-held radios squawked as frequencies synced. Parasails strained in the breeze. Boots pounded down Hilltown's steps, beating their way to strategic spots.

This was it. The city's walls echoed with shouts of encouragement and people mobbed the guardrails high up on the Hill. Cardboard banners danced above their heads. Flags lunged and shivered in the breeze. The air filled with the smells of roasted nuts and fried dough and spicy street noodles.

Through the haze of dust far across the plains, Parbrier College began to take form, a shadow of spines, roaring closer.

Dad sagged against the deck railing, a beer clutched in his hands even though the sun was hardly above the horizon. He looked thin and tired, his hair ruffled up like he'd tossed and turned all night like I had. When I pushed the sliding door open, he pivoted to squint at me, and over his shoulder I saw it: a dark cloud of dust billowing up from the east. Inside the unearthly plume, a knot of shadow made me catch my breath.

Pushing off the rail, Dad came over and wrapped his arm around my shoulders, and we stood like that, watching the cloud grow, feeling the deep rumbling as it shook its way up through the ground, the floor, and into our feet. The warning sirens shrieked, echoing off the courtyard and the surrounding buildings.

The cloud swirled in hypnotizing spirals, coiling up into the sky. It drifted higher and higher, its veil wafting over the sun, blotting it in and out of sight, turning it red as a blister. Beside me, I heard Dad take a trembling breath, but when I glanced up at him, he was grinning.

"Let's get you ready, huh?"

Following Dad down to the courtyard where the motorbike waited, I felt every step jam up into my hip, making me suddenly aware of how my muscles and bones connected to make walking happen. It was such a strange process, walking, I realized; it took so much thought, so much mental work, all of it tucked away in my subconscious, forgotten by ease of practice. But it was a complex movement.

The bike looked fragile in the vague light, patched together with duct tape, its paint pitted, its crevices jammed with dust from weeks of practice. I slung onto it, took the small rubber grips in my hands. Parbrier's approach made the bike's body rattle softly, like it was shaking. I brushed a film of dust from its fuel tank, felt the gentle shushing from my lips before remembering it wasn't a living thing. It couldn't be afraid. It couldn't die.

Dad stood with his hands deep in his pockets, hunched and peering as he paced around the bike. "I checked over everything," he said. "Spent all night making sure it was good to go. It's rock solid."

I nodded, swallowed the muddy spit that had started pooling in my mouth. The rumbling was making me nauseous. I needed to get moving, get distracted.

"You're heading straight up Hill when I go, right?" I asked. He didn't look at me as he stooped to pick at a flake of something on the rear tire. "You'll have a better view up there. And better reception on your clamp, so when I call..."

Dad nodded, stood, cleared his throat. I felt a shudder run through me at the shimmer of moisture in his eye. "Yeah. Yeah, that'll be perfect." He nodded, and I saw his nostrils flare as he glanced up at the sky over the courtyard wall. The dust cloud was drifting towards us now. Parbrier was getting nearer. The fire escape rattled against the building.

"I gotta go." It came out as a croak, and Dad lurched suddenly, catching me up tight in his arms.

"Be careful, okay?" he muttered as he pressed a fast, dry kiss to my cheek and ruffled my hair as he stepped back. "Don't let fear get in your head, but don't do anything dumb, all right?"

I nodded. "Thanks, Dad."

He forced a grin that muffled the wetness in his eyes and threw up his two thumbs. "Go get 'em, kiddo!"

I revved up the bike and the tires spun out on the asphalt, shooting me forward as I wrestled to keep it under control. It was like everything I'd learned, everything I'd practiced had flown out of my head, and suddenly, I needed all my attention just to stay on the bike and keep it going straight.

Swerving around chunks of masonry shaken free from the buildings, I cut through a side street and out onto the plains. The landscape folded flat around me, and I saw it: Parbrier, its spires rising up out of the gloom, its windows glowing in sooty twilight, not more than two miles away.

I gunned the bike to its top speed, thirty miles per hour, forty. The wind filled my ears, its soprano screaming cutting through the roar of the school. I swung out in a circle to get around the worst of the debris cloud. Far to my left, I caught a glimpse of tiny figures scuttling up into the trees at the edge of town, ropes and harpoons dangling like delicate strands of spider silk beneath them. Would they be too close when the college turned?

I shivered and swung out farther. I needed to pass the college in order to get behind it, attack from the rear. The bike engine squealed as it pushed forty-three. A stone stung my cheek. Off to my left, the college formed a cliff of darkness. It was no longer a uniform mass, but a complex of recesses and protrusions, projecting thousands of interior corridors and laboratories and community rooms and private spaces. High up on the spires, silhouettes gathered, waving.

I'll be up there with them tonight, I thought, and yanked down my goggles.

Leaning low over the handlebars, Dad's attack plan raced through my head. I had to keep up the speed to stabilize the bike for the jump. One shot, one jump, one chance. If I missed, I'd land hard and probably scrape off most of my skin, if I didn't break a bone.

The dust cloud boiled ahead of me. It'd be impossible to see inside. I'd have to turn, line up, then drive into the fiercest debris, all relying only on radar.

Overhead, a flash of movement drew my eye, and I watched as a kid with a jetpack raced towards the school, vapor trails streaming behind him. He was almost there when the jetpack's left engine sputtered out in a billow of smoke and he plunged. My heart lurched into my mouth as he tumbled, arms and legs flailing, out of sight on Parbrier's far side.

Then the cloud caught me. Sand sizzled against my windbreaker. I switched on the radar and turned hard. The fist-sized screen started blinking, showing a large cobalt splotch sliding into place ahead of me. My bike jittered over ravaged dirt. I had to focus.

The dust thickened as I gunned forward, barreling towards where I hoped the track was. I tugged up my muffler. The debris burned my cheeks and sand-blasted my goggles, and then I sensed it: a bulk in the darkness, coming up fast. I couldn't hear anything but the bone-numbing roar, the squealing earth, the percussion of rocks. A stone punched me square in the shoulder, making my hand go numb. I yelped and choked on dust.

I aimed into the raging storm. A pebble cracked my goggles. Almost there. Grit stabbed into my eye, blurring everything to the right. I had to jump soon, but couldn't tell where. I couldn't see anything in the chaos, couldn't even detect a shift in sound to find the tread. Rubble flew at me, bounced off. I'd be speckled with bruises later. One chunk clipped my lip, sending a shooting pain up behind my nose. I tasted blood, and felt the knife edge of a cracked tooth with my tongue.

I couldn't get close enough, I realized. Dad hadn't considered how many rocks would be mixed into the soil, that it'd be too dangerous to get close enough to jump. I couldn't see, my goggles were broken, I couldn't breathe!

His plan wasn't going to work. I dropped back to where the dust thinned, ripped off my hazed goggles, and fought back a sob of frustration. This was my boarding story, and this was how would it end? That I'd gotten scared of getting hurt and given up? I imagined riding back to town, weighed down by dust, walking the gauntlet of spectators recognizing failure. Would they laugh? Would they try to comfort me, clap me on the shoulder, say *Nice try*? And then Dad's face, the forced smile, the soothing hug, all the words that would spill out of him trying to convince me it was fine, that there'd be other chances, that sometimes luck just wasn't on our side, but deep down, I'd know—and he'd know—that I'd given up. That when faced with the same terrifying choice he'd made a hundred yards from Wakereach, I'd turned around and run back to safety.

The dust thinned for a moment around me, and I saw the gap between the tracks, Parbrier's underbelly. It looked clearer there. I thought back, searching my brain for some small piece of info, and remembered with a jolt the portholes on the underbelly.

I revved up the bike again and gunned forward, breaking out into the clear and eerily muffled space under the school. Above me, the college was a vast inverted horizon. The size of it gave me vertigo, like I was falling headfirst out of the sky towards the darkened land below.

With a nauseating lurch, my perspective whipped right-side up again as I made out the latticework of catwalks above me. If I could get up there...

Movement caught my eye, a fluttering line, dangling from a grappling hook snagged on a railing. I started towards it, but just then, the college shifted, the right track arching towards me. I veered, and missed the rope. Looking back over my shoulder, the rope was gone. Had it been there at all?

Up ahead, through the broad gap, I could see the buildings of my neighborhood racing nearer. I scanned the catwalks for anything that could help me. There! A broken walkway within reach.

I had to get up and get inside before the debris from town started bouncing around the undercarriage. Ten feet. Five feet. My boot slipped off the saddle as I tried to get it under me, the leather slick with dust. I gripped the handlebars, just as Dad had taught me, and leveraged myself up again. The bike wobbled. I accelerated a little to keep it stable, and then jumped!

I crashed onto grating and felt the twisted metal bite into my thighs. I cried out and shifted to take the cutting weight off my legs, felt hot, sticky liquid soaking my pants. I clawed higher. I could hear the sirens from town again. I had to hurry.

A hand clamped onto my wrist, and I looked up to find a pale lady dangling from a climbing harness. "Welcome to Parbrier!" she shouted, throwing a safety line around my waist. Hauling us up to a stable platform, she unclipped me and shoved me towards four waiting kids.

A concrete chunk buzzed past us, not twenty feet away.

"Inside! Now! We're gonna hit!"

Someone dragged me inside with them, and the woman slammed a steel door behind us, cutting the roaring noise to a whisper that rang in my ears. Then everyone burst out laughing. I sat trembling as someone applied pressure to the gashes on my legs. A girl with black curls hugged me.

"Congratulations! You made it!" She grinned. "Let's get you registered, okay?"

And then it was over. The last chunk of stone flipped up from Parbrier's tracks, and Hilltown felt the roaring subside as the college cut off to the north, its dust cloud once more shrouding it from sight. The city watched, stunned to silence, until one bold voice shouted out in joy and the streets erupted in hoots and howls and Parbrier's fight song which everyone had learned by heart.

Details trickled in, reports from the ground. Of the thirty applicants, eight had gained admittance, ten missed their chance, and twelve perished. The school had crushed two streets deeper than predicted, forcing citizens to scramble to escape. Some didn't get out in time. Parbrier had left its mark on Hilltown once more.

But what thrill! What destruction! It made Hilltown giddy and loud and boisterous. Champagne corks popped, and there was dancing and music and joy and among all that, huddled in dark, quiet rooms, failed applicants and the families of the dead clutched their heads in their hands and wept or stuffed their mouths with bedding and screamed in rage.

The Energy Beetle hummed quietly to itself, pleased to make the strung lights glow, the stereos pound, the griddles sizzle. The town swelled with pride, having launched its seeds of future prosperity at the raging college, and having successfully landed many. For those who failed or died, Hilltown chose to believe if they'd only tried harder or been smarter, if only they'd made better choices, they'd have made it. It was easier that way.

I lay on the bed in my dorm room ,which was little more than a cube with a cot and a storage locker that doubled as a desk. The bulb overhead cast flattening light into every corner, erasing the shadows. I switched it off, preferring the reddish glow of dusk seeping through the slotted window.

On my legs, bandages tugged on the school-branded sweatpants I'd been given in the Parbrier infirmary. Thirteen staples, all told, and filler for my chipped tooth. The painkillers helped, but I was sick with exhaustion and bruised to my core.

I kept waiting for the thrill of triumph to hit, for my version of Dad's victorious whoop to burst from my chest and fill me with joy and pride, to feel changed, worthy. But I felt nothing.

I'd met with advisor after advisor, all of them trying to puzzle out what I wanted to study, what I wanted to do with my life, and I couldn't tell them. I didn't know. I'd never thought about what would happen after I caught a college.

In the end, they signed me up for behemothology. It was the only major I could remember Dad talking about, and lost as I felt, it seemed to make sense to study the thing that had baffled me: this giant machination that came and destroyed and left, without malice or kindness, without explanation. It simply existed, as all behemoths did, without question. Who built them? Who controlled them? But even more, why didn't we question it?

Maybe I was just ungrateful. I tried to conjure up the enthusiasm I'd felt at our kitchen table, but that only made me remember the table was gone. Our plans were gone. Our apartment, our deck, my room, my model of Wakereach, everything.

I thought of the kid with the jetpack spiraling out of control, and my stomach lurched up into my mouth. There'd been four other kids in the medical center when they brought me in, blooded and scraped raw from the ordeal of catching Parbrier. The medical techs chatted around us while they cleaned wounds and patched torn skin. A dozen kids had died trying to board this year. One of the techs said it was the highest casualty count in Parbrier history, and would no doubt increase its desirability.

My wristclamp buzzed with another message from Dad congratulating me, asking me to call, to tell him everything. I stared at its cracked screen, then looked back up at the slotted window. Wind wedged silt under the sill, leaving a film of dust on everything, including me.

Dad wanted my boarding story, the one thing I'd dreamed of ever since I was a kid. But all I wanted to do was sleep. I clenched my eyes shut and tried to squeeze pride out of my heart. How could I feel nothing? How could I not sense how I'd changed?

I'm just tired, I told myself. *Tomorrow, I'll wake up and squeal in delight*, I told myself. *It'll all be worth it*, I told myself, but Parbrier's rumbling engines lulled me to, I was more certain than ever that I was wrong.

See Maggie Slater's story "Catching College" online at Metaphorosis.
If you liked it, leave a comment. Authors love that!
Remember to subscribe to our e-mail updates so you'll know when
new stories are posted.

About the story

If you've read "Catching College," you may think that the first element that popped into my head was the giant, charging college, but actually, Parbrier and all the other behemoths sprang out of another story I wrote almost a decade ago. In that story, the first behemoth was born: a metal aquatic beast that harassed a small fishing town under the guise of helping them.

In "Catching College," I continued this theme, looking instead at the college application process. I was intrigued by the Varsity Blues Scandal, by the willingness of some to risk *everything* to get their kids into certain schools, and the fear that failing to doing so would doom their kids to mediocrity. It got me thinking about higher education as one of those behemoth institutions that we don't always question until things go wrong. When they do, we're at a loss for who to hold responsible or what steps to take to fix them. They just seem too big, too complicated to steer in a better direction. My percolating on all these things grew into Kai and the rampaging Parbrier College.

As with almost all my short stories, I sat on the rough draft of this one for almost a year before I could bear to pick it up again. The core idea was there, but it needed structure and tension. I rewrote it almost from scratch, and it ballooned into a 12,000 word behemoth of its own! Thankfully, I'm a pretty ruthless word-culler, and I managed to wrangle it down to about 8k. Then Metaphorosis showed interest, but wanted a rewrite, so editor B. Morris Allen and I reworked the story through several more drafts, distilling it into the story you now see. It's true what they say, *Writing is rewriting!*

A question for the author

Q: What would your animal totem be?

A: An octopus. I've always loved how smart and yet different they are. I love that their legs can have different personalities. I love that they both look and act like something that maybe, just maybe, slipped through some cross-dimensional fissure and decided that our oceans were comfortable enough to colonize. The only thing I hate about octopuses is how short their lifespans are. I have a growing collection of secret octopus decor hidden around my house. An embroidered throwpillow here. A candleholder there. A door knocker. All subtle enough that they might not immediately stand out, because that's the weird beauty of octopuses, right? They hide in plain sight. I've got my eye on some bookends next...

About the author

Maggie Slater lives in an 1800s farmhouse in New England with two half-tamed boys, a half-trained puppy, her husband, her parents, and at least one benign ghost. When she has an almost quiet moment, she enjoys Haruki Murakami novels, sampling craft beer, and hoarding cheap notebooks.

maggieslater.com, @maggiedotwrites

Escape to Mall B

Theodore Lowry

Brad's first and only memories were of a mall. In time, he came to know it as Mall A, but for most of his life it was simply home. Plastic ferns brushing his face, sofa advertisements dangling overhead, and lime disinfectant squeaking beneath his mother's shoes. Despite the top-ten hits playing in the background, for the first twelve years of his life, Brad hardly noticed music at all. This is the story of how he started listening, and how it cost him everything.

He grew to roam the arcade and toy store, keeping away from his empty home, and later worked in the supermarket to earn mall tokens for Discount Tuesdays in the cinema with candy and other boys yelling along with the latest '80s action flick.

One afternoon, while resting from his labours in the food court, Brad noticed an older boy perched on a nearby stool. He wore a black leather vest inscribed with arcane symbols, and his black boots had left dark traces on the white tiles beneath him. Even from where he sat, Brad caught a rich smell like wet dog, without doggie shampoo.

Brad and his friends had just watched *Too Alive to Die*, starring Chuck Van Willis, and they were acting out their favorite scene. "And then Chuck roundhoused the guy's head into the jet fighter." "Then BOOM!" "Boss goes down!"

Brad stopped listening as the older boy lifted a slender black case onto the square table before him, and slid out a shiny guitar. Brad had only ever seen them in videos. The boy held it, fingers hovering by the strings. The mall's speakers tinkled the current Number 6 song, 'Your Love Hurtz Too Much Much', by The Boyz and Girlz Club. It was slow, but with a dancy chorus. The boy cocked his head, his fingers hovering over the strings.

What came next changed Brad's life forever. The boy played a chord, matching the song. He played another, and yet another, as though he were on stage with The Boyz and Girlz Club themselves. Brad imagined them as tiny people playing somewhere within the mall's speaker system.

From across the food court, a pretty girl glanced over and smiled. The boy looked suddenly shy, and put his guitar away.

Brad blurted out, "How are you doing that?"

"Oh, this?" The boy stopped playing and slouched back in his stool. "Guess you've never been to the Southwest Wing."

Brad rifled through old movie tickets and candy wrappers until he found his bag of mall tokens. "How much do you want for it?"

Brad had traded away all his tokens, three months' worth of supermarket work. He couldn't afford movies anymore, so he spent that time practicing the hits on with this precious guitar. It felt wonderful to have these rhythmic patterns seeping through his mind. As night came, and people went to sleep in their capsule beds, the calls of children demanding candy gave way to still hallways. He played more and more quietly, and sang in a whisper. It was then that Brad softly crooned the slow hits.

At first the flow of music was a trickle, like water through a drinking fountain, then a flow, like the fountain in the food court. Music no longer lived only in the mall's tinny speakers; it flowed through Brad's body, like a special power activated in a video game.

One fine evening, he found himself perched on a column above the meandering crowd, playing along with Hit Number 4. Brad wasn't convinced of the singer's claim: 'My baby makes me so crazy I get lazy'. That guy had probably already been lazy.

"Get down," breathed a low voice.

"That's right," Brad sang. "Get down, get on up." He fumbled a G chord.

"Get down *now*."

Before him was a gaunt face, familiar from many a food-spill debacle. A man who intimately knew every grime-attracting crack of the mall's lily-white hallways. Straddling the top of a ladder, clad in an immaculate uniform, gray hair cropped, Lysol sprayers dangling from two holsters, the Cleaner frowned. "Son, you can't be breathing and sweating up here."

"Why?"

"Moisture breeds mold."

"Mold?" Brad stammered.

"Enemy's first incursion." The Cleaner's hot glare made Brad drop his gaze.

Brad nearly asked, 'Am I mold to you?' But, one: the question was ridiculous. Two: it was obviously true, with the way the Cleaner sneered at him.

The Cleaner's expression lightened. "Pray you never see it, boy. Just keep playing the hits. Y'aint careful, you'll wind up like that good boy who turned into a..." his lips curled, "...*alternative musician.*" In a blur, the Cleaner shoved Brad's foot aside to reveal a smudge, unholstered his weapon, then Lysoled it into foamy oblivion. "You're alright, son. Just don't let that happen to you."

Every time Brad sat still to practice, he imagined the Cleaner coating him with Lysol, then wiping him away. Brad didn't really know what the man was capable of. What *had* happened to that older kid who'd sold Brad his guitar?

In between the hits, Brad would sometimes try out tunes of his own. Fumbling, awkward things, but full with possibility. He knew the Cleaner wouldn't approve, so Brad kept moving. He spent the following weeks strumming and humming on escalators, elevators, and stairs. When he did sit down, people would hush him so that they could hear the 'real songs' playing on the PA. His best spot was a disabled person's bathroom. It was spacious, and the acoustics were excellent.

One fine fluorescent morning, he was sitting on a bench playing his most polished song, 'I Love Dat Lovely Luv' by Dang Dem Witches, the current Number 6 hit. Usually he played for the plastic ferns on either side of the bench, imagining them to be cute girls in his peripheral vision. This time he glanced up, and found a group of people staring at him.

He stood. "It's alright, I'm going."

"Long time since I heard live music." An older woman rubbed her eyes, streaking purple mascara. "Look what you've done."

A boy popped a gum bubble. "Can you play faster?"

"Probably." Brad sat down and played the chorus. People gathered like there was a sale on. It was glorious. For a moment, he was in his own music video.

He'd gotten good. He thought to try out one of his own tunes, but they weren't ready, and he thought he'd glimpsed the Cleaner slipping behind a pillar.

The next morning, Brad awoke to an odd feeling. Something was different. Missing. He couldn't put his finger on it. His sleeper pod was shiny and cozy as always. He was hungry, thinking to get an egg sandwich in the food court.

All normal enough.

Except that the mall's PA was silent. There was no music on the speakers.

Brad had always awoken to music drifting from the ceiling speakers outside his sleeper pod. His parents always went to work early at the Notary Republic, so it was always the music that had woken him. Now he heard only silence.

Was it the Cleaner's doing? This might be a psychological attack against Brad, like the bad guy in Chuck Van Willis' latest film, the one that Brad couldn't afford to see.

The speakers erupted in a cough. A woman spoke, slow and confident, "This is the Mall Mayor. Paging Brad Ashton. Please report to the food court."

Brad's chest tightened. "I'm being taken to court?" Had the Cleaner reported him for playing the wrong songs?

The voice added, "To play today's top hits!"

Brad found himself on a foot-high stage in the food court. He wiped sweaty palms on leather pants given to him by the mayor herself. The guitar was an anchor around his neck, the strings too hard to press.

No one was eating, just staring at him. All he could hear was his own breath. Did they really want him here? This could all be a setup.

"Number Ten," he squeaked into the mic, more gerbil than rock star. "Ten, ten, ten..." like it echoed on the radio. "This one's called, 'Save I Saved my Tears for Years'."

People nodded, watching. There were pretty girls out there.

God, don't let me mess this up.

The A chord came out wonky, his voice thin. The girls looked away. The C chord sounded worse. *Can only get better*, he told himself, and his playing did even out.

At first only a few babies clapped along, off rhythm. Then a pod of football players started singing, and everyone turned on. The prettiest girl sang the loudest.

"Number Nine, nine, nine!" Brad launched into a slow tune, 'Sucky Nights' by Pet Factory.

"Number Eight!" Brad chimed the high notes, swam the sad stretches. "Number Four, Three..."

Number Two was coming fast: 'Your Love's Too Pointy'. This one was tricky. It had this one long, high note at the very end, and Brad had only really pulled it off once. The audience should feel in their bones the cut of his girl's love.

Number Three wound down and he launched into Number Two, feeling exhilarated. He came into that last note ready. Too ready. The note came out happy, like he was a *sucker* for her pointy ways.

The crowd cheered, but not the football players, and not the prettiest girl.

Off to the side, there was the Cleaner, his fingers far from his holster, his grim face satisfied.

Brad was eager to launch into Number One, but the song escaped him. Instead, tinkling, etheric music streamed through his mind. Hardly music at all, but more like the flow from a drinking fountain, mixed with the sound that stars might make as they moved. Not stars as in popular people, but like the ones in outer space in that beer commercial.

A shifting tone trickled from his mouth, another reverberated from his guitar.

The crowd stared at him. The Cleaner's smile fell. The pretty girl looked confused.

Number One landed in Brad's mind. In his voice and his fingers. He started slow and brought it to a messy, gyrating conclusion. The crowd loved it, but to him it sounded mechanical, like a kid pounding buttons on an arcade game.

The Cleaner nodded in approval.

A week later, the Mall Mayor was all over the PA system, asking Brad to play again.

Brad was squatting beneath a drinking fountain by a farflung bathroom, arms crossed, staring at a plastic fern. He didn't know why he was hiding; his concert had gone well. They might ask him to play every week. The pretty girls might smile again. If this was everything he wanted, why did it feel like a trap?

"Brad Ashton, we've paged you many times. Brad Ashton, please report to the food court."

Someone stepped in front of Brad, dressed in immaculate white pants. He squatted, bringing his gaze to Brad's level. It was the Cleaner. "No guitar?"

Brad flinched, trying to press himself into the wall.

The Cleaner cocked his head. "Thought music was your big dream."

Brad made himself hold the man's gaze. "Guess so."

"So get up there and play the hits."

Brad looked up. "Is that all…"

"Spit it out, boy."

"I mean, is there *other* music?"

"Like what?"

"I mean, the songs are all kind of like each other. Is there music that… stretches more, tinkles high like stars, rumbles like… and makes you feel…"

The Cleaner scoffed. "Stick with the hits."

"But what if—"

"I said stick with the *hits*." The Cleaner sprayed a caustic stream of Lysol on the floor by Brad's foot. Something invisible had just met oblivion.

Brad took to late-night roaming of corridors, trying to get away from the Cleaner. Instead of music in his head, he heard threats and the hiss of disinfectant spraying from a bottle, the click of the cleaning cart's wheels gliding over tiles.

Each time Brad found a place to sit and sing, the Cleaner appeared nearby. He was sweeping up any long hairs Brad shed, or walking backwards and spraying both Brad's footprints and his own. Watching, always watching.

One night, Brad went farther than he ever had, trying to get some time alone. It was there, in a far-off region of the mall, that he saw odd marks on the floor. At first he thought they were stickers leading into a nearby store, but when he leaned down to touch one, his finger came away wet. He flinched, looked around for soap, and only then realized just how far he'd wandered from any bathroom. From anything familiar.

Where was he? He'd never seen that shop selling floral syrups, or that one selling camping food.

His finger smelled like that wet dog, or…

Or like the boy who'd sold him his guitar.

These prints didn't lead into any shop. They lead into a long, empty hallway with green flickering lights.

White foam sprayed out of nowhere, coating Brad's fingers.

"It burns!"

"Purified." With a satisfied grunt, the Cleaner holstered his Lysol. A few blurs of the mop, and the odd marks were gone. He handed Brad a white cloth. "Wipe. It's the antidote."

Brad wiped off his hands. The cloth had been soaked in something. Instantly, the burning subsided. His hands still tingled though, and smelled like someone's idea of lemon.

The Cleaner stared into the dark corridor. "If I had my way, there'd be *no* Southwest Wing."

"What's there?" Brad asked.

The Cleaner didn't reply, and in the silence Brad thought he heard tinkling sounds seeping from the green hallway, sounds like flowing water mixed with stars.

"Time to get you back." The Cleaner smiled thinly, glancing between three visible escalators. "Guessing you don't know your way."

For a month, Brad stuck to the safety of the mall, working long hours so he could binge on movies. Then one day, after Brad played the current hits in the food court, the Mayor handed him a bundle of tokens. It was more than Brad could have made working three days in the supermarket. And whenever the Cleaner saw Brad, he nodded his approval.

Brad was safe. More than that, people recognised him in the hallway. A cute girl even told him that he sounded 'almost as good as the radio'.

Yet his thoughts kept returning to the long, storeless hallway. It beckoned to him with patterns of flickering green lights. Each night, he had to pump dozens of tokens into a massage chair just to get to sleep.

In his dreams, the hallway walls were a rich, loamy green. They billowed out and enveloped him with whispered welcomes.

Early one morning he woke up from that dream. Staring at the ceiling of his sleeping pod, it occurred to him that he wouldn't be free from this until he knew what was in that hallway. It was like Chuck Van Willis' wife had said when she'd faced her own sub-main-bad guy: 'You're my nightmare, but I'm your reckoning.' Something like that. Maybe more like she'd said to their son: 'I love you too much to die. I'll be back.'

That didn't work either. None of the action movie lines seemed to work, which just made Brad feel more unanchored.

Without giving himself time to think, Brad got up and, without even getting breakfast, strode toward the Southwest Wing.

As he descended an escalator, he saw the Cleaner coming up, wiping the black banister as he went. Brad grimaced and pressed on. Later, he saw a flicker of cloth on a tile corner. A mop sliding from view.

Brad wove randomly through the hallways until he was alone again. He entered the nearest elevator and hit a random floor. The doors opened, and the Cleaner stepped on.

"Going somewhere?"

Brad was forced back.

Each day was the same, as though the Cleaner had many forms. He held his Lysol like a gun, his mop like a spear, his cloths like garrottes.

Until one day, while Brad was in the food court wondering why he didn't like burgers as much as the people in the ads, the clandestine hand of fate poked the fabric of reality. A soda dispenser exploded, spraying kids, tables, chairs and customers with liquified chemi-sugar.

While everything around him grew sticky, Brad's thoughts grew clear.

As the Cleaner descended with his arsenal of disinfectants, Brad ran. Sprinted past The Screen Zone and The Perfume Panther. Past where his parents worked in the Notary Republic. He thought to say goodbye, but they'd be busy. He ran past shops selling holiday stuff year-round, then into the strange part of the mall, past dangling antiques and boot insoles color-coded by intensity of wearer's mood.

Sinking in an elevator, running up an escalator. Past where the moist footprints had been, then running, *flying* through the storeless corridor.

Silence, save his own footfalls. He ran alone past flickering green lights and fuzzy walls.

Ahead, he saw a sign scrawled in green ink:

MALL B

The lights went out.

He padded on in the dark.

From somewhere ahead, a deep tone unfurled. Then another, much higher, and a third in between. Was it music? It thrummed his bones, while chimes tinkled his mind. A continuum of strings plucked him to life.

Fear filled Brad's gut like a spicy taco, but he couldn't turn back. He glanced up to see cracks in the ceiling, seeping warm and otherworldly light, like the sunset in a chip ad.

Brad stopped. He'd gone farther than he'd wanted. He could still return to the mall he knew. His parents might be home from work. In any case, the soda machine must be fixed by now, and he could sure use some.

But whatever that sound was, it was close. He saw dim green lights up ahead, and had to keep going. The light came from a window, and in that window was the most beautiful thing he had ever seen. Carved from glistening ocher wood, it sported sleek symbols, ethereal and ineffable and maybe kind of Celtic. This guitar belonged in a music video.

He touched the glass and stared in. There were more instruments: carved shakers, cone-shaped drums, and translucent bowls.

Above the window hung a sign. Curving calligraphy read:

SOUND HEALING SHOPPE

Breath caught in his throat, Brad pushed open the door, just an inch. It chimed, and fragrant smoke billowed out. Mesmerised, he stepped into a realm of dreams.

Crystals dangled. Ceramic fairies danced in pentagrams. Rotating carousels showcased books about telepathic whale guides and helpful star systems.

Feeling faint, Brad fell into a chair. Strings surrounding him strummed his spine with spiraling reverberations. His imagination had only brushed the edges of this place. It was much more.

Someone placed an object in Brad's lap, made of cool metal and shaped like a UFO. He pushed it away, and his touch produced a clear note.

"Play more," said a young woman, stepping from behind the musical chair. She was beautiful and strange, like everything here.

"I..." A few more taps on the UFO, and an exotic melody emerged. Brad couldn't hit a wrong note.

The night was young. Brad played three-reeded flutes with rainbow-painted kids, his feet resting on a crystal-powered machine. The translucent bowls that he'd seen in the window, when stroked, sang like Buddhist angels. As evening became night, he lay still while a circle of singers blessed him with songs from before the mall was built. His body was of earth, formed from stardust. As the singers grew silent, Brad knew his purpose: to help the Earth on her grand initiation into new realms of being.

At one point Brad asked, "Was there ever an older boy here? Slick hair, leather jacket, played guitar?"

"There was," said the young woman.

"Where did he go?"

"No one knows. He left one day, said he was searching for more."

That night, he slept on a reiki table with a mobile of planets spinning overhead. In the morning, the girl gave him a pile of CDs. Their covers were full with words like 'overtone', 'meridian', and 'encounter'.

As he turned to go, she touched his arm and murmured, "Remember what music can be."

Brad had never thought of his home as Mall A, just *the* mall. But the Southwest Wing felt like another mall entirely. Going there had been strange, but coming back was stranger. The Healing Shoppe, where he'd been only once, felt like home. He had activated his chakras, had gone on an astral pilgrimage. Now he was back in his sleeping pod in Mall A, comfortable but pierced by loneliness. He hadn't even asked that girl her name.

Later, alone on a bench surrounded by plastic ferns, Brad put *Ancestral Reiki Vibrations* into his discman, slid in his earphones, and closed his eyes. The music drowned out the PA and eased Brad back to the Sound Shoppe.

"Looking mighty content there, son."

Brad yanked out his earphones. "Just the standard amount, sir. I'm loving the hits."

The Cleaner parked his supply cart next to the bench and sniffed the air. "New deodorant?"

"Patchouli, sir."

The Cleaner cocked his head. "Funny, haven't seen that for sale around here."

"Sure is bright today."

"Compared to what?"

"In the supermarket, a light was out."

"Thought I would have known." The Cleaner sat beside Brad and crossed his long, white-polyester-clad legs. "You know, that friend of yours reeked of patchouli, near the end. Stopped looking like the rock star he could have been and..." The Cleaner snatched something from Brad's pocket and held it up. "Had a bunch of shakers, too."

Brad wished he'd hidden it in his pack. "It's from the Halloween Shop."

"Guatemalan, by the look of the engravings on the bulb."

"How do you—"

"Ain't no *Guatemala* in the Halloween Shop." The Cleaner shoved the shaker back into Brad's pocket and lowered his voice so no passing customers would hear. "Don't think I've never been to that place. But you learned the *hits*, boy. You could *be* something in this place." His gaze slid to a tired-looking man toting bags of toys for his son, then back to Brad. The Cleaner's gaze softened. "Don't you want to be a normal father? Someone who can provide for your children?"

Weeks passed. Brad longed for another soda explosion, or for drunk teenagers throwing up, or for an overflowing water fountain, or a messy brawl over addictive candies. Anything to keep the Cleaner off his back while he made a break for it.

Nothing. And always, the Cleaner was nearby, hovering, fingering his Lysol.

Well, maybe Brad wasn't meant to be a rebel musician. He could just stay in Mall A. He could be a music-video rebel, well paid and popular. This was his home, wasn't it? He had grown up here, had developed hand-eye coordination playing those video games over there, had learned about human relations in that theater. His very body was built of burritos from Taco Giant, yet he wanted only to return to the nether region of the mall, and to the Sound Healing Shoppe.

Nightmares held him back: Lysol in his eyes, legs scrubbed clean of flesh. Only one thing in the mall was gathering dust: his adventure pack. He had filled it with all the necessities: fruit rollups, cheese strips, kombucha (weird, but recommended by the pretty musician girl), and, of course, his homely guitar.

One night he dreamt of smooth, white walls with spotless tiles crushing him, buckling inward and bashing him in time with hits playing on the radio. Beyond them, green walls folded outward like a blooming flower beckoning in a bee in a nature documentary. The kind of bee that would return to his hive covered in honey. Or pollen. However that worked.

Brad wanted to be that bee. To hear the tinkling melodies of the flower as they made love beneath an open sky. It was crazy. If he stayed here and kept playing the hits, if he had kids, he'd easily be able to buy them bags of toys and tell them they were from

Santa, like the other dads. He could have a good life. That was like a sweet flower too, wasn't it?

And if he tried to leave... Brad thought of the Cleaner, fingering his Lysol. If he hadn't handed Brad a cloth soaked in an antidote for Lysol, would Brad even still have his hands?

Better no hands than no heart, Brad thought.

As he got up from bed, defiant dialogue from dozens of action movies flickered through his head. "Over my dead body, punk," he hissed to the air. "Or over yours. Something like that."

Brad bought a variety pack of firecrackers and lit them in the children's cereal aisle.

With crackles and squeals at his back, he sprinted from the supermarket... and from his old life. Had he really just done that? Either way, he kept running, his pack and guitar bounding on his back. Past the Notary Republic with his parents doing some kind of work somewhere inside, then past the strange shops, the stranger ones, and into the empty, flickering corridor with its vivid green:

MALL B

It felt like he was falling. Feet slapping tile, guitar bounding on his back. Chest drumming.

Darkness all around. Running. He'd run as far as before. Still, only darkness ahead.

Sensing something ahead, Brad slowed.

Reached out and yelped, a splinter in his finger. With his phone light, he saw no celestial guitar, no singing bowls, just plywood and an immaculately printed sign.

SHOP CLOSED DUE TO UNSANITARY CONDITIONS.

Brad cried out, "It's spelled S-H-O-P-P-E. It's meant to be fancy." He fell to his knees. "Fancy!"

His voice echoed into silence.

He sat on a chunk of broken concrete, too stunned to weep. He would fall forever with nowhere to land. He had no home.

He managed to cry for a while, maybe a long while.

Frustrated, he plugged his earphones into his discman and picked up his guitar. Celestial harps mixed with singing bowls mixed with chords he'd never tried to play, notes he'd never tried to sing. No one could hear him here, so he sang along like a wailing dog. A wet, smelly, rejected dog. Keening calls. Rhythmic grunts. Songs for angels sprouting from the earth, and for whales swimming through constellations on their way to becoming ancestors. No hits. His own music. The world's music.

When the batteries on his discman ran out, he kept strumming and singing something, stumbling over rubble, running fingers over fuzzy walls. He sipped the kombucha, ate all his fruit rollups, and vowed never to return to the supermarket.

Exhausted, he lay on the dusty floor and stared up, singing in darkness. When his throat dried up, he sang on in his mind.

Above him, he thought he saw filaments of light, a spider-web of bright lines. Faint, and seeming to pulse along with his singing. Maybe the walls were singing along with him, in their own way.

This whole place smelled like wet dog. Something sprouting tickled his arm. The Cleaner had used the word 'soiled' like a curse, but this tickling felt kind of good.

Another voice sang too, at a higher pitch than his own. Sad and clear, it echoed through the empty corridors.

A woman's voice.

Brad sipped the kombucha and managed to sit up. Strumming quietly in tune, he approached the singer.

It was too dark to see her, but he recognized that high, clear voice. As he neared, she fell silent.

"This all used to be forest," she said.

"Like trees?"

"Before the mall. I was born in Mall A, same as you, but my grandmother told me." She kicked the ground. "Thought I'd get out some day."

Brad sat nearby on the cold floor. "My name's Brad, by the way."

"Alta."

He sank back against the fuzzy wall with its doggy smell. "I'm homeless. The Shoppe showed me elders, children, ceremonies, stars..."

"Yeah. Festivals, spirits, worship."

"But I've never seen those things, not even in music videos."

"Me neither, just in visions while we played music."

He strummed sad chords, and they sang laments for old-growth forests and cultures, though he barely knew what he was singing.

When their throats fell silent and dry, the songs echoed through the hallways. He gave her his last sip of kombucha.

"That's gallant of you." Alta sipped, and they sat in silence for a long time.

Then she said, "I have an idea."

"For what?"

She pulled him to his feet and led him through the dark hallway, and stopped in front of what had been the Sound Healing Shoppe.

He said, "I hate seeing it boarded up like this." And that was odd: he could see it, even without his phone light.

"Look up, Brad."

He did, then shrank down to protect himself. Light poured through cracks in the ceiling.

Alta was poking at the cracks with a piece of rebar. "Can you help?"

"You crazy? We don't know what's out there."

"So what are you going to do, go back?"

"I... I blew up the cereal aisle."

Alta made an impressed hum. "Might just get in trouble for that."

"Yeah, there's this guy—"

Alta shuddered. "The Cleaner?"

"You know him?"

She shuddered harder, then looked back up at the ceiling. "We've got to get out."

Brad breathed in deeply, and his out-breath was full of friends he'd never see again, video games he'd never win. All gone.

"Alright, let's do it."

It was dusty work. Brad barely jumped aside as a chunk of concrete struck the floor. The cracks widened. Light flooded in.

"Almost!" Alta pried out a chunk of concrete from above her, then a bigger one. She dropped the rebar, shielding her eyes against the light.

Brad stepped back, shielding his head from falling chunks.

When he could see again, he saw a hole just big enough to fit through.

They piled fallen concrete to make a rough staircase, and climbed up. Bashing, stumbling, prying. With a final effort, Alta shoved up and out.

Brad shrank back. Up above, beyond the hole, a brilliant ball hung in the air, brighter than a thousand fluorescent lights, more powerful than the mall's entire electrical system. Maybe it was Brad's imagination, but he heard it crackling and booming in the sky. Its light warmed Brad's skin, like that time he'd gone too close to a burrito oven.

He turned away and stumbled back down the rubble staircase. The Cleaner was right. Brad should go back to where he belonged. He was a mall baby, not made for a huge, intense world. Brad would return to cheese sticks, pop, plants that didn't smell. If he needed variety, let it be in the slow shift of the hits, as old ones slid from the chart, and new ones came in.

"Brad?" she called down.

"What if it's Tuesday already? Big box of buttery popcorn on me, Alta, what do you say?"

"Brad, get up here!"

"What if they don't have normal food out there? Like if there's just grass and shrubs, like vegetarians eat."

"*I'm* vegetarian."

"Sorry, I—"

"Sunlight, Brad."

"You eat sunlight?"

"No, that's what this is called. I remember my grandmother told me. It doesn't seem so bright anymore. Geez, I can see green grass. And trees. Real trees!"

She crouched, peering down through the hole at him. She looked radiant, terrifyingly free. "See for yourself."

She reached down, and Brad withdrew.

"Knew you couldn't do it, boy," a voice resonated from behind.

The man who stepped from the shadows had no cart, no mop or sprays. Gone was his starchy white uniform, replaced by worn overalls. He held a coil of rope in one hand, which he fingered as he had his spray-guns.

The Cleaner raised a hand, reassuring. "What say we forget this little incident? No repercussions. Teenagers do foolish things."

"I..."

"Throw in a year of free movie passes?"

"You could do that?"

"With popcorn."

"All you can eat?"

"Sure as the sun shines, boy."

Unsure, Brad called to his mind a host of action lines to bolster his resolve. "Your reign of terror ends here and now," he said. "You must face justice for your crimes." It had sounded like such a good line, coming from Chuck Van Willis. It didn't even make sense in this context. He added weakly, "I'd rather die than go back."

"Would you?" asked the Cleaner.

"I mean—"

"Ah, heard it in a movie. Out for your freedom, I got it. But what if you get your freedom and then you die?" asked the Cleaner. "Pretty useless freedom, no? Not much protein out there, boy, grazing with rabbits and deer and other... *vegans*." He said the last word like a swear, yet with a tinge of sadness in there.

"I'm sure there's popcorn?" Brad hadn't meant it to come out as a question.

"Not a nibble. I should know, I..." The Cleaner gritted his teeth, silencing himself.

Brad was hungry, thirsty. He *could* return. It didn't even matter whether it was Tuesday; every movie was free to him now! Maybe his parents would finally take some time off from the Notary Republic and they could go together.

As if that would ever happen.

He shoved the Cleaner aside and scrambled up the rubble staircase. "My spirit cannot be bound!"

"Just your body, boy." The Cleaner clambered up behind.

Brad burst onto the rooftop and a whole new world emerged. A meadow of brilliant, waving grass, with trees—real trees!—reaching upward. Some were even taller than the roof of the mall, and geez, the mall was so high that looking down made Brad dizzy. That fall could kill him. Birds stroked the sky in murmuring patterns. Clouds streaked farther in every direction than he was able to see. This was better than any deodorant commercial, even better than that ad for potato chips with the great song. The resolution was higher than the newest TVs, and the smells made the Perfume Panther seem... artificial.

Brad murmured a verse from a poem that had always touched him. "From dirty cuts to clean freedom, Fix-cream's got you covered. Live life without fear, ever untethered."

How would he get down from here? He had seen people make bigger jumps in movies... He bent his knees. Didn't they have stunt doubles and ropes to help them?

"Wondering if it's real?" The Cleaner stepped up onto the roof, his short hair ruffling in the breeze.

Alta grabbed a piece of rebar from the ground. "We can fight him."

The Cleaner's gaze settled on Alta. "Thought you were dead, girl." He tipped his hat. "Guess I'm glad you ain't."

She clutched the metal bar, glaring at him. Then her gaze softened. "He was happier, you know."

The Cleaner grimaced. "Don't tell me what he was."

"Who?" asked Brad.

"Don't you know?" said Alta. "That boy who sold you his guitar—"

"Don't say it," barked the Cleaner. "He's not anymore. I disowned him."

Brad stared at his old nemesis. "The smelly cool kid is your *son*?"

The Cleaner's hand drifted to his waist. The rope hanging there was starting to look more and more like a whip. In a flash, Brad realized that all those hours of action movies had not prepared him for a real fight.

Brad raised his hands and motioned for Alta to back away. "We won't fight."

Alta backed away, but kept a tight grip on her metal bar.

"And not 'cuz we're afraid," Brad added. "It's because this new world shouldn't start with fighting."

He stepped in front of Alta, let his hands fall, and faced the Cleaner.

"Well alright, then." The Cleaner unhooked the rope.

Brad closed his eyes and sang a lines from one of the healing CDs. "I sing of love in times of hate, of hope in times of fate. I sing of boats..."

"They're all times of fate." The Cleaner waved toward the roof's edge. "You going to jump off or not?"

"Is that what your son did?" asked Alta.

The Cleaner winced.

Brad's chest tightened. "Why are you provoking him, Alta?"

The Cleaner looked toward the ground, so far below, and his stance softened. "He would have jumped."

With a sigh, he handed Brad the rope. "If you see him, tell him I closed that damned Sound Healing Shoppe."

A long silence opened between the three of them, a vessel that soon filled with birdsong and wind rustling through grass.

Brad took the rope. It was heavy and coarse. "Thank you."

The Cleaner gazed toward the cluster of trees. "And tell him if he does come back, he'd better have stories to tell me."

"I'll tell him."

Alta was looking down over the roof. "I'll go first."

Brad nodded. "I'll hold the rope."

Feet pressed against the lip of the roof, Brad held the rope tight while Alta scaled down. She was heavier than she looked. His muscles strained more and more, and just when they were about to give, the weight lifted.

He looked down to find her dancing. She looked up. "Wait, how will you get down?"

A hand gripped Brad's shoulder. "Boy."

Brad pushed the hand away. "You going to take me back?"

The Cleaner scoffed. "Like the lady said, how will you get down?"

"You won't let go?"

"Only one way to find out."

The way down was terrifying, and Brad nearly clambered back up. The whole time, he was sure the Cleaner would let go.

When he landed, Brad squealed, "This ground's squishy!"

"Called grass, boy. You might have to eat it."

And with that, the Cleaner was gone. Silently, Brad thanked the man.

They started walking. Alta pulled out a Guatemalan shaker, and found a groovy rhythm. Brad strummed a bittersweet chord. They walked along squishy, pathless ground until they saw, there across the waving grass, a boxy building larger than the one they had left. On one wall, a towering sign read:

OAK MALL

The wall below the sign was broken. People streamed out in twos or threes, yelling and singing. Brad and Alta rushed toward them, adding harmonies. They sang for trees, open sky, and for new seeds sprouting from a worn but fertile world.

See Theodore Lowry's story "Escape to Mall B" online at Metaphorosis.
If you liked it, leave a comment. Authors love that!
Remember to subscribe to our e-mail updates so you'll know when new stories are posted.

About the story

My musician friend inspired this story with his life's journey. He always loved music, but growing up in suburbia, he only heard radio hits. Until a new age shop in Edmonton (a city famous for a huge mall) opened him up to healing music and world music. Brainstorming with my friend, we combined his life with *The Matrix*, the idea that everyday reality is fake, but that clues from the real world seep through, in this case coming as Mall B and the Shoppe there, as well as through the antagonist, The Cleaner. To get to the real world the characters must break out. I also wanted to make fun of both pop music and new age music, as well as mall culture.

A question for the author

Q: What do you think makes for a good story?

A: By inviting readers into strange worlds, a story shows them their own world from new perspectives. However, if the story is too strange, the reader may struggle to enter it. That's where resonance comes in.

A good story contains deep elements that are broadly relatable, even if the skin of the story is unfamiliar. The reader may recognize their own experiences in the story, despite vast differences in context. This resonance connects the reader's own heart to humanity at large and the world we inhabit.

In this way, a good story invites the reader into a world that is both unfamiliar and familiar, challenging them to see things from a new perspective while also resonating with their own experiences. This combination of the unknown and the relatable can make for a powerful story.

About the author

The mall in which Theodore was born sprung up at the confluence of two rivers, rivers who go on to create one of the eastern great lakes. His family migrated westward, so he sprouted up where vast grasslands crash against the western mountain range. Seeking temples, pilgrimage and clear meanings within messy, colorful life, he traveled to the far east to learn in monasteries there. Seeking to link sky to earth, he returned to his home continent to put down roots among the mycelium and cedar of this chilly rainforest. He writes, sings, draws, and helps others do the same.

storypaths.substack.com

Snow Like Pink Pepper

Devan Barlow

It was almost sunset when Albe first saw the girl who understood the snows.

Albe was heading back to the Seneschal Headquarters after her rounds purifying drinking water for the neighborhoods on the city's northern edge. She was running later than she liked, preferring to be back inside before sunset brought with it the risk of flurries, but had been slowed down by a collapsed wagon blocking the streets. And, she admitted to herself, her stride had slowed in the decades she'd served as a Seneschal.

At first she assumed that the girl, who stood on the front stoop of a small house, face tilted upward as if waiting for the snow to begin, was one of the many who illicitly gathered snow to produce extracts. Except the girl had none of the usual equipment, nothing in her hands at all. She was just waiting, though shelter and safety were near.

A spot of light in Albe's peripheral vision confirmed she was running even later than she thought. The sun was setting, and faint flakes were beginning to descend. Snows only fell at night. She swore and picked up her pace, only to realize the girl hadn't budged.

A thought flared faintly in Albe's mind and she looked around, conscious of faces at windows. This was too public, even if her guess was right. Some part of her recognized that this might be a foolish idea, relying on the logic of childrens' stories she hadn't thought about in years. But she didn't give herself time to consider that. With a nervous glance upward, she asked in a soft voice, "What are you waiting for?"

The girl flinched, startled by Albe's voice, and placed a hand on the knob of the front door as if to flee inside. Yet just then, a dusting of snowflakes landed on the girl's shoulders, and her posture relaxed.

"I know what you are," Albe said, though she only half-believed it herself. And then, before the girl could duck inside, she named a place, and a time.

And now here the two of them were, the girl looking grimly reluctant. She had admitted only her first name, Cally, though surely she had known that Albe, as a Seneschal, could easily learn more about her family.

"Finest snow drink this side of the city." The bartender winked as she placed empty glasses in front of them both. Though the place was packed, the two of them might have been the only customers who mattered.

Dozens of bottles rested on the shelves behind the bartender, whose practiced hands flew from shelf to shelf, collecting ingredients. Albe had seen the look that had passed between the bartender and the guard at the door. They seemed afraid that Albe might be the rare Seneschal who dragged themselves out to such establishments for the purpose of actually enforcing the rules regarding Seneschal-approved snow extracts, rather than to partake themselves.

Albe had opted for a plain warm jacket instead of full Seneschal dress, though she had still allowed the bartender to spot her ring. Why? Was she trying to show off for Cally? Hoping to distract herself from how foolish this made her feel, she let the sounds of the bar drift through her mind, pinpointing the other occupants.

Two men were at a corner table, too caught up in one another to notice anyone else. On the other side of the room, a woman in a coat simple enough to be horrendously expensive sat with a figure too wrapped in furs to distinguish, their voice muffled. Albe guessed a merchant, meeting with a client or trader. Maybe even the same merchant who sold snow extracts to this establishment.

Albe didn't think any of the other customers were the Arch-Seneschal's spies, but she kept her voice low anyway.

"Berry wine," the bartender explained as she hoisted a bottle full of pink and orange liquid like captured sunrise, "I can only get a few bottles of this every year." A design pressed into the glass, a bee surrounded by birds, caught the candlelight. From the eastern provinces, beyond the mountain pass. Not one of the finer producers, though Albe didn't inform the bartender. She hadn't chosen this place for the quality of its wares.

"And finally!" the bartender was clearly caught between wanting to show off her fanciest drink and hoping Albe wasn't planning to scrutinize her storeroom too closely. Most every establishment cut costs by buying from unlicensed snow-gatherers, at least until those particular gatherers died or were caught. She pulled down a glass jar, its sides frosted to conceal the contents, and whispered an unlocking spell. Such valuable ingredients couldn't otherwise be so openly displayed.

The blue substance inside the jar was the color of the sky when the sun came out to fool everyone into thinking they were safe. Snow only fell at night in this city.

Albe heard Cally's surprise in the breath she tried concealing. As the bartender scooped out mounds of the stuff with a spoon that had seen better days, Cally leaned closer, eyes searching as if to count the individual blue grains.

Cally knew there was more to the snows than how they could harm and how they could intoxicate, even if no one else seemed to care. Even if she had never dared to tell anyone else what she knew.

The snows of the city, resonating with the effects of long-ago magics, were endlessly dangerous. More than a few minutes' exposure during snowfall almost certainly meant harm to humans, if not death. Even once they were rendered temporarily inert by daylight, careless extraction could still prove toxic, before the proper, Seneschal-approved process rendered the snows down into something luxurious. The snows were also endlessly different, varying in color, shape, and effect based on where in the city they fell.

Cally had been only seven the first time she met a snow creature, young enough that her parents almost managed to convince her the meeting never happened. She'd taken advantage of a moment they were both distracted to linger outside as night began falling, and had seen the way the flakes collected on ground and rooftops and branches, coalescing into shapes that made her think of living creatures.

Suddenly, a curious sound had tugged at her hearing, and snowflakes swirled together into the shape of something winged, perhaps a butterfly. Though the creature had no obvious eyes, Cally was struck by the sense of it watching her.

"What is your name?" Cally had asked, her lips cold enough to mangle the syllables.

The snow creature seemed to understand, wings moving rapidly and its outlines solidifying more than they had before. A few snowflakes landed on Cally's face. She slowly stuck out her tongue, daring to taste the cold shape hovering on her upper lip—

"Cally!" Suddenly hands wrenched her backwards, and she lost the snowflake. She heard harsh curses, and was startled to turn and find her father. She had never heard him speak in such a way.

"You must not heed the voices of the snows," he said once they were inside, his voice still strange to her. "Do you know how fast a snow creature can smother you?!"

She was taught, in no uncertain terms, that the snows were deadliest when they coalesced into shapes, when the magic of individual flakes combined and strengthened the snows already-damaging effects.

You must not heed the voices of the snows. The words followed her through life, yet every time the skies opened up, Cally heard a cacophony of pleas she could never quite fit into the words of her own vocabulary.

Everyone was all too ready to recount to her the horror of the city's snows. While they had originally been summoned by the Seneschals to defend the city, they had quickly overpowered both the Seneschals and the rest of the inhabitants.

Cally had grown up trying to hide her fascination with the snows. Trying to convince herself that she didn't notice the sense of dislocation between herself and everyone she spoke too. That she didn't notice the odd looks or cruel amusement that were sometimes directed her way.

But no matter what she told herself when she was around other people, she always sensed the truth when she was alone. Whenever she dared, and was alone, she would linger outside for a few moments longer than she knew she should and let the snows fall on her. Because that first day, she had almost known the snow creature's name, and every time after that, she sensed she was getting closer and closer to understanding them.

Closer and closer to someone who might finally understand her.

Albe tilted her head back as the blue snow extract hit the orange-pink of the berry wine, and a cloudy smoke rose from the liquid's undulating surface, smelling of burnt rosemary and salt water. Best to keep her mind clear.

Cally, though, let the smoke waft toward her, and closed her eyes in something like contentment. Good. Sharp edges wouldn't help Albe's cause.

The girl took a sip of her drink, then said, "What do you want?"

Albe took a sip of hers and felt the rush of snow extract, both an assault and a caress of the taste buds. This snow was rare, more so than she'd expected in a place like this. Her eyes closed briefly before she forced them back open, fighting the ingredient's strength.

When Albe lowered her glass, she found Cally still staring at her. The girl seemed unaffected by the drink. Surely someone of her age—which Albe judged no more than twenty—and status couldn't have had much exposure to snow drinks, yet she appeared no more affected than she would be by plain, Seneschal-purified water.

Albe had made what inquiries she could without alerting any other Seneschals. This girl was one of many who had inherited the burden of anchoring the city's magic merely by being born here. One of many who would almost certainly never leave.

Cally took another sip. Her eyes closed, evincing that same hint of pleasure, but when her eyes opened again, they were just as sharp. Albe was even more sure she had found the right person.

"We have a proposition for you," Albe said, resisting the urge to have more of her drink, though it rippled temptingly in the confines of her glass.

"We?" Something in the girl's face made it seem like she knew Albe was working alone. That couldn't be true.

"The Order of Seneschals."

The bartender had swung back to their end of the bar to grab something from a high shelf, just close enough Albe saw her twitch at the name.

"I can't think why." The girl was calm, but not the calm of the snow-intoxicated.

"Because the snows won't hurt you the way they do the rest of us."

Cally met her eyes for a few heartbeats, then picked up her drink, downed the remaining two-thirds, and slid off her chair. Without another word, she made for the exit. Albe tossed a voucher at the bartender, which she could bring to the Order for reimbursement if whoever staffed the window that day was in a good mood, and took off in the same direction. She didn't finish her drink.

The first snow Cally had ever tasted, on that day when it fell without hurting her at all, reminded her of pink pepper. She had tasted pink pepper only once before, when her family had gone for a fancy meal after an unusually prosperous season at their workshop. The final course of the night was chocolate, squares dark and bitter, topped with a few finely ground pieces of pink pepper.

Cally soon realized no one else but her was listening to the snow. They *spoke*, they had stories to tell and pains they wished healed. But to everyone else, snows were dangerous, deadly, things that burned through your skin, or paralyzed you, or stopped your heart. Numerous variations in color and shape and viscosity, all ending in one version or another of pain and death. They would all taste different, she knew in her heart, a multitude of flavors.

Whenever the snow she thought of as pink pepper fell, she found it hard to move from the window, that layer of glass keeping her from something almost a friend.

Cally's world was full of whispers, the ones from the sky she wasn't allowed to answer, and the ones from people who saw a strangeness in her, who pushed her away even as she yearned to feel less alone.

The difference was, the whispers that fell from the sky had started, slowly, over the years, to make sense.

By the time Albe reached the street outside the bar, Cally was already disappearing around a corner. Albe fought her way through the increasingly-busy late afternoon foot traffic, elbows out to clear her way, ignoring the occasional shout of dismay this produced.

Despite her own good sense, she hadn't been able to keep from building up a picture of Cally in her mind during the time between their first encounter and their meeting at the bar. Like everyone in the city, Albe had grown up hearing the fables of people who could talk to the snow, who didn't have to be afraid of being stuck outside at night. Before meeting Cally, however, Albe thought she had long since dismissed those fables. She was unwilling to examine what it meant that she now grasped at this possibility so frantically.

She had hoped, many years ago, that if she ever managed to claw her way up the ranks of the Seneschals, she would be able to get out of the city. But all this time later, after having so clawed, achieving everything but the rank of Arch-Seneschal itself, she knew the truth. The Seneschals were as frozen, as *stuck* in this city where the sky could kill, as everyone else they pretended to be better than.

Now, though, she had a plan.

If — and she once again forced herself to remember it was only an if — *if* Cally could communicate with the snows, and more importantly *if* Albe drew her into her orbit before any other Seneschals got the chance, it could be Albe's ticket out of this city.

Snow extracts were the city's most profitable export. But the work was complicated and dangerous enough that few were able to meet the standards required for the Seneschals' stamp of approval, and most of those who made extracts illicitly didn't live long. If Cally could understand the snows, then with Albe's guidance they could produce snow extracts faster and more safely than anyone else in the city. And Albe was willing to bet she'd find herself with more friends once those profits started coming in, friends who could help her manage the treacherous, expensive passage out of the city.

Once she and the girl had worked out a process, she shouldn't have to actually *be* in this awful place where she always had to be afraid of the weather, at least not often. She suspected Cally would insist on a large share of the profits, but since she didn't seem to have any reason to leave the city herself, Albe thought it would work.

"Will it snow tonight?" Albe asked when she finally caught up to Cally, three streets away from the bar.

Cally stilled. "Your Order doesn't know anything about me," she said, looking off into the distance as if waiting to see the first flakes descend. "They'd lock me up if they did."

"I can arrange that."

"Then why haven't you?"

Albe refrained from answering.

Cally's gaze shifted minutely. "So why are you here?"

"Because you're not afraid of the snows. I saw you," Albe said. "Don't you understand how important that is?"

"We turn them into *drinks*," Cally snapped. "The snows hurt us because that's what they were created to do, to wreak havoc on anyone who tried taking the city. But now they're just stuck here like us, and they're *hurting*, but people refuse to listen! Everyone here only cares about processing the snows —" she folded her lips inward as if to take back her words.

Albe saw her chance. "Then help me prove it." She had to stop herself from grabbing the girl's arms and shaking her into agreeing. Cally didn't seem to realize what her gift could mean, but if Albe could get to her through her concern for the snows...

Cally stared back at her, wary.

"The Order doesn't understand," Albe said, keeping her voice low. You could never be sure there wasn't another Seneschal watching, and the Arch-Seneschal would be thrilled by the merest hint of Albe conspiring against the Order. "Help me prove to them what the snows are going through."

Albe wasn't sure if there *was* a way of gathering extracts that the snows themselves would consider acceptable, but she would worry about that later. Yet before she could see whether Cally believed her or not, the air thickened suddenly. Cally looked up, her mouth open as if about to speak to the sky. She paused, looking back to Albe. The older woman saw the calculation in the girl's eyes, but was discomfited to realize she didn't know what it was leading toward.

"They'll only pillage them more," Cally said. "That's all they want, is to take and take and take." There was heat in her words, enough that Albe imagined the heaps of snow around them melting, flooding the city with the force of Cally's emotion. "If we could all stop hurting each other and *listen*..."

"Then make them understand!" Albe countered, forcing confidence into her voice even though she feared the night's approaching snowfall. She wasn't certain she believed Cally's claims about the snows' pain, but, as usual, Albe's pragmatism won out. She could play along with Cally's imaginings if it meant getting her on Albe's side. Besides, Cally might not be so concerned about the snows once the money started coming in. "We can develop a system that doesn't hurt the snows, and save some human lives too. Everyone wins."

Cally regarded her for a long moment, every one of Albe's heartbeats like a warning of the pain that would soon descend on them. Would she burn, here, waiting for an answer?

Finally, Cally spoke.

"Here's what I need."

The next night, the Seneschals were arrayed in front of the Order's main building. Above were the carefully constructed and warded arches of the canopy, a confection of glass doming over their heads, giving sight of the snows they thought they understood.

Cally had requested this hour for her demonstration, as night fell and the first flakes of snow drifted down. She'd insisted to Albe that this would allow the Seneschals to understand the need to listen to the snow.

It hadn't taken long for the others to hear about the demonstration, especially after Albe had encouraged her supporters to spread the news.

The girl was walking past the arch, the last protected area from which a Seneschal could stand and look out at the city.

Albe watched as snow landed on Cally. The girl didn't even cringe, and soon she was enfolded in fluttering flakes, swirling around her and hinting at recognizable shapes.

Moments passed, and Cally neither returned nor screamed out in pain. The air swished and swirled as the other Seneschals bristled and consulted, a small knot of fury springing from the confusion they didn't want to admit to.

What if she doesn't come back? For the first time, it occurred to Albe that she might have underestimated this strange girl.

She glanced at the Arch-Seneschal, a man with many decades carved into his face. She wasn't far behind him in years, but they had never gotten along. Did he know the plans she'd made, and discarded, to unseat him, once she'd realized even his position wouldn't get her what she wanted?

He met her gaze accidentally, shoulders straightening as he wrapped his outermost layer more tightly around himself. Albe smiled, although seeing him disconcerted wasn't as satisfying as she usually found it. He shivered, breaking the connection, as disapproval sculpted his features. They were all frozen in their way, kept within these walls as much as the snow creatures were, once the sun turned them motionless.

She returned to watching Cally, as unease prickled on the back of her neck like stray snowflakes. Reminding herself fiercely that she was safely under the canopy, she still only just managed to stop herself from squirming.

She had convinced herself she might have found a way to escape. But had she, who had told so many lies so successfully over the years, been convinced of an even more dire delusion? She'd thought Cally hadn't seen through her motives, didn't realize Albe didn't care about the snows' wellbeing, but if Cally had played *her...*

Albe saw her plan crumbling, saw herself frozen within the city for decades more.

No.

Albe lunged forward from under the canopy, trailed by the other Seneschals' exclamations. She could not stay here any longer.

Maybe the snows would speak to her, as they spoke to Cally. Maybe all she had to do was trust in this fable a little further, a little more strongly, and she could build her own escape from these terrifying snowflakes. And if she couldn't...

Either way, she was destined to freeze.

Cally opened her mouth, letting a few stray flakes land on her lower lip. Each one was a cold pinpoint, but no more than that, doing no actual damage.

By the time the Seneschals realized why Cally had asked for this, it would be too late. She hoped. The snows would already be speaking through her and then maybe, *maybe*, the Seneschals would listen.

Her conversation with Albe had crystallized Cally's conviction that she didn't want to hide what she could do, what she understood, anymore. Didn't want to continue feeling separated from absolutely everyone, snow and human alike.

She thought she saw a face, an expression, buried beneath the chill and the patterns, endlessly replicated as the sky drifted down. The world swirled until she lost track of up and down and left and right, only floating in the surge of snowflakes.

A touch. Was it a hand? Reaching for her.

Her throat was dry, here in this deluge of frozen water.

She took a step forward, but could no longer tell if the ground remained steady under her feet. The world moved, or she did, or nothing changed at all. But then the face was closer, a question evident in the compilation of the snowflakes.

Up and down and everywhere was the same, but she reached out, felt her hands shape themselves around delicate, fluttering wings.

The snow creature's name was hard to understand, still. That would come in time.

She tasted pink pepper, and heard a voice both familiar and new, speaking from her own throat.

*See Devan Barlow's story "Snow Like Pink Pepper" online at
Metaphorosis.*
If you liked it, leave a comment. Authors love that!
*Remember to subscribe to our e-mail updates so you'll know when
new stories are posted.*

About the story

Amusingly, while I do live in a place with long (and often very snowy) winters, the first idea for this story occurred to me during a hot summer day. I began thinking about how snow sometimes feels like it is actively malicious — making roads and sidewalks more dangerous, slowing down or preventing travel, frostbite, etc. This quickly spun into a setting where the snow did have a kind of agency, which allowed me to think of the city's weather as it own character. Originally, the story focused more on intrigue and the history of how the city it takes place in came to be — there was even an early version where the main plot was interspersed with extracts from an in-universe tourist guide to the setting — but through revisions and edits gradually gained more of a focus on the characters.

A question for the author

Q: If you could have a meal with any character from a classic novel, whom would you choose?

A: Hercule Poirot, from Agatha Christie's mystery novels. I imagine he would choose a delicious menu and we could discuss detection.

About the author

Devan Barlow writes short fiction, poetry, and novels. When not writing she reads voraciously, drinks tea, and thinks about fairy tales and sea monsters.

devanbarlow.com, @Devan_Barlow

Nothing but the Gods On Their Backs

Alex T. Singer

Rekka is sitting by the shrine when the walls start to shake. It's not much of a shrine; decoration more than anything. It's got a figurine her parents bought her at a street fair, two cinnamon sticks, and a plastic dish. The figurine is a little statue of the state god: a polished, red, lacquered statuette clutching the six holy weapons. Each represents a branch of the holy military, amen. She keeps it on her desk and never prays to it. She's studying for her exams. When the shaking doesn't stop, the PA messages start. Not hymns. Evacuation instructions. Rekka looks up, and realizes: That's it, the idiot faithful have finally made it all die.

She sweeps everything on her desk into her emergency bag and makes for the door.

Rekka brings the god with her from the old world, shoved into the lid of her suitcase, rolled into her sweaters and stuffed in her socks. She stumbles into the last train out, dropping her hats and most of her scarves, but though she breaks the wheels on her bag, she doesn't lose the god. She holds the bag to her chest, sticking her elbows out, barely breathing in the overstuffed train car. All she has left in the world: passport, cashbox, three schoolbooks, four dresses, a can of beans, a pan, her mother's rolling pin, and the god. It will be all that's left to any of them as metal groans and smoke billows behind them. The way home closes forever in a wall of falling mortar.

Rekka holds her breath, closes her eyes, and, somehow, survives. She can only hope her mother and brother did the same. Her dad died for the army like a good godly man two years ahead of the rest.

She was never meant for the avatar business — there were plenty interpreters of the faith in the old world. Drill sergeants, captains, colonels, and generals. People in the old world with money, power, or reputation, but the statues they tended were all large and heavy, and bolted into the municipal buildings, huge and grand and now buried and gone.

It's all gone now, from the towering statues to the tiny desk shrines. Anyone who was anyone fell over each other to get out. Rekka's the only one who thought to grab a statue of the god. She will never see her grandparents again, but she will see this stupid little god, so help her.

Rekka stumbles off the train. They herd her to some tents. Then a shelter. Then customs. She seeks out what's left of her family at the border, in a refugee camp set up by some new world relief organization.

She finds them, and finds out where time stopped for them all. Her mother was gardening. Her brother was teaching. Her cousins were at basic training, learning proper religion. It's the same program Rekka refused to attend, after a drill sergeant broke her brother's leg in three places and called him a coward.

Her cousins she hates sneer at the little god in her arms. They were hoping she had cash. "It's one of the knockoffs. Why do you have that? You didn't even serve."

Rekka doesn't care about them. She cares about her mother and brother, shivering behind them. They didn't have time to grab their coats.

"Oh, Rekka," says her mother, in tears. She's clutching a crinkled bunch of herbs under her arm. "It saved you."

In the new world, the god sits on the radiator of the tiny refugee apartment she shares with her mother, her brother, and those two cousins. For the first year, between endless job applications, dishwashing, and night courses, it goes mostly forgotten.

When Rekka gets a job driving rich people to work, she remembers the god. She remembers it the night she comes home late to find her cousins with five friends in the alley behind the apartment. They're laughing and drinking, and kicking over all the crates of old world herbs her mother spent months trying to cultivate. They stick empty beer bottles in the basil.

"Put your garbage somewhere else," says Rekka.

Her cousins laugh in her face. "What's back here? Besides garbage. And you, I guess."

Rekka chases them out with a broom. They laugh all the way out.

"What can you do? Not like you served!"

Like they didn't shove their old uniforms into the trash at the border.

"It's fine, Rekka," says her mother, red-eyed, once they're gone. "They're just boys. It's what they do sometimes."

The next morning Rekka buys used flower pots and a plastic stool. She puts a vinyl tablecloth over the stool. There, among the mass-produced starry print, she plants the little lacquerware god. She leaves a few burnt toothpicks and dried rice cakes. It's the best she can manage on short notice.

"If they start crap again," she says, to the statuette, "eat their souls."

Her cousins come crashing in one more time that week, singing old drill hymns. They bang around the kitchen and trash the living room, but when the door to the alleyway crashes open, their feet stop.

"What's that?"

"Why is it—"

"Shut up."

"Let's just go."

They don't go back there again. They don't care about the herbs and they don't care about Rekka. But they remember the way that god looked when it was 20 feet tall over the training grounds.

The next morning, Rekka finds the rice cakes cleared and a handful of flowers in the dish. She's sure her mother left those, but she won't say.

She finds her brother sweeping up the old cigarette butts. She finds her neighbor adding a few sticks of incense. Her mother tells it about her day. Soon, her mother's old friends are coming by.

"Rekka, can we sit out there for a little?"

"Rekka, do you think these dishes are all right?"

"Do you want another tablecloth?

Rekka isn't sure why they ask her, but she answers: "Only while I'm home. No breakables, please. Sure. A red one would be great."

It's like, all at once, everyone they know from the old world remembers: oh, right. The state god. Oh, right. It's right there, between the tenements.

They come in a lot after that, when Rekka's done driving. Ah, Rekka, can I sit out back for a bit? Ah, Rekka, is it okay if I leave a dish? Her mother's friends. People from the sorting center. People who work washing dishes with her brother. They arrive, sheepish and hopeful, embarrassed they forgot.

“Is the god here? Can we see?”
None of them saved their statues.
“We forgot it.”
“We lost it.”
“It broke.”
So Rekka lets them see the one in her garden. It keeps her cousins out of the alley. She adds a couple of fold-out chairs and some more plants to hide the smell of garbage. She adds some yoga mats when she runs out of chairs. When she doesn’t want to deal with her cousins yelling at each other or her brother, she goes out and sits with them.

They tell stories of the old world. The ones they almost forgot.

“I was a doctor in the old world. Now they only let me wash the floors.”

“I was a writer in the old world. Now I stand in elevators all day, making sure no one gets off at the floors I would’ve once worked.”

“Am I all right? Have I done the right thing?”

“Dear God, I’m so sorry I forgot you. But I’m here now. I’m here. If I remember, will things be better?

They ask Rekka this last part. Rekka’s at a loss. She was a student, in the old world. But their eyes ache for an answer, so she gives them one.

“As long as we’re still here, it can get better. Only thing that’s bad would’ve been stopping, right?”

The doctor-janitor clutches her hand and smiles. The writer-security guard takes a deep breath and nods. They leave, a little lighter and heavier at the same time. Rekka’s not sure she hasn’t just run the biggest scam in her life.

“You really okay with this?” she asks the little god on the plastic table.

The little god just snarl-grins back at her. It starts to rain.

A week later, her mother brings a stained tent cover her coworkers from the kitchen bought together, from a farmer’s market that closed ages ago. Rekka starts to protest the expense, but her mother says they want to visit in the morning. Rekka agrees. She sits vigil over five or six old world women, sitting and chatting about their lives before the collapse.

They leave together, smiling and laughing. All of them have brought an assortment of scented things for the dish.

“And we left the donation out front,” says her mother’s co-worker.

“Eh?” says Rekka, who’s never said anything like that, never even thought about it. The god glares over the woman’s shoulder.

That's how Rekka finds out her cousins have been charging visitors to come see it. They've been taking that money to play poker with their friends.

She kicks them out that night, screaming and swearing louder than she did when she fled the old world.

"How friggin' dare you?" she says, tossing their stuff out the door.

Her cousins chase her, shouting and swearing.

"Psycho bitch!"

"Crazy whore!"

"What the hell, we're just trying to get by!"

"It's a new world! You do what you gotta to get ahead!

"It's new for them too," she says, "What makes you think they're any better off? Get out."

One of her cousins remembers he's bigger than her. He turns and sticks his chin up, a vein in his neck bulging. "Make me," he says. He tries to shove her away.

When Rekka grabs his wrist before his hand can touch her shoulder, she doesn't mean to hold her arm up like the god. She's just trying not to get hit. But she grabs his wrist, and his whole beefy arm stops. Her arm is up. Her other is at her side. Her face is pulled into a grimace, into a concentrated snarl, one that makes her jaw hurt. Her shadow is suddenly very long on the hall ahead of her, and the old world is all around them, here in the narrow tenement hallway.

Her cousin tries to twist away from her. It doesn't work. When she shoves him, he hits the wall behind him. The wrist he cradles has five deep indents seared into them, like a brand.

Her other cousin picks him off the ground, eyes shaking in fear. He tries to play it cool. "C'mon. Let's just go. We can stay with Jules until she calms her goddamn tits."

"My goddamned *what*?" asks Rekka, in a deep, full-chested voice she didn't know she actually had.

Her cousins grab handfuls of their junk and back down the hall. They don't try to come back. She turns to face her mother, huddled at the bedroom door. Her brother, hiding in the kitchen nook.

"Stuff for the garden," says Rekka, without really thinking. She hold her face, until she feels the burning leave the space behind her eyes, and she's entirely sure she doesn't have an extra set of teeth. "If they want to do something for the place. Tell 'em just to donate shovels or window boxes or something. No more cash."

"Thank you," mouths her mother — before looking alarmed at herself, for approving of the cousins' swift exodus. She rubs her face with her afghan. She pretends she just woke up, and didn't see or hear a thing.

The old world lies in fragments, and those fragments are people. They blow around the new world, tossed on the winds of desperation and scant opportunity.

Rekka doesn't wear her driving uniform when people visit anymore. It seems unfair to greet them smelling like gas and smoke. They wait for her to come home before they call on them. Wait for her to change into one of her rescued dresses and her rescued jackets, wait for her to put the old world back on like it's a different kind of uniform. They wait for her to come out and say, yeah, sure, come out back.

The ritual bothers Rekka. She gets why the strangers wait for her permission — there're more of them every day — but her mom and brother do it too.

"You can take them back there, too," Rekka tells her brother, one of the days there's traffic. She arrives home late and there are three very apologetic men and their mother at the door.

"Has to be you," says her brother.

It's rare for him to speak up that plainly. Rekka blinks at him. "Buh? Why?"

"It's your god."

"It's everyone's god."

"Not anymore."

"Okay. Technically true. But —"

"You carried it out."

"Oh, god," says Rekka. Her brother gives her this look, like, exactly, and Rekka realizes a second too late what she just said. "Fine, fine. But the lease is under mom's name. And try to tell them I'm not a priest. If people start expecting sermons from me, I'm closing it up."

Her brother laughs. She asks him why.

"That's not what they think," he says.

"The hell's that mean?!"

He refuses to elaborate. The next morning Rekka discovers another freshly seeded flower box and a line of little wish slips posted on the wall, the kind teachers used to show her how to do when she was six. They're written in crayon. Some of the visitors have kids.

"Dear God, I want a birthday cake."

"Dear God, I want flowers."

"Dear God, I want Momma and Auntie to be Happy."

"Dear God, I want Pop Pop to come home."

Rekka reels at the sheer volume of words that flood her mind. Her eyes ache with them, burn with them, but she doesn't have the heart to tear them down. Instead, she slides down the wall, and puts her face in her hands.

"Why?" she groans. "I wasn't even a corporal!"

The god looks smug and well-fed. She flips it the bird, and cleans off its dish. She doesn't want the rats to get back here. Rats aren't the blood offerings modern gods prefer.

Her cousins must have made some anonymous calls, because men from the city come knocking at their door one night, wearing black vests and tan shirts. They stomp through the tenements, breaking windows and kicking down garbage cans. They break the door. They yell at her mother.

"Who are you?"

"Why are you here?"

"What do you think you're trying to pull?"

They talk so fast her mother doesn't understand them. They take her silence for confirmation. They drag her brother into the street when he gets between them. They throw him down like his drill sergeant, ready to stomp on his good leg.

Which is when Rekka runs in from the back alley, wearing her grandfather's jacket and clutching a candle.

"You leave them alone," she shouts, in a voice bigger than her lungs. "You leave!"

The streets are wet from the rain, but they spark with light. The candle fits in one hand, but the reflection blazes so bright and so wide in the water that it fills up the whole block. The light touches everything, except the shadow at Rekka's feet. This long and wide, and if you squint at the blur, it looks like it has more than two arms, and each one is grasping a weapon.

The arms come down. The light fades. The door's still broken, but the men are gone.

Rekka throws her arms around her brother and cries and cries and cries. The candle rolls into a puddle and gutters out.

The men in vests don't come back after that.

Another man from the city comes to check on the shrine. He knocks on the patched door and asks, politely, if they know about it. Rekka thinks he's going to shut them down, going to nail something to their door, or put a chain up over the alleyway — but he just asks them to move the flammables further away from the vents and not to leave any perishables uncovered. As far as small mercies go, it'll do.

The writer-guard is still a guard, but he works at an art museum now. It's got better hours, better things to stare at during the day. The doctor-janitor hasn't managed to become a doctor again, but he has become the manager of the hospital commissary. It pays better. He tries to give Rekka a few banknotes in thanks.

"No way," she says. "What'd I say?"

He looks at her blankly. Rekka sighs. "The god wants growth, okay?"

So he buys her a sprinkler system for the garden. Still a bit too extravagant, but her mother's started bringing veggies to the local kitchen. She and her women make ready-made lunches for the office folk Rekka drives around. It's not glamorous, but the office workers like their rice bowls and they don't scowl at buying good meals off of old-world hands.

"Look at us," says her mom, squeezing her hands one evening. A new world delegation of IT guys came to the restaurant for dinner. They actually tipped. "Look at you."

"Mom, I didn't do this," says Rekka. "It's a space, okay? It's just a space."

But no matter how many times she says it, no one seems to hear it.

One day, though, when the clouds are thick, and she works well past midnight, Rekka comes home and finds a man crouched under an awning in the thick, driving rain. He's a battered, tattered looking man, in a patched coat. The threads of one shoulder have separated. One sleeve is knotted high against his armpit. The arm that should have occupied that sleeve is gone, like their home.

Rekka recognizes the coat.

"Get out," she says, in anger. It belonged to the men she saw as she boarded the train from the old world, a flash of olive drab and gold buttons. They used to march on TV and stand on temple steps.

"Please," he says.

She starts over. "You could've waited under the canopy in the back."

"I certainly could have" says the man, with a wry smile. "But it's your god, ma'am."

"...ugh, another one." But he's wet and sad, and Rekka's nothing if not a soft touch for anyone who's not a useless cousin. "All right. Let me get you some hot cocoa at least."

He refuses to come inside. He chooses to sit under the canopy in the back. She sits with him. They watch the rain roll off of it in a sheet.

"There you are," he says to the god, as he puts a bouquet of dried flowers on the dish. "That's it, alright. But what a funny little one you've got here. That face is... certainly a revelation."

"Finally, someone says it," says Rekka. "Yeah, I know it's cheap. My folks got it for like five bucks at a street market."

"It came with you, though."

He's not the meathead she expected. She rubs the back of her neck sheepishly, and tries to hand him one of her coats, which he very firmly refuses. "Yeah, well. Kept it on my desk. I liked making faces at it in the morning. Got me all pumped for the hard classes. It was... stupid, okay? I really hope no one told you I was a priest. Because I just set this all up to keep it clean back here. So, uh, sorry if they did."

It's funny. She's heard a lot of old world stories now in this little shrine she made by accident, but this is the first time she's really told her own.

The man nods. He only has one working eye. The other one is made of glass, and drifts lazily in the wrong direction.

"You're no priest," he says.

"Thank you," breathes Rekka.

"But it's still your god."

"I —" Rekka's eyes flick to the little figure, like somehow she expects it to come in and back her up. It doesn't. It just grin-growls like always. It looks almost like it's snickering. "What?"

"Mm. Let me tell you something," he says. "I know I'm not much of anything these days — but back in the old world, I was a soldier. You might have guessed."

"I... kind of had that idea."

"Want to guess my rank?"

"No."

"Why, in the old world, I was a colonel," says the man, and with his peppery grey hair and his smoke-stained teeth, Rekka has no reason to doubt that, though his patched coat is missing all the medals and badges that would've told it more true. "One of the few left, when the old world fell. I'm sure you recall, ma'am, the end happened slow, then fast. We were taking our orders in the Capital Temple by the time we knew the cause was lost. So you see, I'm terribly familiar with this one here..."

He nods to the statue, which seems suddenly very small in his presence.

"Bit... shorter, probably," says Rekka, feeling just as small. Who did she think she was, doing all this? But the sense of smallness passes, replaced by a flashing anger, a hotness behind her eyes. Who does this old bigwig think he is, coming here to lecture her, after he and all those old men made all those stupid decisions, after they brought on the end — slow, then fast. "Look —"

But though she squares her shoulders and readies herself for another world-ending war, he holds up a hand.

"Don't misunderstand me," he says. "I was just told this is a place for old world stories. This one's mine. May I tell it?"

It's not Rekka's right to say no. So she holds her elbows, settles back, and lets him.

"I was standing in the shrine when the sirens started. They had a big bronze statue there, think you probably did see it. It was always in the news. Top brass held their press conferences in front of it — ah, nevermind. I was there, that hour. The lights were off, everywhere except the basin. Was a bit bigger than this little candy dish, a bit more full of fire — but I imagine they don't let you light that out here, do you?"

"Against regulations," says Rekka, stiffly. She hasn't thought about the candle since that night.

"Point is," he says, "You could look it in the eyes, that old god, that old world. When we knew it was the last time we likely would, we all walked in to see it. We all stared up at it. We all wondered, what do you want from us now, at the end of everything? What more can we do for you, my god?"

He gives a sad, misty smile.

"What do you think it told us?"

He's really asking. Rekka downs her hot cocoa and thinks for a moment.

"Survive," she says, with all those shaking swords on her breath. "What's a god without its people, anyway?"

"Is that what it tells you?"

Something about the way he says it makes Rekka grit her teeth.

"Yes," she answers, not allowing herself a moment to overthink it. Her head is full of so many things. The useless cousins. Her injured brother. Her tired mother. The doctor-janitor, the writer-guard. The old women holding hands. The little wish notes from the children, still hanging damp on the wall. "Of course it is. Otherwise, what's the point? We're still here, aren't we? Why shouldn't we be here? Who are we if we don't stay us? Wherever we go, we're still us. So it's still... it."

The old colonel is quiet for a long time. He finishes his hot cocoa. He puts his head down. He doesn't look the god in the eyes anymore.

"You're right," he says. "That makes an awful lot of sense. Thank you, ma'am. I do think you're the expert, these days."

"I said I'm not a priest —"

"No," he says. And with a bit of a wince, he pushes himself back to his feet. "But it's a new world. You don't have to be. I like what it tells *you* more."

He refuses the coat one last time. He refuses food. He won't take money. Holding his coat and his pride to his chest, he limps off into the rainy night, leaving Rekka alone in the light of her little back alley garden.

She stares at the god, like a naughty child.

"What did you tell him?" she asks. "What did you want them to *do*?"

The god doesn't quake or cower in the face of her anger, just meets her gaze as blindly as it always has. And she knows, all at once, exactly what all the men in that temple heard: Fight to the last. Fight to the death. Burn the bridges. Burn the temples. Bring the fires down on their heads. Die with me, so none of us will be alone.

Rekka stares at her tiny god in disgust.

"Seriously," she says.

It offers no answer. No excuses. After all, it was a war god, in the old world. It ate fire and death and countries and politicians.

Rekka has no time for any of those things. "Yeah, I get it," says the woman who stopped going to temple ages ago, even when they were all still standing. "But why did you have me tell them all to keep going?"

And, somewhere in the hurried beat of her heart, she thinks she hears the tiny answer, from what's left of that once great god:

Wherever we go, we're still us.

"That's what I said. Is that what you'd say?"

No, admits the god, in her heart.

But I like your answer more.

See Alex T. Singer's story "Nothing but the Gods On Their Backs"
online at Metaphorosis.
If you liked it, leave a comment. Authors love that!
Remember to subscribe to our e-mail updates so you'll know when
new stories are posted.

About the story

I took a break from working on my horror manuscript to read Marguerite Duras' *The Lovers*, which was recommended to me by my father. It's a wild story, but gorgeously written, and I found myself inspired by its merciless depiction of colonial Vietnam under the French and the cultural displacement felt even on the personal level. I wanted to write a story that felt that stream of consciousness and visceral. I'd recently had an interesting dream I'd jotted down: about a young prophet living in a basement apartment, offering people absolution out of her tiny alley garden. Throw in my own personal feelings about Reform Judaism, and the transformative nature of faith over time as a people's need for it change, and the first draft of "Nothing But the Gods on Their Backs" was done in about a day and a half.

A question for the author

Q: What's a typical writing day like for you?

A: These days, it starts with a (very strong) cup of tea, an omelette for my one year old, and as many words as I can get in before she decides I'm done for the morning. I usually like to take a midday walk to keep from going stir crazy, and if I'm lucky, I can get a few more words at the gym in the afternoon in notepad on my phone. A count of 2K in a day is my ideal, but occasionally, my editorial assistant (see also: the one year old) has words about that.

About the author

Alex T. Singer lives in coastal Connecticut with her wife, daughter, two cats, and too many fantasy books to count. Her grandfather, Loren A. Singer, wrote *The Parallax View*.

littlefoolery.com, @sfeertheorist

The Zoo Diaries

Frances Pauli

Part Six

Previously…

At the Rainriver Zoological Gardens, one escape became the catalyst for a series of unfortunate incidents. The tortoise, Oliver, roamed the zoo as a fugitive, searching for his missing cage mate, Miranda. But when the duplicitous crow led him to the marshland, Oliver's imagined reunion turned into heartbreak.

While the zoo's photography contest broke all attendance records, the crowd's poor behavior heaped extra stress upon the already troubled animals. The spike in attendance boded well for the bottom line, but the zoo was forced to hire armed security to keep the mobs in line.

While Oliver nursed his broken heart, the Employee Appreciation potluck got underway. The alcohol flowed freely, and the party got quickly out of hand. The already-overstressed animals hunkered in their cages, while the combination of booze, armed security, and long repressed instincts set the scene for inevitable tragedy.

Lion Enclosure

Charlie dreams in the night, too. He stalks the tube-gazelles, rumbling in his throat and stepping on death-silent paws. The Savannah mocks him. It has erased the other lions, left him alone with a hollow gut and a herd of nightmare beasts that slip between his paws each time he makes a lunge in their direction.

They squeak and scatter, but Charlie can still smell them. He can smell, smell, smell the meat that is sweet and taught, that bursts beneath his fangs without blood.

He opens his eyes. The scent lingers after the dream has gone. The squeaks become voices, sounds of familiar, barking men. They are too close, too loud. Charlie blinks and gazes toward his trench and the high wall.

They-who-bring-food are at his wire. They have slithered down the wall, perhaps, or entered through some invisible breach in his defenses. They stagger and laugh. There are two of them, pale faces with white teeth. A camera shutter clicks from the far side of the trench. The barking slurs and curses.

The smell of meat is on them. It is there in the night, real and not dreamed of. There is a wire, Charlie knows. Vaguely, he remembers that it bites back. He lowers his belly to the grass, opens his jaws, and huffs.

Confusion.

His head swims. The meaty scent, the voices that almost squeak in the darkness.

Charlie creeps forward. He believes he can leap straight over the wire. He can spring across the trench. He can taste the air. He can stalk and pounce and devour.

The camera ticks like a heartbeat. Charlie tenses, breathes out, and almost changes his mind. The inhale, however, is too much for him. The scent. The meat on the night wind.

He moves without warning. He is a streak in the grass, a lightning strike, a blur sailing over the wire, past the trench, jaws open and teeth showing white as bone.

Zebras

The lead zebra lifts her head, stretches her rubbery nostrils wide, and sucks in a rush of night air.

Something is not right.

She limps a few paces away from the herd. Her left fetlock is bruised. She has forgotten her own advice and stepped into one of the many holes left in her paddock by the native gophers. These do not belong in the zoo, and utterly disregard the respectable order of fences and cement walls.

Tonight, even their soft scritching has died. The ground beneath the zebras' hooves is still and silent. The zoo holds its breath.

Even the clumsy elephant has noticed. The lead zebra can see Shanti's fat shadow by the light leaking out of her shelter. The elephant's trunk is up. Her ears flutter. She listens, as the zebra does, to the sudden, pregnant quiet.

Not even a crow whispers.

The zebra trembles. Her striped skin twitches. She breathes and tenses, and the rest of the herd lift their heads as one, sleepy, hesitant, rigid from flank to foreleg.

For one heartbeat, the night waits. The moment freezes. Then a sound that is not of the zoo echoes out of its depths. It is a primal, wild noise, and even though she has never lived one day of her life outside safe walls, the zebra knows it in an instant.

The herd breaks, wheeling together and hammering the ground in retreat.

The sound chases them. It is all instinct, wholly dangerous, violent, deadly.

It is the lion roaring, and it goes on and on.

The zebras circle inside their fence. They race away from the feeding sound, but the fence brings them back again and again. There is nowhere to go. They streak past the elephant three times before a gunshot fires into the zoo's center.

That sound, they all know. That sound echoes outward.

A stone lobbed through glass.

A heavy step on thin ice.

A bursting heart inside a warm chest.

It remains with them, plays over and over in every mind, in every memory, long after the world has gone silent again.

Elephant Paddock

Shanti counts her own breaths. The night cradles her, dead and black on all sides. She is a statue, a topiary elephant held forever in a moment between action and reaction.

Though everything is silence now, the gunshot lingers. It is branded into her mind. It will live there forever, be with them all forever.

She stares over her fence, cataloging shadows, shapes that register as tree, bench, table. She counts 60 breaths and still her ears hear only the mute shock of 600 animals living their lives in small square boxes.

Oliver is out there. Oliver *was* out there?

Shanti's tail flicks and the spell is broken. She hears the soft hiss of her water faucet dribbling. She hears the zebras shifting position. Hooves against dirt, pelt brushing against pelt. Slowly, they all come back to life.

All but one, perhaps.

Shanti thinks of it, of Oliver and the crow's evil warning.

Someone will be shot.

She let him out. Twice now, she's lifted the fence for her tortoise.

Her trunk drops, heavy and dragging at her face. Shanti counts her toes. Five arch-shaped nails on each foot. She is shaking, rattling in her bones, and weeping, when the first crows arrive.

"Lion." Even their croaking voices seem to whisper tonight. "Lion attack. Lion shot."

Shanti shivers from her trunk to her tail. She is an earthquake, a mountain's shudder, and though the words are tragedy, though the worst thing of all has happened, she is relieved.

Ape House

Gonzo strains against the bars until his knuckles throb. His fists are welded to the steel. His lips sneer in a perpetual, toothy mask that drives his troop to the far corners of the cage and makes him an outcast.

The macaques cringe and shiver in the dark. They long to sneak away, to slip through their square door and hide, but the gunshot holds them in place. Gonzo hears it as a claw against his spine. He knows someone has gone, and he wishes it was him.

He has lost the bean again. It has been given and taken away and now he thinks he will die of missing it.

The night lingers. The most cowardly of his troop slink against the wall, vanish into the safe familiarity of the interior cage. The rest wait, listening with their faces pressed near to the bars and their eyes drifting closed, open, closed again.

A pigeon comes first. It flutters past the bars like an overstuffed bat and lands on the signpost beside the path.

The troop whispers, shuffles, and rearranges the faces at the cage front.

Gonzo resists the urge to lunge at them. He could sink his teeth into a fat, furry body. He could scratch and tear, but it would not bring back his bean.

He waits.

The troop loses patience and whispers to the plump bird who is only waiting to be invited, who has clearly come to tell a story but holds its tongue until the moment is too pregnant to resist.

"What is it!" The troop voices blend into one. "What has happened?"

"The lion has gone mad." The pigeon drops from its perch and marches across the path, puffed up, breast forward. "He's gone mad and attacked They-who-feed."

The macaque troop gasps and tightens its huddle. Gonzo is outside, alone. He hears their gibbering and thinks he is not a monkey. He is not like that. He is something else, something mad like the lion.

"Is it dead?" one of the macaques asks.

The pigeon makes a rolling, cooing sound and flaps its wings. "No," it says. "Of course not. They only shot him with a sleeping gun. But he'll be sold for sure, sent to another zoo or... someplace else."

"Liar." The crow's voice slices between the monkeys and their informant.

She streaks past once, a malicious shadow, then returns in a slow glide and lands on the ledge outside Gonzo's bars. She struts toward the troop, feathers gleaming in the moonlight.

"The pigeon lies," she says. "They've killed him for it as sure as anything."

"Who would trust a crow?" The pigeon puffs and prickles. "Of course, they didn't."

"I saw it," Debra croaks. "I was there at the railing when he flew at them."

"Lions don't fly," the pigeon insists.

Debra clacks her beak, stabbing it at the bars and driving the troop backwards. They cringe from her, and she pivots, paces back toward Gonzo with a gleam in her eye.

"He attacked." The crow sings it, "like a beast, turned on them with tooth and claw."

Gonzo hears her glee at that. Her approval of the horror radiates until she is a small black sun.

"There was blood," she says. "There was screaming."

The slim black body bobs in his direction, one clawed step at a time. The sound of her toes against the concrete seems louder than her words, larger somehow. Gonzo freezes, listening to the tiny scratches as if they are spikes against his skull.

"You're a liar," the pigeon shouts from the grass.

"It's all true." Debra swivels toward her accuser, looks away for less than a breath.

It is all the time Gonzo needs. His fist flies through the bars, opening, stretching. His fingers close around a soft, warm body, and he drags the crow into his cage. He holds her, stunned and squeaking, in a tightening grip.

"I saw it too," the pigeon continues as if nothing has happened. "The gun was not lethal. There was no death."

In Gonzo's paw, Debra makes a final sound, a squeal of protest, an impotent last argument. Perhaps, it is only a plea for her life, but the air has left her, and her words are dead before Gonzo feels the crunching of her bones against his palm.

She is silent, and he thinks it is the only good thing he has ever done.

Murder

The crows call tribute.

They sweep above the pathways, circling from cage to cage, shadows in the night. They sing a song of praise to death itself. They sing for Charlie, for the mad lion, and not one of their own. They have not yet discovered Debra's body, cast into the long grass beside the ape house.

They do not sing of loss but of the great, inevitable cycle, the ending triumphant. The ultimate predator that will come for each and every animal in their time.

Their words are power, dark magic carried forth on streaking, black bodies.

One by one, their clattering voices transport the zoo's population. They sing, and they carry each mind who hears their song, instantly back to a place only vaguely remembered. An instinct. A genetic programming.

The zoo walls fade, becoming shadows too. The trees spread and grow in the wind of the murder's passing. The plastic, oil-tinged air itself, clarifies. The great cellular memory of freedom walks in the crows' wake.

It is the wild. It is the origin.

It takes possession of the zoo, squatting between the enclosures and weaving its spell. In the darkness, the elephant trumpets, a blaring of sound, an homage to death and freedom. From the cat house, an answer comes in the form of discordant rowling.

The apes ook and pound their chests. The bears stretch black lips and let loose a terrible, magnificent roaring.

It is chaos. It is glory. They are no longer here, behind their bars and their trenches.

Tonight, this is Africa. It is Borneo, Malaysia, Indonesia. It is a Nepalese mountain peak, an Amazonian cloud forest. In each beating heart the world shifts outward.

The song spreads. The tribute is called again and again. It is a celebration and a dare. A defiant whisper. "Come for him. Come."

Death walks among them, and for one moment, they are all free.

DAMAGE CONTROL

PRESS RELEASE
RAINRIVER ZOOLOGICAL GARDENS
INCIDENT REPORT

FRIDAY EVENING, DURING AN EMPLOYEE APPRECIATION POTLUCK, TWO INDIVIDUALS BYPASSED ZOO SECURITY AND ENTERED OUR AFRICAN LION EXHIBIT.

ONE MAN WAS HOSPITALIZED WITH NON-LIFE-THREATENING INJURIES AND THE OTHER WAS TREATED AT THE SCENE. BOTH WERE UNDER THE INFLUENCE AT THE TIME.

RAINRIVER ZOOLOGICAL GARDENS ASKS THAT ALL QUESTIONS REGARDING THIS INCIDENT BE DIRECTED TO OUR PR OFFICE.

WE THANK THE PUBLIC FOR THEIR CONCERN AND FOR THE MANY INQUIRIES ABOUT THE LION'S WELFARE.

THE SITUATION IS FULLY UNDER CONTROL, BUT WE HAVE MADE THE DIFFICULT DECISION TO CLOSE THE PARK FOR ONE WEEK IN ORDER TO GIVE THE STAFF AND ANIMALS TIME TO RECOVER FROM THE INCIDENT.

THE ZOO WILL REOPEN FOR REGULAR HOURS ON SATURDAY THE SIXTEENTH.

WE LOOK FORWARD TO SEEING YOU AGAIN SOON.

—ZOO MANAGEMENT

The loss is unprecedented, and the Board panics. PR is in chaos, and the injured employee's family threatens to sue. It is decided to settle out of court. It is estimated this will likely eat through all the profits resulting from the video contest.

Belts will have to be tightened again. Compromises will need to be made.

When a keeper stands up to argue, they are shouted down, reminded that a bankrupt zoo must redistribute or be forced to cull.

They walk a fine line, but accounting believes they can stay open. They can continue to provide the minimum requirements and remain afloat.

They can keep their animals. All but one.

Grizzly Grotto

For three days, Hector refuses to eat his food. Each morning, he trundles from his den, growls at the empty railing, and sniffs whatever breakfast has been left for him with growing suspicion. There is white powder on his food, persistent grains that he can never quite rub off and that give his fruit a taste sharp as a bee's sting.

His belly grumbles, but for once in his life, Hector pays it no mind. He sulks. He scratches freely on the broken stump, and on the fourth day, the miracle happens.

Hector wakes late. His elbows and hips have been aching again, and without his artist to pose for, he sees no point in an early day. He lifts his head with deliberate care only to realize the wall of his den is moving. A tinny, scraping noise has awoken him, and he suffers a twinge of alarm until he sees the bars.

This wall has moved before, Hector remembers, and by the time it retracts fully, he is sitting, waiting for his doctors and their skewers of grapes.

Beyond the wall is a long hallway. There is no cage today, but Hector's doctor is here. She has her clipboard in hand and the smell of grapes is on her.

Hector churrs and raises his paws.

The doctor smiles, making her notes. She has helpers with her, and one of them summons the skewer.

Hector poses.

When the grapes are offered through the bars, he reaches for them, but they are quickly pulled away again. For a moment, he thinks this will be torture. They've only come to taunt an aging bear.

His doctor makes encouraging sounds with her tiny mouth. She claps, and Hector scoots closer to the bars. They let him have the grapes.

One by one, he plucks them from the stick, savoring the ritual, the smiles, and the contact. At one point, his pelt is pricked. They use the long stick with its needle. Hector registers the assault and understands.

He churrs and performs, and when the doctor claps for him, Hector knows suddenly that he is not a real bear. Perhaps, he never was. They-who-clap have made him a dancing fool, a clown. They have shaped him, formed him into a thing that poses.

And though shame fills him, Hector knows he will not eat the bitter food. If he resists, if he waits for it, his reward will be an open den wall, a stick full of grapes, and all the attention, the claps and smiles, a clown could ever want.

Hyena Pen

It takes three days for Rocko to vanish. Alice has not allowed him to mate again, and on the fourth morning, she wakes to an empty cage.

His scent lingers, and she spends time urinating over the top of it. She erases him and is glad when his stink no longer invades her space. Alice climbs to the very top of her stair-step rock and lies, panting and contented.

Her cage is her own. Her water, her food, her rock. She stares out at the empty pathways and wonders if the tortoise has found the aviary. She doesn't exactly miss conversation, but she thinks the reptile was far less offensive than her last companion.

Alice hopes he has found his bird. She hopes that the guns in the night were not for him, and she shivers at the memory of the crows' song.

Liars. Alice remembers that crows lie.

She shakes, cackles, and chooses to believe that the tortoise is fine, happy.

In her belly, Alice carries a new litter. She knows this, though she cannot feel them yet. She will have cubs again. She will make life, make tiny voices, tiny spotted bodies that sing and scamper.

With these cubs, she will not waste time. Alice will teach them her tricks, teach them everything quickly. And when she loses them again, she will know that they are ready. They will learn, and then they will leave.

Alice cackles with her ears flat and her tail twitching. Every instinct in her body says that this is *wrong*.

The stupid cat's voice echoes in her mind, insisting that this is how it should be. She hears Sultan purring again and cannot make herself agree with him. For her sanity, however, Alice swallows her instincts, her need, and her understanding of 'pack'.

Animals in cages do not have room to spare.

Tortoise Enclosure

It takes three days for Oliver to be caught. He spends two of them beside the duckpond, staring at the water while the birds mistake him for a stone. They perch on his shell, preening and flicking their damp tails while Oliver broods and does his best not to hear the occasional, familiar honking from the heron's enclosure.

There are many wading birds here, and the mating noises could have come from any of them.

When he is finally discovered by Those-who-carry-guns, Oliver trundles into the path to meet them. He does not struggle when they tarp and lift him. He does not move while the zoo vehicle carries him back to his pen.

He is done. There is nothing to dig for now, and all he wants is to sprawl beside his burrow entrance and wait for another hundred years to pass.

When the vehicle stops at his cozy, familiar wall, however, Oliver is flabbergasted. As if they have stolen the thoughts from his heart, someone has taken down the heron sign. In its place, beside the plate with his name and picture on it, is another tortoise.

Oliver freezes as he is balanced atop the wall. He reads and reads while They-who-mind-fences scramble to shift and lower him.

As the sign predicted, there is another tortoise waiting. It has occupied the warm spot outside Oliver's burrow. It is smaller than him, less pale and less pyramided. Oliver charges it the moment he is released.

The invader barely has time to brace for impact before their shells crash together. Oliver's legs churn, his fat, spiked forelegs grip the earth. He is wedged beneath the other's shell, and heaves, lifts in an attempt to flip them.

"Invader," he says. "Get out."

"I was here first," the new tortoise, ridiculously, claims.

Oliver stops heaving. They settle, shift inches apart, and glare at one another.

"That's my burrow," Oliver says. "Who did you think dug it?"

The smaller tortoise twists its neck, stretches, and looks toward the wall where They-who-carry-guns are climbing back into their vehicle.

"Humans don't dig," Oliver says. "Stupid."

"Well, where were you?" The newcomer demands.

"None of your business." Oliver lunges again, and this time the other tortoise scoots out of the way. Oliver settles into his place. "Go away," he says. "I don't want a mate."

"Nor do I," the intruder says.

A quiet stretches between them. Oliver feels warm dust beneath his plastron. He smells the reeds and the grass and the water in his shallow pool.

"What's your name?" he asks, finally.

"Arnold," the newcomer answers.

"Sign says you're female," Oliver comments.

"I find that those who make signs often have trouble understanding them," Arnold says.

Oliver stares at him. He blinks twice and then nods his blunt head.

"Arnold, then," he says with a sigh. It is not a terrible name. It is not a terrible thing, to share space, to talk perhaps, to joust and battle. To sit by the reeds or the burrow and not be alone.

Animals in cages cannot chose who comes and who goes. They cannot be selective. Oliver tucks his head into his shell, pulls his legs in and thinks it will be okay to share again.

"Well, Arnold," he grumbles. "You can dig your own hole over there."

Pigeon Hell

Three days after the lion's murder, Peg waddles through the aviary's twin doors. They-who-sweep-and-clean have propped it open with their mop cart and left enough of a gap for an escape. She is almost stepped on as she dodges their shifting feet, and she thinks she sees a finch fly out as well, but she no longer cares about fat, spoiled, tweeting birds.

She is free again, popping like a fluffy cork through the last door and out, into the blissfully dry open.

Peg rushes into a shadow beside the trash cans and catches her breath. She has been to pigeon paradise... and they can keep it.

Regardless, she has stories to tell. She's out now, and her heart fills. Her lungs suck in warm, ordinary air. She smells hot asphalt and cold popcorn and nearly swoons.

When Those-who-clean are not looking, Peg flies, low and with great effort, away from the aviary building. She stops frequently, perching on a rail or a prickly bush, and panting from exertion. The zoo is larger than she remembers, and a diet of rich, free food weighs on her.

When she finally finds her flock, she is out of breath and energy. Peg drops among them like a tossed stone, and they fluff and coo at her.

"Where have you been?" the one called Peter grumbles and cocks his head, taking in her girth. "What has happened to you?"

"I have been to pigeon heaven," Peg announces with less echo than she's intended. She is still surprised by their lackluster reaction.

"We all have," Peter says. "But the Night-Of-Everlasting-Food has ended."

"What?" Peg blinks and forgets she meant to awe them, to brag of her exploits and her daring. "What night?"

The pigeon flock closes in around her. They make a tight circle, just as she'd hoped, but their attention is not on her. They look to Peter, and their beady eyes shimmer.

"A night like none other." Peter's voice booms in an epic, hollow tone. The flock holds its breath, and Peg can't help but lean forward, listening, waiting. "Where the meal is more than a thousand birds could devour. Piles of food lined up for the taking. Mountains of sweet bread, fruit, meats, and cheeses."

Peg loves cheese. She shivers, cooing softly in the back of her throat.

"It was like a dream," he says. "A night of magic and wishes."

The flock bobs agreement, falling into a pensive, reverent silence. Peg's craw tightens. She thinks of the aviary and the sticky air, of the birdseed that seemed to stick in her throat when she tried to swallow it.

She imagines the Night-Of-Everlasting-Food and knows she has missed it. Pigeon heaven came to the flock. It found them here, in the nice dry air, and Peg has missed it.

"Where were you?" another of her flock mates notices Peg, bobbing and scooting closer in the wake of Peter's story. "Where have you been?" they ask.

Peg smooths her gray plumage and dips her head.

"I have been in pigeon hell," she tells them.

The Elephant Paddock

Shanti is counting the zebras when Oliver visits. It has been four days since the gunshot in the night, and she has divided her time since between drawing portraits of the tortoise with her straw and making friends with her neighbors.

The zebra leader is called Alberta, and when Oliver pokes his head free of his tunnel, she flares her rubbery nostrils and snorts.

Shanti stops counting stripes and pivots so that Oliver has room to emerge. She's been guarding his tunnel in the hopes he might need it to get back into his enclosure. That he might pop out of it from the inside has never occurred to her.

"Hello, Shanti," he says.

"Oliver." Her trunk quivers. The long lashes above her eyes dance. "You're back."

"Do you mind?" he asks. "I wouldn't want to bother you."

For a long moment, he retracts, sinking back into his tunnel.

"No!" Shanti's heart stops. "I'm glad to see you."

"You're sure?" Oliver climbs back out of the hole. "I was thinking it might be nice to visit. Since the tunnel is still open."

"I've been guarding it," Shanti says. "So they won't fill it in."

"Thank you." Oliver pops completely free of the ground and stretches his neck out. "How have you been?"

"I've met the zebras," she confesses. "The herd leader lets me count her stripes."

"Wonderful," Oliver says.

"Did you find Miranda?" Shanti watches him closely.

"Yes." Oliver's voice is flat and dry. "And now there's another tortoise in my pen. Would you mind terribly if I visited more often?"

"I wouldn't mind at all." Shanti tries to count her heartbeats, but they are coming too fast. She curls her trunk and imagines talking with Oliver every evening, waiting for him by his hole while the zebras tramp and circle, inviting him into the shed, perhaps, maybe even...

"Would you like to count me?" he asks.

Shanti shivers and drops her trunk low. She believes his bird friend is a fool. With a brief flutter of her ears, she steadies her voice and gives him her best answer.

"I thought you'd never ask."

Ape House

Gonzo wakes from dreams of the dead crow. It has been five days since Debora's murder, but he can still feel the small, shattered body in his paws. The other macaques keep their distance. Gonzo is no longer brushed past or jumped upon.

On the fifth morning, his headache is less sharp, his shaking subdued to its ordinary level of discomfort.

He believes the black cherries were evil. They-who-swept poisoned him, drove him to the ultimate destructive act. Gonzo still hears the crunching when he chews, and has taken to eating last, if at all. He feels better, somehow, picking at the few, mushy scraps the troop determines too poor to devour.

He sits outside while the troop dines, but he only looks toward the long grass twice today. Like the effects of the evil cherry, his guilt is fading.

When the first of his cagemates wanders through the square door, Gonzo swings down from the ropes and circles so that he can slip inside without contact. He waits for the others, but they are slow today. They linger, and he hears excited whispers, the soft screeching usually reserved for something new and confusing.

Gonzo tries to resist their enthusiasm, but despite everything, he is still a monkey.

He passes through the door with his shoulders hunched, with his eyes down and the sound leading him. Inside, someone has lain new straw across the floor. The smell of fruit overpowers the hay, however, and neither are enough to mask a sweeter scent coming from a far corner.

Gonzo lifts his head.

The troop has gathered around a pile of branches. Their poses are cautious, but already one female pokes at the new thing, leaping back when its leaves rattle at her touch.

Not exactly fresh. Not growing. Gonzo's heart still climbs into his throat at the sight. He swings forward, lopes sideways and scatters the troop.

The branches lie in a tangle behind the fruit bucket. They may be slightly shriveled, but they are green and leafy. He smells them with his mouth open, sucking in as much of their air as he can devour.

On the stems no cherries grow, red as rubies and thick as the ticks on a wild hog. Gonzo hesitates, disappointed. His lips peel back.

He remembers the crow, but these branches are harmless.

As Gonzo plucks the first leaf, his troop eases closer. As he fits the thin greenery between his lips, he remembers that he had another troop once. There was a time when he did not hunker and scowl. There was a time when he sat in the branches eating green leaves with his friends.

The taste is flat and stale. The branches are dying, not fresh and alive. The leaves are wrinkled, squishing instead of tearing between his teeth. There are far too many here for him alone. When the bold female reaches for a neighboring branch, Gonzo resists the urge to show her his fangs.

Instead, he chews. He makes a show of it, selecting and plucking a leaf, chewing, and swallowing with little pleasure. For a moment he imagines red cherries among the leaves, but he recognizes the thought for what it is.

Madness.

He is not a free monkey. His troop has long forgotten him. And this one only barely understands what a monkey is.

The others mimic him. They creep in until a circle of macaques sit in a ring. Together, they devour the leaves, and as Gonzo chews beside them, he remembers that they have names, that long ago he learned them, long before he stopped caring.

He helps the oldest male, who is stupidly lipping at the woody bark. Gonzo shows him to ignore this, to focus on the leaves. They eat side by side, and the troop forgets that he was a monster.

Life in a cage is uncertain. He does not know if he will ever taste the bean again, but even without it, he knows he must live.

The troop draws him in, and Gonzo gives up and joins them.

EPILOGUE

The zoo re-opens after seven days. Attendance is spotty at first, but builds over time, though it never quite reaches pre-contest levels. All questions about the lion's fate remain unanswered.

The small, public outcry is short-lived.

In an attempt to recapture their original success, the PR department has cameras installed in all animal enclosures. It is an expensive and ultimately futile venture. Someone is written up for it.

On the whole, the animals ignore the devices. Only the crows seem fascinated by the lenses, and the Zoo-cam feed is overtaken for a week by preening, feathered faces.

Eventually, most are shut down. The crows find new sport elsewhere.

The Zoo-cam website features only one feed, a single camera still streaming. It witnesses the birth of a robust litter of hyena pups. The tiny, spotted babies become internet celebrities for a few, short weeks.

They are blissfully unaware of this.

They have no care to be famous, for their mother has much to teach them, and time is a fleeting hare scrambling ahead of her.

It is freedom, and forever just beyond her reach.

The camera is turned off once they are gone. It misses their mother's grief. It does not witness the courtship of an elephant and a tortoise, the death of a bear, nor the slow integration of one extraordinary macaque into a troop of domesticated monkeys.

Only the birds tell these stories, and everybody knows that birds always lie.

See all parts of Frances Pauli's story "The Zoo Diaries" online at Metaphorosis.
If you liked them, leave a comment. Authors love that!
Remember to subscribe to our e-mail updates so you'll know when new stories are posted.

July

When The Future Calls

Salena Casha

When Derek came down to breakfast, the sight of Savannah at the table stopped him cold. The derm-ate pod attached to his sister's left bicep pulsed with seafoam derm-paynt; she'd gone for *Crustacean Euphoria*, the one flavor that didn't leave an iron tang on the back of Derek's tongue. Except for the elite, no one on Earth had eaten physical food since 2100. The derm-ate feeder pods, embedded in their skin, were all they had now.

"How's work at the Mausoleum at the End of the Old World?" Savannah asked. "Anything, like, interesting recently, or you still cleaning glass?"

That's breakfast ruined, Derek thought.

He gritted his teeth as he rotated his shoulder. His joint clicked. Two days in a row now scraping graffiti off *The Vince Offer Series* at Infomercial Intersection. It didn't help that his dominant arm hosted his own empty derm-ate pod. The graffiti *had* been interesting, but as long as she called his place of work, the Museum of Anthropological Findings, a mausoleum, he wouldn't mention it.

"Aren't you supposed to be an adult and, *like*, get your own food instead of taking Mom and Dad's?" he asked, staring pointedly at her arm and then the front door.

She snorted. "You're the one living at home."

At least his assignment at the Museum gave him a reason to leave the house so he didn't have to hear, for the tenth time, about how what his parents really wanted was steak with bubbled butter in a pan. It didn't matter to them that the last cow had died well before Environmental Reconstruction. Before they were born.

He reached across the table and palmed through the remaining derm-paynt flavors. *Anthropoda Chiffon* and *Imperial Dulse*. Fancy scientific words for 'this will taste like ass and is made from either seaweed or ants'. They were lucky they could afford clean tenth-generation upcycled derm-ate filters. Derek had seen something about it recently on the news: how too many people died from stretching the pods beyond their allocated uses.

"I just don't get how you can watch the same dumb videos every day selling you shit you can't buy," Savannah said.

"You don't need to," he said and reached for *Imperial Dulse*.

If he'd been able to choose his job, which no one did, he'd have gone for his over hers every time. Savannah lived on the other side of Philly with a brutal set of roommates, all of whom waded knee-deep in toxic waste from nine until seven, collecting samples. Plungers sucking up earth muck and what little water there was left, to just spit it out somewhere else that told them it was *no good. Not ready yet.* They'd be lucky if the toxins didn't kill them in the process.

I'm on the cutting edge of post-environmental reconstruction, she'd said once. *They'll upload my words to students one day.* But what she avoided thinking about head on — something Derek thought about for her instead every day — was that the exposure would be the end of her. And maybe, it wasn't worth it.

"You didn't always think the Museum was torture," he said. "Remember 4D?"

She rolled her eyes. "4D?"

"How you can pause a commercial and step into the frozen film frame and mess around. You know. When mom took us, back when we were kids, you went into a music commercial."

"Oh yeah," she said, distracted. Her forehead softened. "I think I tried a piano once."

They had 4D on Infomercial Intersection as well. He hadn't used it in ages, but once, on a particularly boring shift, he'd stepped into a Vince Offer frame. The bars of the recording had fizzled like carbonation against his skin and he had held a Slap Chop in his hand, the seamed plastic cold against his palm.

The memory lingered between them, like the echo of a touched key. Savannah cleared her throat.

"The other day, we were collecting samples on the South Side of the Delaware River, you know, the spot by the old Bristol plant, and Marina caught one of the testers just throwing them out. Dumping the mud we'd spent hours pulling right back into the river. It's all a hoax," she said.

"Did you see them do that?" he asked.

"Marina did."

"So you didn't," he said.

She glared at him and leaned forward. A pimple had crusted above her left eyebrow. She'd been picking at it. Whatever moment the 4D had given them was gone.

"If the Old Worldies had just done the right thing to begin with, we wouldn't be wasting our lives on pointless jobs. I don't get why it's our responsibility to fix their mistakes. We weren't there." She paused and leaned further forward. "We need to resist the tyranny of the past."

The room stopped.

The graffiti. *Resist the tyranny of the past.* Plastered red on Vince's face, on Derek's favorite infomercial of them all.

"Savannah," he lowered his voice. "What did you do?"

"You know it's true," Savannah continued. She took a sip of water.

"You're going to get yourself in trouble," he said.

What he really meant to say was she was making Environmental Reconstruction about herself, again. She didn't want to go on shoveling crap for the rest of her life and, while that was fair enough, it was also tough luck. Her discontent wasn't Derek's problem.

"Why? You going to run to your supervisor and put your only sister in jail?"

His jaw clenched. She was probably on a list already. Actually, *he* was probably on a list now. Typical Savannah, screwing everyone else's lives up without a second thought. He'd been an antibacterialist at the Museum for over fifteen years and wanted it to stay that way. There was something to be said for the comfort of those light-blocking windows, the dark walls, Vince Offer's voice echoing across micah.

She smiled to herself and stood.

"Thought so," she said. "Anyway, got to head out. Need to see if the water is unfucked yet or if we still need to drink filtered piss." She didn't push her chair in before heading to the door.

When he went to work that night, he filled an antique steel mug with beer to keep him company. Drank half before he reached the ruined display. What remained of the graffiti on Vince Offer's *Slap Chop* series was three days old now, and Derek watched Vince bob across the defaced screen, his head wavering in and out of the word *Resist.* His stainless white shirt glowed behind the carmine lens. What Derek would give to be next to him in the infomercial. Saying lines and smiling at the camera, palming the Slap Chop and showing America how to be skinny again. Eating stuff called tuna.

Derek looked at Vince and then down at the scraper in his hand. Savannah and her idiot friends trying to prove a point didn't bring the owners of the museum down to the floor to clean up the mess. He pressed the edge against the glass and began to scrape.

"Stop having a boring tuna, stop having a boring life," Vince said. He slapped his palm down on the white knob of the Slap Chop, the blades slicing dehydrated tuna into cubes.

Derek took another deep drink of his beer. The carbonation crystallized behind his eyes. Vince's teeth looked like bleached ceramic in the dark mica hall.

"Poor bastards," Savannah had said once. "Had no idea what was coming until it was too late. And now, we're so scared of what could happen if we try something new. There's no trust anymore."

"If you knew what was coming, I'm sure you'd do something about it," Derek said to the Vince on-screen.

If Infomercial Intersection was to be believed, Vince had been everywhere. Perhaps even at the same level as Hollywood stars. Everything Vince sold was meant to help people: the Slap Chop, the Schticky, the InVINCEable, the SHAMWOW. Make their lives more bearable. Derek watched as Vince continued slicing and dicing, iceberg lettuce this time. The crunch crisped and tingled the skin below Derek's ear. There was nothing the Slap Chop — and Vince for that matter — couldn't handle.

It was on historical record that plenty of people knew the climate crisis was coming and did nothing, but maybe Vince had been different.

Derek pressed down hard on the scraper's handle. The last *t* was almost gone now. From the smell of it, it was *Russet Scarlet* paynt. Probably stolen from their parents' supply. It flaked onto the floor at his feet.

Vince had pivoted to hard selling, throwing in a free cheese grater if you called in the next fifteen minutes. They'd even add in a cutting board for good measure — what a deal! Operators, Vince intoned, were standing by. Someone had scrubbed the number on the screen to show all zeroes. It blinked in half-assed binary. Somewhere, far off down the hall, an overworked water pipe clanged. Derek glanced briefly down the hall after the noise. Nothing moved except the light playing against black pitch from the activated Offer screen. He needed a walk around, a distraction so he didn't have to think about what Savannah had done. Derek raised his mug and took a long pull of beer. Swallowed. The alcohol was really hitting now, deep in the nerves of his hands.

He stepped away from Vince and felt, more than heard, the video pause. The silence dropped in on him like declining air pressure, and he continued past the Offer series to the videos he often skipped. He went through phases like anyone.

Wandering closer to the Joe Gray series, his fingers tripped across the screen. The infomercial activated.

"This is the only device on Earth that is truly hands free," Joe Gray said.

He wore an absurd headset with a suction cup attached to a 2000s mobile that kept the phone pressed against his head. Derek watched him, his stomach unfurling from its knot. He'd never touched a phone, never even thought about the object glued to Joe's head with any real curiosity. No one used Old World phones or numbers here anymore — thanks to the natural evolution of facial recognition from the 2000s, Derek could just leave a memory note or viz based on the image of a person's face in his mind. So this type of comms device wasn't a part of Derek's every day.

His eyes followed Joe Gray's lips as Joe spoke into the mobile. It was in every shot. Not a piano, but it was an artifact of the beginning of the technological revolution, the base of the exponential advancement curve. Way cooler than a piano.

Derek had tried plenty of Offer products, but not much beyond that. He was in untested territory. It would be a lie if he said he wasn't a bit drunk, a bit lonely. That maybe, it'd feel good to screw around and see how another Old World relic felt. Put his fingers over the numbers of a mobile pad for kicks. There was no one here. He wasn't even sure if his time at the museum would be numbered now because of what Savannah had done. If they knew, what did he have to lose? The only other option was just staring down a hallway at the end of the world, previously known as Philadelphia, in silence.

A thrill shivered down the back of his shirt. He walked to the Gojo Hands Free screen and looped behind the projection. It took him a few tries to remember the order of operations, but he finally managed to turn on 4D mode. Even though Joe Gray couldn't feel it, Derek moved carefully as he untangled the GoJo set from the frozen actor's ear.

His thumb grazed the keypad. He inhaled static. The mobile in his hand was still old enough to have letters above the numbers. 2 = ABC. He turned the phone over gently in his hand. There was a running joke about Old Worlders doing funny phrases for advertising purposes. Vanity numbers, that's what they were called, he remembered. They'd been plastered on billboards all across the corporate wasteland.

1-800-GOT-JUNK to get your old furniture to a landfill, pronto. Maybe 1-800-WEATHER to learn about the forecast. He laughed out loud.

Or even, 1-800-SLP-CHOP. That'd be a good one. He punched in the 1-800 and then 757-2467. Each push prompted a gentle ping. With the number complete, he clicked the button with a pine green, old-style handset on it and lifted the rectangle of plastic and metal to his ear.

The line began to ring, a tiny, sporadic jolt. They'd done the work to make it feel real, he had to give the museum credit for that, at least. He held the mobile a few inches away; he couldn't find the volume button. Apparently, Joe Gray liked it loud.

"Pick up, ya dumb Old Worlder," he said into the speaker.

This was *absurd*. He was about to end the call when he heard someone. At first, he thought it was coming from behind the screen. Grainy, a bit garbled.

"Slap Chop hotline, Bob here," the voice said.

Someone had definitely picked up. Derek's stomach dropped. He pulled the phone away from his ear. Stared at it as if he could see the sound waves coming straight toward him from the speaker box.

"Um, hello?" Derek said.

"Yes, hello?" Bob replied.

"Hello?" Derek echoed back again. His mouth had gone dry. There was someone there. A real someone. Shit.

"Yes?" Bob asked.

"Is this where," Derek tried to find the words, "I mean, do you sell Slap Chops?"

"Yup. That's what the hotline's for," Bob said. This man from the past sounded annoyed. Like he had somewhere to be.

This was ridiculous. Derek looked back down the hall.

"Okay. Wow. Okay," Derek said. His voice was too loud in his own ears. He ran his hand through his hair.

"How many do you want?" Bob asked.

"What?"

"Slap Chops. How many?"

"Do people buy more than one?" Derek asked.

"Sometimes."

"I don't need any," Derek said. He bit his lip, waited a beat. The alcohol tingled across his jaw and he pressed the phone harder to his ear.

"I'm from the future," he said. It came out in a whisper, but Bob heard it.

There was a huff on the line. "Look if this is a prank call, Slap Chop has a policy to take action against you people," Bob said.

"Look, no, sorry, I didn't mean to bother you, it's just, I'm a fan of Vince's. Watched his videos more than a few times," Derek said, trying to play it cool. "We've got a whole museum dedicated to them. Can I talk to him?"

"Vince Offer? You high or something?" Bob asked. "He's not in the call center."

Derek looked back down at the dregs of beer in his mug. Still cold, the froth staining the sides of the tumbler.

"No, not high, but I am a little tipsy," Derek admitted. That seemed, for some reason, enough of an answer to satisfy Bob.

"What did you want to tell him, futureman?" Bob asked.

Futureman. Derek smiled at that. Savannah would *hate* that.

Derek licked his lips. Breathed. "Um, I'm not sure."

"So let me get this straight. You're calling me. From the future. To talk to Vince. And you don't know what you want to tell him."

"No, no," Derek said. He looked back down the hall at the graffiti. Tried to remember back to his history classes of when the Earth started dying. Probably in Bob's lifetime. If Savannah had this chance, what would she do?

"It's going to sound crazy," he started, "but everything they're saying about the climate is true. We survived it, but it's not the same. We lost a lot."

Even though Derek wasn't sure what exactly they'd lost, he felt it in his bones sometimes. He saw it in the deep horizontal line in Savannah's forehead. The monotony. The lack of direction. Maybe that's what she'd meant by 'tyranny of the past', a past they were all still paying for today. Derek glanced back into the depths of the darkened hall. The pitch animated with the looping videos.

"Tell Vince," Derek said. His voice cracked.

The line had gone quiet. Somewhere in another hall in the Museum of Anthropological Findings, a digital counter clocked four AM.

"What the hell am I supposed to do with that?" Bob asked.

Derek wished he had the handless tool that Joe Gray loved so the phone didn't keep slipping down his slick palm.

"Just tell Vince what I said," Derek said again. "He'll know what to do."

Bob snorted. "He doesn't have two brain cells to rub together. And he won't listen to me. I mean, would anyone believe *you* if you told them the world was about to end?"

It took everything Derek had to keep the phone against his ear as panic crested through him like a wave.

"Probably not," Derek said. "I'm not anyone." His arm ached. He looked over at the GoJo, but didn't move to take it.

"Well, I guess time doesn't change that," Bob said. "I'm sorry, but I can't help you, bud. I don't like to rock the boat. Just come in on time, get my paycheck, and go home. No drama."

Derek took another long pull of his beer. He didn't know what to do with his hands except keep the phone glued to his ear, the past breathing down the line. Most of all, he wondered if Savannah would have done a better job. Been more convincing. Said the right words that would have changed history.

"Since you're from the future and all," Bob said. "Can I ask a question?"

"Sure," Derek choked out.

"Did it make a difference?" Bob asked.

"Did what make a difference?" Derek asked. He wanted to reach down the line and shake Bob. *This* was the difference. It was staring at him across centuries down a tenuous connection.

"The Slap Chop," Bob replied. "We've sold over a thousand so far. Did it make a difference in people's lives? I mean, you're calling me about it from, well, the future. So I'm assuming we're famous or something."

Resist the tyranny of the past. The remaining red paint glistened off of the Slap Chop's looping screen a few paces down from him. What Derek did know was posted below the digital display. By the end, Slap Chop had sold 50,000 of their devices. They did not end America's poor eating habits. He'd even heard that one had taken out the last surviving dolphin. Most, if not all, of the Slap Chops were pulled from landfills in the Great Recycling era that predated Environmental Reconstruction. They were dismembered and repurposed, the plastic powering early derm-ate filters that kept what was left of mankind alive.

"They definitely helped things along, one way or another," Derek said.

Bob mulled that one over but didn't press it. "Well, you sure I can't interest you in a Slap Chop or a Schticky?"

"You can schticky anywhere or anytime with anyone," Derek said. The quote from Vince's earlier product lines got him a shocked chuckle.

"What a weird day," Bob said. "I'm going to need a drink after this."

Yeah," Derek replied. "And think it over. What I told you. You could change everything."

Bob laughed at that. "You're not the only one trying to save the world, bucko and, if they can't, I sure as hell won't be able to." He cleared his throat and continued. "Gotta free up the lines for real customers. Take care, futureman."

A lump calcified in Derek's throat, the line cut, and with that, the past slipped back behind a silver screen.

Derek placed the mobile back on Joe Gray's ear. Slid the GoJo suction device back in place. He stepped out of the pixelated box. The static bubbled back across his skin and gave way to the clean, if antiseptic, air of the infomercial runway.

He unpaused the GoJo, watching Joe Gray jump back into a conversation with whatever actor played his mom. Gingerly, he sat down on the floor, crossed his legs in front of him and watched the video loop back on itself, over and over in the dark.

It couldn't help repeating itself. That was all it was meant to do, after all.

See Salena Casha's story "When The Future Calls" online at Metaphorosis.
If you liked it, leave a comment. Authors love that!
Remember to subscribe to our e-mail updates so you'll know when new stories are posted.

About the story

The initial germination of this story came out of a writing prompt from the NYC Midnight competition. If you haven't participated before, this is a sign from the universe telling you to do so. The upside is a writing competition like that will force you to write a relatively polished draft of a story within an allocated period of time, potentially for a genre you're uncomfortable with. Luckily, the prompt that started "When the Future Calls" included science fiction as the genre. While the story evolved dramatically since the initial draft (thanks in no small part to the tireless and detailed feedback of B. Morris Allen), I definitely encourage anyone who is trapped by writer's block — a claustrophobic space I find myself in more often than not — to give writing prompts a try.

Still, why climate change? Why Rich Pacte? Why Savannah? That all gets a little complicated but, essentially, my grandmother was recently hospitalized and when I was visiting her, her roommate watched an endless loop of jewelry infomercials. It was my own personal version of hell. But, the woman who chose to watch them clearly loved them. There was something about the videos on a loop that enthralled her. As I started the story, I brainstormed with my husband and he pulled up YouTube recordings of infomercials out there and led us directly to a few stars on the circuit such as Vince Offer, Joe Pedott, and Billy Mays, among others. Thus, Derek's obsession was born. I thought the infomercials would be even more compelling if it was a medium he didn't grow up with or understand and so, in looking toward the future, incorporating climate change for me was inevitable.

Climate change has been on my mind a lot recently and our tendency to want short-term solutions for long-term problems, to be absolved from our guilt, to buy "green" brands and say, "that's it, I did my part" which I'll be the first to admit I very much participate in. The news talks a lot about what future generations will inherit — and more specifically, what they won't — so I wondered a lot about what a new and changing world would look like where the New England neighborhood I call home would have the climate of Florida in the coming decades. I also thought, relatively cynically, about how even with scientists sounding the climate alarm since the 90s, if not before, we haven't really changed that much today. I wondered if our future selves would understand or despise us for knowing that we had known and did nothing about it. Or, if they'd hoped we were just naive.

Lastly, one of my favorite things to write is dialogue. I think dialogue, when executed well, really ramps up the tension of a story. I mean, just look at how Succession uses it to turn the dial up on its scenes. Bob came first as a character before Savannah and understanding their different voices, what they wanted, how they interacted with Derek, was the most gratifying part of writing this piece for me. Given that I'm influenced heavily by what I read, two recent finds helped give this story life, namely: Cormac McCarthy's set of novels *The Passenger* and *Stella Maris*. *Stella Maris* is written entirely in unpunctuated dialogue. The scenes don't move, it's just a conversation between a patient and a doctor. But it's explosive, it's effused with imagery. Even though the dialogue is untagged, you know exactly who says what. It's powerful to be able to live inside a voice so deeply, it speaks up from the page itself without the author having to describe it.

A final word on the process before I leave you. This piece didn't become what it was until it went through revisions. When I look at the first draft, it's unrecognizable. My husband reviewed it first; he's my most trusted reader and I take his feedback seriously. We ideated through the potential of multiple universes, the conversation between Derek and Bob, what Derek thought of Rich, of his parents. And then, B. Morris Allen provided insight that took this piece to its next level. My advice to writers out there is rewrite means rewrite. Some authors don't even look at the first draft of their manuscript before they begin the second. Be ruthless in your editing. Take that diversion to better understand your characters. Introduce a character, a hint of backstory, a new object. You might find a new theme or a powerful undercurrent that you hadn't noticed before. Maybe the story stays there, or maybe — as we learned — it comes back. All in all, it's where real writing happens. B. Morris Allen helped me take this story to somewhere both new and familiar, and for that, Derek, Savannah, Bob, and I are grateful.

A question for the author

Q: Why do you write speculative rather than realistic fiction?

A: Why do I write speculative fiction rather than realistic fiction, you ask? In general, I gravitate toward speculative fiction because it's my preferred genre to read. All my recent favorites run the wide gamut of speculative fiction from gentle magic realism to dark fantasy and horror. To get to know me and where my writing comes from, explore the worlds of Carmen Maria Machado, Marisa Crane, Emily St. John Mandel, Jennifer Egan, and Haruki Mirakami. They get it. Their stories and word choice gets it. How speculative fiction is sometimes the only way to describe our internal weirdness and spill it onto the page. How speculative fiction gives the space for rumination, for reflection, for, dare I say, speculation and, by its very nature, questioning. Speculative fiction allows me to twist reality into the shape that life feels like under my skin and show it to you and say, "See? This is what I was trying to get at all along." Recently, I worked on a piece about harassment in a workplace. I started writing it as realistic fiction, but the terms on which I could explain it to the readers didn't prove the desired effect, weren't helping me say what I was so desperately trying to articulate: that feeling of walking on eggshells, of being gaslit, of being disbelieved, so I wondered "what if the floor was lava and no one except the main character who was being harassed could see it?" And so, the story morphed into something speculative even if it was about a lived reality. My advice is, always, to let the story tell you where it wants to go.

About the author

Salena Casha survives New England winters on black coffee and good beer. Most mornings when hacking away at a piece in progress, she worries if "writer" is a title she can apply to herself. Whether it's an apt title or not, she's happy that by some kismet combination of SEO and love for science fiction, you've found your way to this story. In her professional life, she has been a literary agent, a math textbook editor, an English teacher, and an IT manager. When not reading, or working, she trains for marathons and tries to remember to stretch. Usually, you'll find her writing at your local brewery.

salenacasha.substack.com, @salaylay_c

When the Oracle Speaks

Albert Chu

One year after the war's end, the royal court welcomed a hundred orphan boys into our ranks. They flew into the city's spaceport by shuttle and proceeded up the hill on the backs of the court's own palanquin-bearers; upon entering the palace grounds, they received the speeches and banquets we held in honor of their noble suffering. The boys, hailing from the kingdom's most war-torn moon, had lost everything, but now their days of hardship were over. They had become esteemed wards of the House of Hassam.

After a few days, though, people in the court whispered of something else. The cooks and dressing girls repeated the same rumor: *Did you hear? One of the new boys can see the future.* The ministers and generals, who should have held themselves above idle gossip, indulged in speculation: *If this is true, could the boy be of use?* And everyone wondered how the king might act. We all knew his strength was the House's strength. If the boy possessed some special power, my father would take him.

So I never had any intentions of turning the boy to my side. I was just curious.

I found him sitting on a bench in the middle of a courtyard, surrounded by onlookers. It was another rainy day, and all the aristocrats had a servant beside them, shielding their heads with an umbrella. Some pretended to write calligraphy or paint—the perfect image of artful nobility, honing their talents as the rain fell around them—while others just stared.

I took in this scene from the colonnade which circumscribed the courtyard. "Come," I said, and my servant chaperone opened my umbrella. "I'm going to talk to him."

We left the colonnade's shelter and entered the courtyard. The boy didn't appear special—he was skinny and looked around the same age as me, and the only thing unusual about him was his uncovered head. Rain plastered his thick, reddish curls to his forehead. They'd be a frizzy mess later; I wrinkled my nose at the thought of it.

Instead of looking up as we approached, he only stared at the rain hammering the surface of the courtyard pond. He'd been doing that, it seemed, all afternoon long. My servant and I stood there, waiting, until the silent lack of recognition grew irritating. Finally, my servant spoke: "Prince Meira Pashel em-Hassam wishes to speak to you."

The boy turned around. His eyes swept over me—my jeweled coat jacket, inlaid with silver; the ceremonial lightgun at my belt; my coiled black locks, cascading to my chest and lustrously shiny. The regalia of a prince was designed for impact. But his face betrayed no emotion—not fear, nor awe, nor muffled resentment— none of the familiar reactions.

As if he expected it all. My irritation grew.

The boy didn't bow, but I refrained from comment; I'd already conceded enough conversational power to this commoner. Instead, I said, "You look wet. Would you like an umbrella? My servant can fetch one."

He shook his head. "I like the rain. It's nice on my head."

The word the boy used for 'rain' caught my attention—a formal construction, not the colloquialism that everyone in the city used. I remembered why he was here. We were both Artani, but I had been born on this moon, Artan itself, while he, like the rest of the orphans, was from Eshtan. Once the crown jewel and proudest province of the House of Hassam, now a dead moon, bombed to a ruin by the Samandirans.

The boy lacked etiquette, but not only was he my House's ward, he'd also lost his parents to the Artani people's mortal enemy. I could hardly reprimand him. So instead, I said, "Welcome, in the name of the House of Hassam, to your new home. Our hospitality is yours to command."

The boy responded to my generosity with only a turn of his lips. I had expected gratitude, and having not received it, I was off-balance. His lips slid back into a level line, and his flat, even stare did nothing to help me regain confidence. I had never spoken to someone like this before.

"What's your name?" I asked.

"Iuno."

"Iuno," I repeated. "Well, everyone is talking about you. I wanted to know more for myself. About your powers."

He sat there, his hands folded in his waterlogged lap, and waited.

My smile grew pained; I'd lost patience for subtlety. "Please tell me about them. How far do you see? What is it like? Can you tell me if someone will be dead in a year, or which side will win a war? Are you ever wrong?"

"That's a lot of questions." Iuno pushed some of his dripping hair out of his eyes.

"And to say that you can see the future is an extreme claim." *And I'm your prince.* "Indulge me."

"If you insist," he said, and I smiled harder to stop my nostrils from flaring. "In the morning, I see everything that I will live through that day. At night, I sleep, and when I wake, it happens again with the new day's knowledge. It's actually fairly simple."

"You must see one of many possible futures, then, perhaps the most likely—"

"No." Iuno spread out his hands, as if to apologize for his gift. "I see exactly what will happen. I am never wrong."

I narrowed my eyes. Was this what he had the entire palace believing? Did people think my father might desire this boy's power?

"I'm going to choose a number." I crossed my arms and allowed myself a small smile. "Zero or one. Which will I choose?"

"Zero." He didn't hesitate.

"Well, I choose one. Didn't you say you were never wrong?"

And then he began to laugh.

For such a small boy, he had a very loud laugh, and it was remarkably ugly. He wheezed like a decrepit minister a week from death. His cackling was unnaturally pitched several tones higher than his normal voice. He occasionally snorted.

Nobody in the courtyard pretended to practice the arts anymore. Aristocrats held their pens frozen in mid-stroke, and servants dropped their umbrellas to cover their mouths with both hands. After those umbrellas bounced off the cobblestones and clattered to rest, nothing moved but the endlessly falling rain and Iuno, who still shook with laughter.

Eventually, he stopped. He reached into his pocket, withdrew a scrap of paper, and handed it to me.

It, like Iuno himself, was completely soaked; I held it delicately to prevent it from dissolving in my hands. After reading a few lines, I understood.

He had transcribed our entire conversation. The trap that I thought I'd laid so cleverly stared back at me from the page: *didn't you say you were never wrong?*

I read the note twice, three times, while the stillness held around me. Everyone marveled at the audacity of this orphan boy, who, by laughing in the face of Prince Meira Pashel, had surpassed even the latitude afforded to a guest. They wondered what I might do to him.

I crumpled the paper in my fist and squeezed it to pulp. "Come with me."

We walked out of the courtyard, followed closely by my confused chaperone. Under the stares of the gathered aristocrats, we passed through the colonnade and into the warm, sunlamp-lit atria of the palace itself. I led him up the silver escalator to the floor with my suite, and when I reached my door, I turned to my servant. "Bring some hot towels for my guest and enough tea for both of us. You may leave after doing so."

The servant wiped the confusion off his face and bowed; he understood my request for privacy well enough. "Yes, Prince Meira."

When he left, I glanced down at Iuno's sandals. With each step he took, he pressed rainwater out of his drenched soles with a wet, squelching sound. A trail of damp footprints followed behind him. "Take those off before your step inside," I said, "and wait here. I'll get you something to dry your feet."

A few minutes later, Iuno, no longer dripping, sat next to me on my divan. The towels the servant had provided lay in a crumpled corner outside my washing room's entrance. He'd changed into one of my spare tunics; the lavender scent of the palace maids' laundry detergent clung to him. We both held cups of tea in our hands.

"It never rained on Eshtan." Iuno held his cup close but didn't drink, content instead to let his eyes bask in the steam. "I knew, today, that I'd feel it for the first time. But I didn't expect how it could mingle with sweat and sting your eyes. Or how it makes the air smell like dirt."

He spoke of his dead home—his parents' grave—so lightly that I wondered if he missed it at all. Everyone knew how to speak to a victim; everyone could console a poor orphan for his loss. But he was different, and scripted gestures of nobility rolled off of him.

When he turned to face me, his steady gaze bordered on a challenge. "You didn't punish me, like they all expected you to."

"No." I ran my fingers around a groove in my teacup. "I didn't."

However aggravating his laughter, however angering the exact correctness of his transcription, he was right. I had told him to prove he saw the future without error, and he had done so. How could I fault him? Perhaps he had laughed so freely because he had seen, when he opened his eyes this morning, that I would not punish him.

Still, I needed to ask one final question. "You lied," I said. "You gave the wrong answer. You say that you know the future, but how can anyone trust you?" How could *I* trust him?

Finally, Iuno took a long sip from his cup. Then, he said, "You wanted to use me to prove that if you knew the future, you could change it. You weren't interested in the truth. I'm not a trustworthy tool, but if you want the truth, I'll give it."

Was he challenging me at all? He showed no attention to the protocols of etiquette and hierarchy; he said exactly what he meant, without hiding his true meaning. What if it wasn't some inscrutable gambit? What if he just wasn't playing the game?

As we finished our drinks in silence, humid air creeped into the room from my suite's open bay windows. Rain blanketed the entire city, and from our vantage point, we could see the swollen, frothing banks of the Azure River, its winding course cutting the city in half.

Iuno placed his empty teacup down. "Thank you for the tea, Prince Meira."

I held up a hand to stop him from leaving. "Before you go," I said. "I have a proposal. Instead of living in the common rooms with the other orphans, how would you like to make this your home?" For a moment, I wondered how to package my motivations —but I had tried, fruitlessly, to maneuver around Iuno for the whole day, and I was tired. "I never understood the tradition of princes having companions. There are dozens of boys from noble families who can fight or paint or just look pretty. The thought of randomly choosing one of them always bored me. But you're different."

He waited before answering; I willed myself to release my held breath. Then, he nodded. "Thank you, Prince Meira," he said. "I accept."

I chuckled. "Well," I said, waving a hand, "if we're going to be friends, you can't call me by my title. My name's Ahpa."

"All right." He smiled—something shy and genuine, the first time I'd seen that expression on his face. "Ahpa, then."

We grew older. While the commoners kept their hair short, the palace stylists knew to trim a noble's hair only enough to prevent split ends. Eventually, my black curls cascaded down to my hips.

Iuno remained my companion. Some ministers, trying to gauge his usefulness, managed to corner him and press him with questions, but they always left disappointed. He had no power; he had no more ability to change the future than an ordinary person had to change the past. And if my father himself ever made a move for him, I never saw it.

We came to know each other. Iuno learned of my taste for dates, and on some afternoons, he surprised me with a plate of them, fresh from the market. "The merchants sell these only rarely," he would say, "but I saw that they'd have them this morning, so I walked down the hill to get us some." And while we finished the plate together on my divan, we talked. Sometimes about idle court gossip or the latest minister to embarrass himself in some political blunder. Sometimes about our favorite pieces of classical poetry. Sometimes about the war.

"On Eshtan, did you ever see them?" I once asked, between bites of date. "The enemy."

He nibbled at his own dates, taking as long to finish one as I did to eat three. "I did," he said. "They occupied my village for some time."

"What did they do?" A scene of Samandiran brutality from the propaganda holovids flashed through my mind.

"Nothing exciting. Mostly, they were ordinary people." Even when speaking of the soldiers who'd killed his parents, his voice betrayed neither anger nor sadness. "They were only there at all because they'd been ordered."

I scoffed. "Samandiran High Command invaded Eshtan in a surprise attack a full day before they bothered declaring war. They killed millions of colonists like you. Shouldn't they pay?"

"How?" he asked. "Another war?"

I blinked. Officially, the war had ended when my father, having turned the tide against Samandir, forced them to sue for peace. But everyone in the court knew that the ceasefire's true architects were key ministers in my father's council; he, to the contrary, had wanted to press his advantage and continue the fight. In recent months, as the peace grew stale, I'd overheard conversations where generals cursed those ministers and whispered their longing for revenge.

I shook my head. "I didn't say that. Still, how can you say they were just following orders?"

He shrugged, reached into his mouth, and fished out his date's pit, still shiny with saliva. "To me, everyone's following orders."

While I digested his meaning, he tossed the pit into our shared waste platter.

One day, some months later, the king convened a Great Circle, where the House of Hassam's princes, ministers, and generals gathered to vote on a question placed before them. A Great Circle could shake lives and turn the fate of the entire kingdom—but nobody knew why my father had called for one. That morning, I left for the Circle, walking blindly into the future, and in the evening, the Circle finished, I returned to my suite.

"Ahpa." Iuno lay belly-down on my rug, a book spread under his head. He craned his neck up to look at me. "Welcome back."

I stood a step inside the doorway and stared out the bay windows. My mouth was dry.

"It was an ambush," I said. After half a day in the throne room, silently watching the Great Circle unfold, the words spilled out of me.

My father had named half the senior ministers in the court, all ones who had pushed the House of Hassam towards a ceasefire at the end of the war. And he named one member of the royal family: Prince Meira Siushem em-Hassam, my eldest brother, his heir. All these men, he said, had committed treason.

His spies produced the evidence. In secret, the traitors had communicated with the Samandiran High Command to negotiate a permanent peace settlement. Its terms—when Meira Siushem took the throne, the House of Hassam would reduce its army to pre-war sizes, with the promise that Samandir would do the same.

A roar went up from the generals in the room. That, I knew, was an act, a front of outrage; surely my father had coordinated with them before convening the Circle.

"He asked us to exile the ministers." He'd been wise, not seeking execution—that was a step too far. "He called for us to disinherit Meira Siushem."

"And you voted to do so."

My mind stuttered. How was he so sure? But then—of course.

"I did," I said. "You've known everything I've told you since this morning."

"I have."

"But then why—"

Why not tell me? It didn't matter; my behavior in the Circle wouldn't have changed if I'd known the king's intentions beforehand. Everyone knew that Meira Siushem, naively chasing peace with the Samandirans, had lost, and there was nothing to do but vote for his disinheritance. Still, something sharp lodged in my chest—betrayal. Iuno hadn't told me.

"You're anxious," he said.

I had every reason to be anxious. With the throne's succession now in question, the king held the right to designate a new crown prince. By disinheriting Meira Siushem, he had invited us, his sons, to compete among ourselves for power, his favor, and a chance to become the next king. Some princes had fought in the war; they could exploit their military connections. Others had mothers from wealthy families; they could purchase influence. And some would eliminate their rivals with poison or lightgun fire—why not, if they could get away with it?

I had none of these advantages, and in a contest of violence, I was underequipped.

"I can see my future." I felt cold, but I resisted the urge to tighten my coat around my shoulders. "Prince Meira Pashel, a pawn in my brothers' succession game. Nobody will notice if I die."

I glanced down at Iuno and felt a spark of hope. I did have one advantage. "But you can help me," I said. "Your powers—I've always thought they can't *do* anything, but that isn't true, is it? When you go buy those dates, how do you ever know that the market is selling them that day? The knowledge just—happens."

"I only see that I buy dates, Ahpa. Then I buy them."

I shook my head. "Couldn't you use your powers to help me against my brothers? To give me access to this hidden knowledge?"

"No." He spoke this simple refusal without malice or spite, but frustration still gripped me. "You don't understand."

"What don't I understand?"

"I could just as easily share with you your doom. What if, one morning, I told you that you'd fall into a trap that day? What if I told you how you'd try to escape the trap, knowing that it was there, and still fail? You already tried to best the future once, Ahpa."

I stared at Iuno and remembered that day, years ago, when he had handed me that waterlogged note.

"Besides," he said, looking up at me with half-lidded eyes. "I have nothing to do with a power struggle between the princes of Hassam."

I bristled. "Even when my life's at stake?"

"It doesn't have to be. You could walk away, couldn't you? If you gave up your title, nobody would have any reason to quarrel with you."

I stepped backwards and curled my lip. Then, without saying more, I turned and walked into my study. The door clicked shut behind me, and silence, broken only by the heavy sound of my breathing, pressed in. My fist had clenched when I'd heard Iuno's suggestion of surrender, and slowly, I relaxed it.

Once, the king had also been a small prince, but when the incompetence of his brother, the reigning monarch, led us to lose half of Eshtan to the enemy, he had seized the future. He took the throne by force. He faced down Samandir's army, larger and better-equipped, and won. He did not surrender to fate.

Like my father, I had my wit. If I played the game carefully, gathering information, cutting deals, and devising plans, I could come out alive on the winning side—a respected prince, with armies and ships sworn to my banner. A small part of me dreamed of winning everything and wearing my father's crown. With Iuno's help or without it, I wouldn't surrender.

For one moment, I heard again his ugly laughter. I quickly stifled its sound.

For months, I had chased a secret.

The thread began with a corrupt customs official, a prime target for me to blackmail and a useful mine of information. One of the secrets he revealed: several months ago, a series of shipments, addressed to a place that didn't exist, had arrived at the docks by the Azure River. After he'd fabricated papers for them at the behest of an unknown party, they'd disappeared a week later.

Gradually, the thread unraveled. Irregularities in the hiring of several dockhands. Strange incidents when the city guard had cordoned off sections of the docks from public access, citing leaks of dangerous chemicals—obvious pretexts. Then the final clue, when I looked into all the companies which had recently filed dock work permits—one company existed only on paper, and they owned only a single warehouse.

When I staked out that warehouse, I found its entrance guarded by a pair of security automata. They were camouflaged to appear commonplace, but I knew better—these were of an elite line allowed only to members of the court. If any trespasser failed to give them the correct passphrase, they would attack, and only a battalion of armed men could hope to dislodge them.

I'd been thrilled. Some member of the court—perhaps even one of my rival brothers—had hidden something inside that warehouse, and now I only needed to crack it open. But at this final step, my progress stalled. I found no leads as to who exactly owned the warehouse, and I had no way past the security automata. I didn't have the passphrase, and without it, I was stuck.

"Something's wrong with you," Iuno said.

We sat across from each other on my rug, a chessboard between us. I'd carved the board and pieces myself and given them to him as a gift, many years ago. He had smiled when I presented them. "But Ahpa," he said, "you always win."

Now, he noticed my distracted play. I leaned backwards on my palms, sinking my fingers into my rug's deep pile, and released a long exhale. "It's a political matter. Nothing serious."

Though we still lived in the same suite and drank tea together, I'd regarded him differently ever since he'd refused to help me on the day of the Great Circle. I needed to secure my future, buffeted as I was by the instability of a House without an heir. What was the point in sharing with him my life of blackmail and backroom deals? If he wasn't helping me, what did he mean to me?

He grabbed one of his pawns at an angle and rubbed circles with the edge of its base against the board; wood scraped hoarsely against wood. "It looks serious," he said. "When you worry, you don't hide it well. At least around me."

"You must forgive me." I strained to keep my voice light; a prince did not allow a barb to offend. "I'm simply trying to open a locked door, but I lack the key. I didn't want to burden you with something that doesn't interest you."

"The key?"

"A passphrase."

"Yes," he said, and I looked up. The confidence in his speech, the flat set to his eyes, the relaxed slump of his shoulders—all familiar. Iuno never cared to feign surprise. "Would you like to know it?"

I stared at him.

"If you go to this door tonight, speak a passphrase, and gain entry, you'll know it's the correct one," he said. "What if you then return and give the passphrase to me? If, tonight, you do that, then I already know it. I can speak it now."

I saw, again, the circles that Iuno drew on the chessboard with his pawn, and I shivered. Still, I didn't understand. "But why help me?" I asked. "You said..."

"I said that I wasn't a tool. That if you wanted the truth, I would give it."

I tensed in apprehension. Was he warning me? Would the warehouse's contents not benefit me? But I couldn't let my doubts and questions dissuade me. I couldn't command the future with a fearful hand.

I exhaled and willed myself to relax. "Give me the passphrase."

He leaned forwards and whispered it in my ear.

After that, we continued our game without speaking; only the clack of pieces against the board broke the silence.

"Ah," he said. I had trapped him in a mate-in-five two turns ago, but he'd kept playing as if he hadn't seen. "You've won, haven't you?"

"I have."

He shrugged and tipped his king over. "I resign. Good game."

"You as well."

I stood to prepare for an excursion to the warehouse, and Iuno began to lay the chess pieces back inside the velvet-lined wooden case that I'd made with the set. Each piece slid into place with an insistent shush.

"After you come back," he said, "we should talk."

The light coming through my bay windows began to dim. Artan's ever-present rain clouds gathered to obscure the sun, and in a few minutes, rain would flow down the city's streets.

"All right," I said. "We will."

I left. Behind me, Iuno continued to place the chess pieces back into their case.

Outside the warehouse, the rain fell in sheets. It whipped the Azure River into a frenzy, and the waters responded with a hungry roar as they swirled past the dock. It pounded the warehouse's loading bay, transforming it into a marshy field of shallow ponds and rocky islands. Nobody, not even a dock worker, was about; the only things that moved were the automata. They paced back and forth, their armor caked with rust, and as they splashed through the watery field, droplets running down their limbs, they showed no signs of minding.

The shadow of a narrow alleyway enveloped me, hiding me from the automata. For a moment, anticipation and fear flickered in my chest, before I exhaled and snuffed them both out. I stepped out of the alleyway, protected by my umbrella. Espionage mission or not, I wasn't letting my hair get wet.

Both automata stopped and turned to face me; the rain filled the void of silence left by their stilled feet. I continued walking forwards with purpose.

One automata raised a hand, its rusted joints creaking as it did. It spoke, in a gravelly, muffled voice: "Halt."

That was the first layer of defense, meant to deter commoners who'd ignored the posted signs against trespassing and somehow wandered this far into the docks. I didn't slow. At first, the automata showed no reaction—those machine minds, hidden to me, recalculated and reconsidered. Then, as one, they both shivered. The illusion of rusted armor fell from them like an unclasped cloak, and now their carapaces, comprised of thousands of scales, gleamed in the rainwater.

"Provide validation." Its voice was as smooth and bright as a stream of molten metal.

I spoke the passphrase from memory: "Clouds aflame. Flower verdigris. In a summer field, a single stone."

The automata pivoted on their feet away from me, like a door swinging open, and I exhaled. "Validation accepted. Enter."

With the rain still pounding my opened umbrella, I walked past the automata's unblinking stares and entered the warehouse.

First it was quiet; then, the overhead lighting turned on with a droning buzz. I held one hand to my brow to shield my eyes from the unexpected brightness, while my other hovered by my lightgun. If there was a trap, they'd spring it now. But nothing moved, and slowly, I relaxed.

I saw what the warehouse concealed, and at first, I didn't understand.

It stood in the middle of the stark white floor, its matte black chassis drawing the eye like a dark stone in a field of sand. Six conical thrust nozzles dangled from the underside; now, they all pointed straight down, but I knew from the holovids how, in combat, they could turn and dance to make the craft fly in impossible ways. On either side of the nose, weapons bays brimmed with missiles, hexagonal ports arrayed like the speckles of a cobra, its hood spread, staring back at me.

A hover-bomber. And as I circled around it, I saw, emblazoned on its side, the emblem of Samandir.

Pallets of sealed crates lined the warehouse next to the hover-bomber; I pried them open at random and examined their contents. Short-barreled rifles, the same ones brandished by the enemy in both propaganda holovids and classified combat footage. Clean-pressed mustard yellow uniforms, the signature mark of Samandiran shock troopers. All the props needed to stage an attack in the city and have everyone in Artan think Samandir responsible.

Such an attack, ending in the loss of Artani life, would surely cause all-out war to resume. But who could have planned something like this? If I discovered the general or prince responsible for this plot, I could ensure they were executed tomorrow morning.

Then I felt the gaze of that hover-bomber, laden with deadly missiles, pressed against the back of my head, and my thoughts came to a choking halt. I knew the answer. Only someone with absolute power, above the reach of punishment, could have set this plan in motion. He had been forced to end his campaign before he'd destroyed the enemy to his satisfaction. Now he would have his glory and his revenge.

My father. I'd misunderstood him.

Night had fallen by the time I returned to my suite, and Iuno was sitting on the divan, a steaming porcelain teapot before him on the parlor table. My room's sunlamps, having dimmed with the onset of night, now emitted a warm, flickering glow. For a moment, I stood inside the doorframe and watched the teapot's shadow dance across the table. The rainclouds had parted; the whole city was visible from my suite. Houses and storefronts and lounges, each a point of light, cascaded down the hill to meet the river.

"You're back," Iuno said.

I sat beside him on the divan, my back straight, and accepted his offered teacup. As I told him what I'd found, the tea cooled in my hands. I didn't drink.

When I finished, I turned to face him. "You knew," I said. "You knew I'd find the hover-bomber there. You've known of the king's plot this entire day."

"I told you." His voice was quiet. "If you wanted the truth, I would give it to you."

Yes, as promised, he'd led me to the truth, and now I found it nothing but a burden. I could only submit to the king's authority and accept that he held the reins of the future, not me. His lie would send millions of Artani people to their deaths, and I could do nothing—nothing—

"No." I stood from the divan. "I won't accept this."

I paced from end to end of my suite, my naked feet padding against my rug's softness. The room's cramped size constrained me; my thoughts outgrew it. "No single member of the court can stop the king, but I can turn consensus against him. And to accomplish that..."

If the votes of a Great Circle fell in my favor, I could avert war.

"I will convince them," I said. "Is honor dead in our ranks? My father's plot makes a mockery of every martyr who died fighting the invaders." I set my teacup, now cold, on the table. "They'll see that my solution is the only path forwards. Quietly, so that no commoners are made aware, the king will surrender his rule to a council of regents. His plan must not proceed."

I saw it all clearly—how my words, carefully crafted, would sway them. How I would gain power over that room. How I could fight and win.

I opened my bay windows and braced my hands against the sill. The night air was cool on my face, and before me, the city's lights unfurled. Something surged inside me. Even as he descended into his own lust for war, my father tried to command fate, and now, I would do the same. I could accomplish something that men in the House of Hassam would speak of for decades to come—how one small prince, given a chance for greatness, had defied a king and prevented war.

I turned around and smiled at Iuno. "You see, don't you?"

As seconds passed in silence, my smile fell.

"You're relying on the court to prevent war." Neither relish nor contempt marked his voice, only a quiet sadness. "But the last time they had a chance, they voted against peace. You did too."

Heat prickled my face. "It's different now," I said. "My father wants to lie. It's *base*. It lacks nobility."

"We're talking about a war." He stared at me. "Nobility has nothing to do with it. You need to look at the situation clearly, Ahpa."

I advanced from the window until I stood only a foot before him. "And what do you mean by that? The sun is almost down; the Great Circle won't happen today. You have no special vision, and you see no more clearly than me."

While I'd raised my voice, his remained level. "But I do. You're a prince of Hassam, and you believe in your House's virtue. You can't see its darkness. You can't see that you won't stop them."

My eyes widened. He truly was the same boy I had first met, a guest who had laughed in the face of a prince and, somehow, escaped punishment. Even as he dishonored the name of Hassam, I found that the lesser offense. "I *won't* stop them?" I curled my lip. "Now I understand. You want me to give up. You want me to be chained to the future, as you are."

"I only want you to accept the truth, Ahpa. The future holds war, and you can't change that."

"Stop *saying* that! When you speak your prophecies, do you enjoy reminding me of what I can't change? Surely it's amused you all these years, watching me fight for the smallest of chances to control my fate. Perhaps, instead of continuing to struggle in uncertainty, I really should live as you do, under destiny's unerring command. Just like a fucking slave!"

Then there was silence, except for a faint ringing as that scream—my scream—echoed off the walls.

Cold air rushed in from my bay windows, raising goosebumps on my arms. My full cup of tea still sat on the parlor room table. There was the bookcase where, on the top shelf, we stored our favorite collections of classical poetry, exchanged as gifts when we were boys. There was the mirror where I had tried to tame his curls with the palace's finest hair products, before giving up and suggesting he shave himself bald instead. There was the divan where we'd sat, side by side, and eaten dates.

"Iuno," I said.

"You have no idea." He was crying. "You've never seen."

I stood there, as anger washed out of me and shame rolled in. I could not remember seeing him shaken before, and now he stood before me, drowning.

"On Eshtan, I didn't always wake up with the day's knowledge. On the days when I did, I was useful. I told the village of a dust storm's approach, and we took shelter. I told the Samandirans that their military police would soon come for inspection, and they hid their Artani wives and children, so the police didn't whip anyone or take any children away. Whenever I saw a disaster approach, I also saw myself helping people. Saving people."

His tears guttered out. He turned his head to look out the bay window, as if his gaze crossed the distance between moons to look on his old home. "But I always liked the days when I didn't see the future better. On those days, whatever I did, I did it because I wanted to, not because I had seen myself do it. I was in control."

He looked up at me from the floor. I couldn't move.

"One day, the House of Hassam's hover-bombers came over the horizon. They hit the Samandiran garrison. I remember the screaming, the fire. Smoke everywhere. I didn't know that I would find *yima* and *yiba* under the rubble." He shook his head and smiled, even as I stepped backwards in shock. "I didn't see the future that day. I still believed that village boys controlled their own destinies. But since that day, I've understood—I have no power. Now, there isn't a morning that I don't see, because I'll obey whatever instructions destiny gives me, just like a slave, as you said. Why wouldn't I? I've nothing left to lose."

Words froze on my lips.

The smile slipped from Iuno's face. He stood, and I smelled my own shampoo on his hair as he brushed past me, and then he was gone, out the suite door.

The rain started again. I walked over to the bay windows and closed them, snuffing out the sounds of the city. Only the rain's pattering remained, fingers tapping on my skull, and I gave in under their weight, leaned against the wall, and fell to the floor. I did not know myself; I was no prince. I was that monster, screaming in rage at Iuno, ruled by my fear of the future.

Look at the situation clearly. I'd always thought myself so clever—I saw through the court's playacted nobility, the propaganda to glorify the House of Hassam. That messaging was for the commoners, not a prince. But I'd bought the same kind of lie as everyone else. Without thinking, I'd assumed that the enemy had killed Iuno's parents, because I didn't understand that a bomb was just a bomb.

I sat there for some time. The sunlamps began to dim, and as the hours passed, reality settled in my mind. Impending war with Samandir. The bleak chance that a Great Circle might prevent the slaughter. Iuno's revelation about his past.

He wasn't here, and I realized that even if Artan burned tomorrow, I needed to know that he was safe now. I stood, breathed, and left my suite.

I searched the common areas of the palace room by room. The few servants still awake cast each other nervous glances, wondering if they should offer help, wondering if I'd gone mad. I'd searched almost three full floors of the palace before I remembered —I was wasting my time looking indoors. I took the escalator down to the grounds and walked outside.

I had crossed half the courtyard before I realized that I had no umbrella, and rainwater was soaking my hair, weighing down the curls until they lost their definition, plastering them to my neck and back—

There he was, lying on the bench by the pond. Only the dim glow from palace windows above us illuminated him.

"I'm sorry," I said.

He tilted his head back to look at me. "You know, when I heard what you would say this morning, I wasn't surprised. I always knew what you thought."

"You knew me better than anyone else in the palace, then."

"You're good at hiding," he said, "but not that good."

I closed my eyes. "Please come inside. You'll catch cold out here. If you want the suite to yourself, I'll find a library for the night. If you want a different room entirely, I'll have it arranged. And if you want to stay here, I'll bring a tent."

"It's all right. I've slept in that suite with you for years. You're still the same person."

I stood there, turning his words over as the rain fell around me, and then I nodded. He took my offered hand to hoist himself off the bench, and together, we made it back to my suite. We toweled ourselves off in silence and stumbled into bed.

I was about to close my eyes when I realized what I'd forgotten to do. "The passphrase," I whispered to Iuno. "Clouds aflame. Flower verdigris. In a summer field, a single stone."

Then sleep took us.

I watched Iuno's face as he woke. I thought to capture the moment when the future's knowledge entered him. But he moved from sleep to wakefulness as easily as crossing a threshold, and his face betrayed neither surprise, nor dismay, nor understanding. His eyes merely slid open, and he turned to look at me.

"Ahpa," he said.

It was still me.

We dressed and ate breakfast together. I asked him about his childhood on Eshtan, and for the first time, he really talked. About the stories the soldiers told of life on Samandir, before they were conscripted. About the nights when he looked up and saw Artan, a blue disk crawling across the sky. About his parents. His *yima*, returning from the day's work, the smell of machine oil wafting off of her. His *yiba*, greeting her at the door with a kiss.

After we finished eating, I poured us two cups of tea. We nursed them on the divan.

"I have been an awful host to you," I said.

His eyes were closed; his nostrils dilated as he inhaled his tea's fragrance. "Yes. You have been."

"Though I have no right, I must ask you for something."

His breath whistled across his teacup's lip. "Go on."

"I will convene a Great Circle today. I will reveal what I know of the king's plan and do what is in my power to stop it."

My hands shook. Here, in the morning quiet, the world was still and ready to shatter at the lightest touch, a sheet of glass spiderwebbed with cracks. Tension pulsed in my temples, and sweat beaded my forehead. I didn't want to step forwards into the future. I couldn't look down.

The treasures and trophies of a prince's life surrounded me—my richly colored rug, the jeweled jacket hanging by my door, vials upon vials of hair cream and conditioner and gel. I exhaled and released it all. In my mind, the rain washed it down the hill to the river, and the waters took it.

"Please," I said, "come with me when I go. Watch what happens. So that you can tell me now, because you already see it, what happens in the Circle."

"And if I see that you fail…"

"Then you should tell me. I will still try. I must."

"You tell me," Iuno said, and I shivered at his words, "why you want it this way."

I leaned back into my divan and inhaled the scent, soaking its fibers, of home. Only darkness lay ahead of me.

"Because," I said. "Whatever happens, I won't hide from it."

Iuno says that we walk into the throne room together. He says—

The throne room is held, like a jewel in a scepter, in the palace's highest spire. As he walks inside, Iuno passes his eyes over the glass floors and walls, shining with reflected light. He can't believe it—we're so high up that we can watch the rainclouds roll over Artan's surface.

The princes, ministers, and generals watch us. The princes, my half-brothers, whisper among themselves. Iuno sees me in them—the curled black hair, the sharp, proud nose, and, in their eyes, the faint, ever-present glimmer of fear. Even in this glass room without shadow, their eyes dart from corner to corner, looking for hidden enemies.

King Azora Meira em-Hassam sits at the front of the room, his generals arrayed on either side of his throne. We kneel before him, and the room falls silent. Nobody knows why I have convened this Circle.

Iuno sees me trembling. After we leave the room, I will tell him that I wanted to run—that the knowledge that he gave me on the divan (that he gives me now, as he speaks) nearly strangled the words from me.

But still, I speak.

I address the princes and ministers in the room. I tell them of the king's plot to instigate another war with Samandir. For a moment, some of their faces break in shock, but they quickly conceal it.

I speak of honor and peace. How many of our bannermen will die in another war? How many Artani conscripts—merchants, students, engineers? How many of the enemy, sent to fight us by powers beyond their will, do we wish to kill?

All for a lie?

I place my resolution before them: the king must surrender his rule. Seconds pass in absolute silence.

Then the king breaks it. When he speaks, anger presses his words into a low growl.

First he turns to the ministers. *Remember,* he says, *when you bureaucrats and administrators feared that the enemy would destroy us? In the shadows, you whispered to me that I alone could save our House. You chose me as your king.* They avert their eyes and nod; half their number is gone.

Then he turns to his generals. *Remember,* he says, *when we took our army's leaders from the academy, not the battlefield? To replace them, I selected each of you regardless of your previous rank or station. I chose you for your strength, and together, we would have achieved total victory, were it not denied from us. Will you fight with me again?*

From the front, they roar their answer with one voice: *Glory to the king! Glory to the king!*

Then he turns to his sons. *Remember,* he says, *my generosity. War is my gift to you. Who among you will drive our armies into Samandir and attain greatness? Who will defend my legacy? I am still watching, and I have yet to make my choice.*

The princes glance at each other, and then they follow their father's eyes and look at me.

Softly, the king curses me. *You,* he says. *I thought you cunning and capable. To act, to war, to command—this is your province as a prince. What has rotted your mind?*

I do not answer him. Iuno understands: nothing remains to be said. I call for votes.

The outcome is obvious. The ministers think of themselves; if any of them vote with me but my motion fails, they're doomed. The generals want war, and they don't care how it comes about. And my brothers crave the power that my father dangles before them: a chance to rule fate instead of being ruled by it.

A minister counts the votes—unanimously, the Great Circle rejects my resolution.

Iuno stands next to me, silent. He watches as the king's hand rises.

I stood before my father in his throne room. Every word he'd spoken doubled in my ears; I heard, as one, the cold clarity of his voice as he spoke in the present, and the soft crackle of Iuno's voice as he relayed the king's words in the past. The uncontrollable tremor in my shoulders, the view of the clouds crawling beneath us —it was all as Iuno had said it would be. I, too, watched as the king raised his hand.

He extended his arm straight from his chest and curled his fingers into a fist, as if he grasped an invisible scepter. I exhaled. It was the Hassamite gesture of command.

"You no longer have power here," he said, "and you are nothing to me. If any power remained to you, I would command you to die—but now, you are beneath even that. So I command you instead to disappear. I will never hear you speak another word, and I will never see you again."

Cracks in his mask of royal calm revealed the contempt roiling beneath. As a child, I'd seen him as a great man. I had fantasized of sharing in his greatness. Now, I turned my back on him and let those fantasies fall from me. As Iuno and I walked out of the throne room, I looked straight ahead, without returning anyone's stare.

I had walked into the future knowing that I would not succeed. In that room, I had seen the great power of the wheels of war. Was my destiny to place my hands on them over and over, failing each time to stop their turning? Then I would do it, if only for the hope of one victory.

Our footsteps echoed in the narrow passageway as we descended the steps of the throne room's spire. My father had not ordered my execution, but he had killed whatever remained of Prince Meira Pashel em-Hassam in that room. A wild and roaring future now lay ahead of me. Perhaps it would carry me to distant lands and lives beyond my small imagination. Perhaps, in a week, it would dash me against the rocks.

We returned to our suite together. I waited until nightfall, when Iuno was asleep, to leave. In the note I tucked under his arm, I was not sentimental. I had forfeited that privilege when I called him a slave. Instead, I only left instructions on how to find an off-moon safehouse, beyond the reach of the House of Hassam and war, though I could make no guarantees.

I had already packed my bags that morning. I slung them over my shoulder, opened the bay windows, and leaned out. In a few minutes, I had rappelled down the palace wall and disappeared into the city.

If I had burdened Iuno with emotion in my note, what would I have said? In my head, I apologized to him for my endless offenses—the arrogance, the fear, the anger—that, frozen in the past, I could not erase. I wished him well as he walked into tomorrow, knowing that the future could not be commanded and hoping, as much as I could, all the same.

The herbal smell of tea bloomed in my nose; a fresh date's thick paste coated my tongue. It tore my heart, and I smiled. I thanked Iuno. It was fitting to remember him by this pain.

I'd made arrangements to leave the city by river ferry. The boat's silhouette, a black shadow punctured by light shining through the portholes, bobbed on the waves. The creaking of the wooden pier overlapped with the rush of water beneath me. One of my men waited for me by the entrance ramp to the boat.

He walked up. "Sir," he said, his voice low, "there's a problem."

I tensed. Not even out of the city, and already beset by obstacles. "What is it?"

"It's...him." By the dim starlight, I saw that he seemed more confused than frightened. "I don't know how he found the boat. Perhaps it's better if you speak to him directly."

And there he was, walking down the boat's ramp.

"Finding shortcuts down the hill has been useful," Iuno said. He yawned. "For things like this. Wherever we go next, I hope we won't have to live in one room for years on end. Maybe we can find some shortcuts together."

I only stared a moment before I burst into laughter. I didn't need to ask him how he'd found me. After a second, his laughter, exactly as ugly as I remembered, joined mine.

Eventually, the gravity of my situation reasserted itself, and the laughter died. "Iuno," I said, "this is foolish. There's too much danger in staying with me. And..."

We locked eyes.

Why would you want to?

"My time in the palace with you was interesting. Complicated," he said. "You were often cruel to me, without realizing it. But you were also kind."

His voice was soft. "I don't know what the future holds," he said, and at this, his lips twitched in an ironic smile. "You may become more cruel than kind, and then I'll slip away some night and walk alone. But I'm not ready for that yet. It's been some time since my life held something I cared not to lose."

I considered the qualities I wished for myself. For so long, I had striven to be nobler and bolder, but now I wanted to ride this boat to a place where I could find humility. Kindness. Where I could be happy to say that I was still myself.

I wanted to argue with Iuno and push him from my path, so that I knew, no matter what happened, I could harm him no more. But I had already harmed him, and here he remained. So, I only said, "Thank you."

"Besides," he said, holding up a lumpy bag, "you forgot your hair products."

"It's actually customary for exiled nobility to cut their hair. Perhaps I should do so before I board." I turned to my man, who snapped to attention. "Do you have a knife?"

Iuno's face crumpled into a pout of mock dismay. "Oh, let's not be so dramatic. That hair shouldn't go to waste."

I smiled.

After I boarded, we walked to the prow together. The boat cast off from the dock, and, gradually, the city's lights grew dimmer behind us. I closed my eyes and surrendered to the night.

See Albert Chu's story "When the Oracle Speaks" online at Metaphorosis.
If you liked it, leave a comment. Authors love that!
Remember to subscribe to our e-mail updates so you'll know when new stories are posted.

About the story

Future sight has been explored extensively in fiction. It's been around at least as long as classical mythology, with your Oedipuses of old failing to avoid the destinies set out for them by mysterious oracles. In contemporary times, we have Dr. Manhattan, seeing into the future with these poorly-explained tachyons, or time travelers from the future who come bearing news of apocalypses ruled by robot overlords. The idea for the story started out from a desire to explore future sight from a slightly different angle—what if, instead of these vaguely worded and cloudy prophecies, someone always knew exactly what was going to happen? They couldn't use this information to alter the future, because their vision is perfect; what they see is what is going to happen. What kind of person would this be, and what sort of life would they live?

Various other bits of media I've consumed over the years got tossed into the ideation blender. The relationship between Iuno and Ahpa is reminiscent of how Madeline Miller writes Patroclus and Achilles in *The Song of Achilles*. The feudal space opera setting is taken straight from the pages of *Dune*—another work which also prominently features future sight. The thematic focus of the piece as an anti-war story came later in the brainstorming process. The concept of an unalterable future often evokes feelings of helplessness or a lack of agency

—something so powerful that it's pointless to even think about trying to stop it. And I realized that such enormously powerful calamities, beyond the reach of any one person to stop, happen in the real world all the time. In the story, Ahpa finds himself in the same situation countless people have experienced in history—he knows war is coming, but there's nothing he can do about it.

Originally, I planned on making the viewpoint character Iuno himself. I was excited to write from the perspective of someone who already knows how the scene's going to play out—the entire first scene between Ahpa and Iuno was going to be Iuno seeing, in the future, their conversation, and then the scene would end with Ahpa actually walking into the courtyard. But the more I sketched the story out, the more I realized that, first of all, it was going to be quite difficult writing from the perspective of someone who is completely resigned to living his life out as a script, and second, the actually interesting character arc is, of course, Ahpa's. His story subverts some of the basic tropes of a hero, who's often expected to take action and change the situation. Ahpa starts out the story feeling entitled to those heroic privileges —he's a prince, after all, taking charge is his thing. So I structured things so I could end Ahpa's character arc with him having some greater understanding of surrender and a lack of power—while still putting a heroic twist on the story.

A question for the author

Q: Do you often include children in your stories? What role do they play?

A: Yes, and they're all teenagers—I have no idea how to write someone below the age of 13. I consumed some of the most impactful fiction to me when I myself was a teenager, and many of those stories featured characters my own age. I loved reading and watching stories about kids in colorful and fantastic settings, facing insurmountable odds, finding their inner hero—stuff that I'd consider a "guilty pleasure" nowadays, but it certainly left its mark. The teenagers in my stories are always heroes; I want them to be characters that I would have wanted to identify with.

About the author

Albert Chu writes speculative fiction out of Seattle, where he currently lives with his wife and a very energetic puppy. His writing transposes the ordinary concerns of his life into fantastic settings filled with lasers and magic. By day, he works as a mechanical engineer. His interests include anime, lifting weights, and PVP games with his wife.

albertchuwrites.com, @chubert_writes

The Princia Prologos

Aaron Zimmerman

Editor's Preface

The order of Gauntleteers requires its members to keep a journal of their experiences. The document you are about to read is such a journal.

Some consider these words fanciful fiction. Others take them as literally true. A group calling themselves the Church of Time has even adopted them as scripture.

While speculations abound, there are some things we do know:

A hunter discovered this text in the northern forest eight years after the events described therein, inexplicably preserved.

No gauntleteer has ever been able to manipulate time.

No one has ever found a river in the northern mountains.

No gauntleteer has ever managed to transport an object from one place to another instantaneously, let alone an entire army.

So what really happened?

I will not prejudice you with my own theories, but I will offer a counter-question: does it matter?

Maybe the value of a story comes more from the questions it asks than the provability of its events. And Miranda Southbrook, whether she means to or not, asks a most valuable question: what is more important, the present or the future?

And the answer? I will let her story speak for itself.

The Journal of Miranda Southbrook

The first day is for sickness
The second is for seeing
The third day brings us power
The fourth sets foes to fleeing
the fifth day is for making
On the sixth, we learn to fly
The seventh brings us wisdom
And on the eighth, we die

That was how my mother sang me to sleep. When I got older, I asked her if the song was true. She told me that one day she would put on the gauntlet, and for eight days she would be a living god, able to fix everything wrong with the world.

"And after eight days?"

"This is the thing about life, Miranda: it requires sacrifice."

I was thirteen when she ascended. I remember her far-away eyes. I cried and cried and begged her not to die. She found me a glass of water, patted me on the head, reminded me that life was about sacrifice, and then flew away.

I can't stop thinking about that song, even though my mother has been dead for years.

Her voice was not trained, it was more croak than croon, but I'd give nearly anything to hear it again.

Oh, gods, I can't believe I just wrote that. I was just kidding, I'm not actually some silly melodramatic child.

I need to start over.

My name is Miranda Southbrook. I am seventeen, a newly sworn initiate of the order of gauntleteers, on my first visit to the septum. I am the twenty-third in line to ascend, to claim the power of the gauntlet.

The first anointed, who is the next in line and leader of the order, gave me this journal an hour ago.

"No detail is too small," he said.

As gauntleteers cannot train with the object itself, for obvious reasons, reading past accounts is our best way to prepare.

It is tradition for new initiates to pass an hour alone reflecting in the septum after taking their vows, and here I am, staring at the gauntlet and not sure what to write about it. What would a future gauntleteer need to know that they haven't already read in the accounts of the gauntleteers before me?

But of course training isn't the only purpose of these journals. They are distributed widely and cherished by historians and minstrels. So really, this journal is my chance to tell my own story, to craft my legacy. Maybe I shouldn't admit such a thing, but my legacy is the reward for the sacrifices I've made along the way.

Asher asked me to go with him to the *Princia Prologos* tonight. It is a delightful play about a clever princess and a wicked queen. I dearly wanted to say yes, but here I am instead.

"The gauntlet's not going anywhere," Asher pouted.

He is a bit dramatic, my Asher. But I love that about him. He's indulgent and spontaneous and all the things I'm not. Perhaps that's why I agreed to marry him.

"There will be time for such things when I finish my training," I told him. And it's true: in a few years I will have all the freedom and means afforded to a fully trained gauntleteer. Unlike my mother, I won't let the order consume my whole life. I'll marry Asher and have a family and everything will be perfect. Years later, I will be called to ascend for the good of the kingdom, but there will plenty of time for plays and Asher before that happens.

And it's not just the gauntlet that keeps me from Asher's company. The Sagian prince is here, in our palace, to swear himself to our princess, and tonight there is a feast to celebrate the betrothal. The entire order will be there, sitting in a line from first anointed to newest novice, as we do for all occasions of state.

We have been fighting Sagia for generations, ever since they stole the other gauntlet, the right-handed one.

I sometimes think, as maybe all initiates do, that I could be the one to unite the gauntlets. I dream of the songs written in my honor, and the smile on people's lips when they say my name.

Miranda Southbrook, the hero whose sacrifice led to a better world for everyone.

But then, what if this nuptial-contrived peace holds?

What if there are no more wars?

I know I should want that. I know from the accounts how terrible war can be.

But my life bends toward the day I put on this gauntlet to perform deeds worthy of the greatest sacrifice of all.

And what could such deeds be, without a war? Shall I give my life to build bridges and mend walls?

Come and hear the ballad of Miranda and the great chimney cleaning?

No, when my times comes, far in the future, I will be a war-time gauntleteer. I will perform deeds worthy of the gauntlet and make my mother proud.

My visitation time expires. I have to dress for the feast. I feel like I wasted my time on wandering thoughts. I will ask for more time and focus on the gauntlet.

Everything is ruined.

I am alone in the sanctum, huddled by a brazier burning low without a chance of refilling.

I stare at the flames and shake my head, unable to move past the unfairness. But there is no changing it, and my obsession accomplishes nothing.

The betrothal was a trick. The Sagians came for the reason they always come: to steal the gauntlet. The king was blinded by his hubris, and now the princess is dead, and the city burns.

After the feast, I asked the first anointed for more time in the septum. He smiled indulgently, saying he remembered his own first night with the gauntlet and granting me another hour.

I hurried down the spiral stairs trying to shake the wine and music from my thoughts.

The door minder, Beatrice, opened the triple lock to the sanctum, let me in, and locked it behind me.

I was staring at the gauntlet, about to start writing a much different reflection than this, when I heard shouting outside the door.

I hurried to the door just as a soldier came running down the circular stairs.

"They've killed the princess," he said, his words all mushed up.

Beatrice turned back toward me immediately. She blinked once, her mouth straightening to a line.

"It is fortunate that you are here," Beatrice said through the locked door. "I honor your sacrifice."

She pulled a lever beside the door. Shells of solid iron dropped from above, sealing off the sanctum.

The last thing I saw was a Sagian soldier, garish in red and orange, stepping around the corner with a bloody sword in his hand.

And now Beatrice and the other guards must be dead or captured. The Sagian soldiers batter the iron shell. They are trying to get in. I don't think they know I am here.

And I have no food, no water, no hope.

I will die in here.

It has only just now occurred to me what Beatrice meant. "It is fortunate you are here," she said.

She meant the gauntlet. It is right there, grey in the fading firelight.

I can prevent Sagia from stealing it.

I can ascend.

It seems obvious in hindsight, yet I've only just now considered the idea.

Part of me thrills at the prospect of being the youngest gauntleteer ever, the savior of Redding, the hero of story and song.

But the price — I knew the day would come but it was always so far in the future it never really felt real. But here it is, eight days away and twenty years too soon. It is one thing to sacrifice yourself in the abstract 'eventually', but quite another to stare that sacrifice right in the leathery fingers.

It is such a tatty thing, like the face of a wicked queen in a play, wrinkles exaggerated to make sure all knew she was wicked.

I put off the gardens and the theatre for when I would have enough time. And now the time is gone. It is hard to believe. Eight days? I have eight days to live.

But I will die one way or another. I might as well prevent the Sagian bastards from stealing the gauntlet.

The constant clanging! It will drive me mad if it goes on much longer.

I will do it now.

I am the thirty-fourth gaunleteer.

There were no trumpets to celebrate, no speeches or ceremonial incense, unless you count the symphony of clanging hammers and chisels on the other side of the shell.

I could find no easy way to break the glass enclosure, so I toppled the whole pedestal. The glass shattered, scattering shards all the way to the wall ten feet away. I looked around, expecting someone to scold me for my disrespect, for my presumption.

I picked up the gauntlet and shook it free of glass. I only hesitated a moment before pulling it onto my left hand. It fit like it had been sewn for me.

The first day is for sickness, as the song goes. All I feel so far is a slight itch.

According to the accounts, there will be body pains, fever, unlike anything I've ever felt.

Morna Evensmith hated the smell of bread. Not the taste, but just the smell of bread baking. What a strange thing.

The itch spreads down my arm like crawling ants.

The fourth gaunleteer, Henry something or other, refused to read anything written down, saying he had trouble understanding words unless someone spoke them aloud. He paid people to read for him until his death.

Such trivial nonsense! I should be focusing on the sickness and its known abatements, and my traitor mind wanders to useless stories!

I cannot take the itching. It feels as if my whole body will shake free of its skin.

I wish I had gone to the play with Asher. The *Princia Prologos*. I wish I could hold his hand and kiss him, and he could tell me everything will be ok.

I think it's been about a day. It is hard to track the passing time. But the shaking itch recedes, so time must have passed.

I still can't believe this is happening: the peace shattered, a battle raging in the streets.

And down here, my life slowly ticks away to the sound of clanging chisels and banging hammers.

Day two is supposed to be for seeing, but I don't see anything. Well, actually, I can see this journal and the ghostly outlines of the sanctum. This must be through a manifestation of the power, as the brazier has long since burned out.

On day two, a gauntleteer must prepare her mind. That is what the accounts say. Day two is the calm quiet before the swell of day three.

But I'm just bored.

What if the power never comes, and I die down here, helpless and starving?

Only I'm not hungry. And there's the seeing without light. So the power must be real.

And my mother wouldn't have lied to me. There was no mistaking the power in her touch before she died.

Her eyes looked distant, sad. She wasn't really my mother anymore. She tried to be, offering me a glass of water as if that single gesture could compensate for years of absence.

I thought I would choose differently, that I would be a parent to my children. But here I am, turning into my mother after all.

By the time I noticed the power, it had been tickling the back of my awareness for a few hours.

"Our world is nothing but ideas and the will to bind them."

That is how Sathia Shoemaker described the feeling in her journal. That is how Will got its name.

The latent power feels like the ache that calls you to stretch after waking — or like the heaving of your belly when you hold your breath past comfort.

I laid my quill on the floor and tried to levitate it, using the trick of thought practiced in lessons: the quill is levitating, the quill is levitating.

And then it was. The feather hovered a few inches off the stone for a heartbeat and then fluttered back down.

I wept for a solid ten minutes. I don't know if it was relief, excitement, or despair. Probably all of them and more besides.

The power is real! I can move things with Will.

The power is real! I will be dead in a week.

I wiped my eyes and practiced. After an hour, it was as easy as breathing to spin the quill in circles and make it dart any which way.

I willed shards of glass from the gauntlet's case into the air and twirled them around each other like snow in a winter wind.

I took a break to record these thoughts.

But the power calls to me.

I am about to leave the sanctum. I am a day four gauntleteer and the power fills me like wine bulging the seams of a wineskin.

I practiced for hours and hours, feeling no fatigue. I think I will never sleep again. Or eat.

The Sagians are almost through the shell. In a moment, I will finish their work and peel back the metal like a curtain proclaiming the start of a story.

And then... I fight. I have never killed anyone before, and I keep imagining it. I am unsure if I will like or hate it, and both possibilities frighten me. I have a lot of fighting ahead. I wonder how long it will take me to rid the city of the Sagians.

I have no doubt I can do it. I am still mortal, but I can deflect an arrow or sword with no more than a thought. I can turn their weapons back upon them.

I try not to think about such things, but my imagination wanders to the future, to the songs written of the battle to come. I imagine the wide-eyed amazement when children hear the story of Miranda Southbrook from their parents over bowls of steaming porridge.

I chide myself for these childish daydreams, but without hope of a future, I can only fight for my legacy.

It is time.

I have done something much more terrible than killing. I have broken the world.

As planned, I peeled the shell away, revealing a half dozen grimy Sagians. They stared at me for a moment and then charged.

As planned, I obliterated them with a hail of metal and stone.

And then it was still.

I choked on my breath, sat, and wept for a few horrible minutes, reckoning with the horror of my actions.

I believe the gauntlet gives more than just control over objects. It connects its bearer to the world in a way no one has ever described. At least for me it does. My violence created — I don't know what — a wrongness, like a pillar of poison smoke disrupting a blue sky.

It seems to me now that all life is connected, part of a larger context, a meta-creature built from every living thing. Killing those soldiers was like cutting off my own hand. I don't mean to say I suffered more than they did. But the gauntlet connected me to this context in some way, and in the aftermath of my monstrous action, I could see the futility of violence with sudden, irrevocable certainty.

I saw only one way forward: I resolved never to kill again.

I was a day four gauntleteer. In my mother's song the fourth day 'sends foes to fleeing'. But I vowed instead to forswear violence entirely.

My nascent connection to the infinite life around me strengthened at my resolution, seeming to bloom in approval.

I marched up the stairs, daydreaming words of friendship.

A dozen more soldiers greeted me as I stepped into the palace. I started my speech, but they attacked before I'd spoken three words. One of them knocked over a pitcher of wine in his haste.

I parried, dodged, repelled, and screamed for them to listen!

But they would not. I was their enemy, and they would not stop.

"Just give me time," I yelled and pleaded.

They answered with slashes and spears and snickers. I deflected each without effort, but I was just one person, and as word spread, more and more of them joined the battle against me. I was still mortal. One mistake and I would be dead.

I wasn't going to convince them.

The blossoming connection to the life all around me turned to a thousand angry eyes and a thousand chiding voices. I felt like a girl again, disappointing my mother.

I deflected a sword, turned a spear, stopped an arrow. I didn't notice the dagger until it was flying by. It missed my head by inches.

I erupted in frustrated impatience.

I screamed for the soldiers to stop, just stop!

And they did.

They stopped moving entirely, along with everything and everyone else.

I keep replaying the moment, searching every detail for an explanation.

A soldier with a dented half-helmet and a mustache slashes toward me, his eyes bulging, his lips curling over yellow teeth. Over his shoulder, a red-haired woman points her elbow toward me, about to hurl another dagger. Beside her, a woman with a shaved head tightens the leather strap of her jerkin, turning toward me.

Beside the shaved-head woman is the wine-spilled table. The red runs in forked rivers to the edge of the table, swelling into droplets on the edge, preparing to fall.

But not falling.

Nothing has moved, not at all.

I think I have frozen time itself.

I don't understand how I did it or how I can undo it.

I have broken the world.

My mother did this to me. I am her experiment.

In search of an explanation, I searched the palace and the city for books, notes, anything.

I found the letter addressed to me in the drawer of my mother's study in the house I grew up in.

Miranda,

There is a river of Will high in the northern mountains. It runs off a cliff, spreading life and time to the corners of the world.

My death approaches, but first, I have given you a cupful from this river to drink. If my theory is correct, it will give you power greater than any previous gauntleteer.

Do not waste this gift. Use your time to the fullest. Make the world better, fix the problems no one else can.

This is the thing about life, Miranda: it requires sacrifice.

Sincerely,

Celia

She gave me liquid Will to drink! I remember the cup, remember drinking, remember the liquid tasting like water. But maybe my memory is colored with grief and anger. Maybe there was a strangeness to it.

Could such a drink have strengthened my power? Is that why I feel the connection, why I was able to stop time?

I feel like a child wielding a too-heavy battle ax.

How could she be so reckless?

I am angry and confused, and this constant stillness is breaking my mind.

I have uselessly tried yelling, "Continue!" and "Resume!"

I have wept and raged and broken things in petty insolence.

My mother did this, and I hate her for it, but I also miss her and wish she were here to hug me and tell me it will be okay.

I thought that perhaps there was some great injustice I needed to fix, and time would unfreeze like some child's tale.

So I set about righting wrongs.

I found every single Sagian within the palace and dragged their statue-bodies beyond the city walls. I swept the floors clean of their boots and threw their swords into the river.

When time resumes, it will seem to them as if they were transported in a single moment.

But my good deed did nothing for time.

I took to the city to find more wrongs to right. I mended a few roofs, and patched a few street cobbles. Nothing.

I found Asher at the fortifications just beyond the castle gates. I think he was to be part of a counter-offensive.

He is strapping on a leather jerkin. I imagine he has been saying things like, "I won't rest until I find her."

I tried to hug him, but it was like hugging a lifeless doll.

I think about the mountains to the north from time to time. I wonder if the river is real. In time, I may set out to find it.

I haven't written in a week.

Ha! A week. What would that mean? There is no sunset, no breakfast, no ablutions, no sleep. My eight-day countdown has been paused along with everything else.

When I feel the inclination, I lie down in my childhood bed in my mother's house. I stare at the overhead canopy, remembering dinners, Asher's touch, laughter.

When I can no longer stand it, I get up. And such I consider a day.

I haven't written because I don't have anything to write about. And why continue writing at all? There will never be another gauntleteer to benefit or a minstrel to compose a ballad.

But still, I feel called to explain, to justify. Maybe it is just naive hope.

I want to write the name 'Celia Southbrook' and circle it again and again. This is her fault. Her fault.

I sometimes see her, my mother, I mean, sitting in her chair with a book in her lap, tunelessly humming to herself.

She asks me what I am waiting for. She tells me I am wasting her gift.

I tell her how I took the sword away from a man about to stab another behind a fish-quarter tavern. I tell her about the coins I took from Shield Street mansions and gave to the poor.

My mother isn't impressed. She says I should keep searching. She says I'm missing the point.

And I tell her to piss off because she is a figment of my imagination.

It has been even longer this time. We could call it a month.

My reeling mind has started to fill in the stillness with motion, to give the frozen people speech and personality and desires.

Their conversation is just my mind's desperate attempt at normalcy. But I hear their voices, so how can I say for sure that they are not real?

There is Benedict, in a green doublet, just outside my house on his way to attend the *Princia Prologos*. He is impatient and grumpy, but in an endearing way. And talking to me always seems to cheer him.

Molly is half a block down the street in a lovely blue and gold gown, with one hand elegantly raised to shield her eyes from the sun. She is austere and elegant, maybe a bit snobbish. She thinks I am reckless and naive. I tell her I'm doing my best, but she never seems to believe me.

And there is Rickon! He is a boy of six or seven, crouched behind a door, about to leap out and scare a passerby. He never scares me, though. I am too wily. His antics always make me smile. Sometimes I bring him a treat, and his eyes widen, and he devours it as only a child can.

Perhaps they are not real, but they feel real to me, and they are all I have.

I visit Asher also, of course. But his voice is the hardest for me to conjure. He is too real in my memory to become imaginary.

I don't know how long it has been. I can no longer tell what is real.

I long ago ran out of things to write in this journal. But I cling to it like a raft in a storm. I trace over past entries with my finger, remembering a world with time in it.

But now I have something to write. I have decided to go north. I feel it tugging on me: my mother's gift, the river of Will. I have put it off because I will either find it or not find it, and both options frighten me.

I've just said goodbye to all of my friends. It was hard, but I must be strong.

Asher's goodbye was the worst of all. He told me he didn't want me to go. He told me that he was afraid I would die and never return.

I told him to be brave and wait for me. I kissed him and hurried away before I could change my mind. He stood still, strong, even though he wanted to chase after me, to beg me not to go.

I think about the *Princia Prologos* a lot — how I wish I could go back and go with him.

The river is dry.

It took an eternity of searching. But I have plenty of time!

I finally found it nestled between two peaks high in the mountains.

The riverbed runs off a cliff, from which Will should fall and spread like morning mist.

But the river is dry.

I followed the riverbed to find the source, thinking maybe it was blocked.

I walked and walked, and somehow I never left the same valley, never escaped the shadow of those two peaks.

This is a special place — a place that doesn't work like other places.

My search was for nothing. I had thought that I could restart time by finding the source of Will. But it was for nothing.

I have explored every inch of this river bed many times over. There is nothing to be done here.

I will return to Redding soon. At least there, I have statue-friends.

Here it is just me.

But there is something about this place. Life is here — a river of Will, passing in a constant current. Or at least it *should* be here.

It is a good place to write stories. I write them on thick, rough papyrus — tales of wicked queens and daring adventures.

Just now, I wrote a story about a tree that kept growing through storms and fires and chopping axes.

The story unlocked an impossible bit of hope.

It is foolish and vain beyond belief, but I still dream of songs.

I sometimes lie down with this journal in my arms, cradled like the child I will never have. It is my only source of hope.

I know what I have to do. The answer has been in front of me all this time. But I couldn't see it. I didn't want to see it.

It came, as perhaps all realizations do, from stories.

At first, I wrote stories as a diversion. But soon, I wrote because it was the only way I could survive. I wrote to inhabit a world that made sense.

I wrote of imaginary people and places, but also, I wrote a story about when Miranda said yes when Asher asked her to go to the *Princia Prologos*. I wrote a story about when Miranda told her mother she didn't want to be a gauntleteer but rather mix herbs into potions in a cottage far away from Redding. I wrote about the many lives I could have had.

Along the way, a realization snuck into my words, waiting for me to find the courage to notice it.

It is my fault. Not my mother's.

I stopped everything because the world would not listen to me. I used my untrained power like a naive child to get the one thing I thought I needed: time.

And now I hold it fast because my secret self clings to stasis.

It is what I always wanted: a chance to sacrifice for the future, to solve every problem there is or will be. I can fix the social inequities, heal the sick, and design a fair system of government. With infinite time, I could accomplish infinite things. And all it costs is my infinite loneliness.

It is an absurd belief. I know that. But I cling to it anyway. And why? I don't have a clear reason. I suppose I am afraid.

I have tried to overpower my subconscious hold on time with shouted declarations and quiet whispers, all in vain.

You cannot lie to yourself, not really.

But I think I have a solution.

There is one thing in my life that binds me to the future, to my sacrifice-strewn legacy.

One thing nurtures my hubris.

One thing that I could give up, if and only if, I genuinely wanted my present to resume at the cost of my future.

This journal.

This journal is the story of myself, told for the benefit of the future.

This journal is proof of my continued choice to sacrifice my present for my future.

I have to give that up, irrevocably and wholeheartedly.

And I will. I will.

I will throw you off the cliff and watch you flutter and fall like a bird without wings.

It will work. I am sure of it.

The wind will stir my hair, and I will turn to see the river rushing toward me.

And then I will be a day four gauntleteer again. My power will start to grow until it consumes me. My life will be finite. What a thing! What a wonder!

On day six we learn to fly. Where might I go? Day seven brings wisdom, but I think I have found that already.

I don't know what I will do with my four days. But even if I did know, I wouldn't write it here. Because I don't need to anymore. I don't care what you think of me, imaginary composer of ballads. You are not my life. You are a lie I told to myself to justify sacrificing every bit of today for tomorrow.

This world will change and change regardless of my little life, and eventually, you will forget even my greatest deed.

What wonders will I miss along the way?

The smell of candied nuts and sour beer.

The calm that settles the trees before a rainstorm.

Asher's hand in mine.

I could agonize about the wasted time, but that would only waste more.

I will have four days. What a gift!

Four days of breathing, of kisses and sunsets.

I would throw away a thousand eponymous ballads for that chance.

Goodbye, my dear, flawed future.

This is the thing about life, Miranda: it is happening now.

Editor's Epilogue

Miranda Southbrook was unquestionably in the septum during Sagia's failed attempt to steal the gauntlet.

The palace was unquestionably cleared of Sagian soldiers in what felt like a moment to all witnesses.

Four days after that sudden victory, the septum was discovered fully restored, with the gauntlet back in its place.

Miranda Southbrook's whereabouts and deeds during those four days remain uncertain.

Many claimed to have seen her in passing or even that she offered some service to them. From such stories, the phrase 'must have been Miranda' emerged as a verbal shrug to an unexplained turn of good luck.

My favorite story, though, is of a young woman matching Miranda's description attending the final performance of the *Princia Prologos* three days after the Sagian retreat.

I imagine her in the third row, her eyes rapt with attention. She weeps and laughs and cheers at all the right moments.

She feels the wind in her hair and snuggles into her companion's shoulder, content and very much alive.

See Aaron Zimmerman's story "The Princia Prologos" online at Metaphorosis.
If you liked it, leave a comment. Authors love that!
Remember to subscribe to our e-mail updates so you'll know when new stories are posted.

About the story

When I get an idea for a story, I add it to a list in my phone's reminders app. The reminder I wrote for this story (probably while running) was, "There is a glove that gives almost unlimited power for seven days and then burns out the body of its wearer". Often ideas sit on that list for months or forever (There are currently 354 such pending ideas), but that one kept popping back into my thoughts, and I almost immediately began writing it. It took a bit of experimenting to find the now-obvious protagonist for such a premise: a young person forced to choose to end their life tragically early to use the power for some greater good. In early drafts, the story followed a linear build of Miranda's power, while at the same time, Miranda grew more and more disappointed with her inability to convince people to stop killing each other. My wife said, "It sounds like a meditation on how you feel like the world doesn't understand you". And she was right. It was a compelling idea, but not really a story. I went back to it and found a better story in Miranda's desperation: a story about the versions of ourselves we are so sure we have to live up to while there are lives unlived just beyond our ability even to see, let alone pursue.

A question for the author

Q: Have you ever wondered whether ideas are thought waves directed at you by an AI supercomputer located in the distant future?

A: In a way, yes. I think a lot about (and my story actually ruminates a bit on) life contexts. Specifically, I think there is a life context that we, as humans, can't directly interact with. It is a context that combines all humans (and other animals) into a meta-life structure with its own motivations, language, and consciousness. It is similar to how human bodies are made up of living cells. In both cases, the components live their lives, many fulfilling a purpose, and then they die without impacting the existence of the higher-order life. This "Sum of all Life" is far beyond our ability, as its constituents, to comprehend. But I think our ideas for stories, inventions, etc, are likely influenced by it. It isn't exactly artificial, but it is certainly foreign (some might call it divine.) And it likely exists within a different understanding of time, so we might call it the future. It needs things from us the way we need things from our white blood cells. And stories are likely a large part of that influence. Look, you humans, it says, I need more of you to start living for the present instead of the future, and out comes a story to try to spread that message.

About the author

Aaron is a writer, software engineer, and musician. When not daydreaming up stories, Aaron can usually be found conducting musicals in the western Chicago suburbs. Love to Katy, Elijah, Oliver, and Arthur.

aarontellsstories.com, @apzimmerman

The Antidote for Longing

Karl Dandenell

Part 1

The soldiers made no secret of their arrival; far from it. The lead pair of riders galloped into the outer courtyard below, scattering the peacocks, who set up a furious and discordant song of complaint. They redoubled their efforts several minutes later when the carriage and rear guard arrived.

I hated the peacocks. Loud, ridiculous creatures. However, they were already established on the grounds when I acquired the house, and my clientele loved them, so they stayed. It was all part of my façade: Lars Bjornsen, courtier and former advisor to Emperor Gustavus Adolphus, retired from imperial service and living a quiet life as an importer of fine victuals. My connections at court—real or perceived—set me apart from other merchants. Beneath this façade lay resentment and worry, for an exile from the imperial court is never truly safe.

I'd been dreading this moment for three years, ever since my dearest friend Fredrik Magnusson, the imperial physik, had hurried me into a carriage in the middle of the night with nothing but a hastily packed bag. "Don't blame yourself," he'd said. "There's no way you could have known the tsar's son was delayed."

"But I should have known something was wrong. Aleksey Mikhaylovich is never late for anything."

The timing of my plan had relied on Aleksey's punctuality and secrecy. I knew his servants followed strict orders to prepare the remote cottage with fresh food and bedding, then vacate the area. I also knew I had a brief window, perhaps half an hour, to add a fresh batch of Miner's Fate to the brandy before Aleksey's current mistress arrived. Miner's Fate was favored by the Soldiers of Night, an anti-Tsarist sect.

"Irina always gave him the honor of the first toast. Always," I said. "The reports were very clear on that."

"Alas, people are not as predictable as machine mage devices," Fredrik said. "What can one do?"

I'd hunkered beneath a nearby bush, visualizing the scenario. When Irina arrived, she would lay out their meal. Aleksey would ride in soon after, and the couple would dine. The poison would take hold gradually, bringing on a gentle melancholy and heaviness of limbs.

When I was sure both of them were dead, I was to leave a letter from the Soldiers of Night claiming responsibility.

But Irina had apparently grown tired of waiting. I'd watched in frustration and fear as she sat on the cabin's step, wrapped in a blanket, drinking a large snifter of brandy.

"I could have acted," I said. "Could have given her the antidote and said I was part of the tsar's secret guard. Something."

"Perhaps. We'll never know."

"No, we won't." By the time I'd gathered my wits together, Aleksey had arrived. It was all I could do to elude capture and make my way back to Stockholm.

"Banishments aren't forever. You'll be fine."

"You're an excellent physik but a terrible liar, Fredrik."

Rather than deny it, he'd clapped me on the shoulder and ordered the driver to make haste.

That was the last time I saw Stockholm.

Now, I barred the door to the solarium and unbuttoned the secret pocket of my waistcoat. Hidden within was a tiny silver flask given to me when I completed my training with the Society of Poisoners.

I kept the flask filled with *Dream Caller*. One good swallow would painlessly stop my heart.

Dream Caller is one of the first compounds taught to poisoners. It has to be ingested, unlike *Angry Falcon*, which is delivered by knife point, so the compound presents less danger to the student. The last time I'd administered *Dream Caller* was four years ago at a Midsummer gala, when Duke Emil had drunkenly referred to the emperor as 'Gustavus the Last'. His bowl of chanterelle soup was the perfect medium: the white pepper masked the *Dream Caller*'s slightly astringent aftertaste, and the broth's warmth improved its absorption.

Duke Emil's death unfolded so quietly everyone thought he'd merely fallen asleep between courses. Just another old man who'd had too much wine.

I added hot water to my teapot, stirring in a handful of leaves from yesterday's delivery: smoked black tea with dried orange peels from Iberia. As the tisane's perfume permeated the room, I reviewed my desk. Just correspondence with distant cousins and invoices. Nothing incriminating, nor particularly interesting: an accurate measure of my life in exile. I would leave behind no spouse or children. No lover would mourn my passing. Ironically, I was the perfect target for an assassination.

I poured myself tea and added half the flask to the cup. The tea was too hot to gulp, so I gave myself a moment. No sense in rushing into the afterlife with a burned tongue. Besides, the oak door was good and stout, made as it was from the timbers of a decommissioned imperial warship. It had held off French cannons; it would hold against fists quite easily.

However, no such pounding ensued. All I heard was a gentle knock and the faint voice of my old seneschal, Pontus.

"General Bjornsen?" he said.

"What is it?" I called loudly, mindful of his poor hearing. Pontus had served in the artillery squads in Iceland.

"A messenger wishes entrance."

I rubbed the condensation from the nearest window. The carriage lacked horses or even harness points. Instead, it was powered by two large, expensive demon jars connected to the front and rear axles. Few in Järna could afford such spellcraft, and they were all gentry. Hardly the sort of people to arrive unannounced.

But then I saw the purple *vimpel* hanging from the carriage's front post. Clearly the visitor was not just a messenger, but someone on imperial business.

"Praise Saint Catherine." I made the sign of the cross, a habit from childhood. Then I dumped the tea into the fire and returned the flask to my waistcoat.

If someone wanted me dead, they wouldn't bother with such theater. Far easier to hire a sniper to put a musket ball through my window, or a knife in my kidney at the marketplace. "It appears I'll live another day," I said.

"What was that, sir?"

"Bring them up!" Hope infused my voice. The appearance of an imperial messenger after all this time might—just might—indicate that Emperor Gustavus Adolphus had forgiven my transgression, or at least forgotten it. The passage of years both tempers our bile and dulls our memory, and the emperor was nearly seventy.

"Yes, sir."

"And Pontus—see that their escort is given some mulled wine." I recalled my own time riding winter escort duty. It was both honor and challenge. You spent hours in the saddle, hunched against the cold, straining your ears for the sudden explosion of hoofbeats behind you. A warm cup at your destination was a gift from heaven.

"Lt. Birgitta Pernillasdotter, my lord," said the imperial messenger with a precise court bow. "At your service." She was young for such a posting, perhaps twenty. Her formal uniform consisted of black boots, trousers, blouse, and a tight-fitting coat with cuffs and collar trimmed with white fox fur. Her hat was bare except for a single ostrich plume. Rather than a court sword, she carried a gold-chased flintlock on one hip and a ceremonial dagger—suitable for cutting wax seals—on the other.

A quarter century ago, I had carried a more functional blade in my boot, its sheath painted with rose buds, one for every Prussian sentry I'd killed on moonless nights. It is strange, the things we take pride in.

"Welcome to Järna, Lieutenant. Be at ease," I said, responding with a salute as smooth and automatic as breathing. "It's just General Bjornsen, now. Retired." I straightened the lapels of my silk manteau and pointed to a chair. "Now, what brings you to my home?"

"The imperial physik sends his compliments," she said, handing over a packet of creamy white paper sealed with violet wax. "And requests you accompany me."

I hesitated over the seal. "Am I to understand this wasn't sent by the emperor?"

"No, sir. I would have said so."

Then it isn't a pardon. "I accept the message, Lieutenant." I tucked away my disappointment and opened the packet.

My dear friend,

Gustavus Adolphus is quite ill and I need your assistance. Please come at once.

—Fredrik Magnusson

*P.S. I have shared your situation with Lt. Pernillasdotter.
She is both clever and discreet.*

Though I recognized Fredrik's exquisite quill work and his favorite cobalt blue ink, the nature of the message struck me as uncharacteristically pithy. Normally his letters ran to several pages. During our days at the Imperial Academy, he loved to fatten his prose with lines of poetry or quotations from Marcus Aurelius. I admit I often spurred him on, especially after a glass or three of cheap brandy.

His brevity now was both plain message and subtle warning about the messenger. *Clever and discreet* was a phrase we used to describe soldiers we suspected of being enemy spies. "Alas," I said. "I am no longer welcome in the capital." Fredrik of all people knew this.

Birgitta informed me the imperial family was not in Stockholm. Rather, they were touring the provinces as part of Gustavus Adolphus's extended birthday celebration. "The emperor and empress are presently guests at Strömsholm Palace, a few hours away. Once the escort's horses are given a brief rest and watered, we can return at good pace. The carriage's demon jars are fresh," she added.

I was relieved. Hiring a machine mage to charge those jars would be ruinously expensive, even if we could find one on such short notice. Järna didn't attract many mages, given the nearest demon factory was a full day's ride away.

I re-read Fredrik's note. Together, we had faced cannon fire and treated our fellow soldiers in bloody field hospitals throughout Europe. In fact, it was Fredrik who'd pleaded with Spymaster Maja Viklund to show mercy, even though my error had almost plunged us into war with Russia.

I sometimes flattered myself that Maja had spared my life because we had once been lovers as devoted to each other as we were to our callings. More likely, though, Fredrik's intercession had simply provided her with sufficient political rationale to stay her hand. Having me executed outright might have raised the ire of the Society of Poisoners.

As far as Fredrik's request was concerned, honor and duty demanded I support the emperor any way I could. Beyond that, I wanted to help Fredrik, for he was the closest thing I had to a brother. Not seeing him these past few years had been one of the most difficult challenges of my exile. "Give me an hour," I told her. "The servants will provide a light meal in the sitting room."

I exchanged my silk clothes for my old field uniform and great coat. Then I shaved off my oiled and perfumed beard, leaving behind a mustache trimmed in the traditional cavalry style. While Pontus put a final polish to my old boots, I secreted several items about my person, including a poniard and a fresh vial of *Dream Caller*. Should this errand go badly, I had no intention of facing the noose.

Thus outfitted, I boarded the carriage after Birgitta, looking every inch the retired officer and not at all a disgraced poisoner.

We rolled away from the peacocks and their complaints.

I tucked a thick embroidered wool and silk blanket around my legs and pulled my plain beaver cap over my ears. Though residual heat from the demon jars leaked into the carriage, winter still gripped my bones. The sun might as well be the moon, for all the warmth it produced. Pontus, an Iceland native, would consider this fine weather. "Tell me, Lieutenant," I said, "what do you think troubles His Imperial Majesty?"

"He suffers from gout and dyspepsia, according to Lord Fredrik," said Birgitta. "The servants have strict orders not to agitate the emperor. Even the musicians are silent, lest they interrupt his rest."

"You don't sound very convinced."

"The stable master is an old friend. He found it odd that the emperor was riding every day without complaint, then suddenly required bed rest as if he were a woman swollen with child."

"Without casting aspersion on the imperial physik, I will acknowledge that he can be quite cautious when it comes to his patient's health," I said. "I'm sure he has matters well in hand."

"And yet here you are, summoned back to court on short notice," said the messenger.

"Lord Fredrik is also an old friend," I said, somewhat testily. "And as such, he has *asked* me to visit and offer what small wisdom I might have regarding His Imperial Majesty's illness."

She inclined her head. "My apologies, General. I meant no offense."

"None taken."

"However, given your former role at court, one can only speculate that matters are more serious than they appear."

Oh, she was a sly one, this messenger. She demonstrated all the hallmarks of one schooled in the imperial court's intrigue. A feint here, a retreat there. Nothing too direct.

I leaned forward and lowered my voice. "Lord Fredrik says you are discreet."

"Discretion is a necessary quality in a messenger, even more so when one serves the imperial family."

"Then I encourage you to exercise that discretion. Am I understood, Lieutenant?"

"Perfectly, sir."

I nodded and sat back against the leather bench. As the miles passed, we settled into silent contemplation of the scenery. At this time of year, the road was nothing but gray stones bordered by gray trees, their branches bare. Even the occasional bird was a welcome respite from the monotonous landscape. As we bumped along, I reviewed Birgitta's news in the context of the larger picture. If I were still at court (if only!) and Fredrik told me the emperor was 'quite ill', I would be closeted away with advisors, preparing for the worst. Especially given that the imperial family was currently far from the relative safety of Stockholm.

Two years before, the emperor's only child and heir, Gustavus Adolphus II, had drowned while crossing Lake Vatten in April. The winter had been unusually warm, leaving behind thinner ice than normal. That summer, when typhus took the empress to her own heavenly reward, there wasn't a church or town square that lacked for mourners. The country was devastated. Ambassadors from across the empire appeared, laden with letters proclaiming their condolences while offering prayers and—according to gossip—offers of marriage.

Once the formal grieving period had passed, the emperor moved quickly to arrange his betrothal to Anna Schlüssen of Prussia, a young, widowed noblewoman known for her archery and fierce chess game. She had also previously birthed two healthy boys, a testament to her fecundity.

Unfortunately, the new empress had failed to produce an heir with Gustavus Adolphus.

If he died now, there was no clear succession. The emperor had—wisely or not—chosen to appease the royals by blocking his stepsons from the throne. That left eight cousins with questionable claims, most of whom had been quietly raising mercenary levies since the old empress' funeral. If it came to civil war, the empire would surely shatter like a rotten log struck by a cannonball. Our enemies would invade, and Stockholm would burn. I shuddered to think of it.

One of the lead riders shouted a warning. I pushed open the window to get a better look just as his horse stumbled and pitched forward.

Above us, the driver yelled, "On the left! Black ice!" He engaged the brake, but not too hard, lest the wheels lock and we slide off the road completely. The heavy carriage crunched the thin layer of nearly invisible ice, coming to a stop a hundred paces later. Birgitta opened her door and freed her pistol.

"Stay here," she said and stepped down lightly, testing the ground. Her head swiveled back and forth as she scanned the forest. The other lead rider, a woman with a long braid tucked into her coat, circled back to take up position close to the carriage. She readied a musket.

I leaned out the open door. The fallen horse lay on the ground, its rear legs kicking weakly. Birgitta was helping the escort to his feet. The remaining riders made slow circles, weapons held ready. Their horses' breath steamed.

"Damn shame," said the driver. "Helvig's only had that mount for a fortnight."

"He seems all right," I said, watching Helvig crane his neck and slap his chest holster and sword belt. I felt that instinct in my gut: after you were thrown from your mount, the first thing was to check yourself and your weapons. Were you wounded? Could you fight?

"Aye, he's a tough lad. Eat a bowl of *surströmming* for breakfast and cut down trees until sunset," said the driver.

"Just stay upwind of him," added the rider.

Birgitta offered Helvig her pistol. He shook his head and readied his own weapon. Very slowly, he knelt and put his hand over the horse's eyes. I couldn't hear him, but I suspect he was whispering to it. Then he pulled the trigger. The report echoed loudly in the relative silence. He and the messenger then holstered their weapons and began unstrapping his saddlebags. In a few minutes, they had stowed everything inside the carriage's lockbox. Helvig took his musket and climbed up next to the driver. Birgitta returned to her spot on the bench inside and thumped the ceiling.

"Make for Rönninge depot!"

"Aye, ma'am!" He unlocked the wheels and we slowly picked up speed.

She said to me, "We'll pick up a fresh mount for Helvig and get you to Strömsholm without further delay."

"How is Helvig?" I asked.

"His backside will be black and blue tomorrow, but nothing a bowl of ale won't fix."

Soon we spied the depot. It was a small place, mostly ancient low stone walls with a newer wooden outer wall. Its *vimpel* barely stirred in the light breeze. Birgitta stepped out as soon as we came to a stop and strode up to a soldier stacking firewood. "What's your name?"

"Private Lundson, ma'am." He dropped the firewood and gave a sloppy salute.

"I'm Lt. Pernillasdotter. Tell your commander we need your freshest horse saddled on the double. We lost one about a half hour down the road to black ice."

"Ma'am. Yes, ma'am!" he said and jogged off. I exited the carriage and casually stretched my legs, trying to work some stiffness out. I observed a pair of sentries at the gate and another walking along the outer wall. Between them they had clear firing lines covering the road in both directions, although they didn't seem particularly alert.

Private Lundson returned in the company of another man, a young captain with dueling scars on one cheek. His flat cap sported a white feather and a jaunty red ribbon. A gift from an admirer, perhaps.

"Hallo!" said the officer. "Sorry to hear about the loss of your animal, but I just can't give you a horse and tack without proper requisition. There has to be an accounting for everything that leaves the outpost."

Birgitta smiled. "Captain...?"

"Nyberg."

"Captain Nyberg—let me remind you that everything in this depot, down to your wool socks, belongs to the emperor. It would be a shame if I had to report that I was delayed because some prissy officer wouldn't give us a fresh mount."

Nyberg put a hand on his sword. "Are you threatening a superior officer?"

"No one is threatening anyone," I said, stepping forward. "However, as much as I admire your dedication to procedure, *Captain*, we have important business that cannot be delayed." I checked my pocket watch. "We're leaving in five minutes."

Nyberg narrowed his eyes, his posture tense. I could see he was considering and discarding his options. As much as he thought he could push around a junior officer, he had no such leverage with me. He'd have to make this a challenge of honor and settle it with steel. After taking my measure, he snapped an order at Lundson, who took off running even faster than before.

"Anything else, sir?" he asked.

"No, Captain. You have the emperor's gratitude."

He saluted. Birgitta said, "You might want to send a squad down the road to collect the corpse before it draws wolves. At the very least, collect the saddle."

Nyberg nodded and trod away with quick, heavy steps.

Five minutes later, Lundson reappeared with a great beast of a black horse, saddled and ready. "This is Baldur, Captain Nyberg's horse. He was getting ready to ride patrol when you showed up." He handed the reins to Birgitta, who passed them to Helvig.

"My compliments to the captain," said Helvig, offering up his hand for the horse to sniff. "I'll take good care of him."

"Anything else, ma'am?"

Birgitta shook her head. "Dismissed."

We resumed our journey. Once we'd made up some time, Birgitta seemed to relax. She drank from a leather water skin and passed it to me.

"Permission to speak frankly, sir."

"Of course." I gulped water as we bounced over a rough patch.

"Would you mind telling me why you intervened back there?"

"I don't like bullies," I said. "And Nyberg is a bully, which is probably why he's commanding a supply depot in the middle of nowhere rather than Stockholm or Göteborg."

"I see." She nodded. "So that wasn't some misplaced display of chivalry?"

She wasn't completely wrong. When I was in the field, few women served in her capacity. "If it was, it was unintentional, Lieutenant." I returned the waterskin. "I'd wager a gold crown you could soundly thrash the captain. If it came to that."

"If it came to that, you'd win," she said with a wicked grin.

The ride became markedly smoother once we attained the main supply route between Malmö and Stockholm. It had originally been laid out by Romans and improved upon and extended by Swedish engineers ever since. It was common in summertime to encounter gangs of political prisoners doing road repair in exchange for reduced sentences.

In another hour, we saw signs for Västerås, which put us close to Strömsholm Palace. The driver rang a warning bell and eased off the brakes, increasing our speed. The outriders spurred their mounts to keep up. Fortunately for the horses, we reached the castle soon enough.

Strömsholm was a cold, dismal place in winter, its gardens nothing but ice-frosted bare bushes, its lake empty of boats. Even the swans had the good sense to be elsewhere.

The driver delivered us through a small gate far from the main entrance while our escort peeled off toward the stables. As the gate closed behind us, I kept an eye on the messenger's hand resting near her pistol. I didn't believe she would arrest me now, but there might be others outside, soldiers with different orders. With careful movements, I loosened my blanket. Should events go amiss I might be able to fling it over her and wrest the pistol away. A lifetime of wariness breeds such thoughts.

We rolled to a stop and the door was opened from without. No jailers waited with irons. Birgitta saluted and leaned back so that I might exit first as senior officer.

With great relief, I returned her salute, grateful for this small courtesy. As my first commander liked to say, anyone can purchase court privileges, but military perquisites are earned.

I winced as I stepped onto the flagstones. Even this well-maintained carriage was a challenge to my knees. All that time in the saddle and too many winter campaigns had taken their toll.

Out of habit, I glanced up at the main tower's flagpole. The rectangular sun and ocean banner snapped in the cold breeze, indicating the presence of the imperial family. And their attendants, including the imperial physik and spymaster, neither of whom I'd seen since Stockholm.

A wave of nostalgia and pride washed over me, quickly followed by a deep sorrow. It was one thing to don the uniform and transform myself into a soldier, but the imperial court was an entirely different, more dangerous battlefield. My heart ached to be part of it once again.

Despite my banishment, I had arrived safely. Perhaps my luck was improving.

See part I of Karl Dandenell's story "The Antidote for Longing" online at Metaphorosis.
If you liked it, leave a comment. Authors love that!
Remember to subscribe to our e-mail updates so you'll know when new stories are posted.

About the story

"The Antidote for Longing" isn't my first story set in an alternate 17th Century Sweden. Before this, I wrote several shorter pieces, including "The Machine Mage of Umea", which explores the demon-powered technology that helped create the Scandinavian empire (think steampunk but with supernatural beings).

My own family traces its roots to Sweden, and further back to Belgium (to the region of Andenelle). There, the Dandenell clan was well known for their impressive silver and iron creations. In fact, they worked on the gates at Versailles.

The story goes that the Swedish king, upon touring Versailles, was so taken with the ironwork that he hired my great-great-etc. grandfather Clas Dandenell (along with various relations) and moved them to Sweden so they could help with the gates at Drottningholm Palace.

At the time, the Swedish military did not have cannons as powerful or accurate as, say, the French. My ancestors helped correct that. So it may be that the Dandenell design esthetic was less valuable than their skill fabricating artillery.

When I sat down to write "Antidote", I wasn't looking to write an action-based military story; I was more interested in the characters who had served a military empire and the personal costs of such service. Plus, I wanted to play around with the idea of court assassins, specifically poisoners. (My interest in poisons was probably inspired by an organic chemistry class in college, well before I abandoned the sciences for the more genteel academic path of Shakespeare, Milton, and Chaucer.)

Finally, I saw the main character, Lars Bjornsen, as something of a contradiction. He was both a military commander and an assassin, representing the open and secret faces of the empire. When he was banished, it forced him to question his past and future. That sounded like an interesting vein to mine.

A question for the author

Q: Do you prefer your SFF as books or movies?

A: That's a tough question. I've always been a big fan of SFF movies. As a kid, I loved the low-budget British stuff and Japanese kaiju films. However, once I joined the Science Fiction Book Club—with its dubiously copy-edited editions and cheesy covers—I was hooked on the printed format. From my early days as a fast-food scullion to my most recent corporate gig, I've always kept a paperback or e-reader in my backpack so I could cram in a chapter or two at lunch. These days, I get more of my fiction from podcasts (which are great for house chores and weeding the yard), but at the end of the day there is something special about curling up with a cat and book.

About the author

Karl Dandenell is a graduate of Viable Paradise and a Full Member of the Science Fiction & Fantasy Writers Association. He and his family, plus their cat overlords, live on an island near San Francisco famous for its Victorian architecture and low speed limits. His preferred drinks are strong Swedish tea and single malt whiskey. This is Karl's third appearance in *Metaphorosis*, following "Comes the Tinker" and "Papa Pedro's Children."

www.firewombats.com, @kdandenell

August

A Wielder Does Not Know Regret

Katherine Karch

You are walking down a winter road that carves a gentle arc through a forest of hemlock and fir. Somewhere, a brook flows along icy banks, the soft murmur of its waters slipping between wide trunks and snow-bent branches. In your hand, a folded square of paper with the following:

A request for the services of a Wielder. Take the western road from the Citadel. Do not look ahead. Do not look behind. Do not lose yourself.

Quantum variations of the message's meaning swirl upon the paper, marking its authenticity. You fold it closed, hold it tightly in your hand.

From somewhere close to the road a songbird chirps a high, two-toned note. *Phee-bee.*

The sound elicits a smile. You stop walking, head tilted toward the tiny creature, and wield. The world bends around awareness, time slowing until it is like cool honey dripping from the comb of consciousness.

Pheeeeeeeeeeee—

beeeeeeeeeeee.

Eternity spirals outward, and in the endlessness of *now*, every possible variation of the bird's greeting is a joy. Delighted, you release the moment. Time flows freely once again.

A curtain of clouds is sliding into view over the treetops to the west. Their grey tones hint at snow. Barely visible behind them, the sun hangs upon a notably low zenith, and even as you hold your mind in stillness of now, nature's rhythms ebb and flow in the biology of your body. A gentle hunger tugs for attention.

It is midday.

Beside the road, a fallen pine lies blanketed in a powdery layer of snow that brushes cleanly from the rough corrugations of its bark. This is a good spot to sit and eat.

The pack you set between your feet is filled with items that invite speculation. With hunger as an anchor, though, it is safe to explore its contents. A blanket roll; wool shirt, pants, and socks. A hunting knife with a keen edge and a worn grip. A small measuring device of tarnished brass with the letters *L*, *R*, and *P* etched into one corner of the dull metal. You pull it from the pack, turn it over in your hands, set it aside.

In a folded square of linen you find several morel mushrooms. Their rich flavor sharpens the hunger in your belly, but a second folded square of linen yields a sizable cash of salted groundnuts.

There is a palm-sized book in the pack as well. Its leather cover is inscribed with the title, *Poems*. You glide your thumb along the soft and fuzzy edges of the book's pages. Words shape and stack themselves upon the paper, but you do not read them. Instead, you tuck the book back into the folds of the pack. It feels right to not spoil their undifferentiated state of totipotence.

The measuring device is cold now from lying on the ground. You use it to check the height of the sun's journey. Today, it says, is winter's solstice. The turning of the year.

With a fistful of snow, you chill the blade of the knife, draw it across your forearm alongside five matching scars. The pain anchors you, tethers you to the present, makes it possible to look beyond its boundaries, to see–if only briefly–how long it has been since you chose to become a Wielder.

Six years. There is a pinching in your chest that feels like sadness. Then, it is gone.

A strip of linen deftly tied is enough to pull the edges of the wound together and stop its bleeding. You roll down your sleeve, wipe blood from your blade, and set off again.

Evening is settling into the low places of the forest now, and a heaviness is building in your legs, a fatigue that implies a long day of walking.

Your left forearm aches.

Ahead, where the road curves and vanishes from sight, a figure stands silhouetted in the gloaming. The distance is too far to make out many details beyond the figure's stance, the wide and staggered placement of feet, the hunched uneven slant of shoulders.

"Hello," a man's voice calls out. "Are you coming from the Citadel?"

You shake your head. "I cannot look backward to answer that question."

The man tips his head like a squirrel at the sound of a snapping twig.

You are close enough now to see him clearly. He is dressed in layers of leather and fur to fend off the cold. His face is mostly hidden by a thick beard, but there is an urgency in the pull of his brows, the shape of his lips, the dark shadows beneath his eyes. He squints. Recognition haunts his features. His shoulders tense.

"It's you," he says.

A simple enough truth. "It's me."

"You are a Wielder, then."

"I am."

"I sent word to the Guild that I needed a Wielder, but..." his voice tapers into a stillness forming between you.

"Then it is good I am here." You hold up the paper in your hand, the words swirling in ever shifting fractals of meaning that only a Wielder can parse.

He tugs the back of his neck with a mittened hand, brow pinched as if in pain. "I didn't expect them to send you."

"Our Guild serves all who have need for our craft."

The light has all but left the world now. A quiet chill settles in as you regard one another—him wary and uncertain, you patient and eternal. Snowflakes begin to drift down through the evening air.

"Are you truly a Wielder?"

You smile at the wonder in his voice. "I am."

His mouth tightens as if to bite back something pressing for release. When he finally speaks, his words are stumbling. "You– I– My daughter. She's sick."

There is more, you are certain, but you accept what he tells you. "I am sorry to hear it."

"I've tried everything, but nothing's worked. I have food. A fire. A bed for the night. Will you help her?"

Such questions. You smile. "I cannot look ahead to see, but I am done walking for today."

His cabin is small but sturdily crafted, the close-set timbers deftly chinked. A season's worth of split wood is stacked beneath the roof's south-facing overhang. Smoke curls from a fieldstone chimney. The sight of it evokes a sense of comfort, of *home*. Inside, it is warm and softly lit, a single open room filled with a table, three chairs, and a wooden chest in one corner. Everything speaks of a hard but good life.

Wordless, you lean your pack by the door, then set to removing your many layers. When done, he gestures for you to sit at the small table and presents a bowl filled with something thick and steaming. It smells of carrots and onions and wild garlic scapes. Between each bite, you take in the smaller details of his home.

A copper pan and cookpot reflect the firelight like lanterns from where they hang on the wall. The wooden chest is a work of art, its edges embellished with decorative carvings that suggest a focused mind and a steady hand. Atop the chest sits a daguerreotype in an oval frame. In the image, the man stands beside a dark-haired woman in a white dress. They're both smiling, but you see whispers of doubt clinging to the edges of the woman's eyes.

"Who is she to you?" you ask.

He turns away and sets to washing the dinnerware. His voice is husky with sorrow when he answers.

"My wife."

Yes, of course.

You pull in a slow breath, noting the myriad scents filling the cabin. Sweat, wood smoke, vegetable stew simmering in the fireplace. Mink oil. Damp wool. A child's sickness, sour and sharp. There is a ladder leading to a narrow loft overhead.

The child is buried deep in a nest of old blankets. Her face glows with fever. Strands of dark hair cling to her sweat-sheened forehead. A necklace circles her throat. Six polished beads hang from its leather cord. The man comes to stand at the base of the ladder but says nothing.

"Let me see what can be done," you say.

Careful not to wake the child, you squeeze in beside her, find a comfortable position, take hold of this moment with your mind, and wield.

Reality stretches into an endless state. The child's life unfurls before you. Strings of possibility vibrate and shine in an iridescent rainbow of colors. Some tangle with your own, a tickling, pleasant sensation. No Wielder possesses the skill to touch infinity, but you can trace many of the girl's strings, heft their weight, gauge their strength and flexibility.

Time regains its linearity. The child's chest rises and falls in labored pants, and a sadness settles into your heart. You cannot resist reaching out to caress her feverish cheek.

Such a sweet young sparrow.

The thought bubbles up, unexpected, a temptation to look away from the present and lose yourself. Worse, lose the magic you possess now. Deep breath in. Slow breath out. The moment passes.

"The child's illness has taken hold deep in her lungs," you say as you climb down the ladder to the man below. "Many of her strings are collapsing."

He looks stricken, eyes shining in the firelight, brimming with tears. "There's nothing you can do, then? She's going to die?"

A silly question. Though the strings of every creature are unique, ever-shifting froths of potentiality diverging in beautiful and limitless arrays, they all share one commonality. With gentle sympathy you answer, "All threads end eventually."

"My little bird. Ever since..." He swallows hard, eyes fixed on the floor. "She's all I have left."

You should refuse. Reversing entropic decay requires perfect focus and an enormous transfer of energy. It is not without danger, even for a Master Wielder. You are only a Journeyman, but the sorrow in the man's voice is evidence of the truth in his words. It is settled, then.

"I can help you."

You settle in beside the child. Her pulse is rapid and weak beneath your fingers as you bring your thoughts to the focal point of the girl's origin. You set yourself like a fulcrum in the space between what is yet to come and what has passed, and *stretch.*

At the very center of the child, where infinite variations of a single life hum and swirl, the strings of reality are thin and fading. It is difficult work, gauging and assessing, finding threads that are both long and stable. Each transfer of energy from one potential life to another introduces uncertainty and invites a spontaneous collapse. Slowly, carefully, thread by thread, you wield. Fatigue is gnawing at your edges, so you release your attention from the girl. Time flows once again.

The angry flush of fever is withdrawing from the child's cheeks. Her pulse is settling, but her breaths sound wet as though her lungs are filled with water.

You activate your parasympathetic pathways. Rest. Recover. Wield. Thread by thread, you reshape the fabric of the child's existence. Rest. Recover. Wield. Again. Again. Again…

Daylight is easing back into the world now.

"The illness is not gone, but the girl has a wild, fierce little spirit," you tell the man. "Her possibilities are strong now."

"Thank you," he says and wraps you in a hug. There is a bed tucked beneath the cabin's loft. You accept his offer to rest, and sleep comes swiftly.

Long beams of sunlight catch in motes of dust that drift and settle across an oval portrait atop a wooden chest. A bed of glowing coals pops in the hearth. The thick aroma of molasses and peppered yams permeates the warm cabin as a man sitting by the fire lifts the lid of a cast iron pot and stirs the contents.

You stretch, rise to dress. From the loft overhead comes the sound of a small body shifting.

"Stay for dinner," the man by the hearth says.

His face gives no sign of threat, though there is a certain familiarity to his features and his voice. As a Wielder, the intuitive sense of knowing this man cannot be examined, only acknowledged.

"Thank you. I am hungry."

His smile falters, but he nods, then turns back to tend the pot above the fire. You slide into one of the three chairs at the table and watch in silence while he retrieves a pan from the wall. The pan sizzles, and the smell of grease and frying chicory root is a delight.

"What's it like?" he asks with his back to you. "The Citadel, I mean."

Your pulse quickens. There are rules that must be followed when speaking with a Wielder, and you are certain that this man knows he is breaking them.

"Why do you ask a question I cannot answer?"

"I'm sorry. It's just… it's good to see you again." He turns to set the food on the table, catching your gaze furtively.

A series of creaks and shifts from above draw your attention upward. The face of a young girl is peeking down from the loft. She is pale, thin, brown hair tangled and dirty, but her eyes are bright and curious. For several moments, long even without your magic stretching the world, the two of you regard one another. She does not speak. Instead, she regards you with an openness and a calmness befitting a member of your Guild.

"Hello, little bird," you say, then look at the man. He's gone still and is staring.

With a startling ferocity, he begins to weep. His broad shoulders sag inward. His head sinks toward his chest, and he collapses into his chair.

"You really don't remember, do you?" he cries.

"To remember is to forget. A Wielder—"

"But you weren't *always* a Wielder. You had a family. You had a *life*."

"Do I not have a life now?"

He shakes his head in frustration. "Please don't leave. You can stay here. You can stay with *us*, Lena."

That name in his voice plucks hard upon a single string, sets it vibrating with a force that bends your awareness towards it. Strings resonate, harmonize, phase with one another. A probability begins to manifest as a memory.

You stand, leave dinner untouched upon the table, retrieve your pack from beside the door. "I must go."

The man's eyes fill with anguish. "It's been six years, Lena."

He is hurting, but this hurt is a thing you cannot heal, a weight you dare not carry, a test. The strings of your reality continue to orient into parallel states, with fewer and fewer degrees of freedom. Your breath grows shallow.

"I am a Wielder. I look neither forward nor back. I am here, now, always. There is nothing to miss."

His grief overbalances, tips into anger. "That's a lie. There *is*! You had a life, a family who loved you! The Guild showed up, and —"

"Stop!"

Without conscious thought or intent, driven by the biology of your panicked body, you wield. Time slows, stops, stretches, expands, elongates, ceases.

There is only *now*.

From the loft above, the girl continues to watch, her eyes calm and without judgment. You smile up at her. She is beautiful in all her various possibilities.

Be well, little bird, you think.

Cold bites at your cheeks as you close the door on the warmth of the space within the cabin and let time flow once more.

The sun is sliding slowly downward on its journey toward the end of day. In your hand, a folded square of paper with the following:

The Citadel welcomes you, Master Wielder. Take the eastward road. Do not look ahead. Do not look behind. Do not lose yourself.

Quantum variations of the message swirl upon the paper, thus marking its authenticity. You fold it closed, hold it tightly in your hand.

As the shadows lengthen, a grey bird hops from branch to branch in a nearby tree. A smile touches your lips at the sight of a pink underbelly as it fluffs itself against the cold, black eyes curious and bright.

Phee-bee, it calls, and your whole existence catches on the sound. The center of awareness shifts, the strings of reality harmonize into the memory of a child's name and of a choice made. The world shivers, tightens, threatens to collapse into something singular.

You draw a slow, deep breath in and hold it. The moment passes, and you remain.

See Katherine Karch's story "A Wielder Does Not Know Regret"
online at Metaphorosis.
If you liked it, leave a comment. Authors love that!
Remember to subscribe to our e-mail updates so you'll know when
new stories are posted.

About the story

I was nearing the end of a cardio session and desperately wanting to stop even though I knew I had the physical strength to finish. Desperate to distract myself, I decided to try to focus my thoughts on. The image of a hushed evergreen forest flashed in my mind, intense and vivid. A snow-covered road cut a path through the trees, gently bending leftward out of sight. Along with the image came a thought: *You are walking down a winter road. Do not look ahead. Do not look behind.* In any case, that mental image and those words turned into a story about the power of mindfulness and the expectations that we and others have of ourselves.

A question for the author

Q: What happens when you hit writer's block head on?

A: When I was younger, I experienced a lot of negative self-judgment whenever writer's block struck. I'd gotten it into my head that if I didn't write X number of words every day then

I wasn't taking myself seriously. I wasn't a "real" writer, whatever that meant. Thankfully, my feelings on the topic have evolved over time. I've become more accepting of myself, I guess. Basically, if I have the mental energy to write and I'm able to do so, then I do. Sometimes, though, the words refuse to flow or the story refuses to reveal itself. Once, I would have tried to hate myself back to the keyboard and brute force my way through the block. Now, when I get stuck on a particular project, I take a breath and turn my attention to something else. Recently, I've started writing flash fiction as a way to cleanse my creative palate when I encounter writer's block. Because the stories are so short, the stakes feel less weighty, and I'm able to explore and experiment more freely. I like to assign genre categories to the numbers on a 20-sided die and rolling twice. Then, I'll try to write a story based on the genre mashup I've rolled. The creative "play" of the exercise almost always gets me unstuck.

About the author

Katherine Karch spent her childhood playing in the woods, frequently with an old copy of Asimov's or Analog rolled up and tucked in a back pocket. She was still pretty young when she started writing her own stories. For nearly two decades she's continued playing in the woods as a biology teacher. When she's not lesson planning or grading lab reports, she's either reading stories, writing stories, spending time with her family, or sitting quietly in nature, just being. You can find her on Mastodon and Instagram.

www.katherinekarch.com, @KarchWrites@wandering.shop

A Life of Color

N.V. Haskell

Last fall's decaying leaves shifted beneath my feet as I crossed the yard. The others watched me come, glancing nervously at the infant held tenderly in the old woman's arms. Moonlight flickered through the barren tree branches and glinted off the baby's delicate skin. Her eyes shimmered with rainbows and nebulae beneath eyelashes so pale they were barely visible. It was because of this tiny bundle that I had been hauled from my cozy bed in the middle of the night. What her story was and where she came from were puzzles that I wished hadn't happened on my watch.

The sleep loss fogging my brain faded as I took in the baby's situation. I swore silently, too quietly for any of the three to hear. The old woman had found the baby in the dingy alley behind her home, wrapped in the paint-stained blanket she still wore. The police officer and social worker had come along later. But after David, my boss at the Department of Magical Resources, woke me at 2 am, it became my problem —magic baby, magic expert. It didn't matter that my expertise was adult crimes, not children.

During my last performance appraisal, David had celebrated my departmental loyalty and hinted at a promotion. Using my desire for advancement, he'd easily leveraged me into the weekend rotations by saying it would demonstrate how effectively I could work outside of the crimes division.

Truthfully, the schedule change hadn't been a huge sacrifice. There was nothing for me outside of work. Relationships had proven to be too taxing, not worth the effort I put in. People always left or died, like my parents when I was three. And though the multiple foster homes I'd been raised in had done an adequate job of feeding and housing me, they'd lacked warmth or encouragement. It was no wonder I still sought approval from figures in authority.

Gazing upon the abandoned infant stirred a sympathy for her.

Hard of hearing, the elderly woman had first assumed the cries belonged to the neighborhood cat in heat again. But after the racket persisted for more than an hour, she decided to investigate and phoned the police immediately upon finding the child. The infant was said to be only a few weeks old.

A magical child abandoned was practically unheard of. The magical communities were notoriously private and, although a few of the larger clans had representatives that appeared in governmental regulation meetings when the situation warranted it, most of the smaller clans avoided the greater nonmagical society completely unless they were called on for required services. Several clans had dispersed into unsanctioned areas, which made it difficult for the Department to keep track of them all.

The baby's pale hair and dainty features made her seem angelic, yet beneath her eyelids danced a myriad of colors. With a small, mournful whimper, tears of sapphire blue paint trickled down her face and further stained the blanket. The oil and organic compounds of the paint's pigment mingled with the other smells of the city, the exhaust from the cars and buses, the garbage, and even the odor of the older woman, who rocked the infant gently. She hummed softly, mindless of the streams of colorful goo running from the child's eyes. The woman's toothless smile matched the baby's as she cooed over her. Maybe caring for children came naturally to her.

As the girl drifted peacefully to sleep, her lips puffed slightly with each breath, and I cursed softly again.

Damn David for making me take these weekend on-call shifts. He was well aware that my specialty was magical crimes, not children. I never did well with anything that required special care. A graveyard of dead plants served as proof of my ineptitude; the succulents lasted a bit longer, but ultimately met their demise as well. The moment they came into my possession, their fate was sealed.

I had hoped to be able to pass the baby off quickly, until the social worker thrust a car seat and diaper bag full of supplies at me while informing me that no non-magical homes would take the infant because of her special needs. It fell to my department to find a placement. Although I argued and threatened her with demotion if she left, she flashed a contemptuous look at me before driving away. All I'd be able to do was mention her name in the administrative meeting, come Monday morning.

I knew that finding placement in any home was a challenge, but magical homes were impossible. Their tight-knit communities were scattered in the countryside, sequestered from the curious eyes of nonmagical peoples and understandably hostile to my historically untrustworthy employer. The likelihood of getting help from any of the clans for a child of unknown origin was slim. Though they were fiercely protective of their own, they were unlikely to take in a stray of unusual magical talents. Which made me wonder where the girl had come from.

When David finally answered his phone, he simply told me to 'handle it' and bring the child to the office on Monday morning. He hinted about the promotion I had applied for being a factor. That advancement would remove me from the grunt work and weekend rotations, elevating my footsteps up the corporate ladder as I'd always wanted. It didn't hurt that it came with a hefty pay increase as well.

The task would have been much easier if this were an adolescent or adult of a known clan. The Department's holding cells were constructed to deal with certain magical elements. Soundproof cells for musical clans. Fireproof rooms with automatic extinguishers for the fire clans. Sterile, metal rooms for the nature clans. But there were no facilities for magical children or infants and certainly nothing specifically built for paint magic.

I watched silently as the detective fastened the car seat in the back of my car. Aside from those swirling eyes, the infant appeared just like any other: probably riddled with germs, but also fragile and innocent.

Even though my stomach knotted at the sight of her, I told myself I could manage. I, Laura Arthur, the woman who always declined to hold all her friend's children—was now responsible for taking care of a magical infant for thirty-six hours. Humanity had continued to exist for many thousands of years, right? Certainly, it couldn't be that difficult.

When I got home, I had no choice but to place the baby's car seat beside my bed, which I regretted when she woke up crying and angry three hours later. Anxiety filled me as I tried to figure out how to put an end to the cerulean acrylic streaming from her eyes, or the loud cries erupting from her small lips. A noxious smell, like a mixture of cat pee and stargazer lilies, stung my nostrils as I unclipped the straps that secured her, distracting me from the yellow and green colors that splattered onto my silk pajamas.

When I placed my hands beneath her tiny hips, liquid squished between my fingers. When I pulled my hands away, they were covered in emerald and lemon paint. My disgust was immediate, causing my stomach to churn and threaten emptying. I'd dealt with messes in crime scenes before, but never anything like this. Another sharp wail made me push aside my revulsion. I rushed the car seat, with the still-screaming baby inside it, toward the bathroom.

I placed everything gently in the old clawfoot tub as paint dripped slowly over the sides of the seat. The colors swirled like a kaleidoscope against the white porcelain, blues and reds turning purple and blending with yellow and green to make an ominous hue. There was no time to consider the mess, even though I knew it would take more than bleach to clean it up. I needed help.

I wiped my hands on a towel and, not knowing what else to do, rushed to my neighbor's house. With her one-year-old twins, I considered Molly to be an expert in these matters, and there was no one else that might help. Though we'd only ever said a few polite words here and there, when she saw the distress on my face, she ran back with me. The inside of the bathtub had splotches of bright yellows and oranges from Iris's spittle that dripped in thin ribbons down the white tub's interior.

Loud protests continued as Molly lifted the pink-cheeked girl in her arms and peeled the wet clothes away. The baby was too small to safely bathe in the tub, Molly said. So, we held her in the sink and washed the paint off with a little soap and warm water. The paint swirled down the drain, leaving only traces of orange and blues on the porcelain. The little one's sobs quieted, dissolving into occasional hiccups as we wrapped her in a towel and put a fresh diaper on her.

Molly didn't ask where the baby had come from. She knew where I worked and knew better than to ask questions. Though the paint had obviously surprised her, she had handled it with more grace than I had, and, to her credit, she didn't chide me for not knowing what to do.

An hour after the mess was dealt with, she returned with a bag full of baby items she had intended for donation. She taught me how to prepare formula and test its warmth. I offered to pay her, but she declined and dismissed my apologies, telling me that no one was born knowing what to do.

Eventually the baby dozed off in my arms, and though my limbs ached from holding her for so long, I wasn't sure how to set her down without waking her. When I awoke later, a strand of my hair was tangled in her fingers. She gazed at me with eyes made of swirling sunflower yellow and sunset orange. She let out a low giggle, like she was the only one in on the joke. I couldn't help but smile back, wondering what I looked like to her. Was I swirls of magenta or blotches of grey cast in sharp angles? Maybe I was nothing more than a blurry figure, if she could see me at all.

I shook away those thoughts, reminding myself that it didn't matter anyway. This would only be my problem for one more day. Whatever foster home she wound up in would surely tend to her better than I could.

On Monday morning, I stumbled into the office with my hair in a mess and a streak of neon pink down one shoulder of my houndstooth blouse. One day of diaper disasters and a broken night's sleep had confirmed what I had always known: I wasn't cut out for parenthood.

I'd hoped that by handing the baby off to the Department researchers they could find a link between her and one of the clans catalogued in the database. That should have been the end of my direct involvement, but when David insisted I supervise, that was my day wasted. We didn't get many adults here and no one remembered a child this young ever being brought in. The awareness of the girl's vulnerability in this cold environment put me on edge.

Dr. Arias was gentler with her than I'd expected when he put her through a battery of tests: MRIs, CT scans, EEGs, and EKGs. The lab technicians handled the whimpering baby with a professional detachment while they lined each machine with drop cloths to protect them. It felt as if she were a specimen they were hastily examining in order to classify. Even I thought a baby deserved better than that.

The phlebotomist tried to extract a blood sample with a butterfly needle, but whatever ran through the baby's veins was too thick for the small needle's gauge and using a larger one would be damaging.

Her wails at the needles' prodding made me queasy and brought back old memories of the testing I'd undergone in the foster system when I was small. I remembered feeling alone and afraid. If that testing had shown any magical talents, perhaps I would have had a clan take me in. I hoped that would be the case for this girl.

Iris 15738—her Department-issued name—was special, of that there was no doubt. If she had been from a more prominent clan, the researchers would have quickly lost interest. But because of the rarity of her magic, they wanted to know how it worked and, more importantly, if it could be useful.

In exchange for government aid and certain assurances of land and protections, the magical clans were legally obligated to assist in certain situations. The nature clans handled natural disasters and farming during times of drought. The fire clans were used for controlling burns and military procedures. The musical clans for entertainment and therapy. But the more physically artistic clans were rare. There were only a few sculptors left, and their creations could only animate for a few seconds, which made them practically useless for most purposes.

Years ago, after reforms were passed that gave the clans more autonomy and less oversight, many of the smaller factions had used the new freedom to quietly scatter. After scouring through the Departmental archives, I found only one reference to a paint clan, from decades prior. Address unknown, the phone number attached to them was ancient. The line crackled when I left a voice message.

Leaving the girl under Dr. Arias' care, I returned to my office to reach out to the small network of approved foster homes with some magical experience. But they each declined. One said they had no room, whereas another honestly said they weren't qualified to handle the babe's issues. I then began the arduous task of calling the larger clans while searching for information about where she might have come from. Then I called a dozen smaller magical settlements within two hundred miles. Eleven had no knowledge of her or her paint magic. The twelfth was the mysterious clan with the ancient number.

David summoned me late in the afternoon, his face somber. Iris slept peacefully in the car seat which was placed in a chair across from his desk.

"Any luck finding a place for her?" he asked, and sighed when I shook my head. "Hate to do this to you, but you'll probably have to keep her for another night or two, unfortunately. We'll cover the damages and I'll add a commendation to your file. Simply fill out the necessary forms and document everything with photographs."

"But—"

"There's no one else, Laura. Jon's got the triplets, and Briana's taking care of her mom. Unless you'd rather give her to the researchers." His lips pursed in disapproval, and he looked away.

We both knew their experiments would turn more invasive without oversight, and Dr. Arias couldn't be there all the time. But there was something else hidden in David's tone.

"What is it?" I asked.

"There's something wrong with her."

My heart sank. Iris stirred in her sleep in the seat next to me. I combed my fingers through her sparse hair and waited for him to continue.

"Her brain activity is abnormal, probably due to hydrocephalus, or whatever it's called with paint." He paused, trying to make sure that I couldn't misunderstand. "Her heart is arrhythmic, most likely working too hard to pump the thick fluid around her body, but without testing her enzymes we can't be sure. There's no cure."

Iris's chest rose and fell, accompanied by an occasional pause or gasp. Petite hands clutched the edges of a pink blanket. It was probably Dr. Arias who had placed a plush giraffe beside her, its head was already covered in mint green acrylic drool. It reminded me of the stuffed horse I'd been given in my first foster home. I'd carried it with me through a dozen other homes, a source of security and something soft to hold in an otherwise hard world.

"Dr. Arias doesn't think she'll make it past a year," David said. He looked at me warily, as if I were going to fall apart at the news.

I tried to keep my expression neutral and steady the sudden throb in my heart. After everything she'd been through in her short life, the girl didn't deserve this fate. Iris deserved to live. I took a deep breath. "Percentages?"

"Eighty percent chance she has a stroke, heart attack, or turns septic in the next six months. One hundred percent within the next year."

My chest deflated as ideas for a solution rushed through my mind. "But if we find where she came from, there might be a chance."

David shrugged. "Only if you can find her clan and convince them to talk to us."

By the end of the first week, I'd resorted to wearing shapeless, faded clothing once reserved for yard work or donation The days were whirlwinds of endless feedings, diapers, and departmental meetings. The sleepless nights left me in a dazed stupor. My home's modern décor had turned into a canvas splashed with bright acrylics and oils. But aside from the damage being done, there were growing smiles and curious hands that slowly tugged at my emotional armor as Iris planted something both unfamiliar and uncomfortably vulnerable beneath it.

There was still no home willing to take her, not once the Department revealed her complications, but the thought of leaving her with the researchers made me nauseous. Adults who committed magic-based crimes were all dealt with properly; I'd made sure of it because I understood how the judicial system worked in those cases. And although the Department of Magical Resources had gone to great lengths to make amends for its past through media outlets and charity initiatives, most everyone suspected they kept certain practices covert.

Without an advocate, Iris might disappear within a month. Though I'd never witnessed anything personally, there were long-standing rumors about experimentation that occurred in the Department's mysterious lower levels. I'd thought that it was all conjecture, but now the fear that there might be truth to it worried me. Iris was more vulnerable than I'd ever been.

The ambitious governmental loyalist that I'd always been began to question everything, including why my other assignments were becoming less important to me when compared to Iris.

In desperation, I reached out again to the magical communities, widening the radius to five hundred miles—with the same sad result. According to one trusted magical resource, the paint clans had vanished years ago. No one knew anything about Iris and after a few brief questions, no one wanted her, either. Despite the Department's considerable resources and informants, we had yet to reach the one elusive clan. But I left another message on their nondescript voicemail and waited.

The following weeks felt like an eternity. My coworkers had been helping with feedings and diaper changes during work hours, but something strange began to happen. Iris would scream hysterically until returned to my arms. Briana nearly dropped the struggling girl when she attempted to change her. And the Department was having to reimburse not only my costs, but many of my coworkers' wardrobes after Iris's messy cries and accidents. With each feeding and diaper change, my coworkers were met with Iris's growing levels of hysteria, until they stopped offering to help altogether. And as Iris's cries grew louder, a subtle pressure began to grow around me. One email complained that Iris was upsetting the office's routine and productivity. Another suggested that if we couldn't find a home for her, the researchers on level 3-B would be happy to study her until she passed away. Level 3-B's enthusiasm at gaining more information about paint magic by studying an ill child was off-putting, to say the least.

David's behavior changed drastically over the same time frame. Where he'd initially insisted that I keep Iris and shown concern for her wellbeing, his tone changed to annoyance bordering on disdain. More than once, he suggested that I consider leaving her at the facility overnight so that I could get a full night's rest, but I heard the veiled demand in his voice. I suspected that the change was the result of pressure from his superiors. When I continued to resist, David asked that I stay away from meetings so that Iris didn't cause a distraction. In fact, I was encouraged to work from home, but refused. I watched helplessly as projects I was vying for were given to less qualified coworkers. Knowing I risked my promotion, I swallowed my anger and frustration, though I wrote down every detail of what was happening.

All hope of finding Iris' clan began to fade away.

One afternoon, David's tall figure filled the doorway of my office, a room now spotted teal and lemon, with the lingering scent of hydrocarbons hanging in the air. His carefully crafted appearance of morality was slipping away with each of our interactions.

"I can practically guarantee that promotion if you will give her up, Laura." His gaze never left mine as he spoke. "The Regional Director is offering a significant raise, too. I'm sure you must be exhausted from dealing with her. Give her to the Department, and rest assured that they will take care of her for the rest of her days."

I sighed and rubbed my eyes, silently begging for the headache that had been etched behind them for the past few weeks to ease up temporarily. For a fleeting second, I considered giving in. But I'd been a child in the system once and Iris deserved no less than what I'd had. A warm bed, a gentle word, patience. David's assurances rang hollow and while caring for her didn't feel quite as overwhelming as it once had, the thought of leaving her alone and afraid made me ill. Iris needed me and maybe I'd needed her to remind me that there was a life outside of work.

"You're okay with her disappearing into the system?" I asked.

David winced at the contempt in my voice while I studied the green and blue staining in the creases of my hands. In the process of giving up rest, personal care, and anything resembling normalcy for the past six weeks, I'd realized that there were some things I couldn't in good conscience do. Even if it was for the agency. I had come too far with Iris to back out now. Fuck him and the Department for asking me to. His face hardened as I said as much. He walked away, taking my advancement with him as Iris began to cry.

My cell phone vibrated at 3 am a week later. I rushed to answer it before it disturbed Iris, scurrying into the living room, now painted in sporadic shades of Tahitian blue, lilac, and burnt sienna.

"Did you call about a baby?" an older woman whispered over the connection.

My voice wavered as I answered, "Yes." Anticipation swelled within me, hoping this was the call I'd been waiting for. "I'm Laura Arthur from the Department of—"

"Don't say it," she snapped. "Tell me what she looks like."

"The baby?"

She took a deep, shuddering breath, filled with emotional restraint.

Flippant words that all babies looked alike nearly left my mouth. But that was old thinking and now felt completely disingenuous. An awkward tension stretched in the silence between us. That she was calling at this time of night with a lowered voice led me to the conclusion that she was afraid of being discovered. Our time was limited. "Blonde hair, round face, colorful, swirling eyes—like they're full of..."

"Paint." Her voice was heavy and raw. "I'll give you an address. Meet me there tomorrow at one pm. I need to see her."

I jotted down the location and the line went dead before I had a chance to ask any more questions. When I returned to the bedroom, Iris had wriggled from one side of her crib to the other, leaving a long squiggle of avocado green behind her. I didn't bother telling David why I wouldn't be coming into work that Thursday and he didn't care enough to ask anyway.

It was a two-hour drive from my home, through the suburbs and into the stark rural countryside. We travelled past fields and small clusters of ramshackle homes set far off the road, many partially hidden behind enchanted conifers and hedges that moved to protect the view of the settlements as I passed.

The address the woman had given directed me to an abandoned gas station, a dilapidated relic of a bygone era. The weather-beaten windows were glazed and cracked and worn chunks of concrete were interspersed with layers of indiscernible graffiti. Generations of spiders nourished themselves on fat insects in all corners of the building. As I pulled my vehicle into the weedy vacant lot, a faint silhouette shifted behind the chipped double doors.

With one hand tucked under the carrier and the other gripping a bag filled with baby supplies and a crusted giraffe, I hesitantly stepped towards the entrance. Hope and dread bloomed equally inside me.

The door groaned in protest as I pushed it open, revealing an interior cloaked in a thick fog of dust motes that were illuminated through narrow shafts of sunlight.

A tall woman stood in the back of the room, her wrinkles betraying her age, and her bright red hair pulled tightly in a bun. Her eyes were made of varied colors that swirled together. She fingered a necklace of glass beads looped around her throat. Most were painted in vibrant colors, but one was plain, as if something were missing.

Fear and reticence filled the air between us, neither of us willing to take a step forward. The woman's eyes darted towards the carrier when Iris moved inside. Her lips quivered.

"May I see her?" she asked softly.

I set the carrier on the floor and pulled down the soft blanket. I cradled Iris in my arms, hesitating. It'd been a long time since anyone else had held her.

"Who are you?" I asked.

"Messina Thawn, of clan Thawn. I'm surprised you found us." Gently, she drew Iris into her arms and swayed from one foot to the other in the rocking motion most parents seemed to know instinctively. A sad smile pulled at her lips. "I'm sorry for making you wait for a response. That number you had is old, set up ages ago for emergencies when our last leader was alive. It's rarely checked; our current clan leader is stricter, doesn't believe in using technology under any circumstances. Not even when it could bring one of our missing back to us." She paused to brush the hair from Iris's forehead. "We've managed to mostly avoid the Department's notice for decades. Ever since their experiments ended back in the thirties." Her look dared me to respond. "I bet they don't teach that in school anymore."

I shifted uncomfortably, understanding what she avoided saying and that reaching out and meeting me was a risk for her. I cleared my throat. "Does she have a name?"

She shook her head, gazing again at Iris. "I wouldn't know it. Gabby, my daughter, ran away when she discovered she was pregnant. Left with a farm boy." Her voice hitched. "I looked for her. We all did. But she was afraid of what would happen. Not everyone in our clan is accepting of the nonmagical mix. They probably thought they'd do better in the city."

Affection swept across Messina's face, but her smile faded into barely suppressed grief. "I knew something had gone wrong. I felt it. As if she'd drunk turpentine and faded away." She sniffed, tried to collect herself before she continued. "Leo, the boy, returned a few weeks ago. He's refused to talk to any of us. Won't even say what happened or where my Gabby dissolved. I can't even add her bead to my necklace."

"Bead?" I asked.

"It's the only thing we leave behind when we die." Messina cleared her throat to cover the tremor in her voice. "A bead coated with our colors."

Iris stirred in her arms, squirming her shoulders against her grandmother's bony chest. Her lashes fluttered open, seeing eyes like her own. Similar, but not the same. It was easier to see the differences when they were so close. One was orderly lines; the other was blurring chaos.

Messina gasped. Blood-red tears welled in her eyes. "Oh, no." It was a soft sound, like whispering down a moss-ridden well.

"The researchers said she was sick. But I thought her clan might be able to help." I choked on the question. "Was I...am I wrong?"

Messina's breath shuddered. Painted tears trickled down her cheeks as Iris's small fingers brushed at them curiously before tangling in the glass beads around Messina's neck.

"There's a recessive gene that runs in our clan. It keeps some of us from solidifying completely. Bones that can't harden turn to mush. The lining of organs and blood vessels eventually breaks down until our colors run together. Dissolving little by little. I hoped that Leo's influence would override..." Her words were knives cutting us both.

"Can't you help her? What about the rest of the clan? There must be someone." At the sudden rise of my voice, Iris turned. Small arms reached for me as she whimpered.

Mindless of the violet paint that splattered the front of her dress, Messina cradled the girl to her chest for a moment and sighed. She shook her head, eyes holding endless depths of anguish as she returned Iris to me.

"One of my sisters died before she was one. My nephew was the same. There's nothing anyone can do." Her fingers glided from one bead to the next before she stroked the back of Iris's head. "All you can do is care for her until she passes."

"Me? She's your family. Surely, you'd want to keep her."

"No one knows I'm here," she said, her voice gone low. The palm she pressed to her lips was covered in Iris's violet paint. Messina closed her eyes for a long moment. As her hand slowly dropped, a bright smear stained her lips and chin. "If she'd been born amongst our clan with that anomaly, she would have been dissolved already. Her life would have been shorter than in your care. Maybe even shorter than with your researchers."

"But I thought the clans... I thought that you took care of your own."

"Laura, even if we were a stronger clan with more resources, nothing could stop what is happening to her. All we have is our limited magic, and after watching so many of our children die over the years, we try to lessen the suffering." Her tears welled again. "If you want her to live a bit longer, it's best she stays with you. Plus, she's already bonded to you."

"I can't care for her. I don't know how to do *any* of this." My voice trembled, and I quelled the volume to keep from upsetting Iris further.

Messina brushed my hair from my cheek with stained fingers. "What do you need to know? Feed her when she's hungry, clean her when she's dirty, bathe her, soothe her, and hold her."

I whispered, "I can't watch her die."

Something within me broke; the veneer of strength I relied on splintered and cascaded down my cheeks. I hadn't let myself cry in a long time. So long that I'd nearly forgotten the initial sting and briny taste of my tears. Messina wiped my cheeks with gentle hands, studying the clear liquid on her fingertips before looking back at me sympathetically.

"Life and love are messy and fragile. No matter how much of either you have, it won't ever prepare you for when you have to let go." She enveloped us in her slender arms, painting my cheek with her sorrow.

Messina said a quiet goodbye as she helped place the girl in the car, stroking her face one last time with tenderness and grief.

My gaze lingered on her necklace as words stuck in my throat. "When she... her bead..."

"Keep it," she said. "It's clan tradition to wear it when someone you love passes away. It will give you something to hold when she's gone. Something to remember the colors of her life with."

Other than pulling over twice to collect myself, I remember little of the drive home. Leaving the dusty gas station, I'd vowed to protect Iris until her very last breath. No matter how much her paint stained my clothing, furniture, and skin, it was a small price to pay to hear her full-belly chortles and breathe in her sweet-smelling hair.

The following day, I found myself in a tense talk with David as I put in my request for a leave of absence and demanded payout for my untaken paid time off and the standard payment for foster parents. Our meeting then transitioned into an extensive virtual conference with the district manager and head researchers. When they attempted to bribe or threaten me, I responded with promises to publicize our exchanges and involve contacts above their heads. I hoped they didn't catch the tremor in my voice. It was half lying, of course, but I refused to abandon this lost child the way everyone else had. The meeting resulted in an extended leave of absence and veiled promises of professional stagnation.

The green and gold of summer were giving way to dusky autumn when Iris finally rolled over. A few weeks later, she discovered her feet whilst gurgling happily on her back. Her peals of laughter shook the house intermittently for days. A month later, Molly and the twins were visiting when Iris sat up on her own for the first time. Molly had become my confidant and biggest asset for all the things I didn't know about babies. She celebrated each milestone with me and stroked my back in my moments of frailty.

Soon after, Iris scooted across the floor for the first time. I no longer minded the dapples of orange and sapphire that seeped between the grooves of the oak planks. Everything could be cleaned or replaced someday.

She delighted in the tastes of pureed peaches and sweet potatoes and claimed a stuffed parrot as a new favorite toy. At eight months—just when I'd hit the depths of sleep-deprived despair—she began to sleep through the night consistently. I focused on celebrating each small milestone as if it were a miracle. Because each breath she took, every smile, each drop of paint—everything she did and each moment we shared—was miraculous to me. I hadn't known it was possible to love like this, knowing it would end.

Iris's attempts to pull herself up were weak, her body unable to coordinate the movement, and each time I raised her to her feet in an attempt to stand, her knees would buckle like a dropped scarf. It was a bleak winter day when fear humbled me enough to reach out to Dr. Arias. He was kind in his response and, under the guise of research, he began to visit us weekly and provide some guidance with her care.

"Her muscles are beginning to atrophy." His voice was strained. He stroked her head gently, his cold professional demeanor dissolved into warmth at the sight of Iris's smile. "Maybe another month or two at most."

It took a long moment for my words to form. "Is she hurting?"

He shook his head. "Not yet. I can prescribe something if you want…just to keep her comfortable."

Iris never spoke in words, but I learned her language of cries and grunts. When I accidentally stepped on toys I'd forgotten to pick up, I didn't curse them. The pain of my body was a temporary distraction to the deeper rending inside me.

I'd never had faith in anything other than science, but there were days of mounting desperation when I found myself standing beside her crib while she slept, and I prayed in the same way one of my foster parents had. Sometimes I would rub the smooth glass bead strung around my neck repeatedly, as if some divine force would notice my plea and take pity. But whomever, or whatever, I prayed to, never answered.

When daffodils broke through the cold ground outside my windows and spring ushered in new signs of life, I'd known for days what was happening. And yet I wasn't ready. I don't imagine I ever would have been.

I'd been steadily increasing her pain medication to make her passing easier. But as I cradled her frail frame against my chest, I felt a weight of sorrow that no amount of preparation could have lightened.

I breathed in Iris's familiar scent. The warmth of her body soothed me as I tried to comfort her. The colors of her eyes dimmed, the slow swirling stilled. Her lips trembled in her final breaths as her tiny frame shuddered. I whispered words of love, fighting back my tears so that the last thing she saw on my face wouldn't be my sorrow. I only wanted her to know my love. There would be time to grieve for years to come.

Her occasional gasps lessened. The rise and fall of her chest eventually stopped. Iris slipped away in a final swirl of sunflower yellow and sapphire blues as she dissolved in my arms.

All that was left of her was a bead painted with beauty and love.

*See N. V. Haskell's story "A Life of Color" online at Metaphorosis.
If you liked it, leave a comment. Authors love that!
Remember to subscribe to our e-mail updates so you'll know when
new stories are posted.*

About the story

I thought about this story for years before I had the courage to write it and I am grateful for the right editor who encouraged me to expand it to what it has become.

Coming from a troubled childhood, I convinced myself that I would never have children. Consequently, when I became pregnant in my early twenties I was overwhelmed with conflicting emotions and had very little support or resources. When I lost that pregnancy, I was devastated. But if I hadn't had that experience and gotten the help that I needed afterward, I'm not sure that I would have had my family or be the person I am today. Although it was a life-altering combination of humbling and heartbreaking, it made me realize that, until then, I'd had no idea what I wanted. It completely changed my perspective and ultimately made me work to become a better person.

Over the last few years, a few friends have suffered miscarriages. Another lost a young child. Grieving with them compelled me to finally write this story.

Although it was many years ago, and my children are now grown, I still occasionally think about the child that might have been. I wonder what kind of magic they might have brought to this world, and, at the same time, I am grateful for the gift they gave me. I only wish that I had something more than words to hold on to.

A question for the author

Q: Do you use critique groups or other resources to polish your writing?

A: I am in three writing groups on Discord with writers at all levels of experience. We regularly trade stories, and the feedback and perspectives of others has been instrumental to my growth as a writer. Plus, after reading other people's work and critiquing it, then seeing them incorporate that feedback to improve a storyline or fill in a plot hole feels great. For instance, one of the smaller groups I am in (there's only five of us) took one person's story and gave deep feedback on what worked and what wasn't clear. That story ended up winning a major writing competition and we celebrated with him when he picked up his award.

I also rely on a couple of beta readers who consistently read over 100 books a year and provide great reactions and questions strictly from a reader perspective. The issues they bring up are often quite different from the writers and provide some interesting insight into how that piece is perceived and whether I hit the mark.

About the author

N.V. Haskell is an award-winning author of speculative fiction who lives somewhere between civilization and the haunted caves of Kentucky with her long-suffering spouse, rescue pets, and too many squirrels and groundhogs that she can't help but feed. When she's not busy writing, you can find her attending Comic Cons or Renaissance Fairs donned in her favorite costumes, running badly, or trying to read too many books at a time. After many years in healthcare, she remains stubbornly (or foolishly) optimistic.

www.nvhaskell.com, @NhHaskell

The Bookseller of Mars

Gaby Brogan

I am where the hurt people go. Not the crying, soft, gentle people. I'm not sure there are any of those left. No, I am where the killers turn when the buried piece of them that is still human reaches out, yearning for the light.

Now there are two killers at my door. Boy-children. I see them on the crackly intercom screen in my kitchen, the red desert stretching out behind them. I will let them in, I'm sure. I always do.

"Guns stay outside," I call through the mic.

They turn to each other and whisper. They look about fourteen or fifteen – the age I was when I first came to Mars over a decade ago, a filthy, scared teenage girl, bundled onto a starship along with the rest of the refugees from Earth.

Originally, thirty thousand of the global elite were planned for those starships. But when society fell to floods, fire, and disease, SpaceCorp took whoever could make it to the launch site in burning California. Beggars can't be choosers during the apocalypse.

The day we landed, I filed out of the ship into the sterile light of the Mars station with the other aching, stinking survivors. We took gear from metal boxes as an armed group of SpaceCorp employees watched over us. The most precious item was a metal cube the size of my fist. If I pressed the button, it would pop open to the size of a cargo container. A ready-made home for the elite's life on Mars; temperature controlled, CO_2 to oxygen conversion, a greenhouse for food, and a drillbug to bore down into Martian rock for water.

That cargo container is where I find myself now, all these years later. Hidden under an outcrop of rock on the edge of the desert, far from the violence and squalor of the settlements.

"We're not leaving our gun," calls the blond kid on my screen.

"Then you aren't coming in." On Mars, everyone's a killer.

The kid kicks the ground, sending up a cloud of ochre dust.

"You don't understand. It's Jay," he gestures to the boy next to him. "His regulator's beeping."

"I'm sorry," I say. "That's a real problem for Jay." If his regulator is beeping, he doesn't have long. That vital metal chip sits in your nostril, creating a bubble of oxygen and pressure that stops your blood from boiling in the Martian atmosphere. Beeping means breaking.

"Fuck," says the blond. He turns to Jay and motions to put the gun on the ground. Jay shakes his head and grips it tighter.

I move a plant's green tendril to hit the intercom button again. "I'm alone here, if it makes you feel better. And I don't have a gun... within easy reach." I look at the stack of books next to my bed. A pistol sits on top.

The blond grabs Jay's shoulders, pleading, but the other boy simply stares into the intercom camera and holds the gun to his chest.

He'd rather die than come into my house unarmed? Jesus. Who knows what they've been through.

I groan. This kid is about to die on my doorstep because of his own stubbornness. I've buried bodies in the rocky ground before, but none this young.

Pushing the button, I open my cargo container's airlock. The boys whip their heads around and scramble in, the door slamming down after them. It floods with air and repressurizes.

On my airlock monitor, I see Jay breathing deeply. Tears stream down the blond's cheeks through the red dust. He scoops Jay into a ferocious hug, gripping his silver jacket so hard I think it might rip.

The kids hold each other like that until I press the button to open the door to my home. They separate, tense and defensive, hurt wolf pups ready to bite. Jay raises the gun, but his hands are shaky, uncertain.

"That was pretty fucking stupid," I say. "Put the gun down. I'm not going to hurt you."

The blond wipes his tears. Jay lowers the gun. That's better.

Martian-born kids. They're slimmer, muscles softer than mine were, growing up on Earth. They walk with a graceful float in their step, no muscle memory of Earth's gravity weighing down their every move. They remind me of birds – hollow bones.

Jay is short, on the childish side of his teen years, with red-brown skin like the Martian dust. His eyes are honey. His blond friend is so pale I can see his blue veins. He's taller than Jay and his wide eyes dart around my home.

I gesture for them to sit at the scrap-metal table. They do, and Jay lays the gun by his feet.

"I'm Melanie. Tea?"

"Uh, yes please," says the blond. "I'm Ben."

I busy myself over at the sink, filling a pot with water and setting it on the thermal pad to heat.

"So, what are two kids doing out in the Martian desert with a failing regulator?" I scoop dried herbs into three mesh metal balls and set each in a mug.

"Got lost on a school trip," says Ben. "We were trying to walk back to our settlement when the beeping started. *Bookseller* is the only thing on the map in this part of the desert. We knew you were our only hope for getting air."

I snort. "I didn't know I was a feature on any maps." Maps of Mars are rarely accurate, anyway, often scrawled on wheat husk paper after a long journey. But if these boys go to school, it means they're from the SpaceCorp settlement – the only place with the resources to build any real infrastructure. The most organized settlement we have. And the most vicious. Perhaps they have half-decent maps. What they definitely don't have, however, is school trips. These boys are liars. And most likely, runaways. "Aren't you lucky you managed to find me."

I feel the cold tip of a gun at my back. Damn.

"Why'd you tell us you were alone?" asks Jay. "I see two plates stacked up there on your drying rack. Two cups. Two forks. You got a boyfriend hiding here?"

I flick a look at my drying rack.

"Girlfriend," I say. "And no. She's gone. Just a few days ago... I – I didn't have the heart to put it all away yet, if you must know."

On Mars, you get used to reading the truth in someone's voice. I guess he hears mine.

"Oh." The gun moves away from my back.

"She isn't dead." I can't stand for this kid's sympathy to be wasted on the idea of Cara. "Just gone. Apparently, life in a settlement is more interesting than here surrounded by badly written books." I slam the teas down and slump into my seat. Jay and Ben watch me warily. "Now, if you're quite done threatening me, maybe we can enjoy this tea."

Ben kicks Jay under the table. "Uh, yeah. Sorry," Jay manages.

"So... uh, you make all this yourself?" Ben gestures around my cargo container home. Masters of conversation, these two.

I look around. He doesn't mean the greenhouse extension, the shelves, or the tins of preserved foods, which, as a matter of fact, I did make myself. He means the towers of books that line every wall.

"They don't call me the bookseller for nothing," I shrug.

"How'd you do all this?" A spark of wonder lights Ben's blue eyes. Now, even in my lonely, heartbroken state, I'm not going to destroy what might be the only spark of wonder currently on Mars.

I sigh. "After the starships landed, everyone in the settlements started acting out the sequel to the earthly apocalypse — real Mad Max shit. I ran out here into the desert alone and popped my cargo container. Raised myself until I got an infected cut and had to venture back into a settlement to trade my food for medicine. While I was there, I met a guy who'd pulp wheat husks and turn it into paper. I came back and traded all my preserves for five notebooks."

"That's a bad trade," says Ben.

"I know," I snort. "But I wasn't in the healthiest state of mind. Anyway, I started by re-writing the classics, from memory, as well as I could. Everything I'd been studying in school on Earth. Some part of me knew they were worth saving and I'm glad I did. They sold first when I went back to the settlement to trade. Then, people started visiting me, threatening me, demanding I write the books they'd left behind. Soon, they realized they'd get better stories if they were kinder. Creativity can't exactly flourish at gunpoint."

They'd wanted the stories so desperately. You see, when your home is burning or filled with your dying family, you don't think to bring your favorite book or e-reader as you escape. You just get your weapon and get yourself to the launch site by any means necessary. And on Mars, there's no infrastructure to build phones or TVs. Our exodus from Earth meant we left all our stories behind.

"People told me plots and I spun them into books. And now, that's all I do, rewriting shittier versions of the books we had on Earth."

"And it's safe here?" asks Ben. "Settlers don't ever raid you?"

"I rewrote *The Handmaid's Tale* for the leader of a raider gang a while back. It's been particularly quiet since then. Maybe she put in a good word for me."

I sip my tea. Indeed, my customers are hard, bitter people. Did you ever see those pictures of a fox or a crocodile or a bear — some creature that is all claws and bite — with a butterfly landing on their nose? They used to put those pictures in cheap yearly calendars. Anyways, the biter closes their eyes and they let the butterfly land, because behind the claws there's a soft warm creature that just wants a nap in the sun. In my little cargo container, killers rest and tell me about their favourite books. They ask me to write a story. And I do, because sometimes, I see the horror and the haunt slip away. Just for a moment.

"So basically, you just hide out here and sell stories to the dangerous assholes who come through?" asks Jay.

"I —" Ouch. "Better than being stranded in the desert on a school trip... or are you running away from SpaceCorp?"

Jay's hand drifts down to his gun.

"Hands where I can see them. Or I won't be fixing that regulator of yours."

His hand shoots back to his lap. "You can fix it?"

I nod. "Put your gun up there, next to mine. On top of that stack of books."

Jay waits for a consenting look from Ben and then stands, placing the gun next to mine.

"Much better. Now, give me your regulator."

He fishes it out of his nose, wipes it on his trousers, and sets it on the table.

"Right, I'll get to it. You guys can wait over there," I gesture to the pile of pillows and blankets that serves as my sofa. I tell them they can help themselves to whatever food or books they want, as long as they're quiet.

They busy themselves raiding my shelves. Ben munches on some dried carrot chips I made last week. Jay stares out the kitchen window at the endless red ocean.

I open my box of tools, grab the magnifying glass, and get to work. But a few minutes in, I lean back in my chair.

"Who made this regulator?" I ask.

"Does it matter?" Jay snaps.

"Kind of. It's a piece of shit."

It's more than that. This regulator isn't like the one I took from the SpaceCorp boxes when I landed, built to last a lifetime. It's flimsy, designed to break after a few days. Why would anyone make this? Nothing on Mars is disposable. Every scrap we have is precious, used carefully, made for a reason. Sending someone out with this is a death sentence.

"Can you fix it, though?" asks Jay.

"I don't know. It's going to take me a little longer."

Ben sat up. "How much longer? We uh... we need to get moving soon."

"Why? Someone coming after you?"

He looks at the carrot chips in his hand.

"Fine, don't tell me. But I need at least a day or two on this."

"Shit."

"Up to you."

The boys whisper to each other in the corner.

"We can't pay you for fixing the regulator. Or for letting us stay while we do," says Jay, finally.

"Oh." On Mars, nothing is free. "Then you can help out here – the greenhouse needs fixing up and I've been meaning to repair the shelves."

The boys nod, relieved. I set them up with their tasks and then spend a few hours tinkering with the regulator. In the evening, I warm up some soup for dinner and they sit on the blankets, flipping through my handwritten books and asking questions. It feels good to speak to someone, again.

The next morning, I go back to work on the regulator. The Martian time slips by, quiet and red.

"*To Kill a Mockingbird*?" asks Ben, in the afternoon. "What is it, like a guide?"

"Sure, it's a guide. But not one to do with birds," I say. Jay looks up from the old drillbug he's trying to fix.

"I don't get it," says Ben.

"Sit and read it and you will," I say.

"It's long."

"Ah but it's worth it. Books are more nourishing than you know."

Jay and Ben share a look — a hint of a laugh, a twist of embarrassment on my behalf. Not quite an eye roll, but nearly. I smile. My little brother and I shared that exact look about the nearest clueless adult countless times. He didn't make it past the first wave of sickness back on Earth.

I shake my head. "Take it."

Ben's eyebrows shoot up and he looks at Jay. Jay smiles.

"Well, thanks." Ben holds it gentler now, flipping softly through the pages.

That book is worth three weeks of food in a trade. I can practically see Cara in the corner, chastising me about economic irresponsibility. Well, she isn't here.

Ben reads my rehashed version of *To Kill a Mockingbird* and I watch him out of the corner of my eye. It's one of the few books with words I know I've written right. The lady who commissioned the first copy had the text tattooed on her shoulder, "*I wanted you to see what real courage is, instead of getting the idea that courage is a man with a gun in his hand. It's when you know you're licked before you begin, but you begin anyway and see it through no matter what."*

I always liked that quote.

The next day, the intercom buzzes like a yellowjacket. I flick a look toward the screen.

Now, these are the kind of guests I'm used to. A man and a woman stand tall, decked out in cobbled-together desert-gear and heavy-duty boots. Their faces are obscured by rags. Guns hang from their shoulders and grenades from their belts. Raiders or SpaceCorp, I can't tell. All the same, anyway — grizzly bears.

"Good morning," I say over the intercom. "You've reached the bookseller."

"You seen two boys out here?"

"Hard to say. Who are you?"

"Retrievers, from the SpaceCorp school. Those two students killed a member of staff and ran away. We've come to ensure they receive proper punishment."

Shit. I take my hand off the intercom and spin toward Ben and Jay.

"Is that true?" I don't want trouble.

Ben shakes his head. Jay nods.

"We each killed a guy," says Jay. He talks fast like he can see I'm spooked. "But they made us, as part of our training. That's why we ran away."

"Training?"

"It's not a school. They're training kids as soldiers and planning to take over the other settlements by force and form a proper country, led by them. They haven't come to punish us. They want to stop the truth getting out before they're ready."

This is huge. Finally making the settlements into one city, united, makes sense. Resources could be shared. A society could be built. Well, that's what logic says. In practice, the one settlement that SpaceCorp already runs is brutal, with settlers fighting over scraps from the people at the top. A takeover is going to be violent. And bloody.

The intercom buzzes again.

"Bookseller," says the man on the intercom. "Did you see the boys?"

I press the mic. Ben's hand twitches on *To Kill a Mockingbird*.

"Yes," I say. "I have seen the boys." Jay scrambles to grab his gun. "They passed through here a few days ago and left. Said they were heading to the northern settlement. One of them had a broken regulator. I doubt they'll have made it far."

The man and woman nod. This is no surprise to them. They know those regulators don't last.

"So you just let them go?" says the woman.

"Obviously. I don't need two more mouths to feed. If they want to get themselves killed in the desert, that's on them."

The man and woman scuff around in the dust, whispering to one another.

"On behalf of SpaceCorp, we're requesting entry to your home, bookseller. To trade for supplies," says the man.

"I've got nothing to trade but books."

"That'll do."

He's clearly not coming in for books.

I consider my options.

"Guns stay outside. That's my policy."

On the little screen, the man nods and hands his gun to the woman. She takes a few steps back, looking at the perimeter of my house. No doubt making sure no figures escape as her colleague searches inside.

Behind me, Ben and Jay's panicked whispers fill the air. I usher them under my bed and pass them my pistol. Their wide-eyed faces disappear as I throw a blanket over the bed.

Pushing the button, I open the airlock and the man walks in. It repressurizes.

It's not ideal. If he finds them, then what? Can I feasibly say that I didn't know they were there?

Another press of a button and the man is in my home. He lowers his mouth rag. His face is pitted and scarred, like the surface of our new home.

"I'll take a look around now," he says. He's done us both a favor by dropping the pretense.

"Go ahead," I say.

He walks along the towers of books, and I look at my home of over a decade with fresh eyes. Not many hiding spots. The bed is glaringly obvious.

The man drops to his knees to check out the entrance to the greenhouse. He stands and cocks his head, reading the spine of a book on a precarious stack. My rendition of *The Catcher in the Rye*.

"Interested?" I ask.

"No," he says. "I've heard your prices. I'm not in the market to waste three weeks' worth of food on a book." His eyes linger on it, though.

"Well, they take me a long time to write. You read this one back on Earth?"

"Uh, yeah. As a matter of fact, I did."

"Go on then, what did you do, before? Office guy?"

He considers me. "I was a teacher in New York," he says, finally. "Math. Always liked that book, though."

"Bet it's a bit different now, working at SpaceCorp."

His face clouds over and he looks away. Wrong thing to say. Don't remind killers of what they are. I've become too used to the truthful simplicity of my conversations with the boys. This feels like a deadly chess match that I'm being forced to play once again.

His eyes catch on the three mugs in that damn drying rack. The plates. He sighs and walks towards the bed.

"Don't you miss stories?" I ask.

He turns back. "Let me just get this over with, lady."

I ignore him. "There's no TV here. No cinema. I think that's why people like my books. Medicine for the mind – a way to get lost."

He blinks. More people need a mental escape on Mars than they're willing to admit.

"If only there were a way for you to procure a story without having to trade your hard-earned food."

I take *Catcher in the Rye* off the stack of books and hold it out to him.

His face is a mirror-image of Ben's when I gave him *To Kill a Mockingbird*. On Mars, you only own what you need to survive.

Slowly, he reaches out to take the book. He holds it in both hands, eyes roving over Cara's illustration of the cover. It's beautiful, like everything else she created. He flips open the first page, gently.

"So... have you found what you're looking for?"

"Perhaps."

His eyes flick to the bed again. What's the price for two kids' lives?

"Take another," I say. "For the road."

He spins around and looks at the stack of books next to him. *Percy Jackson and The Olympians*. He pulls it out quickly and stuffs both books into the inside of his jacket pocket.

"My students used to love Percy Jackson," he says. "Back on Earth."

That's the thing about my sanctuary – even killers have an inner child. And stories help them find their way back out.

"I bet," I say and indicate the airlock.

He nods. I push the button and he walks out into the Martian desert.

I rush to the intercom screen. Outside, he gestures, talking to his colleague. She questions him. He shrugs. She tips her head, and they kick around in the dust for a while. Then, they turn and go.

My hands are shaking, white.

"You can come out," I say.

The boys scramble out from under the bed. Ben runs at me and hugs me. Jay hovers behind. "Thank you," he says.

Ben lets me go and I exhale all the tension.

To think, Cara left because of how quiet life was here with me, how slow.

We collapse at the table.

"So, you guys ran away from SpaceCorp. No destination in mind?"

"Not exactly," says Jay. "A few weeks ago, these girls from the year above broke into the SpaceCorp offices. They read through a bunch of documents. Plans for the new country, breakthroughs in terraforming. The girls stole the papers and a bunch of supplies then ran away to start a new settlement. A hidden one for Martian kids, where we can try to build something better."

"And you're going to follow them. How do you know their regulators didn't break?"

"These girls are smart. Their regulators didn't break."

"Do you even know where they are?"

"They've gone to the western mountain." Jay's face looks young, hopeful.

I consider these two Martian kids. They aren't killers. They don't have claws and fangs. Maybe they're the butterflies on the predator's nose. Or I'm confusing my metaphors; I said they were hollow-boned birds, right? Either way. They are a thing with wings. And they see a future on Mars, one away from the suffering and the violence.

"Well, then I'd best get that regulator fixed up for you," I say.

The boys spend the evening browsing my shelves while I tinker and process the impending doom of a SpaceCorp takeover.

An unfamiliar noise fills my home. I look up. It's the boys, laughing. They're reading bits of a book to one another, acting out scenes with big, exaggerated movements. I tilt my head. *The Hitchiker's Guide to the Galaxy*. How strange, to hear laughter. Not the broken half-hearted chuckle of a killer. Not the condescending bark of a lover who's sick to death of my company. No, laughter like... in a family's home.

I squeeze my eyes shut against a wave of unwanted emotion, and the tears that threaten to follow. What is wrong with me? If I didn't know better, I'd say I didn't want the boys to go.

The next morning, after breakfast, I spend a final few hours on the regulator. I reinforce Ben's too, for good measure.

"Alright," I say. "Your regulators are ready. Time to go. Quick."

"Why quick?" asks Jay, eyes darting, back on alert.

"I'm kicking you out. And myself, too."

"You're kicking yourself out?"

"I'm coming with you," I try to sound confident, like when I used to lead my little brother in the games we played. "You need supplies and a plan if you're going to make it west. I can provide at least part of that. Anyway, this hidden settlement will need books."

I clamp my lips shut against the confession that threatens to follow. That I can't stand to write here alone again, speaking only to killers and characters. That SpaceCorp won't allow a writer to live unmanaged, out in the desert alone. That one of their retrievers knows about me harbouring two fugitives and a bribe only lasts so long.

Ben tilts his head, looking at me with squinted eyes, like he hears my thoughts. He looks at Jay.

"You're right," says Jay. "The new settlement will need books. I hear they're very nourishing."

I exhale.

We spend the day packing supplies and planning our route. Finally, when we're ready, we insert our regulators. Then, we step out into the light of that faraway sun.

"Ok," I say. "Let's go."

We walk under the rocky outcropping and out towards the vast western horizon. I turn and look back at the little cargo container that has been my world ever since I escaped Earth. My refuge, filled with other people's stories. Now it's time to write my own.

*See Gaby Brogan's story "The Bookseller of Mars" online at
Metaphorosis.
If you liked it, leave a comment. Authors love that!
Remember to subscribe to our e-mail updates so you'll know when
new stories are posted.*

About the story

"The Bookseller of Mars" was inspired by a daydream about what would happen if someone sensitive, creative, and totally unequipped for the apocalypse managed to get herself onto a survivor spaceship heading to Mars. Where would she be ten years down the road in a lawless new settler society? She'd find herself a peaceful little nook away from the violence, most likely. So, in my mind, this character became a writer and bookseller, catering to the other survivors' need for stories. After a few years of this, I thought this character would be used to dealing with hardened survivors and would become an expert at walking this line between sensitive and guarded. That would be her life. But this just takes us to where the story begins.

When my sister and I were 10 and 11, my parents had two more kids — boys — disrupting our comfortable little all-girls club (+dad). My brothers changed my life with the energy they brought and now, even though we're over a decade apart in age, they're fantastic friends to me as well as great people. Drawing on this, two boys show up at the bookseller's door — changing her comfortable life and giving her a new perspective on family, as well as forcing her out of her shell and towards bold new decisions that shape who she is forever.

A question for the author

Q: What are you reading now?
A: *Other Minds: The Octopus, the Sea, and the Deep Origins of Consciousness.*
If I'm being honest, I've never had enough patience with non-fiction. I would much rather get lost in fantastic new worlds than read more about our own (isn't that what the news is for?!) However, this book was a gift so I was determined to give it a try. And I'm glad I did. The ocean is a fantastic alien world in itself. A few chapters in, I have found a profound new respect for our underwater friends. The idea that intelligent minds, so different from ours, have evolved on our planet is fascinating and tells us more about our own consciousness. Not to mention how inspiring this not-quite-human-intelligence is for a speculative fiction writer! The book is written by Peter Godfrey-Smith, a philosopher of science and scuba diver. As someone who also enjoys scuba diving, his insights have given me a new lens through which to view these explorations.

About the author

Gaby Brogan was raised in the UK and Italy on a steady diet of pasta and science fiction. Usually based in Amsterdam, she's now traveling and working from the road as a freelance copywriter. Whenever she can, she scribbles poetry and fiction, practices yoga, and goes out to explore.

The Antidote for Longing

Karl Dandenell

Part 2

Previously… Lars Bjornsen, the disgraced Swedish imperial poisoner, has been living in exile for the past three years because he failed to assassinate the son of the Russian tsar. One day, a messenger brings a letter from his old friend, the imperial physik Fredrik Magnusson. Fredrik informs Lars that Emperor Gustavus Adolphus is deathly ill and they believe him poisoned, though they cannot be certain. They need Lars' skills to determine a possible antidote before word gets out and triggers a succession crisis since Gustavus has no heir. Lars decides to assist Fredrik and fulfill his duty to the emperor, despite the threat of imprisonment and death that hangs over him every step of the way.

I considered the nondescript servant's entrance of Strömsholm Palace. As much as I wanted to see the brilliant gold-leaf plasterwork of the main doors again, I could appreciate the caution of this approach. With a deep breath, I straightened my cap and pulled the door open, revealing Fredrik Magnusson. He squinted against the daylight. "Lars, is that you?"

"Who else would it be, you old goat?" I said. The imperial physik's white hair and large, droopy mustache were a welcome sight, momentarily pushing aside my worries. His wool coat was dyed a simple green, although his tailor had added intricate patterns of gold thread along each cuff. "For the love of Saint Catherine, Fredrik, let's go inside before my nether regions freeze off."

"You southerners are so delicate," he said.

"Denmark is hardly Iberia."

"*Valkömmen*, my friend!" His strong arms embraced me. "The emperor's condition has not improved," he whispered, his mustache tickling my ear. "I'll tell you more once we have some privacy."

"It's good to see you, too." I held Fredrik a moment longer, then followed him through one of the kitchens, where he handed me a serving basket.

"Get us some *kanelbullar*, would you?" he said in a deliberately casual tone. The nearby tables were covered with trays of marzipan cookies, dried apple tarts, and rolls still warm from the ovens.

"I've never seen so many sweets outside Jultid." My mouth watered. I'd eaten only a spare breakfast and missed lunch due to the messenger's arrival.

"It's been like this for weeks," Fredrik said. "The emperor demands pastries at every meal, and between meals, and sometimes in the middle of the night. No wonder his dyspepsia has returned."

I filled our basket and inhaled deeply. "Oh, I've missed these." Järna's bakers, while skilled, were mere epigones to those of court.

Fredrik appropriated a coffee carafe and porcelain cups, then took me to a small chamber assigned to him. It was warm, with a cheery fire, a writing desk and chair, a bed, and two familiar items: a chaise lounge and a large chest of drawers holding his medical tools and herbs. As a member of court, Fredrik was allotted a large travel allowance of personal baggage. "Not up to the standards of Drottingholm, but comfortable."

"More comfortable than my first fortnight at Järna, I assure you." It had taken me months of wooing patrons before I could afford to replace my furnishings or even adequately heat my house.

He closed the door and poured coffee. "That will put some color in your cheeks."

I hung my coat by the fire. "So, you started a rumor the emperor had dyspepsia and gout?"

"It was Spymaster Viklund's idea," replied Fredrik.

"An excellent idea. Maja's always been clever." Dangerously so. I raised my cup and sipped. "Once the story made the rounds, I suspect the nobles and their respective entourages fled back to Stockholm as soon as they could make their excuses." Gustavus Adolphus's tolerance for fools was low at the best of times. Under duress of illness, he lost all sense of decorum and became the very model of the irrational autocrat his enemies imagined.

"Indeed," said Fredrik. "With only the family servants, guards, and a few senior advisors still in attendance, we may be able to resolve this problem before it becomes a public crisis." He sounded confident but chewed his mustache nervously.

I was once well-acquainted with the emperor's inner circle and maintained a well-annotated mental map of political relationships, much like I had organized my battalions in the Prussian campaigns. Yet it had been three years since my last appearance at court, which meant my intelligence was woefully outdated. As much as I hated to admit it, I had depended extensively on Maja's insight. She'd whispered secrets across the pillow rather than words of love. Now I was left only with Fredrik's gossip. I sighed inwardly. "When did the *actual* illness start?"

"About a week ago. We've been touring the provinces, as one does, taking the measure of the nobles, before the official birthday celebration a week after Epiphany."

I tore a roll in half and dipped it. "I remember Gustavus's sixtieth. Quite the fete." The entire event had been so expensive that every noble was assessed a special levy above and beyond their expected 'gift' to the emperor.

"This one is much worse," said Fredrik, shaking his head. "Days on the road. Nights filled with feasts, concerts, dances, and parties. Even the strongest veteran from the Scottish campaigns would have found the pace challenging, let alone an elderly man who sleeps with eight feather pillows."

I said, "His Majesty used to jest that if the Society of Poisoners could find ways to prolong men's lives as easily as end them, we'd all be rich as Croesus. You poor physiks would have naught to do but pull rotten teeth and treat the pox."

Fredrik frowned at the barb. "As I was saying, His Majesty's personal servants called upon him at the usual hour but could not rouse him. Fearing illness, they summoned me.

"My examination found only a slight fever, though his heart sounded like a newly captured bird flinging itself against its cage. With some reluctance, my suspicions turned to poison."

"As wonderful as it is to see you, my friend, you risked your reputation"—and possibly my life—"by bringing me here. Wouldn't it have been easier to consult... Lord Anders?" I couldn't bring myself to say the *current imperial poisoner*.

Fredrik folded his hands. "Most definitely not. Anders Selberg is dead."

"What?" I set aside my roll, my appetite gone.

"Josef, one of the footman, found him collapsed at his writing desk, a suicide note under his hand."

"Poor *gubbe*." As much as I'd disliked Anders—he'd always been a status-seeking popinjay—he'd been a member of the Society. At the end of the day, he deserved the benefit of the doubt. I spoke a short prayer to Saint Catherine.

Fredrik said, "My thought is the villain tried to poison the emperor and having failed, took his own life to avoid a lengthy and painful confession at the hands of the spymaster before his eventual execution."

"That's one possibility." Maja might have been a gentle and kind lover, but her public persona lacked mercy. "Another possibility is a larger plot, but Anders wasn't part of it. When he discovered it, the assassins killed him. Or he took his own life out of shame. I probably would." Poisoners swore on their lives to obey and protect their sovereign.

"If that were the case, why didn't he say something?" Fredrik scratched his beard. "*Oj!* There'll be time enough later to invent conspiracies. What we have to do right now is treat the emperor."

"Agreed. I'll need to examine him."

"Ah," said Fredrik. "That might prove difficult. I'm the only one allowed to see him. Spymaster Viklund's orders."

"Where is the emperor now?"

"In the winter guest bedchamber."

"We are in luck, then," I said. "Come with me."

Fredrik set a cocked beaver hat with a gold brooch on his head and followed me down several hallways, passing liveried servants, until we reached a gallery of large tapestries and oil paintings. The entire space was quiet as a church, confirming Birgitta's report that the strolling lute players were idle.

I stopped before a depiction of Vilhelm the Conqueror astride a white warhorse and pointed out the thread's vibrant colors. You could almost see the wind whipping the animal's mane.

The demon lamps cleverly positioned to either side cast almost no shadow, creating an overall effect of afternoon summer light. "The Duke of Uppland spares no expense to display his artwork," I said.

"Or perhaps he brought them in special for His Majesty's visit," said Fredrik. "There's old soot on the wall over here that smells of whale oil."

An older bewigged servant strode through the gallery, his wooden heels clicking against the stone. As he passed, he paused and bowed toward Fredrik. "Good morning, Lord Physik. Do you have a question regarding the tapestry?"

"No, no, I'm fine."

The servant turned to me. "And you, General?"

"None, thank you."

"Very well. If you need anything, please don't hesitate to ask. My name is Oskar." He bowed.

"Wait, I do have a question," I said. "Are you familiar with Madame Torstenson's restaurant near Ulriksdal?"

"I have dined there," said Oskar.

"Tell me," I said, "does she still have a private room for cards?"

"Very much so." He lowered his voice. "Though I am sad to inform you she now requires a fee to play."

"Scandalous!" I dug in my pocket for a silver stag. "Here," I said. "Please partake the next time you're there."

Oskar nodded. "Many thanks, sir." He continued on his way. I waited a good minute, listening carefully to his departing footsteps and my pounding heart.

"Why did you do that?" asked Fredrik. "I thought you wished to remain inconspicuous."

"I gave him a coin and no name. Such transactions are anonymous." There was some risk, admittedly, but it had been so *long* since I'd heard any gossip from Stockholm that I couldn't help myself.

"Let us proceed." I felt the wall along the tapestry's edge until I found a familiar slot. "Here we are." I pressed the recessed keys in sequence. There was a soft click and a panel swung inward, revealing a hidden passageway. "Quickly! I'll be right behind you."

Fredrik ducked under the edge of the tapestry. I slipped in and closed the door behind us. "Bide a moment." On a shelf adjacent to the door, I located a patch box with a goodly supply of char cloth and beeswax candles. A minute later, I'd coaxed enough flame to light a candle.

"Where does this lead?" said Fredrik.

"Several places, including the winter bedchamber," I replied. "When I trained here with Maja, she used to bring secret couriers through or arrange assignations, depending on the visitor."

"You trained with the spymaster herself?" He sounded impressed.

"She wasn't the spymaster then," I said.

"Surely you don't expect me to believe that was the only thing you did together," said Fredrik.

"I will say only we shared common interests," I replied. The Society had taught me the best poisoner is an amalgam of physik and spy, and Maja had been quite willing to explore those territories with me. "Best we keep quiet now."

We soon arrived at a plain wooden door with a dusty brass knob, which I took as a sign that no one had passed this way recently.

Fredrik pressed his ear to the door. "I hear nothing," he whispered, and slowly turned the knob.

We emerged into a room dominated by a large, canopied bed. Upon it lay Gustavus Adolphus, Emperor of Scandinavia and Northern Europe, including Prussia, Austria, and the Netherlands.

Small demon lamps and a banked fire cast a soft glow over the scene. "We're alone," Fredrik said. "Go ahead."

I quickly examined my sovereign. The years since our last meeting had not been kind. His face was thinner and more lined, the skin pale, almost waxy. His pupils were dilated and did not shrink when I brought a lamp close to his face. I also confirmed he was breathing shallowly, though his heart was indeed working harder than it should. *What had they done to him?*

With great care, I tilted the emperor's head and exposed the tongue, which had a peculiar dark coating. Taking my kerchief, I rubbed it over the tongue to get a sample. Finally, I straightened the bedclothes, noting the old man's aroused state.

We returned to the secret passage and I directed Fredrik to another exit that opened into a book-filled chamber: the emperor's traveling library. The glowing coals in the fireplace did little to chase away my chill.

"I fear God will have the emperor all too soon unless I devise an antidote," I said.

Fredrik chewed the edges of his mustache. "You think it's a poison, then."

"It's not one of the Twenty Nine poisons, but it certainly has the *feel* of one," I said. Something about the emperor's condition resonated in memory like a distant church bell, familiar yet quickly fading.

"If you can't recognize the poison, nor I the disease, we are lost," said Fredrik.

"I would give my best winter coat to talk to Lord Anders right now. I'm sure he could enlighten us."

"If you could talk to Lord Anders, the bishop would burn you for a witch," said Fredrik. "However, we might divine something from his room."

An old woman wearing a stained, shapeless dress and worn leather shoes was sweeping up shards of pottery and glass as we entered Anders' chamber. A tall young footman stood nearby, feeding the fire with pages that he tore from a notebook.

"Javlar!" shouted Fredrik. *Devils!* "What's going on here, Josef?"

The woman dropped her eyes and bent into a stuttering curtsey, her joints crackling. Josef said, "The chamberlain ordered this chamber cleaned, Lord Physik," and ripped out another page.

"Did he also tell you to destroy imperial records?" I spoke with as much authority as I could muster. "Get out, both of you."

The woman picked up her bucket and broom.

"Leave the bucket," I said. She bobbed her head and departed, followed by the footman, who offered the tattered notebook to me with the barest of bows.

Fredrik closed the door behind them. "I advise we search quickly."

"See what's in the desk," I said. "I'll peruse the wardrobe."

The wardrobe's main compartment held neat stacks of clothing: silk shirts, body linens, and hose. When I dug through the pockets of a sky-blue brocade jacket, I discovered a poisoner's flask, which I pocketed.

On the wardrobe's top shelf, I found Anders' poison kit. Inside lay neat rows of stoppered glass vials. Three vials were missing.

I scanned the remaining labels, deciphering the Society code. "Fredrik, have you found anything?"

He had laid out the desk's contents on the gilt blotter: spare candles, new quills, a small trimming knife with a bone handle, bottles of ink, and a novel. "Nothing interesting, unless you have a fancy for *The Sailor Returns to Tønsberg*." He fanned the pages and found a scrap of parchment serving as a bookmark. "Apparently," said Fredrik, skimming the page, "the titular character is fascinated by the baker's daughter, whose breasts are described in great detail. Ah, the agony of young love." He closed the book. "I'll bet you all the butter in Småland this was written by some poxy clerk whose only experience with women is gazing upon a statue of the Blessed Virgin. Useless. What of the notebook?"

I flipped through the remaining pages. "Mostly the words 'I have failed' and 'forgive me' and some scratched out lines. A draft of his suicide note, one presumes. The fire has the rest.

"Bring over a candle, Fredrik." I borrowed a pair of leather gloves from the wardrobe and carefully shook out the servant's bucket. Fredrik held the flame close, nearly singeing his beard as he leaned in. I picked through the glass until I found the poison kit's missing labels. "Something is amiss."

"How so?"

"This is *Ottoman Madness*, which is quick but agonizing. A poor choice for suicide."

"Perhaps he panicked and made a mistake," said Fredrik.

"Unlikely. A good poisoner always keeps a personal dose of *Dream Caller* or *Cloudless Sky* on hand to avoid capture." *And inevitable questioning.* "And even if Anders didn't, he had *Umber Sorrow* and *Autumn Sunset* in his kit." I shook my head. "As a member of the Society, Anders took an oath to protect the emperor at any cost. He would have given his life to fulfill that oath." I swept the glass into the bucket and stripped off the gloves. "I believe he was silenced to cover the attempted regicide."

"So they may try again," said Fredrik.

"It's what I would do," I admitted. "If His Majesty hadn't banished me, I would have returned to Moscow to finish the mission."

"Lars, please, we must focus." He squeezed my shoulder. "What poison would have manifested such symptoms in the emperor?"

"*Mad Monk* would explain the heartbeat, but the deep sleep is more akin to *Miner's Fate*." An old memory arose, tinged with nostalgia, but I couldn't quite hold it.

"Could we not try treat the emperor for both to be sure?"

"That's not a wise course," I said. "Honestly, I am at loss." My stomach growled.

" 'Hungry is stupid'," said Fredrik, quoting one of our old academy lecturers. "Let's get you a proper meal and then perhaps things will make more sense."

"You're probably right." I picked up the notebook. Fredrik winked and grabbed the novel.

Once we were safely ensconced in Fredrik's chamber, he put the novel on the desk and tossed a log on the fire. I eased onto the chaise and pulled my shoulders back, everything cracking and popping. "Damn that carriage."

"They are difficult on one's bones," said Fredrik. "Do you want a brandy?"

"After some food."

"I'll scavenge something once I check on the empress." He poked the fire. "The fewer people who see you, the better."

"We've been lucky so far," I said. "Why are you seeing the empress? Is she also ill?"

"Tired and irritable. Not sleeping well, apparently," he said. "Until recently, Empress Anna has been visited by her husband most nights on this tour. So says her maid." Fredrik rose and brushed a bit of ash from his trousers. "Throw the bolt behind me. I'll give the academy knock when I get back."

I rapped the chair frame with my knuckles: a six-beat staccato signaling a proctor was patrolling the dormitory.

"Perfect," said Fredrik. "I'll return forthwith."

I bolted the door as instructed, then stretched out, thinking a short rest might restore my wits. When I closed my eyes, though, all I could see was Anders' face stretched in agony after consuming *Ottoman Madness*.

In Lapland, there was a monastery called the Eternal Crevasse. As part of my Society training, I spent an autumn there studying the monks and their astonishing immunity to seventeen of the Twenty Nine poisons. The key, they said, was an ancient breathing practice and daily recitation of an eight-word Norse prayer handed down by the gods themselves.

For years, the Society had tried to reproduce this secret knowledge. How much easier would assassinations become if the poisoner could drink from the same cup as the target?

The monks taught me the prayer and sat next to me for hours, working my belly like a bellows to infuse me with freezing air and divine presence.

My efforts failed, like the other poisoners before me. Fortunately, my compatriots were able to administer the antidote before the swallow of *Miner's Fate* froze my lungs completely.

Since then, I had occasionally returned to the breathing practice when fatigued or struggling to face another day of false smiles and empty platitudes from my patrons.

I set the candle close by and placed both hands on my belly. With an eye on the flame, I filled and emptied my lungs as forcefully as possible. After two hundred breaths, a great sense of calm descended on me, reminiscent of my first taste of *Dream Caller*.

Dream Caller.

I retrieved Ander's flask from my pocket. When I unscrewed the top, the odor that emerged was not, as I expected, the copper and rosemary of *Dream Caller*. Nor was it the earthy petrichor of *Ottoman Madness*. It was something else entirely: thickly sweet like honey or burned sugar. It was the aroma of Christmas dinner at the Imperial Academy with its giant gingerbread castle and caramel-mortared battlements.

Someone knocked at the door. "Not now!" I rummaged for my kerchief. Held it close to my nose, inhaling deeply. Closed my eyes and slipped into memory.

A party. Music and drunken laughter. Students in their finery, handing out goblets of punch....

The knocking repeated. Six beats.

The memory vanished. "All right!"

I threw open the door. Fredrik stood there, balancing a tray piled with cold meats, breads, cheeses, and more pastries.

"Help me, will you?

I took the tray. He bolted the door, then cleared a space on the desk.

"I bear good tidings!" From his coat, he produced a bottle of brandy and two tiny glasses. "The empress is with child!" he whispered fiercely. He uncorked the brandy, practically dancing.

"Most excellent tidings, sir," I said. "Thank Saint Catherine."

"Indeed. I can't wait to tweak the spymaster's nose. Once the emperor is well, of course." He filled our glasses. *"Skål!"*

"Skål." I drank, then proceeded to layer cheese on bread. "What tweaking would this be?"

He snagged a slice of ham. "She confided her worry that the emperor might be too old to father a child. She hinted—with all the care and subtlety you'd expect from her—that there might be something I could do."

"An aphrodisiac?"

"Clearly." He raised his glass. "I informed her that I was the imperial physik, not some weird woman huddling over a cauldron in the forest. If God wanted the emperor to have another child, He would provide." Fredrik chewed noisily. "The best thing I could do was encourage husband and wife to cleave unto each other. Which they have been."

"Apparently our Lord agreed with your suggestion." I broke open a roll, releasing scents of marzipan and burnt sugar. It smelled like Gustavus's mouth.

"Fredrik?"

"Hmm?" He said, topping up his glass.

"How long has the baker been making extra marzipan rolls? And the other sweetmeats?"

"I'm not sure. Perhaps a few months."

"*After* you had this exchange with Maja?"

"I think so, yes," he said.

The facts were starting to form a worrisome pattern. "When I examined the emperor earlier, did you happen to notice his state of arousal?"

"I took it as a sign of his general health and vitality."

"What about last night, and this morning, before you sent for me? Was he the same?"

Fredrik frowned. "He was, though I fail to see how that matters."

The hairs of the back of my neck rose. "And you're positive the empress is gravid?"

"I wouldn't make a proclamation in Stockholm's central *torget* just yet, but yes, she is. What has the blessed event have to do with the emperor's illness?"

"Because he's been poisoned," I said. *Anders, you fool. What were you thinking?*

He fixed me with a serious look. "But you said it wasn't one of the known poisons."

"I said it wasn't one of the Twenty Nine. Strictly speaking, it's hardly a poison at all. But it is known within the Society." I took a bite of my sandwich. "We call it *Sweet Agony.*"

See parts I and II of Karl Dandenell's story "The Antidote for Longing" online at Metaphorosis.
If you liked it, leave a comment. Authors love that!
Remember to subscribe to our e-mail updates so you'll know when new stories are posted.

September

That Lonesome, Restless Feeling

B. Morris Allen

Outside the house, a placard swung slightly in the twilight breeze. To and fro, to and fro, never making any progress as it moved in complex helices at hundreds of meters per second through the solar system, or hundreds of kilometers per second through the galaxy. Motion was a matter of perspective.

The house had never moved. It stood where it always had, where it had stood throughout their marriage. It would never move, until the great Northwest earthquake finally came and flung it toward the Pacific. Then, at last, the closets would open, the drawers would break, and there would be chaos until the tsunami came and washed it all clean.

It had always been clean, of course. Always spotless, always ordered, always neat, until she returned from a trip with her dusty luggage, her tacky gifts, her long-winded stories. Madhup had cleaned them up, labeled them, put them away for future use. Madhup had always known where they were, what they were for, when they'd last been touched. And she, Bettina, had relied on that, let her own memory atrophy. She'd wiped it clean with every arrival, left it empty to be filled again, on her next trip out to Centauri, or Aldebaran, or some unnamed new system, with unnamed new planets.

She'd left her memories here, in this dark house, on the grey Oregon coast, stored away with bookends and croquet sets and nameless artifacts. Madhup had stored them, kept them, known that without them, Bettina was not Bettina, was not the galactic traveller, the intrepid explorer, the feted hero.

"Without you, I'm nothing," she whispered to the gloom of the hallway. It was hardly a room at all — just a wide space where real rooms came together. The stairs to the dormitory, seldom used; the doors to the laundry, the guest bath, the library, the guest room.

Grand names for empty spaces. And this plain hallway, with its entries and exits and its shallow linen closet. Hardly a room at all. And yet it had a ghost.

"You always were thorough, Madhup." After the funeral, when she'd unpacked, when she'd had time to look around, when she'd looked for something to fill her time, she'd found the folder, neatly labeled, in the middle of the library desk. Doctors, crematoria, wills, accounts, utilities, passwords. Everything was there. Everything but Madhup. For that, there were the ghosts.

She hadn't seen them, at first. She'd stared down at the folder, watching it blur and blur until the ocean broke her walls and spilled out all over the neat, printed label, turning 'After death' into a confusing, smudgy mess of ink and paper.

She'd cried and cried, curled into a corner of the tiny library, face pressed into the books until she realized she was pushing them out of line, and then turned the other way and cried some more. When at last the sea was empty, her heart wrung tight until it hurt, she let it go, let it curl like a wounded animal in the cage of her chest, wanting and fearing to be free. That was when she'd seen the ghost.

It wasn't ghostly. It was Madhup, solid, stolid, serious. Working with her files, with a softscreen hung from the windowsill, a keyboard at her fingertips. Spreadsheets, documents, investments — dull things, important things. She didn't moan or shake or turn to mist. She didn't look up, not even when Bettina scrambled to her feet, launched herself bodily at her wife, scrabbling, grabbing, gabbling.

"You're not... you're here... you're alive!" But of course she wasn't. She was a hint of ashes spread across the beach, blown into the surf, eaten by molecrabs or sand hoppers.

And yet, she'd sat there, solid, unmovable, typing her figures, scrolling her documents. Dutiful and unresponsive. Lost in her own world, as she had liked to say, 'without even leaving the house.'

Bettina had sat there for hours, watching, holding, feeling Madhup's dead heartbeat. She'd cajoled, entreated, threatened. She'd tried to take the keyboard, to stop the fingers, but ghosts were stronger than hope, it seemed. They played by their own rules.

She'd stayed for days, taking catnaps on the floor, or on the desk itself, half-curled on the corner still available. Frightened at every waking that Madhup would be gone again, and she'd be alone for real. But always the ghost was there, still typing, still working. It wasn't a loop, that she could see. Not a creation of the holojector she'd brought back from Tarsis IV as her first big find, the one that had bought them the house, paid off the loans, let Madhup do her research, Bettina her exploring.

Ghost Madhup did different things, used different files. But they were old, irrelevant. They said nothing to Bettina. Most of them she barely recognized. It was not until the second day that she noticed, finally looked carefully at the softscreen. At the upper right, a small icon — a little blob of text. The ghost never touched it, never tapped it. But the space was always clear; however the windows and desktops shifted, that one little icon was never covered.

The workspace was still there, of course, still stored on their little server, its passcodes carefully spelled out in Madhup's perfect, awful folder. Bettina pulled her glasscreens from her pocket, settled them on her nose, logged in. The desktop was bare, clean, save for one little icon. It did nothing when she tapped it, had no hidden information in the properties. At last, she zoomed the screen, and then she got it. It was just an icon, a tiny image of black text on white — a poem Bettina had written for Madhup, back when she'd thought she was an artist. It had been terrible — painful, hackneyed promises of love they'd both laughed about, agreeing that maybe Bettina should stick to exploring and adventure — the things that she was good at.

She'd cried a little more, then, but only a little. There were only so many tears a body could make, so much emotion a soul could take. She'd hugged the ghost again, and staggered out to fall asleep on the soft covers of the guest bed — always fresh, never musty, seldom used.

When she woke, the ghost was there. A younger ghost, a younger Madhup. A little chubbier, a little less grey, a little less certain. She stood in the doorway, looking in at the bed. She smiled, she shrugged, she flirted. She laughed, all soundless. She looked happy, then troubled, then happy again. And in her eyes, a hunger seemed to burn, that made her look lost and brave and vulnerable all at once.

Bettina had lain in bed and smiled, waved. Basked in this memory of the younger Madhup. Had called her over, knowing that the ghost would not respond, could not respond, that these were passive ghosts, for all they moved and acted. And despite entreaties and enticements, ghost Madhup never left the doorway, only glancing away from time to time when the troubled looks came across her brow.

After a while, Bettina had gotten up, stood next to the ghost, hugged it. It felt warm, comforting. It was just like the real

Madhup. It was Madhup, it seemed, when she'd been younger. From close up, she could see the lack of grey, the fainter wrinkles. Five years ago, maybe seven. Bettina had been gone a lot, then. She'd been exploring around Rigel, had always been on the point of the next big find, in promising ruins that turned out to be natural crystal formations, or in deep caverns that held nothing but ice. She'd barely been home at all, for about two years. They'd talked via long videos back and forth through courier bots. Madhup had never complained, never said how lonely she was, though Bettina had seen it in her eyes.

She'd realized then, standing next to the ghost, what she should have seen at first. It wasn't Bettina the ghost was looking at. Why would it be, lying in the guest bed? She'd never slept there, until today. It was a guest, of course. A guest who'd flirted, cajoled, entreated. A Madhup who'd laughed and giggled, and felt guilty.

Bettina had been angry then, confused. She hadn't known. Couldn't remember who'd visited then, or whether anyone had. That was Madhup's department, all the social arrangements, the friends, the schedules. Bettina's job was to find things, Madhup's in part to put them in their places.

She'd been alone. For years at a time, sometimes.

"But you never complained!" And why should she have? That was the way things were, the rules laid out by Bettina, the active one, the famous one, the one who got her way.

She sat on the bed, got up again, feeling the invisible, intangible presence of the other ghost, the one ghost-Madhup was winking at.

"Why this? Why show me this? Why save *this*?" For there was no doubt Madhup had done this, had selected these memories, had arranged her own haunting somehow.

Bettina turned to leave, to go… somewhere, to think. And yet, as she came to the door, to the sly, leering, potentially unfaithful Madhup, she paused. For this was Madhup too. This was her, and what she'd done, and what she'd felt. It was honest, as Madhup had always been honest. Even after death, when her ghost itself was an illusion, she was honest.

The ghost was always in the doorway. Just on the threshold. It never came inside. Never sat, and smiled a sultry smile, never ran a gentle hand along the leg that wasn't there. It burned with passion, but it burned alone.

That was the message, she supposed, and it was true. She'd left Madhup alone, and trusted her. She, out among the stars, with a ship and its robots as companions, had been focused on her work. It had never occurred to her that Madhup, alone among temptations, might feel lonely. Not in a real way. They'd talked about it, joked about it, but it had never really sunk beneath the surface of her mind. Yet it had happened. And Madhup had acted on it, or she had not. Either way, Bettina had contributed. And either way, it didn't really matter. What mattered was that there had been more to Madhup than she'd known, more than she had ever thought to explore.

She'd stumbled out to the kitchen, hungry and confused, and hurt by her own actions and inaction. There was food, of course, tidily labeled containers of frozen food she'd cooked herself, and that Madhup had divided and packaged and put away.

It had always surprised people, that Bettina was the one who cooked. 'I thought you were the' this type or that type, they liked to say. People liked to label things. Like Madhup, she admitted. Madhup had liked to label things, to organize them, to put them into boxes.

Her ghost sat now, on her little stool beside the pantry, where she'd always sat while Bettina cooked, marking pen in hand, wet wipe in the other. As Bettina's meal defrosted, ghost Madhup labeled and packed, sorted and cleaned. She wrote new labels on in her terrible handwriting, wiped old ones off with her little cloth, so that smudges of ink always got on her fingers, and they looked liked she'd contracted some dread disease.

'Something you brought back from Zubenelgenubi,' she always said, because she liked the name so much, couldn't believe it was a real star. 'A deadly alien virus from one of your gadgets.'

Because the gadgets weren't always obvious. They usually weren't. There were only a few that Bettina had immediately understood, had seen the use of, once she'd, via robot, pushed all the buttons, pulled all the levers. Most of them, she brought home to Madhup, to classify and test and send to experts. That was where most of the money came from — the little day-to-day sums that paid for the food, the utilities, the fuel for Bettina's ship, the lawyers to make sure the rights were locked down. She'd have to manage that on her own, now, or hire someone to do it. There would be names in Madhup's folder, a plan, step-by-step directions.

She ate in the kitchen, from an immaculate little bowl, a bean curd lasagna that she'd made weeks ago, before another trip, before she'd known about the cancer.

She watched ghost Madhup label spices and cereals, little plastic containers of frozen goulasch, big bags of alien gimcrack. For a while, she sat against her dead lover's knees, telling her all the stories again.

"I found that one in a city of broken crystal spheres. I cut my suit open, but I got a patch on in time. The city was all smashed into shards and powder, but it was beautiful, with the light from a blue sun refracting through the bits and throwing rainbows everywhere.

"That one was from a little satellite out in the middle of nowhere. It's incredible I found it; there was no system there at all, just a ring of dust with a radius of about 10 AUs. The satellite was right in the middle, right where a star should have been. Not really a satellite so much as a three dimensional metal frame, really. I felt bad about taking it, after. Maybe it was just a monument, or a piece of art.

"This one was from the same sector where I found the holojector, about 32 light years away. I thought at first it was the same folks — see how it has sort of that same filigreed cylinder look? But I could never figure out how it worked, so maybe it was someone else's.

"Ooh, that one. You remember that one, you got it working. The molecular needle, you called it, cause it makes stitches so small, and out of anything. You said it pays the property tax.

"This one..." She talked and talked, and ate again when the ghost moved back to foods and rolls of tape and carefully sorted cables. It looked happy, or at least content. Had it sat there, had Madhup sat there when Bettina wasn't home? Had she done familiar things to pretend Bettina was there, or had she had some other life, with different habits, different places? Whichever this was a memory of, it wasn't unhappy. That was enough.

She slept that night in the master bedroom, with its French doors open to the sound of waves, and the fog floating in through the screen. She curled around the warm, solid figure of Madhup's ghost, in its camisole and garish, ludicrous pajama pants. It felt alive. Its heart beat, its lungs breathed, it fidgeted. Mostly, though, it slept, and it snuggled. Sometimes in the back, curled up to face Bettina, so that she could lie facing its closed eyes and slightly smiling face, ghostly in the moonlight, or push herself back against it and imagine that its other arm wound around her, crossed between her breasts so that she could kiss it as she slept. Mostly it lay the other way, and Betting curled around its question mark shape, spooned like big dipper and small. 'Always with the astronomy,' Madhup had complained. But she'd come out to lie on the beach with Bettina anyway, to look where she pointed and to ooh and aah about invisibly distant stars she would never visit.

'I'm happy where I am,' she'd said. She'd visited Bettina's ship, the Lightfoot, one time. 'It's so cramped,' she'd said. 'And so

... plain.' As if a scoutship had room or mass for decorations and luxury. 'I need my beach and my eagles, and my garden, and my deer. I need seals, nasturtiums, whales, bluejays, crows, garlic, sand, surf, blackberries, rain.' All of which were right here, outside the house and sometimes in it. She fell asleep with her face deep in ghost hair, her hand tight against soft ghost belly. It was still there when she woke.

She ate pancakes with the cataloging ghost, shaking pancake mix from a labeled container, dropping in frozen huckleberries from the garden. She didn't tell any stories as alien artifacts passed through dead hands, only watched as they were slid into padded containers and labeled with scrawled but detailed notes, due to be replaced later with machine printed ones that a person could actually read. When the ghost started packing fresh blueberries into plastic freezer containers, she kissed it on the head, and went to wash.

The bathroom was a horror. In the tub, chest deep in steaming water, a wasted ghost shivered as it wiped loose grey hairs from its mottled scalp, and set them apologetically on the rim. It smiled, a horrific rictus of thin lips and skin, and held its bony hand out for help. Dripping wet, it staggered out two steps to the toilet, and retched and retched and retched, until the water was pink and the bowl streaked with crimson.

Bettina held the ghost Madhup's hair, what was left of it, and wiped its face clean while she cried. It looked at her with a depth of devotion so absolute that she felt her heart begin to tear within her chest. She left before it came completely loose of its stitches.

She showered in the guest bath, whose ghost did nothing worse than brush healthy gums and draw little hearts on the steamed-up glass with M + B inside. She avoided it and left to sit on the master bed. Beside her, a healthy dead woman slumbered and drooled a bit from a slightly open mouth.

After half an hour of blankness, her mind empty of coherent thought, she was no further along. With a trepidation that bordered almost on fear, she went back to the bathroom to face her memories.

For hours, she bathed the ghost, and held its hair, and wiped its face, and helped it stand and sit, in a long and painful cycle with no defined start or end. It washed and dried, and vomited and defecated, all with a look of gratitude and love that broke her heart over and over and over, until she felt there was nothing left but dust.

It was the most painful of memories, brought back from the dead, condensed to relive as often as she could stand. She stood it until evening, alternating bouts of guilt with anger and despair.

She left again for dinner, some nameless stew of lentils and vegetables that Madhup herself had made. It was solid, filling, flavorless. She ate it in the living room, where Madhup sat reading and watching birds out the window and feeding the non-existent fire, just as she had in life.

When the stew was done, she did the dishes, wiping the marker notes off the plastic stew container with careful hands that trembled as she prepared herself for the bathroom again.

That was why she was here, it was clear. That was how she was haunted, how at last the ghost followed classic rules of fear and horror and disgust. Disgust with herself, for leaving Madhup alone, for failing her. Fear at the future before her, of an endless round comforting an eternally dying ghost. Expiating her guilt for as long as she lived, or worse, as long as she could stand it until she left and built up more guilt, more moral debt.

The bathroom ghost smiled its familiar, fragile smile at Bettina's invisible past. She remembered this one, she found — this particular smile, this particular moment, so recent, so painful. They'd come back from a trip to the beach. Walking slowly, the wheelchair disdained for this one last excursion. 'Our last exploration together,' Madhup had said, and Bettina had denied it, pretending there would be many more, knowing Madhup would die that night, or the next one. It had been three nights. Three days cooking elaborate purees of this and that when Madhup was sleeping after vomiting up the last one. Three days spent sitting just here, on the edge of the tub, holding her hair and bathing her sunken frame.

She started to recall the other smiles, the other gestures, the other looks. She remembered them all, made a puzzle of placing them all in context, nicely labeled the way Madhup would have liked it. She fell asleep by the side of the tub, holding the ghost's frail hand.

The cycle was still going when she woke up. This was from the day before Madhup's death, when she was so weak Bettina had had to carry her in to the toilet and the tub, had had to change the sheets. And all through it, Madhup had smiled and joked. She was making one now, Bettina saw.

'Let m stand for an unknown,' Bettina mouthed with her. 'No, we need something bigger. We'll use n.' It was Madhup's favorite joke, a relic from her days as a mathematician. She'd told it that day just to see Bettina roll her eyes. Bettina remembered doing it.

That was the point, she realized. She remembered all these moments. She'd been there. She'd held the hand, wiped the bottom, cleaned the hair from the rim of the tub. That was Madhup's message. Not 'I died and it's your fault,' because it wasn't. It was cancer's fault. Madhup was saying instead, 'I died and you were here for me. I died and you took care of me. I died in your arms, and I was happy. Don't forget this. Don't block it out. It was important to me, and it's important to you.'

Maybe it was wishful thinking. Maybe Madhup was a classic vindictive ghost. But only if dying made you a different person. She chuckled through the tears. That was a joke Madhup would have liked.

"Only if dying makes you a different person," she said, and the ghost held out her hand for help getting up.

The next morning, she woke early. She had breakfast with a silent ghost, then went upstairs to the dormitory. As she had expected, it was full of Madhup. Madhup rolling around, racing, turning somersaults among the beds. Madhup playing with the nieces and nephews, with borrowed dogs and cats to which Bettina was allergic. The ghost laughed its silent, exuberant laugh, played peek-a-boo with babies, board games with youngsters, sat silent and comforting with teenagers, napped on the sunlit floor with cats on her legs and dog heads on her chest.

And now the hallway, at the base of those tall steps, with the irregular one painted orange, at the confluence of doors and travel. And here, in the shadowed gloom, was one more ghost. Madhup, in middle age, in the comfortable jeans and cotton blouse that made her look a little dumpy, with her arms out waiting to be hugged.

She hugged and was hugged, kissed and was kissed, looked into small brown eyes that looked into hers. Remembered and was, perhaps, somewhere, remembered. Loved and was loved in precious memory.

She'd made the calls this morning, and the agent from Madhup's folder had put up the sign that afternoon. She could just see it from here, through the glass of the front door, swinging aimlessly in its circular, spiral voyage that went nowhere at vast speeds around the galaxy.

She knew now, what she'd find in the laundry room. No shelves of carefully cataloged mysteries. They would have been packaged up, sold, donated. There would be an intent, happy ghost, doing the work she loved the best — putting together puzzles, solving problems in her little workshop. And on a desk or a workbench would be a little filigreed cylinder that was like her holojector after all, that somehow made memory solid, or made the past solid, or something. A device that Madhup had figured out, a puzzle she had solved. Just as she had solved the puzzle of what to do with Bettina's grief, how to hold her wife's hand even after death, how to bring her through the grief and guilt and the 'if I had only' moments to give Madhup the credit she deserved, to remember that it had been a partnership, and they had both had what they wanted most, and had paid a price.

"It was worth it," Bettina said as she found the cylinder, read the careful directions, and twisted it just so. "It was worth every minute," as she put the cylinder back and a ghost slowly faded out of sight. And though tears rolled down her cheeks, for the first time in weeks, her heart beat free in her chest.

She'd walked through the empty house, left the door unlocked behind her. She would go out again, into the night, to lose that lonesome, restless feeling in the space between the stars. She'd go further than she'd ever gone — exploring, as she'd always done, in her cramped, plain little ship, with only memory for company.

See B. Morris Allen's story "That Lonesome, Restless Feeling" online at Metaphorosis.
If you liked it, leave a comment. Authors love that!
Remember to subscribe to our e-mail updates so you'll know when new stories are posted.

About the story

Many of my stories are sparked by song lyrics — whether or not correctly heard. In this case, I'm fairly confident I got them right, and the story draws on Gordon Lightfoot's song, "Ordinary Man". I'm not usually drawn to ghost stories, but I liked the line about "a ghost in every room", and, since I write SFF, made it a science fiction ghost created by an alien artifact. The ending draws on a lyric that's a little less obvious — a line from Herbert Grönemeyer's beautiful song, "Der Weg", about going on ("Hab' meine Frist verlängert") even in the face of tragedy.

Arborify

Cadence Mandybura

Bang.

Yvonne flinched at the pop of the anti-drone cannon. She rushed to the nearest tree, placed her hand against the papery bark, whispered, "It's okay." In the past seventeen seasons of working at the arborification facility, Yvonne had typically only heard the cannons go off once or twice a year. Now they sounded at least a dozen times a day.

She caught one of her subordinates staring at her as he walked past, but he flicked his gaze downward immediately. Yvonne narrowed her eyes as he quickened his pace away from her. From her co-workers' perspective, the drones weren't dangerous, just Shut It Down fanatics angling to get footage of the arborification process, looking for abuses that didn't exist. But the trees didn't know that, and the violence of the cannon noise might be distressing to them. Yvonne comforted them where she could.

Her colleagues were only worried about the safety of their pension-clad jobs. That fear was too big to be sharp for Yvonne; imagining life without this career was an ungraspable blankness. She had been eight when Ms. Moyo had explained to her that the birch trees outside the big kids' entrance were from the government's arborification tree-planting program, and so some of them might have once been people. When navigating playground friendships became too difficult, Yvonne would retreat to the trees, wishing she could root herself more fully to their calm presence. It felt safe to her, that people could become trees; that the chaos and questions and pain of life could be quieted into the simplicity of sunlight and sap.

Another cannon boom, a whipcrack echo.

Yvonne winced, moved to another tree in the grove to murmur reassurances. Inside, she cursed Malcolmson, that young thug, for being the first to attack the trees, for inspiring the Shut It Downers, but she didn't want her charges hearing her anger. This batch was about six weeks old. Planted to mid-calf, with their linen clothing starting to melt into bark, their human faces were still recognizable, but with clear signs that arborification was underway: the thinning lips, flattened ears, and eyebrows tugged away by the wind.

She walked among the trees, checking for parasites or other signs that growth wasn't progressing normally. She noticed, weightlessly, the marks of the trees' former lives. Many had tattoos, some of them gang markers in cheap prison ink; one tree had needle scars on its forearm; another had suicide attempts racked into its wrists. Most, though, were just old, frail creatures, now at peace, alchemizing light, water, and air.

"Hello, my friend," said Yvonne to one of them. "Don't be afraid of the noise. You're safe here." A bulb of amber liquid glimmered at the corner of the tree's left eye. Yvonne dabbed it away; the eyelid fluttered at the contact, a reflex to be expected at this early stage. Yvonne still had a print on her wall that she had bought as a teenager: a famous photo of the weeping trees. The work of a muckraking journalist back in the early days of arborification, the image had sparked the first wave of protests. The scientific community had done its best to quell the outrage with beige reassurances. There was no evidence of consciousness at the weeping stage. All clients gave their full consent prior to the procedure. Within minutes of the injections, all human brain activity ceased. The occasional blinking and lip twitches were automatic gestures that faded as the clients' anatomy transformed.

Public opinion hadn't truly swung until a pop megastar announced her choice to arborify at the end of her struggle with ovarian cancer. Other celebrities took up the cause, championing arborification as a compassionate and sustainable process. Today, people were content with the status quo, mostly ignoring a government program that, over decades, had quietly eased the strain on social systems. Some outrage remained, but it had narrowed to the margins.

Until Malcolmson. Yvonne squeezed her eyes shut, bit her lip until she cut through to the salt-iron of blood.

Yvonne could still see the news reports from the event, forty-one days ago: yellow hazard tape flapping at the edge of a stand of birch. At least two trees fully felled, others gashed and keeling over in pain. A close-up of the stumps, the broken trunks splattered with a rust-brown liquid. Yvonne's first thought had been of cough syrup, the gross, medicinal kind. It had turned out to be cow's blood.

And the kid behind it: Rawling Malcolmson, legally an adult at eighteen, but still in high school. Revulsion had slithered through Yvonne as she consumed his features: smirking, even though it was a mugshot, smirking for god's sake. His tight cap of dark hair started far down the nape of his neck, creeping to a widow's peak that skewed left. His face was shiny and thin, spotted with a few pimples, with wide-set slug-coloured eyes.

He had been easily caught and didn't have anything to say; he clammed up on the advice of his lawyers and everyone was still waiting for the gears of justice to establish his guilt and pass sentence. Just another maladjusted youth, some speculated, lashing out for attention. Others saw him as the forefront of a renewed campaign against arborification. Yvonne didn't know which was true. She hated him regardless.

Yvonne's watch buzzed. Town hall in ten minutes. Reluctantly, she left the grove and followed the dirt path through the fields back to the main building. As always, her hand drifted up from her side, finger pads towards the trees, as she repeated her usual silent greeting.

Hello. Hello, my friend. Hello.

" 'Dear class,' " the substitute begins in her scratchy voice. Yvonne hates going to school now, but today's a good day. Today they get to hear another letter from their teacher, Ms. Moyo, who's been gone on medical leave since February but has written a letter to the class every week during her absence. Yvonne sits at the back edge of the classroom carpet, scratches even-branched Ys onto her frayed corduroys, not sure why her stomach is twisting so much. She desperately wants to hear the letter. She also doesn't.

" 'This will be my last letter to you,' " the substitute continues. Yvonne freezes. Her face becomes a knot, her throat and chest, too, as the tangle of her emotions cinch tight.

She sobs. Too loud. Frankie O imitates her, his friends giggle. Yvonne covers her face.

The substitute clears her throat starchily; the boys quiet down. She continues Ms. Moyo's letter to the class.

" 'This is my last letter to you, but I'm not going away forever, and at the end of this letter I'll tell you how we can stay in touch.' "

Yvonne's darkness sprays with shapes as her palms press into her eyes. She sniffs, puts her hands back in her lap, and listens hard.

Town halls were bullshit. The deputy minister's office had only started hosting them when people began quitting because of the Shut It Down harassment. After the initial Malcolmson incident, when it still seemed like an isolated case? Nothing.

Yvonne tucked herself into a corner carrel, plugged in the headset, and fished out a notepad from the top drawer. She doodled as the meeting got underway. It helped to scratch out her frustration.

Today's town hall was about the increase in drones. First, an assurance of their safety—the military had set up additional cannons and radar, not even a horsefly could get through, hur hur —but the meeting soon morphed to offers of transfers, temporary leave, psychological support. Blah, blah, blah. The deputy minister had no good answers for how the division would take care of the trees with a reduced workforce. Yvonne fractalized the heavy Y she had drawn into the pad, repeating the pattern in smaller increments.

During the Q&A, people asked what would happen to their jobs if the facility shut down. The deputy minister didn't seem to think of it as a real threat; the protests were loud, he acknowledged, but the silent majority was content with arborification. Everyone knew it had been one of the greatest successes of the past century, addressing challenges in health care, homelessness, addiction, and the environment all at the same time. Still, if the facility closed, employees would be offered positions elsewhere within government. No one would be left out in the cold.

Except for the clients, Yvonne wanted to say, jerking her drawing to a stop as her pen ripped a furrow in the paper. Without arborification, where would they go?

Halfway through Ms. Moyo's letter, Naima raises her hand. "I thought only bad people were borified," she says.

"Arborified," the substitute corrects quickly; Yvonne does the same under her breath. "Who told you that?"

Naima shrugs. "Like, it's for criminals and stuff."

"Whoa, wait, is Ms. Moyo in jail?" says Frankie O. Yvonne wants to hit him, but he's too far away.

"No, no. Ms. Moyo is very, very sick," the substitute says, glaring at Frankie, before turning back to Naima. "There are people in our justice system who sometimes choose to become arborified. That might be what you're thinking of. But it has nothing to do with being good or bad. It's just an option for people who are ready for a different sort of life."

Naima looks uncertain. "So... Ms. Moyo... because she's so sick..."

The substitute nods. "Incurable," she says. "It's quite common for people in her predicament. Yes, Ricardo? Speak up."

Ricardo's a shy boy; Yvonne was friends with him for part of first grade until he got mad at her for borrowing his toque without asking. She was going to give it back, but he didn't understand when she tried to explain. Now, whenever she looks at him, she has an ugly, bubbly feeling, even when he's being nice.

"Are the doctors making Ms. Moyo arborify?" he asks now.

"Of course not. It's always a choice. This is what she wants. In fact, if we keep reading, the next sentence says, 'I know this may seem sad, my young friends, but I want you to know that this is not an end, just a transformation...' "

Yvonne looks away from Ricardo, thinks of Ms. Moyo instead, her soft nose, her big laugh, her bright lipstick. Of course, Ms. Moyo wouldn't just end. She wouldn't do that to Yvonne.

"Shut! It! Down!"

Yvonne hid her head between her knees as her car glided past the perimeter fence. There had always been a few tired protestors at the edge of the arborification grounds, but since Malcolmson and the copycats, the numbers had grown. Now Yvonne's car had to crawl past a crowd that seethed right up to the ribboned line watched by extra security guards.

"This isn't the help we need!"

"Stop coercing the elderly!"

"Rehabilitation, not lobotomies!"

Yvonne put her hands over her ears. She had nothing to do with client intake, consent, last wishes, but she knew the process was thorough. The lawyers had to provide every possible parachute, escape hatch, eject button, and knotted sheet, legally speaking, before the client's arborification was approved. But these shouting people acted as though she were murdering clients, when all she was trying to do was care for them. She knew just as well as the protestors that life might have been hard on arborification clients. That was *why* it mattered. Why couldn't they see that?

She knew she'd get in trouble, maybe even fired, if she shouted back, but it was hard to quiet her mind. *DON'T YOU KNOW THEY'RE PEOPLE*, she thought at top volume as she passed a chant of "Shut! It! Down!" *LET THEM REST.*

Bam bam bam. One of them had got close enough to rap a palm against her window. Yvonne shrank. Whoever it was got pulled back quickly, but had left a smear on the glass. Back home in her carport, Yvonne tried to rub the handprint with her sleeve, but that only made it worse. Exasperated, she glanced around to see if anyone had followed her, then hurried inside.

Yvonne heated up some noodles for herself and got drunk on coverage of the attacks, new and old, as she did every night. Trees hacked and splattered in the Malcolmson style. Trunks tagged in dripping neon. Scoring and scratch marks. In one case, a knife was buried in the tree, birch sap trailing from the wound. Someone had even tried to burn a grove and almost set the neighbourhood alight.

Because Malcolmson himself wasn't saying a word, the copycats interpreted his vandalism however they liked. "Arborification has been wrong from the start," a young man with eerily calm eyes pronounced into a microphone. "Just because we *can* do something doesn't mean we should."

Another clip, this time a woman scowling as the wind kept blowing hair into her face. "The science of arborification isn't our primary concern," she said. "What we question is the vetting process involved. Who gets sent to these facilities, and why? Is it truly consensual? Are they well treated? We keep getting the government runaround about privacy. What are they keeping secret?"

Yvonne stayed locked to the news as light faded from the world, only going to bed when her watch chirped a reminder that she had to wake up in four hours.

" 'Now, some final thoughts for each of you. Giselle, I want you to remember...' "

Ms. Moyo has sent the class a letter once a week throughout her medical leave. Every time, she ends with a few sentences for each person in the class, the same way she's given everyone their own special job in the classroom. Naima makes sure everyone's outdoor shoes are tidy, for example, and Ricardo is responsible for getting all the classroom books put back on the shelf.

Yvonne is in charge of the plants. This is her second job with the class. Her first was to make sure all the scissors were back in the bin at the end of the day. But one afternoon when Frankie O wouldn't give his pair back, Yvonne twisted it out of his hand, scraping a long red line down his thumb. Ms. Moyo shuffled that job to someone else, but asked Yvonne to stay late the next day and walked her through caring for the line of plants at the window. One lesson at a time: water, fertilizer, spraying for mites, how they like it when you talk to them. Now, whenever Yvonne feels upset in class, wants to shout at a classmate for misunderstanding her, or balls up homework sheets she's struggling with, she takes a breath and thinks about the plants, about every new leaf and bud that is quietly growing, about how they need her.

The substitute is droning on, the words mushing together for Yvonne as the letter goes through students one by one. She waits to hear her name. Surely she will be the next one... the next one... the next...

The next day after work, Yvonne changed into an oversized hoodie that she hoped would shield her face. She didn't think anyone would recognize her, but if there were protestors at the grove, she didn't want to take any chances.

The deputy minister had advised them to avoid visiting arborified sites, but hadn't made a specific rule against it. His words had the opposite of the intended effect on Yvonne: she felt ashamed that she hadn't been brave enough to visit any of her local groves since the protests had begun.

The whole way to the park, she raked her teeth over her bottom lip, squeezing the pinpoint of pain where she had broken the skin the day before. What would she do if there were other people there? Worse, what if it was too late, if the trees were already marked and abused? And if this grove was okay, what about all the others?

The grove she chose was hidden in a generous suburban park. Yvonne stared at her sneakers as she followed the cedar-chip path into the thin forest. Luckily for her, it was a snippy day for summer, with heavy cloud cover and a mean wind. Not many people out except lone dog walkers.

In her peripheral vision, the poplars lapsed into birch. Yvonne's head snapped up before she could think better of it—

before she could decide for sure if she wanted to look or not and prepare herself for the worst—

—to see the grove quiet, gloriously intact.

The clean, long-lived trunks drew a relieved sigh from Yvonne.

Too late, she saw that there was another woman standing at the edge of the grove. She turned to smile at Yvonne.

"You were worried too," the woman said. She was about Yvonne's age, but better presented, with smooth hair and a fancy scarf.

Yvonne gulped and looked back to the trees as she nodded.

"The news has been awful," said the woman. "I don't think people understand…"

Yvonne shifted from foot to foot, the wind stinging her ears. She wanted to go up to each tree and greet them, but she knew that her behaviour would look odd to the other woman, so she held her place and touched each tree with her gaze instead. This was an old grove, planted before Yvonne had been hired, branches wide and venerable.

"My great-aunt's one of them," said the woman.

"Wait—one of these?" asked Yvonne. "How do you know?"

"Well, I don't, I guess," the other woman said, sounding a little embarrassed. "They don't release those records. They don't even track them, apparently. But I followed it as closely as I could, and it's the right age, at least."

Yvonne opened her mouth to tell the woman that it wasn't likely—that even back when this grove was planted, most plantings weren't in municipal parks but went to reforestation projects far from the public's eye—but the woman went on.

"She was a bit of a kook, you know, but she was very sure about this. Look, this is going to sound a little weird, but could you take a picture of me?" The woman held her phone out to Yvonne, even though they were still standing several steps apart.

"Why?" said Yvonne.

"There's this thing I saw online, people are tying ribbons around trees and taking pictures, to counteract the violence, you know?"

Yvonne didn't know, but she nodded anyway. Her screens only seemed to come up with pictures of groves that had been attacked, not whatever this woman was talking about. Her arm was still outstretched, hovering in the expanse between them. Reluctantly, Yvonne stepped forward to take the device.

The woman smiled her thanks and walked to the closest tree, laying her fingers against the white bark.

"But you don't know if that's her," said Yvonne. "Your aunt."

The woman pulled a blue ribbon out of her purse. Yvonne's throat caught. "Of course," said the woman. "But any one of these trees *might* be her, and that's good enough for me." She started winding the ribbon around one of the branches. Yvonne felt as though the loops were roping her own forearm.

"There," said the woman, tying a careful bow before turning to Yvonne with a camera-ready smile.

Gingerly, Yvonne lifted the phone to head height, the screen blurring as it tried to focus. The woman stood beside the tree, the blue ribbon companionably at shoulder height. As Yvonne's thumb hovered over the snap button, a wind gusted, freezing her ungloved hands and flattening the ribbon loops into whipping lines. The woman kept her smile in place but squinted, lifting a hand to tidy her hair.

"No, no, you can't!" exclaimed Yvonne, rushing to the tree's side and shoving the phone into the woman's chest. Yvonne began picking apart the bow with stiff, panicked fingers. "I know you mean well, but—you can't tie up a tree just for a picture—it'll choke." She unwound the ribbon from the branch. "And this feels synthetic, too, so if it fell off it wouldn't biodegrade, or it could affect other wildlife, didn't you think of that?"

The woman stepped back as Yvonne scrunched the ribbon and wheeled towards her. "Okay," the woman said, her hands in front of her, palms down. "Okay, yes, I hear you, I hadn't considered that."

But Yvonne, expecting more resistance, carried onwards. "And for a picture? Just a picture? You don't even know where your aunt is, and it doesn't matter anyway, they're all at peace now, don't you see that it's the whole grove that we need to love, that a ribbon won't protect anything?"

She took a breath as a new realization hit her. "Actually, most people probably don't even know that this is an arborified grove, your ribbon would tell them, and then they'd know, *then they'd know* and they might attack this one too, we just have to let them be, they've escaped everything that could hurt them, just leave them alone..."

Yvonne's head hurt. Some hair had escaped her ponytail and flapped across her face; she clawed it behind her ears, unsuccessfully.

"Okay, you're right," the woman said. "Let's just leave the trees as they are."

Yvonne nodded and sniffed. She yanked the drawstrings on her hoodie to hug the cloth around her face.

"I'm going to go now," said the woman in a delicate tone, although she didn't move. "Did you know anyone arborified here? Or—wherever."

Yvonne swallowed. A stiff nod. Yes. Someone. Yes. All of them. Yes.

The woman said a soft goodbye and walked away at last, her question a thorn in Yvonne's mind.

Then she realized that she had been twisting the ribbon between her hands this whole time. The woman was out of sight already. Not wanting to throw the ribbon out, Yvonne carried it home, stuffing it at the back of a junk drawer so that she'd never have to see it again.

" 'To Yvonne,' " the substitute teacher reads out at last. Yvonne's breath catches and her face blooms hot. " 'You have a great deal of kindness inside of you. Remember that when you feel angry. Take care of the plants.' "

After the encounter with the woman at the grove, Yvonne looked up the ribbon campaign, and it upset her almost as much as the vandals did. Everyone was missing the point.

She started polite, advising people against tying foreign objects to trees. But when people called her names, her responses got angrier, telling them they were empty do-gooders who were only fuelling the Shut It Down movement. Only at 3:00 a.m., when a network of lonely neighbourhood dogs started to chorus, was she able to blink the screen's glare from her eyes and step away.

Two days later, her director called her into his office. He was about ten years older than her, a man with a comfortably worn demeanour. Not a bad guy, Yvonne had always thought, but the grim line of his mouth set her heart racing.

He had printouts for her, spread on the desk between them. All of her after-hours comments. More of them were in all caps than she remembered.

"Yvonne," he said, gently, after letting a silence pool between them. "Are you okay?"

"It's just..." Yvonne gestured helplessly. "They don't understand!"

"I know," he said. "But you know our media policy. My boss told me that I should suspend you for this."

"No! You can't—"

He held a hand up. "I told her I wouldn't, that she'd have to fire me first. We need you, Yvonne, but I have to know that you're okay to do your job, and that you'll delete all of this." He tapped the pile.

"But if they... I have to do something, they're talking about cancelling the whole program. Closing the..." She couldn't finish.

"The most important thing you can do is what you were doing before. I don't disagree with you, you know that. But getting angry doesn't help anything. We already have people arguing our side, through the right channels."

He sighed and leaned back. "The truth is, these things are bigger than us, Yvonne," he said. "It's noisy right now, but this will die down. Comms says that it's already waning. We just notice because we care."

"But everyone should care."

"Sure. These people do, even if they think differently than you."

"That's not the same."

Exasperation crossed the director's face. Oh no: she was going to lose him too. His tone soured a little. "Yvonne, I'm not going to suspend you, but this has to stop, okay? Forget about these people. You're here for the clients, right? Focus on that."

Yvonne looked down from his annoyance, her hands cold. Yes, of course, he was right. The trees. She was here for the trees, and she hoped to be there for them for the rest of her life.

" 'I'm sorry that I wasn't able to finish the school year with you, my friends, or see you grow into future grades and beyond. I hope you will visit me sometime.' " The substitute teacher frowns, but her brow clears as she continues reading. " 'Now, it's true that I won't be planted in public for a few years, and even then, you won't know which tree is me. So I have a favour to ask from all of you. This is how we can stay in touch. Whenever you see a birch tree, say hello. Touch the trunk if you're able. You never know. Someday it might be me. And if it isn't, a friendly hello is a precious gift to share.' "

By the time Malcolmson was sentenced almost two years later, the public had lost interest. Yvonne enjoyed the news privately, having learned not to expect much from her colleagues. At the facility, job anxiety had smoothed back into complacency as the Shut It Down tagline went stale, a slogan chained to a receding year.

The judge gave Malcolmson a hefty fine, four hundred hours of community service, six months of prison, and a thorough upbraiding. *What you've done is inexcusable and unforgiveable,* she had said. *It's as though you defiled a grave, or burned a canary alive in its cage. I hope you examine your actions and decide how to be a better human being.*

Yvonne cheered the condemnation, although it wasn't how she would have put it. The trees weren't a grave, or a cage. If anything, they were more like... angel wings, unfurling in a thousand fresh leaves every spring. It was freedom, not bondage; life, not death.

It was too late for the trees Malcolmson had killed and scarred, and for the many other trees injured in the surge of anger that followed his attack. Still, the harsh sentence would serve as a template for the other vandals, all waiting their turn.

That day Yvonne told the trees, with conviction at last, that justice was served. They were safe. And she could continue to care for them for the next ten, twenty...

...thirty years. When she had time, Yvonne still liked to witness the new arrivals. She'd begun to think about which season would be her last—and she knew the staff wondered too. She resisted making retirement plans, but she was slowing down, and even part-time work was getting harder with her arthritic hands and knees.

Yvonne took her breaks in the small patio enclosed by benches and planters, deadheading the annuals with only her fingers and thumbs as snippers. It made her look busy when the client vans pulled up.

The white vans hadn't changed much over the years—just that there were more of them—and neither had the security guards, an endless replication of fresh-faced youths. She knew they weren't the *same* young people, of course, just like the intake team had changed over many times in her career.

There—Yvonne ducked behind a geranium—the clients, shuffling off the van. Her future charges. Grey heads. Some younger people, but not healthy ones. Thin, muted, haunted. Soon soothed by soil and sunlight.

Yvonne frowned. Something about the group snagged her thoughts as she scanned the individuals from her oblique vantage point. Nothing out of the ordinary, really—one tall man, youngish, in his fifties, maybe, a skinny neck craning forward, exposing the long smudge of his hairline...

She gulped, her fist twisting a flower stalk, as she remembered the broken trees, the blood-spattered stumps.

Rawling. Rawling Malcolmson.

She hadn't thought of that time in years, her mind always skipping away whenever the memories floated back. Demonstrations against arborification were unheard of these days.

What was he *doing* here?

She stared at his aged appearance before he disappeared into the reception centre. A few days of procedures, medical and legal, and he would be on her field, in her hands.

The rest of the day, Malcolmson was all Yvonne could think about. How could she face him, even in his arborified state? All the hurt and betrayal from his actions years ago stewed inside her, interfering with her need to do her job properly, tend the untended, care for the unwanted.

She was shocked that no one else had recognized him—the clerks and lawyers had access to his full name, even—but when she stopped to consider it, she couldn't think of anyone who had been working here in the Shut It Down era. It had been more than thirty years. Most of her colleagues had been children, or not even born, the last time the facility had been threatened.

As soon as she got home, without even bothering to change, she huddled on the couch and scraped up all the old coverage she could find. The bloody trunks, the vandalism and graffiti, the protests, counter-protests, Shut It Down flyers, the ribbon campaign. The long editorials and then, abruptly, the slide back into irrelevance. She was surprised at how small it seemed now, a brief media sizzle that had quickly gone flat.

Searches for Malcolmson himself had paltry results. A mention in his mother's obituary. An out-of-date contact for what might have been a pyramid scheme. A listing in the back of a long-dead community plan. When her increasingly esoteric searches came up with nothing one time too many, she smashed her fist against the screen. As it rainbowed from the impact, she pulled her hand to her chest, her eyes itching with tears.

The day of the planting, Yvonne woke up knowing that she would have to face Malcolmson. His mind would be calmed. He would be clad in undyed linen, pliant, barefoot, awaiting the peace and care of arborification.

She called in sick.

No one gave her a hard time, and she knew that her chief was more than capable of overseeing the work. They didn't realize how monumental this was. Yvonne had never missed a planting, not once in almost fifty years.

Of course, there was nothing physically wrong with her. But thinking of his features felt like a cold slime under her skin: his dejected form, the way he had slouched into the reception centre, the bunched architecture of his face. That same sinister hairline.

Avoiding work was as bad as going. She never knew what to do with herself when she had a day of forced inactivity. Spurting restlessly between watching TV and housework, Yvonne couldn't tear her mind away from Malcolmson, what he had started, how he had threatened the very existence of arborification. And now he was back, wanting it for himself!

Scrubbing her kitchen sink: how could she tend him—*him*—the way she did every other person who came into her care?

Scrolling irritably through sitcoms: but was his case different from anyone else she had helped in her long career?

Descaling her showerhead: no doubt she had assisted others who were guilty of worse crimes, or who were blighted with thoughtless sins—cruelty, greed, self-absorption.

Peeling carrots: now the thought of him would contaminate his entire cohort.

The next day, Yvonne rode into work past the familiar lines of birch, their clean perfection hurtful. The newest trees were like any other freshly planted grove she had tended. From their constellation of origins, they had all converged here: forty-odd souls who had agreed to the simple release of life as a tree.

Yvonne glimpsed him immediately as she walked up to the new grove. That long, close-cropped head. She looked away. Her chief was reporting on the planting—minor concerns here and there, nothing to be alarmed about, a good healthy group all around—and Yvonne did her best to pay attention. She was creating a bubble around Malcolmson, erasing him. She would not see him, or touch him, or connect with him the way she did with every other tree. Her secret vengeance. It would have to be enough.

"Whoa, Yvonne, are you okay?"

Yvonne regained her balance after stumbling into her colleague. It was what's-her-name, the new girl, newish, new two years ago. Her eyes flickered with concern, her hands wide as though to catch Yvonne.

"I'm fine," said Yvonne. She pulled her hat on more snugly and glared. "Just the heat, I think."

"Do you need a break? I can get you some water—"

"I said I'm fine!" Yvonne turned away to walk along the grove she had been inspecting. It hadn't been the heat, although springs seemed hotter than ever these days. She had been avoiding looking at Malcolmson and hadn't seen where she was stepping.

She thought she'd been bricking up her hatred, but the more he changed, the more irritable she felt. He'd progressed smoothly over the last ten weeks, and soon he would be indistinguishable from the others. Even though she knew where he was planted here at the facility, one day he would be mingled with other trees and shipped out, his identity lost for good.

Yvonne paced down the line of trees, a few steps beyond Malcolmson, then swinging back to pass him again. Leaf-shadow speckled her feet.

How dare he think he deserved arborification, after what he had done?

Her pockets jostled as she turned and paced back again, catching against her leg. She reached in to rearrange the items—keys, clippers, communicator.

She stopped in front of his tree, looking at it properly for the first time. Wormtrails of sweat tickled her neck.

A good, healthy tree, no different from the others.

She pulled out her clippers, squeezing and releasing to open their half-moon blade.

Disgust rose in her throat. She couldn't go another day, not another hour, even, without—without—*something*.

For a moment, she thought of stabbing the tree, tearing at the new wood, making him as ugly as she knew him to be.

But no. That was excessive. She didn't need to be violent.

Before thinking any further, Yvonne knelt. She might have been tying her shoe. Holding the clippers at their crosspiece, she touched the point to the tree's fresh bark, only a few inches from the ground.

Baby flesh. She paused to let the thought drift away. Then, ready again, she pressed the blade a little harder into the tree, feeling a soft pop as it punctured the outer layer. Somewhere inside her, groundwater level, she knew she was making a mistake.

Too late: she was slicing a vertical line. It was unnervingly easy, the newly grown skin parting smoothly under the blade.

Her first thought had been to carve an M into the tree, an ugly zigzag to suit the degenerate Malcolmson. But after scoring the first line, the memory of her grade three teacher, dear Ms. Moyo, floated back, her beautiful looping handwriting, the sunny afternoons Yvonne had spent caring for the class plants. Swallowing, Yvonne changed course: an M wouldn't do. Instead, she added two branching lines to turn the mark into an even-armed Y, her own secret symbol.

"Yvonne?"

She jolted at the interruption, dropping the clippers into the dirt, *paff.* "What?"

It was the new girl again. What was her name—Emily? "Sorry. Margot's looking for you. In the east field."

"Fine," said Yvonne, grabbing the clippers, then standing and brushing dirt off her pants. She tried to position her legs so that they blocked the carved mark from Emily's view. "Anything else?"

"Uh—no," said Emily, but she didn't move. Her gaze wandered past Yvonne to the trees behind her. Yvonne's breath froze in fear.

"Yes?"

"It's such a beautiful thing, isn't it?" said Emily. She took a step toward one of the trees—not Malcolmson, thank god—and placed her palm on the trunk. "You get used to it, working here every day, but it hits you sometimes... such a beautiful, beautiful thing..."

"Don't you have a job to do?"

It came out more rudely than Yvonne intended. As Emily stammered a reply, Yvonne backpedalled with a hasty, "Thank you, Emily."

Emily was already walking away, but she paused to say over her shoulder, "It's Emma."

Yvonne waited until Emma/Emily was a safe distance away before she turned to check Malcolmson, scuffing away the depressions her knees had left in the dirt. The Y mark was weeping sap, but from standing, it was barely noticeable. It would do.

As she left, her hand automatically reached out towards the trunk—but she pulled back before she made contact.

It was a small thing, that mark: three scored lines, less than an inch across. In all the wide, deep, rich world, just three little lines!

But when Yvonne closed her eyes, it was all she could see. Those lines were giant to her. They had obliterated Malcolmson's whippet neck, his damp eyes, his cruel mouth. Now he was three sap-filled scratches, gashing every thought she had.

Yvonne became more distracted at work. She directed the wrong field to be fertilized on Tuesday, forgot a meeting on Thursday. Arrived late on Friday because she had left her pass at home. Distantly, she knew they were building the case for her senility, and how could she tell management the true cause of her sloppiness?

When she closed her eyes at night, memories pressed into her darkness. The carnage of Malcolmson's attacks, the Shut It Down hysteria. Her past director confronting her with piles of her online shouting. A long red mark on Frankie O's hand. And a sliced Y, one that was scarring her as much as it did Malcolmson. More, perhaps.

Shame tunnelled deeper into Yvonne. The years hadn't healed her—they had only fooled her.

She knew what she had to do.

By the time Yvonne was sitting down with one of their in-house lawyers, Benni, the envelope containing her last wishes was already thumbed with worry. It had taken her three tries to set it down correctly.

She had requested this lawyer specifically because Benni had a reputation for empathy, more interested in the spirit than the letter of the law. Yvonne was surprised to find how generously staff accommodated her arborification request, allowing procedural exceptions to help smooth the process. She didn't have to arrive in a van, of course, and she could complete the paperwork at any time, although she would still receive the injections on the same day as the rest of her group.

Benni went through the paperwork as she would for any other client. All the rights that Yvonne would relinquish. What would happen to the possessions she left behind. Next of kin: none.

Yvonne barely listened as the lawyer described every nub and nodule of the law, waiting for the moment when Benni paused, her eyes warm, and asked if Yvonne had any questions.

Yvonne lifted the envelope from her lap to the table.

"Just one special request," she whispered.

No one spoke in the waiting room. Yvonne had never been to this part of the facility before. It was restricted, and she never had any reason to come. This wasn't the main reception space—she had skipped that phase—but the smaller waiting room, the one before clients were called away to the private session with the doctor.

The man beside her cleared his throat. The oxygen tank on the woman in the corner hissed and sighed, a soothing sound in the sterile space, almost like the pulse of ocean waves.

Yvonne was one of them now. Wherever they came from, her fellow clients, they were here now, haphazardly together. A someday grove. Yvonne's fingers floated up a little from her knee. Absurd here, of course, but she felt her familiar refrain. *Hello. Hello, my friend. Hello…*

"Yvonne?"

Her turn. Yvonne stood, followed the nurse, and disappeared.

Benni took last requests seriously. The tree in question—the tree that had once been Yvonne—was in the far corner of the grove. Benni had visited her several times earlier in the transformation. Week by week, Yvonne's face had smoothed into the fresh skin of birchbark; her frame winnowed to a slender pole; branches and leaves sprouted skyward.

No time to dawdle today. Benni found the tree, dropped to one knee, and pulled out a paring knife. She touched the blank spot where she would leave the symbol that Yvonne had requested. Benni ran a finger through the dew pearling the soft bark, tracking the even-armed Y, remembering Yvonne's old brown hands, her skittery gaze, her clumsy, earnest voice.

The air was fresh here in the groves. Benni took a deep breath, then started to carve.

See Cadence Mandybura's story "Arborify" online at Metaphorosis.
If you liked it, leave a comment. Authors love that!
Remember to subscribe to our e-mail updates so you'll know when new stories are posted.

About the story

This story began about five years ago with a few paragraphs describing a woman tending to planted people. I was fascinated by the core concept of a government program that lets people choose to become trees (perhaps because I was working in government at the time), but was frankly intimidated at how to turn the idea into a meaningful story. I'm a worldbuilder to a fault, so spent much of my writing time thinking through the ramifications and moral greyness of such a program—is it compassionate or wildly dystopic? How would citizens respond to such a program? Would good intentions fray into corruption over time?

Ultimately, I wanted to leave many of these questions for the reader to contemplate rather than have the story provide definitive answers. "Arborify" ended up being a much more personal story about Yvonne's relationship with the trees, exploring themes of care and neglect, innocence and guilt, and what connects us as individuals and as a society.

A question for the author

Q: Do you use music for inspiration? If so, what do you listen to?

A: Absolutely, music is a key part of my process when I'm generating new writing. (For revising, I need quiet.) My go-to writing playlist consists of oud music by artists like Anouar Brahem, Le Trio Joubran, Faran Ensemble, and Naseer Shamma. I usually start with Brahem's "Conte de l'Incroyable Amour," a gorgeous ten-minute piece that helps me settle into my writing. I also love Western classical music for writing (Bach, Dvořák, and Rachmaninov are perennial favourites), and if I'm trying to tap into a particular mood, I turn to ambient sounds, such as swamp noises or a looped version of the Sardaukar chant from *Dune*.

About the author

Cadence Mandybura writes speculative fiction with a fondness for both beauty and absurdity. She works as an editor and is the associate producer of the fiction anthology podcast *The Truth*. To unwind, she enjoys drumming, including taiko and a range of Latin and West African instruments.

www.cadencemandybura.com, @cade_bura

Astrid Underwater

J.J. Eskelin

The day Sigun lost her son in the water, it was unusually warm, even for August. She had driven with him up the Olympic Peninsula to a park just over the bridge, on the western shore of Kilisut Island. The little island had been created some fifty years before, when a ship canal was dredged through a backwater marsh, severing the land from the Olympic Peninsula.

Now, a sand bar, bleached and desolate, edged the deep canal. The sand bar was littered with empty shells and strewn with bone-white driftwood tumbled smooth by water. In between the sand bar and the rocky shore of the little island, tidal rivers wove through the sand and rock. Beneath their sparkling waters every surface was generously carpeted with life; the rocks were sharp with oysters, dressed with purple sea anemones, slippery with green and brown algae.

Sigun, tall and strong, carried Erik easily as she waded through the seawater streams, stepping gingerly over the life-encrusted rocks, out towards the sand bar. Once there, Erik set about busily reorganizing the driftwood into a fort. A constant monologue accompanied his work, demanding no response. She was lucky in this, that he could play alone.

Erik had been terrified of the water all summer. Sigun had not been able to get him to even dip his beautiful pink toes into the sea. Swimming lessons had been a complete disaster. Erik had taken a particular dislike to the last swim instructor who had attempted to force him into the pool. Before Sigun could intervene, Erik had started screaming. "I hate her! I hate her! I hate her!" His cry had echoed like a curse in the vaulted chamber above the indoor pool.

Sigun had been ready to concede defeat when the director of the Aquatic Center himself had emerged from the water. While the swim instructors had been barely out of childhood, the director was a man with closely cut hair and a stiff beard of shining silver. He was short, smaller than Sigun, but his presence was commanding. He was perfectly formed, every muscle outlined by his black shorty wetsuit. The skin of his exposed arms and legs was smooth bronze, his face ageless. A trident would not have looked out of place in his hand, Sigun had thought, amused at the image.

"Come, Erik," the director, Mr. Merehinen, had ordered in a low, even voice. He was devoid of the false cheer and friendliness that often seem a prerequisite for working with small children. Yet Erik had not hesitated; he had taken the man's cold hand and stepped willingly into the water at last.

Sigun had never been afraid of the water. She was an excellent swimmer, and an even better sailor, having grown up sailing her father's boats. She loved the water, but she understood the danger of it, the vigilance and respect it commanded. So, even if she had good reason to believe Erik would not touch the water, she did not intend to close her eyes while he played so close to the lapping waves of the deep canal.

As she watched Erik, her back rested against a driftwood log, warm from the sunshine. Sigun slipped her feet out of her sandals and anchored them in the coarse sand. Erik had been awake in the night again and Sigun was deeply tired. Keeping her eyes open against the onslaught of the sun and sparkling water was unbearably painful.

Suddenly, Sigun was jolted awake. A cloud had eclipsed the sun, the rocks were gray and cold, and the trees above the shoreline were dark emerald, almost black. She was shivering.

"Erik?" she called out, leaping up. "Erik!" she screamed, running around the piles of pale dead wood, raking the black water with her eyes, her stomach accelerating through the bottom of her feet.

"Erik!" There was no answer. Even in the summer, the Salish Sea is deadly cold. It takes only a few seconds for a child to drown. Shame and guilt broke into a torrent beneath her terror. The loss of another child would be unpardonable. Unbearable. She wanted to tear her heart out from her body.

Too much time had passed, but Sigun ruthlessly repressed her panic. If she was to have any chance of saving him, she had to keep her head. She bounded out into the water, the sharp shells cutting her feet, until she felt the seabed drop into the deep, icy canal. The surface of the sea was unforgivably still. The world was colorless. The trees were black against the grey sky.

Then Sigun heard splashing behind her, and Erik's laughter. She turned and scooped him up into her arms, every dear, precious, inch of him soaking wet. Sigun crushed his cold, damp body against her racing heart. She was filled with a mixture of relief, joy, and rage so overwhelming she was speechless. She felt sick.

"Erik, where were you?" she whispered hoarsely, holding him tightly against her breast as she carried him back to the barren sand bar, over the slippery stones and the rocks sheltering spiney assemblies of black-purple sea urchins, until he struggled to wiggle free of her arms. She was shaking as she set him down on the bone-dry rocks beside her backpack. "You know not to go into the water alone!"

"I wasn't alone," he answered unconcerned, but his lips were blue. She dug into the backpack, pulling out the extra set of clothing she always carried for him. She helped him dress and handed him a tart green apple, which he happily accepted. He bit into the crisp fruit, the juice running down his sea-damp chin.

"If you can't see me, I can't see you." Sigun didn't want to make him afraid again, and she was careful not to sound as terrified and angry as she felt. "It is good to be in the water, but you *must* have someone in with you." Sigun was strapping her bleeding feet back into her sandals and packing up their things. She lifted Erik up, and tucking him under her arm, forded the tidal rivers back to the shore. Their car was parked, dusty and alone, on the gravel underneath the long arms of a giant Madrona tree, whose red bark had peeled back to reveal smooth wood that glistened like tanned, wet skin.

Sigun settled Erik into his car seat, fastening the harness. "I wasn't alone." He handed Sigun the core of the apple. "She was with me."

"Who was with you, Erik?" Sigun asked as she fastened her seatbelt, glancing up at his reflection in the rear view mirror.

"The mermaid," he said. Sigun pulled away from the park, and drove quickly up the gravel road and over the bridge. She was still fighting the afterburn of terror, and in its place shame and anger were settling into her body. She, Lars Havegrimm's daughter, had almost lost her child in the water. It was unforgivable.

"Did the mermaid have a tail?" Sigun's heart rate was returning to normal. Maybe Erik had seen a harbor seal, or some other creature swimming below the water, and had been curious, as Sigun would have been. Sigun was a marine biologist after all, or at least, she had been one.

"No," Erik laughed as if her question had been ridiculous.

"Well, what did it look like, then?"

Erik was kicking his legs into the seat in front of him. "Like you," he said, "Her eyes were green, but brighter. Her hair was long, but darker. Her teeth were whiter—" He had his hand in his mouth, feeling his own teeth. "—and sharper."

She glanced at him quickly in the rearview mirror to see if he was as disturbed as she was by his imagined encounter, and was struck as she was every now and then by how impossibly dear he was to her. He looked healthy and unconcerned, as if he had not just been pulled, blue-lipped, out of the cold sea.

"You know her, Mama. It was Astrid," Erik said, his angelic brow furrowed in frustration, his foot kicking the back of the seat with renewed vigor. "She found me."

"Astrid?" Sigun jerked the car back into her lane just in time. A truck sailed past on her left, its honking horn distorted by the speed of their near collision. It took all of Sigun's concentration, then, to drive safely home.

Astrid, Erik's twin sister. Astrid who had lived only eight days. Astrid who had been sedated, wrapped in tubes, and placed in a glass box, floors above Sigun's ravaged body. Astrid who had drowned, not in the water, but in the air.

Unlike Erik, who had been born looking like a shriveled elf, skinny and jaundiced, a tiny wizened old man with pointy ears and a piercing scream, Astrid had been born beautiful and healthy looking. But she had been born second, pulled, violently, feet first, out of Sigun, unwilling and unready. Her lungs had never made the transition from the liquid world of Sigun's womb.

The sky was darkening and little drops of rain began to hit the windshield as she drove over the bridge onto the large island where they lived. She wound her way carefully down to the southern tip of it, the roads dark and narrow, lined with towering trees. It had begun to rain in earnest, and it was hours before Tom would be home from the city.

When Tom did come home, he was soaking wet, having biked back from the ferry in the worst of the downpour. He was exhausted, but the shadows under his eyes did not diminish his good looks. If anything, Tom was growing more handsome. Sigun almost resented it, that his beauty was increasing as she felt hers to be fading. Her hand moved involuntarily to the silver streak that ran through her dark red hair. It had seemed to appear suddenly, the day she finally came home from the hospital without Astrid.

Motherhood had changed the geography of her body inside and out like an earthquake, a volcanic eruption. The cost of it had fallen on her physically, heavily. Sigun, enveloped in grief, had experienced so little of the joy of it.

She had once been sure of Tom's desire, but now she was no longer confident it was under her sway at all. Although the truth was, for some time she had not cared. Sigun felt much less like a siren than a fury.

It was only at the beginning of the summer that she had finally weaned Erik. She had been warned she might suffer a sort of withdrawal; her body had been a factory of calming hormones. Perhaps that was why she felt a storm building inside her, a tumult swirling in her blood. Perhaps that was why Astrid's apparition felt so unsettling, a sudden burst of turbulence when she was already in the middle of a storm.

Later that night, as Sigun and Tom lay in bed together, he asked her about her day.

"It was fine. We drove to Kilisut Island."

"Did you see anything interesting?"

"Well... Erik thought he saw a mermaid."

Tom laughed. "I shouldn't have taken him to the Olde Curiosity Shop."

The shop was on the wharf near where the ferry left the city for the big island where they lived. Among its curiosities had been a 'mermaid', a taxidermist's chimera of fish and monkey, its sharp little teeth bared in fury at the customers below. It had seemed obscene, even in Sigun's childhood.

Sigun rolled onto her back, hesitating. "But the strangest thing was... Erik called the mermaid Astrid."

Tom stilled beside her. "Astrid? Do you and Erik talk about Astrid?"

"No, never. Do you?"

"Of course not. But Erik is like a little sponge. He must have heard us mention her name." She turned away from him, onto her side, and he curled around her. She couldn't bring herself to share how close she had come to losing Erik, the terror and shame of it. Not yet. Sigun could feel his body settle as he fell quickly into a deep sleep, the privilege of the exhausted and the innocent. Eventually, and with great effort, she followed him into oblivion.

The next morning Sigun set about with renewed determination to get Erik swimming lessons with the director of the Aquatic Center. If nothing else, she could make sure Erik learned to swim.

"He doesn't give lessons anymore," the scheduler at the Aquatic Center said, sounding   bored. Despite Mr. Merehinen's flat affect and lack of good cheer, which some parents found disturbing, he had a reputation on the island for being able to teach the children to swim in a fraction of the time of other instructors. After one of his students had gone on to compete in the Olympics, the clamor of families wanting to work with him had become an annoyance, and he had stopped teaching altogether.

"Would you please ask him to consider it?" Astrid persisted. "He is the only person who has been able to lure Erik into the water."

To the obvious surprise of the Aquatic Centre's scheduler, her request was granted, and on the following Tuesday, Sigun and Erik set out for his first lesson.

As they stood at the rim of the pool waiting, Erik held her hand, leaning hesitantly towards the water.

"Are you ready, Erik?" said a gruff voice from the pool. Sigun turned and met the gaze of the director standing in the water. His hair was glowing metallic in the light that filtered down from the skylights in the high cathedral ceiling. His eyes glinted like pale green sea glass in his copper face.

"Good morning, Mr. Merehinen." Sigun was careful to politely keep her eyes on his face, above the collar of his skin-tight neoprene suit. He nodded tersely and held out his hand past her, unsmiling, to Erik.

"Come, Erik," Mr. Merehinen said. Once again, the small boy took the man's hand and jumped into the water.

When Mr. Merehinen brought Erik back to the steps of the pool at the end of the lesson, he cast an assessing glance up at Sigun. He stepped out of the pool after Erik, water dripping off his body.

"We can continue lessons for now." Mr. Merehinen didn't seem pleased or displeased. Sigun felt relieved, as if they had passed some sort of test.

"Thank you. This is important to us." Sigun blushed. She sounded overly earnest even to herself.

But Mr. Merehinen had already turned away and quickly disappeared, past the showers and the nurse's station, into the bowels of the swimming hall.

The next morning, Sigun and Erik took the ferry across to the city to visit her father, Lars, and her grandmother Tulikki, her mother's mother, who had helped raise her. The plan was for Sigun to accompany her grandmother to a long-anticipated art exhibition while her father and Erik walked to the Ballard Locks to ogle ships and boats passing up and down between Lake Washington and the Salish Sea.

Sigun drove first to Tulikki's little yellow house, northeast of Green Lake. A giant birch tree dominated her front yard, towering over the house. This was Tulikki's Yard Tree, and following the old customs, she gave it offerings: coffee, milk, vodka, and occasionally, Sigun suspected, blood.

Most people had forgotten such traditions, but not Tulikki, who had been raised by her own grandmother. After Tulikki was orphaned by the Winter War, she and her grandmother had been sent from Finland to live with cousins north of Seattle. They had shared a little bed in a closet, more indentured servants than family, until Tulikki had saved enough money for their escape.

Even in Sigun's childhood, the Yard Tree had been a massive, flourishing thing, a testament to Tulikki's archaic superstitions. Sigun had said as much to her father one day as he had collected her from her grandmother's house. She had been looking back at the tree, so tall she could not see the top of it from the pickup's window.

"It's not your grandmother's witchcraft that makes that tree grow," her father had growled at Sigun, irritated. "It's her damned sewer line." Her father's angry dismissal had surprised her. Over time, Sigun had learned to be careful not to share Tulikki's little eccentricities with him. Sigun glanced up now at the tree as she walked beneath the green canopy and up the uneven stone steps to her grandmother's red door.

Tulikki popped, grinning, from the front door before Sigun's knuckles reached the red-painted wood. As Sigun helped her grandmother settle into the car with her packages, a magnificent smell of cardamom and butter emerged from her parcels. She had brought a basket of pastries, of course. She never visited Sigun's father without them. They were her special tithing, a penance for her daughter's desertion of Lars when Sigun was just a baby.

Lars was waiting outside when they pulled up to Havegrimm's shipyard. The shipyard had been founded a hundred years before by Lars's grandfather, Torsten Havegrimm, a master shipwright, and his younger brother who had come over from Norway together. The original sign for Havegrimm's Shipyard still dominated the front face of the office, carefully maintained and restored, like the old wooden boats within. On the sign, a wizened seal balanced a sailboat on its right-front flipper. Erik, as was his habit, greeted the seal happily, and it grinned back at him with a knowing twinkle in its eye.

The habitual glower of her father's weathered face broke into a smile as he took Erik's tiny hand. Lars was just over six and half feet tall and he loomed over little Erik and tiny Tulikki like a giant. His tousled, white-blond hair was a tangle beneath his old fisherman's cap, and his clothes and boots were dusty from work. After exchanging greetings, Lars and Erik set off eagerly for the locks, and Sigun and Tulikki turned east toward the museum.

The museum was newly built, a monument to the ideals of rational, Scandinavian modernity. As they entered the white curving walls, Tulikki said, "Do you remember when I read that children's version of the Kalevala to you?" The exhibition was of a Finnish painter, Akseli Gallen-Kallela, who was famous for his depictions of scenes from the epic poem. The Kalevala was the national epic of Finland, and it had been composed from bits of songs and spells collected throughout Finland some two hundred years before. Sigun vaguely remembered the strange tales: wizards battling through song, women forged from metal, jaw bones turned into harps.

"Of course," Sigun assured her, but Tulikki was already moving briskly between the paintings, pointing out this and cooing over that. Sigun trailed in her wake, happy to follow her irregular course as Tulikki paused to examine each work. Sigun liked best Gallen-Kallela's later paintings, finished after the death of his daughter, with their bold black lines and anguished figures. Her favorite was his depiction of the witch-woman Louhi, as a monster with the body and wings of an eagle, vicious talons, and braided red hair, hovering above a long ship sharp with spears.

They had seen almost everything, and Tulikki had finally begun to slow her pace, when she sailed right past the large triptych, three canvases enclosed in a massive, intricately carved and gilded frame. Sigun, curious, stopped to take a closer look. The object of the paintings was a young woman, pale and passive, naked in the last two panes. In the central painting, she was half in the water, twisting away from a man with a long white beard who was reaching out from a wooden fishing dory with grasping hands.

A bony hand gripped Sigun's arm, startling her.

"Do you know this story?" Tulikki said, not looking at Sigun, but at the painting with narrowed eyes. "It's the story of Aino, from the Kalevala. Her brother bargains her away to Väinämöinen, the old wizard, and her mother happily agrees to give her away in exchange for her son's life. Aino escapes by drowning herself and turning into a fish."

Where was the anger on Aino's face? Sigun felt it for her. The girl in the painting was a hairless creature, pale and innocent and as inured to loss as a wooden madonna in a medieval church.

"The model in this version is the painter Akseli Gallen-Kallela's own wife. A little bloodless, don't you think?" Tulikki cackled as she patted Sigun's arm. "It makes you wonder, doesn't it?"

"Shall we go outside to wait for the boys?" Sigun needed fresh air; she was already moving toward the door.

"Of course," Tulikki assented and took Sigun's arm, patting it again. Sigun had at least a dozen inches of height on her grandmother, and she checked her stride carefully to match Tulikki's as they moved down the ramp into the soaring entrance of the museum.

As they reached the towering entrance hall, the darkened glass doors parted to reveal her father, a dusty giant, out of place amidst the sparkling glass and high white walls of the modern museum. He held Erik in the crook of his arm, a beaming cherub riding on a thundercloud.

"Just on time!" Lars boomed, pleased as always by punctuality, his fearsome face breaking into a smile of large white teeth.

Their little procession stopped at the shipyard's messy office. Tulikki conjured her cardamom rolls from beneath a linen tea towel. A silent contentment fell over them, amidst the bliss of butter, sugar, cardamom, and coffee, until Erik, with crumbs on his face, demanded they get to work on the boats.

It was the end of the summer, and the shipyard was starting to fill up again. Boats were straggling back in from spending their summers in the archipelago, or from traveling up north to the raucous shores of the Canadian coast, where they had wandered past waterfalls crashing into the sea, orcas breaching the surface of hidden bays, waves lapping fondly on their wooden hulls. Havegrimm's dealt only with the upkeep and restoration of wooden boats. These boats, costly and difficult to maintain, were the obsessions of their owners; they sounded different in the water, more magical, more alive. Now they were home to be coddled over the winter at great expense.

Her father was working on a boat that had not been on the water that summer, nor for several years, by the look of it.

"Has this boat just been purchased?" Sigun asked, running her hand over the wood with its flaking paint.

"Nope. It's been with the same family since the beginning. But now someone finally has the money to restore it." Her father sounded pleased. He was carefully scraping off the peeling paint. "It will take some work to make it seaworthy again." He turned to Sigun, a sly look on his face. "Do you know who built this boat?"

She did. Even without recognizing the lines of the elegant little sloop, she would have known by the sparkle in her father's eye. "Grandpa Torsten," Sigun smiled back at her father.

"Otherwise I wouldn't have taken it on. But I know I can get this one back out on the water." He patted the wood fondly. "When's the last time you were out on a boat?" Lars did not look at Sigun, his gaze still fastened on his work.

"Oh, I don't know. It's hard to find the time." After college, Sigun had chosen to work on a humble research vessel rather than continue to graduate school; she hated desks. She had planned to work on that ship right up to giving birth, had dreamed of returning to it with a baby strapped to her back. Carrying the twins, and then the difficulty of keeping either of them alive, had put an end to those fancies.

"I had a friend once," her father was saying. "Used to fish with me in the summers. Excellent fisherman. Even better card player. He was good with numbers. One day he fell in love with a girl from Magnolia." Her father waved his hand derisively towards the South, where a hill reared up, its western sea-facing side graced with dignified houses. "He went to college, got a degree—fished every summer to pay for it. And then he got a job at the bank downtown. The one in the black tower. He was good at it, too, but he gave up fishing. He couldn't find the time to be on the water." Lars was scrapping something off the hull of the boat now, his face hidden.

Sigun barely managed to stifle a sigh. Her father's stories had a way of irritating her.

"I'm getting to the point, girl," he said tersely. "The point is, he loved the water, and he gave it up. He didn't fight for it, and he was miserable. Then one day, something went wrong down at the bank, and he shot himself."

Sigun dropped the piece of wood she was holding. "Dad!" She turned, looking for Erik, and spotted him up in a wooden sloop on wheels a few boats back. Not close enough to hear, he was busy talking at Tulikki, who was smiling up at him from the solid ground.

"And his wife, she was devastated. She moved up to Alaska," Lars paused to look at Sigun from under his bushy, white-gold brows. "The point is, she really did love him after all. He didn't need to be slaving away in that dark tower for her. He should have found a way to stay on the water, to stay alive. The damned idiot."

He turned back to his work. Picking up a can, he began to paint something over the scraped wood. "Got to get your feet off the land, girl. I can see it in your face."

"I was just on the ferry, wasn't I?" Her father let out a derisive scoff.

Sigun had picked up a little chisel and was testing its sharpness with her finger.

"What is it?" Lars said, straightening up to his full height and looking down at Sigun with a concerned glower.

"Nothing, really. Erik thought he saw a mermaid under the water, near Kilisut Island, and he talks about her still..."

Her father made another dismissive snort and returned to his work. "Well, when you were about his age, you declared you were going to marry a harbor seal." He let out a rumble of laughter.

"I don't remember that."

"Well, you did. You used to speak to him over the edge of the boat. He was very friendly. A big fellow. I told him he had to wait at least another twenty-five years." Her father chuckled, a deep, rough, almost uncomfortable sound. Children will imagine all sorts of things, after all, and it was a comfort to have her father dismiss her worries.

When it was time to catch the ferry home, Sigun drove Tulikki back to her little yellow house. She could see the birch tree long before they turned onto her grandmother's street. Sigun thought of mentioning the mermaid to Tulikki, but she hesitated, saying instead:

"I think Erik's swim instructor has a Finnish name." Tulikki turned to her, curious.

"What is it?"

"Merehinen."

"Merehinen," Tulikki rasped thoughtfully. "It's a little unusual, but then when people immigrate... Anyway, it's a good name for a swimmer," she laughed. "It would kind of mean a merman, you know, although maybe that would be *Vetehinen*."

"Is that like a *näkki*?" When Sigun was just a little girl, Tulikki had taught her a charm for protection against näkki, something to say before entering the water, and the words came quickly back to her tongue: "*Näkki maalle, minä veteen,*" It was a simple charm: *näkki to the land, I to the water.* She and Tulikki would say it, tossing a stone into the sea before touching the water, like politely knocking on a door before entering a room. Tulikki had always insisted, in her lighthearted way, on reversing the spell as they left the water, to avoid angering spirits. It had been a comforting ritual in Sigun's childhood summers.

"A näkki is a little nasty thing, like a nixie," Tulikki was saying eagerly. "Always after children. You can find those tales all over. Vetehinen is an older thing. My grandmother used to say they weren't good or evil, but sea folk trapped as the land began to rise when the weight of the glaciers lifted after the last ice age. As the land rose up, bays became lakes, islands turned into peninsulas, water was separated from the sea... No one likes to feel trapped. Still, one had to be careful with them, too, so that boats wouldn't capsize, so the fishing was good, so that women weren't lured into their wild arms..."

Tulikki brushed something invisible off of her long skirt. "So maybe Merehinen would be like a Vetehinen, but one that was never caught. Or one that had escaped." She chuckled. "Anyway, it could be a Finnish name." She cast a sideways glance at Sigun. "Be careful. Don't be like your mother."

Sigun felt as if she had been slapped. "I'm not my mother." Sigun managed to keep her voice calm. Erik was in the car, after all.

"We can't help who we are," Tulikki added casually as they reached her driveway, the little yellow house glowing beneath the towering birch tree. "Think of Erik."

"That's practically all I do," retorted Sigun, her eyebrows drawn together in annoyance.

On the ferry ride home, Sigun and Erik joined the tourists on the south side of the ferry's top deck, where they were gathered to take photographs with Mount Rainier looming over the city behind them, a live volcano and one of the most dangerous in the world. Its snow-covered dome was illuminated by the warm light of the setting sun, a white-haired giant's round sleeping head nestled in the green mountains. Someone on the deck yelled excitedly "Look! Killer whales!"

Erik's feet were on the railing high above the sea, and Sigun held her body pressed against his as he leaned back into her. She pointed out over his shoulder to where four fins were slicing through the water, moving fast northwards toward the archipelago. Four bodies breached the surface, dressed in dashing black and white. Not orca whales, but *Phocoenoides dalli,* Sigun thought. A shoal of Dall's porpoises flying through the water. Sigun felt the crazy urge to dive into the sound after them, but she kept her arms wrapped around Erik, her hands curled tightly around the steel bars of the railing. Her father was right; she had been out of the water too long.

That Friday, Erik had his last swimming lesson before the start of school. He slipped into the water as happily as a duck, pushing off the side of the pool and reaching out his arms to Mr. Merehinen, who waited for him in the water.

When the lesson was over, Merehinen brought Erik back to the rim of the pool where Sigun was waiting. He stopped by the stairs, half in and half out of the water. He was looking up from the pool, and yet he managed to have the air of a king granting an audience, or a judge gazing down from his bench. When he finally spoke, he asked:

"Who is Astrid?"

"Astrid." Sigun repeated, turning away to wrap a shivering Erik in his little hooded towel, emblazoned with fire trucks. It meant something to have her daughter's name on her lips. Sigun had learned early on not to speak of her. It made people uncomfortable. Her grief frightened people. They had worried about Erik, too, but there was no reason, now, to hide her from Erik's ears. "My daughter." Sigun was toweling Erik's hair. "Erik's twin sister. Who is dead."

"I see." Mr. Merehinen considered Sigun, not with pity or compassion, exactly, and then turned to Erik. "Good work today, Erik," he said finally.

"Thank you, Mr. Merehinen," Sigun replied carefully. "For the lesson. Say thank you, Erik." Erik did, and they turned and left the man, still standing in the pool.

Sigun waited until they were home, until after lunch, until Erik was busy building.

"Did you see Astrid today?" Sigun finally asked casually. She was lying on the floor, looking up at the ceiling.

"No." He was concentrating on fitting two pieces together. "But I heard her singing under the water in the pool. She was far away, like a tickling in my ear."

Sigun closed her eyes for a moment.

"I'm learning to swim, so I can be with her." Erik added calmly.

What would a good mother do, believe him or tell him it can't be real?

Her own chest was pinched with longing to hear Astrid, to see her. Sigun imagined Astrid as a creature sewn together from the ocean itself. Eyes of sea glass, fingers made from crab legs, a heart of blood red coral. She could not bring herself to be terrified of such a daughter, even if such a daughter would have cause to be angry and jealous of the living.

Astrid, manifested or imagined, had not hurt Erik after all. It was Sigun who had been the danger to him, who had failed to keep her eyes open, as she had once failed Astrid.

On Saturday, Sigun, Tom, and Erik drove to the northern edge of the Olympic Peninsula and hiked down through the evergreen trees until they reached Dungeness Spit, a long sandy arm curling out into the water towards Victoria. They met another family with a boy and a girl close to Erik's age and the children began playing. Soon they were sharing buckets and filling them with wet sand to build a sandcastle.

Sigun knelt down beside them. "Do you want me to teach you a Finnish spell for making sandcastles? My grandmother taught it to me."

"Yes!" The girl replied, clapping her sandy hands together. Sigun glanced quickly at the girl's parents. One never knew who would be disturbed by these harmless little things, but they were talking animatedly to Tom, oblivious. Sigun helped the children tip their full buckets over. She began to tap on the bottom of a bucket with a tiny shovel and the children mimicked her, chanting:

"Älä tule paha kakku

Tule hyvä kak-ku!"

It was an order: *Don't become a bad cake, become a good cake!* They smacked the buckets in rhythm to the rhyme and, laughing, carefully lifted them to find perfectly neat sand-cakes standing proudly below. Sigun glanced up again at the boys' parents, but their mother was smiling, charmed.

The children eagerly set about filling their buckets again. Erik ran towards the surf to gather water and Sigun followed. She thought of her grandmother's charm for entering the water, but she held her tongue back, kept her lips from whispering it, just as she restrained her hand from tossing the smooth granite stone she was grasping in her palm. It was all too easy to get attached to little rituals, comforting bulwarks against the tides of fate.

Looking at Erik playing joyfully at the edge of the waves, Sigun wondered if there wasn't something cruel about ordering a creature out of the water, in removing something from its element without its consent. Anyway, she had never told Tom about the charm; he'd never heard her say it.

She glanced back at Tom, who was still speaking with the other family. The afternoon gilded his dark hair with bronze. He looked happy at a distance, painted gold by the sun, washed by the sea wind, apart from her. Free. Sigun knew her loss, her worry, her sorrow, were not hers alone. And yet, somehow the labor of keeping Erik alive felt more hers, however imperfect her skill at it.

Sigun looked back to Erik, then, just in time to see him being pulled underwater, black tentacles twisting about his legs.

"Erik!" She leapt across the sinking sand, the tide pulling at her feet. He was completely under the water now. He hadn't come back up. She could see the bright white of his striped sun shirt as he was pulled away from her, gliding west into the ocean. She lunged for him and, grabbing him around the waist, dragged him up into the air. He was too shocked to cry or even take a breath.

"Help! Tom!" Sigun screamed, but Tom was already running towards her. Long, thick rubbery strands of kelp wound around Erik. They were still pulling on his little legs as the heavy ball of kelp root rolled away on a receding wave. Sigun tore at the kelp and it tangled around her own legs. "You cannot have him!" Sigun growled at it, weeping with fury.

"Sigun," Tom said sharply, as if he had said her name many times without her hearing. He was holding Erik now, curled against his shoulder. Sigun hurled the mass of kelp roots away, far into the tide. When she turned back to Tom, he was looking at her intently over Erik's shoulder, and she could see him absorbing her words, the madness of them. She looked down, abashed. A piece of kelp was still trailing from her hand, its large floating bulb filled with gasses the alga had breathed into it. *Nereocystis luetkeana*: mermaid's bladder. She dropped it into the water as if it had scalded her hand.

On Monday, Sigun drove Erik to his pretty little preschool in the forest for the first day of school. As she watched him, he hesitated on the threshold, and looked back over his shoulder, a grave look on his face. But then he turned away to greet his teacher, and she escaped.

All summer she had been waiting for this moment when she was no longer responsible for him, when she was alone. Other parents were celebrating by going out for coffee, or rushing back to work; Sigun had a swimsuit on, hidden under her pants and an old fleece jacket.

She drove home under a gray sky heavy with clouds, and, after grabbing her bicycle, pedaled down the street toward the steep paved path that would take her through the seaside park to a remote little beach. This path was why they had chosen the house, but she had learned after moving in that a boy, out on a lark one night, had died when his bicycle had sped off it and over the cliff to the park below. Many parents moved to the island for safety, but perfect safety is impossible.

Down the treacherous path she flew, past the ruined wharf where the cormorants stood sentry as usual, brown-black and iridescent as an oil slick. When she reached the little beach, she did not use Tulikki's charm; her whole purpose was to meet whatever was in the water.

Sigun left her things on the shore and waded through the muddy shallows. Peach colored blood worms fled in frantic fringed spirals from her giant feet until it was finally deep enough to swim. The water was unbearably cold, but as she began to swim, she could no longer feel it, just the pleasure of floating in the water, the weightlessness, the grace that always came to her there.

She swam with long strong strokes out into the channel and let herself feel all of it, the longing, the grief, the anger. If some part of her daughter were there, in the dark water, lost, suspended in the old boundary between worlds, alone, vengeful even, Sigun would find her.

I love you, my daughter. Come to me. Whatever you need, take it from me.

After Erik was born, Sigun had been rushed to an operating theater by yelling doctors with shaking hands. They had tried one last time to pull Astrid out from where she had been curled beneath Sigun's heart. Sigun could feel her panicked struggle against the grasping hands before Astrid went horribly still inside her. Later, Astrid had been wheeled past Sigun, one small, perfect, plump hand lifted, waving from the bouncing speed of the trolly.

For days they had not let Sigun touch her. "She is sleeping," they had said. "She is in too much pain," they had said. Her legs had been dark with bruises. Sigun had nursed skinny, wizened Erik constantly, but she had struggled to express her scant, rich first milk into a tiny plastic cup for Astrid. The night nurse had thrown it away. "It had blood in it," she had said. As if Sigun's painful effort had spoiled the colostrum. As if a drop of her blood could contaminate what was part of her own body, her cells, her antibodies, the dissolved proteins of her tissue.

"Wake me, wake me when she is awake, even in the middle of the night," Sigun had begged. But the night nurse never had. Sigun could understand Astrid's rage because she was still full of it.

Sigun's body drifted, floating like dead wood in the channel. She had stopped shivering and her breathing slowed, as had the blood in her veins, the beat of her heart. If she drifted far enough, she would be in the path of the fast ferry to Bremerton, but she didn't lift her head to look.

Worse than the rage was the guilt. Once, when she was taking Erik to an appointment at the children's hospital, she could not help noticing the many sets of twins lurking in the waiting rooms and elevators. Twins with reconstructed skulls, twins with parents grey as ghosts, twins with tiny arms bandaged from where blood had been drawn from their little veins, their mother weeping over them as she nursed them. Sigun had not been jealous. She had thought: *I am lucky.* Even now, the guilt engulfed her, that she could feel, even for a moment, such a horrible loss to be a blessing. She thought of the ancient tales in which women leave their babies in baskets to drift on the water, or fathers abandon twins on the banks of rivers to be nursed by wolves. What if she was like them, what if she could have done more? How could Astrid ever forgive her?

I love you, my daughter. Can't you feel it? Come to me. Come for me. Take what you need from me. Devour me. I loved you.

I love you still.

Sigun felt something then, surrounding her, a longing that was hers, but not hers alone, a question. Her eyes were closed and she rested her weight on the moving sea. She nestled this presence closely to her chest. This was how it should have been, a child born in water and held over her bursting heart. She held the feeling of it, like a sea otter holds her child fast to her belly, floating on the surface of the ocean.

Just as Sigun became fearful of its end, hungry to keep it, the sense of deep communion began to release her, to leave her, to dissolve in the cold current of the channel, into the sea dark with pollution and storm water and life.

Part of Astrid was alive, after all, swimming inside Sigun's own body. Astrid's cells would live inside Sigun's blood for years, as Erik's would. To become pregnant is to become a chimera, no longer made only of yourself. Across the channel the sea lions were trumpeting again. The water was noisy with life. The sea was our first mother, and we are still made of it.

Suspended in the water and part of it, Sigun imagined she was a shapeshifter, a dragon. She was Charybdis, daughter of a sea god, a maelstrom that could capsize her family in her discontent, her anger, her sorrow, her desire. It wasn't Astrid, but she herself who was the monster. It would be easy for what was left of them to be torn apart like a brittle wooden ship into so much flotsam and jetsam, broken and scattered. It was a terrible responsibility to keep them all afloat, to keep them safe from the furious currents inside her.

A responsibility, an ability, a power that was hers alone. She would honor it. To withstand the thirsty cyclone inside her, to not allow it to swallow them up, to withstand it and to live, that would be a worthy feat of honor, a battle deserving of glory, if only in Sigun's own heart.

But Sigun had been drifting dangerously long. Her dark hair trailed out behind her in the water like the swirls of a fractal, her skin was blue with cold. The sun was somewhere up above, blanketed by the wet gray clouds. She twisted onto her belly to swim back, her eyes open wide in the dim water, but she couldn't make out the shore, and she couldn't quite feel her arms or her feet. It was as if they had vanished and she had been transformed into a salmon, silver-cheeked, bound to live forever in the watery underworld.

She felt it before she saw it, something large and fast swimming towards her beneath the slow current of the channel. Here, after all, was the sea come to claim her, Sigun thought, but her blood was so cold, her heart so slow, that she could not rise in panic. She closed her eyes instead.

Only when arms wrapped around her did she realize the animal swimming towards her had not been a whale or a seal or a shark, but a man, who rolled her onto her back and lifted her head out of the water. She was pressed by the gentle waves against his body, his black wetsuit as slick and velvety as seal skin. He pushed his diving mask up into his silver hair: Mr. Merehinen.

She noticed that his eyes were not actually green, but a cold storm grey, the pupils rimmed with a halo of gold, like the last glimmer of the sun on the crest of a winter sea.

"Sigun! You are alive." It came across not as a question, or statement even, but a stern command. His deep voice shivered across the calm water.

When she made no move to escape, he embraced her, one arm curled beneath her knees and the other wrapped around her chest right below her left breast, holding her to his chest. As they reached shallow water, he picked her up out of the water easily and carried her as if she were still weightless, despite the awkward neoprene mittens that hid his hands, the flippers on his feet, which slapped in the shallow water of the muddy beach.

"Yes, I am. I am alive, thank you," Sigun said, or she thought she said, her lips were still blue with cold. She was filled with gratitude, and she felt as if she could have left her forehead on his shoulder forever, but it wasn't only solace she felt.

She wriggled from his arms like a fish, and stood, towering over him.

He stood very still, his chin up as he contemplated her. There was a quality to his stillness that was transfixing. His attention was so focused on her that Sigun felt heat flood her cheeks. She was blushing and she was so surprised to feel it, she found it so delightfully mortifying, that she had to stifle a chuckle of mirth. Instead, she lowered her eyes, in an attempt to appear demure, remembering her grandmother's rules of etiquette when encountering strange creatures in the forest, unsettling men in parks, animals rising out of wild water: to be respectful and polite, to move away quickly.

"I could help you," his voice was quiet now, a low whisper, "to learn to swim in this water. If you want."

"Not today, but thank you, Mr. Merehinen." Her cheeks flaming, she risked one last fleeting look at his face and was almost sure she saw a flicker of expression there, that his eyes were crinkled at the edges with amusement, that the golden rings around his dilated pupils glowed. Sigun turned, hurriedly towards her bicycle, careful not to chance even a glance over her shoulder. Her skin was still blue with cold, but she felt remarkably revived.

When she finally reached it, Sigun leapt onto her bicycle and raced back through the park, past the old wharf, now empty of cormorants except for the one, streaked red with blood, vanquished below the talons of a bald eagle that was piercing the midday with its incongruously beautiful cry. She hurtled up the treacherous path, pedaling ferociously, her blood (Astrid's blood, Erik's blood) heating again, her lungs burning, to where her house perched precariously on the steep hillside above the water.

Grief is not something that can be nailed in a wooden box and buried, and neither is desire. They ebb and flow like the tide; one has to learn to navigate them. There is no perfect closure, and to believe in one would be a perilous delusion, a mirage, like an island of perfect safety, a sea without monsters.

She sped, cutting off from the paved road and bouncing down the short-cut through the woods where blackberry branches stretched out across a dirt path with monstrous, spiny arms that lashed her bare skin and pinged against the spokes of her furiously spinning wheels.

The air was heavy with the sweet ferment of August berries as Sigun burst out of the forest onto to her ordinary, paved street lined with houses. As she put her hand on the door latch, it opened from within, and Tom was standing on the threshold.

"I left the office early—I wanted to go with you to pick up Erik..." His eyes wandered over her, taking in her red cheeks and the cold, blue skin of her arms, the seaweed in her hair, the hermit crab clinging, terrified, to her swimsuit, which was all she was wearing. She had left her clothes at the beach. He lifted a hand out towards her, gently removing the hermit crab and placing it aside.

She raised her eyes to his face, unsure of what she would find there. At some point, Sigun had lost her confidence that Tom could know her and still love her, let alone want her as she stood now, her hair beribboned with seaweed, her arms red with scratches and tiny drops of blood from the pricks of the blackberry brambles. Sigun thought suddenly of what must have been the exact moment she had fallen in love with him. It was soon after they had met and she had taken him out sailing in one of her father's boats. Tom hadn't grown up around the water, and he was awkward in a boat. She should have been careful with him, but she was overjoyed to be out on the sea again. The wind was strong that day, and had picked up even further to a fierce gale. Sigun hadn't been able to hold back, and she had been laughing as they ran with the wind, the spray of the water hitting her young, grinning face. She had looked back at him in her wild joy, suddenly unsure of what she would find. He was seeing her in her element, unrestrained in all her terrible power and glory, but he met her eyes, not with terror or anger, but admiration. He had trusted her, putting his life in her hands as they flew over the water.

Now, Tom smiled down at her from the front step, with wary affection and longing in his eyes. "You look like yourself again," he said.

"I feel alive again," Sigun said and she found herself grinning back at him. She took his warm, dry hand in her cold, salty one, and placed it over the cool damp skin above her heart. "I don't want to be late to pick up Erik," she said, "But I need to warm up before we go..." Then Tom was pulling her through the door and Sigun was pushing the door shut. They were laughing as they raced up the stairs, her long arm wrapped around his and their hands tangled together.

Sigun's skin tingled almost painfully as her heated blood flowed into the last edges of her body, flushed to the tips of her fingers. She could feel everything again and the return of feeling was a stinging effervescence. She was a pulsing medusa, venomous, bioluminescent, ephemeral. Sigun could feel in that moment, haunted and monstrous though she might be, not only the anguish of living, but also the joy and pleasure of it. She could feel the triumph and the fragility of it, the grace and good fortune of being there, terribly, magnificently alive.

See J.J. Eskelin's story "Astrid Underwater" online at Metaphorosis.
If you liked it, leave a comment. Authors love that!
Remember to subscribe to our e-mail updates so you'll know when new stories are posted.

About the story

When I embarked upon writing "Astrid Underwater", I did not set out to make a story that drew upon Finnish art and myth, but as it evolved, Finnish myth bubbled up in to it. In the story, there is an exhibit of paintings by Akseli Gallen-Kallela. His images of Finnish myth are among the most iconic. Years ago, I used to live near his house, a little Jugend castle on a bluff above the sea, and once I even went to a smoke sauna in his turf-covered sauna, an ancient building, older than the house and built into the hillside on the shore of Laajalahti. However famous he is in Finland, I don't think Gallen-Kallela has ever had a major exhibit in the United States, at least not in my memory. At one point, I thought I should take his paintings out of the story altogether, but I couldn't bear to do it. There was this resonance, not only with his work as I went back to look again, but with the myths underlying it. That resonance kept me going when this story was unruly and difficult. It was the blood running underneath the bones of the story. However, the most unexpected thing to me was that, as I was challenged to go deeper through the editing process, how I saw his work, and my relationship to the underlying myths was transformed. One of the last things I added to the story was Sigun looking at Gallen-Kallela's painting of Louhi. In the Kalevala, Louhi is the chief antagonist, a frightening woman with magical powers. She is also a fiercely protective mother. The juxtaposition of Louhi and Sigun felt like something I had been missing all along. Seeing Louhi through Sigun's gaze, my own interpretation of her was altered. Now, when I look at Louhi, a hostile monster hovering above the boat that is stealing away her treasure, I see her differently; I hope she wins.

A question for the author

Q: Do you generally start with mood, title, character, concept…?
A: When I start to work on a particular idea in earnest, it is because I have a strong feeling about it. I often feel a sense of urgency to capture it, to try to convey a particular image or scene, a voice. If it is an idea that has been haunting me for a while, I will have a clear

concept of the beginning and the end. Even so, there is usually something I only uncover as it develops, some underlying secret that surprises me. To help evoke the particular feeling of a story, the texture and sensation of a particular piece, I have started to write out every word I can think of that captures the feeling I am trying to communicate. I write these not as a list, but by hand as a free-form, organic, cloud of words. Maybe this sounds silly, but sometimes I see something there I have been missing; something I have been struggling grasp rises to the surface. Writing for me can be like being caught up in a wave. I won't pretend to have a great control of my process; I am still learning to find a way to let my subconscious do its work, and to not be afraid of the outcome.

About the author

J.J. Eskelin is a writer of speculative fiction currently living with her family on the Central Coast of California. She has lived in Finland, England, and the United States, and is a dual Finnish and American citizen. Nature and place are important to her, and, no matter where she is, she tries to escape with her giant dog to commune with wilderness on a weekly basis.

jjeskelin.com

She Was the Universe

Damian Stockli

Feb. 1st, 2030

Night shift in the facility always began the same.

Arni woke at 7:00 PM, on the temper foam mattress that had once belonged to Governor Björnsson. He used the governor's shower, his electric toothbrush, and the wool clothes hot from his personal laundry machine—Björnsson wasn't there to protest, was he?—and finally clicked his watch into place. Shower-teeth-shirt-pants-watch, in that order, every night, invariably. The final item of the routine was in the bottom drawer, hidden in a wad of socks: the diamond ring, from when Arni's parents were in love. He pushed it deep into his pocket.

At breakfast, the empty cafeteria echoed with every spoon clink of his Rice Chex and soy milk. Arni explored the grooves of the diamond as he ate. It wasn't fashionable to propose in your twenties, not in Iceland, but Arni had no illusions about it. It was a sure thing, and he needed a sure thing. She would understand.

"So this is, potentially, a kind of stupid question. A potentially, a kind of, a— No."

After breakfast was hydroponics work: managing nutrient levels in the soil, testing to ensure the fungal infection in their wheat didn't escape its quarantine cell. Every time he looked down at the floor, he imagined the ring falling between the bars of the plastic grate and getting lost in the irrigation pipes. *Mamma* had given it to him when he was eleven, after his father had taken a head-on collision along Route 41. She'd said one day he'd make his own home with it. He was careful to keep his free hand cupped over the right pant pocket.

"I figured this is a sure thing. We could all use a sure thing, in times like— No."

Tests came out negative. Plants healthy.

At 10:00 PM, Arni jogged the long way around the facility to reach the south exit. The quiet corridors exploded with the sort of high art graffiti he used to see in Reykjavík: a small girl reading a book under a maple tree, a family of magic tortoises, a woman's hair folding into ocean waves. Good exercise, good view, and it was best to avoid the dormitories, so Arni took the long way every night, invariably.

"Is it open season for—? Siggi, can I ask you a real—? Ugh, Christ."

He nabbed some of their industrial-grade salve at the worker's closet, then thought about Siggi as he applied it to the cold-cracked skin of his hands. It wasn't fashionable to propose in your twenties, but who was around to judge them now? On went two more layers of wool and polypropylene so not a square centimeter of his skin was exposed to the air. Still his nose hairs went solid as he rotated the exterior lock. He hiked up his neck-buff.

It was a clear night, the Reykjanes basalt frosted over and glimmering with starlight. Arni retraced the path of a thousand frozen footsteps from the shelter to the power plant. The blood returned to his face on the way inside, where he resumed his role as one-man control room operation and maintenance crew. Most of the night was spent monitoring corrosion in the injection wells, doing freedom tests on the stop valves, and, when necessary, stepping into the wide turbine room for visual checkups and mechanical repair. Tonight he noticed a single aberration in a control valve's response time, but it didn't persist.

6:00 AM—there always comes a time to put the work down and go home, *Mamma* had said.

But not quite yet.

Arni suited up and spun the exterior lock. The silhouette of the old Reykjanes lighthouse cut a dark thumb out of the starry horizon, and that was his guide to the shore. He didn't look at Jonas's corpse, frozen stuck along his path. When he reached the shore, he plopped onto the ice-crusted ground under a million stars. Each night Arni marveled at the galactic disk, arching horizon to horizon like spilled cosmic milk. The black background of space only appeared as cracks in the light.

He slid his hand between his layers, searching for the pocket. When he found the ring, it looked baby-sized in his double-gloved hand.

"Hey, um, Siggi. There's...." His voice was hoarse. "I have something I need to tell you."

No. Siggi wouldn't be charmed by theatrics. He would have to try harder, be a little more original.

He cleared his throat. "Is it open season for stupid questions? Because I have... one... Fuck. So, is it open season for stupid questions?" He huffed through his neck-buff. "You sound like an asshole, Arni."

He found a more comfortable position, sat up. Chest out, right? Confidence. "Okay.... Hey, Siggi, so, can I be serious with you for a second? I have to say something, and it has to do with something I sensed you weren't too keen on in the past, but I guess I figured, maybe, this was... maybe—"

Arni let himself fall back onto the ice. "Shit."

He figured he'd get it before the sun rose.

Aug. 6th, 2026

"I'm just trying to get you out of that, y'know, that *place*," said Erik, gesturing to the opposite end of the bar. "This could be something good for you. It's been a year, man. Live."

Arni peered left halfway through a swig. The bar was circular, in the middle of the place, so a row of Svedka was just eclipsing her face. She was mixing a drink while she talked up Júlia and Helga. "I have a lot of good things," said Arni. "My therapist has me keep a gratitude journal now."

The trio was framed against a wall of paintings—a nude woman on a beach, a weary fisherman with shining boots, a wintery village. Last week, she had had him guess which was hers, and he got it on the nineteenth try: the little girl reading under a big red maple. She had given him a print of it after, and when he got home he put it in a drawer and not on the wall, because he thought that would be creepy.

The volume of Erik's groans usually depended on how many drinks he'd had. Tonight he'd had quite a few. "I'm not talkin' about job, I'm not talkin' about mortgage, I'm talkin' about *living*, Arnar."

"Don't call me that."

"What? *Arnar?* You only get to be happy Arni once you're living again."

It was an unusually lively weeknight at the Ölstofa, and the scene was beginning to wear Arni down. He had hoped to drink quietly and watch the news for developments on the story going around the water cooler. He hadn't anticipated everyone would be there for the same thing, laughing and cursing each other out and building stacks of cash at the bar and every table. Through a jumble of bobbing heads, he saw the image on TV. It was a true-color reading from the Hawaii observatory, showing an elongated blue-white flare on a background of stars. The 'alien thing' was getting a name tonight, and three options appeared in a list: *Eos, Shamash, Phaeton.* Everyone had a bet.

"You two doing okay over here?!"

Arni froze. Sleeves rolled up, freckles and a silver ponytail. Her name, *Sigrún,* was sewn into her shirt in cursive lettering.

"Just giving my friend a little therapy!" said Erik, over the noise.

She grinned, shining a glass. "Parents fucked you up, huh?"

Arni's head got heavy.

"... sorry, did I say something?" she asked.

Erik waved the concern away. "He's just getting over something. Don't—how about this? What do you think about the alien thing? We're definitely gettin' invaded, right?"

" 'Present fears are less than horrible imaginings'," she said, in practiced English. "But hey, I want to know what the science guy thinks." She pointed to the stitching on Arni's own work uniform: *Arnar Ívarsson | Reykjanes Power Station | Mechanical Engineer.*

He laughed. "Caught me."

"What's the prognosis, then?"

"Well, it's on a heliacal vector, so it's probably going to burn up or get captured by the sun's gravity. As for whether it's aliens..."

"*All*-right, this is where I check out," Erik said, giving Arni one last squeeze on the shoulder. "You two have fun with this gripping conversation." He slid through the forest of bodies then took a seat by Júlia, who beamed and hugged him.

Arni sighed. "Sorry. Are you actually interested in this?"

Sigrún shrugged, but didn't break eye contact.

"Okay. So, it's a high velocity object of extrasolar origin. That's what we know. Aliens are always the last hypothesis."

"Always. Of course."

"But the cool thing is the ionized particles making the light. See, that's not what comet dust looks like. And the reason people are *saying* aliens is because there's a hypothesis going around that it's the effects of a fusion—"

A curse split the noise, commanding everybody to quiet. The whole bar shushed and turned to the anchor on TV. The suit looked down at his tablet, and drew out the last word of each sentence: "The votes are innn... Here we gooo... and the name, is..."—a pause for optimal effect—"Phaeton!" The noise around them swelled to a pitch, and the stacks of cash were distributed appropriately. Erik, apparently a winner, fanned his face with bills and pretended to faint into Júlia's arms. Laughs all around.

"Get another drink out of him while he's feeling gracious," said Sigrún.

"Eh, some of us need to work tomorrow," said Arni, pointing to the stitching in his shirt.

"Don't I know it. But he's right, I think you could live a little," she said. She was juggling the conversation with another order now. "You only get away with the brooding because you're cute, and that won't last forever, Arnar."

His stomach sank. Her eyes bored straight through him. "You —you heard?"

"You get good ears in this business," she said, filling a glass with the house brew. "But listen. It sounds like you're getting over a breakup, and I'm not handing out rebounds."

"My mother died."

Sigrún handed the patron his drink, then froze. She didn't look back at him. "Sorry," she mouthed, too quiet to hear over the noise.

"You couldn't know," he shouted. "It's okay. I'm in therapy and all that." The regret was burning in his forehand. He searched for a way back. "But listen. I'm warning you now that my power plant salary isn't as high as most people think, if that's your angle."

"Curses, foiled again," she said. "Do you want to start this conversation from the beginning, Arnar?"

A familiar rush snuck up on him. Something good? "Call me Arni," he said, pointing to the stitching in his shirt.

"Siggi," she said, pointing to her own.

"So what are you up to tomorrow night?"

Siggi's smile widened like light breaking. "Mondays are better for me."

Feb. 2nd, 2030

7:00 PM on the governor's bed.

Arni washed and brushed. He grabbed the ring from the drawer and slipped it in his pocket.

He ate his Rice Chex in soy milk.

And tended to the crops in hydroponics.

He avoided the dormitories.

An eventful night at the plant. The faulty control valve had failed to trip while he was gone, so the turbine was spinning so fast it would disassemble within hours. Arni unhoused the valve actuator to work on it, steam piping into the turbine room. When the valve shot closed on his left pinky and ring fingers, he discovered it was an electrical hiccup in the governing mechanism, not the actuator itself. His team would have stopped him from making the assumption, if they were there.

He flipped the emergency release and pulled his fingers out of the steam, ignored the swelling and burns, fixed the electrical bug, then proceeded to the shore.

Ring in his hand.

"Is it a cliche to say you make everything worth it?"

Jan. 31st, 2027

When Arni was six years old, his father had dug a hole in their backyard after they found hot groundwater breaking the surface there. They had let the water fill the hole, and set up a rain gutter to let it run down the hill. The empty house was for vacation now, so when they made the trip out he insisted Siggi give their manmade hot spring a try.

Phaeton-3, the third object of its kind, happened to cross Earth's orbit close enough to be visible in the northern hemisphere in daytime. With his face just above the water, Arni watched the pale white streak in the sky.

Siggi, slowly floating from the opposite end, finally collided with his arm.

"What are you thinking?" he said, to break the quiet. "You okay?"

"Every time you ask me that, do you think this will finally be where I say I'm leaving you?"

"It's a habit, isn't it?"

" 'Words like violence, break the silence. Come crashing in. Into my little world.' "

"More English poetry?"

"Yes."

"Ah."

"So what are *you* thinking, *elskan mín*?"

A cloud passed over the white streak, and a gust of wind nipped Arni's nose. "That coming back to this house is easier with you. It's funny. *Pabbi* used to joke that I'd bring a girl here one day."

She frowned. "You haven't told me much about him."

Arni shook his head. "He was here until I was eleven, and then a car accident. It's old news, really. But at the time, it... I don't know. It's like it broke the world."

"Only tell me what you want."

A world of memories broke the surface. He pushed them out. "The thing I remember most was my mother. I couldn't let her leave my sight after that. It was like... Schrödinger's *Mamma*. Ugh, God she'd slap me for that one."

"What do you mean?"

"Every time she left the room, she could be gone. I just couldn't... *not know*. I had to *know*. That she was still there. Does that make sense? So I had problems going in to school. For a year, I went in late or I didn't go at all. They sent me work to do at home when I could, and the only subject I stayed ahead in was math." He laughed. "There's always an answer in math, right?"

"Including a financial answer, which you of course have found as well."

"Yes," he chuckled. "I was attached to her for a long time. And a year ago I finally lost her too, and this house went empty. Orphaned, at twenty-five. Whenever I pull in the driveway, it feels like she'll stick her head out the front door."

She frowned. "I'm sorry, *elskan*."

"But it wasn't as much a shock as *Pabbi*, you know? *Mamma* had MS for years, even when he was alive. I think it's uncertainty that gets me. I can't not know what's going to happen next."

Siggi sat up, staring at the clouds with sullen eyes. "I think I'm the opposite way."

"Really?"

"People on this island," she looked at him with that stare, "settle into lives early. I think that's like death. When nothing changes, when you know everything that's coming at you. It sounds crazy, but dying in bed at 90 scares me. Knowing that I could get shot tomorrow? That helps me sleep. Because I know it's not all going one place."

"So you wouldn't grow old with me?"

She tilted her head. "Arnar. Come on."

He let his head fall back into the water, and watched the clouds drift past the snowy edge of the hole. Siggi placed her wet hand on his chest, and her face appeared above him, eyes now gone soft. "Just answer me this," she said. "Am I the girl you were always supposed to bring here, or am I me?"

"I don't understand."

"She was a vision your father created. Am I her, or am I me?"

"Of course you're you."

With a smirk, she said, "Don't forget it," then held her nose and went under the water again.

Feb. 3rd, 2030

Wake up at 7:00 PM.

Get dressed. Grab ring.

Breakfast.

Make sure the crops are healthy.

Avoid the dormitories.

Can no longer ignore burns and swelling in fingers. Probably broken. Apply topical ointment and splint.

Work at the plant.

Pass the corpse. See the stars.

The ring.

"I asked you once if you'd grow old with me. Now I have a sequel to that question."

Aug. 30th, 2028

"Is it competition on the job market?" she asked, looking down at him in his spot at the kitchen table. "Is that the problem?"

"No, no."

"Is it English? Are you afraid of having to use English for your job?"

"My English is... fine."

A letter had shown up in their mailbox a week prior—Siggi's fellowship. They were both ecstatic at its arrival. Only now was he losing his footing. Siggi had cleared the books from her desk, and the letter had sat there since. Arni found himself avoiding it.

"London is going to be harder than Reykjavík, I know that, but from everything you tell me, you're good at what you do and your position is *in demand.* In my field, I can't just pitch a tent wherever I want in the developed world. You can."

"Siggi, the industry is more complicated than that."

She drew out a long breath. "Don't pull that with me. You know I know what's what."

"Can we just give this more time? Maybe we're not ready for that yet."

"That's..." Another breath. "That's not how a fellowship works, Arni. I can't defer forever. I'm..." She looked down at her empty palms, then up at him. The stare. "I'm trying to make *this* work right now."

"What if we end up there forever?"

"What is keeping you *here*? God help me, I'm struggling to figure out *what* is keeping you here. Do you have *anything* here?"

"Really? You're going there?"

"Oh, Arni. You know that's not what I mean."

"Then what do you mean?"

"Arni..." She glanced out the window, drawing another breath, but it came staggered. "I love you, but I have to take this." She rubbed something out of her eyes. "And because I love you, I don't want this to be an ultimatum."

He shook his head. "I don't know that word."

"A final decision."

"It feels like that's what this is."

"I can't—" she said, hands in her face. "I'm bad at this." She grabbed her jacket from a kitchen chair. Then she snagged her keys from the counter. Arni was standing before he realized it. *Where are you going?* he would have said next, but she read it on his face. His face gave everything away, she always said. "I'm going to my family's house. I'm not punishing you, I just... I just need to think, I want you to think too, okay? I'll see you tomorrow. Okay? Okay."

There was a *creeaak-BANG* on the door, then quiet. Arni was alone again.

Feb 4th, 2030

7:00 PM.

Grab the ring.

Work.

Avoid the dormitories.

Burns not healing. Discoloration. Possibly exposure to cold.

Sit on the shore anyway.

The ring.

"You always say the only constant is change. What about one more constant? Just one more?"

Sep. 30th, 2028

Arni's feet were propped on the ottoman, silhouetted against the TV screen. A sharp ache stabbed at his knees, since his legs had no support, but he didn't dare move them. Siggi had fallen asleep with her head in his lap. She smelled like alcohol and bar food. Her bare feet were at the edge of the couch, veins bulging, bright red blisters around her ankles. Arni held her acceptance letter in his right hand, stroked her hair in his left.

The TV made its noise: "This marks the *thirty-ninth* object that has entered our solar system since last year. Astronomers expect Phaeton-39 to follow a similar pattern to each one that has come before it, being captured by the sun's gravity and entering a low-solar orbit. We'll continue to provide updates…"

Arni placed the letter by his feet, then remembered, in *Mamma* and *Pabbi*'s house, the ring in the bottom left drawer of their dresser.

Feb. 5th, 2030
7:00 PM.
Ring.
Work.
Avoid the dormitories.
Burns still not healing. Dark purple.
Jonas is really frozen solid.
Ring.
"There's just something I need to get off my chest. And I promised myself I'd do it."

Nov. 4th, 2028
Tonight was the night.

On the old king bed in his parents' house, Arni laid two tickets to London Heathrow International—and their diamond ring. "You're going to ask her before the sun rises. She'll say yes. You make your—It'll be fine. Fine." He dropped both into his jacket pocket and spritzed himself with cologne.

The plan was dinner on the back deck. The food was almost out of the oven, the table was set, and the night was clear. The aurorae borealis were out in a flood, jittery green ribbons being towed across the sky from some uncertain point beyond the mountains. There was a soft green glow on the deck and table setting. Nature had been kind to him.

Siggi pulled into the driveway at 7:00, looking confused by his outfit. "Should I have worn my work uniform?"

"No need, since I'm waiting on you today. Come out back."

She reacted with the surprise he was hoping for, but there was a sense of urgency underneath which—he thought—they could both feel. It was all a romantic gesture, but she must have wondered, and he knew she must have wondered: *Why?* Before carting out the wine, he told her he had something for her. She was still smiling when her brow furrowed, but when he reached into his jacket, and told her to close her eyes, she frowned. In that second while her eyes were closed, he thought he might have guessed what her answer would be.

"You can open."

When she saw the boarding passes spread on the table, her shoulders relaxed. She put on a happy frown, and met his eyes. "Thank you, *elskan mín.*"

"Call it the appetizer. Now, the rest!"

The night ran away from there. They talked about the old days at the bar, Erik and Júlia's on/off relationship, Arni's obsessive boss, and of course, the life that waited for them in England. He admitted to her he was scared, and he was going to need to brush up his English, but he wanted the best for her. They were going to make a new life.

When the meal was finished they took their clothes off and went back to the spring Arni's father had dug. He kept the ring balled in a tight fist under the water as they floated and watched the aurorae in the sky, green glow scattering off the surface and lighting her face.

"Siggi."

She kept her eyes on the sky. "Yeah?"

So you wouldn't grow old with me?

He felt the hard diamond between his fingers. If he squeezed tighter he'd bleed. "Siggi, I need to ask you someth—"

"Wait. *Elskan*, have you seen this before? The sky."

The aurorae all seemed to thin at once. First, the accents of blue and violet at the upper edges dissipated. Then he watched as the green glow in the water around Siggi dimmed. "No," he said. "Never in my life."

The ribbons, all the way to their origin beyond the mountains, dimmed until they were gone. The moon's face shifted, gradually, from its bright white to a dull gray, and they watched it until it too dimmed into a black disk. Then the stars came out. A thousand new points of light broke through and twinkled all at once, more than he had seen in his life. The black of space became cracks in the light.

"What just happened?" she said.

He tightened his fist around the ring. "I don't know."

Feb. 6th, 2030
Ring.
Avoid the dormitories.
Amputated fingers.
Shore.
Ring.
"You knew it was coming."

Nov. 6th, 2028
Arni took a dixie cup from the water cooler back to his desk, and stared at the clock on the control room wall. He'd give himself ten minutes to zone out—what passed for a break now—and then he'd go back into the meeting with Magnús and Anna and the rest. He was on his fourteenth hour and third energy drink. His team had never been this busy before.

The clock: 6:59 PM.

Two days. 48 hours. The night had lasted 48 hours. The banality of it was unsettling, but also misleading. The lights in their houses still worked. Their electricity and plumbing was still there. Cars still had gas. The internet worked. As far as anybody could tell, they had entered eternal night, and that was it. It was just sustained darkness. Arni knew better.

He did the math.

1 day: avg. global temp 14 degrees C, immediate cessation of photosynthesis worldwide, lives lost negligible

7 days: global avg. temp 0 degrees C, all grass and cereals dead, halted supply chains ~10 million lives lost

30 days: global avg. temp -30 degrees C, complete ecological collapse as scavenger species die off (cats in Reykjavík), emergency stockpiles near depletion, ~5.4 billion lives lost

365 days: global avg. temp -75 degrees C, frozen oceans, long-range radio comm unusable due to ionosphere deterioration, only people left are who we manage to save

4,000 days: global avg. temp -130 degrees C, air begins to condense into snow, shielding required on facilities to protect survivors from exposure to cosmic radiation

7:09 PM. Break over.

Arni's watch read 7:08—a minute slower than the control room's atomic clock. He twisted the minute-hand a hair forward, then wound it. Only seven minutes later, he found himself winding it again.

Feb. 7th, 2030
Ring.
Three frostbitten toes amputated.
Shore.
Ring.
"With a thick enough jacket, we could ice-skate to anywhere in the world now. Ha. How does that sound?"

Dec. 1st, 2028
"Sir, you're not priority," the guard said to Erik, his breath a white fog.
"What the fuck does that mean?" said Júlia. She stuck an arm out toward Siggi and Arni. "We're their friends. You have to."
The guns had finally come out. Route 425 was barricaded a mile and a half out from the plant. Just behind Erik and Júlia, cars on both lanes, backed up all the way to the airport. Somehow the word had spread. Things were getting tense under the stars.
"Why can't they come?" said Siggi.
"Mr. Ívarsson is priority, and you're his plus one. We're at capacity until more of the shelter is constructed."
"They'll take you on the next round," Arni said to his friends. They looked between him and the guard, bundled under blankets, fear-stricken. "They will."
"You're sure?" said Erik.
"I'll see you soon," said Arni.
"O— Okay," said Erik.
"Okay," said Júlia.
The guards pushed Erik and Júlia back with the rest of the bundled squatters along the road. Arni put his hand on Siggi's back and they walked together to the shuttle bus, windows glowing yellow in the darkness. When Arni looked back, Erik was still watching him go.
"They're going to get in, right?" said Siggi.
Arni stuck his hands in his pockets and shivered.
"Arnar, they're going to get in, right?"

Feb. 8th, 2030
   Ring.
   Avoid the dormitories.
   Shore.
   Ring.
   "You've read my mind plenty before, haven't you?"

Dec. 21st, 2028
   Anna, now a project lead, scribbled the equation on a napkin and shoved it in his face. "Negative sixty-two celsius: with only one jacket that's hypothermia for you in under ten minutes. Remember Jonas? There will be no more dead engineers on this team. Put. On. Your. Jacket."
   "There's no time."
   "Mr. Íva—"
   "No time. I need to get the modified fuel to—"
   "You have time to put on your jacket, Mr. Ívarsson. You do not have time to argue with me."

Feb. 9th, 2030
   Ring.
   Avoid the dormitories.
   Ring.
   Take as long as you want, elskan.

Oct. 3rd, 2029
   The walls of their shelter were made with an ICF process modified for insulation in subarctic temperatures. The interior-facing polystyrene blocks were sheeted with fiberglass paneling cannibalized from the state building and other power plants, making hallways of hospital white gloss. This was a problem Siggi had led the initiative to fix. When Arni walked to the south exit for work in the plant each day, the halls were covered in springtime vistas, psychedelic cascades, and animals the children had done.

In Dormitory 02-02, Arni and Siggi's Sistine Chapel, two plane tickets were wedged in the frame of a wall mirror. The plaster walls and ceiling had become a baroque sky-scape, the circular mirror its rising sun emanating light beams. Siggi dabbed her brush with more yellow, and dashed a beam with definition, carefully avoiding the tickets. Arni lay in bed, mesmerized by the precision of each brushstroke.

Siggi mumbled as she flicked her brush. "Tyson sphere? Dagursson sphere? *Dyson* sphere." Then, in her soft English: " 'Darkness had no need of aid from them—she was the universe.' "

Feb. 10th, 2030
  Avoid the dormitories.
  Ring.
  Schrödinger's dormitories? Ha.

Nov. 21st, 2029
  Sitting at his terminal, Magnús sent a diagnostic request to master control, and it produced pages of text in less than a minute. Arni and each person on the control team read it individually, then gave Magnús the okay. He sent in another diagnostic request, and the same process followed. They repeated this action at least five times. When it was clear that the plant would stay in perfect shape for at least another 24 hours, Magnús stood at the front of the room. He took a deep breath.

"Alright everybody, good work. Before we... close the book... on this place, I just want you to know how proud I am of all of you. I don't want a single one of you to think that we failed here. Maybe we can't say the same for the botanists..."

Weak laughter.

"... but the engineering staff... You did what shouldn't have been possible. I especially want to recognize Arni Ívarsson and Anna Jónsdottir for their work developing the conduction system running from the plant to the shelter. We were lucky enough to have Iceland. But we were even luckier to have Arni and Anna on our team. Your work was a godsend."

Lucky to have Iceland. The geothermal vents were their salvation. Everyone with the means had drafted plans for nuclear powered bunkers, but couldn't stay ahead of the chaos. On the newscasts around the world they had seen many bright orange flashes in the darkness die slowly and give way to the starlight. The radio signals had gone one by one, the last a persistent communication from Nishiyama, just lost a month and a half ago with the last of the planet's ionosphere. Iceland might have been the last man standing.

Even then, a blight in their hydroponics had gotten them. There'd been no genetic diversity in their fruit and cereal farms. The fungus tore right through one cell, then leaked into the irrigation pipes and took out the rest. Dr. Gunnarsson had led an expedition to the Svalbard Seed Vault to prevent that very thing from happening, but found that the E.U. people had already stolen the seeds and taken them back to Germany. Some good it had done them.

The engineering team suited up under all three layers, then Magnús led them across the ice to the shelter for the last time. Arni and Anna walked together in silence.

"Did you tell your husband about... you know, the dinner tonight?" he asked.

Anna shook her head.

"It doesn't feel right," he said, "making this decision for everyone. I don't know."

"With Kristján..." said Anna. "He'll fight to the end. But that's exactly why. It's just better that some people don't know."

"Yeah," he said.

"But you told Siggi about the dinner?"

"Yeah," he said. "She— It just— I knew... that she'd want to know."

Anna put a comforting hand on his back. "All good things, Arni, all good things. Take one more look at the stars before we go in."

There they were, like always, fixed. At the end of the night, maybe the humans would be gone, but the earth would keep turning, and they'd still shine down, and all of it would keep on moving like they never existed in the first place. There was an interesting feeling there. If he asked Siggi, she could probably cite a poem or a painting or a book about it. He wished he had had the time to read them.

"Don't feel humbled by them," said Anna. "A few trillion years, and they burn out too. The little green guys that stole the sun? Don't know what they're gonna do then. It all trends toward stasis. We just made it to the Big Freeze a little early." She nudged his shoulder. "Like ants who nested in some nice-looking lumber."

He wasn't sure how the idea gave Anna peace. As she took in the stars, he didn't see fear on her face. For the rest of the night, right up until the last moment he saw her, none.

Arni helped prepare the last supper, but he and Siggi didn't eat, knowing what they knew. Most of the facility's inhabitants weren't clued in as to why Governor Björnsson had called for a feast so large it nearly depleted their store of luxury food, but they didn't question it. The people were hungry, many of them emaciated. Some of the youngest children had swollen bellies, a mark of protein deficiency. Until three months ago, Arni had never seen children that looked like that with his own eyes. The facility's main cafeteria echoed with thousands of happy voices. A sadness pulled him down as he watched them all devour their food, but this was better than starvation—and the violence that accompanied it. The governor had made the right call. He was tearing into a steak not twenty feet away.

The night came to an end when a profound tiredness fell on all 5,402 Iceland survivors. Each cafeteria was cleaned, and everybody shuffled through the corridors to go sleep.

Around 10:00 PM, in their tiny unit, Arni sat on the edge of his bed with Siggi. Had the light been turned on, he might have gotten a look at their Sistine sky, but only a thin bar emanated below the door. Siggi was gaunt and fragile, her freckled cheeks sunken, the silver color in her hair now only down to the tips. He wondered if that meant the Siggi he knew was gone away, or if this was who she always was, underneath, waiting to come out. He wondered that about everybody.

Her hand felt like a vice around his. He thought she might have been scared.

The ring was in his pocket, still there, waiting.

She kissed him. "I love you."

"I love you."

She produced two capsules of pentobarbital. He could have mistaken them for multivitamins, or antibiotics. "Are you ready, *elskan mín*?"

But the ring.

He cupped his hands over them. "What if we didn't?"

She looked sad. "Arni..."

"I know there's one hydroponic cell left. I know that's enough to sustain five people for life, and I know I can maintain it *and* the plant alone if I need to. It won't keep the species alive, but it'll keep us alive. It would just be us. It could work. I know it."

"Arni... That won't be living."

But the ring. What about the ring?

"Stay here with me," said Siggi. "Please."

It wasn't supposed to go like this.

"Okay," he said.

A smile. A kiss. She pulled his hand off and slid the pill into her mouth. He did the same.

Siggi swallowed.

Arni felt the capsule roll around on the roof of his mouth, but he couldn't push the thing back. It wouldn't work. Something in his mind, his jaw, his tongue—it wouldn't let him do it. The pill stayed there, even as she fell into bed with him and brought the sheets over. He held her bony head to his chest.

The ring. In his pocket.

"Siggi?"

"I'm here, *elskan.*"

"I— I— I have to— I…"

"Shh. Stay with me. It's okay."

The mean pill sat there, pressed between tongue and gums. The not knowing, he decided, was what kept him from rolling it back. The never-ending not knowing, and the unknowing. If he could say something. If he had the time. He could not let the world slip into that box. He could not let her slip into that box. He would not.

Arni pulled the covers off his body and felt his feet touch the cold floor. Spit the pill in the trash. Across the room, he pulled the door to the hallway open.

He had to wipe the water from his eyes to see. Had to steady his breathing. The light from the doorway reflected off Siggi's pupils. Drowsy, she raised a single finger to him. "*El... Els—*"

"Good night, *elskan mín,*" he said, like every night, then closed the door and went back to work.

Feb. 11th, 2030

The ring.

Arni sat on the shore, looking out at the ocean. Where once the waves had crashed, there was now only a flat and dull expanse, all the way to the twinkling horizon. The air bit. It had taken fingers and toes. Still, he sat on the shore, because he had to.

"By the water again," he said. "Your favorite."

Thanks for reminding me, Arnar.

"Sorry," he said. He began again. "So I know we have, um, multiple layers of gloves on right now, but... think you can fit *this* on your finger?"

Awful. Not as charming as he thought.

"Can I show you something I've been saving?"

Too forward.

"Fuck. Fuck fuck fuck fuck FUCK!" He wound his arm back and hurled the damned thing into the ocean. It made a clink when it hit the ice, and skidded along until it came to a stop against a small crest, glinting diamond unmistakable.

There was a tight jolt in his chest. He forced the sob down. Tears came out, but crusted on contact with the air. He couldn't feel his cheeks, or his toes, or his fingers. Arni turned back towards the lights of the shelter, squat on the rocky plain. There always comes a time, *Mamma* had said, to go home. He took four steps in that direction.

But the ring was behind him. Sparkling there.

"Where did you go?" he whispered.

I think you kn—

"No. No. *No.*"

He rushed across the ice to grab it, but lost balance on the bad foot. He slipped once. Ran. Slipped again. With the three fingers of his left hand, he fumbled it into his right, then trudged back to the shore and found the same spot.

Arni took a deep breath.

"Siggi," he said. "Will you—"

It caught in his mouth.

Arni sat still for a while, rolling the ring between his fingers, eyes stuck on the horizon. He figured he'd get it before the sun rose.

*See Damian Stockli's story "She Was the Universe" online at
Metaphorosis.
If you liked it, leave a comment. Authors love that!
Remember to subscribe to our e-mail updates so you'll know when
new stories are posted.*

About the story

The first iteration of this story was written when I was 18, and dissatisfied with how human-centric alien invasion stories tend to be. I figured the only thing an interstellar civilization could want from us was the sun—making us the "ants in some nice-looking lumber"—and that idea stuck with me. The story's current form took shape during the height of the pandemic, where I revisited the idea for a Zoom class on writing about catastrophe. It reflects some of my own experience with loss and neurosis. In that way, you could probably frame it as a COVID story.

Some of the works in my head as I wrote it include the poem "Darkness", by Byron, which is where the title comes from; Ingmar Bergman's classic film The Seventh Seal; and a melodramatic pop song called "As the World Caves In" by Matt Maltese.

A question for the author

Q: How does writing speculative fiction affect your daily life?

A: I definitely don't think normally. My brain is always looking to relate some mundane observation to a gestalt, even when there is none. I'll hear a friend pronounce a word in an interesting way, and sixty seconds later I'm daydreaming about dialect variations in the NYC metro area. Then, at some point, I start speculating on fictional anthropologies. That leap is where the SF writer comes in, I suppose. My writing teachers always taught me to take notes on the world around me and use that in my writing. It's been good for making SF, but in my daily life it probably manifests mostly as inattentiveness.

About the author

Damian Stockli is a writer and graduate student from the Hudson Valley, in New York State. When he isn't doing thesis research on the grammatology of virtual semiotics, he's pursuing that childhood dream of writing a space opera—and all the short stories currently on deck. He hopes to finish them before age 30, or maybe 40.

damianstockli.wixsite.com/stockliblog, @DamianStockli

The Antidote for Longing

Karl Dandenell

Part 3

Previously… Lars Bjornsen, the banished imperial poisoner, has returned to court in disguise, where he is reunited with his old friend, the imperial physik Fredrik Magnusson. Together, they investigate the mystery of Emperor Gustavus' illness and the apparent suicide of the newest imperial poisoner, Lord Anders. While the clues point to a possible coup attempt, Lars begins to suspect that Lord Anders has been feeding the emperor an aphrodisiac known as *Sweet Agony* to ensure a new heir. And for an old man like Emperor Gustavus, *Sweet Agony* can be a deadly poison.

I told Fredrik the story of the *Viktoria*, an imperial warship that patrolled the fjords around Oslo. Two score years ago, a strange sickness had struck *Viktoria*'s crew. Following an extended refit in Tønsberg, her sailors began sleeping through their shifts, and they repeatedly raided the captain's store of sweetmeats despite the heavy punishments meted out to restore discipline.

One boatswain and a cook, both of middle years, died without warning. Emil Krog, the imperial spymaster at that time, believed the tsar's agents had contaminated the ship's water barrels and called upon the Society to investigate. His suspicions proved false.

The Society eventually traced the crew's illness to a spiced wine served at the Lusty Mermaid bawdy house. When questioned, the owner admitted she'd hired an unscrupulous physik with the goal of 'fortifying the desires and increasing the flow of heart's blood' of her customers.

"The name *Sweet Agony* was said to have been coined as a salacious jest by the owner, but that part of the story is likely apocryphal," I said.

"An ingenious method to fatten one's purse," said Fredrik. "Still, why would Anders implement such a ploy, knowing it had killed several men?"

"We tested *Sweet Agony* and found it fatal only in extremely high doses. Very impractical, and thus, never formally adopted by the Society," I replied. "However, in repeated low doses, *Sweet Agony* increases fertility as well as desire."

"I hope that wasn't part of the Society's tests," said Fredrik.

"Oh no. The evidence came to light during an imperial tax audit of Tønsberg's orphanages," I said. "One of Gustavus's reforms provided a small stipend to women who surrendered their unwanted newborns."

Fredrik nodded. "It's certainly better than abandoning them to nature."

"But the audit found an unprecedented cluster of bastards appearing eight to nine months after the *Viktoria* left port. Turns out the Lusty Mermaid's girls contributed more than their usual share. Far more," I said and cleared my throat like a lecturer at the imperial academy. "Given all the evidence, I am confident we're dealing with nothing more than a simple overdose of *Sweet Agony*."

"Impressive deduction," said Fredrik and gently applauded.

His praise brought a flush to my cheeks. "This isn't my first encounter with *Sweet Agony*. Nor yours."

"What do you mean?"

"Do you remember the awful punch they served at the academy's Christmas parties?" I said.

"Gah," he said. "Half molasses and half *akvavit*. It did enliven the spirit, though."

"That's because the Society sells *Sweet Agony* to the senior students."

"That's terrible! Poisoning the best and brightest!"

"'Twas no more deadly than the *akvavit*. Besides, the profits go to the church." I tapped the cover of the novel next to me. "Anders is—was—a much younger man, so his memories of the academy were no doubt fresher. And this romance became his Mnemosyne."

I trimmed a quill and found a piece of foolscap. "Fortunately for His Majesty—and the rest of Europe—there is a simple counteragent." I inked my quill and commenced writing. "You'll need these herbs."

Fredrik came behind me and read over my shoulder. "Yes, yes, I can manage this from my stock. How do I prepare it?"

"Grind everything into a fine powder and add it to a tisane of dried mint flowers and honey," I said, annotating my list. "Put a spoonful under the emperor's tongue every hour until he consumes a teacup's worth. When he fully wakes, give him another four full cups, or until his piss turns clear. Then he can have some broth."

"What about sweetmeats?"

"I think his cravings will be eased by then," I said. "He should be fit for court in a few days."

Fredrik began selecting jars from his chest. "I'll have the cooks steep some beef bones and onions with a pinch of white pepper." He turned to me. "Anders' heart may have been in the right place, but he did us no favors."

"I suspect Anders did not take this road without encouragement," I said. "The spymaster can be very convincing." Maja had almost convinced me that she didn't love me.

Gustavus Adolphus coughed again.

I crouched behind the dressing screen, peering through a gap in the painted panels as Fredrik held a cup to the emperor's lips. "Please drink some more, Your Majesty. It's only mint tea and honey."

"How long was I sick?" asked the emperor, his voice gravelly.

"Five days. You're over the worst of it."

The old man's eyes flicked around the bedchamber. The demon lights burned bright as the noonday sun. "Where is my valet? And why is it so damn quiet?"

"I thought it best you remain undisturbed, given the nature of your illness."

"Nonsense! You're an old hen, clucking over nothing." He coughed again and accepted a swallow of tea. "Just my stomach, is all. Too much cake. Nothing to worry about."

His dismissive tone crushed the small hope I'd been nursing. Most men sailing so close to death might see the world with different eyes, but not Gustavus Adolphus. He'd always considered himself the empire incarnate: powerful and unbending.

"Not anymore, no," agreed Fredrik. "You *were* very sick, though. So much so that I called in a trusted colleague for a consult. I'm sure he could explain it better than I." He glanced toward the screen. "Perhaps if Your Majesty feels up to it, I might arrange a brief visit."

I shook my head, even though Fredrik couldn't see me. An hour ago, before the emperor began to stir, Fredrik had suggested that we reveal my involvement in his recovery. I'd agreed, eager to seize this singular opportunity to regain his favor.

Now the plan struck me as foolhardy at best. The emperor's gratitude was a coin rarely spent, and certainly not wasted on men who failed him.

"Later, perhaps," said the emperor. "I'm starving. Have someone bring me food."

Fredrik rang the small bell on the side table. A moment later, the heavy oak door swung open and a servant entered.

"Some beef broth for His Majesty," said Fredrik.

"At once, my lord."

"And close the door behind you."

The servant bowed and departed, dragging the door closed with a solid thud.

"Help me sit up," said Gustavus. "I'm not an invalid to sup lying down."

"Of course." Fredrik arranged the feather pillows and refilled the emperor's cup. "Your Majesty, I have good news. Empress Anna is gravid."

"Finally. That woman was burning through the candle of my patience." He sipped more tea and grimaced. "Tastes like grass."

Two quick knocks announced a servant, who bore a silver tray with a matching bowl and spoon. He arranged the tray on the bed and stood at attention.

"Out," said the emperor, wielding his spoon with a steady hand. That, combined with his obvious energy, gave proof to the efficacy of the antidote. It was a small comfort and I clung to it.

"Gently, Your Majesty, gently. You haven't eaten for days."

Gustavus narrowed his eyes but set aside his spoon. "All right, Lord Physik. Tell me of the empress."

Fredrik's demeanor immediately brightened. "From all appearances she is quite healthy, and I anticipate no problems," he said. "Though it might be prudent if she were to return to Stockholm as soon as possible. Bed rest is normally called for, even though it's not her first child."

"Fine. See to it personally. I will join her after I have dealt with matters here."

"Yes, Majesty," said Fredrik. "And now that the poison is purged from your body, your usual vigor should return in short order."

Gustavus finished his soup. "Poison? Nonsense. Everything I eat and drink is inspected by Lord Anders or Lady Maja. Too many sweetmeats, that's all."

A braver man might have pushed aside the dressing screen and revealed the conspiracy, but my legs were weak. In that moment I was overwhelmed by my memories of Gustavus's anger when he'd learned of my blunder in Russia, and his swift order to banish me.

I crouched lower.

"Oh course, Your Majesty, of course," said Fredrik. "It's as you say, nothing more than overindulgence."

Gustavus closed his eyes. "Send for my chamberlain. I want a fresh dressing gown. And more food."

"Just some bread, if you please, Your Majesty."

"Yes, old hen. Bread. *And* butter. Now leave me."

Fredrik rose, bowed. "Yes, Your Majesty. I shall fetch the chamberlain."

When I emerged into the traveling library, two men were waiting for me, flintlocks pointed at my chest. "Hello, gentlemen," I said. "Oskar and Josef, if I remember correctly?"

"General," replied Oskar. He pressed a barrel to my forehead. Josef turned out my pockets, relieving me of poniard and flasks, then prodded me forward. "Downstairs, sir."

"I know the way," I said.

The dungeons at Strömsholm were much smaller than their counterparts in Stockholm, though no less disheartening. Chill dampness permeated everything. The Duke of Uppland's largess with demon lights did not extend this far below the castle; what little light there was came from lamps redolent of rancid whale oil. A tiny brazier burned desultorily beyond the iron gate of my cell and the thin blanket on the straw-covered pallet did little to soften it. I shook it out and wrapped myself, wishing for my great coat.

I sat and shivered, reviewing my mistakes. If I'd truly considered the risks involved, I might have hidden another weapon —or at least another flask—in my boot. If I'd been more alert, I might have heard Oskar and Josef in the library. Might have fled back into the secret passage. Might have disarmed one of the guards.

Might have made my escape.

It's particularly damning when the arc of your downfall is rooted in one clearly defined failure. Mine was Russia. If I'd successfully completed my mission then, I would mostly likely now be sitting by the fire upstairs with Fredrik, gently laughing over the ridiculous preparations for the emperor's upcoming fete. We might have had a game of chess, or a round of One and Thirty with the spymaster and the imperial machine mage, while dozens of functionaries kept the business of empire running smoothly around us.

But I hadn't succeeded in Russia. I'd been more concerned with getting home safely than with risking a second attempt. Now, my breath steamed in this frigid cell.

After a time, the corridor brightened with the warm light of a demon lamp. Maja Viklund entered the chamber, accompanied by my guards. Oskar hung the lamp from a rusty hook while Josef fetched a stool and placed it close to the cell's iron bars.

Maja turned her head slightly. "Wait outside." Then she perched on the stool.

I stood and doffed my hat. "Maja."

A flintlock appeared in her right hand. With her left, she gestured to the pallet. "General Bjornsen... have a seat."

She wore no rings or jewelry, nothing to indicate she was an influential member of court. Even her firearm was plain, with a patina of frequent use. Very unlike Birgitta's pistol. I lowered myself with deliberate slowness to my scratchy mattress, keeping a close eye on her finger as it floated above the trigger.

"You look well, Maja." She possessed a fierce beauty that still attracted me, even now.

"I am the same as I ever was, General... loyal," she said. "*You* however, appear very tired. Life in the country has... not agreed with you."

So it is to be titles and formality, I thought. *So be it.* "I never stopped being loyal, Spymaster. His Imperial Majesty needed me, so I am here."

She nodded. "You're loyal to your friends, at least. I didn't think the... imperial physik would be so bold as to contact you. Fortunately for me, Lieutenant Pernillasdotter understands her... duty. She has given me a full... accounting." After all these years, Maja still spoke as if she were just discovering the words. I remembered when I'd found the habit charming, like watching a child sounding out the pages of a storybook.

"Where's Lord Fredrik?" I said.

"My men are holding him in his chambers. I will have a conversation with him... presently." Her smile did not reach her eyes.

"Are these the same men who faked Lord Anders' suicide? Because they did a poor job of it."

She ignored my barb. "None of this would have been necessary if your successor had been more... cooperative. When His Majesty began nodding off at court, the imperial poisoner refused to... dose him any further."

"I presume that didn't stop you," I said.

"Indeed, Lord Anders left excellent notes. That and my own... training were sufficient to recreate the formula," she said. "I added the syrup to His Majesty's evening cordial, much like you did with Aleksey Mikhaylovich. Or rather... his mistress."

My faced burned with shame.

"But all that is... behind us now. The empire will soon have a proper heir, and nothing else matters, yes?" Maja pursed her lips. "It's a pity about Lord Anders, though. He was a raconteur, much like you... once were. I will inform... His Majesty that the young man fell into madness and took his own life. It... happens, does it not? All that time spent with poisons."

"I've seen it only once," I admitted. Which is why *Cracked Stone* is always prepared in a room with open windows.

"This may be another... such occurrence." She shrugged. The pistol didn't waver. "At the end of the day, I doubt the emperor will give the matter much thought. He has ... other concerns now. A birthday. A child."

I wanted to reach though the bars and seize her hand. Try to make her feel that connection we once had. But such impulsiveness would probably earn me a pistol ball and a quick trip to gallows for Fredrik. Instead, I focused on my words. "His Majesty is an old man. He could have *died*."

"But he didn't," she said, matter-of-factly. "And even if he had, there are contingencies. Empress Anna and... a few well-chosen regents could guide the empire.

"My duty lies to the empire itself, General. Not the man. Everything and... everyone is secondary to that."

"I understand that now." The truth, so obvious now, pierced me. The woman I'd loved didn't understand honor. Perhaps that's why she'd never understood me?

"In the meantime... I find myself in need of a new imperial poisoner," she said. "Someone willing to do... what is necessary. Without question. Do you think the Society can direct me to such a... person?"

I hung my head, resigned to hear the price of my redemption. "I swear on my life I will protect Gustav Adolphus against his enemies and carry out his will," I said, repeating my Society oath.

"Good. There is value in... keeping oaths. Swear another one now. Swear to silence. You will never speak of this. Not to me. Not to anyone. Ever."

I swallowed against a dry throat. "I swear. Please, spare Lord Fredrik."

"I have no quarrel with him."

Relief flooded me. "What else do you want from me?"

"Nothing." She turned toward the corridor. "I'm finished here!"

The guards entered, pistols drawn. "Your carriage is waiting," Maja said, standing and tucking away her flintlock.

"Where am I going?"

"Home, General Bjornsen, where you belong. Home to your tea and your... peacocks."

"Wait! You said you need a new poisoner!" I hated the sudden desperation in my words. "I *saved* the emperor. I have earned the office."

"Yes, you certainly saved His Majesty from dyspepsia and... gout," she said. "I'm sure this will be taken into... consideration when the subject of your exile comes up. As far as an important court position is concerned..." She shrugged. "I have changed my mind. Good day." With a graceful incline of her head, she left.

I stood there for several minutes, eyes shut and fists clenched, fighting back tears, until Oskar cleared his throat. I stepped away from the cell door and he unlocked it.

I accompanied them through the castle, my back ramrod straight, eyes forward and lips clenched. They took me through the main gallery, the ballroom, and the reception hall. Though my escorts said nothing, there was a subtle shift in the genteel voices and gestures as we passed. A clear signal that I was unworthy of their rarefied company.

At least my silence will buy Fredrik's life. I held that thought close and prayed Maja would keep her word.

At the front gate stood an ordinary coach. Its frame and doors were painted a dull red most often associated with common houses and barns. This was the meanest sort of conveyance, something a yeoman secretary or *glädjeflicka* might hire on a rainy night.

Even the horses had dull eyes.

The driver, his head covered by a thick wool cap, climbed into his seat.

I shivered in the evening air and spoke for first time since leaving the dungeon. "May I have my coat?"

Josef snapped his fingers. Another footman stepped from the castle and handed over my great coat. I thanked him and clasped the familiar garment to my chest. "Your flask," said Josef. I turned.

He poured out most of its contents before tossing it to me. "The spymaster does not wish you to act rashly."

"Never again." I seated myself on the cold wooden bench. No demon jars or blankets to warm me here. The driver clucked his tongue. As the horses strained forward, the first tears came.

No one had offered the barest courtesy in farewell. No salute, no blessing, not even a tipping of their cap. They had dismissed me like a villain without rank or station.

I pulled the shades and inspected the great coat. The pockets were completely turned out and empty. My poniard was gone as well. Maja had apparently not wanted me to open a vein, at least not until I arrived home.

With shaking fingers, I opened my flask and drank the remaining drops. As the *Dream Caller* took effect, I vowed I would someday devise an antidote to purge my heart of this longing and loneliness.

I woke to the mocking calls of peacocks.

See parts I-III of Karl Dandenell's story "The Antidote for Longing" online at Metaphorosis.
If you liked it, leave a comment. Authors love that!
Remember to subscribe to our e-mail updates so you'll know when new stories are posted.

October

Any Day Now

K. E. Redmond

She pushed the intercom button and waited, taking in the sprawling brick pile that was the Unadilla Senior Living Community. It could have passed for a grand manor or a country club, but the ramps at the doors were a dead give-away, even if she hadn't seen one or two geriatrics, bundled to the eyes, cruising the grounds with their walkers. She wondered where they were going. There wasn't anything around for miles.

She'd driven out from Boston, taking the Interstate west, then backroads where despite GPS, Unadilla's entrance eluded her. Finally, she found it, nearly hidden in the undergrowth; two stone pillars with a non-descript sign and a chain link fence stretching off through the woods on both sides. The razor wire was unexpected, though, and driving up to the main building she noticed discreet security cameras at intervals. Somehow, she wasn't surprised when hers was the only car in the lot. Walking to the front door, she looked to the north where the sky looked threatening. It still hadn't snowed this winter; it was certainly cold enough. But any day. She hoped it would hold off until she got home. She hated driving in the snow.

The intercom crackled. "May I help you?"

"Yes. I'm here to see Professor Cervine. Professor John Cervine. He's expecting me." The first lie. A small one. His reply to her email requesting an interview had been more of an open ended, 'We'll see'.

"Your name?"

"Kat. Kat Dobrovolsky. But he called me Dobs. I mean, that's how he'll remember me."

"One moment."

Behind the glass-paneled door, a shadow crossed the room.

Kat recalled another time she'd waited to see the Professor, outside another door. It had been the beginning of her sophomore year, outside his department office. Through the frosted sidelight, she had been able to make out two shadows inside. One of them she knew was Trey Tottenger, the only sophomore to ever make the varsity team, he of the blinding smile and chiseled torso, catnip to cheerleaders everywhere. She'd met him once at a freshman mixer. He'd draped an arm around her and told her she had nice eyes. She reasoned, accurately enough, that he was both drunk and competing in the ancient and fraternal sport of bagging the homeliest frosh. She was reluctantly prying him off when he spied a more viable target and staggered away. Anyway, outside the Professor's office, he'd walked by like she didn't exist.

"No exceptions," the woman on the Registrar Desk had told her. "The Professor interviews all students for his Astronomy 101 course. Don't worry," she said with a grimace. "He'll be quick. Good luck."

So she sat, listening to the low murmur of voices inside the office, although the conversation sounded one-sided. Abruptly, the door swung open, and Trey Tottenger stomped out, red to his ears. A voice called after him, "I'd recommend basket weaving. You'd at least graduate with a skill." A pause. "Next!"

Kat sidled in. The only chair was positioned directly across the desk from the Professor. He was older than she'd expected, snow white hair in waves to his shirt collar, the hand that waved her in flecked with liver spots. But his eyes, when he looked up, were blue, bright, oddly intense.

"Major?" he barked as she slid into the chair.

"Uh, English."

"I see." He rapped the desktop with his pencil. "Let me guess. You needed a science credit and decided my course wouldn't be too much of a heavy lift."

She nodded, then quickly shook her head.

"Well, which is it?" he snapped. "Yes or no?"

She felt a hot flush rise. He was trying to fluster her; that pissed her off. "Yes, I need a science credit. But I really want to know more about the universe."

"Is that so you can write odes to the summer's full moon?" He waved his hand languidly. *'Art thou pale for weariness, of climbing heaven and gazing on the earth, wandering companionless, among the stars that have a different birth.'* He snorted. "You're wasting your time. Wordsworth did it better than you could ever hope."

"Shelley." Kat returned his stare with a bland look. "That's Shelley. Not Wordsworth."

The Professor grinned. "Speak truth to power, my dear. I stand corrected. Alright, for entry to my class and all the marbles, tell me what you think is the most significant advance humankind has made in space exploration in the last one-hundred years." He leaned back, closing his eyes, lacing his fingers across his paunch. "I'll warn you," he murmured, "your predecessor in that chair thought it might be warp drive. I hope you can do better."

Kat thought for a moment. "Voyager," she said finally.

He sounded bored. "I imagine you're referring to the television series. Or, lord help me, to that benighted movie with the aliens who couldn't spell? Vegan? Verger?"

"V-ger. No. The Voyager space probes."

He opened his eyes; she thought he almost looked surprised. "Explain."

"Because when we launched the probes we looked outward, not in. We said, hello, is anyone out there? We didn't just look up and wonder. We took the leap. We hoped." She stopped, embarrassed.

The Professor closed his eyes again. "Acceptable. Pick up your books in the bookstore. There will be two papers and a final. Do not be late for class. Next!"

A buzz, a click, and she was back waiting in the cold. The door opened. A muscular man in scrubs and a high fade stood inside the entry, a small bare foyer behind him. She noticed there was no reception desk, no chairs. They really didn't get many visitors. He motioned her in.

"Miss Dobrovolsky? I'm Frank, Professor Cervine's health care aide." He looked her over. "The Professor didn't say anyone was coming today. Is he expecting you?"

She gave him her most engaging smile. "He said come anytime, so here I am. I hope that's okay. It was kind of a long drive."

"Oh? Where are you coming from?"

"Boston. I was back in the area visiting and thought I'd drive over to see my old professor. I was a huge fan. Well, me and about a thousand other students. He's—was—just an incredible lecturer. Getting into one of his courses was cutthroat. I did his introductory course, and I was hooked. Not that I went into the sciences. No brain for numbers. But I've always loved astronomy. And he was one of my advisors on my senior thesis. Sorry," she stopped, blushing. "I'm babbling." Lie number two, well-buried. But it had done the trick. Frank's wary look faded to polite boredom.

"That's okay. He's feeling pretty good today, so you're in luck. Follow me, I'll take you to him." They headed down a long brightly lit corridor with tasteful bucolic reproductions on soothing pastel walls. At regular intervals on both sides, they passed numbered doors. At her Nana's facility, all the residents decorated the doors to their rooms. Photos of grandkids. Artwork. Political signs. Holiday wreaths. Not here. One door was like the next. Uniform. Regimented. Frank stopped outside Room A219, his hand on the knob. "What was your thesis on, if you don't mind me asking?"

"Uhm. Cultural acceptance and acclimation to scientific progression through mass media saturation. Yeah, it's a mouthful. I was an English major."

"The elevator version?"

"Basically, figuring out how often people need to read or hear about some scientific breakthrough before they actually believe it."

"And did you? Figure it out?"

"Not really. People are hard. They believe stupid things all the time for their own reasons. And once they do, it's hard to shift them."

"Everyone thinks they've got the inside track, huh?"

"That's right."

He didn't move to open the door. "So, you're a journalist?"

Her smile tightened. "Not quite. Science writer, slash editor. I translate what the science guys write into something actual people can understand. Those who can't do, write, I guess."

"Working on anything now?"

There was no point trying to get by him, she had to play. Lie number three coming up.

"A children's book. Introduction to the giants of astronomy. You know, Newton, Copernicus, Galileo."

"Professor Cervine?"

She shook her head. "He's big, but not quite in their league. I was hoping to run the list by him though, see if I missed anyone. And catch up on how he's doing, of course." Lie number four.

He took the hint. "Right. He tires easily, so I'll ask you to keep your visit short." He opened the door and stuck his head in. "Professor? Your guest is here. I'll be down the hall if you need me." He stood aside to let her in. She could feel Frank's eyes on her back for a long moment. Then, quietly, the door closed behind her.

The room was like any university professor's office: crammed bookcases, drifts of paper, professional journals stacked in corners, and a desk barely visible beneath the detritus. All typical, apart from the hospital bed near the window. Its occupant turned his head on the pillow to regard her, his eyes overlarge in a skull pared down to a few strands of white hair and skin thin as tissue paper, sallow, and wrinkled.

"Professor Cervine? Remember me? Kathy Dobrovolsky."

He raised a bony hand from the crisp white sheets, immediately dropped it, as though the effort was exhausting.

"Well, come in. Don't stand there gawking. Find your seat. I can't stand late arrivals. Disrupts my chain of thought. Disrupts the class. Hurry up." The tone was testy, but the voice was nearly as she remembered, giving the lie to the frail form.

She scurried over to the chair beside the bed, throwing her coat across the back, and sat down, setting her handbag at her feet. He stared hard at her. She stared back.

"Do I know you?"

"Yes, Professor. We spoke. Well, we texted. I was one of your students at university. You knew me as Kathy Dobs. Well, that's what you called me. I've come to say hello."

"Have you?" He looked away. She followed his gaze. Outside the windows, an aide pushed a wheelchair containing an elderly man bent nearly double in the seat. "I don't do outings, if that's what you had in mind."

"We don't need to, if you don't want. I brought you the last print copy of the British Astrophysics Journal. I thought you'd like it."

He turned back, looking peeved. "The last?"

She shrugged apologetically. "They're going online. Save the trees."

He made a noise between a snarl and a sneeze. "Continuous publication since the 1800s and now it's some mishmash on a computer screen. What depths will we plumb next? Lego models of the universe? Well? Give it to me."

She handed it over. "I was in Oxford looking at Sir Isaac Newton's papers. I was writing a piece for a magazine there. The editor said he knew you. I think he was one of your graduate students."

Frankly, she'd been surprised by the assignment. Out of the blue, the magazine had reached out to her, all expenses paid to the U.K., top dollar for an article any hack could have written. Who did that?

The Professor flipped open to the table of contents, running a finger down the titles. "I can't be expected to remember the names of all my students. And Newton was at Cambridge. Wrong place entirely."

"Yes, I know. But the Bodleian had a recent acquisition from a private library. An amateur astronomer. Contemporary of Newton's."

"May is still banging on about cosmic dust, I see," he grumbled, flicking the journal page with a finger that looked too fragile to take that kind of abuse. "I told him to move on, but he never listens. It's dirt! Get over it. What were you saying about Newton?"

"One of his contemporaries. It turns out, they exchanged several letters. That's what I was looking at in the Bodleian."

He flung the journal down on the bed and fixed her with a glare perfected during eons of oral exams and faculty meetings.

"In my experience, correspondence between such intellectually mismatched individuals as Sir Isaac Newton and some dilettante in knee pants is useful only as mulch. I see you hesitate. Let me guess, this unknown pen pal told our boy Newton he'd transmuted lead into gold."

She smiled. "There was some of that."

"Why am I not surprised."

"Not all of it. One of Newton's letters was interesting."

"Was it? You sound pleased with yourself." He scowled at her. "Don't be coy. It's boring."

"Newton wrote to this friend about an astronomical observation he'd made. He described it as, 'A most wonderous sight. Three nights standing.' Based on his notes, he was describing something near or possibly from the star Elnath, in the Taurus Constellation."

"I hadn't realized our English department was churning out qualified astronomers these days. Elnath? That's 100 light years away."

"131. He reported it in 1700."

"I know when Sir Isaac lived," he retorted. "I'm not senile. Yet." His fingers beat a tattoo on the sheet. "And so?"

"So?" she repeated blankly.

He clicked his tongue against his front teeth impatiently. "Does this particle, this mere mote of information carry some earth-shaking import? Elnath, as far as I am aware, would not be described as a wonderous sight. Giant star. Blue-white in color. Nothing to write home about, so to speak."

"True, but it made me curious. What did he see exactly? Who else saw it?" This part always excited her. She couldn't help it. "So, I started digging. Did you know that one hundred years before Newton, Copernicus studied the occultation of Aldebaran? Also, in the Taurus Constellation."

"Oooooh, I'm getting goose bumps. Two astronomers studied stars in the same constellation. Rewrite the textbooks!" He rolled his eyes.

She fished in her handbag, pulled out her phone, holding the screen up for him to see. "I found a note he made, marginalia, about the star Alcyone. He wrote, and I quote, *'Trinitas in tenebris. Mirabilis.'* 'Trinity from the darkness. Wonderous.' Trinity. Three. Just like Newton's three nights. And wonderous. Obviously, they saw something similar."

He sighed. "No, obviously you are in thrall to an illusion peculiar to our ignorant times, my dear. That there must be a causal connection between two completely unrelated events."

She ignored him. "I kept digging. I went back in history to observations by Chinese astronomers. Year 1054, the supernova in the Crab Nebula. Incidentally, also in Taurus."

"Let me guess," he sighed. "Three sightings or events or however you're mislabeling them."

She ignored that too. "I couldn't believe it. Three unique observations that can be traced back to some part of the Taurus Constellation. Professor," she leaned in, lowering her voice. "I think there's a pattern. I think this is contact."

He snorted. "Contact? I presume you mean some alien intelligence signaling to us from across the universe. Based on what? Three random observations? Do you have any concept of the distances you're describing? How vast? No. You were probably watching cat videos on your little phone when I covered that topic in class. I'll put it in terms you might understand. One light year is 5.88 trillion miles. Rounding up so even you may comprehend, six trillion is 6 with 12 zeros behind it. Alcyone is 370 light years away, the Crab Nebula is, let me see," he paused, but only for a second, "6,523 light years away. Multiply either number by a 6 with all those little zeroes and you'll realize you're talking complete nonsense."

She edged her chair closer to the bed. "But Professor, I've found others."

"Paleolithic cave drawings?" he scoffed. "Some daubing of stars on rocks."

"What about the WOW signal? August 15, 1977. A signal was detected by Ohio State University's Big Ear radio telescope for 72 seconds. It came from the Sagittarius constellation."

"Discredited. Never detected again. Or do you imagine your aliens are playing some intergalactic game of ring the doorbell and run away? Besides, you're mixing your constellations. Or are you simply throwing anything into the pot to prove your point?"

She sat back, silent.

"Have I stymied you?" he sneered. "Good. Next time, get your facts straight before you bother me with nonsense." He shifted in bed, closing his eyes. "I think I've had enough entertainment for today. Go away."

"Humor me. One more."

He opened his eyes to object but saw the mulish look on her face. "In 1945," she began, "a graduate student at our old university—who will remain nameless—observed a signal originating from Alpha Tauri, 65 light years away."

"Odd, I've never seen anything published. That would have been quite the coup," he said.

"It was rumored the War Department suppressed his paper in the interests of national security. They probably thought they had enough problems with a world war here on earth without worrying about extraterrestrials."

"You're citing rumors now! The true hallmark of a failed argument," he said. The contempt in his voice stung her.

"He was—is—a dedicated and brilliant astronomer. He believed in rigorous scientific observation."

"Sounds like a swot. Did your Bodleian friends tell you what a swot is?" he asked sweetly.

She leaned in, lowering her voice. "Also, he was a little anal about keeping stuff. I know, because I helped him pack it up. Books, notes, drafts. He squirreled everything away. In time, I imagine, he completely forgot he'd kept a draft. It happens. A lifetime of stuff piles up, retirement rolls around. Who wants to go through all that paper? Just box it up and shove it into the archives. Forget it. Practical obscurity."

The door opened. Frank stuck his head in. "You ready, Professor?"

Cervine who had been lying in bed, immobile, nearly levitated. "Get out! I'll tell you when I'm ready. Get! Out!"

Frank's head disappeared; Kathy sat back.

"Oh, don't look so worried," the Professor growled. "I haven't thrown you out. Yet." But the outburst seemed to have drained him. He lay back against his pillows, his breathing labored. He took a deep breath.

"This feels like explaining fission to a sleep-deprived toddler, but let me try," he said. "In terms of the Earth's development, all 4.5 billion years of it, our pathetic human civilization is but a blip. Less than the last half-second on the timeline. For an exceedingly small portion of that time, barely 60 years, we have actively looked for others of our kind, although I am at a loss to understand why.

We don't get along with the neighbors we have. Regardless, we've listened for signs of intelligent life in the universe. And do you know what we've heard?"

"But…"

He held up a hand, forestalling her. "Nothing. We've heard nothing. Of course, techno transmissions may be exceedingly rare. Maybe none have crossed our path in the last 60 years. Maybe they only transmit to our part of the universe every 100 years or so." He chuckled. "The other equally valid possibility is there are no transmissions to receive."

"Carl Sagan said…" Kathy interrupted.

He groaned. "Dear Carl. Let me guess: 'The universe is a pretty big place. If it's just us, seems like an awful waste of space.' Spare me."

"We're finding earth-like planets every day. Based on dozens of factors, one researcher estimated an intelligent civilization would be at most 17,000 light years away. And that was in a peer-reviewed publication," she added quickly.

"Pie-eyed optimists. And how do you suggest we talk with them? We have no technology that can transmit to those distances. And what would be the point? Our message, optimally sent at the speed of light, reaches them; they send one back. Do you really believe there will be anyone here to receive it? As a species, we'll be lucky to survive into the next century."

"But that's my point, Professor. They're not sending a message. They're coming here. Look at it: Crab Nebula, 6,523 light years away; Alcyone, 370 light years; Elnath, 131; Alpha Tauri, 65 light years. Every time, they're getting closer."

"Please listen to the voice of reason. I'm sure I covered this in one of my lectures, it was certainly an exam question. The Space Shuttle travels five miles a second. At that speed, optimistically, how long would it take a person—or an E.T., if you insist—to travel one light year?"

"37,200 years," she replied. "I got it right on the exam."

"I'm sure you did. And yet, you believe these intergalactic interlopers, these E.T.s, are traveling hundreds of light years within the span of our own written history. It is not possible. Do the math. It should be well within even your limited capabilities."

"But suppose they can travel faster than light?"

"Impossible!"

"They said men flying and the Higgs boson particle were impossible, too. How else would you explain the signals? They're leap-frogging across the universe."

"I've always envied the latitude writers have to wax poetic when they fail to understand basic science," he murmured. "I sincerely hope you're not thinking of writing about this wild theory of yours. You'll be finished, professionally. Unless you enjoy being lumped in with the crazies and conspiracy nuts."

He waggled a hand in the direction of the carafe on his nightstand. She jumped up to pour him a glass of water, waiting while he took a sip. As he handed the glass back, he held her gaze.

"Do you remember what I wrote on your thesis?" he asked. She looked blank for a moment, then her eyes widened. "I see you do. You always were a bright one. My final affirmation of all your hard work. Do not disappoint me now." He slid down in bed. "Trying to reason with you has been exhausting. Thank you for coming. Leave."

Frank was waiting for her in the hallway. "Good visit?"

She nodded. "So-so. I think I upset him."

"Believe it or not, he was in a good mood today. Get everything you need?"

"What?" She wished Frank would shut up so she could think. Her thesis, where had she packed it?

"Did you talk to him about the book?" He stopped beside the front entrance, watching her. "You said you needed to talk to him about your children's book."

"Oh. No. We got off on a tangent. That's okay."

"Yeah? Say, about your thesis. You said the Professor was one of your advisors. I'll bet he had some good comments. He always has a lot to say."

"You know him," she replied, going over in her head the boxes she'd stored in the attic at her parent's house. There wasn't much room in a studio apartment. The thesis had to be in there somewhere.

"So, like what?" He was waiting, all friendly curiosity. But his persistence made her wary.

"I'm not sure," she said slowly. "Something about science needing more scribes." Lie number five. She was getting good at this.

"That's harsh." He opened the door. "Have a safe trip back. Looks like the snow's holding off. But any day now, it's going to get here."

She nodded. It wasn't until she was back on the Interstate that she thought about Frank's questions. How had he known the Professor had asked about her thesis? She checked the rear-view mirror and sped up.

In his bed, the Professor waited. He could practically predict the next move. So when the phone on his bedside table rang, he let it ring itself out. In the quiet, he felt the sweet pull of sleep. The phone rang again, jarring him awake. This time he picked up.

"I'm sleeping," he snapped, then listened in silence. "No, I don't see any need for concern. A tissue of conjecture and twaddle. Yes, I told her that," he replied. "I have no idea if she'll listen to her favorite professor, as you so unctuously phrase it. I can tell you she's bluffing about my papers. I went through them all myself. As I'm sure you did." He listened again with a bored look. "Your threats are wasted on me. You harbor the mistaken belief I care what you do to me now. And tell that useless blob you call my aide not to disturb me." He hung up. The phone remained resolutely mute. Still, for a long time he kept watch on the driveway, alert for comings and goings. After a while, darkness obscured the distant tree line, then gathered itself up to fill the room. The stars appeared. Tomorrow maybe there'd be snow, but tonight the sky was clear and cold.

He looked up at the twinkling lights, seeking out the constellation Taurus, the bull. Catalogued by Ptolemy in the second century, known since the Bronze Age. In the Northern Hemisphere, the constellation passes through the sky from November to March but is most visible in January. That was a lift from one of his lectures. What had she called it? Leap frogging. Inelegant, but accurate. He preferred a skipping stone. The Crab Nebula, Alcyone, Elnath, Alpha Tauri. Closer and closer. And the last one, from his red dwarf, 8.72 light years away, the signal he'd detected when he'd nearly given up hope, just before his abrupt and unwilling retirement. In terms of the universe, 8.72 light years was practically next door. He hadn't bothered trying to publish this time. He was too old and tired to fight them now, but he wasn't going to let the knowledge die with him. When she'd asked him to be her senior thesis advisor, he'd agreed, already plotting. If the universe teaches you one thing, it is the long view. Signing off on her thesis, he'd written the signal coordinates for the red dwarf as though they were random scribbles. His way of telling her, when she finally put it all together, that she was right.

He'd counted on them discounting her. Wrong major. Wrong sex. Why did they always underestimate women? But she was bright, and she'd always been stubborn. He'd known she'd figure it out eventually. With his help, of course. All the breadcrumbs he'd strewn in her path. The draft of his so-long ago graduate paper, his notes on the red dwarf, left where she had to find them, packing up his office. The magazine assignment he'd finagled for her. Little nudges. Trusting to her curiosity to piece it all together. And with the internet, social media, she had resources he'd never dreamed of. This time they'd have trouble stuffing that genie back in the bottle. Let them try. Speak truth to power, indeed.

He recited it over and over like a mantra. Crab, Alcyone, Elnath, Alpha Tauri, 6,523, 370, 131, 65, 8.72 light years away. Getting closer. He almost wished he'd be around for it. In the dark, he chuckled. They'd run in circles screaming. He could just hear them. The stock market would have a seizure, if it didn't crash. The arrival of extraterrestrials would certainly take the shine off capitalism. Not to mention organized religion. Where do little green men fit in God's great plan? Do they get their own image of the Deity, their own Savior? Their own heaven? It would almost be worth it to hear how they worked aliens into Creation. Countdown: 6,523, 370, 131, 65, 8.72.

He smiled slyly at Taurus. "Any day now. Any day."

See K.E. Redmond's story "Any Day Now" online at Metaphorosis.
If you liked it, leave a comment. Authors love that!
Remember to subscribe to our e-mail updates so you'll know when
new stories are posted.

About the story

The idea for this story came while I was reading about the search for life on other planets for a course on the mysteries of the cosmos. It struck me that alien life is not as improbable as it might seem. In fact, it's downright probable. Of course, then I wondered what the official reaction might be here on Earth to signs of intelligent life. "Any Day Now" was the result.

A question for the author

Q: Do you make art other than prose? What kind, and how is it different?

A: Do I make art other than prose? Isn't that hard enough? But yes, I paint and sculpt, in addition to my writing. My painting is old school representational. I like the effort it takes to really see something as it is. On the other hand, my sculptures tend to be fantastic. I identify with that mythology of creators breathing life into their creations. It's just something about the malleability of clay.

About the author

K.E. Redmond writes about the extraordinary possibilities of our everyday world, that interstice shared by mystery and hard science.

Salaatu

Lisa Short

After two days of the carriage's relentless jolting, Darya felt battered to the point of numbness. She fixed her own eyes on her hands, clenched tightly together on her lap—she still wore her librarian's smock and kirtle, ruched at the neck and laced down the sides, the fabric bunching up under her curled fingers. That lacing seemed to tighten up hourly, and the fleeting handful of stops over the past two days had not included time to bathe or change. She itched now, miserably, and surreptitious squirming did nothing to ease it.

Outside the carriage door's single small window, the sparse pine forest that dotted the flat, still winter-brown landscape jolted past, nothing like the rich glory of trees that grew in the foothills of the Imperial capital. But this landscape *was* familiar, drearily so— though Darya had not returned home since her grandfather had won her the appointment to the Imperial Library five years before. The school had been grueling, the few holidays granted librarial students mostly given to sleeping off the exhaustion of constant work-study. And after graduation, her place in the Library had been so new, she hadn't wanted to seem less dedicated, less *aspiring*, than any of the other newly minted underlibrarians—

—and, all other variously true excuses aside, she hadn't wanted to go back home. She *had* missed her grandfather, the measure of her love for him increasing nearly every day she had been away, discovering anew every hour what joy she found in the sheer volume of scholarship and knowledge suddenly available to her in overflowing measure. She *had* missed him, and would have loved nothing more than to speak to him of her studies, of all the Library's books and maps and registries, a love she knew well he shared.

But she hadn't missed the rest of her family, and she hadn't missed her home village of Korshun. She *certainly* hadn't missed the seashore, nor the sea, nor anything living *in* or *on* it—and perhaps, if she insisted on it long enough, it might even become the truth. Darya jerked her gaze away from the window and back down to her white-knuckled fists once more.

The driver's muffled shout was barely enough warning for Darya to grab for the bar beside her head; the carriage jounced and shuddered to a halt. Seconds later a guard, large and expressionless, pulled the door open and held out his hand to her. She blinked down at it in surprise; he took her hesitation for reluctance and caught her wrist up in one rough hand, pulling her up from the seat and out the door.

The other carriage, in spite of its greater size, had beaten them to this chosen campsite—its outriders already had a bonfire built. The fire dazzled Darya's eyes; she looked away, blinking, and her gaze fell upon two men standing some distance back from the fire, deep in conversation. The taller of the two looked up, and Darya had a moment of mere cataloging without identification— silver hair, cut like a soldier's, long thin face, narrow lips—then those lips turned up at the corners, and the shock of recognition drove the blood from her head in a rush.

She hurried forward and dropped into deep curtsey, a prelude to full genuflection, but he shook his head briefly at her as she bent lower still. "There's no need for that here, *Maya* Darya." Was it only the firelight that made the lines carved deeply around his eyes and mouth sharper than they had been just a few days before? "My physician"—a nod in the other, younger man's direction—"insisted we stop for the night." Darya tore her gaze from the Emperor's drawn features to his companion's, startled to find he was already staring at her—*glaring* at her. She recoiled involuntarily, a movement she tried hard to disguise as a shiver in the chill night air. The Emperor followed her gaze; his mouth compressed in fleeting annoyance. "Do be courteous to our guest. If nothing else, she is expanding our knowledge of the natural history of our own lands. I would have thought you'd be pleased by that, at least."

"Sire, this isn't knowledge, it's *mythology*. These sea demons —" Darya bit back a hiss of protest, clenching her jaw to remain silent. "—or whatever they are, if they even exist—Sire, your own reforms, the medical colleges you created in the first years of your reign, a half-century ago! were designed to eliminate the charlatanry and yes, *dangerous* ignorance of these backwater beliefs—"

"The *salaatu* aren't myths," said the Emperor, mildly, though his gaze had narrowed on the young man's half-averted face. "The *maya* could doubtless show you where in the Imperial Library to find the many historical references—documented evidence—of their existence." His annoyance softened into obvious affection. "Truly, Aison. My father had some dealings with these sea people—*not* demons—in his oceangoing days, before he was designated my great-uncle's heir."

So the young man was Aison—*Loro* Aison, a fourth- or fifth-degree relation of the Emperor himself and, she'd heard gossiped more than once, fanatically devoted to him. Then the Emperor waved her away, not unkindly; she obediently hurried backwards, once more out of earshot, though judging from Aison's passionate expression the argument still continued. One of the servants scurrying past thrust a bundle into Darya's arms; shaking it out, she found herself in possession of a roll of thick quilts. A quick glance around confirmed that several of the guards were clambering awkwardly into their own, not even removing mail shirts or boots. The outriders were erecting a tent, for the Emperor and likely *Loro* Aison, Darya supposed. Well, the air didn't smell like rain was imminent, and anything was better than sleeping sitting up in miserable snatches in the carriage. She shook her bedroll out too and after some experimentation, managed to squeeze most of herself inside it.

The brackish, muggy edge to the breeze, carried westward from the still-unseen ocean, pricked at her even as exhaustion pulled her down into the oblivion of sleep. The shadows behind her closed eyelids gradually morphed into dreams of the sea, obsidian swells limned with phosphorescence under a pallid moon.

Darya had been seven years old the summer the *salaatu* had come to Korshun. She'd been playing near the shore, hot and listless; she had heard them before she'd seen them, a singing like the ocean wind blowing over the shells the queen conches left scattered along the shoreline. She'd squinted up at the horizon, seen something dark bobbing upon the waves in the distance, not quite the right shape to be one of the village fishing boats.

The singing had grown louder, oddly compelling—then, between one blink of her eyes and the next, the shadow on the horizon had materialized into a long boat larger even than the village headman's, the biggest in the fleet. A tent had been lashed to its deck; as Darya gaped at it, an enormous woman wearing nothing but a headdress of coral-studded feathers strolled leisurely out onto the bow.

"*Ha!*"

The cry, shockingly close, had startled Darya into stumbling backwards, her foot coming down hard on a rock, her ankle twisting painfully. Rough warm fingers had clamped around her wrist as she fell sideways with a cry of her own.

Yanked neatly back onto her feet by those same fingers, Darya had found herself staring up at a stranger's distressed face. That in of itself had been an astonishment—no strangers had ever come to Korshun in her short lifetime. This one, perhaps a few years older than Darya, was barefoot and barelegged, her shirt a mere strip of cloth tied around her narrow chest.

"Are you all right?" She'd spoken strangely—Darya had never met anyone for whom Imperial Oun was not their first language, and the musical rippling of the girl's speech fascinated her. Then the girl looked down at Darya's dress, her heavy dark brows drawing so far down they nearly met over her nose. "Why are you wearing so many clothes? Are you cold?"

The girl's name, Darya discovered, was Sayu—nothing like any name Darya had ever heard, as Sayu herself was nothing like anyone she'd ever met. And the rest of that summer, for the first time in her life, Darya had been grateful for how little attention her family paid her. They cared nothing if she disappeared for hours, as long as she was back in the manor by supper.

"But you can't swim?" Sayu had asked in astonishment, the third morning they'd met at the shore's edge. "*Babies* can swim! Perhaps you've just forgotten how?" Assured that was not the case, she'd sputtered, "But what have you been doing instead?"

Not knowing what else to say, Darya had muttered something about liking to read. "Read?" Sayu's lips had pursed as she'd rolled the word over her tongue. "*Read.* It sounds ugly. Does it hurt?"

It had been Darya's turn to laugh and then explain, though Sayu's puzzlement hadn't seemed much eased. "Oh? Well, it sounds lonely. Swimming's far more fun. I'll teach you!" She'd looked enormously pleased by the idea.

The *salaatu* had sailed up and down Oun's northeastern coast on their own inscrutable business, frequently returning to Korshun for a few days' or a week's rest—and whenever Darya sighted their boat, bobbing gently against its beachrock moorings, she ran as fast as she could to the shore, likelier than not to find Sayu already there and waiting for her. But finally, the day after the autumn equinox, Sayu had clasped Darya's hands tightly enough to hurt and had said abruptly, "I have to go."

Darya hadn't protested, but she hadn't been able to stop the tears that had welled up either. She'd opened her mouth, meaning to say something stoic and brave, and had sobbed aloud instead. Sayu had pulled her close, resting her cheek against the top of Darya's head, and they had stood like that until her sobs had ceased. "But we'll be back," Sayu had said, her voice muffled against Darya's hair. "Next summer. I promise—"

Darya awoke to something poking her shoulder. She pried her eyes open, squinting in the dull gray light of dawn, to the unwelcome sight of a guard crouching over her. "We're leaving," he said flatly, and withdrew as soon as it was clear she'd understood him.

The sparse scatter of trees outside were thickening, the ragged evergreens now interspersed with fatter, paler trunks, lightly dusted with the first leaves of early spring. *Home... Grandfather.* She had treasured, still treasured, his handful of letters to her over the years, his obvious pride in her accomplishments in the Imperial capital—she flinched a little at the thought of those letters, abandoned and unsecured in her small clothespress in the underlibrarians' dormitory. Losing them would be a blow; hopefully nobody would find them interesting enough to steal.

The winter after the *salaatu* first sailed away, Darya had crept into the manor library, determined to assuage her now-unbearable loneliness by finding out more about the *salaatu* themselves. Her grandfather had happened upon her there one evening, her nose buried deep in an encyclopedia. She'd been too young to understand then how the rest of the family had feared his scholarly and acerbic wit—to eight-year-old Darya he'd been no more fearsome than any other member of the household, all seemingly alike in their disdain for her existence.

She understood far better now, his awkward and stilted enthusiasm at the sight of anybody other than himself voluntarily opening a book. She'd told him willingly enough of her curiosity about the *salaatu,* and had shown him what little she'd found about them in the library. "But I'm sure they aren't *sea demons,* Grandfather—"

"Indeed not," her grandfather had agreed with some indignation, and bent down over the open encyclopedia far enough that his nose nearly touched the pages. "Let me see that—

"Hmph!" He straightened back up, flipping the pages rapidly backwards until he reached the very front. "I should have known.

Sornois wrote this. Incompetent *and* a coward." Darya had blinked up at him warily—he hadn't appeared angry at *her*, at least, though she had no idea who Sornois was. "Likely he was writing it to pacify the then-emperor—this edition is over a century old." Her grandfather abruptly clapped the book shut, causing a small geyser of dust to erupt from its binding, then gazed narrowly down at Darya. "I'm delighted to see that you aren't credulous enough to believe everything you read." He paused. "And that you chose to try to find the answer to a question about the natural world in a book."

He'd seemed to be waiting for a reply, so Darya had gathered up her courage and ventured, "I, I *do* like books, Grandfather. But —" she did her best to ignore the beginnings of the lowering frown on his brow, because she really did want to know, "—how do you know which books to believe, and which not? If you want to know something?"

His eyebrows lifted, erasing the frown lines as if by magic; Darya, who had been quailing inside—questions were generally not encouraged, at least not her questions and not those put to an adult of the household—was heartened by the sudden gleam of warmth in his dark eyes. "Now *that* is a question of worth, Granddaughter." She started a little; it was almost as if he'd seen what she was thinking. "And it's a very important one. Come, let me show you something."

He had gone on to show Darya a great many things—not only the marvelous stories hidden in his books, but the science of the books themselves—how they came to be written, how to understand the meaning beneath the obvious words, how to search for additional books to verify (or refute) the contents of any other. Her grandfather's library, it had turned out, was as full of joyous surprises as the summer had been with Sayu.

Darya's first sight of the village outskirts now, through the carriage window, made her stomach clench tight. Even the meanest shack had at least one guard stationed at its door— unable to help herself, she glanced up at the manor house looming silently atop its hill. Guards manned both front doors, and likely were standing at the postern gate as well. Her gaze darted to the grounds—yes, she could still see the faint, blackened remains of the old stillroom. Her grandfather had refused to rebuild it there, had insisted on moving the new stillroom to its own building, completely out of sight of the manor. She had heard him shouting at her mother one night as she lay sleepless in her bed, wracked with the pain of her burns—her grandfather, who had never before raised his voice in her hearing—

But there was no reason to suppose that all the manor's inhabitants weren't perfectly all right. She understood why the Emperor would want to keep his presence, and especially his purpose, an absolute secret. The fact that he was taking such pains to keep everyone ignorant of what might be happening outside their homes was evidence enough that he intended them no harm in the long run.

Once again, the Emperor's carriage had outpaced hers; after they'd jolted to a halt, the stone-faced guard from the day before escorted her straight to the Emperor's tent. Once inside, Darya curtseyed, darting lightning-fast glances at the Emperor's face to gauge whether he wanted her to skip full genuflection once more. It was still rather unreal, to be standing nearly within touching distance of him—close enough that the scent of his cologne tickled her nose, to see the shadows like bruises etched deep beneath those ostensibly friendly eyes.

"So, *maya*. How do we contact the *salaatu*?"

Darya took a deep, fortifying breath. "We don't. Not from the shore." She had tried to explain that before, back at the palace. "They came themselves, in the summer, in their own boats. We never summoned them."

The warmth in his eyes dimmed. "Then how do you propose to bring them here?"

Darya's frantic, scurrying thoughts during that first sleepless night in the carriage had finally settled on a possibility. "There is a place I used to go with," she took another deep breath, "one of them sometimes. A few leagues out to sea. When we were children." And a bit older, too, but there was really no need to elaborate on that. "I can swim out to it. It's in their territory; they may realize someone is there, even if they aren't sure who it is. They're likely to investigate." *Eventually.* Well, it was the best idea she'd been able to come up with.

"Swim out to it? By yourself?" The Emperor's face had gone very still; his lips barely moved as he spoke. "Why don't we take the village boats to it? *All* of us?"

Darya flinched. "It's underwater. A fair bit underwater. Even if any of your guards or servants—or yourself, or *Loro* Aison—are unusually strong swimmers, you probably wouldn't be able to follow me there." It was hard to force out the next words. "I...have some ability to swim the way the *salaatu* do." Her fists clenched, hidden deep in her skirts. "I did tell you, Sire, that you might not want the healing—it doesn't leave you unchanged, from what you were before."

The Emperor's dark blue gaze shifted from her face to a point beyond her right shoulder. "Aison. The *maya* says she must swim out to sea, underwater and alone." He smiled, thinly—his smile at her the night before had indeed held genuine warmth, because by contrast this one held none at all. "I recall that you did some sailing as a boy, with your father—why don't you take her out that few leagues, so she doesn't dangerously tire herself reaching this meeting place?"

"Certainly, Sire," came *Loro* Aison's voice, behind her—she hadn't even heard him enter the tent. She curtseyed deeply once more and followed Aison back outside.

Aison had commandeered someone's yoal. He handled it, and its simple square sail, well enough, which was a little surprising— the yoals were unique to northeast Oun, she'd learned during her very first year in the Palace library. Had his father hailed from here?

"Tell me when we're far enough out." Aison's voice was rough; startled out of her thoughts, Darya's head jerked up. His face was averted, but a muscle jumped in his jaw. Clearly he wanted nothing more than to shove her overboard, preferably bound hand and foot. "Are you even listening to me?" he snapped, still staring determinedly away from her.

That almost surprised a nervous giggle out of her—and what terrible timing that would have been; he probably *would* shove her overboard if she laughed in his face. "Yes, I'm sorry—yes, we're out far enough."

Aison lashed the sail down firmly, locked the yoal's single wide oar into its ring, then turned around to look her full in the face. "Who paid you?"

The words made so little sense that for a moment she almost thought he wasn't speaking to her at all—but they were quite alone in the tiny yoal, the calm sea stretching out for leagues in all directions save for the now-distant shore. "What?"

"Who paid you to carry this tale to the Emperor?" Two spots of color burned high on his cheekbones—he was fairer than the Emperor, than Darya herself, fair enough for his temper to show through his skin. "Was it one of his daughters' husbands? Or a great-nephew? You should know they have no care for the tools they use—they're far more likely to discard them than reward them, once their purpose is served. If this is as ridiculous a story as I think it is, I recommend you drown yourself down there before coming back to shore empty-handed. And if you *don't* come back, don't doubt I will look for your body, and if I don't find it, you'd best not show your face anywhere in the Empire. I *will* find you."

Speechless, Darya stared back at him. There was nothing more she could say in the face of such seething hostility. It didn't matter that she herself hadn't been the one to carry the tale of the *salaatu*'s healings to the Emperor; she'd even downplayed every aspect of it that had reached the Emperor's ears, as far as she had dared without causing offense to him, who had been so desperately delighted to hear it at all.

Darya inhaled deeply; Aison shifted back, shoulders stiffening, but she only exhaled hard, then inhaled again, then a third time; his eyes widened, as blue as the Emperor's, the rich deep color of a summer sky in evening. Those eyes were the last thing she saw as she squeezed her own tight shut and thrust herself off the side of the yoal and down into the dark waters.

The shock of the frigid water was painful and the rushing roar of bubbles around the deep impact of her body deafened her. She sank quickly, the weight of her now-soaked smock and kirtle, underlinen and boots dragging her down far faster than she could have swum alone. She began to struggle out of her clothes, shoving the sodden handfuls down and away as fast as she could.

With nothing but her boots left in her hands, her descent slowed to almost nothing. She was deep enough that the daylight world above had shifted into an eerie dimness; she could just make out the bottom of the yoal far above her head, barely the size of the pad of her thumb. She tilted her head down, to look at the pale brown of her arms and legs that were slowly acquiring a smooth, reflective sheen. Her braids waved gently as she drifted in the twilight haze, the weight of the water an implacable cocoon around her.

But she couldn't stay there forever, as weirdly comforting as it was—the tightness in her chest, the need for fresh air, was growing more urgent. She closed her eyes again and focused on the nearly imperceptible shift of tide and temperature rolling over her, as Sayu had taught her to do all those years ago. Yes—*there* was the current that led to the caverns honeycombing the beachrock scattered across Korshun's inlet.

Darya quickly discovered she was no longer as hardy and limber as she'd been as a girl—her muscles, all of them, were burning after a mere ten minutes of steady swimming, and the starved sensation in her lungs had become torture. She whipped her head around, back and forth, searching with eyes that saw more and more clearly the longer she remained submerged—*there*, that deep wall of shadow just ahead—

Darya dove deep, swimming hard, and reached the familiar, seemingly unbroken mass of rock below the shelf just as she thought her lungs were going to burst. She scrabbled at it, awkwardly pulling herself up hand over hand until her fingers abruptly broke through into empty air, then frantically paddled the last few feet up. With a desperate surge of strength, she flung herself up over the shelf, head and shoulders finally breaking the surface of the water.

The stone was icy against her bare flesh, gouging into her as she wrenched the rest of her torso atop it, dragging her shaking legs up after her. She rolled over onto her back—for a long, terrible moment it was as if she'd forgotten how to breathe, but then her lungs spasmed convulsively and she sucked in a deep lungful of air. The damp rock walls rising up around her sparkled in the phosphorescent glow of the moss that coated the cavern's stone ceiling, or perhaps it was only in her own eyes—her vision was dimming as the shakes that racked her body grew more violent, then abruptly faded to black along with all conscious thought.

Darya regained consciousness slowly, drawn by a pervasive feeling of warmth; she opened her eyes to a softer, yellower light than the soulless green glow of the sea moss. Someone had built a small fire near the edge of the shelf she'd so laboriously pulled herself upon.

Her vision blurred, cleared, then blurred again; she rubbed her eyes, wincing at the bite of salt. Her head throbbed sharply as she levered herself up onto one elbow. A shadow blocked the firelight; she flinched back, then stilled, eyes opening wide at the sight of a face she hadn't expected to see again in her lifetime. Though she wasn't sure why she hadn't thought Kel might be the one to come—perhaps she hadn't really believed anyone would come at all.

"Thank you," she said, then spat to clear her mouth. "For the fire."

"You're welcome." His accent was heavier than Sayu's had been—though of course Sayu had had every summer for nine years to practice her Imperial Oun with Darya, and Kel had only had the one. He settled back against the stone wall behind him, his eyes fixing on a point past her head.

Darya found herself unable to tear her gaze from his face and entirely missed the next thing he said. "I'm sorry, what?"

"I said, I thought you'd resolved never to return?" He was looking at her once more—she thought, though she'd never been good at reading him, that he might be wary of her in spite of the sardonic edge to his voice.

Darya swallowed against her tight throat. "I need to speak to the *Alii*. If that's possible." She swallowed again and forced herself to meet his eyes. "The Emperor of all Oun desires it."

He grew very still; the firelight reflecting from the few wet drops remaining on his bare shoulders shone like jewels, unmoved even by a breath. "Well," he said, after a long pause. "The *Alii* it is, then." He began to rise to his feet.

"Wait! Is—who *is* the *Alii*, now?"

He stopped, then lowered himself back down beside her, legs crossed. Something about the question had pleased him, or reassured him—Darya couldn't fathom why, and her head had started to ache again, enough to blur her thoughts. She closed her eyes, and didn't even start when she felt a feather-light touch on her matted braids.

"Rest," she heard him say. "You're still tired. You've been too long away from the sea. When you wake up will be soon enough for the *Alii*."

She obediently laid her head back down; the rock floor didn't seem so unforgivingly hard now. She found his touch inexplicably soothing—and that was very different than it had ever been; once, his touch had unnerved her, then excited her, then finally driven her to a kind of despair when she had finally accepted that he could never be *just* hers, *only* hers—but it had never before soothed her. Exhaustion, or simply the slow march of time across the years and leagues of hard dry land that had separated her from him—she didn't know, and was too weary now to care.

Kel—Kel had come ashore with Sayu the year Darya turned sixteen. She'd had more trouble slipping out of the house to meet the *salaatu* on the beach that summer than ever before. Her grandfather, as obviously fond as he'd grown of her, never troubled himself about what she did when she wasn't directly before his eyes, but her mother had finally remembered that she had a daughter on the cusp of womanhood. Endless lessons in the kitchen, the buttery, the stillroom—she'd been left little time for Grandfather and the manor library that spring, and she'd been determined that her summer with Sayu wouldn't suffer the same fate.

But Sayu hadn't been alone, that first morning Darya managed to escape the manor. That stopped her in her tracks, on the very edge of the shoreline, because Sayu had never brought anybody else along before. And it was a boy—a few years older than she was, she thought, closer to Sayu's age—but *why?*

Sayu looked uncharacteristically disgruntled. After their usual embrace of greeting, she'd stepped back, scowling over her shoulder at the newcomer. "And this is Kel—who didn't believe I had an Imperial friend! And who was finally brave enough to come with us on the summer journey."

"Only temporarily," the boy said—he seemed unfazed by Sayu's mild hostility. "Just to see the far lands, and the foreign creatures!" He'd grinned unrepentantly down at Darya, then neatly dodged Sayu's shove.

"They're not *creatures*—"

"Well, I admit, she doesn't look like a *creature*. In spite of her odd attire, she looks as if she could—" He hadn't dodged quickly enough a second time and ended up sprawled on the ground, laughing up at them both.

He hadn't come ashore every day with Sayu, but he had more often than not—he'd been openly delighted with everything on land. The beach, the forest, the village—and Darya, it seemed. He'd never done anything inappropriate, never touched her in any unseemly way—but still he *had* touched her, light fleeting strokes of her face and bare arms, shocking her into stillness each time, to his obvious amusement and her deep embarrassment.

Sayu had grown more and more irritable that summer; finally, it had occurred to Darya what the reason might be. She'd stuttered and stammered over asking it. "Is it—do you *like* him, Sayu?"

"Like him?" Sayu had said distractedly. "I suppose—he's well enough—*oh*." After a second or two of astonishment, she'd burst out laughing. Darya smiled back, relieved, but also puzzled as to what was so funny. Then Sayu sobered abruptly. "No, but he likes you." Darya's face had heated. "Yes, he does! And it can't *be* anything and I wish he'd leave you alone. Darya—our men, they're not like yours. Your people—there's a man, and he marries a woman, and that's it, isn't it?"

"Well," said Darya, who had read most of her grandfather's books by then, "that isn't how it *always* goes—"

"It isn't like that at all for us. Ever. Kel—he has his *hoalli*—" Her lips had flattened in frustration. "There isn't even a word in your language for it. Not brothers, not lovers—but yes, that too. Lovers. Sometimes one of them *does* attach himself to a particular woman—but the rest of the *hoalli* won't accept what they can't share in, not for long…you don't understand a word I'm saying, do you?"

"I do, though!" Darya retorted indignantly—but she hadn't, not really.

And then the rest of that summer, and its dreadful, fiery end —her dozing thoughts skipped quickly over the worst of those memories—followed by a fever dream of a gently rocking boat and Sayu's voice in her ear, promising the *salaatu* would make her well, *could* make her well again. Except that it hadn't been a dream at all, as she had realized upon her first awakening, all those years ago, on the distant beach of the *salaatu*'s true home.

It had been night, the sky an enormous black bowl arching overhead. She had levered herself up on her elbows, awestruck—she had never seen the sky so unbroken by anything but the endless expanse of dark, rippling waves below it. The ground beneath her bare arms had been soft as powder, gleaming palely in the starlight—it was sand, but not the rough golden-brown of Korshun's shore; it was as light and fragile as winter snow. The breeze had caressed her face, her bare belly and legs, deliciously warm—she had started to sit up, suffused by a sense of well-being so overwhelming she nearly laughed aloud from the joy of it. Then she'd stilled as a dark silhouette rose from the surf lapping gently against the shore, shaking a silver-black spray of water from his long, fair braids.

Kel.

She'd looked down at herself again, in sudden terror—but the burns were gone, her skin as smooth and clear as a baby's. The *pain* was gone. The relief of it rolled over her in a wave of pleasure, an almost physical caress, and when she looked up again, she found Kel had stepped ashore and was gazing back at her, for once without a smile. She'd shifted her weight to begin to stand, delighting in the effortless movement of her body, then had stopped in startlement as a familiar hand had clasped hers. "Wait," Sayu had whispered into her ear—had she been there all along?

But I feel newborn, Darya thought—*I feel like I could do* anything—*anything I wanted, now*—

"Our people are very different." Sayu's grip had tightened. "And yes, you're different now too. But not inside—not in *here*—" and her fingers had lightly brushed Darya's temple.

Darya started awake. The *salaatu*'s beach was gone, replaced by the damp, ugly cavern walls, though it wasn't Kel beside her now. A woman bent over her instead, thick black hair cropped short—cropped for the *Alii*'s headdress, though she was bareheaded now. Eyes as black as her hair gazed down steadily at Darya, expressionless in the flickering light, set in a face with starker bones than Darya remembered. Then the woman smiled ruefully and she was Sayu again, the Sayu that Darya had run to all her life, until the day she'd run away from her instead. Darya closed her eyes against a sudden rush of tears.

"So you've returned," she heard Sayu say—and it *was* Sayu's voice, half-forgotten, but now so familiar in lilt and tone that she could hardly believe she hadn't remembered every nuance of it.

Darya forced her eyes open, blinking hard to clear the unwanted tears away. "That's what Kel said. More or less." She was at too much of a disadvantage, lying curled on her side—she struggled upright, trying not to grit her teeth too obviously at the shrieking protest of every muscle.

"Why?"

Just like Sayu to cut straight to the point. Darya decided to return the favor. "The Emperor wants to meet you," she said, and lifted her gaze up to meet Sayu's once more and surprised a fleeting look of shock lifting her heavy dark brows. "He's ill." As little as the Emperor wanted that fact bandied about, there was certainly no reason not to say it now, here, with Sayu.

"So? I'm sure the Emperor of all Oun has a dozen physicians, or perhaps a hundred. What has that to do with us?" Sayu was fully back in control of herself now, the gleam in her eyes only ironic. "What has that to do with *you*?"

"He's dying," said Darya, starkly; it was harder to say aloud than she had realized it would be. It was nothing anyone had yet said openly in her hearing, and in fact would never have dared, not if they had wanted to go on living themselves. "I don't know of what. I don't even know if it's something you could heal him of. It isn't just old age—he *is* old, of course, which also might pose some difficulty—"

Sayu waved that away, gaze intent. "And so you approached your Emperor—with a fantastic tale of my people, and our great and terrible magic—"

"No." Darya jerked her face away and stared at the pitted, muddy wall behind Sayu's head; the light of moss was washed out by the firelight, rendered dull and ugly in the sputtering flames. "I wouldn't have told him. It would never have occurred to me to tell him. I barely even knew he was ill, much less—anything else. Hardly anyone does." She sucked in a deep, shuddering breath. "I got drunk, one night a few months ago." It was impossible to explain why—she hardly knew it herself; she had never taken too much wine before in her life. She'd been restless, perhaps—more and more restless; her librarial studies had satisfied *some* part of her, the part she had always thought of as the most important part —she had been unused to having time on her hands, as she sometimes found herself having since graduation. "There was someone—someone I was interested in. I doubt he'd had any real interest in me, of course, at least before that night. We were all drinking together, and somehow he and I ended up in a corner alone, and I told him…not the *entire* story, or even much of any story at all…" She trailed off, barely able to speak for shame. "Of course I know why he seemed so fascinated *now*—he was the son of a high-ranking Imperial courtier, he must have known something, overheard something of the Emperor's illness—and of how all conventional treatments seemed useless. *Any* chance of a cure must have seemed worth the chase to him, and after all, what did *he* have to lose by it? So… he began to pursue me." Lightly, casually, yet with enough of an appearance of real engagement behind it that she had fallen for it. Like the most unutterable fool. "He managed to pry rather more details out of me after that. And then *he* went to the Emperor."

The silence that followed was quite miserable, at least for Darya. "I see," she heard Sayu say, finally—but she heard no anger in that voice; startled, she met Sayu's gaze once more. "Well…it wouldn't be an entirely *bad* thing, to have Imperial Oun in our debt." Sayu's lips were faintly curved "Perhaps I should thank you." Darya's own lips parted; her *What?* had no breath behind it—but Sayu understood it well enough. "Let's also say—I think I owe you this. For if your Emperor's *not* healed, it won't go well for you, will it?" She read the answer in Darya's expression. "So." Sayu rose with effortless grace from her crouch, strong slim hand locking around Darya's wrist and pulling her up to her feet as well, steadying her as she swayed a bit. "My mother warned me not to fool around with the Empire, all those years ago, you know. I defied her, for you. I let Kel indulge himself with you—"

"You tried to warn me." Not warn her that Kel could never love her, no—but that no man of the *salaatu* could ever love only one woman, could ever love *anyone*, alone, without his *hoalli*. And she hadn't understood anything, until it was too late.

"Not hard enough. Because I *did* want you to stay with us." She squeezed Darya's wrist lightly before letting go. "Come on. Let's see what we can do to salvage this."

Darya wondered what they thought, the Emperor and all his men, when they spied the *salaatu* fleet on the horizon—she didn't know, because she kept her head firmly down and her eyes on the slick dark wood between her bare feet, gripping the edge of the lead boat with white knuckles. No single trading boat, this; the *salaatu* had come in force. A small force, compared to the full military might of the Empire—but still carrying a good three times more *salaatu* than the Emperor's entire camp of followers.

Darya finally dared to peek upward, as the handful of *salaatu* who had jumped easily overboard ran the lead boat to ground. The Emperor and *Loro* Aison stood surrounded by the guards and outriders, their finery strangely artificial-looking under the bright, featureless glare of the overcast sky. Sayu had donned the *Alii*'s fantastic headdress of coral and feathers, and a woven cloth shift that fell halfway to her knees to appease Imperial sensibilities; she graciously accepted the helping hands of her crew as she stepped down onto the beach. Darya felt clumsy as a bear clambering down behind her.

Certainly now was the time for full and formal prostration; the tension emanating from the Emperor's guards was nearly palpable. Darya pushed her way forward and edged around Sayu, who stood proudly in front of the phalanx of *salaatu*. The sand was icy, a thousand tiny sharp knives cutting first into her knees, then into her thighs, belly and chin—she'd had to borrow one of the same thin shifts Sayu now wore, leaving far too much of her skin miserably bare to the elements.

"Sire," Darya said into the sand, muffled but determined. "As you ordered, so I've done—the *salaatu Alii* Sayu stands before you." Sayu had been quite explicit in her refusal to prostrate herself before Imperial Oun.

A long, thick pause, then— "Rise, please, *maya*." The Emperor's voice was noticeably hoarser than it had been before—surprise, or yet another turn for the worse of his health? Darya pushed herself to her feet and fixed her gaze on the Emperor, who thankfully had no attention left to spare for her. The deep mahogany of his flesh had an oddly chalky cast to it, only emphasized by the bejeweled glory of his Court dress; the sleeves of his ornate robes trembled.

Fingers bit into her arm, nearly startling a shriek out of her. Aison was staring down at her with slitted eyes, his mouth barely more than a line bisecting his rigid face. She jerked her head away, though she didn't quite dare do the same with her arm, and fixed her attention back on Sayu and the Emperor.

"—must take place upon our boat," Sayu was saying. *Though better if he came back with us altogether, and stayed for at least the season, just as you did,* she had said to Darya with unusual seriousness, during their boat ride back to the Emperor's camp, *but I think he won't. You agree?* Which had also meant that Sayu wouldn't be able to sing him back to health alone as she had done for Darya, not so far from the *salaatu*'s home, not in the sort of timeframe the Emperor would certainly expect. Hence the boats, plural, of the *salaatu*, in numbers likely never seen before within the boundaries of Imperial waters.

But aside from a brief hesitation, the Emperor seemed unfazed by this comparatively mild demand. "You'll leave your young friend here with my men," he said, with the briefest glance at Darya. Aison's grip tightened brutally on her arm and Darya clenched her teeth together.

"Of course," said Sayu serenely. She offered her hand and the Emperor took it, managing to do so in such a way that almost seemed caressing. Darya didn't think she imagined the appreciation in Sayu's smile. "But—" Sayu's heavy arched brows quirked upward, shifting her smile from pleased to pained all at once, "—she mustn't come to any harm, while we're away?"

"She will not," said the Emperor. "My word on it." He cast another lightning-sharp look back at them—at Aison, this time, Darya realized. She had thought Aison couldn't possibly look more upset than he already did, but she'd been wrong. Her arm throbbed painfully under the vicelike clamp of his fingers—Darya supposed that degree of harm didn't count.

The Emperor followed the *salaatu* to their dinghy. Minutes later they'd reached the *Alii*'s vessel; three of the *salaatu* assisted the Emperor up its rope ladder with quick light touches and bowed heads. Then he ducked under the low-hanging edge of the *Alii*'s shelter and abruptly vanished from sight. Aison made the faintest of muffled sounds—Darya glanced up at his face, but he'd already turned away and an instant later was hauling her back to the Emperor's tent.

As soon as they reached the half-opened flaps, he thrust her inside, then wheeled around and stalked away, leaving her alone— well, not *entirely* alone; two of the Emperor's personal servants stared round-eyed at her as she stumbled inside. Sand cascaded from her bare legs and feet onto the rich, jewel-toned carpets lining the tent's floor; one of the servant's stares followed it down, then back up, past her short plain skirt to her hair, completely unrestrained and curling wildly over her shoulders and arms from wind and saltwater. Darya turned her back on them and stalked across the tent to the pile of cushions in the farthest corner from the door.

Sleep would have been good for her, but it would not come, even as the light streaming in through the tent flaps gradually faded and the breeze drifting inside the tent took on a cool, bitter edge. As the tent's interior grew darker, one of the servants lit a lantern—just as it flared to life, Aison pushed his way into the tent.

"Out," he said flatly to the servants, who fled without so much as a murmur of protest. Darya recoiled as he strode across the tent and crouched down in front of her, close enough to touch. "If the Emperor doesn't climb back out of that boat at dawn, entirely in one piece and at least as healthy as he was when he first stepped aboard it, you won't die quickly."

Darya was genuinely afraid of the Emperor, whose power over her very life was both whimsical and absolute; she had been genuinely afraid that the *salaatu* wouldn't come to her, in the cavern—but she couldn't fear any such impossible scenario as Aison was clearly imagining. Though at least the reality of their existence had clearly freed him of any conviction he'd had before that she was the agent of some ambitious Imperial relation. "He will," Darya said, spurred into unwilling sympathy for his obvious misery. "Why would they hurt him? What could they possibly gain? The might of the Empire would grind them to pieces if they ever dared show their faces anywhere along the coasts of Oun, ever again."

"You—and *they*—are using him! Using a great man's fear of the only enemy he can't defeat by his strength of will alone—"

The injustice of that was the final straw. Darya's temper, usually mild, had been sorely tried by the events of the past week, and it abruptly snapped. She surged to her feet, kicking the muffling cushions aside, and glared at him. "Oh, yes, they're *using* him! That was their plan all along, when they encamped themselves outside his throne room and forced their way into his presence—"

"*You* were a far more effective messenger!"

"I wasn't any kind of messenger at all! I never wanted to tell his Imperial Majesty anything—I had never so much as *spoken* to him before—"

"And that's what made it all the more effective," Aison ground out. "A whisper, a rumor to amuse him, about some girl nobody knew anything about—carried by a son of the Chancellor himself —"

Darya couldn't help her flinch, or the heat that flooded her face, though if anything it made her even more furious. "Yes, I was a fool to say anything to *anyone,* you can't possibly despise me for that more than I do myself." That part of her that Kel had so thoroughly awakened all those years ago, somehow escaping the iron control she'd kept it under ever since—"You can't think that *this* is what I wanted to come of it!""

"The harm this journey alone has caused him—"

"Then perhaps you should've done a better job of healing him yourself, physician!" she snapped. "Then he wouldn't have been tempted to resort to this, this *charlatanry* in the first place!"

Aison took a single step toward her, his fists clenched, one rising, but Darya was in no mood to indulge him now. *"The Emperor's word!"* she hissed, and he recoiled as if she'd struck him instead of nearly the other way around. His fist dropped back to his sides and anger—and perhaps shame—reddened his cheeks, leaving the skin around his mouth white.

"Whatever lies you told him to convince him of this folly—"

"I only *ever* told him the truth—perhaps he *is* a great man, far greater than you, and knows it when he hears it!" A sob, harsh and ugly, tore itself out of her throat—she'd started to cry, and hadn't even realized it. "I can't prove the healing—they did far too good a job of that—but I can prove to you the price of it. You'll need to know anyway, as the Emperor's *physician*." Her voice dripped scorn. "Take hold of me, and pinch my nose shut and cover my mouth."

He was taken aback enough by this that his flush faded a little, his hands loosening at his sides. "What?"

"You heard me." He stared blankly at her. "*Do it*, you coward!"

That was enough to spur him; Darya barely had time for one deep breath before he gripped her shoulders roughly, then whirled her around and slammed her back against his chest. His fingers clamped down over her nose and mouth, as unyielding as steel bands.

Her lungs spasmed as the shock of impact tried to force a gasp out of her, and for a long panicked second she thought that perhaps she couldn't do it after all, here on dry land. The change had been easy and painless after she'd jumped from the *yoal*—her body, cradled in the deep implacable grip of the sea, had simply responded to its natural element. But now—

Her lungs spasmed again, then abruptly settled. She relaxed back against Aison, her pulse slowly subsiding in her own ears as her vision began to blur. The seconds ticked past, then a minute— two minutes—her skin grew slick as oil against his hands, wrenching a revolted grunt from him, but his grip didn't loosen. Three minutes—four minutes—five—six—by then, even with her lack of physical exertion, she could feel the first faint burn of starvation in her lungs.

Then he released her. She turned slowly around to face him, gazing up at him with eyes she knew looked utterly inhuman, unbroken ovals of shining pearl like a queen conch's inner shell. Aison took two careful steps away, his own eyes wide and unblinking on her face. She looked back at him for several seconds, still utterly unbreathing—then gently, deliberately inhaled.

"You see," she said.

Shouts outside the tent awoke her—Darya struggled up from the deep carpets, raking the salt-dried mess of her hair out of her face to squint at the tent flaps—still closed, but the light of dawn was creeping in through the gaps in the lacing. A quick glance around the tent confirmed that she was alone. She pushed herself creakily upright; every muscle in her body had stiffened during the night and now screamed in protest. The shouts had ceased, the silence outside the tent now ominous—she staggered over to the flaps and fumbled them open.

The glittering gold reflection of the sun on the ocean briefly blinded her, then resolved into two forms stepping onto shore—a tall, thin man, his hair blazing silver in the sunlight, and a woman nearly as tall as he, long-limbed and graceful, the coiling ends of her headdress whipping around them both in the chill morning wind.

A flurry of movement in Darya's periphery resolved itself into Aison, running forward and stopping abruptly several feet away from the Emperor, who had raised his hand palm-out to halt the headlong rush. "I'm well," said the Emperor—his voice was strong, resonant. The same vibrance that newly infused his voice had infused his face as well—he might have been a man in his fifties, not his seventies. "Aison." The last word was strangely tender. The rising sun shone mercilessly down on Aison's face, now wet with tears.

"Let me examine you, Sire," said Aison. *"Please."*

The Emperor smiled faintly. "Of course." He released Sayu's hand—Sayu was looking at him with an expression Darya found very difficult to read, because she could not believe it. The Emperor and Aison headed for the tent. Darya hurried forward, noting the abortive moves of a few guards towards her, but a dozen *salaatu* suddenly emerged from the surf to plant themselves directly behind their *Alii* and the guards backed away.

"An interesting man, your Emperor," said Sayu, her expression a shade too solemn as she gazed down at Darya's face. *"Very* interesting." Her dark eyes crinkled up at the corners.

Apparently Darya hadn't misread her expression at all. "How *could* you," she said, very faintly, and then, to her complete surprise, choked on a giggle. "He—you—he's *old*, you know—"

"A very Father Wisdom," Sayu agreed serenely. "Just like the Imperial tales you used to tell me."

Then Sayu held out her arms, and Darya fell into them. "I've missed you," Darya said, struck nearly insensible by the truth and strength of it, her voice muffled against Sayu's shoulder.

"And I've missed you." Sayu's voice was very soft. "I didn't know how much I would, until I knew you were gone for good."

"I didn't know if you'd come."

"Always," said Sayu. "I'll always come." She paused. "If you're where I can even reach you. Darya, perhaps you ought to stay with us, this time?"

"I understand why you're asking," Darya said slowly. "And...I can't promise that I won't have trouble now, going forward." Her mouth twisted. "Perhaps I'll become a favorite of the Court—"

"Or perhaps you'll end up dead." Sayu's lips flattened. "Consider—"

"No," said Darya. "I can't."

"That Kel," Sayu muttered. "I *told* him—" Kel hadn't returned to the Emperor's camp with her and Sayu. She'd been glad and sorry, hurt and relieved, and supposed dismally that she'd never truly get over him.

But— "It isn't just what happened with Kel." The Imperial library—she thought of it now, dry and warm with its hundreds of shelves of books, paper and ink, the infinite well of knowledge and discovery contained within its depths. Of her grandfather, his arms around her, holding her burnt and seeping body as if it were fragile as glass, carrying her to the *salaatu*'s boat in the dead of night so the rest of the family wouldn't try to stop him. "I can't—too much of me is here." Her chin jerked involuntarily over her shoulder, past the tents, towards the manor house looming silently on its hill. "In the *Empire*. I *can't* leave that. Not for good. Not forever." Darya took a deep breath. "But I was stupid to try to do the same with you—to leave you, leave the *salaatu* forever, leave... myself, what I became. As much as anything else, *that's* why I ended up being dragged back here, and then dragging *you* into this, this Imperial *mess*—"

"Now *that*," said Sayu, dark eyes alight, "is...what is the word? Irreverent? Or no, you don't actually worship your Emperor, your dives into the sand at his feet notwithstanding." She sobered abruptly, keen gaze searching Darya's. "But I do hope that means what it sounds like." One corner of Sayu's mouth curved up.

"Because I may have suggested to him that he should return here himself, every year or so…just for a brief visit, just to monitor his continued health—and that he should also perhaps bring someone along, someone familiar with my people, when he does so—"

Darya's lips parted, but no sound emerged. Could it be that easy? *Could* she return, every year—with Imperial favor, even approval…? She thought of Aison and shivered involuntarily—she didn't think *he* at least would let everything go, let bygones be bygones…but he would never oppose the Emperor's will. She was sure of that.

Sayu nodded once, sharply, then gave Darya's shoulders a final squeeze before she released her. Darya stepped back as Sayu turned away and waved her *salaatu* into their dinghies. They all rowed out to the *Alii*'s vessel. She watched the smaller boats flock to its side, like chicks to their mother; then the broad triangular sails caught the sharp morning wind, the forest of oars splashed down and churned, and it surged away, a rapidly shrinking silhouette against the risen sun.

See Lisa Short's story "Salaatu" online at Metaphorosis.
If you liked it, leave a comment. Authors love that!
Remember to subscribe to our e-mail updates so you'll know when new stories are posted.

About the story

This story actually takes place in a secondary fantasy world I created—Metaphorosis published the first story I wrote in it ("The Season of Withering", October 2019)]. Though the Emperor of the country the characters lived in is only briefly mentioned in that story, I became rather interested in him, then interested in setting more stories in that world, and even in the exact same time frame, just geographically separated. I have another short story (possibly a novella) in the works set in the southwestern reaches of the Empire (same time frame, though, again) and my in-progress novel is also set in this world and time, though on an entirely different continent. The Emperor is still only a secondary character in "Salaatu", but we do become more acquainted with him as seen through the eyes of the story's protagonist—and I also wanted to write a story that included a non-subjugated people coexisting with a large, heavily structured political entity, and not the story of their subjugation either—a story that demonstrates their strength and independence from the looming behemoth of Empire.

A question for the author

Q: What other writers inspire you?

A: Authors that inspire me—when I first started to answer this question, I realized about halfway through that what I was listing were authors whose stories I loved—not that there's anything wrong with that! But not necessarily authors who inspired me. Now, I do love the following authors' stories too, but their work also leaves me daydreaming for hours and aspiring to emulate their levels of creativity, artistry and/or originality: Octavia Butler, Rivers Solomon, Joan Slonczewski, Robert E. Howard, Barbara Hambly, and Tanith Lee.

About the author

Lisa Short is a Texas-born, Kansas-bred writer of fantasy, science fiction and horror. She has an honorable discharge from the United States Army, a degree in chemical engineering, and twenty years' experience as a professional engineer. Lisa currently lives in Maryland with her husband, youngest child, father-in-law, two cats and a puppy. She is a member of SFWA and HWA.

lisashortauthor.com, @Lisa_K_Short

Hard Sunset

Sam Griffin

The Curator hummed as they descended to the Archive's power core. A jolly song that mimicked the chirping legs of dancers in a sunlit square, and the whirling of lovers on a faraway summer afternoon. Days so warm and long there was nothing to do but weave sound until their feet ached and burned with the joy of life.

The Curator detected smoke. Detected a fresh imbalance in their position. They looked down at a basement floor mottled with subsidence, and new sun-bright cracks of breaking planetary crust. Smoke rose from the Curator's six mismatched synthetic feet.

Oh.

On the far side of the impassable surface, the reactor cast a pale glow, etched with impossible numbers of coolant spirals. Dim compared to its former brightness, but the Curator suspected it would nevertheless outlast everything else here — by at least several seconds. Remaining down here served no purpose, the Curator knew, and they still needed feet. One leg at a time, they backed up onto the stair, one of their feet already melted beyond repair.

"There's nothing to be done about it, and no reason to make a fuss," the Curator said to themself and left it there.

Back on the upper levels, the Archive's walls juddered, as erratic and out of tune and tempo as their guardian's failing voice. A stack of crystals tumbled loudly out of a storage bay, into the aisle, and rolled to a stop around the Curator. No librarians scuttled over to retrieve them. *All is as I expected, under these circumstances,* the Curator mused, and out of habit, picked the crystals up to place in the return chute. Below, on the sorting tables, the data solids tumbled out over data solids, rolling to a stop among piles long abandoned by the last half-working librarian.

The Curator took the only working elevator towards the reading room. It shuddered and whined between the floors, lights flickering from amber to white to red as it stalled, disrupting both the Curator's journey and their song. This would be an unfortunate place to spend their last hours, after a millennium of planning a few formal words to mark the demise of the Archive. It was true there wasn't much point to such an announcement — the last remaining librarian-clerk processed nothing but indices, and there was nothing to be gained by making a speech to the Curator's Assistant, as all but the most rudimentary of its cognitive functions had long since expired. Nevertheless, the Curator was expected — a duty of their position — to do such a thing, and they tapped again at the elevator's control disc.

With the keening wail of a failing structure, the elevator ejected them onto the upper mezzanine. Final function performed, it slid down the shaft and shattered on the ground thirty seconds and three hundred floors below. The Curator thanked it quietly for its long service and limped to the reading room.

There, the Curator collided with the Assistant, as they had every morning for as long as the Curator remembered. The Assistant whistled as it polished the blank screens with cloth, meticulously wiped down the seats and disinfected the auditory probes. Dust lay in sedimentary layers on the silent flutes, faded iridescent books, and everything else. The Curator queried the necessity of the Assistant's actions. At this, the Assistant cocked its heads on one side with a sigh.

"You never know," it said.

But the Curator did know, precisely, how improbable any hope was.

The People had been an old species in a young universe, and all evidence suggested no other vibrant, thinking, creating, beings existed in the cosmos. An entire civilization — even now the Curator shuddered the word — *alone.* And the hives had been dying — no children, no tradition, no kin. The People had reached towards the future, built the Archive on an empty world orbiting a binary star, and entrusted all they were to the Curator. To *eternity.*

There was enough left of the stairs for the Curator to warily make their way up a level — to the outside viewing platform — and gaze up at the hole in the sky. *How strange for there to be no tomorrow.*

The Curator stopped humming their song, reflected on the oddness of the thought. *Should I feel sad?* they thought. *Even anger would be appropriate.* But they'd shed their biological body eons ago, to fulfill a duty deeper than flesh, and any emotion was impossible. Nevertheless, they had long been aware of a certain *emptiness*, a lingering sense of having *failed.* Just as they had failed to keep another promise made on a distant summer afternoon for the sake of another fruitless dance.

Over the millennia since that day, one half of the stellar binary had tumbled towards its hungrier, heavier twin. Now, beneath the swirling, glowing disc of particles that had once been a sun, no eternity remained. Instead, the Archive world surged and bulged with liquified rock as it broke apart. The last dawn had come and gone. This evening, the sun would inevitably set for the last time before it — and the world it had once supported — became dust.

No one had come to the Archive. The People were forgotten, and the Curator's life had — at the end of everything — been in vain. *Today is proof the universe cannot abide forever.*

"I am, perhaps, the last sentient mind in the universe," the Curator said, dutifully dictating the speculation into the records, for no-one to hear.

"Thee was most totally, never," said an unexpected voice.

It took the Curator several seconds to interpret the signal as a mutated, clumsy, single tone form of their own language. Confused, they looked around, traced the sound to a shape in the doorway. A figure with an unfamiliar number of limbs, sealed inside some form of... exoskeleton? Environment suit? Surely the shape was the hallucination of a wishful thought; just a damaged circuit in the depths of the Curator's worn out and patched brain.

"Greetings, Formal Neuter," continued the strange creature, bending awkwardly in the middle. "Canyons of >ERROR, NOT FOUND< with taking an excess of forward transition."

The Curator could not believe the reliability of the sensory input they received. *Is this an alien? Here? Now?* How had it got here? The Curator accessed the Archive's sensors and found — in the static of overloads and exceeded parameters — an outlier datum in the vicinity of the roof, barely minutes old. *A ship!*

"Do give me a moment," said the Curator, calmly and politely. Somewhere in the recesses of the Curator's mind, they hoped the Visitor had some technology or magic to save the Archive. They struck up the cheerful hum again. "I need to compensate for linguistic drift and your frankly terrible accent."

The Visitor gestured with its upper limbs in a way that did not seem threatening, and the Curator hastily processed. Systems unused for a billion years responded to the Curator's summons, and a side routine brought light to the reading room and images to its long-dull screens. The Assistant's yelp of surprise carried through the conduits. Below, the reactor shuddered in time with the convulsing planet, and gave all it could.

"I'm sorry I took so long," the Visitor said, as the Curator accommodated the transformed words. It lacked tonal nuance, but that was also to be expected.

"I am sorry too," said the Curator. "The Archive is at your disposal, comprising seven thousand physical artefacts, plus six hundred and eighty-four billion zettabytes of data."

The Visitor tipped what might have been a head upward at the particulate sky. "I don't think I can stay that long."

"You have storage? On your ship? You can take much with you…"

"I … can't. The drive takes up so much space. It has to — to resist that." The figure waved a limb toward the bright ring and its dark core.

The last of the Curator's hope shattered in that moment. *Then why did you even come?* the Curator thought, only to realize too late they had spoken it aloud.

"I wanted you to know you weren't alone," the Visitor said. "To tell you I've followed pieces of your history across a thousand planets. I wanted to promise that your people are remembered."

"But not all of us. Not everything," said the Curator. Overhead, brilliant white gasses swirled towards oblivion.

"No," said the Visitor. "Not everything. But perhaps you could choose something special?"

The Curator thought for many milliseconds. They thought of science, biochemistry, anatomical structures. They thought of brilliant crystalline buildings that murmured in the heat of a warm day. But the laws of the universe were universal, bodies had ceased to matter long ago, and the houses were long gone. Then they thought of a sunlit afternoon and a lover's chirping limbs as they whirled around the square, and a promise unkept.

"I wonder," said the Curator, eventually. "If you would have time to visit the music section."

The world ended exactly six hours and thirty-eight minutes later.

The Visitor had, some three thousand seconds ago, climbed into its ship, humming the song the Curator had taught it. They watched it go, watched engines of unfathomable design carry the People's last wish in the form of as many crystals as the Visitor could fit in the pockets of its suit — to a young species in an older universe. One song, one thousand years of music, and one lover's gift, never given, on a faraway summer day.

The Curator found just enough energy inside themselves to crawl down the crumbling stairs. They left a leg or two behind — but they didn't need to patrol anymore, didn't need to pay attention to counting. Simply one final duty to keep.

In the disintegrating remnant of the reading room, the Curator (the first and the last) contentedly delivered their terminal speech to a half-working librarian and the Assistant. The Assistant stopped polishing, for one long second, to applaud. Flared brightly for a second more as the particles that had once been the Archive, and the Assistant, and everything else, began their final and near eternal descent into the black hole.

The Curator hummed contentedly and returned to dance in the warmth of the sun.

See Sam Griffin's story "Hard Sunset" online at Metaphorosis.
If you liked it, leave a comment. Authors love that!
Remember to subscribe to our e-mail updates so you'll know when
new stories are posted.

About the story

The first version of the story came from one of the creative challenges my partner (graphic/web designer and photographer) and I sometiimes set each other. Write a story in an afternoon, and they'd come up with some kind of art for it. This prompt was 'sunset'...

I like to subvert prompts — I'm annoying like that — and I'd been watching a science documentary about the universe. Can't get much more sun or setting or going down than a black hole!

From there on, a swirl of Brian Cox, Arthur C. Clarke, Douglas Adams and a sniff or two of a certain long running Brit SF show led to the Curator, the Archive, and a tale of the last day. But that's only where it began.

In the four years between the first version and the published version, I'd finally received a decent level of cPTSD therapy. In edit for *Metaphorosis*, I could properly engage the Curator's emotions. Now the story is consciously infused by neurodivergence, loss, purpose, legacy, finding peace with the past, and making sense of endings. And hope, of course, which rarely looks quite how you expect...

A question for the author

Q: Do you live near where you were born? Have you traveled much?

A: My home in the North West UK is less than 60 miles from where I was born, which is probably not far enough (or close enough!) to be interesting. Home contains my partner and my cats, with the luxury of a big garden and a nearby beach, so no complaints!

My travelling is mostly of the mental variety … which is a) cheaper, b) more disability friendly, and c) comes with less (but not zero) chance of losing my passport. Also, many more possible destinations, unconstrained by space, time, or reality. Honestly, I have been on exactly two aeroplanes in my life and hated it — I'm not a fan of being up anywhere. Luckily I do like rugged scenery, rain on canvas, history and lukewarm weather, as I'm spoiled for all those in Britain. If everything aligned for a big trip, I'd love to go to Norway (for the Aurora), but until that time bring on the words!

About the author

As a neurodivergent, queer, and disabled author of speculative fiction, Sam is many things. An academic, creative, middle-aged rebel, a problem solver and chaotic mess. Her/ their recurring themes include liminality, becoming, entropy, being truly seen, and sex.
www.unquietwords.co.uk

Translations for a Dead Sea

Corey Farrenkopf

Laura struggled to hold a half dozen nails between her lips. She'd found the hammer under the sink, along with several rudimentary tools her father had used for cabin maintenance. He had never been very handy. She used her knee to balance the plywood, galvanized steel chilling her tongue. Once the wood was aligned over the first window facing the sea, she leaned a shoulder onto the salt-worn surface, pressing it in place as she drove a nail into the casement. The hammer clatter reverberated in light fixtures and summer screens, a metallic chittering not dissimilar to cicadas.

She repeated the process until the graying wood was tacked in place.

The next board waited beneath the deck. Her father had cut each to the exact dimensions of corresponding windows, eight in all. The only window he left unadorned was the leaky, western-facing skylight. Even though the roof wasn't steep, her father hated ladders, so it was left bare to view every winter snow and swelling Nor'easter. The cabin was only meant for three season habitation, the insulation thin. Everyone in the area boarded up for winter, to keep out storm winds and the freezing spittle rising off the ocean.

"Isn't it a little early to be putting up the boards?" Ray asked from behind her. Ray was in his early forties, a thick brown beard covering his face, eyes the color of the sea, wardrobe composed of nothing but flannel.

"Definitely not," Laura replied, words struggling around the nails.

"I'd say we have at least a month of good weather ahead. Won't you miss the view?"

Laura didn't know how to answer honestly, so she lied.

"It'll help me concentrate when I'm translating. If I spend too much time looking at the water, I'm going to get nothing done."

"How is the writing going?" Ray asked, moving to her side, steadying the plywood with a callused hand.

Ray lived in one of the large renovated ranches across the street. He worked as a maintenance man for the stretch of cabins crowding the road, for summer people incapable of fixing toilets or hooking up propane tanks. They'd known each other for years, only growing close after his wife passed, leaving him with their twin daughters and the ever encroaching sea.

"It's going," Laura replied. "A few more weeks and I'll be pretty close to the end."

"Your dad would have been proud, finishing it up for him like that," Ray said as Laura hammered another nail. She slipped, aim off, spilling a cascade of galvanized steel across the deck from her toolbelt. Laura swore as the two bent to retrieve the sharpened metal. She'd heard too many horror stories of thin soled sneakers and lockjaw to leave the nails for long.

"Who's to say? I don't think he even knew if it *should* be finished," Laura said once the stray nails were gathered.

Ray looked at Laura askew, then shrugged, going back to holding the wood.

"Well, I'm sure he would be," Ray said.

Her father's cottage was identical to the fifteen other white, clapboard cottages strung along the road in North Truro, one of the towns farthest out on the Atlantic-wrapped peninsula. Neighboring roads repeatedly washed out with sand, blacktop giving way to soft shoulders, desert-like. Sparse forests of scrub pine pressed up to the dunes, the scent of sap always on the air.

Each building was a single story. Turquoise shutters framed windows. Chimneys divided rooflines. Over their shoulders was Cape Cod Bay, a thin stretch of beach on the opposite side of a concrete seawall. When storms rolled in, roiling waves kicked about front steps, the buildings more aquatic than terrestrial. In October, most were abandoned, the seasonal economy come and gone for the year.

Ray said only eccentrics stuck around.

Laura welcomed the epithet. She had a goat tattoo on her collarbone, had given up dying the gray out of her bangs. She used to stitch patches of band names to leather jackets, fixing studs to shoulders. She was getting too old for that, though, she told herself.

Laura had lost her previous lease in Boston when she could no longer afford the rising rent. It was hard to afford anything in the city when you were single, and after an unpleasant divorce in her late twenties, owning her own place always seemed like a distant daydream. The cottage was her only option, the mortgage already paid. All she had to worry about were taxes and insurance. After the prolonged pandemic, her job, like many, had cut hours and gone remote. The cottage got decent wifi. It was enough to continue her graphic design work, sketching logos for organic juice shacks, crafting tri-folds for some corporation's overpriced healthcare package.

Her job didn't really matter anymore. It paid the bills, kept the heat on, provided enough for takeout twice a week, but little else. It was her nightly task that propelled her days. Her father, an armchair academic after a lifetime of marine biology, had left behind a poetic text he believed held the secret to many things. He had believed the words could provide hope, a tipping point, some great revelation and unveiling. But he also believed the inverse, possibly one of the reasons he hadn't made it through the sheets of paper now piled on Laura's writing desk.

With the boards up, her view was gone, the ocean curtained by plywood, the desk lit only by the warm glow slipping beneath the lampshade. Now the windows only peered at the backside of graying boards, several dark knots like wide eyes gazing back at her while she wrote, fingers tracking through dictionaries, unheard voices muttering in her ear.

She hadn't wanted to cover the glass, but she didn't have many choices.

They'd get in if she didn't provide a barricade. From the noises she had heard, her sunless rooms were a small price to pay to sequester her from what came in the night.

Laura had written a pros and cons list for finishing the translation of her father's found poem.

CONS:

There are still a few trees.

Cori and Mark. Diane. Russel and Taraneh. Cashel, Daria, Ralph. Gabrielle.

Art's thriving.

There are still guitars. Concerts every weekend.

All those retired ladies at the conservation trust.

The girls.

> *Ray*
> PROS:
> *There are only a few trees.*
> *Most people disappoint me.*
> *Most people don't care about other people, or animals, or plants…especially not plants.*
> *Colony collapse disorder.*
> *Rising ocean temps.*
> *The Sixth Extinction.*
> *Death hornets.*
> *Favorite Indian restaurant closed.*

Laura's father, while being good with words, had never been the best translator, hence the unfinished manuscript and the age-muddled line he believed could be understood in one of two ways:

> *Once rewritten, all will be calm and well*

or

> *Once rewritten, none shall remember calm that well*

Laura looked at it as a fifty-fifty chance. Pleasant improvements or vague unpleasantries? She didn't know the scale, what extent of healing or joy or despair would come from the fractured lines. The way things were going, those were decent odds. Speeding up the apocalypse wasn't a great option, but continuing on the same trajectory would lead to blight, emptiness, and very little potable water. Laura wasn't very good with knives or machetes, so defending the only clean waterhole for miles seemed like a grim prospect. She'd read the emergency reports, the UN's 2029 predictions and warnings. Local governments were already talking about placing water restrictions on communities, about storing surplus runoff in newly constructed holding tanks isolated from the public. It was never too early to think about where your next drink might come from, her father had always said.

The thought was never far from her mind.

Her father had bought the crumbling papyrus from an indoor flea market in Maine. He'd found it nestled in a poster-tube between a taxidermied armadillo and a glass case containing antique pearl-handled revolvers. It was in Greek, the language of his great-great grandfather. Laura had sprung for the Rosetta Stone app for the two of them, promising they'd learn in tandem. It was a point of bonding. He hadn't been doing well since her mother passed, and the daily lessons gave them an easy entry point for conversation. Once she became fluent, her father had promised he'd bring her to Athens.

They had been at the translation for four years, moving between a pile of dictionaries and the app, before lung cancer caught him.

Now it was up to her to figure out the words left behind.

Once dusk had settled, a resonant thud quivered through the plywood. Laura's eyes left the half-composed paper, drifting to the hammer she'd left on the table by the door. The door itself was the only point of entry to the cabin. She couldn't board it up and still make it to the store when she needed eggs and milk and basic human contact. She had to hope the new twin deadbolts Ray had installed would hold. It had been a strange request to make, needing two, but Ray seemed to understand the fears of a woman living alone.

There was also the unprotected skylight, but the thing (things?) outside seemed to have no skill in climbing, so Laura pushed the second point of entry from her mind. It would have been even weirder to ask Ray to install another latch up there, or some heavy-duty screen, though she knew he'd be more than happy to do it for her. Ray seemed more than happy to do most things for Laura and that made her glad. After her divorce and five years of on-again-off-again online dating, she had begun to wonder if there were any decent guys left out there.

Decent was only one of many words Laura could think of to describe Ray.

Another thud snaked through the boards, followed by the sound of claws dragging along their surface. Something circumnavigated the outside of the cottage, slender fingertips mapping the borders between her life and theirs. She was still trying to figure out if there was more than one. A flock? A gathering? A parliament? Laura didn't know. She'd only caught glints that first night before she put up the boards. Only the teeth stayed with her, the sight of moonlight catching on enamel.

Either each night they grew more determined at forcing their way in, or there were more of them. More claws scraping at boards, more feet/flippers/tails scuffing along the deck. Whenever she made progress on the translation, the clamoring grew worse, as if each new word called to them more persistently.

The real problem was whether they were the hero or the villain of the story. Had they come to stop her from finishing the manuscript, halting her from destroying the world, saving the human race from an endless dark horizon? Or were they something else entirely?

Her father's field of study had been mollusks.

"They're nature's healers," he'd once said to Laura over Thai food, a dinner date of broken Greek underway. "Did you know that one oyster can filter fifty gallons of water a day? We've been trying to find a way to use them to clean up waste in the bay."

"I didn't know that," Laura replied, though she had. It was her father's favorite factoid about his work, most of which was too jargon-heavy for her to follow. But the oysters she understood.

The oysters were one of the reasons her father had fallen so hard into the translation. Their shells were growing thin. Ocean acidification ate away at them slowly year after year. If the trend continued, they would eventually become translucent, like pebble ghosts scattered across the floor of the bay. Then a year or two after that, they'd be dead.

"So you want to save the world for oysters?" Laura asked him one night as he hunched over his papers, lamp bleeding green through its banker's shade.

"What's good for oysters, is good for fish, is good for gulls, is good for us. It's all connected."

"I think I'm going to blame vandals," Laura said as Ray examined the shreds of plywood heaped beneath the bay-side windows, a harsh tear dividing the top of the wood from the bottom.

Wind was heavy off the water, a salt sting in the air, their skin peppered by sand. A tumbleweed of a hydrangea head rolled into the dunes, the once blue bloom now decaying brown.

Ray picked up the larger half of the plywood, fingers running along the gashed surface.

"Vandals?" he asked. "Would have thought me and the girls would have heard something. I guess the ocean's been pretty rough lately. Hard to hear anything over all those waves."

"Yeah, let's go with vandals. Who else would do this?"

Laura knew very well who would do this.

Or vaguely well.

Or just vaguely.

She hated lying to Ray, but didn't know how else to explain her current circumstances, poetry summoning potential demons and all.

"If the vandal was a tiger, maybe, but we don't have many of them out here," Ray replied. "I chased off a pack of coyotes a few weeks back, but nothing bigger than those guys."

"So, if it wasn't vandals, or tigers, or coyotes, what would you put your money on?" Laura helped him slide a new piece of wood from the back of his truck, hoping that Ray might know more than he was letting on.

"Have you pissed anyone off lately?"

"I haven't talked to anyone besides you and the girls and a few people at the grocery store in the last month. I might've pissed off one of those retired bagging ladies who's never careful with my eggs, but otherwise, nope."

"Do you have a gun?" Ray asked.

Laura almost dropped her end of the plywood.

"Do you think I need one?"

"Whatever ripped this guy down," he said, gesturing towards the scrap wood, "is big. Biggish at least. People in the Outer Cape get eccentric sometimes. Who knows if someone bought an exotic pet and it's been getting out at night. You know, real Tiger King shit. That's the only thing I can think of. Would you like a gun? On loan of course."

"Can you legally give me a gun?"

"Don't worry, cops aren't going to come around to bother you. In the off season, they're on call, mostly. And if you shoot something, I'll come running and say I did it. Problem solved. It's not like I'm going to miss a gunshot in the middle of the night."

"Is it safe?"

"Of course. Do you think I'd keep guns in the house around the girls otherwise?"

"Well, if that's the case, yes, I'd very much like a gun."

"It's all yours. You sure there's nothing else to tell?" Ray said, pointing to the wood. "I really can't imagine sleeping through all this."

"Earplugs do wonders," Laura replied, unable to meet Ray's eyes, pretty sure he'd never glimpsed what slipped from the sea nightly.

Later that night, Laura lay next to Ray beneath the covers of his queen-sized bed, staring out towards her cottage through the open window, waiting for inarticulate shadows to swarm her doorway. She hadn't left her translation inside. She knew better. It rested in her backpack by the bedroom door. A copy of the first page lay on her writing desk back in the cabin, the lure hopefully singing to those amorphous shapes slouching from the sea.

The night was still early, the girls having gone to sleep after an impromptu ping-pong tournament with Laura. They'd fallen into the custom of batting the hollow ball back and forth most evenings, something to unwind after a long day of school (for the girls) and dread (for Laura).

Somehow, Laura and Ray managed to keep their sex quiet, never waking his daughters, for which she was thankful. Ray's work-toned body was slick with sweat beside hers, one damp arm slung around her waist as he snored into their pillows. He had fallen asleep quick. He'd been rebuilding a neighbor's deck all week. She didn't fault him. It was just nice to not be alone for a few hours, to hear someone else's breath besides her own.

Laura's mind tracked to her pros and cons list, all that would be lost if she were wrong, Ray's name down there at the bottom. The girls. She always wrestled with the same issue before sleep. It was only after dark she doubted her purpose, fearful of mistakes, of losing those she loved.

But those she loved would be lost anyway, just on a later date when tides had risen and cannibalism wasn't so frowned upon.

Laura thought of the sections as cantos; she'd been obsessed with Dante's *Inferno* when she was an undergrad and always liked to think of section breaks in poetry as such. She knew that wasn't accurate, but who was there to correct her? Ray wasn't the reading type and the girls hated anything that resembled homework.

According to Laura's calculations, she was on canto twenty-two of thirty.

It went like so:

By the water I have written.
Several days have passed.
They swim far out. Farther than I might swim.
I don't swim.
I fear what I see on the surface.
I fear what lies below.
If there is no name, it doesn't exist.

I fear I will find the words to describe it.
To call it into life, plucked from my head,
dropped at my feet, writhing limbs and teeth.
I'm often tempted to lay down my pen.
To forfeit these lines.
But it is also these lines that keep them in the water.
But it is also these lines that call them ashore.

Laura kept the gun within reach. She left the hammer by the door. She'd seen many horror movies; she knew to tuck plenty of weapons away. A crowbar by her bedside, the tire iron from her trunk beneath the pull-out couch, a scaling knife behind the television. Two steps and she could be at any hiding place. She wasn't sure most of the objects would do much against what she'd seen through the cracked plywood, but it was better than nothing.

The night she had spent in Ray's bed, the creatures had left her cabin alone, as if they knew she wasn't inside, as if they knew she wasn't dragging pencil across paper, thumbing through dictionaries for difficult adjectives. Was it the words that called to them or the work that led to the words? Laura hated not knowing, hated the uncertainty of every aspect of her life, both environmentally and romantically speaking. She didn't know if Ray saw her as anything more than a fun hookup, if he imagined they had a future together, if he'd willingly do all the macheteing to keep their joint water supply safe.

She was trying to work up the nerve to ask, but the timing didn't seem right.

Nothing really seemed right anymore.

Three days later, the moon hung nearly extinguished above Laura's cabin, a pale sliver in the overshadowed sky. It cast enough light to make out the teeth, the slap of gums, a tongue tasting the air as if premeditating its next meal. The thing (things?) had pulled down one of the boards, wrenching the nails from their tired hold. The creature lingered for a moment before moving to the next window, talon-fin-fingers scrambling at the boards as if it were blind, as if some other sense guided it to her home.

It gave her comfort to think the creatures weren't intelligent. They had the opening, the glass right before them, her soft skin just beyond that. But instead, they moved to the next window, repeating the previous process. Laura promised herself she wouldn't shoot until they broke through, until she could smell their breath, feel the heat on her neck. If she shot now, she'd have to explain the thing's corpse to Ray, and the police, and every gawker who swarmed the cottage once a photo landed online. If that was the case, she'd have to confess what she was doing, and someone more knowledgeable would take it out of her hands. Laura didn't want that.

The translations were the only thing that made her feel close to her father anymore, the only thing that gave her life purpose. Designing Kale Chip flyers for her day job certainly wasn't cutting it.

As Laura dropped to the next line of text, which she roughly translated as *There will be joy once collapse. Different joy, but joy nonetheless*, she felt as if her father's hand pressed her shoulder, cold fingers gripping her collarbone. His negative image reflected in the glass, his thin face and beard tinted gray, translucent. Laura reached her free hand up, to place it on his, but there was only gooseflesh coursing down her neck, the call of the wind rushing outside, the stomp and drag of the creatures' movements across the deck. His face slipped from the glass, dissolving back into the writhing night beyond, back into her insomnia-addled memory.

At some point after midnight, Laura heard a splash, something dropping back into the ocean. She had put her pen down moments before and retreated to the mattress, pulling the blankets up around her ears. She prayed sleep would come.

There were only three more pages to translate. Two more cantos.

It wouldn't be long until she knew which version of her father's predictions was true.

"Tigers again?" Ray asked.

It was the fourth time he'd helped rehang the plywood. It was December. The Cape was quiet and gray, the sky low, beach grass freezing in the dunes, their brittle skin snapping like tin bells on windy mornings.

"I think of them as cougars, but that's just me. Tigers are expensive. Cougars are the value point big cat," Laura replied, nails under her tongue.

"Don't you think you should winterize the place, move somewhere inland? Maybe the tigers will leave you alone."

Ray had offered to call the police, or animal control, several times. Each time, Laura refused. She couldn't risk interruption to her work, no more than she already added with her visits with him and the girls.

She'd started to hear her father's voice, reading over the lines, suggesting changes. They were close. Another few days and the oysters wouldn't become living ghosts, another name relegated to the endangered species lists.

"That's not going to help," Laura said.

"You could always stay with me," Ray replied, looking back towards his own home. "The girls would love that."

If she said yes, she knew she'd never finish the translation.

"I'm fine here. For now anyway. Who knows what the future holds? For now, if we fix the windows, that should be enough. The pattern's worked so far. I just need another week, tops, another week—"

"Another week for what? You want to tell me what's going on?"

Laura bit her lip. "It's nothing. Just another day or so and I'm done with dad's old translation, that travelog from the Greek monk I told you about. It's mostly recountings of wildlife, lots of utopic scenery and descriptions of tropical fruit."

Ray nodded uncertainly, as if her words had slipped past him too fast to be believed.

"And what does that have to do with your little night visitors?"

Laura froze. "They must love poetry. It's in high demand."

She tried to laugh off the comment, but the forced mirth died in the air between them.

"I see," Ray replied, eyes drifting back towards his house where the girls were playing basketball in the side yard. He began backing away, moving towards the road. He didn't offer to hold the plywood like usual, leaving Laura to use her knee and shoulders. She thought about calling after him, explaining everything, but she didn't want Ray to become a greater deterrent, one of those halting forces, a potential casualty.

But she also didn't want to drive him away, swept out of her life by a torrent of unhinged speculation.

Ray paused before he crossed the street.

"Are you still planning on joining us for dinner tonight?" he called to her. "We're doing lasagna."

"If I can get enough work done," Laura said, a spark of hope floating in her chest. Maybe everything really could be healed, happy endings not solely relegated to fiction.

"Door will be open. Just come over around six if you can. The girls will miss you if you skip out."

Laura had found her father, weeks after the diagnosis, crying before the aquarium in his living room, a holdover from lab days. The bottom was cluttered with mollusks: oysters and clams, mussels adhered to pieces of driftwood in the corner. Streams of green kelp drifted in the artificial current. The buzz of the filter burbled over his sobs.

His forehead was pressed against the glass when Laura pulled up a chair.

"We're definitely not going to make it to Greece," he said.

"We can still go. There's plenty of…"

"Not if I'm going to finish the poem."

"I thought you weren't sure whether that was the right move?"

"I need to leave something behind. Something that will help, otherwise it's all been a waste."

Laura's hand moved to her father's shoulders, rubbing circles into the fabric of his shirt.

"You did plenty of good, Dad. Think of the bay cleanup. Or the dovekie rehab. Or the plover monitoring sites. There's quite a list."

"But it's not enough," he replied.

"Is there ever enough?" she asked.

"I'd hope so."

They remained seated in the dim light of his living room, listening to the burble of the fish tank, observing the subtle movements of the mollusks, her father's entire life's work condensed to a single fifty-gallon tank and a stack of pages.

Laura hadn't left the lights on, certainly hadn't left the door unlocked, not with the completed manuscript on the desk, those final lines ready for recitation. But the cottage was wide open, light bleeding through the skylight and the singular window whose boards had been partially sheared away in the night, the things having left before shattering glass, only tearing the screen to tatters.

It was the closest they'd come to getting in.

Laura had a half dozen donuts clutched in one hand, a bottle of hand-pressed grapefruit juice in the other. She figured she deserved a treat before the end...or the beginning, whatever came after her reading by the water.

The manuscript was exact in its instruction:

These words must be spoken in sight of the sea,
over waves,
carried on tides,
washing low to all ears.

Did oysters have ears? she'd wondered as she wrote, a skip of joy in her throat. That joy deflated as she hesitantly opened the cottage door, holding the donuts before her like a shaking, gluten-heavy shield. She wished she had the gun, or the hammer, or the knife, anything beyond a box of cheap baked goods.

Ray sat on the couch, manuscript pages stacked neatly besides him, the last left in his hand as his eyes traced the remaining words.

"How'd you get in?" she asked, putting down the donuts on her small dining table.

He raised a keyring from his lap without looking up from the page. "You gave me the spares when I installed the locks, remember?"

"That tracks, but why are you here? It's not like the pages call to you like they call to them," she replied.

Ray lifted a small shoulder bag with a patch depicting a goat-headed god and the name of a metal band sewn to the fabric. "You left this last night."

Laura hadn't been able to resist the lasagna.

"Can you just put those down? I worked really hard on them and I can totally explain what they all mean and..."

"I don't know if there's much to explain. The text is pretty straight forward on our options," Ray said, finally looking up, eyes red as if he'd been crying moments ago. "Are you actually going to read this? Have you thought about what it might mean for my girls if it's real? What it means for you and me?"

"If I don't read that, your daughters are going to be murdering neighbors for a bottle of water. Do you really want to be looking over your shoulder the rest of your life waiting for someone to do the same to them? There's no more ping-pong in the apocalypse. No sleepovers. No love. That's what's ahead."

"You don't know that," Ray replied, hand slowly moving through his beard. Over her shoulder, the sun had begun to set, the shortest day of the year only a week away. Winter's chill rushed through the open door, the lap of the sea failing to soothe the tension.

"Some people don't believe science, but I'm not one of them. Neither was my father," Laura said.

"There's always hope…always other options. Your father was real big on hope."

"This was the last thing he wanted." Laura didn't know how true that was, but the words came with confidence. She had to do this for him, after that night by the fish tank.

Before Ray could reply, the sound of something sloshing out of the water crept through the open door, wet and bulky, shifting its weight through the sand. Laura swore, rushing back to the door and slamming it shut, turning the twin deadbolts in place. Ray and Laura held each other's gaze from across the room before their eyes drifted to the unboarded window. A shadowed figure stood there, dripping seaweed from its massive frame. Laura didn't really know what she was looking at. The thing's body was amorphous and many limbed, barnacle-crusted, its head too high to view through the small opening.

"Not tigers," Ray said, eyes wide.

"Not tigers," Laura replied.

"Do you still have that gun?"

"What? Like I'd throw it in the ocean or something with this thing hanging around?" she said, hurrying to the small table beside her bed, unearthing the revolver from within.

"So, I'm going to shoot it and we're going to run back and get the girls. We'll get out of here and go read that poem. That will fix things, right?" Ray asked, gesturing for Laura to give him the gun.

"You want to read it together?" she asked, brain snagging on the implications as she handed over the weapon.

"Sure, I wouldn't let you do it alone. I…"

The sounds of something else sliding across the deck cut him off. There were a second and third body moving over the boards, others dragging their skin over the cement seawall, pressing through beach sand as they scaled the incline. From the noise, it was hard to pinpoint an exact number. It was safe to say many, all drawn to the final iteration of the poem, far more than the eight bullets in the revolver could handle.

"What do we do?" Ray asked, eyes traveling from one boarded window to the next.

"We wait. This happens every night. When the sun comes up, they usually just go away. They're kind of dumb, if I'm being honest."

"But what if they're not dumb this time? What if they get in?" Ray said, pointing to the only unobscured pane of glass, the seaweed-wrapped creature outside, pawing at the portal.

"Then we go back to your first plan and hope they can't run fast," Laura replied, retrieving the knife she'd stashed behind the television.

Ray nodded, moving to stand next to Laura before the window. The last gasps of sunlight sank into the sea, casting a final orange blear across the creature's waterlogged skin. Then the evening's shadows were all consuming, everything through the slim portal fading to grayscale. Laura could smell the sweat wicking off of Ray, could hear his heartbeat pulse in her ear. She was glad she wasn't alone on her last night in the cabin. She was glad at least one of her questions had been answered.

Together.

Not separate.

Now, all that was left was to find out what the poem would do to their world. If the words would tear some rent in the ocean floor and suck down all the sludge and smog, the pollutants and plastics and chemicals that never should have been...or would it vomit up more and more of the blind creatures who stalked about her home, scraping at the boards, hungry for what hid within.

Laura tightened her grip on the knife, leaning into Ray's side as they waited for morning to come.

It took three hours for the creatures to pull down the boards, leaving only bare glass between Laura and Ray and the gathered horde outside. The light from within made it hard to see much beyond their own reflections. Fangs bled through, and seaweed wrapped limbs, but there were so many bodies pressing against the cabin's walls, it was impossible to separate one silhouette from the next or see the ocean beyond. The single bullet and run plan was looking grimmer with each passing moment as the cabin's frame quaked under pressure. Then a window cracked in the eastern wall, a spider web of fractals creeping through the glass.

"I'm saying the skylight's our only way out," Laura said, pointing to the ceiling and the water stains ringing the aperture. "We've got to push the couch over."

"I thought you said waiting was the best option," Ray said, nervously chewing his lip, eyes darting from one exposed window to the next.

"I don't think there've ever been this many. We need to improvise or we're screwed," she said, bending to wrap an arm around the old sofa, pushing it across the hardwood. Ray bent to help as they aligned the furniture with the lowest point of the skylight. The ceilings weren't high, but they needed an added step if they were going to get out.

Laura stood on the back of the couch, Ray steadying her thigh with his free hand. She twisted the knob, opening the skylight to the chill night air. The mechanism was old and rusted and fought her at every turn as her home continued to shiver under the press of the creatures' mass. Eventually the skylight opened wide enough for their bodies to slip through, once Laura pushed the screen out of the way.

"When I'm out, hand me the pages," she said, pulling herself up.

Ray did as he was asked, pushing the gathered poem through the skylight once Laura steadied herself on the roof. Then he followed, revolver tucked into the waistband of his pants, metal cylinders clinking against one another, reminding them of the eight bullets, the eight chances they had to clear a path through the swarm.

Swarm was the only way to describe the gathering. Laura looked out over the sea of huddled bodies stretching down the beach as more and more emerged from the ocean. She looked over her shoulder to see if they were approaching Ray's house down the road, but most seemed to orbit her small cabin, never wandering far from her sun-like pull.

"There's no way…no way we're making it to the girls," Ray said.

"There's one way. Maybe. I'm still not sure, but I don't think we have another option," Laura said, sifting through the pages as she climbed to the cabin's peak, the moon's glow barely enough to make out the words written there. "We're close enough to the water and I can clearly see the ocean. The tide can carry these words to whatever ears it wants to."

Below, the creatures continued to dismantle the cabin, pulling shingles from the walls, dragging nails from boards, shattering glass. Laura didn't know how much longer the building could remain upright, how long before it pitched over and tossed them into the throng of grasping limbs and gnashing teeth.

"How long will it take you to read it?" Ray asked, hurriedly flipping on the light of his smartphone, aiming the beam over her shoulder so she could see.

"I don't think that matters anymore. This is either going to work or it isn't."

"Can't you just tell me it will? I need something to go on. Something—" Ray said, words seizing in his throat. His eyes turned to his home and the dim glow filtering through his front windows, his girls somewhere within, possibly unaware of what their father was facing, possibly hiding in fear for what lurked beyond their front porch. Laura didn't want the last thought she left Ray with to be one of despair, so she lied.

"Oh, it's totally going to work. A hundred percent. No doubt in my mind. Just hold that light steady and we'll be fine."

As Laura began to read, the creatures gathered below stopped pushing against the cabin, stepping back, tilting their heads towards the sound of her voice. It was as if the words were familiar, as if they were waiting for what came next. Laura didn't know what the final canto would bring, but their stasis gave her hope. The cabin wouldn't collapse after all. Maybe there was still a chance to be the healer her father sought. Maybe the oysters and the fish and the gulls and everyone else weren't doomed.

Laura flipped to the next page, the words unspooling from her tongue as if they'd always been waiting there, waiting for the right moment to slip free.

See Corey Farrenkopf's story "Translations for a Dead Sea" online at Metaphorosis.
If you liked it, leave a comment. Authors love that!
Remember to subscribe to our e-mail updates so you'll know when new stories are posted.

About the story

When I first moved back to Cape Cod after failing to find a teaching job after college, I worked for my uncle's fireplace company installing gas stoves. We did a lot of work on the Outer Cape, particularly in Ptown and Truro. The cabin this is based on is one of the dozens that you can see from the side of Route 6 when you head out towards the tip of the peninsula. We installed a few stoves in these over the time I worked there, usually freestanding propane units to take over for old, nonfunctioning woodburning hearths. These little shacks are kind of an odd, iconic segment of Cape Cod. They're tiny and sell for an ungodly amount of money and during moon tides are practically underwater. Picture a really waterlogged shed with a chimney. It seems like the owners are constantly fighting the sea, just dumping money into something they can't actually fight, which really matched up well with a climate change narrative. I wrote a number of stories set in and around these cabins, but nothing fit quite like "Translations for a Dead Sea". Being a person who is very obsessed with fixing problems and also being a person who has a ton of anxiety surrounding climate change, I always imagine what it would be like to figure out some way to make things better. If only I could find some forgotten Greek manuscript at an antique store, then we'd be all set. Remember, always keep your eyes out at flea markets and community swap meets. You never know what you'll find.

A question for the author

Q: How often do you think about writing during a day?

A: Until I've done it. Basically from the time I get up until the point I've gotten at least a handful of words down on the page, I'm thinking about what I should be writing. I usually get between 500 and 1,000 words done in a day, and once those are out of my head, I get a little euphoric bliss and can let myself play video games or something for a bit. Most weekdays I write during my lunch break, but often times its later in the day...and those days where I can't find the time at all, the words haunt me from sun up to sun down. Those are the worst days :)

About the author

Corey Farrenkopf is a writer of strange speculative fiction living on Cape Cod with his wife, Gabrielle, and their tiny dog, Ooli. He works as a librarian focused on spreading the good word of SF/F/H and Weird Fiction. He is also a member of the Blue Marble Librarians, which is a New England based group of librarians focused on climate change education and helping other libraries run environmental programs. He is also an active member of HWA.

@CoreyFarrenkopf

November

The Fool Who Sings You to Your Grave

Katie Cervenec

I'm not superhero fodder. The cape, the muscles, the dewy-eyed drive to save the world while sweeping back Ken-doll hair? That's not me. I'm a mediocre Great-Clips visit, brown hair, graying at the temples. I'm a pudge that hangs over my seatbelt, especially when I cram into the jeans I wore years ago in community college.

I've got my window down; it's a warm, windy day in November. My stomach flops when I stop at the next red light and look to my right. Cavill aka 'Cav' sticks his trucker-tanned arm out the window of his red Chevy pickup and gives me the head-bob nod from the second lane over. His eyes literally twinkle when Robert Plant starts up on his radio, singing about that lady and her stairway. I'm surprised it's Led Zeppelin and not Alan Jackson or something with achy-breaky twang.

Over the chug-chug of his idling V8, Cav belts out the words. Holy wailing rock-band, Batman, he cannot sing worth a wet crap. Mouth wide, he looks over at me with eyes that crinkle against the sun's setting light.

They're always light-drenched and full of joy, the ones that listen to old rock songs. I fit my nails to the divots in my Mazda's gray speckled upholstery and force my lips into a tight-lipped smile.

The same song plays on my radio too.

We sing together, terribly, then the light turns green. He gives his head a shake, grinning at me from ear to sunburnt ear. As he rolls away, I hear him whoop out the next verse.

My hands shake.

At the next light, I pull over and hyperventilate in a Rite Aid parking lot, because I saw it all when the song started. I know his name; I read it in the air, but there's more after that. It hovers before my eyes, bolded text, backlit by the lowering sun. An obituary. Tomorrow's.

Cavill Watts Johnston, age 47, died in Sevierville, Tennessee on November 16, 2022.

He is survived by two children, his fiancée and his beloved dog, Callie. He was preceded in death by his parents, Watson and Cherie Johnston, and his sister, Joanne Durnst, née Johnston.

In lieu of flowers, the family requests donations be made to the National Institute for Occupational Safety and Health (NIOSH) Construction Program, or the Golden Retriever Rescue Society.

Three months ago, I called into one of those dumb radio contests. Didn't win. But the static that came over the line right before I hung up? Ear-splitting, stomach-wrenching. Something happened, something wrong.

Ever since, I've been singing radio lullabies with the imminently screwed.

Not sure why this ability attached itself to me; I don't want it. Don't want to talk to or sing with or help anyone; don't want anyone helping me.

I do best on my own.

A tap on the driver-side window pulls my head from the steering wheel.

"Are you okay in there, mister?" a young woman asks.

She's holding tight to the hand of a toddler.

"Just...narrowly missed a fender bender, scared the sh—" I look down at the kid. "Shook me up. I'm fine now."

"Do you need help? Want me to call anyone?"

"No," I answer, more gruffly than I mean to. "I'm fine, great."

Because it's easier than saying I just witnessed a stranger's last earthly moment of joy. It's easier than explaining the truth of my lonely superpower. Every time I hear the same song as a stranger and we sing along together, I know right then, they're going to die that day. *Yeah, I'm great as hell, lady.*

She hurries away. I lean back against the headrest.

At first, I didn't realize what was happening.

There was the couple, just over the state line. I was on my way back from a parts-inspection in Kentucky. I'd stopped at a gas station for a piss and a bag of M&Ms. The couple were in the next parking spot over. White paint all but covered the back windows.

JUST MARRIED
Bryan and Kira 4 EVA
XOXOX
Heart heart heart

An x-rated stick figure drawing someone had tried to smudge off the window

I grinned.

Four or five Ale-8-One aluminum cans tied to the back bumper.

I was mumbling along to "Brown-Eyed Girl" playing on the radio and casually glanced over. They had started making out, like gophers trying to propagate the frickin' planet. I glued my face to my phone, still bopping with Van Morrison.

I flicked my eyes back up to check up on the crazy kids before backing out of the parking spot. But they were full-grin-staring at me through the driver's side window. Bryan had a lipstick-stained smirk as he *la tee da-ed* with me. But Kira 4 EVA was belting it out so loud I could hear her voice through the glass. Not half-bad, even at enamored-bride volume. Head back, her natural curls bounced against the top of their car.

We sang the last verse, the three of us, the newlyweds and the stranger. When the song was over, the girl jumped out of the car and ran over. Bryan scratched his head then opened his door. Wiping my melted-chocolate hands on my jeans, I got out too.

There's something about silently sharing music with a stranger. The hush. The inhale. Watching their mouth form the word you're singing. Connection: delicate and cloud-shaped, through two panes of tempered automobile glass.

I asked them where they were from. They asked me where I was going. Kira wiggled on the balls of her Keds-sneakers-with-lace and told me about their honeymoon plan. She wanted to line-dance in a real Nashville bar; he just wanted pancakes somewhere. They both had to be back at work at the factory on Monday. I gave them five bucks and my congratulations. I meant it.

I live alone. I eat alone; I work alone. But singing with them, I felt connected. Somehow that song tied us together for that moment of humid-Kentucky time.

That first time, there were words, names, burned like an afterimage wavering right outside my windshield, but I didn't pay much attention. Just thought I was tired. When their photos popped up on the evening news — *overturned semi on I65 kills two* — I remembered their names and put my fist through the wall.

After that, there was —

Martina Marie Sanchez-Brumheld, age 34, passed away surrounded by family after a courageous battle with ovarian cancer, in Knoxville, Tennessee... We sang "Despacito" together. She'd glanced out of the passenger window through the rain, drawn and huddled in a fleece pullover and caught me with a thin smirk as I stumbled through the Spanish chorus.

And —

"Happy Birthday" with Ajay Dubois, age 6...

Dammit. I had no idea why that song was playing on my radio, until I turned the corner and saw the wreck.

I held Ajay's hand, 'cause there was no one else left alive by that time. Just a grocery store birthday card playing the same tinny tune sprawled across the broken window, six green balloons in the back of the smashed SUV, and

...happy birthday dear Ajay, Happy Birthday to you

I tried to stop it from happening.

My car radio refused to turn off, so I smashed it. And yet it played. Pried it out and hauled it to a dumpster behind the Burger King. Next morning, there was it, brand-spanking-fracking new in the dash.

I tried working from home so I wouldn't have to drive. Oh, I thought I was onto something then. I wore earplugs when I had to leave the apartment. But do you have any idea how many doctors' offices and stores have Spotify radio playlists turned up to eleven on loop? All it took was one head-bop, one mouthed word and someone was grinning at me.

I used to think it was ridiculous, Batman swooping in on a crime right as it happened; Captain America just hoisting his shield when the bad guys get up to something. But that's how it is:

the universe lines us up, puts us in each other's paths, these doomed people and me. It turns out the only thing harder to avoid than a snippet of a melody is a damn flicker of connection, that briefest moment when a stranger and I align our fates for a few notes. And I don't want it.

This morning, I'm taking the bus to a new job. Amazon is always hiring during the holidays. My folks are gone, have been since I was twenty. Not too interested in all the ho-ho-ho and family sing-along stuff, so I won't mind pulling some overtime sorting boxes.

There's a spit-layer of snow on the ground when the bus pulls up and I get on. Next to me, the dreadlocked Black man's headphones start to play the same song that was in my head so loud that I can hear it.

"Let It Go" from Disney's *Frozen*

Not falling for it, universe, not today. Go pick on some other schmuck.

I forget myself and mouth three words of the chorus. He nudges me and smiles as he sings along in a baritone fit for Broadway.

Before I know it, a single word flashes in front of me, then another, then a line of words, like defiant poem stanzas between the trees and bridges and buildings as the bus chugs along.

Jeffrey Alexander Whitson, age 44, passed away in Catlettsburg, Tennessee on November 23, 2022. Mr. Whitson was earning his culinary degree and spent his free time volunteering at Big Brothers Big Sisters of America. A BBQ dinner will be served for all family and friends in the Springs Baptist Church basement at 4 pm on Saturday following the service.

I ride the bus till he gets off and follow him into a bank, like a lunatic sidekick. It's my first day on the new job. But screw it.

He laughs when I tell him what I know, when I beg him to go home and stay home the rest of the day. "Are you kidding? I've got a girl to propose to tonight."

"You don't understand..." Briefly, I think about asking the bank teller to help me make my case. But what would be the point? No one would believe me; no one will help me save him.

I've got to do this on my own.

The man laughs again. Then he gets mad, because what sort of jackass goes around proclaiming imminent death on a random Tuesday?

When security hauls me outside, I cry. Jeffrey Whitson, the guy who grinned at me on the bus with a mouth full of braces and Elsa-angst is going to die today, and I can't stop it.

I make it to my new job, three hours late, eyes red-rimmed. Mercifully, they're slammed, so they still need me.

I wrack my brain for ideas while I sit through the safety orientation at Amazon. Hell. I'm not going to even open my mouth except to order a Big Mac no onion or to tell off the fruffy politicians spouting their lies on cable TV as I slouch in the comfort of my plaid couch. I just want these strangers to stop dying.

After my shift, my lips sticking together from staying sealed all day, I slink into the suburban library near my apartment. Libraries are quiet. You play a song in there and some owl-eyed librarian will kick the crap out of you.

I like the library.

There's a girl here: Sophia, her name tag says, with blonde hair and skin so pale it's almost translucent. Freckles like a stripe of stars across her nose. I think she's taping barcodes on new books.

I watch her through the half-open workroom door as I pretend to read a fraying Tom Clancy. Holy patriotic good ol'boys, Batman, Clancy loves to hear himself write.

I put it down after about thirty minutes and look at Sophia. Each spine, she aligns with narrow-eyed precision. Each book slots into alphabetical order. All of a sudden, she jumps up, lets out a moaning yell, and her chair crashes to the floor. She shakes her hands in front of her, over and over, over and over.

The librarian sitting at the circulation desk slips into the workroom from the other door. Sophia hits her head with her fist, and I bite my lip. Staying away, keeping quiet is the plan now, but I've got to do something for this woman. My hands shake as I stand up. I pray there's no random song from a phone, or a car blasting its radio outside. I come closer and just stand there. Maybe standing counts as showing up? What the hell do I know?

The librarian, her nametag says Esme, touches her own cheek, then scoots into Sophia's line of sight. Esme's hands move: sign-language. Sophia shakes her head and gives a thumbs-down with the hand that's not striking her head.

I ease into the room, keeping quiet, but Esme, without taking her eyes off Sophia, says, "We're okay. Sophia's deaf, and we're okay. She gets upset sometimes when barcodes get stuck together."

All the while, her hands are moving, talking without words, to Sophia. I toe the rubber base on the wall next to the door. My shoulders relax when Sophia stops hurting herself. She gives a quick thumbs-up and sits cross-legged on the floor, her back now to me.

Esme offers me a small smile then says out loud, "Would you like a drink of water, Sophia?" Her hands move, signing the same words to Sophia, I assume.

I stand there till Esme raises a brow at me.

I'm dense as crap.

In a minute, I'm back with a paper cup of water from the drinking fountain near the bathrooms. I bump into the doorframe, feeling like a praying mantis with too damn many arms and legs.

I place the water cup near Sophia, back up to the door and ask Esme to tell Sophia with her hands that she's doing a great job on the books. I haven't said a word all day; my voice comes out all froggy.

Soon, Esme goes back out front to help a patron. Sophia's still on the floor, so I edge into the workroom again. I slide down the wall and sit so she can see me out of the corner of her eye. She doesn't look at me, but I see her mouth turn up in a small smile. I give her a thumbs-up, open my Tom Clancy again and stay for another hour.

All is calm, all is bright...

I knew this moment would come, didn't know it would be in the library parking lot with a radio Christmas song. It's my day off. Been coming here every few days, when I can. I figured with my new rock-solid commitment to never open my mouth, I could risk driving today. It was just so snowy and cold. I dig into the nail-indentions in my car and glance over at the bubble-gum-pink-haired girl with warm brown skin in the VW bug next to me. She's into the song, big-time, even got that Elvis lip-curl going.

Slee-eep in heavenly peace.
Silent night, holy night...

Her pink phone vibrates on the dash and she picks it up, turning down the radio. I fiddle with the dial on my car's stereo, trying to lower the volume. It's playing the same song.

She steals a glance at me, then covers her face, talking into the phone. Whatever it is, it's not good news. It's been longer for me than I'd like to admit, but I know a break-up call when I see one. Poor kid.

My radio chooses that moment to blast full volume.

I see her mascara trailing down to the corners of her mouth. See her mouthed words through both of our rolled-up car windows.

Shepherds quake at the sight
Glories stream from Heaven afar ....

She pauses in the song; my radio's thrumming Elvis's words too.

She points to her dash radio, then motions between her car and mine with a teary smile.

I shake my head pretending I don't know what she's asking even though I know she wants me to sing with her.

"Please?" she says, the word silent in my ears.

Even though I don't understand why, I know it's all up to me. I feel her red-rimmed eyes on me as I turn away without joining in her song. I feel like a monster as I'm saving her life.

On my way home, it starts to snow again. Just windy flurries. That girl, the Christmas Elvis lover. I think I just saved her; I think I did it, and all on my own. When I get to my apartment's parking lot, I get out into the cold night air and stare at the streetlight. Flakes fly like mini-tornados, only visible in the cone of the light. I grin, 'cause it's kind of beautiful in a clunky suburban way. Then, the snowflakes smash together like magnets. They form words.

Cassidy Vinnie, 19, died December 2, 2022 in Knoxville, Tennessee. She was born February 28, 2003 in Augusta, Georgia. Cassidy is survived by many friends and her paternal grandparents, Lilly and Gavin Vinnie, who raised her. A memorial service will be held Wednesday, December 7th at Victor Ashe Park. Donations may be sent to The Trevor Project, website included below.

I lock myself in my apartment. Forget the new job. Forget the library. Forget Sophia with the stars on her face, though I have to admit that'll be harder to do. I'll never leave again. The image of Cassidy's pink hair burns in my mind when I'm awake, when I try to sleep.

When I finally leave the apartment, days later, I pretend I'm going to get the icy hell out of Dodge, make a beeline for someplace where no one listens to music, wherever that is. But those words in the snow already know where I'm going, and I do too.

I drive to Victor Ashe Park in Knoxville, smashing the pedal to the floorboards. I don't know what I hope to find. Her grandpa sitting on a park bench? A place to sign my condolences in a mild-colored notebook with the Target barcode still adhered to the back?

A shock of bubble-gum-pink hair among the maple trunks?

I don't know how long it takes for the last notes of a soul to flee on still air. I don't know where a person's melody goes. Does it trip over itself like the highest-octave keys or is it more of a *Five-Finger Death Punch* throw-down-type-thing at the end?

Even if I couldn't save her, I've decided to believe that Cassidy's song — her soul — goes somewhere. Somewhere calm and bright.

I rush among the leaf-less trees and trails. At the edge of a small pond, I see a deflated balloon and a wilted bunch of sunflowers. Her name on a program, her picture with that hair, pink as hope.

The service is over, but Death has time to wait.

I feel dumb as shit, but I queue up Elvis's Christmas album on my phone.

Looking out towards the muddy pond, I sing Cassidy every damn word of that damn song.

It's cold.

The wind cuts through my t-shirt and whispers to me what I know, what I've probably always known: I can't stop it.

If I wave my hands and shout, they don't listen. If I follow them, they think I'm crazy. If I don't sing... they still die. I thought it was up to me, but I'm helpless. Stuck in this loop of melodies and words signaling the end of someone's life. It's not me killing them, but they keep dying anyway.

The next day, I sit in the library with Sophia again for four hours. I don't read. We don't talk.

The day after, I go again. And the next.

After about a week, Esme brings me a stack of books, not a Tom Clancy among them. A couple of thin Scholastic copies of Shakespeare plays, one fracking-thick Shakespeare anthology, and a book on American Sign Language.

"You got the wrong guy if you think I want to read all of—"

"Sophia set them aside for you," Esme interrupts.

Sophia scratches her nose.

I find my spot on the floor and open the sign language book.

It's Tuesday, two days before New Year's Eve. I've got no job, nowhere to be. The library and its silence haven't let me down yet, so I join Sophia in the workroom. She expects me now; that feels good. Sometimes I tell her about the book I'm reading. I hope, someday, in her own way, she'll tell me a thing or two as well.

Today she's standing at the end of the table, trucking away at her barcodes as usual. I sit down, still clutching that same Tom Clancy, but I'm bumbling through *The Tempest* now too, on good days. Not today.

"I'm sad all the time," I tell her. It feels strange to really talk to someone, but I'm tired of going it alone.

She watches the words leave my mouth. I know she knows what I'm saying; it's just, words don't mean the same things to her as they do to some other people. I kind of like that.

My story comes out, a few words at a time, in between the paragraphs I read silently to myself about Jack Ryan saving the world.

"I thought not singing with them would save them, but it doesn't work like that. Instead I stole something from her, from Cassidy Vinnie age 19."

Sophia's hands move over the books and barcodes. She stacks one book to the side every now and again. But her eyes stay on my mouth. She's listening, but I can tell it's hard for her. I need to dig deeper into that sign language book.

I mash my palms to my eyes. "Singing with someone, it's fun. Just a little zing of connection in this shit-assed world."

With that, I clamp my mouth shut. She's never going to believe my story anyway; why did I get carried away talking to her like that? We usually just share silence together. I scratch my head and find my place in the book again.

Sophia stacks two more books to the side.

She puts a barcode on a children's board book, but it's a little crooked.

She looks at me and bites her lip; her hands make fists and rise into the air.

I lean back in my plastic chair, stretch my arms out and give her the biggest smile I can find, then I yawn. *This ain't no big thing, Sophia*, I try to tell her with my body language.

Her shoulders relax, her fists unclench.

She gets back to work.

"You're a damn cool cat," I tell her. "Would you like some water?"

She nods.

I hear someone humming to themselves as I walk back. I don't know the song, but I rush away anyway.

I can't stop them from dying. I'm no savior. I'm just the fool who'll sing you to your grave; I'm just one last smile before death's final kiss.

After I place the cup in front of Sophia, I raise my fingers in a *W* at my chin and sign water. And it's probably hokey to hope she wants to spend time with me as much as I want to spend my time with her, but I don't want to miss anything she has to say, no matter how she says it.

She looks up at me and rubs those freckles on her face again. And we stare at each other. Worlds and oceans of sentences, thoughts, songs — I can see them behind her eyes. I stare a moment longer and a dumb thought pops into my head. I could get used to this. Me and Sophia. If I can't sing with her —

She shakes her head, almost violently. I'm convinced she can read my thoughts on my face. She pats the floor where she has spread out a handful of books. My knees creak as I crouch on the library carpet.

She points at the books, left to right, one at a time and gives me a look I can't understand.

I shrug.

Sophia makes a noise, and her fists clench. She grabs my hand, makes my pointer finger stick out.

Like the beats of a song, she moves my finger over the pages. Different place each page, down the line of books, ending on the hardback cover of The Book Thief.

I'm so lost; I want to understand. I just don't. This is on me Sophia, I don't get it.

She does it again. Again. Each time, she lands my finger on Thief, the final note of her song.

Same places each time.

Oh. I'm dumb as shit.

"The ... robbed that ... smiles, steals ... something from... the ... thief," I say, reading her words, her song, to me.

"Shakespeare's *Othello*." Esme has peeked her head around the corner of the workroom. She's putting on her coat. "I haven't come by a Shakepeare play yet that Sophia doesn't know mostly by heart. We close in 10 minutes."

She taps the doorframe and disappears.

My finger starts to move again, led by Sophia.

Not Thief.

She punches my own finger into my knee.

Not Thief.

She's telling me it's not my fault. Not my job. I'm not a superhero; I don't have to be.

"All those people, they were going to die anyway," I say. It hurts, but it feels true. It isn't a job I have to do right. It's a gift, a gift I was given to give back to them in the face of death. Connection, light as a cloud, as invisible as a tune, soft as freckles across pale cheeks.

Thought I had to do this all alone. Turns out, I was the one who needed saving. I feel like Sophia knew that all along.

She smiles.

"You're right, Sophia. I got to smile at that thief Death for as long as I can."

I'd be lying if I said I wasn't choked up.

On the way home, my radio starts up. Three ascending horn notes. *Do-dodo*, that 60's beat. A Domino's delivery woman pulls up beside me in a Toyota Camry, with that illuminated blue and red beacon on top. Neil Diamond starts singing about that girl, "Sweet Caroline".

I'm already crying again. But I nod my head to the beat anyway.

Our windows are rolled up, but the delivery driver turns her head to me, already singing along. When she sees my mouth forming the same words, I watch her say "No way. No way!" and then we're singing together again. I don't even know her name. Not yet.

I'm just the musical finale number, big hands, big dance, the last hoorah. The last smile.

So I make it a good one and smile in spite of that thief. Picturing Sophia's grin helps. And she was right; joy floods me. It almost makes me giddy.

We're hamming it up at the red light. The delivery woman smacks her palm against the window, and I lunge over the center console to tap my fingertips to the passenger side window. Neil's singing about hands, touching hands.

We're pointing at each other, pointing at ourselves. My vision is a sea of red swimming brake lights. She's crying now too. It's just a moment so silly, so dumb.

So full. Worth every note. Worth the smile in the face of Death.

I sing to her, and she sings to me.

Sweet Caroline, bum bum bum....

The light turns green. I wipe my wet eyes and look to the road.

A pair of headlights, blinding my eyes, blinding my brain, speeds straight towards me. Crunching metal drowns out the sounds of Neil Diamond. And for a moment, I'm confused. The universe messed up, got the wrong guy. I've just figured things out. I'm not the villain, certainly not the hero, just the singing fool.

The air freshener tag on my rearview mirror flies off, thumps me in the shoulder. I get a strong whiff of pine and then watch it land in the empty passenger seat beside me.

And then I understand. That woman wasn't hearing the same song as me.

I think of Sophia, her barcodes, her banner of stars. She showed me I don't have to be the hero. I'm just an ordinary guy living his life.

Ordinary people die every day.

Neil Diamond and the Domino's delivery woman, sending me out, full of joy and a song.

I heard the same song she did. And I sang along.

See Katie Cervenec's story "The Fool Who Sings You To Your Grave"
online at Metaphorosis.
If you liked it, leave a comment. Authors love that!
Remember to subscribe to our e-mail updates so you'll know when
new stories are posted.

About the story

I think writing is an intensely personal and soul-baring activity. I wrote "The Fool Who Sings You To Your Grave" when I shallowly felt like the grind of daily life was getting under my skin, but also during a season of hard times in my family where doing the little things felt like a big thing. There's a great sadness in living, and, I believe, there's great hope too. It's all there together. The light, and the dark.

I always like the idea of exploring some very, very ordinary person who suddenly found themselves shouldered with a super-power, which is sometimes just another way of saying — a heavy responsibility. (Which, side note, is kind of all of us.) We'd all love super-human patience, or strength, or persistence, but here we are just doing our best with our ordinary, mortal shells. And the crazy thing is, there's a deep beauty in that.

In "The Fool Who Sings You To Your Grave", the main character, who isn't named, finds himself always singing the same song as the person he's pulled up next to in traffic. And, wouldn't that be fun? What if, while you were belting out Elvis or Beyoncé with the radio, the person in the car next to you was too? I think little moments of connection like that remind us that we're a part of something bigger. But the main character soon finds out his innocuous "superpower" of singing the same song as someone else, has a sinister turn to it. And he's completely helpless against what happens next.

Since I was personally feeling the same about situations I couldn't change, I thought, what can this poor guy do to combat his lack of control? And, like writing often does, it flows answers onto the page that you didn't even realize were there. What do you do? You focus on the small things, the present, the stolen moments of joy. You wring the absolute life out of those times and take hold of the abundance of them. So this is a hopeful story about the beauty of an ordinary someone who shows up, does his best, and sings his song. The rest is out of his hands.

A question for the author

Q: What work of art has been the most inspiring for you?

A: Hands down, the work of art that has inspired me the most is the painting *Mystery and Melancholy of a Street* by Giorgio de Chirico. It's a bizarre, unrealistic painting that has fascinated me ever since art history class in college. There's a term called "chiaroscuro", which sounds stuffy and pretentious, but really just means areas of light and dark in a painting. When I look at this painting, it reminds me that the same holds true for a lot more than just paint colors on a canvas. In writing, in stories, goodness, even life in general, sometimes it's the darkest corners and deepest shadows that make the bright daylight mean more. That's pretty inspiring to me!

About the author

Katie Cervenec is an ear-buds-in writer in the evenings and a commercial interior designer by day. She enjoys sushi, learning about trees, and dabbling in vegetable gardening. She aspires to read 50 books a year but has never quite made it. She's an active member of the Lexington Writers Room and lives in Lexington, Kentucky with her husband and teenage triplets.

katiecervenec.wordpress.com, @ReadKaCerv

It Thaws in Spring

Brittany M. Perkins

Lena lived under the ice. She might have always been there, or perhaps she had lived on the surface once. It didn't matter. Lena could not remember a time when she had not floated in the still waters below the frozen pond, a time when she knew things other than damp and cold and dark.

The under was a vast expanse of water, which, with an effort of great concentration, could be molded into ghostly rooms or objects, though these structures were easily dispersed with a wave of the hand. Impermanence was the way of the under, and it was the way of the ice children as well. There were only four of them now (Lena and Edna and Rebecca and Julian), and every winter began with the uncertainty of how many would remain.

Winter was all Lena knew, all she could experience and remember. She never saw the pond melt in spring, although Edna assured her that it did. Edna never saw this either. Instead, Lena and the others awoke each winter, the ice above them firmly intact, aware that time had passed, but unsure what had happened in the interim. And sometimes, when winter came, someone would be missing.

There had once been more of them, but Lena had not seen Raymond in four winters and Matteo in seven. Lena didn't remember much past twelve winters back, but she had heard other names, of children who had disappeared before her memories began: Cindy, Lola, Isaac. After Raymond hadn't come back, the other children grew more and more distant, until the under became a silent place, and Lena worried that one day he too would be only a name to them.

Lena was drifting through the under, thinking of those who were no longer with them when she spotted Edna, sitting in a chair. A swirling current that had not quite solidified made up its curving frame, and an elaborate tea set was suspended in the space in front of her. Many winters back, before it had become just the four of them, Edna had often talked with Lena, but, lately, Edna rarely acknowledged her at all. Lena approached the girl who had once taught her how to spin up towers and tea sets from the water around them. In the old days, Edna would brighten at Lena's approach and immediately invite her into a story or game she had come up with, but that never happened anymore.

Today, Lena hovered beside Edna, studying her, while the other girl hardly seemed to notice. "Can I join your party?" Lena asked, conjuring a chair of her own, more solid than Edna's, and sitting across from her former friend.

Edna glanced at the teapot and the cup in her hand as though seeing them for the first time.

Lena waited a moment before continuing: "What are you playing? Are you a princess? Or a society lady?"

Edna looked at Lena, opening her mouth as if to speak, but no sound emerged.

"Why don't you talk to me anymore?" Lena asked. "Why don't any of you ever want to play?" Lena rose from her chair, and the structure dispersed into the depths around them. "You used to be fun," she said. And then, softer, "You used to like me."

As Lena withdrew from the girl she had once considered a friend, she thought she heard Edna speak, a barely audible rasp: "I'm sorry."

One of Lena's earliest memories was of Matteo, and it was really more of a feeling than a memory. The memory was a single image of Matteo, pushing a ball made of water toward her. He was laughing. And the feeling was of excitement and joy. That was the best way to describe Matteo: joyful. But the winter before he disappeared, something had been different.

Once, that final winter, Lena had approached the watery rocket ship where Matteo had resided for going on three days. She crept through the half-formed hatch, careful not to disturb the structure's fragile architecture, and inched upward toward the boy who had once filled the underneath with such light and laughter. As Lena neared him, she could see that Matteo was in constant motion, wafting back and forth across the small space at the top of the rocket.

"Matteo?" Lena called up to him.

He did not answer, an eerie smile dragging up the corners of his mouth, as if against their will.

"Are you alright?" she asked. "Do you want to play a game?"

Matteo floated in a slow circle to face her, and although his eyes met hers, they were cloudy and seemed not to see her at all. Then his right hand shot out, grasping for her. Lena couldn't remember what had happened next, but she knew that she had left, and the next thing she could picture in her mind's eye was talking to Raymond.

None of the ice children knew how old they were, but Raymond had always felt older than the rest. So when she told him about Matteo's unresponsiveness, Lena expected an explanation.

Instead, she received a shrug. "That happens sometimes," Raymond said. "Matteo is very social, and it's been hard on him not having new children to play with."

"But I asked him to play, and he wouldn't talk to me," Lena said. "Why does he need someone new if I'm right here?"

Raymond sighed, not meeting Lena's eyes. "I don't know, Lena," he said, the slightest edge of frustration creeping into his voice. "I've tried to tell them—all of them—to be grateful for what we have here, but they always want more. I can't make them happy, and I just..." Raymond clenched his fists so hard and fast that a small current swirled around them. Then he looked at Lena. "You're happy, right? Even with just the six of us?"

"Of course," Lena said, though she wasn't sure that was true. She remembered that feeling of joy from years ago, but she couldn't think of the last time she'd felt it. "I'm very happy, Raymond."

When Matteo didn't come back during the following winter freeze, Lena had been confused. She was the only one who hadn't seen it happen before. Lena had searched for Matteo, and when she was nearly sure but not quite believing that Matteo was gone for good, Lena had asked Edna where he was. She received only a slow shake of the head in response before Edna drifted away, leaving a trail of silt in her wake. Lena soon learned it was taboo to talk about the disappearances, which was why she only had the whispered names of those who had already gone. But Raymond was different. Raymond would talk.

One night, Raymond appeared beside the bed Lena had willed together out of water droplets. The ice children never slept in winter, but they did rest, and sometimes, they dreamed. Lena had been dreaming. In the dream, a girl, whose face Lena could not see, hovered above her, near the ice. Lena was falling away from the girl, as though sucked into an undertow. The girl's hand reached toward Lena, and Lena reached out in return, but their fingers never met. As the distance between the two increased, Lena saw a sunray peek around the girl's head, but she soon faded away, leaving Lena staring into the blaring sunlight.

As Lena tried to call after the girl, she felt algae tickling at the sides of her mouth. She thought it was only part of the dream, until a hand lightly brushed across her shoulder. The coldness of Raymond's skin, which was blue with chill and slightly slimy, like they all were, startled her. Before she could call out, Raymond put a slender finger to his lips. "You want to know what happened, don't you?" He did not wait for Lena to respond. "Do you ever feel alone, Lena?"

Before she could think through the action, Lena nodded.

"We all do, and sometimes we feel so alone that we can't stand it. Sometimes during spring, we get so lonely that our ears are searching, even if we are not. And sometimes our ears find them: the children of the surface. We might hear a laugh or a splash, but it's enough, enough to wake us and call us upward."

Lena's eyes moved back to Raymond's. "Does that mean the others went to the surface?" She sat up, sending loose bubbles and mud flying as her pillow lost form and dispersed. "Is Matteo up there now?"

"We used to have many children," he said. "And for a long time, it wasn't like this. We were happy. We played games. We weren't just... quiet."

"But if they were lonely, why did they leave their friends?" Lena's bed flittered into nothing as she floated upright.

"They were bored with just us," he said. "They needed *new* children—new friends. They got greedy, and now they're all gone."

"Are they on the surface?" Lena's voice was pleading.

"No. We can't live up there. We can't go back, not once we're here."

"Go back?" She thought of the girl from her dream, reaching out to her from the surface.

"More of the surface children used to play on the ice in winter. They would skate and sled, and sometimes, they would fall through. After a while, I guess they decided it was too dangerous."

"What happened... when they fell?" Lena thought she knew, but she didn't want to. She wanted to be wrong. At the edge of her memory, she heard the scrape of blades on ice.

"The ice children would save them. But to save them, we'd have to *change* them, get rid of who they were before. When the surface children stopped coming in the winter, the others still wanted to save them. But that doesn't work in the spring. It only works with the ice. In the spring, they just drown, or they swim away. And if we go after them, we disappear." He took a deep breath, and the water swirled around his mouth. "We're barely here in the spring, not even ghosts, and when we go up there, we're nothing."

"What if we go up in the winter?" Lena asked.

"We don't."

"Why not?"

"Because of the ice." And he turned and drifted away.

Lena was lonely, under the ice. She missed Raymond and his stories about how things used to be. She missed Matteo and his games and high spirits. And it was on a very lonely day, when the sun breached the ice and lit up the underneath, that Lena first heard it: a child of the surface laughing.

Lena soared upward, the water's temperature seeming to rise as she ascended, and stopped just in time not to hit her head on the ice. As she arrived, something thumped above her, and she saw a blurred shadow cover the ice above like a rug. Then the laughter came again, followed by a faint call: "Claire! Claire, get back here. It's too dangerous. Come back to the shore." The caller's voice was like an icepick driving into Lena's brain, and she suddenly felt scared and cold.

"Okay." This voice was closer, clearer, and somehow warmer as well, taking the edge off of Lena's fear. This voice came from the shadow, and as Lena realized this, the shadow moved, became smaller, and began to recede toward the edge of the pond, the water cooling in its wake.

Lena followed the shadow as fast as she could. Claire's shadow quickly outpaced her and was gone, taking the laughter with it. Lena continued her pursuit until she came to the pond's edge. She pressed a hand against it, mud wafting around the point of contact. She tried to grab a chunk of the muddy bank, but it was too tightly packed. Lena let go and wandered back toward the middle of the pond.

When she returned, Lena saw two structures, and she could see the occupants of each through the water that comprised them: a cottage with missing bricks and a crooked chimney (Edna) and a ship that was cracked down the middle, with only half a flag dangling from its too-short mast (Rebecca and Julian). Lena burst into the cottage where Edna sat in a one-armed armchair, a plate balanced on her lap, in front of a fire that would have been roaring had the flames been more than water held in shape by Edna's wishes. When Lena reached her, she stood in front of Edna's chair, blocking her view of the heatless flames. "So, what do you think happened to Raymond?"

Edna choked on her water droplet toast. "What do you mean?" she rasped. Edna looked older than Lena, but not by much. Lena knew Edna remembered longer, though, and knew things the others did not.

"I mean, where is he? And Matteo? Where did they go?"

"It's best not to—" Her voice was clearer now, though still sharp around the edges.

"Raymond said they got lonely and bored and that you think they go to the surface and evaporate."

"Lena."

"I saw someone today."

Edna's eyes brightened for a moment. "Where?"

"She was skating on top of the ice. A surface child." Lena paused, deciding whether or not to go on. "Raymond said there used to be more of us. He said surface children would fall through the ice."

Edna closed her eyes. "Yes," she said. "That was the way. But not anymore." Edna placed a hand on Lena's cheek. "You used to be so warm," she said, and Lena felt a chill run through her, though she wasn't sure if it came from Edna's touch or her words.

Lena recoiled and turned to face the fire, wishing it and its heat were real.

"I wish you still were," Edna said, reaching toward Lena again, her fingers barely brushing Lena's forearm before Lena fled, not wanting that chill to spread elsewhere on her body.

Lena hovered briefly above the cottage, rubbing her cheek. Then she entered the ship, where Rebecca and Julian were clapping their hands together, chanting nonsense rhymes and giggling. The two moved their hands in a circle and spun up three small dolls from the bubbles around them. The dolls hung near Rebecca's head, and she giggled again.

"What are you playing?" Lena asked, moving closer to the pair. "Can I play too?" Lena could remember a time when she had played with the two—Edna called them twins—but that was long ago, when Matteo and Raymond still occupied the underneath. "When you clap like that," Lena added, still feeling Edna's cold handprint on her cheek, "how does it feel?"

The twins did not look at her. "Did you hear something?" Julian asked Rebecca, not breaking the rhythm of their clapping.

Neither seemed to wince or react in the slightest to the other's touch.

"It's the dollies," Rebecca said, inclining her head toward the bubble creations suspended to her left. Lena wanted to reach out and slap one of their hands to answer her own question, but instead, she departed the ship. Once free of the twins' rhymes, Lena willed herself her own structure: a twisting tower, like you would find at the top of a castle, but without the castle.

Lena surged to the top of the tower, which nearly brushed the ice, and as she sometimes had over the past four winters, closed her eyes, and spoke to the only friend who had ever been truly honest with her. "Raymond," Lena said. "I saw someone today. It was a surface child, and she was on top of the ice. I heard her laugh, and I heard someone calling her, and then she got away. I tried to catch her, but she—" A voice seemed to call from somewhere deep within Lena, jerking her sideways and sending pieces of parapet flying. It was the voice that had called Claire, except it was calling for her instead. As Lena shook away the imagined sound, something drew her eyes upward. She looked from the ice to her hands, feeling like they had not always been blue, and almost, but not quite, remembering what warmth felt like. *Claire would be warm.* The thought came, unbidden, and pulled Lena's gaze upward again. Claire would come back. She had to.

After what could have been three weeks or two months—Lena had never been good at measuring time—the light shifted overhead, and Lena felt the slightest kiss of sunlight on her cheek. She flew toward the surface, and, through the icy blur, Lena thought she saw skate blades gliding overhead. She watched for a moment, in awe, and then panic set in. What if this was her only chance to have a friend again? Dizzy at the thought of losing Claire forever, Lena raised a shaking fist and rapped on the ice. In what seemed like an instantaneous response, the figure above collided with the ice with a thud. The shadow filled the patch of ice above Lena, but this time, there was no laughter.

Lena was quick. She pressed her face against the ice to one side of the shadow. Lena rarely ventured this high in the pond, and the solid dryness of the ice always surprised her. "Hello?" she said. "Claire?"

For just a moment, Lena saw blurred eyes in a dark face. Then she heard a muffled scream as the figure jumped up, and the shadow quickly receded toward the shore.

Lena pursued, this time keeping pace for nearly twice as long as before, but still, when the figure reached the shore, Lena could not follow. Lena buried her face in the muddy bank and screamed. As she did, she again heard someone calling her name. It was less of a call and more of a shriek. And then it was all shriek and no words.

The possibility of seeing Claire—she was sure it had been Claire—again filled Lena with such desperation that her stomach ached. The other ice children either ignored her or took from her, but Lena sensed that Claire had something to give, and Lena had not been given anything in a long, long time. Lena thought that if she could talk to Claire, a bit of warmth and joy might make its way into the under, and maybe things could be how they once were. So she hovered under the patch of ice, waiting for Claire's return. She did this every time she could see sunlight, and did not retreat until all light drained away, occasionally scratching or tapping on the ice above to feel closer to Claire and the surface. Lena wondered how many ice children had waited like this. She wondered who had waited for her.

She was engaged in such thoughts when the shadow returned. A soft thud sounded above Lena's head, and she moved as close to the ice as she could.

The blurred face appeared above her. "A-are you still there?" It was Claire's voice.

"Claire?" Lena said, and Claire recoiled. "Wait. Don't. Please."

Claire's face returned. "Sorry," she said. "You're a little bit scary." Claire paused. "Say, how do you know my name?"

Their conversation was muted, as through a tunnel, but Lena could understand her clearly. "I heard someone calling you," Lena said. "The first time I saw you." She paused. "You didn't see me that time."

"Oh," Claire said. "That was my mom." Every word Claire spoke was like a little ray of warmth through the ice, and sometimes, the warmth burned.

The burn at the mention of the screaming woman from their first encounter was too much; Lena needed to change the subject. "Do you like to skate?" Lena asked, and she could almost feel herself gliding smoothly over the ice.

"What? Oh, yes. I do."

These words muted the heat, now more of a comfort than a burn.

Claire continued: "It's just my mom thinks it's dangerous. She doesn't trust the pond to hold out, says I'll fall through."

Lena heard a cracking sound from the corner of her memory and winced again, but it was less intense this time. "Are you afraid?" she asked. "Are you afraid you'll fall?"

Claire laughed, and Lena moved closer. The ice between them made the laugh sound far off, like it was coming from somewhere Lena couldn't quite reach. "No. Nothing scares me. Well, except you." She paused before adding, "But not anymore." Claire's shadow shifted. "Besides, I just come when she's sleeping. Mom sleeps a lot during the day, actually."

Lena didn't know how to respond to any of this. She was overwhelmed and excited and somehow afraid of what Claire might say next.

"I'm sorry. What's your name? I didn't even ask you."

"Lena."

"Huh," Claire said. "My mom had a sister named Lena."

Lena shuddered.

"They used to live where we do now. We moved to the cabin to help when Grandma got sick. She died a few months back."

The feeling of lying under a quilt, safe and warm, filled Lena's mind for a moment until the face of an older girl invaded the vision, scorching it around the edges. "What's your mom's name?" Lena asked, inching closer to the flame of Claire's voice.

Claire's shadow shifted again, and Lena worried that she'd upset her, that maybe she'd leave now. "It's Margaret," she said, finally. "But everyone calls her Maggie."

The name set Lena's thoughts afire. "What... happened... to... her sister?" she asked, needing a break between nearly every word.

"She died. Or they think she did. She must have. They never found a body, though. Mom was a lot older, and she was supposed to have been watching her. Mom and Grandma fought a lot after that." Claire trailed off before asking, "Hey, what *are* you?"

"I—I don't understand."

"Like, how did you get down there? There aren't even fish in this pond anymore. Are you a mermaid or something?"

Raymond had told Lena that there used to be fish. They had disappeared a long time ago, though. Even Raymond hadn't known why. "I'm just down here," Lena said. "I've always been down here. I—I'm an ice child."

"An ice child?" Claire asked. "I've never heard of that." Claire moved her face closer to the ice. "I can't see you very well," she said.

"Not much to see," Lena answered, dragging a fingernail across the underside of the ice and sending a curl of frost receding toward the pond's floor. She didn't want to explain herself anymore. She didn't want to tell Claire about the other children. She just wanted Claire to keep talking, because even though the warmth of her words hurt, they made Lena feel more *real* somehow, and Lena needed that.

"Listen," Claire said, "I have to go. Mom will be up soon, and she'll never let me out of the house again if she knows I've been here."

"Wait—" Lena started. But Claire was already on her feet, skating for shore.

"Do you remember that surface child I told you about?" Lena asked.

Edna was silent, still as the water around her.

"She talked to me, asked how I got down here."

Edna closed her eyes but made no move to speak.

"Was I one of the children who fell? Like they used to? Claire's mother had a sister: Lena."

Edna opened her eyes, pain filling the icy blueness of them. "You were mine," she rasped. "Yes. You fell too. You were skating, but it was too thin." Edna's voice caught a bit. "It shouldn't have been so thin, but it was."

And as she said this, Lena could almost remember. It felt like remembering the feeling of a dream, but not knowing what it was about. "And you saved me."

"Yes. To save one, you have to take out the warmth. They can't live down here with that. But with the warmth goes the memory. Everyone starts over down here."

Lena took a breath. "Did everyone come from the surface? All of us?"

"I think so," Edna said. "I can't know that for sure. I can only remember the ones who came after me, and most of them are gone now. But I remember you, and I remember Rebecca and Julian. They came down together. I remember when Matteo fell. I don't remember a time before Raymond. I think he's the one who saved me. But that was long ago."

Lena still could not remember. Only the shrieking was left, but excitement quickly overtook it. "Maybe Claire will fall," she said.

Edna's eyes brightened. "She might."

"Claire would be new. She could make things good again."

"Would you do that?" Edna asked. "Would you save Claire for us?"

"Of course," Lena said. "I'm tired of alone."

Claire spread out on her belly on the ice. She had not visited in what seemed a long time, and Lena had been antsy. "Sorry," Claire said.

The single word left Lena slightly singed, and she wanted more.

"Mom's been having a hard time. She always does in winter. I think it's—"

"How old are you?" Lena had not spoken to anyone since her conversation with Edna, and her voice came out rushed and clipped.

"Uh, twelve, but I'll be thirteen next month." Claire paused, dragging a gloved finger through the frost covering the ice. "How old are you, Lena?"

"I—I'm not sure..." At the fuzzy edge of something like memory, Lena saw an older girl, someone who loved her and protected her. "Say, how old was your mom's sister when she...?"

"Well, Mom was nineteen, I think, so that would've made her sister eleven."

Lena felt herself swoon slightly, certain now that she was also eleven, and that she had been eleven for a very long time. "Are your friends twelve, too?" she asked a little breathlessly.

Claire sat up, her blurred face blending into the rest of her shadow. "I don't really have any," she said. "They just kind of stopped coming around once my grandma got sick."

"But they could visit," Lena said, nervously scraping the ice with a nail. She imagined how warm they would all be, Claire and her friends. "They could skate with you. You could be friends again."

Claire's shadow shifted slightly. "I don't think so."

"Why not?"

"It just doesn't work like that," Claire said. "We don't talk anymore, and I had to change schools. And Mom doesn't really like visitors. Even before everything… happened, she liked to keep to herself.”

Lena was overwhelmed with the feeling of a shy, reserved presence. She sighed, working the edge out of her voice. “That’s okay,” she said. Then a thought occurred: “We can be friends, then.”

Claire shifted again, hesitating. “Th-that’s sweet of you.”

“You should visit more often.” Lena paused, as though deciding something. “It’s lonely when you’re gone.”

“Is it just you down there?”

“Yes,” Lena lied. “There used to be others, but they went away.”

Claire’s shadow was still for a moment. “Lena, did you ever have a sister?”

Lena shrank back from the ice. “No.”

“It’s just, my mom’s sister, she drowned, and I was wondering —”

“It’s just me,” Lena said. “And I’ve always been here.”

“Listen, I have to get back. Mom will be waking up soon.” And before Lena could respond, Claire’s shadow began to move away.

When Claire was completely gone, Lena again slid a fingernail along the underside of the ice. Pressing harder this time, she scraped off a thin mist of shavings. Claire didn’t understand how important it was for them to be friends, but she would. And so, Lena lingered there, scraping at the barrier between her and the warmth of her new friend until the sun was gone.

That night, just as Lena was nearly to dreaming, Edna appeared at her feet. Lena sat up, dispersing her sleeping mat and waiting for the other to speak, but Edna floated silently, staring down at Lena.

“Edna?” Lena said at last.

“Yes,” Edna said, her voice a slowly clearing rasp. “Did you see her today? The girl from the surface?”

“I did.”

“And will she be back? Do you think she’ll fall?”

“I—I think so,” Lena said. “I told her we could be friends.”

Edna’s eyes widened, a hungry look growing in them. “When will she be back?”

Lena shrugged. “Edna, is it okay to… to *help* them fall?”

Edna’s blue-tinged ear twitched. “Do you mean to thin the ice?”

“Uh, yes. I guess so. Would that—would that be bad?”

Edna moved closer, close enough to touch. "We used to do it sometimes, just when we needed more friends. Matteo did it a lot. Raymond was always very mad when we did."

"So, it is bad, then?"

Edna looked away before placing a hand on Lena's forearm.

Lena shivered.

"My hands are colder than yours," Edna said. "Did you know that?"

Lena shook her head.

"You think that we don't talk to you because we don't want to, but really we can't remember how."

"I don't—"

"Raymond said that the other ice children disappeared because they were lonely, that we saved the surface children because we were bored, but that was never it. He didn't understand. You don't either, Lena, because you're the newest, but you will, soon."

Lena retreated slightly, putting distance between herself and Edna.

"I don't remember how to start talking anymore. Someone has to talk to me first, and then I can, but I can't start it. Rebecca and Julian—they were twins before, on the surface, always together—they can only remember how to talk to each other. To save a surface child, we have to take away their warmth, and the longer we're down here, the colder we get."

"And with the warmth goes the memory," Lena said.

Edna nodded. "Yes." She advanced toward Lena. "Do you remember that you used to sing?"

Lena gave her head a single shake.

"You did. All the time, but now it's gone. Sing me something."

Lena tried to think but could not find what singing was. "I can't," she said.

"Because you forgot. And you'll forget more, the colder you get." Edna began to drift back and forth in front of Lena, as though pacing. "Matteo and the others didn't leave because they wanted to bring back children; they left because they were so cold that they forgot they couldn't go. You can't be warm and live down here, and once you're here, you can't go back.

"The reason we saved those children and helped some of them fall was because new children help us remember what it's like to be warm. When the new children stopped coming, we couldn't remember anymore. But Raymond always said it wasn't fair. Not fair. Not fair."

Lena drew her limbs close to herself, as though afraid that Edna would take them from her. "If Raymond saved you," Lena started, "then he'd have to understand."

Edna shook her head. "He was different. Raymond was always different."

"Who saved Raymond?"

Edna shrugged. "We never knew, and he wouldn't say. I think maybe Raymond saved himself. I think maybe he was the first."

"But Raymond left. He must have been cold too."

"Maybe," Edna said. "Or maybe he knew what he was doing. Maybe he didn't want to watch us forget anymore." Edna closed in on Lena again, grabbing her by the collar. "You have to save Claire," she said. "We need her, Lena. You have to save her. I—I'm cold."

And it was true. Lena could feel the chill through her frayed shirt.

"You're the newest, Lena, which means one day you'll be all alone. Alone for real. Things didn't used to be like this. We used to have fun. We used to be happy. You're still warmer than I am, Lena, but touching you is like remembering my name. Touching a surface child would be like remembering who I am. Claire can help all of us."

Lena pulled back, breaking Edna's loose grasp. "Okay," she said. "I'll save her."

"Thank you," Edna said, and she wrapped her arms around Lena tight enough to hurt.

Lena felt a chill run through her, a chill that she was sure would stay there now, for always, although she couldn't remember why.

Whenever the sun broke through the ice, Lena raced toward the surface to wait for Claire, and each time Claire did not arrive, Lena worked at scraping the ice. She would drag her nails back and forth, shaving off the thinnest layers until by the time Claire returned, their patch of ice was noticeably thinner.

Claire arrived this time not in skates, but in boots, and she squatted over the patch rather than lying on her belly. "Sorry, Lena," she said, and her voice sounded hoarse, not quite warm enough to burn just yet, and Lena ached to get closer to her. "Mom's been really bad lately. I think she knows I've been skating on the pond. She won't say anything, but she hid my skates."

As Claire said this, Lena almost felt that it had happened to her instead. Lena had found her skates, though, hadn't she?

"Listen, Lena," Claire started, "I don't think that I'll be able to come back. It's getting late in the season, and Mom's probably right that it's not so safe now."

"No," Lena said. "You have to come back." Lena remembered falling on the ice, someone carrying her, a sprained wrist. She remembered an arm around her shoulder and a kiss on her forehead. "If anything happens, I can save you," she said.

"That's very kind, Lena," Claire said, but her voice did not have the same warmth as her words. "I just don't—Oh no."

"What is it?"

"I think my mom is outside the cabin. I think—"

And then Lena heard it, the screaming woman: "Claire! Claire, come back!" Lena imagined that voice—Maggie—calling her own name, ordering her down from a tree branch or away from a ravine.

"I have to go," Claire said, straightening up.

"No. You can't leave. I have to save you."

The light shifted as Claire turned to go, and Lena pounded her fist against the ice. A sickening crack echoed through the under, and with the crack came a flood of heat. In seconds, Claire was submerged in the water, Lena catching her in her arms. Lena could feel Claire's warmth, and she suddenly had the urge to sing. She knew what singing was now. And then Lena felt a hand tugging at first one leg and then both. Lena looked down into the depths to see Edna's hands around her ankles.

The heat from Claire's body was almost unbearable, but Lena could feel it draining, little by little, and as Claire became colder, Lena began to fill with warmth. She looked at the girl in her arms and saw not Claire but herself, and Edna holding her. Lena remembered the struggle to break through to the surface and the fear as she was pulled down. Someone above was screaming, but that too was fading as Lena descended into the depths, Edna's hands leaching the warmth from her body.

That was when she heard it.

The shriek.

Maggie screamed for Claire, just as she had screamed for Lena back then.

Lena looked at Claire's face and saw her lips beginning to go blue, and she felt the tug of the other ice child at her ankles again.

"Let go," she said, kicking at Edna.

"Save her," Edna rasped.

Save her. She would save her, but not for Edna and the ice children. She would save her for Maggie, Maggie who had always looked out for Lena but still couldn't save her all those years ago.

Lena closed her eyes and kicked against the water. Edna fell away, and Lena felt the light and warmth of the surface. And then she felt air and snow-covered ice. She thrust Claire's body onto the ice and pulled herself out. Lena could feel every part of her wanting to float away, as though she, like most everything else in the world beneath the ice, were formed from fragile water droplets. She willed herself together and scooped Claire into her arms. Lena began to sing. She couldn't remember learning the song, but still, she knew every word: "Oh my darling, oh my darling..."

Lena walked. She pointed herself in the direction of the shore, and she moved. "Oh my darling, Clementine..." Lena felt her feet begin to fade away and saw that her hands were losing color and shape, but she willed her arms to stay together, just for a bit longer. "You were lost and—" she could see the woman on the shore, frozen to the spot like she had lost her own warmth as well "—gone forever."

What was left of Lena's feet stepped onto the shore. "Dreadful sorry..."

"Claire," the woman breathed, interrupting Lena's song. Then she followed the arms holding her daughter. "Lena?"

"Maggie," Lena said. And as her legs and arms and face dispersed, she remembered all of it.

See Brittany M. Perkins's story "It Thaws in Spring" online at Metaphorosis.
If you liked it, leave a comment. Authors love that!
Remember to subscribe to our e-mail updates so you'll know when new stories are posted.

About the story

I wanted to write a story that takes place in a 'secondary world', and the first line of the story popped into my head: 'Lena lived under the ice.' I didn't know what it meant or what the story would be, but I loved the image and the alliterative nature of the line. Shortly after coming up with the opening line, I went to visit my boyfriend. It was on the car ride to his house that I started internally 'writing' the story. I came up with the scenario, the characters, and even some of the language I planned to use. This was back in November 2022, and at the time, my boyfriend and I would do something we called 'co-work', where we would both work on projects we needed or wanted to get done while keeping each other company. During this visit, we co-worked, and that's when I wrote it. I wrote almost the entire first draft of the story in one sitting, on my boyfriend's couch, while occasionally scratching his Labrador behind the ears. It's evolved quite a bit since then, of course, and I expanded on it a lot during the following months, but that was how the original came about, and it's ended up being one of my favorite things I've ever written.

A question for the author

Q: Q: Do you ever feel bad for what you put your characters through?

A: Honestly, yes. I was the type of kid (and somewhat embarrassingly am the type of adult) who worried about hurting a hairbrush's feelings by not using it enough or throwing it out. So, obviously, I feel bad when I have to bring harm or hardship to a character I've created. When I was younger, this aversion to harming my own creations led me to avoid unpleasant fates for my characters, even if that was what would best serve the story. As I've gotten older and have matured as both a reader and a writer, I can accept that sometimes a character has to suffer for the good of the story. While this may not have been what Stephen King meant when he advised us to "kill your darlings," I think it holds true in this context as well.

About the author

Brittany M. Perkins resides in not quite a small town but definitely not a big city in the Southern United States with her three well-behaved cats and one horribly-behaved cat. Since childhood, she has had the habit of disappearing into imaginary worlds. As an adult, she has yet to outgrow the habit of playing pretend. While she enjoys writing in many genres, she has a penchant for all things speculative.

Rosalind Dreams of Aersea

Travis Burnham

Rosalind was eleven when she got her first hammer, an 8-ounce, Estwing ball-peen. She thought it was the most beautiful thing she'd ever seen, though her Dad had frowned the whole time she unwrapped it. Rosalind's father's first disappointment had been that Rosalind wasn't a boy—he was a carpenter who'd dreamed of a son to follow in his manly footsteps. Rosalind couldn't remember a time when she hadn't wanted to be a carpenter—to be a builder, a maker of places people could call home.

When she was thirteen, she ran the third leg of the 400m relay at the State Track Meet. Second only to carpentry, she loved running—the warm burn in her muscles and the feel of air brushing against her skin. And she loved the companionship, telling wild stories to her teammates, the shared training and hard work. The team was depending on her points for the meet. On the starting line, her toes were tingling—she thought it must be nerves. But at three hundred meters, her left foot went numb to the ankle and she stumbled to the track surface. Scraped and bleeding, she pulled herself up and hobbled across the finish line. It would have been easier to bear if her teammates or coach had been angry.

That night, she had her first seizure, opening a gash in her forehead on the way down to the yellow kitchen linoleum. Nearly the only thing she recalled of the experience was the gentle voice of her older stepsister, Muriel, trying to talk her through it. When, five weeks later, Rosalind was diagnosed with Taeka-Storovski Syndrome, she was told she'd be lucky to make it to her 17th birthday.

This was Rosalind's father's second disappointment—and he didn't stick around for a third. Rosalind's mother stayed, but was never quite the same after. She'd always been somewhat mousy, and the abandonment drained something vital from her, making it seem like everything she did was just going through the motions.

As Taeka-Storovski dismantled Rosalind's body, she raged against fate. She cried, she screamed into her pillow, she shattered plates in the kitchen and smashed her favorite 'Dark Side of the Moon' record. One morning, she woke to her throat still raw and her vision bleary from crying the night before. She could barely feel her right hand. Down in the kitchen, she poured some milk into her Lucky Charms with her shaky offhand and looked over the room with exhaustion. Her eyes fell upon the fold at the top of the milk carton: SELL BY 10/26/23. This milk would go bad in five days. Her eyes fell back to her soon-to-be-soggy cereal as she realized she, too, had an expiration date, and would most likely be dead in three years, maybe less.

She didn't want to spend her remaining days in complaint and misery. She would try hard to be grateful—the disease was destroying her ability to do many things, but it left her imagination intact. She had always told stories to her teammates, or for invented tales for herself about strangers she saw, but what if she were more ambitious? That night, she began constructing an entire world she'd call Aersea in her mind.

Aersea began as a single, floating stone. Rosalind perched on it with her beloved ball-peen hammer—which she knew was not the best tool for the job—to pound and chip the floating boulder into shape. Made of cloudstone, the stone was a white, porous mineral, flecked with mica and lighter than air. When she needed it, another chunk of cloudstone would appear. Rock by rock, stone by stone, boulder by boulder, amid oceans of clouds, the archipelago of Aersea came together. She was a carpenter of worlds.

The construction of Aersea wasn't flawless. Sometimes the wrong stone would appear, a piece of dense granite or quartz or marble, and it would fall, shrinking into the unknowable distance. Sometimes, she would swing the hammer wrong and a piece of cloudstone would shear off and spin away. She'd hew a forest from cloudstone and breathe life into it, imagining it as verdant green, but as life flowed into it, the leaves would resolve to mother-of-pearl, and the bark become noctilucent.

As Aersea grew, she'd gaze out over what she'd created. And it was then she'd notice geographical features she *hadn't* created— a range of low slung hills, an achingly clear lake filled with cloud-white trout, a forest of cloud firs festooned in white needles.

By that time, Muriel had been offered a dream job working for *Destinations*, a travel website with a monthly magazine. She didn't want to accept it, as she knew it would take her away from Rosalind. Their mother and the nurses were good caretakers, but they couldn't be big sisters.

The night before Muriel had to make the decision on the job, she was stretched out in bed with Rosalind and they were staring at the glow-in-the-dark stars on the ceiling. "I don't want to leave you, Rosie." The quiet gasping of the respirator was a constant background noise. Rosalind depended on it more and more of late. Being on the respirator was terrible, like she was constantly drowning. But it was even worse without it—like running the 100m with a pillow strapped to her face.

Rosalind took a deep, raspy breath and said, "I need you to see the world for me, Murzie. Please." The more of Aersea she built, the more Rosalind realized she was going to see none of her own world. Rosalind would miss Muriel terribly, really couldn't imagine what she would do without her, but even worse was the thought of both of them losing their dreams. She buried all the selfish thoughts that would keep Muriel home.

From the pillow next to her, Rosalind took a tattered, pink, stuffed bunny and tucked it into the crook of Muriel's arm. "You can take Energizer with you. It will be like I'm there, too."

Muriel turned away for a moment, blinking back tears. Rosalind offering the bunny was a gut punch—a reminder that her little sister was just a little kid dealing with much more than she should have had to: dying with dignity.

In the end, Rosalind begged for Muriel to take the job, and Muriel relented.

Muriel sent letters and postcards to Rosalind. She texted photo upon photo upon photo of herself and Energizer—from the altiplano of Colombia, with the little stuffed bunny wearing hiking boots and riding on Muriel's shoulders, or of the stuffed bunny perched on the walls of Monsaraz Castle, looking out over the lake-spattered plains of the Portuguese Alentejo. Yet another of Energizer wearing swimming goggles and being held above the Klein-blue waters of Rota in the Mariana Islands. One postcard from the Marianas read:

> *We dove with sea turtles! Okay, Energizer saw them from the dive boat, but still! I'll bring back loads of dive pictures to show you. My love for you is deeper than the Mariana Trench!* ♥ *Murzie*

Many of the landscapes Muriel described would find their way into Aersea.

Time flowed differently there. Rosalind would doze off and a day would go by among the clouds—but when she woke and looked at the clock, only an hour had passed.

But the creating was becoming harder. More and more things she hadn't created herself began appearing. It seemed the worst injustice that she was losing control in both worlds. She did her best to reframe the losses in a positive light. Small towns dotted the landscape. She thought of the movie *Field of Dreams* that her dad had made her watch when she was eleven—the main character kept hearing a voice telling him that if he made it, they'd come, or something like that. There were people living in Aersea. Had she given them a place to live? It had always been her ultimate goal as a carpenter—to provide shelter.

When Muriel wasn't working or traveling, she was home with Rosalind. Muriel was never negative—she didn't want to waste any of her precious time with Rosalind with complaints. They'd talk far into those nights, reminiscing. Muriel told tales of her travels—the Great Wall, the Great Barrier Reef, the Great Ocean Road—and Rosalind about the changes happening in Aersea, where she was spending more and more time. Muriel was fascinated with the depth of detail Rosalind had for her imaginary Aersea.

"Do you remember when we made war clubs that winter?" Rosalind asked. "And then smashed sheets of ice down on the Merrimac?"

Muriel laughed. "You mean those war clubs made out of poison sumac that gave us rashes so bad we missed a week of school? And my left eye actually swelled shut?"

"It was worth it though, wasn't it?"

"Yeah." Muriel smiled, and squeezed Rosalind's shoulder. "Worth every minute of itchy torture. And time with you. Though I remember Dad refused to come near us, afraid we were contagious."

Rosalind asked, "Do you hate Dad?"

"Yeah." Muriel quirked her mouth to the side, thoughtful. "I mean, I don"t want him to die, but I hate him for being such a coward and leaving you. Us. How about you?"

"I did for a little while. Now, thinking of him just makes me sad. But he lent me his dreams of building beautiful things, so I don"t want to waste time hating him anymore."

On the next trip abroad, Murzie met Dylan. He was wanderlust personified, with striking eyes of green sea glass, a disarming smile, and an unfortunate love for the 80s band Styx. By the end of what became a shared trip through Torres del Paine National Park, Murzie knew she was in deep.

Finally, Aersea wriggled free of Rosalind"s creative grasp. She was still able to effect small changes—sweeten a mug of cloudberry wine, darken the feathers of a *jordmow* in flight, change the shape of a distant stratocumulus cloud—but she was no longer the architect of Aersea.

She often felt her life had become an exercise in settling for less—less magic, less running, fewer breaths. *No,* she'd tell herself. *Not settling for less, but embracing what remains.*

The next postcard read:

Hiking the Torres del Paine Circuit. Rained all day. You (Energizer) and I got drenched, but Gray Glacier is amazing. I love you more than the height of Cerro San Valentín! PS: I think I've met someone. ♥ *Murzie*

And so Rosalind traveled, too, ranging across Aersea, a pilgrim in rough clothing trying to squeeze what she could out of every minute she had left. What she'd loved about running, she poured into hiking and exploring Aersea. She studied the electric-blue icebergs that slid along the surface of *Tarn Screar*, and immersed herself in their blissful silence. Wandering among the massive cloudwoods of *Gruluth Mons*, she wove garlands of their arm length pine needles. She explored the *Gor Sezu* foothills, and passed between the jagged *Hasaped Loam* mountains.

And then, when Rosalind thought she must be somewhere in her late twenties in Aersea years, she also met someone. Heliotrope was a blacksmith with an incongruous, delicate name. Hels, as she preferred to be called, was most certainly not fragile. She was forge-baked and had the low deep laugh of a bellows. When Rosalind was in her strong arms, she nearly forgot about home and her dying body. Rosalind learned Vobidian, the language of the southern *Farth Girchead* peninsula, and the most commonly spoken tongue of Aersea, while Hels picked up a bit of English.

Back at home, a postcard from Portugal read:

Took a wine tour in the Baixa Corgo of the Douro River. Forgot sunscreen. Terribly sunburned. But you (Energizer) and I got buzzed on vinho verde, so the pain is minimal. I love you more than the number of bridges in Porto! Dylan says hello. ♥ *Murzie*

Muriel found Rosalind more and more detached with every visit, and her health in exponential decline. She began to wonder how Rosalind could possibly still be alive in her wasted body. Muriel hesitated to tell Rosalind about Dylan's proposing atop one of the towers of Kinnity Castle under an Irish sunset.

"I'm super happy…for you," Rosalind said, wishing that she'd be there for the wedding, but knowing she wouldn't be alive that long.

"I love you, Rosie. You're the best little sister I could have possibly asked for." Muriel never missed an opportunity to tell Rosalind she loved her, because she never knew when it might be the last time.

In Aersea, Rosalind poured every last bit of her creation magic into two items: a small cloudstone sculpture of intertwined flowers—a rose and a cluster of heliotrope. And a key that she hoped would do what she asked it to do.

Hels asked, "Where do you disappear to, when you leave me?"

Because when Rosalind woke in the real world, she disappeared from Aersea. How do you tell your lover that you're from another world, and that your body is dying? The tears spilled out of Rosalind. "I want you to know how much your love has meant to me. I never expected such a gift in the short time I had." It felt unfair to Rosalind: she had not one, but two worlds to lose.

"You make it sound like you're dying," Hels said, fear in her voice.

"I had a life before you. And I fear that life will soon take me away." Rosalind handed her a small package wrapped in white linen.

Hels gave a small laugh and handed Rosalind a delicate and intricate pounded copper box in return. Hels said, "Looks like you're not the only one giving gifts." When Rosalind lifted the box's cover, she found a fine silver mirror in the felt-lined interior. In the mirror, she thought she caught a flash of Murzie, Dylan, and Energizer, looking out over a serpentine river edged with small, terracotta roofed houses. The image disappeared quickly enough that Rosalind thought she'd imagined it.

Then Hels unwrapped her present to reveal the cloudstone sculpture of intertwined flowers. Rosalind said, "And I also want you to have this," handing Hels the well-loved and well-used ball-peen hammer that Rosalind's father had given to her. Or at least the version she'd created to design Aersea. Was it only a facsimile? When was the last time she'd seen that hammer in the real world?

The next morning, Hels woke to an empty bed, while Rosalind woke in her gaunt and skeletal body.

Muriel was there and heard Rosalind mutter, "⟨unintelligible script⟩."

Muriel asked, "What was that?" Muriel knew words in a dozen languages, and could at least recognize a dozen more languages. And this was nothing she'd heard.

Rosalind drew in a ragged breath and said, "I think ... I said ... I love you, ... in Vobidian ... language of Aersea." Muriel then knew that Rosalind was probably measuring her life in days, and maybe less. Rosalind's words hadn't sounded like gibberish, but couldn't have been anything else. Muriel was now with her constantly, afraid to leave her bedside.

The next morning, Rosalind managed to force a whisper out: "... love you ... Murzie ... you're ... best ... big sister ... I could have."

"I love you, too, kiddo. Please don't leave me." But Rosalind didn't respond, lapsing into an unmoving silence—her breath shallow, her heartbeat slowing, slowing, slowing.

Then Rosalind took her last breath on Earth—

Muriel held onto Rosalind's hand until it went cool. She'd cried herself dry—her eyes felt raw and her head ached. Finally, she stood, and then she caught a glint of silver and white in Rosalind's left hand. She was certain it hadn't been there before. How had she missed it? Leaning over, she opened Rosalind's fingers to find a white stone skeleton key with a ball-peen hammer emblazoned on the shank. It was so light it practically floated on her open palm.

—and then Rosalind, just one moment later, took her first true breath in Aersea, opening her eyes to see Hels, a worried expression on her face.

A postcard rested in Hel's hands.

You (Energizer) and I are leaving on the first plane out of Kalispell tomorrow. I'll probably beat this postcard back, but can't wait to see you. Love you to Aersea and back! ♥
Murzie

As Muriel approached the bathroom sink, she couldn't imagine how she'd live in a world without Rosalind. She splashed water on her face and looked at herself in the mirror. She looked terrible. But then, for just a moment, Rosalind's face flickered in the reflection. The mirror shimmered like mercury and a small keyhole appeared on its surface. Muriel hesitated, wondering if any of this was real. Could all of those things that Rosalind had told Muriel about Aersea be true? Maybe this was a portal to oblivion—Rosalind had died. Would Murzie be joining her? And if she left, what about Dylan? Pulling Rosalind's cloudstone key from her pocket, Muriel weighed it in her palm. Looking up at the keyhole, she saw that it was smaller. Almost imperceptibly, it was shrinking—there was a diminishing window of time to decide.

Muriel lived a whole life in a few stretched out moments—she married Dylan, they bought a tiny blue bungalow to live in. They got a little pup, a Portuguese podengo pequeno they named Azores. Then they had two daughters, Harper and Isla, born a few years apart. They wrote, they traveled. They loved.

Though Muriel thought she'd cried herself dry, a tear slid down her cheek as a single sob was pulled from her. Then she took two deep breaths, three. Back in Rosalind's bedroom, in one of her desk drawers, Muriel found an envelope and wrote Dylan's name on it. Slipping the engagement ring from her finger, she put it in the envelope and put the envelope on Rosalind's nightstand. She kissed Rosalind on the forehead. "I love you to Aersea and back, Rosie."

Standing before the mirror again, Muriel took out her phone. She stopped herself before she scrolled through pictures she and Dylan shared and instead she opened her messaging app. Tapping on Dylan's name, she typed:

> *If you truly love me, Dylan, you won't come looking for me. I know it sounds far too crazy to be true, but I've gone to Aersea.*
> ♥ *Murzie*

She hit send.

Setting down her cell phone, she put her hands on the edge of the sink to steady her trembling hands. Closing her eyes, she pictured Rosalind in Aersea.

Then, opening her eyes and reaching forward, Muriel slid the key into the mirror's keyhole.

See Travis Burnham's story "Rosalind Dreams of Aersea" online at Metaphorosis.
If you liked it, leave a comment. Authors love that!
Remember to subscribe to our e-mail updates so you'll know when new stories are posted.

About the story

I wrote "Rosalind Dreams of Aersea" to a prompt about building worlds, but the true heart of the story is from my own dream that our lost friends are out there somewhere in the universe. And at some point I'll meet up with them again, maybe in a fantastical world of their own design. There are personal memories of my own lost friends scattered throughout the text, so the story is also something of a home for them. I'll leave it up to readers to find those memories or maybe create their own.

A question for the author

Q: What distracts you?

A: Beauty. Travel. Prose. That's the short list (that isn't the obvious ones of baby animal videos, stress, artistic Instagram reels, and video games). As an international teacher, I'm extraordinarily lucky that I can indulge my love of travel and beauty on a daily basis. Where I'm living now, Montenegro, is chockablock with stunning views. As for the final "distraction"? By staving off the obvious, true distractions mentioned above, I can write. I have a ritual I try to follow when it comes to my final love: early morning, ocean sounds played on my headphones, a timer to keep me on track, sometimes a word-count goal, and a turned off internet. But life is really just a series of distractions and it's up to us to choose the distractions that matter.

About the author

Travis Burnham is a speculative fiction writer and science teacher. Originally from New England, he's lived in Japan, Colombia, Portugal, Malta, and the Mariana Islands, and currently teaches science at an international school in Montenegro. He's a bit of a thrill seeker, having bungee jumped in New Zealand, hiked portions of the Great Wall of China, and gone scuba diving in Bali. He's got some novels looking for homes and can be found online at travisburnham.blogspot.com.

Saving the Whales

C.J. Erick

Niemi misses the whales.

She misses the bowhead, the fin, and the southern right. She misses the grand blue, the understated minke, and the elegant sei. She misses the way water bulged like candy glass over their backs when they rose to the surface, and how it broke into liquid shards. She misses the billowing rainbows of their exhalations on cold mornings, and the percussion cannons of their tails when they announced their preposterously powerful dives-to-be.

She didn't always miss the whales. Once, she watched them, idolizing them, yearning to be with them grokking the water and not rocking in her rowboat or rolling in her Zodiac.

It is hard now, to crinkle her eyes at the sun setting on the washboard Pacific, the delicious smells of crusty sea salt and delicately rotting seaweed in her nose, the shoosh of waves not in her ears, but somehow over and around and through her, feeling the voids where the whales should be.

Her first summer post-junior year, she spent wet through her suit and behind her ears. She spent hours leaning over the side of the inflatable with an aluminum pole like a lightning rod, plunging it into the galvanic water. Algae-laden, the water was tarnished green, like corroded bronze.

At the end of the rod was magic, a flashy new hydrophone — analog, since this was 1975 — hard-wired to a plastic-wrapped tape recorder the size of a suitcase large enough to hold her entire wardrobe of jeans, tees, tanks, hair clips, and caps, and the three Lycra one-piece swimsuits she rotated throughout the summer. Behind her, the annoying drum of San Diego, a million miles from the farm in Illinois, interfered with the recording.

She couldn't hear the sounds they were recording. She and her research partner, Floyd, whom she'd picked because he was gay and she could trust him not to use her exuberance like a date-rape drug as one professor had tried to. The voices of the grays were well below human hearing, but she'd manipulated them through the miracle of mid-Seventies sound manipulation, applied in the biology department's sound room. Now their eerie songs, replayed through the stereo speakers, touched something primal within her, like a deep siren call, the come-hither seduction of sensuous clicks and thrums and moans exotic and otherworldly.

Her senses, once piqued, would never rest.

Whales went missing.

First, the pods of minkes that frequented the central Pacific failed to arrive that year. Biologists blamed it on the failure of the last major shelf of Antarctic ice, a diversion in the ocean currents, red tides, overfishing, and even sunspots.

Niemi knew better. But her suspicions were confirmed through a chance encounter. She'd been following a small pod of the slender gray creatures at a distance, quietly rowing after them, letting the airfoil sail of her little sun-bleached white sailboat push her along as much as possible.

Lights appeared in the sky. Two silent machines the color and size and shape of pre-World-War dirigibles lowered as one imagined the carcass of a whale might fall into the lightless deep. The craft settled into the waves, kilometers from shore, well away from the sight of land. Great doors opened in the vessels' ends, and whales swam into them two by two. And then the great craft closed their doors and lifted steadily into the sky, their lights extinguished, until they grew as small as sailing ships curving away over the horizon, and disappeared.

Niemi had watched, asking herself why these ships were taking the whales, and why the whales were boarding without a struggle.

In the weeks that followed, she contacted every agency she thought would have interest in her sightings, in the disappearances. But what agency would have the authority to investigate? The California State Police? After three calls and visit to the headquarters in San Diego County, they refused to speak to her. The CIA? Probably weather balloons, was all they offered, and dismissed her. A young biologist from NOAA, the National Oceanographic and Atmospheric Administration, met with her briefly, but tried to push her observations toward illegal whaling operations, probably by Chinese fishing companies, which were suffering as ocean stocks of fish collapsed further from the unrecoverable levels in the 2020s.

Lights in the sky. Alien visitors harvesting the world's cetaceans? No one would believe her.

She lived on the ocean, helped conduct whales counts. She pursued a degree in marine biology, cetacean focus, and manhandled her way through a Ph.D. The degree and her well-taken thesis on cetacean language led to grants, and the grants led to the books published, the ones that sold at last after so many rejections and failures to launch: *Living with Earth's Smartest Beings* and *Love and Sex Among Krill and Plankton*. She became a name then, cited in oceanographic journals and doomed environmental legislation. But the writing wasn't about credibility or notoriety; it was about money, the money she needed, and there were many things she needed.

The world turns on coinage. She turned hers into a submersible, a truck-sized, two-person submarine. Electric. Quiet. Loaded with sensing equipment that beat most space missions.

She called it Grayfin.

Her mother died, the woman she most loved, but feared as the one most likely to lead her back to 'a practical career, Niemi'. And then seven months later her broken-hearted father passed as well, a man she'd never liked, but in whom she'd found a kinship in their complex, seldom-spoken feelings for her mother and each other.

Her brother and sisters divided the estate among themselves, leaving her out, since she was obviously more well-off than they were, though they knew nothing of sleeping on a wave-soaked dock, or spending one's own money on teaching supplies, those costs even a prestigious West Coast university passed on to untenured professors.

But seven years after she had seen the lift of the minke, had seen the lights dropping to the ocean again and again, she had her machine, her mechanical stalking whale, her way to find out why.

The sky ship, dull gray and oblong, dropped like a deflating helium balloon from the tortured sky toward the open waters of the Pacific. Silent, even several hundred miles from Baja where no one was going to hear it. It descended slightly butt-heavy, angled like Grayfin powering across the surface at full throttle, which was about to happen. Timing; timing.

The whales were out there — five hundred meters by the radar, lolling and spouting vapor in the waves. Four big blues, three females and one male. No calves, despite it being birthing season, which was sad and one explanation for all this.

Niemi's hands felt numb and twitchy on the controls.

The alien vessel leveled out and settled into the water. A white wave spread outward from the hull. After a few eternally long minutes, a vast door opened in the end facing the whales, like the mouth of an earthworm about to consume a bit of cornmeal sprinkled into its bait container.

The whales circled and then lined up two by two and swam toward the craft, but still a good two hundred meters from it. Niemi waited.

The first two spouted mightily, as if kicking the dust from their sandals, and entered the maw of the ship. As the second pair moved within a hundred meters, Niemi grasped the control handles and willed her sub to life.

She was thrown back into the seat as the nose came up. Four-thousand electric horses leaped ahead. Past the side-view screens flowed dirty green water, plastic junk, rust-colored debris, and the broken skeletons of maritime equipment. Her machine was stealthy quiet, but still the whine of the motors was in her ears like Triassic hornets. The rangefinder counted down the numbers. Four hundred meters. Three. One fifty.

The vessel's door closed, and the ship lifted from the waves, streamers of water falling from its sides like dishwater from an aluminum urn. It lifted into the sky just like the first two she'd observed, shrinking slowly, sailing over the horizon of the darkening sky.

"No!" She heard the ragged rage in her voice, the childlike cry of frustration and abandonment.

And then the light paused, descended, grew. The gray craft, now charcoal in the late twilight, touched the water, and the great doors opened again. It stood in the water, motionless, as if anchored by rigid pilings to the ocean floor two thousand feet below.

She eased her submarine forward, passing into the black mouth of the ship, watching the stars covered by a sky-colored sheet. The doors closed behind her ship, and all was dark. She could barely breathe.

She assumed they lifted into the sky, although she couldn't tell because there was no sense of motion, no acceleration, no feeling of changing momentum. She struggled to find a term for the beings who had taken her into their ship. Calling them 'extraterrestrial' would be Earth-centric, as if her planet were the center of the universe of intelligent species, when in fact the very existence of these beings and their ships proved otherwise. 'Space travelers' would imply they'd come from the endless void out beyond the wispy extremes of the atmosphere, when she had no idea where they'd come from, and almost certainly they'd not come from the void itself. And 'aliens' wasn't just human-centric but also politically disrespectful, since humans were at least as alien to these beings as the other way around.

So she settled for the Visitors, which seemed to cover just about anything nonhuman.

They allowed her to rock in the hull of the ship in complete darkness. She began to wonder if they expected her to navigate by sonar. She remembered her sonar then, and, risking offense, pinged around her ship, finding it rolling gently in the center of a large tank with featureless walls, shaped like two bathtubs stacked one upside down over the other. Two whale tails disappeared from the far end of the tank, rising upwards through a porthole into another chamber above her, apparently. Once they were through, dull blue lights came on and another door opened in the ceiling above her. Her submersible eased through it with no action on her part, rising into a smaller, egg-shaped chamber where metal rods protruded from the walls like fingers pushing through a balloon, cradling her ship gently as if holding a shiny black pouch of stingray eggs. Water drained from the chamber in seconds.

"Join us," said a voice. It was female, brash and harsh, brassy like someone speaking from a conch shell. A voice she disliked when she heard it in taped interviews; her own voice.

The main hatchway of the sub slid into its recess with a barely audible hum. The air that flowed in through the open door held all the taste and smell of boiled water. A metal walkway pushed out from the wall and stuck to the ship just below the port, dull like aluminum, soft like plastic as she walked along it step by step.

Beyond the doorway was a small chamber, surrounded on all sides and the top by clear glass, the walls of water tanks all around. A woman stood with her back to Niemi, and she knew it would be herself, even before the hologram or whatever it was turned to gaze at her over its shoulder, assessing her so closely and with such human intensity and expression that she couldn't convince herself the image wasn't real. She fought back the urge to touch it.

"You believe they are beautiful," said the woman. Beyond her, the four blue whales floated in an infinite pool, rising slowly to breathe, then sinking slowly under the surface. The otherwise colorless water was foggy brown with krill, and occasionally one of the whales would open its great beak-like mouth to allow the rich water to fill it.

"I do." She was overwhelmed as always by the beauty of the whales. The impending loss struck her like a migraine, twisting at the bones in her forehead. "Why — ?"

"All of us are different, and yet we are the same."

The woman explained that consciousness existed beyond the physical boundaries of the brain and of the body, and that all touched each other. When the predominant beings of a world — she didn't use the word 'planet', as that excluded many places where rational beings lived — were able to harmonize, a stable tranquility could bloom, one that could last for thousands of years.

"These beings," said the Other Niemi, "they are special. They have a gift and a yearning for harmony which we've never seen before. Such a shame you humans don't recognize this, and you harm them."

"Some of us cherish them," said Niemi.

The Visitor said, "We have observed and, at times, sought to promote harmony on Earth, as is our calling. But despite these efforts, humans have not harmonized with your world, with the other rational beings there, such as the primates, the cephalopods, the avians, and of course, the whales."

Niemi said, "But we do achieve harmony — sometimes. We organize. We achieve great things. We help each other during crises and natural disaster. We even harmonize in song, just as the whales do."

"Truth. But political and resource organization is a sad caricature of the true, deep connection of a harmonized world.

"Your race has been given enough time. And these beautiful beings are needed elsewhere."

"Where? Why?" asked Niemi.

"Every world seeks harmony. These beings can help. And they deserve better."

The woman told Niemi they were telling her this because she was one of the few who listened — sometimes. If there was hope, it lay with her or others like her.

"Are you taking all the whales?" she asked.

"They speak across entire oceans," said the Other Niemi, shaking her head, perhaps preoccupied as she was with the whale's beauty. "No, we will only save the ones who wish to go. The orcas and some dolphin species have chosen to stay. Their food supplies are doing well for now, and they like interacting with humans. We will come back for them if they call."

"Will you bring the other whales back, once their work is done?"

"No."

Niemi paused, frozen by an aching she couldn't explain or readily locate.

"May I go with them?"

"No."

Nothing else. No explanation, no conditions. Just no.

Niemi wasn't allowed to protest or plead or fall to her knees and beg. One minute she was standing talking to this Other Niemi, or a diagram that looked and sounded exactly like video and audio of her, and the next she awoke in her submersible, washing back and forth in two-meter waves in the open sea. The ship and the whales were gone.

She sat and rocked and wept for as long as it took.

Niemi convinced a department head to support her for another grant, and she used it to finance expeditions to record whale song, and computer time to translate. She followed the herds, playing their own recorded voices to them. She paid for seeding of plankton and devised outriggers for Grayfin to scoop waste from the bleary seawater, and when that didn't make a dent in the floating and sinking trash, she had automobile-sized drone submarines built, rigged with nets to catch trash. But they did little except tangle with fish and turtles and jellyfish. The entropy of waste was pervasive and resistant.

Whale sightings and counts continued to dwindle, pointing to cataclysmic losses. Scientists and politicians and fishermen argued not over the why, but over whether this was a good or bad thing, since whales were known to reduce fishing trawler yields, and feeding the world was hard, so hard, so bloody hard to make profitable.

She spent much of her time following the orca pods, continuing to journal and sketch individuals, just as she'd done since her first whale watching excursion as a young teen on a school trip, the prize for winning a climate science award. Now, she had Grayfin, where she lived most days.

One day, she languished like an empty water bottle in calm waters well off San Diego, where one couldn't see the land and where few boats ventured. She was there because bright lights in the sky had been reported for several nights over the previous month. She turned the sound system off, the sonar sensors, the radar, the infrared thermographs, the radio.

Was it harmony she felt then, alone, like a dead piece of kelp being nibbled by tiny crabs? The harmony of the carcass of a sei whale stinking the water with the promise of food and habitat for months, before sinking into the lightless depths to provide fodder and shelter for blind eels and tube worms and beaked fish that would never see a rainbow? Or was it just loneliness, alienation?

Her eyes were to the sky, and she didn't notice them until they were nearly upon her, black and white looping shapes in the water, a dozen or more, bulky cetacean missiles, moving silently as one body, as only beings who knew each other well could. She didn't move as the pod of orcas approached and circled her. She kept the hydrophones off to avoid spooking the pod, but their clicks and whistles resonated through the craft's thin titanium shell.

They flowed around her in an intricate swirl of day-and-night bodies, then away into a funnel, leaving her. She was drawn to them as into a whirlpool. She touched the controls and followed across open water, following their bulging rhythms and infrequent breaths, to where she didn't know, and suddenly didn't care, but when they arrived it was obvious why. An old container ship, sunk so that its deck lay just above the surface, flat and open like an ice floe. It wasn't on any maps she knew of, but sonar showed it anchored to the bottom by strands of fishing net and cable, probably communication cables mistakenly dredged up, spelling its doom.

On the ship were dozens of sea lions, letting the afternoon sun broil their skin to a fearsome pink, like monsters from some children's anime film. Niemi breached Grayfin a hundred yards away, and climbed out to watch, a small hand-held camera ready.

Three of the orcas stormed the ship's deck, landing on their bellies with only their tails in the water, each grasping a mature sea lion in its mouth, wiggling their water-wet bodies back into the water, shaking the lions and dragging them down through the broken pane of the ocean's surface, down into clouds of red, before disappearing out of sight. The lions scrambling on the deck roared and retreated to the center of the ship, crushing smaller females, pushing others off into the water, where some didn't make it back to the safety of the ship's deck before being sucked down by domino torpedoes.

She knew she should record this event, but she lacked the strength to raise and point the camera. For whom would she take the pictures? For whom capture it on video? For some vulgar wildlife reality show, another outlet for those who enjoyed the violence of nature, never seeing the necessity or reason for it?

Niemi lost track of time watching the orcas circle the ship. The lions crowded together in a wary crush of gray-pink bodies. Niemi was wondering what she should do next, knowing it was already too late to return to the harbor before night and not caring much about that either.

A single orca approached, a large female, with clean lines as if painted, her shorter female's dorsal fin curving at the end, and a gray marking shaped like a human hand at the end of her left pectoral fin. Niemi remembered this whale woman, a mother she'd followed for three breeding seasons, one who'd raised three calves with brutal efficiency and care. She'd named the woman Mileva, for reasons she couldn't remember.

Mileva swam to Niemi's vessel and spit a melon-sized chunk of sea lion flesh onto the sun-beaten hull of the sub, like a grill chef dropping a slab of cod onto an aluminum fry pan. It sizzled.

Mileva rocked her face in the waves, blowing breath expectantly. Niemi eyed the fatty mass and gray hide on the hull, and her stomach grumbled.

Mileva whistled and blew a geyser of hot vapor toward Niemi, showering her in acrid spit.

Niemi scooted to the edge of the sub, scooped up the flesh, and sat holding it, feeling her throat tighten at the glowing, shiny meat, which seemed to pulse in her hands.

She bit, chewed the jelly-like flesh, tasted blood and rank oil and noxious umami; gagged and swallowed.

She swallowed another bite. She vomited into the water. She bit again, swallowed. Vomited. Her head rocked, vision blackening. She fell to her side on the hull, unable to rise.

The orca eased alongside her sub, its black eye almost invisible against its ebon skin, the large white patch above it like the luminous white eye of a phantom. The whale's gray saddle patch curved about her back like a knitted sweater. It turned, swirling, and lifted a flipper and swept it away from the craft, the gray hand patch at its tip beckoning.

Niemi thought about her snorkel gear, donning the wet suit over her thin cotton shirt and shorts, and the flippers, but instead let her body slide from the sub's hull into the cold water. Immediately her nausea passed, and she bobbed easily in the infinite soup of ocean, her clothing clinging to her like tissue paper. Mileva's head bobbed in the light waves. Was this a nod? The great black and white being slid away like a ghost, her flipper rising once to beckon again. Other orca had gathered at a distance, blowing steam, whistling, pulsations of sound tapping at Niemi's skin.

Mileva, now twenty yards from the ship, whistled loudly.

Niemi pushed away, settling into an easy swim — she could swim for hours without tiring, so much time spent in the water. But it was cold, and she was thin and would chill quickly in the Pacific water.

She came within ten feet of the huge woman whale. Mileva stroked her tail to ease away. Leading her away.

Niemi swam. Her submersible Grayfin fell away behind her.

Mileva played this game several times, letting Niemi approach, then pulling away. Cat and mouse? The other whales swam with them, to each side, remaining yards away, like spectators at a long-distance race, following the runners.

Then, after a hard, muscular thrust of tail, Mileva dove and surfaced facing Niemi, blocking her path, just ten feet in front. She waited.

Niemi paused, then swam toward the whale woman. She was at the whale's mercy, hundreds of yards from Grayfin, more vulnerable than the sea lions Mileva's pod had attacked earlier. She stopped just outside touching reach of the whale's black and white snout, which bobbed like a marker buoy, shiny as rubberized paint. The whistling of the other whales stopped. There was only the sound of the ocean around them; the susurrus of the waves, the clicks of sea creatures, the bellowing of the sea lions on the rogue ship, the screes of gulls and shearwaters scavenging the remains or hunting the small fish drawn to the blood.

Mileva swam to the side, around Niem. She turned, opened her mouth, and gripped Niemi by the chest. Teeth dug into Niemi's skin in a hundred places. She closed her eyes.

Mileva held her in her mouth, pulled her, brushed her stomach with her great sandpaper tongue. Niemi fought the urge to push the whale away, to throw a fist at Mileva's eye. Mileva raised her partly from the water, swam in a circle, as if showing this prize to the others.

Then she opened her mouth and released Niemi. She swam ten feet away and waited, lolling in the waves, once again a dark phantom with ghostly patches.

Niemi felt the sting of seawater on small cuts on her side, her arm, her belly. She could breathe, but she wanted to vomit again.

What did the whale want from her now? It lay expectantly in the water, waiting. She could swim back for her sub, if the currents weren't taking it away from her, beyond her reach. But that would be returning to who she had been before this night, this act of connection from Mileva. That's what it was, surely. The whale could have killed her, but hadn't. The pod could have ignored her and swum away, but remained, the others again swimming in a circle around her and Mileva, whistling, blowing breath.

They were asking "Are you one of us?"

Niemi leaned forward, stroked the water with her cold arms, feeling the stings, the chill, the touch of microscopic stingers from tiny krill and squid, how her skin loved the water, the caress as it passed over her arms, her shoulders, her back.

She reached Mileva in a dozen strong strokes. She gripped the flipper nearest her, the one with the shape of a gray human hand. She gripped the end of the flipper in her teeth, held it there, pulled.

Mileva's small black eye, two feet away from hers, studied her.

She held the flipper in her teeth as long as Mileva had held her body, then released and kicked away. She placed two fingers in her mouth and blew air, spitting water, phlegm, giving a harsh rasping whine at first, and then a loud clear whistle, which cut the air and breeze, silencing the birds and the other whales.

Mileva nodded, whistled back.

She swam to Niemi, leaned over to allow the woman to grip her dorsal fin. With Niemi clinging, Mileva snapped her tail, suddenly a whistling steam ship plowing the waves. She covered the quarter mile to Grayfin in a few moments, Niemi holding tight with both hands.

At the sub, Niemi, suddenly very tired, eased back into the water, swam to the boarding ladder, climbed onto the sub's hull and knelt there, too tired to stand. Mileva, head pointing straight up, spun twice like a great black and white top, then swam away, pausing once to turn back, before disappearing beneath the dancing moonlit surface, leaving hardly a ripple in her wake.

They should, all creatures, leave the world that way, with barely a ripple marking their passage.

The next two times Niemi met Mileva and the whales, she ate of what she was offered, sea lion meat, or seal, or chunks of raw tuna or shark, she vomited. After that, she didn't vomit again.

Two calves were born, in one of the new 'conservation' sea parks, "Whales Forever," just south of San Diego, from one orca female, twins, an almost impossible miracle. A sign, many pro-captivity lobbyists said, that their programs were needed and helpful. The foundation would preserve the remaining whales through reproduction and nurturing programs, funded by interactive aquariums, agility and skills displays, swimming with the whales events.

It was harmony, of a sort, with the underlying dark shadow of corporate profit driving the enterprise.

Niemi was running a monthly educational program at middle schools, along the West Coast of the US and into Canada usually, but sometimes invited to progressive districts near Chicago, New England, even Austin and Minneapolis. Her theme was simple — "Whales are People." She was loved or hated, invited or banned. And always, always threatened. For her own protection, she became a licensed firearm carrier, and hated the need.

At the news of the miracle birth, she paused her program, spending more time on the water, her Eden, the garden she'd been pulled away from too often as she taught and wrote. Even she had bills to pay, and the grants came less often. She was too controversial.

Miracle calves, young whale children who would be raised wrong, never learn what they needed to survive in the sea, never know the true joy of pod life.

Never learn to kill for food and survival.

She requested a meeting with the sea park administrators, on the premise of being allowed to produce multi-media works for promotion of the twins, watch their lives grow. It would be like an orca version of the Hollywood film *Truman*, lives lived in a virtual-sea. A morning swim and simulated hunting. Whistling conversations with the head keeper, other staff, and virtual pod-mates. Games and entertainment with their mother and the other aquatic residents. Fun for all. And all the funding they'd need for the next ten years.

Her work was known then, over a dozen books, webinars, sea-cliff retreats for the well-heeled. She wasn't despised as much as she would be, not yet labeled an 'ultra-libertard', an 'ocean-head', a 'whale groomer'. The foundation accepted her request.

The offices where they met were located on the harbor. The ground floor conference room in the white-pillared mausoleum-like box was all windows on one wall, with a clear view of the newly-built aquarium sitting near the water, like a silver domed cosmetic box pushed there by some great hand and left to face the surf. It was a white concrete monument, not a home for sentient beings. Yet these people thought they understood cetaceans.

She'd come alone. They'd brought video-documentarians, local politicians, corporate sponsors.

After introductions, she listened through two hours of effusive promotional ideas, their vision of a grand cooperative union between human and orca, an experiment in sustainable harmony, cooperation, and mutual benefit. After this, as her patient silence endured, their enthusiasm flagged, their voices one by one fell quiet. The room's attention shifted unconsciously to the foundation's director, Mrs. Delilah Fernace, founder and CEO of God's True Foods, an organic testing and services corporation, a woman who Neimi might have liked, had she not been so much the aggressive charitable type, for whom altruism was just another arena.

At the end of the presentations, Mrs. Fernace asked Niemi, "What do you think?"

To which, Niemi said simply "It's been tried."

"But not like we intend. This isn't just a sea-zoo we're planning. This is to be a real, working environment. Humans will not make all the decisions. The orcas and dolphins here will be voting members. And we'd like you to show us to hear their voices."

A pang of earnestness struck Niemi, and she almost fell for the spell. Mrs. Fernace was a gifted visionary. One wanted to believe in anything she set forth.

"As long as there are walls," said Niemi, "this will be not a zoo, not a 'zoological garden'. It will be a prison. And the whales will not speak truly. You have been blessed with a miracle birth of fully-sentient beings. You must let them go. Back to the sea, now, while they can still adapt. If you don't act now, they will die.

Perhaps not physically, but emotionally. They will not live as they would wish."

Mrs. Fernace sat silently for a moment, her face reddening.

She said, at last, "We respected you and offered you our hand in cooperation. But you've come under false pretenses, with no intention of joining us. This meeting is over."

The construction of the facility continued, larger tanks, natural plants and settings, like nothing ever built before, and the orca twins and their mother seemed well. They were allowed to interact with orcas in the wild — at least at a distance, since the wild ones stayed away. The captives grew less healthy, less vocal, eating less of the farmed fish they were given, more prone to lethargy.

Niemi was asked about these events during one of her podcasts. Her words were few. "They have heard the voices of their cousins, and they know of the true world they are missing."

Two months later and six months after the miracle birth, a summer strain of Covid virus swept through, this strain virulent among most mammals. The mother and calves were stricken, and only one calf survived. After two months of anti-viral treatments and round-the-clock care, it was a thin version of itself, alive but hardly thriving.

Niemi was asked to speak at a contentious panel discussion on ocean farming, which many felt was the only way to address food shortages among the world's eleven billion humans. Each panelist was allowed closing statements, and Niemi requested to be the last to speak. Rather than reiterate her feelings that ocean farming must be closely-controlled to prevent exploitation and environmental damage, she made a plea.

"This is to the director of 'Whales Forever'. Mrs. Fernace — give me the child. If you truly believe in God's work, give me the child, or it will not live."

Days passed, and then Niemi received a terse message from the foundation's matriarch, delivered in person by a young woman oceanographer, one who had attended several of Niemi's webinars.

The handwritten note read, "The child will be placed in your hands. My messenger, Ms. Montez, will help with the arrangements."

In Grayfin, Niemi led the foundation's vessel carrying the young orca in a watered sling. She hadn't seen Mileva's pod for weeks, but they found her within two hours of the ships leaving the San Diego harbor.

Niemi entered the water first, in scuba gear. The young orphaned orca, a beautiful female called 'Seaflower' by the institute, was lowered into the rolling waves. Niemi and Tanya Montez, the whale's main caregiver, moved with her as she slipped from the harness into the open water, eyeing Tanya wildly, and Niemi with suspicion.

The pod drifted slowly in like ghosts, quietly clicking, two young females moving closest. Fights between orca pods were rare, and strangers were generally accepted or ignored as the extreme. DNA evidence showed that orca females rarely mated within their own pods, so interactions were common, if only for biodiversity.

But there were no certainties.

Seaflower clicked and then one of the wild females whistled. The poor young stranger tried a soft whistle. And then the two females swam in a pattern before the newling, and she followed, away into the ocean gloom.

Would Seaflower tell them of her life among the humans, her illness, the loss of her mother and sister? Was their language so richly sophisticated?

Mileva appeared then, a dark slow-speed torpedo. Tanya started to retreat, but Niemi waved her fear away. The orca swam closer, passing gaze on Tanya, then paused near Niemi, before swimming away with a rocking motion, disappearing after the others. The pod's whistles and clicks grew more distant.

The following week, Tanya joined Niemi's inner circle.

Following the publicity around Seaflower's release, scientists from China and Finland contacted Niemi with a proposal they said she would find attractive. They met secretly, in an abandoned fishers' shed, with two of her assistants knocking around outside on the aged and warped pier. The researchers had a proposal, one that would have intrigued anyone who worked with the few whale species still observed in the wild.

They sat away from her, as if repelled by her natural odor. Dr. Wen Zhang allowed Dr. Hern Ruminen to speak first.

"We have a process. We can place a living human brain inside the skull of a young juvenile member of Orcinus orca."

He explained how they intended to bio-splice the nerves to the medulla oblongata, microsurgery involving elaborate medical robotics and supercomputer AI. The rest of the details bulged like a tide and bowled into Niemi, where she sat in the small office of a fish market south of the city, one of the last places in the USA where one might avoid observation. She knew what they were proposing, even without the details. She would become a whale.

"Of course, the transition," said Dr. Zhang, in a precise voice devoid of accent, "will be very similar to a new birth. Every aspect of living, breathing, swimming, eating, must be learned from the first day of life. There will be no parallel experience. No amount of empathy or living among the subject species will prepare the human participant for this irreversible process." When she didn't react, he cast a side glance at the rigid, gray-templed form of Dr. Ruminen. His voice lost some of its enthusiasm. "This is why it is necessary to place the human brain into the skull of a newborn specimen."

They knew of her writings on inter-species connection, the potential for biological harmony, the only way for the tortured modern world to survive, and then thrive. All living things were part of the same biome, the microcosm bound only by the limits of the atmosphere, and perhaps not even that.

And yet these scientists, these researchers, although sympathetic to her cause, they felt this process, this experiment, this exploitation would be attractive to her. This was the best idea they could bring to her.

"Where will you find a recipient?" she asked, without inflection. Her voice sounded brassy and alien, echoing in the small shack. She had grown to dislike speaking. She had taken to humming along with her many recordings of whale song, those wondrous voices now lost, like the songs of ancient humans.

"It will be necessary to capture a mature, pregnant female and extract a late-term fetus."

Niemi nodded. She choked back her rage, told them it was a very interesting project, and thanked them for considering her. She would respond within a few weeks.

She followed the research through spies she'd placed at their institutions. Months later, after they'd given up on her repeated postponements and found a willing participant, a young military scientist, when the capture ships were being stocked and prepared for the initial hunt, she and three assistants used guided drone submarines to attach deep sonic beacons on the ships' hulls, near the drive units. She was able to track them at all times, and so were the orcas.

Their efforts to capture a pregnant female were unsuccessful.

They came after her, of course. Not the researchers, but the others she was angering the most; international fishing corporations, whose ships were increasingly assaulted by marine life; major religious institutions, whose spiritual messages she was subverting with her drive for harmony and unity through nature, the message that humans lived within nature and not above it, that all living things were citizens, not resources; governments, whose citizens more and more refused to pay for the privilege of citizenship, who were choosing to join the growing movement to an untethered oceanic community, a community that wasn't just universally human, but for all creatures, all living things.

She and many of her followers gathered on handmade rafts and platforms, offshore from San Diego Harbor. They were harassed occasionally by military aircraft, but they were loose, able to deconstruct their floating base in minutes, allow the currents to scatter them, with the occasional help of friendly orcas.

'Humans First' movements hated her the most, and she found great satisfaction in that.

More than once, vigilantes from anti-whale groups attacked them, with weaponized drones and small helicopters. Such attacks were never surprises, always given away by internet traffic, monitored with little effort by friends of Niemi's following. By the time the drones arrived, the flotilla would have vanished, dispersed as if it had never been.

Save one vessel, a small submersible, floating among the black and white bodies and vaporous spray of orcas. If the attackers had looked closely, they would have seen that the largest orca female had a gray marking on one fin, in the shape of a human hand. When the drones fell upon them, they dove straight down, gone in seconds, beyond the reach of weapons and soon beyond the reach of air-based radar and sonar.

The attackers waited. They must rise for breath. They pursued did rise, single whales rising to breathe and dive again in dozens of locations miles apart, and Niemi's submarine was not among them.

But the orca attacks on fishing ships became more sporadic, the losses less important.

The scarcity economics that spread in every continent brought more famine, more disease, and more anger. The world was coming to war, and Niemi's pesky social experiment was forgotten for a time. It became a dim, distasteful memory to most. But to some, a legend.

Her following, hidden in ocean shadows, continued to grow. And with less food competition from other whales and sea predators, the numbers of orcas and the few dolphin species grew with her following.

On a day of gray skies, Mileva lingered by Grayfin, not venturing out, not blowing vapor well up to splash on Niemi where she ate her sea greens, not following the others as she had come to do, watching the younger ones hunt the seas and return to the old grandmother with a hunk of flesh. The time had come for her to pass on, and knowing it was coming still hadn't prepared Niemi.

Twenty-five years had passed for them together. She had loved this whale woman more than her own mother. The connection between them — this was the fabric of heaven, the hope of eternity, the bond of hand to flipper, bodies, worlds, universes.

Mileva — a Slavic name meaning 'gracious'.

Mileva's steamy breaths came slower and shallower, until they just ceased. Her body rocked against Grayfin's hull, as against a lover.

Soon, several big females came to grasp the elder mother by her fins and pull her away, to where Niemi never knew.

Niemi had not wept in many years. But with this loss, she remembered how.

The years passed, like cool ocean waters passing over the skin, leaving the sands and stings and memories of great swims.

They are thousands now, living on a floating island caravan just within sight of the coast, where lay the war-damaged cities and their damaged people. Ropes of kelp and knots of barnacles and coral cling to the old fishing nets and foam plastic balloons lashed beneath, providing ballast, stability when storms rage against it. Gardens spring from the sand and dirt they've collected, seeds and feces dropped by birds, thousands of them. Shimmering fish pinwheel in swarms around and beneath the island. The caravan moves on the wind, nudged at times by those who built cloth sails and turbine masts, holding it in favorable waters.

Guarded by orcas; guided by the moon, the stars, the sun.

It is a warm night.

Niemi climbs from the tarnished and dented and welded hull of Grayfin to gaze upon the caravan a quarter-mile away. A floating city-state it has become, nothing she ever imagined or wanted, a thing sprung from the harmony of being, the harmony of beings. She may have inspired it, but she isn't part of it, is she? Haven't they come for themselves, thinking of her as an idea only? She walks among them sometimes, the hushed tones as she passes, the orcas ever-present. The symbol of the mother orca Mileva is sown into many of their sails, with the gray, human hand pattern on her fin.

The night sky is brilliant, bisected by the pale ribbon of the Milky Way. Her sense of smell is going the way of her body, her sight, her strength, yet the sea air is alive with salt and life, and the hint of death, the ultimate certainty. There is harmony even in the smell of the sea.

How many worlds out there have lost their harmony? How many have lost their whales?

This is the ocean; a pool of interaction, living and passing on, woven lives and minerals and elements. Harmony, in a word. One cannot escape it, not without leaving most of oneself behind, in the infinite song that bounces from shore to shore, island to continent, depth to sky.

Come back, lights, bring our people back home.

The sky remains quiet, the lights do not come. They stopped coming decades ago.

Away over in the colony, flutes and horns, stringed boxes and deep drums begin to play a lilting song — not a song, really, more a feeling, a yearning, a reaching out for ears and jaw teeth to hear. Wailing, whistles, clicks of wood and stone and metal rod. Language in every form, every pitch, vibration in every frequency.

Beneath her, the orcas speak, respond to the music, join the conversation. Niemi has listened to their voices for so many years now, decades, that their language has become her own, like it was her first. She hears every sound, every idea, every dream.

They are thousands now, on hundreds of floating pods in every sea and ocean, around and near every port, the human-orca communities, in salty seas all over the planet, patrolling the shoals, monitoring the sea farming, keeping it within sustainable boundaries. There is spill-over, communities on land springing up, the harmonizing of humans with other primates, elephants, even forests, nearly doomed at one time, but sprouting back to life. The movement was now a tidal wave.

It all started with a few real believers dipping into the water, a ritual they all performed now, to leave the security and technology behind for a short time, to become one with the sea, one with the orcas, to be completely vulnerable. To have a faith like no other, the faith in the impossible community of living spirits. They didn't call it a baptism. The didn't call it anything.

The pain hits Niemi again, this time too hard to ignore, the malignancy that spread from her lungs — micro-dust sarcoma, doctors explained, a condition even bathing in the nurturing salt waters can't cure, so many afflicted with it now. If only she'd had more time to build the sky pods— communities of humans and birds, to patrol and scour. She tries to breath, but great invisible hands crush her from both sides.

"Niemi?" Tanya hears her fall, rushes from Grayfin's cabin, is there, grasping her shoulder.

"It's…huh…time, sister."

"No —"

"Yes. I need…to be…in the water."

Dark fins cut through the ocean soup in the twilight — they always know somehow, the tall black fins of the males, the shorter, sometimes curved dorsals of the females. And there among them, Seaflower, tulip-shaped patches of white on her flippers. They always know, these great beings, these wise ones of the sea. They know when one of their own is about to pass.

"Help me…get these off." Niemi struggles to unbutton the shirt and trousers, but Tanya is there to help.

Many more orca come, as Tanya helps her ease into the cool water, so nice, so delicate a caress on her skin.

"Where…are the lights?" Niemi studies the sky, knowing they are coming, coming to bring their friends, their other peoples back home. The world is better, ready for them. There is harmony now. Isn't this enough?

"What, Niemi? I can barely hear you."

No matter. She can't draw the breath to talk. The whales are around her in the water now, buoying her up, nuzzling her, holding her up to the crisp air as they would a newborn calf. Funny that the air bites her lungs so. Funny how the sky darkens. Is a storm coming?

There. Lights in the sky, moving across the stars, no satellite or abandoned space station. No, these lights are falling, growing brighter as they sink through the miles of atmosphere. Great tankers of water, carrying the children of those huge beings who left before. They are coming. She has done enough.

Her peoples are coming home.

See C.J. Erick's story "Saving the Whales" online at Metaphorosis. If you liked it, leave a comment. Authors love that! Remember to subscribe to our e-mail updates so you'll know when new stories are posted.

About the story

"Saving the Whales" was a coalescing of several themes or concepts that rolled around in my head for months. The first was the idea that consciousness isn't just a network of complex chemical reactions in the brain, but is an energy field that extends beyond the physical boundaries of the skull. This field is influenced by other people around us, environmental conditions such as air quality, and other internal processes, such as our internal biome, including bacteria, viruses, and parasites. From this idea came the concept of 'harmonizing', how all living things and perhaps natural elements come together in a universal conscious community.

Another theme expressed in this story is that of the responsibility of humans above all other creatures to lead the stewardship of the planet. Of all living things, we have the greatest power to alter, manipulate or destroy the living environment. If this is true (and it may not be actually) then we must accept the responsibility to protect and preserve. Failing this, we risk losing it all, bringing about cataclysmic upheaval and mass extinction.

The title "Saving the Whales" seems to invoke the existing lobbies to preserve the cetaceans through ending whaling, better control of pollution, and restricting fishing and naval techniques that harm them. But the title really refers to the alien visitors who step in to protect the whales when humans have failed. The visitors see the true unique value of the whales in 'harmonizing' the world's living biosphere, and move to preserve the whales so they may rise to achieve their calling. That only the 'killer whales' choose to remain among humans is symbolic, and seems very timely with the recent increase in orcas attacking small sailing craft in several places world-wide.

Also, this story started with a line of text, the melancholy first line of the story. "Niemi misses the whales." From there, my mind took off into 'what if' land.

A question for the author

Q: What was your favorite children's book?
A: Excellent question, and I had to go back to memory lane.

I'd like to mention two books. The first is *The Little Engine That Could*. I loved this book because even as a young child I was a lover of underdogs, and those who achieve great things beyond the expectations of others, by the sheer force of self-belief. The second book could be any of the early Dr. Seuss books, but I'll say *If I Ran the Circus*. I loved the zany adventure and creative acts, the bravery of doing something strange as an occupation, and, as with all of his books, the wonderful words!

About the author

C.J. Erick writes in multiple genres, publishes novels in a space fantasy series, and dabbles in poetry. He lives in Dallas area with his wife and their rescue superhero dog Saber-Girl, calls his sourdough bread starter "Ursula" (K. Le Guin), and cooks crazy-good Cajun food for a Midwest Yankee.

www.cjerickfiction.com, facebook.com/cj.erick.9/, Instagram: cee_jay_erick

December

Visions for the Independent City of New York

Cidney Mayes

Addie Bell was six years old when she first held colored drawing pencils between her uncoordinated fingers and made marks on a crumbling map of the old, flooded tunnels beneath the city. It was a typical pastime for a child of her age, but looked different depending on what district of the Independent City of New York the child found themself living in. If Addie had resided in the Cloud District, she would have colored with a stylus on a tablet, swiping in a palette of pixels to drop red into the waiting outline of an apple on her device. Her street would have been clean, her clothes pristine, and the top of her house would have reached like a golden chapel into the sky. If she had lived in the Mids, Addie would have sat in a clump of other children her age, sharing supplies, and fighting over who would get to use their orange pencil to color in the sweet fruit on their alphabet worksheet. Her father would have had a blue-collar job and kept things in the Cloud District running smoothly. He would have been compensated well for his services. Instead, Addie Bell was one of the few children in the Deep, the level of the city that sat closest to the polluted water, to own such a nicety as colored pencils and thought herself very lucky to have such a treasure.

Addie's father, Charlie, was a weathered man with gnarled, arthritic hands who walked the dank streets collecting all manner of items. An accident on an oil rig had robbed him of good posture, unable to perform the necessary heavy lifting out at sea, so he walked the streets and shores looking for things to sell, objects dropped by those who lived above or washed up on the street banks with the tide. Items that would fetch a good price with the junkman were quickly sold, but occasionally he would bring home a gift to his daughter. It was just the two of them who lived in a city-appointed, wooden shack that could not keep out the damp.

When he saw the pencils on a grimy street corner, fallen through a grate in the scaffolding above that held the rest of the city aloft, he pocketed them.

His daughter's rise to fame, and subsequent tragic fall, was not something he anticipated when he handed her the mildewed, tattered box of half-used drawing pencils.

Addie was fascinated with her new colors. Boxes, scraps of paper, and even the walls of their shack became her canvas, filled with faintly drawn shapes and lines. She knew that it would be very hard for her father to find more of the magic pencils, so she used them lightly, delicately, leaving whispers of luminous color one might miss unless they looked carefully.

The day after her father had given her the pencils, Addie went with her neighbor, Mrs. Martinez, while her father went off to pick through flotsam. Together, Addie and Mrs. Martinez walked for half an hour up the winding, unsteady steps to the lower Mids to take their usual spot. While Mrs. Martinez, a short woman with ink-black hair and a kind face, thrust her wooden cup into the path of passersby, pleading for alms, Addie entertained herself by drawing on the cracked concrete, relishing the soft scratch of her pencil against the pebbly surface. Mrs. Martinez's benefactors were quick to give Addie a bit of their change, too, amused and maybe a little wistful that she knew nothing yet of life's hardships and cruelty. Addie accepted the coins shyly, placing them with a muted *clink* into her dress pocket.

She dutifully gave the coins to her father that night. She didn't need them. She had her magic pencils. Besides, her father used the money to buy them something good to eat. Slices of not-too moldy bread and pale cheese, which they toasted over their stove. Addie drew a picture of herself and her father, eating their cheesy toasts together, which he accepted with wet eyes and pinned to the wall of their shack.

Everything changed the day a city official, clothed in white and carrying a tablet that glowed blue, meandered down the street. He stopped occasionally, making notes on his screen, and commiserating with his assistant about the poor conditions of the Lower Mids. Addie watched out of the corner of her eye and noted that the hem of his pristine robe was smeared with dirt. He mumbled to his assistant, something about 'real change this term'. He stopped in front of Addie's spot and cocked his head, staring at her with the curiosity of a cat watching a fish floundering in the shallows.

Addie kept her eyes fixed on her work. She drew faces of people on the street with surety, tiny birds who rummaged through the trash bin with realistic detail, and the market streets of the Mids with captivating perspective. Her drawings had a strange, bright quality due to her odd color choices. Addie felt the hair on the back of her neck prickle as the man watched her. Finally, he cleared his throat, and asked, "Child, what is your name?"

"Addie Bell," she replied, not looking up from her work. People around them grew quiet. Mrs. Martinez clutched her wooden cup and took a few steps closer to her charge.

The city official, more astute than his peers who had never left their borough in the skies, sensed the uneasiness at his presence. The citizens were wary of his pointed interaction. "Well, Addie Bell, might I commission you to draw something for me?" He held a silver coin between two fingers. It caught the light, and the small crowd grew larger.

Addie looked up from her work then, sensing the shift in the air. Her face pinched in confusion. She had seen men in pristine, pale clothing walking in the streets every once in a great while, but never had any of them spoken to her. Nor had she ever seen a silver coin before. "I only trade for 3 coppers," she said nervously.

The crowd tittered as the city official flashed a toothy smile. Addie's cheeks flushed; her stomach flipped. She felt suddenly self-conscious. Everyone was looking at her.

"I see. This is worth two hundred coppers. If you draw what I ask for, you are welcome to keep the extra." He kept the smile plastered on his face as his assistant withdrew a smaller tablet and held it in front of her, capturing the interaction on video.

Addie looked to Mrs. Martinez for confirmation of this sum, who gave her a tight nod. "Okay. What would you like me to draw?"

"Have you ever seen the city from a distance away, where all the buildings can be seen together, reaching into the sky?"

Addie shook her head as her eyes pricked with tears. She didn't understand what the man wanted, and everyone was still staring. All she knew how to draw was what she saw, and she had no idea how to draw what he wanted.

"Let me show you." The city official swiped his fingers around his tablet and flipped it around for her to see the photo of the city's skyline.

Addie stared at the picture for thirty seconds, taking in the shapes and details of the buildings that stacked on top of one another, clawing for purchase, trying to escape the rising sea beneath them. "Okay," she said, once she had memorized all she needed to. She spread a clean sheet of paper on the concrete and began to draw, now oblivious to the swell of people around her. Addie grabbed colored pencils, seemingly at random, as the buzz from the crowd fell into the background. She used her whole arm to draw wide swaths of color, painting the sky in a frenzied rainbow, then placed the buildings against it, exactly as she had seen in the photo.

When she was done, she stood and placed her hands on her hips, scrutinizing her work. Satisfied, she handed the drawing to the city official as his assistant took a photo of the exchange. Everyone clapped politely. The city official handed the silver coin to Addie, who thought it felt very heavy, and left with his drawing. The crowd dispersed, and Addie and Mrs. Martinez bought a hearty dinner to bring home, as well as a sealed box of brand-new colored pencils which Addie clutched tightly to her chest.

The video, artfully edited by the official's press team, went viral the next day. The drawing was posted to the city official's website with the tagline *a vision of what the Independent City of New York could be*. Cloud District citizens, as well as Upper Mids, loved it. The comments poured into all social channels, hashtags trended, and approval ratings went up, up, up.

Addie was unaware that anything had changed. The next day, she and Mrs. Martinez returned to their street corner and went about their business as usual. They did not know that the city official was very astute and knew just how to keep the buzz going. He made some calls and secured for Addie Bell a scholarship to a prestigious STEAM Academy where science, technology, engineering, art, and mathematics students studied to become the next generation of city leaders.

More men wearing cloud-white uniforms appeared that afternoon, stepping out of a black car. Addie felt her stomach twist into knots as they approached. Mrs. Martinez stepped in front of her, blocking her from their view. It took some convincing for Mrs. Martinez to move aside and let them talk to the young girl. They asked where her father was, and when she told him, one of the men scrunched up his nose like he'd gotten too close to the Deep's standing water. With Addie leading them, they descended rickety stairs to the banks of the Deep.

Her father stood, arms crossed and shabby clothes hanging from his thin frame, as the official's men showed him a piece of paper with a shiny seal. They spoke of moving, of government allowances, of giving Addie *opportunity*. Addie's father stood as still as stone, distrustful. He believed it was all a sham until they showed him the viral video, and asked Addie herself. "Wouldn't you like to go to school? To take some art classes?"

Addie's eyes grew wide. She nodded, unable to speak. Mrs. Martinez often spoke of school. It sounded like a wonderful place.

Seeing Addie's face, her father finally set down his collection bucket, grabbed his daughter's hand, and followed the men. Mrs. Martinez and their neighbors watched them go, with smiles that did not quite reach their eyes.

Another video aired on the city broadcast. It was a compilation of quick cuts set against an uplifting song, showing Addie accepting her scholarship, moving into a house on the outskirts of the Cloud District with her father, and walking past the gates of the STEAM Academy. Her life, compressed into a forty-second press piece, could not convey the unbridled joy she felt as she stepped into her first art class, how her heart fluttered against her ribs, how her fingers itched to draw.

In the Academy, students sat in a ring, their heads bowed like acolytes before their easels. Each flicked their eyes towards the center of their circle, observing a bowl of fresh fruit set before them. A white-robed instructor sat Addie before an easel and told her to draw. The next two hours flew by in a blur of color and shape. Addie had never known such peace, to sit and draw undisturbed, listening to gentle music.

At the end of the class, the work was critiqued. Addie listened as students commented on one another's shading techniques, use of color, or perspective. Addie's drawing was last. It left the class speechless. She did not simply draw the fruit and the table on which it sat like everyone else. She drew her view of the whole room, including the instructor as he paced between easels, the students at worship before their own art, the sweeping pillars that held the ceiling aloft, in her signature display of churning color.

Addie twisted her hands, nervous at their silence. Tears stung the corners of her eyes as her fear and shame grew. Her art did not look like everyone else's.

"It is extraordinary," the instructor finally declared, and students began hounding Addie with questions. They clapped her on the back, praised her composition, and marveled at her color palette. Addie smiled so wide that her cheeks began to hurt and felt as if her chest could burst from happiness.

After that, people began to call Addie Bell *singularly talented, visionary,* and *genius.* A month went by, then two, and Addie settled into her new life. She and her father took to spending their weekends in the park, taking picnics of fresh fruit and bread. Addie like to draw her father sitting in the grass, running his hands through it, marveling at its softness, head tipped to welcome the sun on his skin. In the Deep he'd always been hunched, plagued with coughing spasms. A visit to the doctor had finally cleared the ailment in his chest, and he now breathed much more easily. While Addie went to school, he got a job in the Mids sorting scrap metal in a factory. It wasn't glamorous work, but he made a decent wage and was home in the early evening to share supper with his daughter and listen to her talk excitedly about her day.

As she grew up, Addie became the most celebrated artist in her school. Requests for her artwork poured into the Academy from Cloud District citizens, for everyone with taste wanted a Bell original for their homes. Her instructors encouraged her to examine the world around her, noting the line, shape, and shadow of her environment. Addie drew and painted, observing her subjects closely. And the more she saw, the angrier she became.

It started with small things, trivial points of friction with her classmates. The other students who grew up in the sun and sky knew nothing of the damp that swallowed those who lived below them in the Deep. They teased her for being an outsider, then grew jealous when she stole all the attention of her art teachers. She did find friends, and enjoyed spending time with them, but they could never understand where she had come from. When she tried to tell them what it was like growing up in the Deep, she was met with uncomfortable silence. Such things were not talked about. The news did not even mention any happening south of the Mids. "Well, you live here now," they would say, and the conversation quickly moved on to shopping and crushes.

Her father did not like to linger on the past, either. Addie could not bear the pain in his eyes when she tried to bring it up. So, the picture in her mind of the Deep grew faded and fuzzy, time softening the harshness of her memory. But she always thought fondly of Mrs. Martinez and wondered how she was doing. It did not seem right to bury the past so easily, so she kept the dulled shards of her memories, the jabs from her classmates, their lack of understanding, pressed tight against her ribs where they pricked her heart when she lay in bed, trying to find sleep.

On the day of her sixteenth birthday, the dulled shards of her pain were sharpened to razor points when she saw the news. The broadcast played on the screen in her room as she dressed for school. There was no way to change the channel. The broadcasts came at scheduled intervals, morning and night, regardless of if they were wanted or not. The reports reminded them all how lucky they were, and the dangers of what happened when one strayed too far from the confines of the Cloud District. This morning, the broadcast was a tale of the latter. A report on a crackdown of panhandling in the lower Mids, an effort for city-wide improvement.

Addie watched in disbelief, hairbrush halfway through her tresses, as Mrs. Martinez flashed across the screen. She, and a few other faces she recognized, were moved off their street corner by Cloud guards. The old woman's hair was streaked with silver, the lines of her face deep with dismay, her back hunched, but there was no mistaking her. Time had not been as kind to her as it had to Addie.

With trembling hands, Addie tied her hair into its neat twist. She hugged her father goodbye, slung her bag over her shoulder, and marched to school. Her thoughts were in tangles. At the beautiful gates where she had nearly wept with joy upon first seeing them, she felt her cheeks flush and acid creep up her throat. Her feet were cemented to the sidewalk. The sight of Mrs. Martinez's face had rattled something deep within her, and Addie could not make herself go inside. Instead, she turned on her heel and began the very long walk out of the Clouds.

Addie strode past the towering, gilded homes to the first flight of stairs made of cement and iron. Down she went, minutes turning to hours, descending to the Mids. The smell of standing water filtered up from the Deep even here. It stung her nose and sharpened those memories that had gone as soft and blurry as blended pastels. Her shoes were dirty and stained by the time she reached the corner where she'd spent her days drawing on the rough concrete. Mrs. Martinez was nowhere to be found. There were very few people around and the street was oddly quiet, given that it was midday. Addie hadn't really expected her to be here. She took a long breath through her nose, adjusted her school bag, and took the rickety stairs back down to the Deep, ignoring the strange looks from passersby.

The shack was smaller than she remembered. Addie rapped on the rough wooden door with her knuckles, and a faint voice called through it. "Who's there?"

Addie spoke past the lump in her throat. "It's Addie, Mrs. Martinez. Addie Bell."

The door opened a crack. Only Mrs. Martinez's wide eyes were visible. "Oh, mija, it's really you. Come in, quick."

Addie stepped inside the shack and took the offered seat on a three-legged stool. Mrs. Martinez sat on her bed with a groan. "Mija, what are you doing here? Don't you have school? A smart girl like you shouldn't be missing your classes."

"I came to see how you were doing." Addie decided not to tell her that the reason for her visit was because she had seen her on the broadcast, and that she wanted to relieve herself of the invisible guilt that she carried with her. She had thought that seeing Mrs. Martinez would make her feel better. It only made her chest ache.

Mrs. Martinez's eyes darted to the door. "That's very sweet, but I think you should go back home." She inhaled a wet, raspy breath and coughed, her body shaking under the attack.

Addie stood, alarmed. She sounded worse than her father ever had. "You should see a doctor," she said, once the coughing had subsided.

"No doctor will see me," Mrs. Martinez croaked.

"Why not?"

"I don't have insurance."

Addie narrowed her eyes. "What's insurance? You're sick. Papa saw a doctor and ..." Addie stopped at the sad look that passed across her former caretaker's face. Her cheeks burned, mortified. Of course, her father had only seen a doctor when they moved into their Cloud house. "I'm sorry," she said softly.

"It's okay. I'm glad you came to see me. I've missed you, but you really should be in school."

Addie stood and gathered her bag. "You're right. I'm happy I got to see you. Bye, Mrs. Martinez." She gave the old woman a careful hug and left. Instead of heading towards the shaky stairway, she walked along the damp, grimy streets of the Deep, stopping when she reached the sickly lapping of the water's edge. Had it always been this far up the street?

She stood, gazing out past the gloom of the rusty beams that held the city aloft. The water sloshed in and out, reeking of sewage and decay. A dead seagull, wings akimbo, floated nearby.

Whispers of dissent had been bubbling up from the Deep for some time. She had overheard her classmates, the children of government officials, share stories in hushed voices. They spoke of strikes, protests, retaliation. The ember of anger that had ignited in her chest this morning turned into a roaring flame. The sea was eroding homes, eating away at their crumbling foundations, yet the Mids did not welcome the people who lived in the Deep into their level of the city. Addie could not imagine the Clouds ever doing anything to help.

She looked at her shoes, stained from her trek. Shame made her eyes prick with tears. She'd been so blind; dazzled by the sparkling life she'd been given. Why had she been chosen, out of all the people here, to move up to the Clouds? Addie felt, suddenly, that she did not deserve it.

That night at home as she lay in bed, unable to sleep, she searched for her own name on her tablet. She found a video that had aired after her first art class. A reporter had taken a short clip of Addie with her still-life drawing, the one she'd been so proud of on her first day. When asked about the nature of her composition, she replied that she'd drawn what she saw. She scrolled and found the video from the city official, the one with the tagline, *a vision of what New York could be.*

Addie pushed herself out of bed and hastily cleared her worktable. She grabbed her colored pencils and began to draw a copy of her own artwork. She drew it nearly identical to the original, with swirling colors and the city skyline. Only this time, she added a slashing line of blue: the ocean rising to swallow the city, bodies floating in the water. She scrawled *a vision of what New York WILL be* across it in jarring red.

By the time she was done, the sun was just beginning to rise. Addie readied herself for school, ignoring the broadcast that played yet another cautionary tale. She placed her newest piece into her portfolio, tucking it safely between other drawings. Addie hugged her father a little tighter than usual as she said goodbye.

While everyone else was in their classes, Addie stole away to the workroom. She made dozens of copies of her newest piece, printing bundles of flyers which she shoved into her bag. Lastly, she made a large banner, wider than her arms and half as tall as she was. Perspiration beaded on her brow as the laser printer did its work, rolling out her print one inch at a time. It finished just as morning classes were dismissed. Her heart pounded in her ears as she rolled up the giant banner and marched back out the school gates.

She walked, head held high, straight to the heart of the Cloud District. At every corner, she tossed a few flyers from her bag, marring the pristine streets. She moved quickly, not stopping to hear the shocked murmurs at her behavior, or the fearful whispers of rebellion. A little drone began to follow her once she was three blocks away from her destination. She broke into a run, anxiety making her swift.

On the steps of the capital, Addie dropped her school bag and rolled out her banner. The drone had caught up with her and was now beeping shrill commands. Heavy footsteps sounded on the marble steps, but Addie did not look up from her work. She pushed the paper until it unfurled across the stairs. She stood, hands on her hips, studying her work. She could not hear the shouts above the sound of her own pounding heart, but she felt hands grab her roughly at the elbows. She was steered into a car that hovered off the street by Cloud guards, their faces obscured by helmets.

Addie did not feel scared until they escorted her to a windowless, white room that smelled of antiseptic. Her stomach clenched in fear as they pinched her arm with a needle that put her to sleep, and set about dissecting what had given this girl from the Deep the audacity and to paint the world in such colors.

Addie Bell's fall from grace was a brief news headline on the evening broadcast. Too many people had seen the flyers for the incident to not be addressed. It made for a wonderful cautionary tale. Clouds sneered at their screens and removed their Bell originals from their walls in shame, for the little girl from the Deep had no real talent at all. It was, in fact, a horrible anomaly of her vision that distorted her way of viewing the world. For Addie Bell was colorblind and did not perceive the world as those with all their proper eye cones did. She had been picking colors blindly, scribbling nonsense onto her canvases. There was no real *vision* there at all. And her vulgar art did not paint the whole picture, the effort the city was making to stem the rising seas, to help clean up the streets of the lower districts. The Clouds washed their hands of her and went about their lives.

Addie was questioned. The government wanted to know whom she was working with, who had given her orders to destroy her own art. Her answers were simple, and honest. After a few hours of questioning, when they had given up trying to extract names of other dissenters from her, they left her alone in a cell.

Her father watched the nighttime broadcast in stunned disbelief. He couldn't believe that his sweet, gentle daughter had done something so rash. He pressed his gnarled fingers to his mouth as images of her face flashed across the screen. He had no idea the rage she had carried inside her. His own anger had burned down to ashes long ago. He shrugged back into his jacket and walked under the golden glow of streetlamps to city hall.

No one could tell him where his daughter was. There was no record of her or where she had gone. He was turned away politely the first three times. On the fourth day, armed guards escorted him down the pristine marble steps where Addie had unfurled her banner, forbidding him from asking again.

In a last effort, he traipsed back down to the Deep, as Addie had done a week prior. He knocked on Mrs. Martinez's splintered door, and was welcomed in. She gasped wetly for breath. Her skin had the telltale gray tinge of lung sickness. When he told her of what had happened to Addie, fat tears slid down her cheeks.

"But you should be proud," she said as she dried her face. "She's a very brave girl."

He wanted to feel pride. Instead, he felt hollow. He thanked Mrs. Martinez for her time and began his long trek home, heart aching. Addie had given him something he could not give her in return: safety, and a place among the Clouds.

After the first few weeks, Addie lost track of how long she'd spent in the prison. She wondered if it had done any good, spreading her message through the streets. She hoped her father could forgive her, even if he never understood why she'd done it. Over time, her face paled, regaining the ghostly pallor of her girlhood. Her days dragged on in monotony, devoid of sun, art, and companionship. Sometimes, Addie found her fingers curling delicately, as if embracing one of her pencils, the habit hard to shake. At night, she fell asleep with a soft smile upon her lips and dreamed of a sky stained with a kaleidoscope of color.

See Cidney Mayes's story "Visions for the Independent City of New York" online at Metaphorosis.
If you liked it, leave a comment. Authors love that!
Remember to subscribe to our e-mail updates so you'll know when new stories are posted.

About the story

I typically write my short fiction in 24-48 hours. If I am feeling very passionate about an idea, it's best for me to get as much onto paper as possible, even if that first draft is incredibly messy. My first foray into short fiction was through 48-hour contests, so I think my brain has been trained to operate in this way.

A lot of inspiration for this story comes from the housing crisis where I live in Portland, Maine. I have been increasingly struck by the sight of homeless encampments that have appeared, and continue to grow, here. Every few weeks, the city will break up the encampments and people will just move their tents to a different park or underpass. In contrast, more and more real estate is being built to attract wealthy buyers to sparkling waterfront properties. In a city of only 68,000, this disparity is shocking.

Expanding this polarity of socio-economic status into a giant city, set in the future, provided the foundation for this story. Addie is from the Deep, a place where her home is slowly being eaten away by rising seas, and the government doesn't really care about what happens to her or her neighbors. They're only concerned with aesthetics and in keeping up their idea of luxury, even though their wealth is literally built on the labor and lives of the people who live directly below them.

A question for the author

Q: If someone wanted to make an animated series out of your work, based on the title or recurring themes, what would it look like?

A: My favorite thing about this story is its setting. I envision the levels of this future New York City to have distinct designs, aesthetics, and color schemes. The Deep is dark and bleak, with steel ocean-gray tones. Old, rusted fire escapes create a lattice above the rotting buildings on this lower level, holding up the rest of the city. The Mids are an amalgamation of culture, color, and sound; much like present day New York. Though, they don't receive much natural light either. Their light comes from artificial sun lamps, and coveted real-estate is on the outer edges of the city where light can pierce the gloom. The Clouds, the upper level of the city where the wealthy and powerful reside, is a soft, airy place. Greco-Roman architecture, the best in new technology, salt-kissed breeze, and blinding sun abound. The clothes are sleek, soft-edged, and pale, much like wisps of clouds.

In an ideal world, the storyline for an animated series adaptation would focus on different characters who live here. Addie, the main character in this story, had one vision for New York; but this is a behemoth of a city. What would the lives of someone from the Mids or Clouds look like? How could their stories interweave to create a larger picture of the city and show how it evolved from the New York we know today into this one? In my mind, I have a lot of backstory on who governs the city, how they rose to power, and how they are battling not only the rising seas, but other power-hungry politicians as well as a populace on the brink of collapse.

About the author

Cidney Mayes is a middle school librarian from Portland, Maine with a passion for anything magical. When not writing, she enjoys giving tarot card readings, walking outdoors with a good audio book, or playing board games with her husband and friends.

cidneymayes.com, X/Twitter: @CidneyMayes. Instagram: Cidney.mayes

The Final Face

Norah Lovelock

There were seventeen people left between Dia and the end of her commission.

Failed colonies were too expensive to run, difficult to maintain, and so her commission had sent her here to collect up the stragglers, put them into cyro, and take them back to the homeworlds. FC3-268b, dubbed Rija by the locals, was the last planet on her very long list. There were seventeen people left for her to collect.

And when it was over, she'd have to return to Central. She was old and damaged. She could make an educated enough guess: they'd decommission her. Upload her memories to some storage somewhere and forget she ever existed: the fate of most custodians, useless until they weren't.

This colonist's house was away from the others. Against the general backdrop of neglect, it was stark in its upkeep. The front door was painted an obnoxiously bright yellow, the brickwork repaired instead of crumbling. Dead bushes wilted below its wide bay windows. Dia gave herself a moment. She was tired. She had done this thousands of times, yet it never grew easier. Then, finally, when she could wait no longer, she stepped close and knocked.

It took a minute before it opened. A pair of eyes squinted suspiciously at her from the narrow crack between the wood and frame. Then the stranger noted the ruins of Dia's faceplate, her torn plastic skin and exposed, stained circuitry, and said, conversationally, "You look like shit, don't you?"

Dia did look like shit. It had been a long time since she'd had maintenance beyond what she could do for herself. Working on planets several hundred lightyears away from Central did that to a robot. Her plastic skin had been torn by a particularly aggressive mammal on a desert planet, her faceplate ripped out by a colonist with a vendetta. Once, she might have been able to disguise herself as human—convince the humans, as immoral as it was, that she could understand their plight, making it easier to take them to the sleepship. Maybe—and the thought alone felt traitorous—she might've been able to run: find a nearby space station, hide herself among the humans, as innocuous and invisible as any of them. Maybe it was a childish dream. Sometimes, it felt like it was all she had.

But her visible circitry betrayed her and there was no way for her to repair herself. She would have to wait until she returned to Central to see what they'd do to her.

"Thank you," she said dryly, inclining her head. The humans never greeted her warmly. "May I come in? I'm a custodian. I'm here to help."

After another moment of suspicious squinting, the woman pulled the door open wider and stepped aside. "All right."

The house was cluttered. The walls were filled with photos, competing for space against framed prints, children's drawings pinned into the drywall. Belongings filled every empty surface: magazines, crocheted pillowcases, blankets, coasters. Considering how beloved the woman appeared, it was fascinating that she lived here, alone in this big house, removed from the rest of the remaining colonists.

The woman led her through the chaos to an equally chaotic kitchen, where she sat at the table. After a moment of deliberation, Dia sat too.

"I'm Dia. What's your name?"

"Alma," the woman said, leaning forward, elbows on her thighs. "You here to convince me to leave, then? Homeworlds decided that Rija isn't worth supplying anymore?"

Dia immediately knew this was not a conversation she could win. Her spiel had been ready: her polite, well-practiced, 'I'm a custodian from Central. Due to cost-cutting measures, we're asking the residents of Rija to relocate back to the homeworlds via sleepship. You *can* choose to stay, but the food packets will stop, and you'll be disconnected from the network.' Alma had beaten her to the punch.

"No," she demurred. "I'm just wondering who'd want to stay behind."

Alma snorted. "Only ever known this place, haven't I?"

She'd heard that excuse hundreds—thousands—of times before. It was no longer compelling. "You are aware that Central will set you up on whichever of the homeworlds you'd prefer? That you'll be cut off from food packets and the network?"

"Of course. I don't want to leave, though. Not gonna pack all my stuff—" and, waving an expansive hand, it was clear she had a lot of it, "—into a suitcase for the sake of some mandate I didn't even choose."

Dia still asked the question, as rote as it had become: "Don't you have people who care about you? Friends who'll miss you if you stay behind?"

Alma scoffed. "Ain't no-one here who gives a damn about me."

It felt like a lie, but Dia didn't know enough to argue. She didn't want to argue. She wanted to leave. "I take it I won't be able to convince you."

"No," Alma said sharply. Then she paused, her lips twitching with sudden mirth, and added, "And anyway, I like the weather."

There wasn't any weather to like. Rija was a miserable planet. The buildings were grey; the scant vegetation was muted and dull. Only far out at sea did the planet gain colour: the deep green of algae, the planet's primary source of oxygen.

And here, beside the shuttle, the rest of the town was collapsing into the ocean. From afar, the tide was foam-tipped; closer, just below where Dia stood, the waves gnawed hungrily at the ruins of houses. Overhead, it was drizzling: fine, thin, terrible stuff that made her want to shield her ripped forehead with her hand to try and stop the water from reaching her electronics.

Trust her final assignment to be on a wet planet. With her broken faceplate, it was the last thing she needed.

"Hello?" a voice called. "Are you from Central?"

She turned. It was a family: three adults, an infant, huddled against the rain. Her processors sparked with recognition: she'd seen them on the info sent from Central. "We saw the shuttle," one of them said, his eyes roaming her face. "You've brought a sleepship, haven't you?"

"I have," she said gently. It was up in orbit, waiting for its final passengers. "You want to go up?"

They did.

Once the humans and their luggage were inside, Dia set the autopilot, leaned back in the pilot's seat, and watched out the window as the planet grew small beneath them.

Her thoughts drew back to Alma; Alma, who seemed so bizarrely possessive of this ugly, backwater planet. Sure, it had a breathable atmosphere, but that was hardly rare. Even from the sky it was monochrome. Only as they entered orbit did it gain beauty: the grey cut by great swathes of white cloud, the ocean revealed to be swirls of deep navy and dark green. She couldn't help her cynicism. The miracle of orbit could make anything beautiful.

And in orbit, too, was the sleepship, dignified against the backdrop of stars. In the back, the humans were talking, nervous but quiet. She'd be nervous too, if she were human.

Inside the sleepship, there were rows upon rows of cyro pods: thousands of them, patiently waiting for the person inside to wake. She had recited her explanation so often that it no longer held meaning: each pod was a cryo system. It would freeze them but would feel like taking a very long and timeless nap, and when they woke up, they'd be in Central.

They were scared. They also couldn't go back now. When all were all settled, she sealed the pods. On her custodian node, she set the countdown and the commands; watched as the drugs kicked in, and, one by one, as they fell asleep. Eventually, the lights in their pods turned off. They began to freeze.

When she had first received this sleepship, she had been a different custodian with a different name. The ship had been empty. She'd been excited.

And now she'd sat through near a thousand cycles of travel, been to deserts and mountains, valleys and moons, and all she wanted now was to go back to Central. She didn't care if they decommissioned her; not anymore. She wanted this done. She wanted to rest.

Without any humans around, the room slipped into darkness to conserve energy. She didn't bother wishing them sweet dreams. They couldn't hear her anymore.

She took the shuttle back planet-side. There were just three families left: two bigger families and Alma. The thought of collecting them exhausted her, but the end was in sight.

According to the intel she'd been given via custodian node—and she did *not* envy whichever custodian had been tasked with reconnaissance—the families occupied a single row of houses, well-kept in comparison to the abandoned building. Despite the drizzle, she went on foot, angling her head down to try and keep her internal components dry.

Whoever had done recon had done a good job, because they were right. Three terraced houses huddled together against a long row, the front gardens overfull with exotic fauna: bright orange, luminous purple, stark in the gloom.

And Alma was outside. She was leaning against the doorframe, chatting to a man inside, her tone light and cheerful.

It was awfully coincidental that Alma had claimed no-one here liked her, yet here she was, conversational—warm. Then she turned and her expression narrowed. "Here to spirit this family away too, then?"

"No," Dia said, and pressed her hand against her still-attached forehead plate to try and shield the worst of the rain. "They went voluntarily."

"Only because you bullied them into it."

The man interjected with a valiant, "Alma! Don't be mean to it!", but it was clear Alma would not be deterred. She waved her hand at him, scowling. "Go look after the kids, Mailer. Tell 'em I'll give 'em electronics classes next week—if you're still here."

Dia wanted to retort with something sharp—that keeping them here would serve no purpose but their deaths; that Alma's determination to stay didn't grant her the right to trap everyone else here, too; that it certainly was strange that no-one cared for her, but she was giving electronics classes. Then the feeling faded. Arguing wouldn't help. It very rarely did.

Alma turned on her heel and began to make her way down the road. Dia paused—then, deciding Mailer was a future problem, followed. She fell into step. "Electronics classes?"

Alma shot her a sharp glance. "None of your business."

"I never suggested it was," she responded, purposefully mild. "You don't have to tell me anything you don't want to."

That earned her another sidelong glare—and then, after a moment of silence, a sigh. "A long time ago, I used to be a custodian technician."

A technician? They were rare to find outside of the Central homeworlds—near impossible to find on any of the planets Dia had ever been deployed to. Hope, sudden and terrible, rose in her chest. Maybe there were options beyond decommission. "You could replace my faceplate."

Alma stopped walking. She stared up at her, squinting through the rain, the droplets catching on her lashes. "Why d'you think I'd help you out?"

It felt so obvious to say it was nearly painful: "I need help, and you're the first technician I've encountered."

"Obviously," Alma grumbled. "I just dunno why you're coming to me. We're not friendly."

They weren't. But right now, that didn't matter, because Alma had something Dia needed—needed so desperately her electronics ached with it. "What do you want from me in exchange?"

"I don't want anything from you." She began to walk, expecting Dia to fall back into step, then said, tightly: "Fine. I'll do it. How bad's the damage on your internal circuitry?"

It was that easy? And she didn't even want anything in exchange? Dia spoke quickly before either of them could change their minds: "I can't smile properly, but I'm sure you've already noticed that. Anything else I wouldn't be too sure about."

"Thought you new models could self-diagnose?"

"I'm not a new model," she said wryly. "Can you do it or not?"

"Of course I can *do* it." Alma said it quickly, like it was a point of pride. She pushed open her front door, stepped inside, then turned to survey Dia properly: a long, slow look up and down. "All right. My workshop's in the basement, and it's drier down there than up here."

She had been expecting a small workshop—maybe enough for a single table, some spare parts. She hadn't been expecting a full workroom. There was a table in the centre for the custodian to lie on, whilst the walls were lined with shelves containing every part Dia knew she contained and then some.

Out here, so far from Central, there surely weren't enough custodians to warrant this level of set up. Rija was a backwater planet in a backwater system. While custodians were everywhere, there couldn't ever have been enough work to be able to make it into a *career*.

She turned to Alma, eyebrow raised. "You've been hiding this down here?"

"Not hiding," she retorted, but folded her arms and shifted her weight. "Everyone already knows. Kept up with it even after I retired." She looked back at Dia, then said, curt, "The face plates are up there. Choose one."

She did as instructed, depositing options on the table, trying to hide her delight. She could be whole once again. There were faces of every size and shape, colouring and structure: brown eyed, purple eyed; freckled or scarred or neither or both. With every face, potential opened before her. She plucked through them until one felt *right*: dark eyed and dark skinned, similar to the plastic skin on the rest of her body. "This one," she said, and pressed her finger to feel the way its—soon to be *her*—cheek compressed. She looked up at Alma. "Do I wanna know how you got it?"

Alma plucked it up in deft hands. "I bought it." Her fingers skated along its still cheek. Some deep tenderness shone through in her face, enough to wipe away her sullenness—but when she looked at Dia she was surly once more. "Do you want to power off? It'll be uncomfortable if you stay awake."

"I don't mind."

"Lie down," Alma instructed, and turned away to a metal chest of drawers to bring out her tools.

Dia lay. The table was cool against her back and neck, but not unpleasantly so. She couldn't see what Alma was doing, but she had been repaired enough to take a guess at what she could hear: Alma was pulling out a wheeled stool to perch on; the way the metal bolts and screws clinked against each other as she plucked them out of the drawers and into tiny bowls. She got out a drill and a set of screwdriver attachments, prepared a cotton swab and rubbing alcohol.

Finally, she was ready. Alma flicked on lights bright enough to blind a human. "Are you sure about this?"

Well, it wasn't like she could mess Dia's face up any further. She shut her eyes. "Yes."

Alma began by unscrewing something below Dia's chin, soft skin against her sensors—and then those same hands darted up, unscrewing something else near her temple. The touch was overwhelming, too fast for her to meaningfully process—fingers on the wires in her face, knuckles against the inside of her skull, and Dia knew she didn't need to breathe, but it left her breathless anyway: the terrible intimacy of it, this woman inside her, taking her apart.

Then, finally, a part of her face came away. She heard it hitting the little table next to her, metal and cold. Next, she knew, would come the specific servos to support the musculature of the face she'd once worn; the tiny processor that made it move.

She hadn't expected Alma to need to wriggle it out. Every careful nudge of those fingers felt like an earthquake. It left her tense, every fibre of her locked into stillness, Alma's knuckles warm against the inside of her face—that terrible face; the one she hated to have, hated to see, the touch burning like fire.

"Are you alright?" Alma asked, voice low. "I'm about halfway through. Do you need a break?"

"I'm fine," she said. Her voice, the traitor, didn't even quiver. "Are you okay to keep going?"

Alma paused. "Yes," she said finally, and the wriggling resumed.

Dia lay there and tried not to move; tried not to use her processor in thinking how Alma's hands were so hot inside of her, removing and discarding the parts of her that no longer functioned. And then, quite suddenly, it was too much: this room, the overhead lights, the feeling of someone poking at the exposed parts of herself. "I need a break," she breathed, and this time her voice shook.

"I'm almost done," Alma groused. She wriggled the processor sharply, and Dia stopped processing data entirely.

And then, finally, it came out, and Alma's hands withdrew, and Dia could *think* again. She sat up, jerking up without the excess weight of her broken faceplate, itching all deep inside like a wound she couldn't touch.

Alma didn't even have the grace to look at her. She was poking the ancient parts on the tray, turning them this way and that. "Hope I didn't ruin any of the prongs," she murmured to herself. She glanced up at Dia and, with characteristic brusqueness, said, "Lie down again. We're not done. Need to put the new one on."

Could Dia lie down? Could she tolerate even a moment more of that touch, so terribly invasive? She wasn't sure, but she had to. Walking around with no faceplate would be worse than a broken one. There would be no future for her at all. She forced her body back down onto the table and lay utterly still, not even letting her hands clench into fists.

But what had been difficult was now easy. She kept an eye on her internal chronometer as Alma worked, watching the minutes count down. Alma did the same in reverse to the new face: attached the processor, plugged in the circuit boards and servos, and made it align with the rest of her head. None of it took very long, even if Alma's hands were burning hot; even if Dia wanted, just a little, to crawl out of her own skin.

Slowly, hyperaware of her new eyelids, she opened her eyes to let them focus and unfocus. And finally, as Alma cleared off the finishing touches, Dia installed her new drivers.

Alma's hands drew away. The overhead light flickered off. "There," she said finally, quiet. "We're done."

Dia sat up. The weight of her new face was unfamiliar—heavier, but welcome. When she brought her hand up to touch, there was no longer the tangle of wires and circuits, but flesh—a little cooler than human temperature, but *hers*. Her nose; her lips.

"Want a mirror?"

"Please," Dia begged.

Alma held one up for her. If Dia had had a heart, it would've stopped—because it was her, Dia, but she wore a stranger's face. Unfamiliar, but not for long. She stared at herself and made faces, stretched her mouth and crinkled her nose in an attempt to remind herself that this was her, now. She checked the groove between her neckplate and faceplate and, if she hadn't known, wouldn't've been able to tell there was a seam at all.

Hope, sudden and terrible, rose in her chest. The suffering felt suddenly worth it, like she had gone through something terrible for something redemptive at the other side. And her discomfort hadn't entirely been Alma's fault. She could allow a little praise. "I'm not sure a Central technician could've done a better job."

"Thanks," Alma said, watching Dia's face. Then she turned away, putting away her tools, her shoulders a tense line.

Dia got to her feet. Even though she knew it may ruin the silent truce between them, she had to ask: "You really don't want to go with them?"

Alma didn't even turn to answer. "Go with them *where*? Some sterile homeworld? Where there's traffic and people and noise?" She snorted. "I'd rather stay here, thanks, even if that means dying."

It was human idiocy of the highest order; the derision, the belief she'd be fine even when Central would essentially starve her out. "Stay, then," Dia said, and took the stairs two at a time in leaving.

The man Alma had spoken to—Mailer—caught her on her way back to the shuttle. "Custodian," he barked.

He was heedless to her anger. "Yes?"

He paused, fixated on her new face for a split second before he said, "We're leaving. Network's been turned off, and I suppose we didn't realise what we were signing ourselves up for." He grimaced. Humans really did love to revel in their own misery. She wished she had that luxury. "All the rest of us are coming, apart from…"

"Yeah," Dia snarled. "I'm aware."

"We want her to come. It's convincing her that's the problem," he said, shrugging.

She knew what a good custodian would do. She would go back to Alma—explain to her, softly and patiently, that everyone else was leaving, and hope that it would jolt her into leaving too. Dia would point out that they did care about her. Maybe she'd even get Mailer's children to come along. She wasn't above emotional blackmail.

But Dia wasn't a particularly good custodian. She didn't want to face Alma's grumpy expression, her short words. She wasn't sure she had the patience. Some spiteful part of her wanted to leave Alma here; wanted her to stay here, alone, and understand just the choice she was making. But mostly it sounded like too much work.

"Alright," she said instead of something tight and unkind. "I'll take the rest of you up in the morning. You've got tonight to pack—to say goodbye."

He nodded. "Thanks." Maybe he meant it.

It rained that evening, hard and heavy. She sat in the shuttle and listened to it thunder on the roof. Once, she would've been forced to worry about the electronics in her face degrading. Now she didn't have to worry at all.

That didn't mean she was happy about it.

At least the colonist situation was improving. She'd be able to round them all up before her final due date—bar Alma, of course, who would stay unless Dia convinced her otherwise. And Alma *would* stay alone if she had to.

Her chronometer told her it was dawn when she heard a knock on the shuttle door. She slid it open to reveal the rest of the families, carrying suitcases and pet carry cages and whatever else they needed to bring with them. She ferried them up, settling them into their sleep pods, and they went easily—painlessly. She drank in the sight of them as they shut their eyes and dreamt of whatever world they'd wake up in.

And then, finally, she was alone, and Dia could put it off no longer.

She landed the shuttle near Alma's house—because now there was no need for politeness. The drizzle had stopped, the air thick and grey, and she walked through it and felt the rain smudge against her face, whole once more.

She could have knocked. She didn't bother. Instead, she pushed the yellow front door open, wiping her shoes on the mat, and stepped inside. "Alma?"

A low grumble, then: "I'm in the kitchen."

It was just as cluttered as her previous visits. No attempt had been made to clean—to bring away things Alma might want to transport with her. She was ferociously stacking plates, her shoulders drawn.

"I'm going," Dia said simply, "and I'm taking everyone else with me."

For a second Alma paused, and then her expression narrowed. She ever so carefully put down the plate, almost soundless, on the counter. Her voice was poisonous: "You don't understand."

It was an absurd, impossible claim. However old Alma was, Dia was far older. "At least I understand how short-sighted you are. You could teach the kids electronics classes anywhere—"

"Short-sighted?" Alma laughed unhappily. "No—really. It's you who doesn't understand." And she stepped forward and took Dia's hand in her own—and between them, a custodian node flared to life.

Dia froze. Data flickered through her, images layered upon images: Alma's deployment here, generations ago. Rija had swelled and swelled with more and more people who accepted her, universally, unilaterally, as human. How terrifying that had been. How wonderful.

And how she'd had to hide. How she'd been able to confide in only a few, but how that was rare; how she had learned to maintain her own faceplate, do her own updates, because otherwise someone would work it out—they'd tell Central, and she'd have to return to the hell that was custodian work. How she didn't want that. How she'd rather stay here, alone—rot and fade and disappear—than return to the purgatory of reality.

Or at least at first. How the days had become monotonous without something to structure them. How alone she was around humans, hiding amongst them, unable to relate to them; unable to have them relate to her in turn.

Dia's broken face at Alma's front door, and Alma's terror at knowing she was going to be taken back to Central.

Dia staggered away. She knew it was programming—knew it was the facsimile of some human emotion—but her knees felt weak with sudden, terrible understanding. "You're not—"

"No," Alma said, and her anger had faded to something quiet, something sad. "I'm not."

She could see no evidence of a seam or seal in Alma's earnest face, although that was the point of them, wasn't it? It was what Dia herself had delighted in scant hours before: that if you didn't already know, there would be no way to tell they were anything other than human.

"I've maintained myself as best possible with a single pair of hands," Alma continued. "And when I saw you—I thought the ruse was up. Thought it was all over; that you were here to take me back to Central."

"No. I doubt Central even knows you're here. I thought you were just another human." Her words stumbled out, unwieldy in the wake of her understanding: "I mean, now I know, I can leave you here..."

But Alma shook her head. "I'm tired of this: of hiding from Central, of being on a backwater planet, living in fear, being lonely. I don't want to be this person anymore."

Dia didn't say anything. She was tired in a similar way: tired of being the good custodian.

"What do you want to do?" Alma asked. "Because with a second pair of hands, you could change your faceplate too. You wouldn't have to be a custodian anymore. You could disguise yourself as human—could be anyone you wanted."

It was nothing she hadn't thought of before—but somehow Alma saying it made it sound impossible, a reality she'd never be able to achieve. She knew what she wanted. She could feel hope surging up inside her, fragile and tentative. She just didn't know whether it was justified. "What do *you* want to do?"

Alma paused, then said, "I want you to ask the question you need to ask."

It was enough to make Dia fumble, almost forgetting the point of all this: "Will you come up to the sleepship?"

"Now I know you're not going to tell Central about me... of course," Alma responded, and smiled.

The flight that had seemed so boring gained an odd magic with Alma as a passenger. Dia set the autopilot and together they stared out the window. They watched as the ground gave way to the town, then the jut between land and ocean, and finally just cloud cover, Rija no more than a sphere hanging, weightless, in the infinite dark.

"You alright?" Dia asked softly.

"Fine," Alma said, nodding jerkily. "What happens when we get up there?"

"I... don't know."

"Dia," she said, and her voice was heavy—weighted. "I notice you didn't answer my question. What do *you* want to do?"

The shuttle thrummed as it piloted itself into the sleepship. What did she want to do? More than anything, she wanted to be honest. "I... don't want to be a custodian anymore." Saying it aloud was terrible, a truth that felt awful to admit, yet her relief was stronger. "I don't know what else I can do, but... I don't want to go back to Central." She didn't want to be uploaded onto some databank somewhere, forgotten about, her memories rendered into files.

Alma's smile was small and warm, and enough to make Dia surge with sudden, desperate hope. "With two of us, we don't have to go back to Central. Being alone and scared was what made me stay. But we could—"

"We *could* leave," Dia interrupted, her hope turning from a trickle into a waterfall. "We could repair each other; cover for each other. I wouldn't have to do this anymore. You wouldn't have to hide on some backwater planet in case Central comes looking." It was like an invisible weight was being removed from her shoulders: she wouldn't have to carry the burden of these people; of their frustration and joy. She'd done her job as best she was able. She hadn't let anyone down. And, most importantly, with Alma's help, she could leave.

"We should take them most of the way," Dia added. "The humans. Let's find a planet—a station, even—and set the autopilot to take the humans back to Central. Then we can run." They could hide among the humans, invisible among them. They'd have to be careful, but careful was better than decommissioned.

Alma was still grinning. "Yeah. Alright, then," she said, like it was easy. "Think I can live with that."

Dia knew she didn't have a stomach—just metal and wires— but it flipped anyway. Together, they could be anyone. They'd have to hide from Central, would never be able to stay anywhere long... but she'd been doing that for a long time under their orders. She'd rather do them under her own.

Around them, the shuttle fell to silence. Then Dia took a deep, unnecessary breath. The universe was unfurling before her, every possibility suddenly within reach. She'd collected the other sixteen people from Rija. The seventeenth was offering her something she hadn't even dared to dream of: an escape from oblivion.

"Okay," she said, smiling back, wide enough that it near ached: "Yes. Okay. Let's do it. Let's see what's out there."

*See Norah Lovelock's story "The Final Face" online at Metaphorosis.
If you liked it, leave a comment. Authors love that!
Remember to subscribe to our e-mail updates so you'll know when
new stories are posted.*

About the story

"The Final Face" originated from a question I had about a lot of sci-fi: if there are all these people going in and out of cryo-freeze all the time, who's the person putting them there? I then decided it would have to be someone; asking people to voluntarily do something without any external pressure or help is generally a recipe for disaster. I decided she'd have to be a robot, as she would therefore not be susceptible to being frozen herself, but she'd have to look and behave human enough that humans would be able to trust her—and that's where Dia, the narrator, was formed.

I quickly also realised that she needed something to be in opposition to; it wouldn't be a story if she just put people into cryofreeze without anything to rally against! That was how Alma came into being. Fundamentally, for them both, I was very interested in writing about the idea of them looking and behaving in very human ways—and yet, despite that, being indefinably "non-human" in some way that is impossible to remedy. Alma can disguise herself as human, but for Dia, the task is impossible. Even when returned to a human appearance, the colonists see her as other, a label that's impossible for her to escape.

Setting-wise, I was heavily inspired by the Atlantic Coast of Ireland. Although I love to live in cities, I enjoy writing about isolated natural environments. I found the very stark, grey ocean very beautiful—and very cold to swim in!

A question for the author

Q: What inspires you?

A: People! I'm a character-driven writer and like to imagine how people might behave in imagined futures. I don't think we'll change much!

Generally, my ideas come from building a character (or characters) in my head before working out what kind of situation that character may be in and generally run from there. Sometimes these characters appear fully formed, but more often than not it involves piecemealing traits together: that person I spoke to the other day who told me about their partner, that character from another piece of media I really enjoyed, a personal experience that I'd like to write about... Ultimately, I'm a writer who is most interested in and inspired by character and people above all else.

About the author

Norah Lovelock is a speculative fic writer from Manchester, UK.
https://norah.love

When Darkness Falls on Edinburgh

C.J. Erick

It was Gavina's favorite image of Edinburgh: the spire of the gothic Scott Monument rising above the skyline of rainbow-colored shop fronts on Victoria Street, with the setting sun lighting the monument's peak in golden fire. The colored shop facades marked Thomas Hamilton's redesign of the original Bow Street in colorful Flemish sensibilities, the renaming when the queen ascended the throne in 1837, and a salute to gay pride. Or, for Gavina, white light manifested as a spectrum by the faceted glass of an aged oil lantern.

Walking down the curving narrow street was like walking backwards in time, perhaps to the era of the witch burnings. The smells of food and wet stone, sounds of hawkers and music, and light dazzling in the mist were spectra for the senses. Moist air oddly blowing from the south brought mist, pale as her translucent skin where it peeked from beneath her dark cloak. Her pale skin spoke of delicacy, fragility, something precious. She hated her skin sometimes.

Victoria Street led to Forrest then High Street. She paused there, looking west toward the Castle. The brownstone buildings on each side of the street were like hands reaching up, with shops like bracelets around their wrists. In the valley of their open palms sat Edinburgh Castle, lit to golden red by electric lights, the turbulent deep turquoise and gray sky above it like ocean water. One expected great fish and whales and mythical creatures, perhaps selkies, to swim in great grand circles above and around it.

She reached the shop, hers now, an old one, hardly noticeable among all the other tourist traps along this street. The sign above the door was faded just to the appropriate shade of ambiguity: Miss Aileen's Mysteries and Potions.

Suddenly, she felt tired, as if gravity was pulling her into a smaller, squatter version of herself.

Gods mighty and fay, I miss you, Aila. We need you now more than ever.

Dusk was giving way to night when she unlocked the door with the old skeleton key, which seemed to warm when it found its home in the old brass lock. The only light in the shop was coming from an old Oban whisky sign on one wall, the one Captain Petr refused to throw out. The light was good, though. It kept her from barking her thin shins on the displays and counters as she wended her way back to the old office.

Petr was there, even though she'd told him to take a few days off to enjoy fishing or hiking. He missed the Highlands like the raven he was. But he was a lovable raven, one with a snaggled beard and feathery hair grayed by more age than he would admit. At times, one might see a shadow clinging to him as if he were a spirit afoot. Darkness took no pity on the poor man, Aileen had said, which was his punishment for defying it.

Petr sat hunched at their big wooden desk, snoozing over a leather-bound book older than he was, probably. She picked up his plate with breadcrumbs and bits of cheese and the glass with dribbles of milk, and took them to the tiny kitchen at the back of the shop. Not much of one, really, just an old one-burner gas range with an oven too small for even a loaf of soda bread, a sink too small for a decent-sized pot, and a tiny, grungy window that looked out on the alley behind it.

When she returned to the little alcove they called the office, he'd awakened and poured himself a short glass of brown, oily liquor — whisky, reeking like a bale of wet peat. He offered her the bottle, but she declined. She fancied a wee dram now and then, but not at the moment, not with so much on her mind.

She slumped into the wooden rolling chair opposite his, the one worn smooth by decades of polishing by Aileen's self-proclaimed iron butt. Like the door lock, it always seemed warmer than expected. The captain pushed the old book he'd been reading across to her. The black leather cover was worn at the edges, but otherwise well-kept.

"What's this?" she asked.

"Something the lady wanted me to give you. At the right time."

"Right time? For what?"

"I dunno, lass. Maybe it will become apparent after you have a look."

The book looked sturdy and heavy enough, but she felt it might explode into black and yellow dust if mishandled. Inside the front cover lay sheets of folded paper, newer than the book, a few years old at most. She unfolded them and found words in Aileen's hand, two pages, one a few lines of verse and the other a personal note addressed to her. She felt a quiver.

"How long have you had this book, Petr?"

"Long enough. And that's all I'll say about it."

"Why didn't you give it sooner? Like three months ago when she passed?"

"Like I said, Gavina, the lady told me to give it to ya when the time was right. She said I'd know when. She was right. And you know it too, don't you, lass?"

"I don't know what you mean."

"Yes, you do."

Yes, damn him, she knew. Look for the chill wind coming from the south and not the north as it should. Watch for flocks of dark birds riding high in the evening wind. Feel the tremor in the earth like a deep growl rising from the bowels of it. She'd noted all these things in recent weeks, but the wind was an odd, late season cyclone. The birds were flocks starving after fires on the mainland of Europe, crossing the Channel in search of food. And the vibrations she felt — construction work around the palace, rollers and shovels and cranes moving large sections and blocks. Nothing unnatural in any of that, all explained by known things.

"The signs will always seem to be usual, Gavina," Aileen had said. "The ominous will always be hidden in common things."

"She said you must read the notes," prompted Petr.

She slipped the pages out of the book, unfolded them and pressed them flat on the desktop. But to read Aileen's words would bring the heartache, resurrect the pain that had plagued Gavina in the hard weeks since she and Petr had held Aileen's hands where she sat in the big upholstered chair, where she'd insisted they place her. They'd watched Aileen's slowly shallowing last breaths.

Gavina chose to read the letter first. Aileen's writing was still strong and straight. Not the hand of a woman dying of cancer.

Dear Gavina:

I must start by saying I am sorry. I hoped to deal with the coming storm myself, but it was not to be, and I must think this is the way the gods wanted it. My powers, once strong, are now weak, too weak, and so my time as the guardian has come and gone. I would not have it this way. I would not force this great responsibility on someone as young and bright and full of potential and promise as you, but...

Here, Gavina imagined Aileen pausing and trying to find the best words, perhaps wiping a single tear away, full of memories of love and conflict and sorrow that she'd rarely spoken of, even to her ward and mentee Gavina, whom she treated like her own daughter.

…this decision is not mine to make. You came to me by providence because you are the chosen, and there is nothing you or I can do about that. May the gods lay their miserable and spiteful eyes upon you with mercy.

Evil comes in many forms, and likewise the ones chosen to fight it. Our way is the rare way, the light of night. For we walk in the shadowy streets and wait for when we are needed. That time is again upon our land, and so upon you, my lovely girl. We are the way of the lantern, the glass, the burning wick. But we are also connected to the Earth, as those who come are, those who come to claim that which is not theirs.

They will come as three, the children of my foe, Madame Griselda. Trust not their youthful smiles. Griselda and I were sisters once, in the Coven at North Berwick, along with Petr, whose time in merchant marine was past. But the Satanic Panic in the 1980's forced us to disband, and left Griselda bitter. She called me a fool of the light. This sentiment she will have passed on to her children. They will regard you coldly.

Be brave, lovely girl, for you know within yourself where your strength lies. Your enemies are powerful, but you are greater.

Be brave. I will be with you.

Love,

Aileen

Aileen had spoken often of the gods she believed in, the evils that fought for chaos, the followers of the Gaelic devil, Black Donald, in his quest to corrupt all the peoples and cover the land in ash and dark snow. She'd spoken of the power of the lantern and the glowing coals, the mirror and the prism and the faceted glass. These were all magical things, she had said, and beyond Black Donald's power to corrupt.

But was any of it still powerful in the modern world?

So Griselda had taken to the dark side alone, pushing away the way of light, forsaking duality and balance. When freedom and respect could not be achieved through cooperation and service to the people, it would be wrenched from the hands of non-believers via force.

Petr was watching Gavina now, his brows knitted and eyes pinched. He didn't speak much of the anti-paganism he and Aileen had endured as they fled the mob from North Berwick, but Aileen had hinted at his bravery. How easy it would have been for he and Aileen to follow the way of darkness, as Griselda had.

Gavina took the second sheet of paper, the one with the verse, and spread it before her. The words were Gaelic, and she struggled to translate them.

Chan eil dorchadas an taobh eile de sholas; tha e dad.
Chan eil an taobh eile den dorchadas aotrom; tha e a h-uile dad.
Nuair a bhios solas agus dorchadas a 'tighinn còmhla, faodaidh a'
bhuil a bhith mar rud sam bith.

"I can't read this, Petr."

He took the sheet from her, his eyebrows rising.

"It's an old one, Gav, something spoken even before the Druids walked the lands to the north, before the pagans built their mystic stone observatories.

"The opposite of light is not darkness; it is nothing.
"The opposite of darkness is not light; it is everything.
"When light and darkness converge, the consequence can be
anything."

He handed the paper back to her.

"I don't understand it, Petr. A Book of Genesis reference? But the last line…"

"I could guess, but that would be of little help to you. You must seek your own meaning. Aileen gave this to you for these times, so your understanding is important."

"What could be coming? When she spoke of the dark times in the past, her words were always allegorical and inscrutable. Things about the children of the deep earth and forest, the creatures of the night, the spirits of the shadows — crazy talk. Weren't they just silly tales meant to keep them children in line, not real-world evil?"

"There isn't any difference. The stuff of nightmares speaks of real evil."

She reread the verse.

"It's just a puzzle, an enigma. 'The consequence can be anything.' Something outside the real world, like dividing by zero? Or that old saw about an unstoppable force striking an immovable object? What is infinity divided by infinity?"

"Nothing. Everything. Or perhaps just… one."

His hands raised from a sketch he'd been fiddling with while he listened to her ranting, a doodle. She recognized it as the Celtic quaternary knot, infinite loops forming four points. It represented many things: the four primary directions; the four elements of nature; the four seasons; or the four Wiccan sabbats, the fire festivals. The last of them, Samhain, was three days away. Some called it Halloween.

Samhain marked the end of the season of light and the beginning of winter, the season of darkness. In that transition, the veil that separated the physical world with the spirit world faded to ethereal thinness. In that time, the spirits, both good and evil, might leave the spirit world and walk the earth again.

Fia cast the stones on the gray tile board, careful to keep them on the surface. Stones that left the board might fall either way, toward power or weakness, like smoke drifting from a wisping pipe or smudge-burning sage. Better to remove uncertainty and control all that was within one's grasp. That had always been Griselda's advice.

She studied the six pieces, each one a different shape, size, number of facets, shades of gray and black. There was a pattern, and a surprise, a good one.

"The woman is truly dead," she said. "The stones confirm it."

Mairi, sitting opposite her at the table, lifted her thick black brows. Dorn, whose full name was Dorn Dubh, Black Fist, hardly moved from where he sat on their one sofa, staring at his hands. They were very different, the three of them. How could they have crawled from the same womb within minutes of each other? Fia, as the first born, had become their leader, by ancient covenant.

Fia added, "She is childless."

"Then it's done," said Dorn. He stood, leaving a depression in the dark red leather. He moved about the room in a slow-motion dance, touching things; the dark shade of a brass lamp that cast its light only downwards, tinted glass jars of minerals and ground bone, a wide book of ancient maps with its charcoal leather cover turned open to one they'd been surveying for the three months since Griselda's death, the map of inner Edinburgh, the city fifty miles away from their remote, little-known castle, the place that was the subject of their thoughts every day since Griselda had wheezed her last malodorous breath and cursed them to bring the night down at last.

"Why do I still feel tension?" said Mairi. Mairi — The One Who Is Bitter. Bitter at being the youngest? "I feel the woman's powers still present."

"Nonsense," said Dorn. "If the old hag's dead, her powers died with her. The time is now ours to claim Castle Hill as the witches' hallows, and all the death-shrine that lies in the bloody soil beneath it. Hundreds died there because of people's fearful hatred. It's all ours now. The witches will reign." He used the Gaelic word for witches, buidsichean.

Fia felt her sister's bitterness, like the darkest of chocolates, burnt blacker than black. She also felt her brother's excitement, his lust for the power that had so long been denied her kind, the promises of the dark angel, Black Donald. He was the Breaker, destroyer of the non-Wiccan, builder of the dark age that was to come, fulfillment of the prophecies. When the power of the deepest earth would rise to sweep over the land like the wings of a great dark bird.

Three days until Samhain, November 1. One of the four fire festivals, and the most powerful, the beginning of winter. The dark winter they had all dreamed of as the followers of Griselda, The One Who Dwells in a Gray Castle. Their mother.

Gavina slept little for the following three days. She ran the shop during the four evening hours it was open, to maintain the routine, to keep curious eyes from gazing too deeply through the windows and into the shop's shadows. And of course to keep them fed. But all night and into the morning, she pored over the books of handwritten notes and observations, verses and incantations, everything Aileen had guided her with, spoken of, made her practice. She still didn't know whether most of it held any real power or, even if it did, whether she knew how to invoke it.

She was deeply lost in the special book Petr had given her days before, the thick, leather-bound volume of special quotes and verses, each one meant for a different day.

The verse for Halloween read this in ancient Gaelic, which Petr had translated:

As the hours fall
So shall the veil
The dead and wicked will walk
And the two worlds shall be one.
Until light breaks in the east
And the spirits must rest again.

Petr cleared his throat behind her, breaking her mood, so unearthly quiet when he wanted to be. He reached around her and turned the book's cover closed.

"This will do you no more good tonight, girl."

"Then what will, elder? All of this —" She waved her hand toward the piles of books, scrolls, notebooks, and envelopes big and small, all old. "I don't know what I could need and what's just a waste of time. I don't even know the enemy."

"Yes, you do. The enemy is darkness, all those things you are not."

"It's dark now. Is the night our enemy?"

"Not now, but it could be. I'm not talking about the time between sundown and sunup. I'm talking about the eternal darkness that rises from the world, not that which falls from the sky."

"Then how will I know it? How will I fight it?"

"What did your friend and patron call you, when you were morose or when you needed a good chastising to take this all seriously?"

Gavina couldn't answer for a moment. When she did, her voice was tight and brittle.

"Gavina, of course. Little White Hawk."

"That's your spoken name. Its meaning comes in the day, when you're challenged by the physical world. What did she call you when you were challenged by the ethereal?"

"Lantern Girl."

"Yes."

"It always felt silly, like she was making fun of me."

"Think on her name. What does it mean in the physical world?"

"Aileen. Ray of Sunshine."

"Aye. Not many were brighter than she, Gavy. Do you know her spirit name?"

"No. She never spoke of it to me."

"But you know it. The same as yours, at least when she was young. Lantern Girl. A title passed down from olden times. She didn't choose your spirit name by chance or whim. When she found you with the homeless urchins, lighting trashcan fires for the bums, she recognized your way. You are the way of the wick, the burning flame, the faceted glass, the light which guides carriages and ships and people through the night, through the underground."

"I don't feel that."

"You will when you need to."

"I feel something, a shadow, like a black hemorrhage coming over the land. And I don't know how I can feel it."

"What you need now is rest. Get some sleep, Gavina. Darkness is not evil in itself. All living things need it, for renewal. Just as you do."

"But there's no time. I don't know what we're facing, or how to prepare."

Petr said nothing for a moment, measuring his words.

"Gavina, you are the way of fire, not the fire that burns and destroys, but the fire that lights the way and enlightens the soul. You are the way of the lantern, the glowing ember, the fire that warms and heals. Did you think Aileen found you by chance? Nay. She was drawn to you as a kindred spirit. You are both the way of the lantern, the vessel of fire one may carry. And that's the weapon you must wield."

He urged her to her feet and guided her toward the sleeping area in the back of the shop. But her mind refused to rest, roiling with images and fears so that she didn't know if she slept or merely lay awake with her eyes closed, haunted by visions.

Dorn led his siblings up the rising streets toward Edinburgh Castle, leaping ahead of his sisters as he had done when they were younger, usually to Fia's annoyance. Age and cynicism had molded him into the snarling young man he'd become in their isolation in the old castle, a more demonstrative counter to Mairi's quiet moroseness. His unbridled enthusiasm seemed to have returned. Beside Fia, Mairi seemed if anything even quieter. But even in her, the spark of adventure and anticipation had come to life, like a tiny struck match.

It was late afternoon, cloudy, dead calm in the street, almost stale, but strong winds high up, driving the mottled gray and indigo clouds. October 31; Halloween to the laypeople, who totally missed the true meaning, the fire festival, disrespected as a barely remembered pagan event. High Street was populated, more than the last time Fia had walked it, six years earlier. When her mother had dared to bring her, just the two of them, leaving Dorn and Mairi with a school acquaintance in Aberdeenshire.

Griselda's words echoed in her head:

"The Castle Hill, Fia. That's where you'll make your stand. The blood and power of all those who were unjustly murdered there remain. It is time for the children of darkness to take back that power, and to take the land to where it was always meant to be. Time for the influence of those of us who see a better future, to overcome the fools who only see the naïve innocence of lightness."

Students moved around the street, primer age in white and black uniforms, no tribal tartan allowed. Older higher school boys and girls, itching in their skins to become adults, wore everything and sometimes nearly nothing, some already in costumes, many of haunted things or demons, some absurdly in those of celebrities or food items or political characters from the news, but some in dark goth clothing that made Fia laugh. The gay human enthusiasm for the pagan holiday, these would-be Wiccans, or followers of some other order they knew nothing about. The need to identify themselves as different, outside the norms of proper society. *Oh, be patient, young souls, your time will come, so soon now. That which is odd will become common. Those who are outcasts will rule.*

So comforting that all the tools she and her siblings needed were in their trendy red and black shoulder bags, easy to bring to this place without suspicion. Their gray and black clothing blended in well with the students, even the older ones, the university gems, who thought the world revolved around them even more now than when they were primer age. Perhaps Fia, Dorn, and Mairi should just leave everything as it was so these pretentious elitists could find out how little the world cared about them.

They worked their way west, uphill, climbing the cobblestones past the tourist shops. At the corner of Forest, Fia paused. Something felt strange there, like business left undone, like an oven left burning or letters unsent. Dorn was halfway up the next block before he realized she'd stopped. He loitered where he was, didn't return to where she stood. Annoyed, she gathered Mairi, who'd stopped to watch her from the doorway of a bookseller, looking unperturbed.

"I thought we were in a hurry," said Dorn, when she and Mairi reached him. "Were you looking to hail a cab?"

"I felt something disturbing, black head," Fia said, using the Gaelic, ceann dubh. The old language was creeping into her speech more and more, as if she were channeling her mother and her kin. "We're not alone here."

He huffed. "With the woman dead, no one else matters now. The grounds are ours for the taking."

"It's not the grounds I'm concerned about. It's the very Earth. And arrogant complacency is a danger we cannot afford." She paused to listen and feel, but she felt nothing and heard nothing beyond the sounds of people and traffic and the rising wind in the high wires and towers. Even the light from the castle seemed subdued, as if expecting them. "Maybe I'm overreacting. But let's prepare our things as soon as we can."

They entered the open yard leading into the main entrance to the castle, the esplanade, where the annual Fringe Festival was held. The thought of dozens of traditional and modern bands playing there and tens of thousands of sweating people in that small slanted concrete platform made her skin crawl.

Mairi cast a cloak of mist and shadow over them, and they passed the gates just before the castle was closed for the evening. The landmark workers and the real soldiers walked by them without notice, as if they were invisible spirits. Though they weren't of the spirit realm, after this night they might live for ages, the guardians of the damned souls who had been murdered here. So many witches and innocent laypeople had been caught in mob hysteria that descended on this place.

May it all be made right in the night, and in the many days of blessed darkness that will follow.

They walked around the winding walled streets of the castle, up past the parade stages, around the tabernacle and hall of heroes, to the highest observation lane, the best vantage point over the city. Ancient black cannons pointed outward at the sea, the land, the forests below, and toward Arthur's Seat, the hill in Holyrood Park, another site of witch burning. They were surrounded by places of power the spirits would occupy over the days ahead.

Mairi laid her pack down, withdrew a small stone pot the size of a grapefruit, and filled it with herbs and organic matter. She cast a spell of protection and isolation, warding off any of the night guard from coming to this high, stone-walled avenue. This was her work for the night, to keep her pot smoldering with the pungent leaves and bracken and moldy peat while Fia and Dorn cast bigger things. When her incantation was complete, she settled onto a seat on the high wall where she could watch them.

Dorn swung his pack down and removed six black-glazed bricks, cut into twelve halves on their long flat sides. He laid these in a circle about a half-meter across. In this he laid short rods of stainless steel he'd made for this occasion. The rods formed a grating in the bottom of the brick circle. He placed pieces of kindling from his pack on the grate, along with some paper as starter, and lit it with a red plastic wand lighter. With all of this, the pack had weighed three or four stone. But Dorn had the strength of the earth behind him and had carried it as one might a pack of duck feathers.

Dorn represented the earth, Mairi the restless sea, and Fia the sky. And now they had applied the flame to wood — fire, the fourth element. The circle of physical and ethereal energies was complete.

Fia laid her pack near the expanding fire, taking in the pleasant smells of burning wood. She could feel the terror of the ones burned at the pyre on the flat ground just over the wall far below them, hear their cries and wailing, hear their flesh and hair sizzle, smell the stench. Anger rose within her, but she held it in check. In anger was rashness, and she needed a cool head. The darkness was not emotional; it was calm and relentless, and so must she be as well.

She drew leather pouches from her pack, thirteen in all, herbs and bones and insect hives and the skin of reptiles. These things were not magical in themselves, but in the things they represented, the magic that had been ingrained in them by Fia's mother, and her parents and grandparents before her. The items were hundreds of years old, some of them irreplaceable. Some Griselda had brewed, others Fia and Mairi had concocted from the old journals, exactly as had been done generations before by those who had never seen ships and cars and television and the computer age. Had the world been a better place back then when things were simpler, as Griselda had lamented?

Fia added these things to the fire in the order Griselda had taught, reciting the learned words. One by one, the ingredients of the eternal darkness, the endless winter, charred and burned in the low flames, sending gray and green smoke upward into the darkening sky, up toward the flying clouds. Yet the smoke did not blow away in the wind, but rose as if in its own invisible chimney toward the sky.

As she added the last ingredient, the smoke paused for a few seconds, the air seemed to halt its elemental motion, and Fia couldn't breathe. Dorn's eyes widened and his mouth opened and closed like a fish's or like a clenching fist. And then the moment passed and the smoke doubled, dark and beautiful, like the mane of a mighty black horse. It rose in a twisting column up to the flying clouds, and then turned into an eerie mist, rolling back down over the city. This blanket of gray mist flowed from the castle, following the streets like coiling snakes.

There was little to do but watch and wait, for the dark fog to complete its consumption, for the veil between the worlds to dissolve for the night, for the real work to begin, the building of a new time, a new world.

But the fog had concealed the approach of another, the presence she'd sensed as they'd walked up High Street. From the lower part of the castle, two figures came up the stoned street, both dressed in dark hooded jackets and dark clothing. One was a hulking form, bent over probably from age, face hidden. The other was smaller, about Fia's size. They walked to where Fia and her siblings waited, all watching them now.

The two set down their own backpacks, red and black leather, the best colors to hide at night. The small one pushed back its hood and revealed a young woman no older than Fia, with dark hair and moon-pale skin. Her huge eyes were haunting, like an owl's or hawk's. Fia felt she knew this woman, even though she had never seen her before.

"You're the old woman's daughter," Fia said.

The woman seemed taken aback by that, as if this were something she had never considered. The bigger figure pushed back its hood, revealing a gray-haired man with a wide forehead bent like his back, and small eyes dancing with blue fire.

The strange woman gazed at the sky. The blackness from the sea had crossed halfway now, engulfing the circle of darkness from the fire smoke. Dorn ignored the woman and her elder companion and added more wood. Mairi sat on the wall and kicked her feet. Her little pot continued to sizzle, although the need for it seemed to have come to an end.

"Very nice," said the young woman, continuing to gaze upward.

"I'm glad you like it." So ludicrous that this one would come now, when it was far too late for an intervention. The elder man waited beside her, like a trite legend. "I'm Fia. And your name?"

"Gavina." Her own name sounded strange in her ears.

Below the castle, the people of Edinburgh didn't realize something very wrong was happening in the sky, that the darkness falling was more than just a heavy cloud layer moving over the setting sun. Random sirens twee-dee'd below, but in no greater number than a normal holiday evening. Across the expanse of foggy air, crowds were gathering on top of Arthur's Seat. Not the safest place to be, probably.

"Gavina? Hmm. The White Hawk," said the young woman who'd called herself Fia, which meant Dark Peace. That name brought a fresh chill to the air. "Are you the old woman's daughter?"

A pang, not heavy or deep, but sharp.

"No."

"She is," said Petr. "By any measure that matters."

"And you are?" asked the young man, who'd stepped forward.

"Your nightmare," said Petr, meeting his eyes coolly.

"My brother, Dorn," said Fia, "and this is our sister, Mairi."

"The Fist and the Bitter One," said Petr. "Appropriate."

"Well, this has been *so* nice," said Fia, "but as you can see, we're rather busy. Why are you here?" Her eyes flashed with malice.

Gavina removed from her pack a small metal lantern as tall as her outstretched fingers, with straight glass sides set in a hexagonal shape. Then she took out a white paint pen and hesitated over the side of the lantern.

"Which one, Petr?" she asked.

Petr eyed the three young people marveling at them.

"Make it the triquetra. There is worthy power in that one."

The triquetra, symbol of interwoven trinity, of body, mind, and spirit, or the elements of land, sea, and air, or the three stages of life; child, adult, elder.

She nodded and drew a simple Celtic knot with three points on the metal base of the lamp. The pagan symbol shone boldly white against the dull gray steel of the lantern and seemed to sparkle with its own internal energy. Such ancient beauty in it, and hidden power. Next, she pulled a lighter from her pocket, chanted quietly, lit the lantern, and set it on the stone at her feet. Immediately, it flared, pushing white light from the lamp, brighter and brighter. Resting on the stone, it resembled a model lighthouse from a child's electric train set.

The light expanded in a bubble of clean air, wider and wider, pushing wisps of dark fog away from the castle street.

Fia's brow furrowed in dark shadows. "Dorn, crush that thing."

Dorn stepped forward and stomped the lantern, leaving it a tiny hulk of metal and broken glass. The flame sputtered and died, and the wisps of fog reappeared.

"That wasn't it," said Gavina. She took an identical lantern from her pack. "Maybe the triskele?"

"Worth a try," said Petr.

Dorn stepped forward to seize the new lamp, but Fia stayed him with a gesture. "Let her try again. This amuses me."

Gavina drew a design with three spiral swirls connected to a central hub, then lit the lantern and set it on the pavement. The triskele, another symbol of trinity, this one associated with movement, a moving forward, a hope that it would touch the three foes before her with light and enlightenment. Again, the flame came up and brightened, and the dark fog cleared away. Again, Dorn stepped forward and crushed the lantern with his heavy black boot. The flame died, and the fog returned.

"Nope," said Gavina. "What next?"

"We tire of this game, White Hawk," said Fia. "The time for your ways is gone, and our time is here. Dorn, see them out."

"Gladly." He stepped toward Gavina.

"Not a good idea," said Petr, not moving from where he stood at Gavina's side.

"Get out, old man. You're moving on. We'll let you live in a dank old castle out in the fen somewhere."

He seized Petr's elbow and shoulder and shoved, but there was hidden power in Petr he hadn't counted on. They struggled and grappled, but the younger man was the stronger and moved Petr back down the street toward the castle entrance.

"I'd hate to kill another witch on these haunted grounds," Dorn said, "but I'll throw you over the wall, I swear it."

Petr leaned away, pulled a dark device from his pocket, and pointed it at Dorn. There was a harsh electric buzz, and Dorn staggered back, fell to the ground, and rocked in tremors. A Taser. Petr had not told Gavina about that.

Petr said, "Remember, young 'un, old age and treachery beat youth and skill."

Gavina pulled another small lantern from her pack.

"You're wasting your time, little bird," said Fia. "Your weak powers are nothing, even if we don't destroy your little matchlights."

"Three of you, for the basic elements, correct?" said Gavina. "Let me guess. Dorn is earth. Mairi is sea. And you, Dark Peace, are the sky."

"Astute of you."

"But no one to represent fire."

"We use it as we need to, as you can see." She pointed to the smoldering cauldron and the brick fire and its column of black smoke, which was thicker and more violent since Petr and Gavina had arrived.

"I see that you use it," said Gavina, "but you don't really understand it." With the white pen, she drew another symbol on the lantern, a single spiral. She chanted quiet words as she drew it. She set the lantern down and lit it, and like before, its light bloomed and pushed away the dark fog and gloom.

"The simple spiral," she said, "symbol of ethereal energy. The symbol of the flame. The fourth element, the one that is mine."

Fia eyed Dorn, who was now lying bleary-eyed on the stones, panting. She shook her head, then stepped toward the lantern. Petr moved to block her.

"Let her come, Petr. We can't guard the light every hour of every day."

He allowed Fia room to pass. She walked to the lantern and reached to pick it up. As her hand closed, white light flared from the glass and she jerked her hand back. She swore. She curled her hands into fists and let them burst open, and a great breeze rose and swirled about the lantern, catching and casting leaves and dirt and dark smoke from the cauldron. The wind rattled the lantern, pushed it so that it leaned as if about to topple. But the flame swelled like when one blows on a campfire, and the lantern remained upright. The gloom and smoke retreated further. The black column of smoke seemed to bend away.

Fia swore again. She waved her sister forward. "Mairi, quench the damn thing."

The younger sister, kicking her black shoes and looking unconcerned, jumped down from the wall. She placed her fingers on her lips, then opened her hands and chanted inaudible words. Immediately, rain fell on the castle, as if an umbrella that had been protecting them had been stolen away. Gavina and Petr tightened their cloaks, but the cold water struck their faces and ran down their necks into their inner clothing. Driving, the rain struck the lantern with a great hissing and billowing of steam, and the lantern rattled on the stone like a carnival popcorn popper sounding off, spinning in a tight circle.

The flame dimmed, but only for an instant before it found its shape and grew brighter again, punishing the offending wind and rain for challenging it. The gloom and smoke and darkness retreated further from the landing, as if a great white moon were hanging above and painting it in pale white light. Mairi stood with her unusually long arms hanging at her sides, like one wilted and washed in the rain, which had not touched her.

Dorn had recovered at this point and rushed the lantern, but the ground under his feet rumbled and buckled, and he fell to his hands and knees several feet away. He cursed and thrust his scraped, bleeding hands into his armpits.

Gavina, the white hawk... no, really a white dove, but also the Lantern Girl, just like her spiritual mother before her, the shining Aileen, lifted the still-burning lantern by the thin metal ring attached to its top and hung it on a hook in the courtyard's wall that seemed to have been placed there for just that purpose.

The rain had quenched the cauldron, and the smoke from it was white and weak; as Gavina watched, it fell to nothing. The black column of smoke from the pit fire was now just a wisp, lolling and squirming like a thin black snake writhing in the refreshing breeze that had risen from the east.

"Hmmph," said Fia. She'd walked over to lean over the castle wall overlooking the city, and the revelry growing louder. "A fair spell. But too late. The veil has been lifted, and the spirit world has entered Edinburgh." She crooked a black-nailed finger downward.

Gavina and Petr rushed to the wall. Below, the Halloween revelers were still milling about, moving between shops and taverns, which were all open and lighted. The noise of shouts and firecrackers and songs swelled as a fire may when blown. From several place, the sound of things breaking came, glass shattered as if dropped, hard blows against wood, car-horns honking. As they watched, a group of dark-clad youths blocked a car, waving their arms.

It all seemed mostly harmless pranks. But some of those who moved in the crowd carried with them odd shadows, like barely visible shrouds. The others around them paid them no more heed than they did the others. But these shadowed ones moved with purpose, and where they went, the pranks grew louder, more insistent. One such figure led a group of youths to throw rocks at a shop window, breaking the plate glass, then moving away in wicked laughter.

"Dark spirits," muttered Petr. "They lead only mischief now, but worse will come. I should know."

Fia said, "The weak minded are easily led to evil. When the spirits walk free, the people will know that evil exists in their pretty little world, and they will need us, need those they've forsaken and oppressed, to help them. And our power will rise."

Gavina ran and seized her lantern from the hook. It glowed strongly, none the worse for its trial. But she was feeling tired suddenly, as if she were the fuel keeping the flame aglow.

"Come, Petr. We must go to the streets and try to drive the spirits back to their home."

Fia chuckled. "Good luck, little hawk. You can drive some away, surely, but you can't be everywhere at once. And the spirits now walk throughout Edinburgh. And as you can see, even in the places beyond." She waved her arm to indicate the lands around the city, the hills across the water.

Petr and Gavina ran from the high courtyard, down the winding streets of the castle, through the gates and over the sloping esplanade, where a marching band was playing and costumed revelers danced. Among them were shadow people, whose looks were more real and not disguise; tall men in soldiers' uniforms, real weapons at their sides, thin-armed women with pale skin like Gavina's, whose expressions were centuries older than their skin; pale children stealing candy and garments and then running into the crowd, their eerie shadows passing with them like thin cloth caught in the breeze of their passing.

Everywhere Gavina went, the light from her lantern drove the spirits away. They shrank back into the real shadows of doorways, shops, and alleys, disappearing in the liquid darkness. But Gavina's legs had used their last strength running from the castle, and every step was like wading through dark mud. When they reached the crowd on Market Street, she moved to the entrance of one empty, dark shop to catch her breath. Petr joined her, eyeing the crowd with suspicion. The shadows of spirits moved within, a frightening number of them from where she stood.

"She's right, Petr." She paused to breathe. "I can't walk all of Edinburgh's streets with my lantern. I can't be everywhere at once, and the spirits will merely slip away and cause chaos elsewhere."

Here knees grew weak, and her head swam. Seeing her distress, Petr helped her reach a window stoop where she could rest.

"If only there were more of you," he said.

"One of Aileen was always enough." Around them the young people moved in singing and laughing groups, dressed in every manner of disguise, from zombie and sexy vampirellas, to toothy monsters and killer clowns. And among them, only recognized by Petr and Gavina, real evil spirits moved and cajoled and led the celebrants into more and more destructive pranks. The sounds of screams and things breaking and evil laughter were a grim counterpoint to the music coming from all directions.

"If only I could recruit help," she said. Around her many of the partiers were carrying lights of their own, small flashlights, cell phones with bright screens, and a few the colored wands that glowed with chemical fluorescence when the internal sections were broken and joined. She and Petr offered glow-sticks in her shop, always a big seller during nighttime outdoor events.

She couldn't be everywhere at once, but perhaps her fire could. The light from the sticks did nothing to drive away the shadow spirits, but what if that fire were hers?

"Petr, run to that shop and buy as many of the glow sticks as you can carry."

He looked puzzled. "Glow sticks?"

"Yes. Quickly, please, while I summon my strength."

Without hesitating, he left her and ran to the shop she'd pointed to, a book store and emporium that, like many of the others on Market Street, carried seasonal holiday items, including Halloween accessories. She sat and focused, drawing energy from around her, the frenetic movements of the people, the shaking of the earth beneath them, the wind blowing over her.

She heard a raven's call and looked toward its source, the castle wall, high up. There, the three young witches she'd fought stood, looking down at her. They lifted their hands and the wind rose and hard ice pellets began to fall. The ground beneath her vibrated. The partiers in the street around her took this all in-stride. It was October in Edinburgh, for god's sake, and the weather would do as it was wont.

Petr returned with dozens of pale white glow sticks in his arms, each about a foot and a half long. Between puffing breaths, he said, "I bought all they had, miss. I hope this is enough for what you're thinkin'." The raven's call came again, and he looked up where the three witches were casting spells against them. He muttered a dark curse.

"Thanks, Petr. Hand them to me one after another when I'm ready."

She stood and held her lantern before her, passing her finger over the symbol she'd written there, the simple, single spiral. The element of fire, the maker for the worthy, the destroyer in the wrong hands. But tonight, the illuminator. As she drew her finger over the symbol, the lantern flared and burned in a prism of pastel colors. People around her gasped and laughed, except for the few shadow spirits, who snarled and disappeared into the dark.

"Now, Petr. A glow stick please."

He placed one of the sticks in her outstretched hand. It felt cool and hard, lifeless like the wand of wax that it was. As some around her watched, she eased the tip of the stick into the lantern's flame. There was a flashed and sizzle and the smell of burning wax, and then the stick flared at its tip. She pulled it out and it glowed at the end with a beautiful, prismatic flame. She held it high for all around her to see. Many clapped. A lone spirit looking over the crowd moaned and slipped away.

"I want one of those," said a teenage girl in a pirate costume near her, turning as if to go to a shop to buy one.

"Take this one, friend," said Gavina, handing the glowing stick to her. "Take it all over the city, and light the way for others. Pass the flame."

"Cool!" The girl fairly danced away, showing her prize to all those around. Other partiers pushed in to where Gavina and Petr stood. She lit one stick after another, each one glowing with a different flame, different colors. With each, Gavina asked the person given to run through the city, lighting the way for others. In minutes, she had lit all the sticks and given them away, and the circle of light they emitted seemed to grow and brighten the street. There were no shadow spirits in sight. The three figures on the castle wall stood motionless, watching.

She was exhausted, as only a flame could be. But when she and Petr walked toward their shop, others had heard of her, the woman with the little lantern. Young people came to her from all directions, asking her to light their glow sticks as she'd done for the others. She found that she could light even the sticks that had given up their chemical life, now dead rods of wax. The light she gave them was no less than the light from the sticks that were new.

The night passed, and despite her fatigue, her death on her own feet, she and Petr walked the town. They had to make the light grow to take the whole city, and the lands beyond. And they needed to stay awake and light the way until morning came, when the veil between the worlds would close, and the spirits be back in their world.

Days passed, and Gavina spent an afternoon doing something she had grown to love, walking all the streets of Edinburgh in the winter snow. But it wasn't a dark snow. The overcast sky was lit from above by the moon and the stars and heavenly bodies she couldn't name. The threatening sky on Samhain had been written off by the media as the result of an unexpected bomb cyclone off the coast and wildfires on the continent, even though the meteorological scientists proclaimed neither of those causes credible. In the beautiful, ethereal lightness of being that followed, no one cared.

She chose this day to walk the length of the Princes Street Gardens, admiring the rounded shapes of powdery snow over the hedges and brambles and trees of all sizes and shapes, like phantom ghouls caught out in the open on All Hallows' Ev'n and frozen there, trapped until the thawing of the spring equinox, the Wiccan Eostar. From there, she circled the castle from low down and found the magical place where she caught a glimpse of her little lantern hanging from the wall, hidden in plain sight, unbothered. For weeks now it had burned continuously, without oil being added, without her hand to adjust the wick, without someone to clean the glass.

She headed back east to the modern shops and businesses and the weekday afternoon bustle they raised, citizens of Edinburgh moving in concert, like a choreographed dance on the walks and in the streets. In many cities, they might grumble and hunch their shoulders in this breezy snow, but not here. There was a lightness and life to the city which the sky's gloom couldn't quench, but only fed.

As she approached the shop, a small figure dressed in drab gray clothing moved from a doorway shadow toward her. In a croaking, elderly voice, the figure said, "Might I have a word with you, young woman?"

"Yes, of course."

The figure pushed back its gray hood to reveal the face of a young woman.

"Fia," said Gavina.

"That was an impressive spell," said the young witch, in her normal voice, youthful, with a bit of sneer, but also a note of respect. "We won't be victim to that one again."

"It doesn't have to be a new war, Fia. We — you, me, your sister and brother — are all not very different. The past murders of witches hurt us as if we were the ones lost on the pyres. But I will never let the world burn or hide in darkness because of that shame and guilt. And you don't have to follow that path either."

Fia shook her head. "So poetic and uplifting. And naïve. We've tried the way of acceptance and outreach for hundreds of years, and the result is always the same. Promises made, but in the end, there is only persecution. My mother and the others like her have long since tired of the dream of acceptance."

"I can't deny the tragic history for our kind. But I can't give up hope. But you and I need each other, like the two curves of the Gaelic yin and yang, the symbols of balance and complimentary strength. We are two poles of the spiritual magnet, just as your mother Griselda and my ward Aileen were. Without each other to balance our ways and power, we can be nothing but a danger to our own people to those who don't follow the craft. Don't you see that?"

"I see only a fool who thinks things will ever change by doing the same thing."

"This isn't 1597," said Gavina, "the time of the great witch hunt. Nor is it the Satanic Panic. We have new ways to communicate now. Many witches are reaching out on social media. Many are joining us. We no longer have to hide in the shadows."

"Oh, that sounds dandy. It really does. But look more deeply into the media traffic and you'll find the new panic, fool. They're called conspiracy theories, and the ones spreading them don't need churches or traveling evangelists or television. They have QAnon and other haters doing it for them. You feel safe and cozy here in Edinburgh, but they'll be coming for you, for your little cute occult shop. The true evil ones will never give up their persecution."

Gavina reached in her pocket and found a business card. On the front was the name and address of her shop, Miss Aileen's Mysteries and Potions. On the back was the symbol of the simple spiral. She offered it to Fia, who took it with suspicion.

Gavina said, "Each alone, we are only one way. Together, we can change things. You three are the ground and the earth and the air of which all things are made, but I am the spark which can give it all life. Together we can do anything."

Fia held the card up, and it disappeared in a puff of smoke.

"If I need you, I know where to find you."

Fia pulled her hood back over her head, once again a nondescript elder doddering through the streets of Edinburgh. She soon disappeared into the darkness of an alley.

When light and darkness converge, the consequence can be anything.

Back to High Street and to the shop and in the door, shaking her cloak and knocking her boots together, donning the leather slippers she kept in the alcove at the door. Petr was there, dusting potion bottles and spell books.

Gavina said, "Have you noticed? Such a lovely afternoon." She cleared papers from her desk and moved a ledger Petr had apparently laid there, open to yesterday's accounts.

Was she a fool as Fia said, to only feel the light, ignoring the dark which gave the light its purpose?

She really did need Fia, the dark one and her siblings.

"Petr, it's only three weeks until the yule. Before it comes, there are quite a few things we must do."

See C.J. Erick's story "When Darkness Falls on Edinburgh" online at Metaphorosis.

If you liked it, leave a comment. Authors love that!
Remember to subscribe to our e-mail updates so you'll know when
new stories are posted.

About the story

This story was inspired by a brewing cauldron of ideas and events. I've been fascinated by witchcraft and magical realism for some time, in how they offer alternate ways to see the world, and in fact true alternate realities. Beliefs in the occult or magical in any form are the reality for the believer.

The varying and personal nature of witchcraft intrigues me. There are no formal hierarchies or governing bodies for the Craft, as it's sometimes called, so personal experience and creativity are important in one's own journey. Stones, herbs, and talismans are sensually appealing, pricking all the senses. And as a lover of all cards and card games, I was drawn to tarot — I own four decks now and several references — studying the origins of the practice and the arcana, or archetypes of the cards.

I've spent time in Salem, Mass several times visiting a son, obviously the site of the most famous witch burning in US history, and later enjoyed a trip to Edinburgh, a beautiful city in a beautiful county and nation for inspiring story ideas. Edinburgh's history of witch hunts in the Sixteenth Century and beyond are a grim reminder of the depth of human hatred and brutality, and a warning that we "modern" humans are not above similar injustice. That these "hunts" were often used as a vehicle to oppress women, and especially poor women, makes them doubly sinister.

A question for the author

Q: What's your favorite *non*-SFF book?

A: "Favorites" are always an evolving concept, based on stages of life and experience. But I'll give it a go.

Non-fiction first: *The Complete Idiot's Guide to Music Composition*, because I like to spread my modest creative talent as thinly as possible.

Fiction: The novel that sticks with me although I read it several decades ago is *The Reivers*, by Faulkner. An accessible tale by one of the country's most complex writers, and master of dense multi-page, stream-of-consciousness prose.

Honorable Mentions: *Interpreter of Maladies* by Jhumpa Lahiri, *The Lone Ranger and Tonto Fight in Heaven* by Sherman Alexie, *A Good Scent from a Strange Mountain* by Robert Olen Butler.

About the author

CJ Erick writes in multiple genres, publishes novels in a space fantasy series, and dabbles in poetry. He lives in Dallas area with his wife and their rescue superhero dog Saber-Girl, calls his sourdough bread starter "Ursula" (K. Le Guin), and cooks crazy-good Cajun food for a Midwest Yankee.

www.cjerickfiction.com, facebook.com/cj.erick.9, Instagram: cee_jay_erick

Useful and Beautiful Things

E. Saxey

This suburb has rows and rows of identical 19th century houses, but when any single home is opened, it can contain wonders.

It's late in the hot afternoon when I report to the address the Guvnor sent me. A mahogany behemoth is escaping through the ground floor sash window: a George III wardrobe with claw feet. A remarkable piece of furniture, requiring a gang of four sweaty men to wrestle it through the window.

"Frankie!" I recognise one of the men as the Guvnor, the gang's coordinator. He's hauling at a claw foot, struggling with the weight. "Give us a hand, girl?" I step in and take some of his burden, protecting the wardrobe from damage as we bring it down to the ground. The men are thankful, if confused. I'm stronger than I look. The Guvnor slaps me on the back. "Ta, Frankie. This is a hell of a house. There's so much bloody junk, we've only got half of it out."

I follow him up the garden path. The back of his T-shirt reads 'St Lucian 'till I die', providing his own provenance. Alongside the path, I see marvels: a Chinese *famille-verte* floor vase, which shouldn't be standing up on the uneven lawn like that. I lay it gently on the grass. Sheltering under the hedge is a herd of six dining chairs, Queen Anne style, two of them stacked awkwardly, like animals mating.

"Sorry about your Ma, Frankie," calls the Guvnor. "You doing alright?"

I catch his anxiety and reassure us both: "I can work solo."

The Guvnor beckons me indoors, and upstairs to a sunlit study. "This place is a total hodgepodge, Frankie." He flaps his hand at walls, which are lined with shelves. Most are packed with books, but one shelf holds statuettes of gods, a dozen of them, an international pantheon. "It's a bad scene."

I wonder why he sounds dejected. There's death, here, certainly, I know the signs. This house was a man's home, he was the gravity which kept these objects together. Without him, they spin off and spill into the garden, and get damp and chipped. But estate sales are bread and butter to the Guvnor; he's a genius at house clearance, he can strip a place in a day. He helps to mitigate the tragedy of death by finding every item a new home.

"What have you found?" I ask him.

"We put it over the back, there. For safety."

Pushed to one corner of the study is a small low table. My discernment stirs: the table is circular and wooden, satinwood, 19th century—yes, 1860s—with a *pietra dura* marble chess board in the centre. My skills still function, thank goodness. Despite the worries of the last few months, I can do my job.

A chess set made of stone is laid out, ready to play.

I stop dead in the middle of the room. I can't intuit anything about the chess set.

I recognise the shape of the pieces—the nobs and planes of the ultra-traditional Staunton design—but little else. I suppose the translucent pieces could be rock crystal from South Asia. Too vague, much too vague! I try to keep my heart from tick-tick-ticking in panic. The set is slightly uneven, the pieces not symmetrical. Handmade, perhaps by an amateur; such objects are always hard to identify. The dark pieces are carved from malachite, dark green with vivid spots like moss or mould.

"What's wrong with it?" I ask.

"Three of my boys couldn't put this bloody thing away," the Guvnor informs me. "I'll show you what it does." He plucks the dark green queen from the table, blinks, puts her back, nods. "Here, I'll show you." Picks up the queen again and replaces her. He remembers nothing, resetting before my eyes. "Wait a mo, I'll show—"

"You showed me."

"Damn! Did it mess me around, again? Well, you get the idea."

"What do the other pieces do?"

"Not a clue. But one lad who touched them was acting so funny, I had to send him home. It's all yours, if you want it. Usual terms? You take it away, fifty-fifty if you sell it on?"

That's fair, so we shake on it. The Guvnor leaves me to my work. I slough off my backpack, tie back my hair. I don't go back to the chess set, at first, but poke through the bookshelves in case there's a box for the set, or any provenance or context.

"Hey! You can't take any of those."

I jump back. I overlooked the person frowning at me from the far corner of the study, because she wasn't part of my jurisdiction. I take her in: rounded, wearing dusty dungarees, about three decades old, but people are hard to date. Her dark brown hair, in a shaggy bob, is a couple of inches longer than when we last met, and her expression is more combative.

"My employer has an agreement for the books," she says. "I work for Sotherans. I'm Tamsin Zhang."

"I know. I mean, we both worked on the Griffiths estate, in Portslade. I'm Frankie Cornish."

"That was woman with you, an older woman. She got the *Mabinogion.*"

"My colleague." My mother. Yes, she took the *Mabinogion*, an 1880 edition, lavishly illustrated, cloth-covered in green. What a memory for an object Ms Zhang has. I recognise a kindred spirit. I need to reassure her. "I'm only taking the chess set."

She walks closer. Her spectacles are round, with faux tortoiseshell and strong lenses, and I think I come into focus for her because her frown relaxes.

"Oh, yes! I remember you. Why are you in my books, then?"

"Looking for anything related."

"The dead guy had a secretary, who took all his papers."

I sigh at the news. She could go back to her work, but she lingers, perhaps regretting her initial hostility. "What's so important about the chess set?" she asks, peering down at the pieces. She is 5'3", not as high as my chin. "They carried it in here like it might explode."

"I'm disposing of it."

"You're throwing it out? Can I have it?"

"No! Sorry. I mean, I'm taking it away with me. To evaluate."

"Are you taking any of this other stuff? This house is ridiculous. What was he doing with all these?" She points at the shelf of gods, where a fist-sized blue baboon (sixth century BC) hides in his newspaper wrapping from a bronze leopard (17th century, probably stolen in the sack of Benin City). Some of the gods are genuine and some are replicas, and nobody will want the whole mismatched collection, but the Guvnor will find each god a new owner.

In the second during which the gods distract me, Tamsin reaches for a chess piece.

"Don't!"

"I can be careful. I handle fragile books, that's my job." Tamsin is so sure of herself, so indignant, that I pause. She plucks up the green queen, places her down again, blinks and resets. "I'll be careful." She picks the queen up again, puts it down. The possibility of danger overrides my manners, and my hand shoots out to grab her wrist, to stop her third attempt. But Tamsin is already drawing back, and my hand closes on empty air. "Ooh, that's weird. That's *clever...*" She touches the head of the green queen, blinks a few times and laughs in astonishment. "Bloody hell."

"You have to stop. It might not be safe." I sound priggish. She doesn't seem to take offence, but does give me a hard stare, eyes huge through her distorting spectacles.

"Did you know it would do that?"

There's no chance of bluffing, she's felt the weird effect herself. "I knew it would do *something.* That's why the Guvnor called me in."

"Does this kind of thing happen often?"

"To me, yes." She looks at me with avid interest.

"So how does it work?"

"I don't know." I have a handful of hypotheses. "I have to take it away and test it."

Her frown returns, similar to when she mentioned the *Mabinogion*: unwilling to let go. "Wait! I have something that might be connected. We can investigate!"

I am so used to working with my mother that the offer of collaboration is a comfort.

The owner's name is Magnus Owens. Earlier that day, Tamsin found his diaries, which were shelved with his books and thus escaped the notice of his secretary.

"Check these out," Tamsin says. They're half-bound in Moroccan with blind tooling. "Bit creepy, other people's diaries. Not my area."

She passes me a volume. Diaries are the most personal, the least transferrable objects. I know these ones may not find a buyer, despite their fine bindings. "Are there family members who might be interested?"

Tamsin shrugs, indifferent. "Dunno. Owens doesn't mention having a wife or kids, in the parts I read. He was mining graphite in Sri Lanka, obsessed with his collections. He lists all the things he buys, there are cross-references to a stack of auction catalogues, I showed them to the Guvnor." I'm glad. That will help him re-home the objects. "But look at this." Tamsin stands close to me, turns the pages of the volume I hold, and points to the notes and number at the foot of each page: *Won in 22, Sicilian Defence, Smith-Morra Gambit. Lost in 10, Dutch Defence.* "This is the main thing, apart from collecting, that he bothers to write down. It's a record of chess games." She flips forwards, backwards. Numbers on every page.

"He played every night?"

"Yeah, almost. So, do you think he made this freaky chess set to confuse his friends? To win more games. Maybe to win money?" I admire the leaps of her logic. But there's no money mentioned here, only a tally. I flick the pages, find a month when things improve for Owen: *Won in 12. Won in 10.* Only a week before, I find a description of his chess set arriving from Rajasthan.

As soon as I read the place-name, I am flooded by images of Rajasthani stone-carving: Jali screens framing the sky in a lattice of stars. A provenance! I feel it like a delicious cool wave. My heart calms. And the diaries have proved useful, after all.

Tamsin quizzes me, as I take photos of the relevant diary pages

"So do you ever get called in to deal with books? Books which do weird things?"

"Sometimes."

"Magic books?"

"Not magic."

"Alright, *freaky* books. Do you have any? Could I see them?"

"Thank you, but I'm not planning to sell any. You're with Sotherans? I'll think of them, the next time I have one." She looks a little annoyed. I suppose it would have been a professional coup, for her to bring in an unusual tome. I pick up the green queen and stow her in my backpack.

"Hey. Frankie!" She touches my arm, suddenly agitated. "How can you touch the pieces, like that?"

I've made a foolish mistake. Normally I'd wear gloves, to keep up appearances. "I have a high tolerance."

"For freaky stuff." Tamsin's eyes shine. "It doesn't do anything to you?"

"I'm not very sensitive." The room is too hot. If I were staying, I'd throw up the sash windows, invite a breeze in to ruffle the packing paper. But I'm leaving.

Tamsin asks: "If you're not *sensitive*, how will you find out if the other pieces do the same thing?"

She notices too much, and she thinks too fast. I look at the ranks of chess nobility, slightly askew as if drunk, gazing over their pawn army. Each piece could be hazardous. Normally, my mother would test the pieces, at her workbench back home, with great interest and care.

"I'll help you," Tamsin offers.

"You can't."

"I can. They won't do me any real harm, will they?"

"One of the Guvnor's boys went home, sick."

"He might have skived off to enjoy the weather. I'll help you find out."

I have a book of contacts, from my mother, listing trustworthy people who buy strange things. I have storage facilities, and a network of folk (including the Guvnor) who put interesting artefacts my way. What I don't have is someone to do what my mother did: interact with objects, and let them work on her, demonstrating their properties. The nervous ticking fills my chest again.

"I won't *steal* them," she protests. "I'm a *book* person!" I think she's teasing me. I find her hard to read.

"Maybe, thank you. Yes." I make one stipulation for safety: "But not until the house is empty."

For the next few hours, Tamsin works at the far end of the study, chatting with me between periods of intense concentration. She asks me again about unusual books, and I describe a handful that I've seen, and their hazards. I tell her in the hopes she will respect my expertise, as I respect hers, but she seems unsatisfied.

At six in the evening, the shouts and crashes downstairs die away. The Guvnor hands me the keys, and the house is silent.

"So I pick the pieces up," asks Tamsin, "One at a time?"

I hold my notebook and pencil ready. "And tell me the effect."

"Just the greens, or do you think the whites do anything?"

I try to think like Magnus Owens. "He wouldn't want to disadvantage himself."

"Yeah, but could the white pieces do *positive* things?" She puts herself in the shoes of the dead man, so easily.

"Perhaps. Let's try them first." I sit on the floorboards, cross-legged by the chess table. In my experience, it's better not to have too far to fall. Tamsin sits down, not across the board where an opponent would be, but on the adjoining edge to me, our knees almost touching.

I can see how deftly Tamsin must handle delicate books. She walks her index fingers with care along the heads of the pawns.

King's pawn: "Nothing." Knight's pawn: "Nothing." I write, for both: *No effect.*

Bishop's pawn: Tamsin sneezes violently. Her bobbed hair falls forwards. "It wasn't the pawn! It's dust." *No effect/allergenic?*

Rook's pawn: "I feel calm. Really chill." *Relaxing?* Then she looks about the room and sighs. From up on the shelf of gods, the small blue baboon watches us. "This damn house. Why don't I have a house like this, a collection like this? Oh, hang on." She throws the pawn from hand to hand. "It's this piece. It makes me feel like I deserve everything."

"Confidence?"

"Entitlement. Resentment."

Queen's pawn: "Oooh. This one feels *nice.*" Tamsin clutches it to her chest. "Satisfying. Like dumplings. Maybe I'm just hungry." She lifts her arms over her head, savouring the stretch, and regards me with a catlike smile. *Sense of wellbeing?* "What do you want?"

"Sorry?"

She's taken out her phone. "Wonton soup?"

"Dim sum," I say, for the sake of appearances.

"It'll be here in half an hour, you owe me a tenner." Her fingers take three last steps along the front rank of pieces: rook's pawn, bishop's pawn, knight's pawn. "And these are all duds. You could let me have one as a souvenir."

"I have to keep the set together." But perhaps I should pay her half of what I make from the set, because her evaluation will inform me about how to sell it. Not on the open market, of course, but using my mother's list of trustworthy collectors. I would have to stay in contact with Tamsin, to arrange payment. The prospect cheers me.

Tamsin plucks up the white bishop and squints at a bookcase, more than three metres away. "I can read all the titles." She takes off her glasses. "Hey, my eyesight's fine. Holy crap! Has this thing fixed my eyes?"

"It may have optimised how your brain works with your eyes." *Positive minor visual effects*, I write.

"Wow. Can I buy it, seriously?" Her glasses have left a pink dent on each side of her nose. "My eyes are so rubbish, this would be a life-changer."

"We don't know how it works. It could be doing terrible damage to your brain."

White bishop is grudgingly replaced, as are Tamsin's glasses, and she scoops up the white knight. "I feel confident." She chuckles. "No, I feel *lucky.*"

"Shall we test it?" In my pocket, I find two dice and hand them over.

Her expression is sceptical, but she sends the dice rattling across the floorboards. Two sixes. I retrieve them, and Tamsin rolls them again. Double sixes. I write *positive effect, good fortune* while she glares at the white bishop, its eyeless face and aghast mouth.

"So this little blobby boy is actually affecting the world," says Tamsin. "But double sixes are a completely arbitrary symbol. How does it know that they're lucky? Wait, are those dice loaded?"

"I can give you a coin to toss, if you'd rather."

She stands and paces back over to the bookshelves. Impossible questions are grinding together in her mind. She's probably going to leave, now. I may not see her again, except at contentious estate sales, at intervals of years. That's alright. People are allowed to relocate themselves.

Tamsin uses both hands to unshelve a large dictionary, Bosworth and Toller's Old English, cloth-bound in burgundy, and carries it back to me. She opens the cover carefully. Inside, the pages have been hollowed out to hide a flat bottle of Talisker 25 year single malt whisky. "I found it this morning. Isn't it tacky?" She upends the bottle into her mouth and there's an audible glug. She hands it over to me.

"I don't know if we should combine alcohol with…"

"We totally should, because people are going to play with these pieces when they're drinking sherry, or what-have-you, and you need to know how bad that would be." She folds her legs up and re-joins me on the floor. She's misjudged our proximity, and now her knee presses mine. "I bet Owens got his friends drunk, the filthy cheat. Why do you have dice in your pocket? Does this kind of thing happen to you a lot, eh?"

"I have some cufflinks which work the other way. Gold with blue enamel." Translucent lapis blue over hatched engine-turning. They're in my mother's permanent collection, never to be sold. "Fabergé."

"Unlucky cufflinks?"

"Three owners found them… difficult." I realise I'm showing off. I shouldn't. It's dangerous to invite her to look closely at my life.

"Wow. *Terminally* difficult? And you kept them? William Morris wouldn't like that." She prods my shoulder and takes back the whisky bottle from my hands. I want to share her joke but I can only think of William Morris' floral patterns, looping across mid-C19th sofas.

"Why would he care about my cufflinks?"

"He said you shouldn't have anything in your house that you don't know to be useful, or believe to be beautiful. But your house is full of *awful* stuff, by the sound of it. Am I right?"

I think of my mother's workbench, and all the artefacts my mother restored and rehomed. Then the wall of strongboxes, one of which will hold the chess set. I picture the peace that will fill me when I close the lid. "It's a very useful place, overall."

"Oh, Frankie, you should have a beautiful house!" This time it sounds less like a scolding than a wish: Tamsin thinks I deserve a beautiful house. Before I can ask her, she adds: "What's your favourite thing that you own? Is it a book?"

I've never thought of that. I don't truly consider the objects in my collection to be mine. They're only resting with me because nobody else can own them, at present. "I don't have a favourite."

"Not even that *Mabinogion* you snatched?" Another nudge on my shoulder. "Was it freaky? What did it do?" It could be a joke, but perhaps her excellent memory for books is supported by a great capacity for grudges. I shake my head.

White rook: "Nothing. No, wait." She holds out her wrist. Should I admire her bracelet of 1970s cloisonné beads, patterned with bats? "My pulse. Feel it."

I touch her warm soft wrist, and the flicker I find there slows and slows. "You should put the rook down."

"But I feel really calm. Really on top of things..." I pluck the rook from her hand. *Induces catatonia?* "Spoil-sport," she accuses, rubbing her wrist where I touched it. "The queen's got to be the most powerful one, right?" She lowers her fingertip onto the milky crown of the white queen. "Oh. I'm the most important person in the world. Anything I do for my own benefit is just fine. Cool." *Solipsism?*

White king: "Wow. The board just lit up." Tamsin sits bolt upright. "I can see all the moves. I haven't played chess since I was ten, but I can see every way it could possibly go..."

She turns her gaze on me, and lapses into silence.

I write down *strategic foresight.*

"How do you get into a job like yours?" she asks, still staring.

I write *overly curious,* because I know she's reading it.

"No, but seriously. It can't just be because you're *insensitive.*"

Persistent intrusive questioning. I shouldn't have shown off about my cufflinks. I need to turn her attention aside. "Is there more whisky?"

Tamsin reluctantly relinquishes the white king. "I can't keep it?"

"It might give you something like concussion."

"But you're still going to sell the set?"

The list of people I would trust with them has dwindled with each piece, each power. "I'll see."

"Or get rid of them. Throw them away."

"No! Don't say that!"

"Why not? God, you sound like those people who get sentimental over books being chucked out. Do you know how many terrible, waste-of-space books there are? You can't hang on to *everything*, you can just bung stuff in the bin…"

I shake my head, over and over. I worry I might scream.

A chime rings round the room. Tamsin springs to her feet. "Food's here!"

Tamsin thunders down the stairs, and the vibrations set one of the shelf-gods wobbling. I nudge it further back, to safety. I would love to have a day to hold each of the small statues in my hands and know who they are, where they come from. But they're not dangerous, so they're not my business.

I should be wary of Tamsin. She lulled me into thinking of her as my work partner, but I didn't choose her. She keeps teasing me and touching me, but I should keep a level head. I hear her chatting with the delivery man, which gives me time to pluck up all the pieces we've tested and stash them in my bag, away from temptation.

When Tamsin returns, her face is somewhat pallid. "The delivery guy told me that Owens *died* here. In the house."

I remember the Guvnor saying this was a *bad scene*, and wonder if he meant the manner of Owen's death. "It's understandable." People die. Things endure.

"It's grim." Tamsin lays the pots of food out on the floor. "Hey, where did the white pieces go?"

"They're safe. What do you think Owens was like?" I ask, to distract her from my tidying, and from the fact that I won't eat the dim sum. And because I want to know her opinion.

"An English man collecting colonial curiosities to make his Englishness more interesting." She puts herself in Owen's place, then puts him in his place, too.

"Did you get that from his diaries?"

"I got that from his book collection—lots of international publications, lots of uncracked spines. Don't be sad! All the better for my bosses, to have pristine Bengali poetry. *Gitanjali* will end up with someone who appreciates it."

I wait until Tamsin wrangles a steamed dumpling into her mouth. "The green pieces," I say. "I shouldn't let you test them."

"*Let* me, hah." She can still argue with her mouth full.

"The green ones may be terrible."

"No, because look…" She swigs her coke. I've hidden the whisky under my backpack. "They can't be that godawful, or nobody would ever play chess with him twice. They're not going to make you cough up your lungs, are they?" She's three moves ahead of me. "And *you* need to know how they work. Don't you? To be a good caretaker."

I need to know the full extent, to judge what to do with the set: who might safely buy it, or more likely, how I can store it. Whether to seal it in clay or submerge it in running water. But must I rely on Tamsin?

"Let's just do the pawns," she offers, as a compromise. "They're only small."

The pawns will perplex us both.

King's pawn: "Nothing." No effect. "It's not doing anything at all." She chuckles slyly.

"Tamsin, are you lying?"

"Nooo, heh-heh." I write *Induces duplicity/hysteria?* Tamsin shivers. "Holy hell, that was stranger than the eyesight thing."

"And it made you lie?"

"It didn't do anything! I was fine. Heh-heh."

I reach to take back the pawn, and she makes a fist, twists and turns, play-wrestles my fingers with her own. I don't like to look strong, and she's wily and enjoying herself, so the fight goes on for longer than it needs to. When the pawn is out of her hand, she asks: "Why would that help Owens win? I suppose it would encourage his opponent to cheat."

Bishop's pawn: Tamsin sighs. "I'm rubbish at this, anyway."

"At chess?"

"At everything." *Hopelessness.*

Knight's pawn: "I want to bet you a lot of money that I'm going to win." *Risk seeking? Over-confidence?* "What happens if—" Before I can stop her, she's palmed two pawns simultaneously. "Ha! I think I'm going to lose and I don't care, I still want to bet on it! I wish you could feel this!" Her grin is contagious, her eyes are alight. This is all irresponsible, reprehensible. I should be working alone.

"Stop. Please." Thankfully, she does.

Queen's pawn: "It's telling me just do anything, move wherever, don't overthink it."

Hazardous rashness. "Does it have a voice?"

"No, it's just a feeling. Do some things have voices?"

I think of the rooms in my mother's house—my house—filled with items that charmed and berated her, to which I am blessedly oblivious. We were perfect colleagues. "Sometimes."

She leans in closer to me. Does she want to be hugged? I could do that. She swipes the whisky from under my bag. "Queen's pawn makes you thirsty."

Rook's pawn makes Tamsin jump to her feet, knocking over the remnants of her takeaway. "Sorry! I can't sit still." *Restless.* "Why does he get all this stuff? How can anyone deserve…" *Psychologically restless?* "I feel small. Do I seem small?"

"Not more than you—no."

"You're not taking me seriously!"

I should have said something kinder, more respectful. "I'm sorry. Put the pawn down?"

Instead, she sweeps up more pieces, handfuls of them, stuffing them into the pockets of her dungarees, and runs.

I lunge at her but she's quicker. She's off down the stairs, almost flying, bursting out of the back door and vanishing into the overgrown garden.

I have to follow. It's dusk, and the trees cast deep shadows. There's a pale path, but as I run down it, chasing her, I feel thorns catch at my clothes. I hear Tamsin, rather than see her, ahead of me. Please let her not be hurt. Let her not drop anything, either. Let me not have to hunt for the dark green chess pieces amid brambles in the dark.

My eyes adjust and a movement draws my gaze to Tamsin standing in an old wooden gazebo. I should jump at her, pin her arms, make her release the rook's pawn. But I can't imagine hurting her.

"Come on! Take them off me." She raises her fist and waves it from side to side. "This is most the important thing, right?"

It is an accusation, but it is true. People pass, things endure; my responsibility is to things. While I hesitate, I see a quick arc in the dark, her arm as she flings the pawn of low self-esteem far into the garden.

Her penitence is instant. "Oh, God, sorry! Shit! I'll find it!" Her face glows in the light of her phone. "It went in that direction…"

I have a keyring torch, and I spot the pawn before she does, resting in a patch of dandelions. I turn my back to Tamsin before I stoop to pick it up. I need to keep it secure. I dust off the dirt and place it on my tongue, force myself to swallow, feel the nobbles as it slides down my throat.

"Found it," I call.

"I've found something else." Tamsin has her phone light trained on a flickering tail of plastic tape in the bushes, with lettering: POLICE LINE DO NOT CROSS. "I think he died in the garden. Owens." Tamsin stares up at the house, the sash window glowing with light. "Maybe he jumped out of the window of his study. Do you think the chess set killed him?"

I thought not: he should have known its properties. But what pieces might he have touched by accident, in what combination? Did he grab recklessness, self-doubt, and foresight all in one hand, and throw himself away? And now all his possessions have followed him, flung outwards, dispersing.

Tamsin, standing beside me, says: "You'll get rid of it, won't you?"

"Don't worry. I won't pass it on to another owner."

"No, I mean you should trash it. Smash it up and bury it."

I dislike this line of thought. I dislike it very much. Inside me, things tick painfully fast.

The horrible plastic police tape dances about in the wind. I am seized by a pang of fear. I'm not mourning Owen, or thinking of the ways he might have died; I'm empathising with the objects he's left behind. I never want to be wrapped in a rug, left on a lawn. I don't want to be forced to seek someone new, someone who appreciates me enough to keep me.

My internal mechanisms are spinning wildly. I need to be calm. I remind myself: I may not have an owner, but I have a place in the world. I have earned it.

I duck into the gazebo and sit on the bench I find inside. "You can't throw an artefact away," I say. "Just because you don't have a use for it at the moment." I'm speaking to myself more than to Tamsin.

She hears me, though, and shouts back: "But you can't hang onto it indefinitely, either. Not if it's toxic!"

"I'll keep it safe."

"But you won't live forever, will you?"

I don't know the answer to that.

Tamsin stumbles into the gazebo and joins me on my bench, pulling out her bottle of coke (into which, it occurs to me, she has poured a lot of the whisky) and drinking deeply.

"Let's do the rest of them quickly," she offers.

I shake my head.

"But we're almost done." She points to her dungaree pocket. I see the bumps of the stolen pieces through the denim. "You get them out."

I work my hand into her pocket, ignoring the warmth of her body, and retrieve them. I line them up on the bench, within arm's reach, and lay my torch alongside, to light them. I take out my small notebook and pen. I can complete this quickly and depart.

Green rook: "I shouldn't be here," says Tamsin.

"The same as the rook's pawn?"

"No, that was just twitchy legs. This is: I need to get away, right now! Shit, do you think this is the one that killed Owens? Sit on my feet. Come on, it'll slow me down if I try to run off." She's tucking a foot under the bend of my knee, wriggling it until it's wedged. "There, like that."

Need to be elsewhere? Self-destruction? My handwriting is not neat.

Green bishop: "Do you ever wonder what you're for?"

I did. I do. Has the bishop given her telepathy? If so, does she know how conscious I am of her wriggling foot?

"Go on, write down *existential doubt.* Or *moody cow.*"

Green knight: "I want to fight you. I hate you!" She wrenches her foot free from under my leg, but falls backwards to the floor. I spring up, hit a gazebo pillar and shake down cobwebs and dust onto both of us. I want to help Tamsin stand, but her arms are flailing, she is still furious at me. She takes a wild swing. The chess piece flies from her hand. "Gah! Vicious little horse bastard!" she cries.

I crouch down to pick up the knight, and quickly swallow it, to join the pawn. I am the safest temporary store for small, wicked objects.

Before I can stand, a hot hand lands on my back. I hear Tamsin's breath. Her hand slides up, she slips her fingers into my hair, to stir deliciously against my scalp.

"You're a very attractive—whatever you are. A very cute curator."

Her voice is low and tender, all her rage boiled away, and her heat warms me. But only one of her hands is in my hair.

She's holding the green king in the other.

It's not fair to let this go on. I twist around and prise her fingers open as gently as I can.

I know it's worked when I hear her swear, and she pulls away from me and stomps to the other side of the hut.

I eat the green king. I focus on finding my notebook. I write: *Emotional connection?* A euphemism. The lust-inducing king is even less explicable than the rage-knight. Would desire distract your opponent? It's distracted Tamsin, who is holding her head in her hands.

"Is that the last one?" she asks, flatly.

"There's only one piece left, and we know what she does. The green queen. Amnesia, or confusion."

We are confused enough. "Yes."

Tamsin raises her head, sucks in the night air. The aphrodisiac effects of the green king have disgusted her. And I'm to blame, I wanted to impress her by my association with wonderful things. My back feels chilly, now, where her hand had rested.

Tamsin raises her head, sucks in the night air. "Is that the last one?" she asks, faintly.

"There's only one piece left, and we know what she does. The green queen."

"Oh! Her." The monarch of forgetting and re-setting. Maybe Tamsin would appreciate some amnesia.

I look back to the house, and through the back door glimpse floorboards of rich golden oak. Carpets fade and moths consume them, but wood goes on for centuries. Until you burn it. Even then, it's useful.

"You have to get rid of them all," Tamsin instructs me. "Apart from the one which fixed my eyesight..."

"White bishop."

"You could give that one to a doctor. All the others, though, they need to go! You can't let people use them to start fights, or win elections. Or as a bloody truth drug."

I can't read my notebook, so I double-check my mental list of the pieces; none of them worked as a truth drug. Her anger's making her exaggerate. "I'll keep them away from anyone," I promise her, as I pick up my backpack. "I'll use my best strong-room."

"But you could fall under a bus tomorrow. They'll get out into the world again. Why not destroy them?"

Tick-tick-tick, my heart stutters, faster than I've ever felt it. I can't speak my objection.

"They're lethal!" she insists. "They might have killed their last owner!" I know the fuel for her hate isn't the self-destructive bishop, or the aggressive knight. It's the green king, the piece that made her want me. "*And* they're ugly! They're failing the William Morris test on both fronts."

"I do believe that almost everything can find a new owner."

“Really? How long have you been hoarding those murderous cufflinks? Objects have to earn the space they take up in the world! Things have to be useful...”

And to my surprise, tears well up in my eyes and drip onto the golden oak floorboards.

“Not you! I didn’t mean you! Oh, damn...” She scrambles across the bench to wrap her arms around me. “You’re remarkable.”

“Am I?” My mother did a lot of work to make me appear ordinary. “Is it obvious?”

Tamsin continues her clumsy hug and clumsy reassurance. “No, no, not unless you look really closely.” People don’t usually look at me closely. “I’d never have noticed, except the white king made me understand how things worked. Oh, and then you ate those chess pieces.”

I clear my throat. “I’ve lost my mother.” My co-worker, the one who restored me. Almost all my memories are from after she mended me. “She died, two months ago, she died.”

“I’m sorry.”

“This is the first job I’ve been on, without her. I need to know I can still do the work, that I’m useful.”

Tamsin loosens her grip and I think she’ll let me go but she settles into a more sustainable embrace. “I understand. Everyone wants to be useful.”

“But every thing *needs* to be useful.”

Tamsin shakes her head very hard, brushing her face against mine. “No, no, no. You don’t need to be useful.”

“I do.”

She is trying to think of arguments against all her earlier pronouncements. “Beautiful! You could be beautiful, instead.”

I want to correct her: no, someone else must *believe* I’m beautiful.

I want to ask: does she believe I’m beautiful?

Instead, I ask: “Which chess piece makes you tell the truth?”

Tamsin buries her face in my shoulder without answering. It is the green king, then. I study her cloisonné bracelet in the dimness and listen to the tick-tick-ticking of my heart.

See E. Saxey’s story “Useful and Beautiful Things” online at Metaphorosis.
If you liked it, leave a comment. Authors love that!

Remember to subscribe to our e-mail updates so you'll know when new stories are posted.

About the story

My most obvious inspiration was all the magical objects in fantasy fiction. Some of them are owned by a sinister religious order or kept in a secret government warehouse, where they can sit for decades. But if an object is in private hands, it would probably come back onto the market when the owner died, so how would the antiques trade handle it? I thought it would require a small team of specialists, taking the proper precautions to nullify curses or contain startling powers. The specialists would be well respected, but not showy, brought in by word-of-mouth recommendations.

What pushed the story onwards was the essential strangeness of collections, and their need for an owner to give them meaning. If I look around my study, every object makes sense to me; they're an external map of my interests and experiences, past and present. If I die, then it's just a roomful of junk. Nobody will be able to tell: did I love that book, or had I never got around to reading it? Where did that pebble come from? The key has been lost, the message is meaningless. I became fascinated by the restorative work of finding a new owner for an object, a new home, and thus a new meaning. Something as mundane and brusque as house clearance becomes a very kind, respectful process. I combined these two concerns — handling magical objects, and rehoming things as a restorative act — and together they conjured up my main character.

A question for the author

Q: What do you think is the single most important quality for a good writer to possess?

A: I think a writer's most important quality could be the capacity to stand back from the work and evaluate how it will be read by others. It's an incredibly difficult work of strategic amnesia — you know what you wanted to convey, but you have to forget that, to see whether your meaning actually comes across from what's on the page. And you also know what's going to happen next in the plot, but have to evaluate whether you've laid enough groundwork, or over-egged the pudding. Reading groups or partners are invaluable, because they're genuinely fresh eyes, although you have to get past the exchange of polite compliments and ask really big basic questions: what time period do you actually think it's set in? Did you notice that this character confessed to murder? And you can't get readers in at every sentence. So being able to do it alone is necessary, and ten times harder.

About the author

E. Saxey is a queer Londoner who works in Universities and volunteers in libraries. Their current writing desk used to belong to the Ancient Order of Druids.

thelightningbook.co.uk, @esaxey

The Beast-Consul

E.C. Dorgan

It's the best day of the year for a Consul. Five hundred guests invited to the national day reception, and most of them are here, clapping while the Consul climbs up to the stage. There's the host-country Foreign Minister, the Chief of Protocol, the Dean of the Diplomatic Corps. The Consul spies a little girl in the second row, in a grey dress. She makes a mental note to approach the girl later, and tell her she too, one day, can be Consul.

There's a hush while the audience waits. By some miracle, every cell phone is silent. The Consul touches her helmet—her hair, and pushes down her doubts.

"Esteemed guests."

A bird with black, indigo, and orange feathers flies over the stage. The Consul's voice trails while she watches it. By the time she remembers her guests, cell phones are ringing and everyone's talking. The Foreign Minister's chair is empty. Her audience lost, she starts to speak.

She sits in her office after the reception, watching birds out her window while her staff bring her papers. She writes 'approved' and signs her name without reading. Two years at post, and she still doesn't know how to be Consul. Her bunions ache and her nylons chafe. She's dying to take off her sharp heels and cracking makeup but she's wanted at a dinner. They're always the same—her diplomatic colleagues laughing and clinking glasses with their more gregarious counterparts, the Consul alone with her plate.

The other diplomats attribute her silence to some national quirk, but the Consul knows better. She's still that strange little girl from the woods north of the capital, under the cover of helmet hair and a title she'll never be fit for.

It's past dark when she returns to the Official Residence. She needs both hands to take off her heels. Her husband meets her in the kitchen, wearing fuzzy socks. He holds out a colourless rose.

"Our anniversary." He kisses the top of her head.

She tells him she needs air.

She steps outside to the garden. Her bare toes breathe in the night. The garden is the only part of her job that she likes. During the day, it's all vehicle exhaust and traffic. But after dark, it's magical. She can smell the night-blooming roses, touch their tender petals.

She feels her cheeks and finds them wet. The next instant, she's sobbing. She doesn't need to look up to know it's the moon. She cries every time it's full. Some nights, she doesn't stop until morning. The moon reminds her of her childhood, how she spent too much time alone in the woods, reading. How she lost herself there. She wishes she could remember what part of her is missing.

She tastes dread when she wakes up in the morning. Steels her toes for her pointed heels and her face for the camouflage of makeup. It's too much. She takes out her phone and searches until she finds a forest. Brings the screen to her nose so she can smell the plastic and see all the thumbprints. That night, instead of staring at the ceiling unsleeping, she watches the trees until morning.

The next thing she knows, she's skipping receptions and sending 'regrets' to dinners. Googling trees during meetings. One day, she's in a tough negotiation when she has a revelation. The thought rocks her entire being. She stops the session and rushes with her phone to the bathroom. Locks herself in a stall and zooms to make the screen big. Presses her nose into the forest, utterly certain, for once, what would fix her—to learn the secret name of trees.

All day at work, she stares into the phone. In the evening, she closes herself in her home office and watches the forest some more. Her eyes strain. She misses deadlines and neglects to eat. She forgets her son's birthday. And something stranger—she remembers things.

At first it's nothing—bright colours, indescribable smells. They come to her when she's signing documents, or watching her trees. Her husband asks if she's okay. Soon she's seeing whole scenes—forests, dragonflies, pine trees. She gets flashes while giving speeches. She has to grip the podium with both hands now. One day, she draws a dragonfly on a document. She scribbles over it, but her staff bring it back to her, seeking clarification.

She's in her office one night, toes in the rug, bunions aching, when a memory returns in a rush. When she was still that little girl in the forest, long before she was Consul, a monster and the moon came down to her. She can still see the shine of the moon, reflecting so bright it burned her eyes, and the sound—how could she forget it—of that stretching of her heart from forest to sky. The sound of it snapping like gum, the monster with its teeth dripping red.

She buys gum and puts all five pieces in her mouth at once to try to make sense of it. She chews and smacks and stretches the gum between her teeth, but all that she feels is emptiness.

One night, sitting in her office, the Consul gets a call from headquarters. It's the Head of department—the Consul's boss. She instructs the Consul to report back to the Ministry by the end of the week for 'consultations'. The Consul makes the arrangements. She knows it's a euphemism, like everything in diplomacy.

On her first day in the capital, the Consul wears a grey power suit and slips on her sharpest heels. She puts on two layers of foundation, and sprays extra hairspray on her hair. She looks in the mirror, but she doesn't see a diplomat.

She spends the day in meetings. People in ashen suits call her 'Consul' and take notes when she speaks. It's stultifying. Her nylons itch. Her mind is on the forest in her phone. She touches her helmet-hair and wonders how she became this thing.

There's the hanging threat of a working dinner, but the Consul needs to breathe. She leaves the Ministry and walks two blocks to a park. It's nothing fancy—dying grass and a pond that's more of a puddle. The Consul walks around it. The uneven pitch of the grass hurts her bunion, and her pencil skirt limits her step.

She walks in circles and loses track of time. The sun descends behind buildings, and the nearby road quiets. She looks up and sees ducks in the water. Their necks are bright green, and when they swim, their rears waggle. The Consul smiles. The next time she looks, the sky is dark and the ducks are long gone.

Her phone buzzes and when she checks it, she sees five unanswered calls. She's missed her dinner. She returns to the hotel and kicks off her shoes. It feels good to throw her nylons in the garbage, though she has another pair laid out for tomorrow. She studies her reflection. Her helmet hair's held, but her foundation is cracked and all she can see of her makeup is lipliner.

For the first night in weeks, she doesn't pull up her cellphone forest. Instead, she looks up ducks. Each search leads to another query. Two hours and many Internet wormholes later, she finds herself making an appointment for a therapist. She has no idea how googling ducks has led her there.

The next day, she finishes her meetings early to get to her appointment. A blast of essential oils hits her when she walks into the therapist's office. The scent might be pine, but it burns her nostrils—it's nothing like the imagined perfume of her forest.

The therapist exudes confidence—she would make a good diplomat. She asks the Consul about her job. The Consul tells her she signs papers. She asks her about her marriage. The Consul says her husband remembers anniversaries. She asks about her son. The Consul describes what he's reading. The therapist asks if she's happy.

The Consul looks out the window. There's no bird outside to save her. She wants to tell the therapist she's a fake, that she doesn't know what to say at dinners, or what to do with all those papers. She wants to tell her how she doesn't love her husband, and how when she looks at her son, she doesn't know how to be a mother.

Instead, she tells the therapist the one thing she promised herself she wouldn't share. She tells the therapist how she cries under the moon, and how she lost herself so many years ago, when she was just a little girl in the forest. She tells the therapist how she knows what would make her better, how she'd throw away every diplomatic privilege and title, just to taste, for one fleeting moment, the rounded syllables of the forest's secrets.

The therapist's eyes widen. She opens her notebook and writes. At the end of their hour, she declares they'll need more sessions. The Consul says she'll check her schedule. She walks out of the therapist's office and resolves never to go back.

Back at the hotel, the Consul peels off her godawful nylons and rubs the budding bunion on her foot. If only she could throw her heels out the window...

Her phone buzzes with an incoming message. She reads it and wants to toss her phone away too. Instead, she pulls out another pair of nylons and reaches for her heels. Stares at her cramped toes in the elevator, wishing it would descend slower. When the doors open, her husband greets her. He holds out a grey rose. His face, as usual, is blank.

"Surprise dear, I'm here."

Her son steps out behind him. His face says he'd rather be reading.

They go to a restaurant. Her husband says their son spent the day choosing it. The Consul doesn't believe it. Her son's like her. Even now, lingering over his pasta, his eyes are elsewhere. Her husband's the sentimental one. The one who wants this facade of family. He reaches his hand out to touch her. She doesn't pull away. She forces a smile—that's what diplomats do.

Her eyes start to tear after dinner, when they're waiting for the bill. No need to look outside to know it's the moon rising. She excuses herself to go to the washroom. When she looks at her reflection, the tears are already streaming.

The Consul's most important meeting is the next day, with the Head of department, in her office on the executive floor. The Consul has never been up there. When she steps out of the elevator, the first thing she notices is the different carpet. It's the colour of smoke, and it cushions her toes, even her bunion. When she steps, her heels are silent.

She arrives at the Head of department's office and sees the Head of personnel is there too. It makes the Consul uneasy. The Head of department doesn't acknowledge her. She types and hits send on an email, then picks up the phone to ask about a briefing note. Her slate suit is designer and her helmet's immaculate.

The Consul looks out the window and waits. After ten minutes, the Head of department points to the mints on her desk.

"Take one."

The Consul complies.

The Head of department takes off her glasses. She finally looks at the Consul. "How are you doing, really?"

An impossibly orange bird lands on the outside ledge. The Consul's eyes follow it. The Head of personnel opens her notebook. It hurts to look away from the bird, but the Consul needs her wits. The Head of department watches her, unblinking. It occurs to the Consul that these 'consultations' have nothing to do with bilateral relations and everything to do with how she's doing 'really'.

When the Consul starts to speak, the Head of personnel picks up her pen. She writes more notes than the therapist. At least the Consul avoids mentioning trees. Precisely twelve minutes after it's started, the Head of department declares the meeting over. She picks up the phone and says she needs that briefing note. She doesn't look at the Consul.

The Consul comes away with an extra five days of leave and instructions to 'decompress'. The Head of personnel escorts the Consul out of the office. She tells the Consul she cares, but she's looking into her phone and typing a message when she says it.

Her husband finds a cabin in the woods north of the capital. The Consul can't work the kettle, and she's afraid of the propane-powered stove. But the setting's incredible. Those ducks from the city are nothing like the birds in these woods. On her first day, she sees an enormous blue bird with a magenta beard, a bright orange and black bird with a yellow stripe, and tiny purple bird whose chirp sounds like a dragon or a train engine. And the trees—each time she looks outside, they take her breath. Her little forest on the screen pales in comparison. And their perfume, evergreen, is so much more than that she ever dreamed.

Their first morning in the woods, her husband makes her breakfast in bed: homemade scones, blueberry jam, and hot coffee. By the time she gets dressed, he's back in the kitchen, making a batch of brownies. Her son is in the woods, probably reading. Growing up, she was always in the woods too, with a book. She wonders if he watches birds.

Her husband hums while he mixes batter. The Consul watches him and pours a second coffee. He's always been a different creature. Nothing like her and her son. At least he bakes.

He pours the batter, and for a split second, the tune he's humming wavers, and his sleepy eyes go sharp. The Consul blinks, and he's back on-key, his eyes are once again soft. The therapist said she had imagination.

The Consul can't figure out where the days go. Her husband makes a different pastry for breakfast every morning. He bakes more brownies than they can possibly eat. In the evening, he barbecues hamburgers. One night, he gets mustard on his shirt and they laugh like a family. When the sun goes down, he makes a campfire and they roast marshmallows and listen for loons. Her son surprises her with his knowledge of them. The moon rises, but she's surrounded by trees, so she only cries a little bit.

By the fourth day of her 'decompression', the Consul's had enough of watching her husband bake. She puts on boots—so much better than heels—and pulls her hair into a ponytail. She takes a compact out of her purse and squints into the glass. It's been days since she's looked in a mirror. There's powder stuck to the glass, it makes her face soft and hazy. She looks decades younger without her helmet.

When she steps outside, the first thing she notices is how the soft earth cushions her feet, even her bunion. She breathes in spruce and pine, and regrets spending the previous days indoors.

She walks out to the trees, and takes in a world beyond that pond in the city. Her night-time garden pales. To think, she wasted all that time staring into that screen. *This* is a forest. Her fingertips brush on silken tree needles while she walks. She's never touched anything so soft. The perfume wafts up from her fingers. It makes her light-headed, almost giddy. She marvels at the clubmosses and lichens. She used to play with them when she was little, in these same woods. Dragonflies flit, bright reds and blues. She didn't know the world contained so many of them.

She stops in front of a towering pine. Can't even breathe when she looks at it. The whole universe is there in its branches. When she touches her palm to its bark, it thrums electric and vital. She closes her eyes and asks for its name. She waits, then continues walking. The forest keeps its secrets.

She only knows it's past dinner when the moon rises, glimmering behind pines, and the tears start to flow from her eyes. She should go back to the cabin. Her husband will be worried. Her son won't know she's gone. But now, reunited with dragonflies, the thought pains her. She could spend a lifetime here. There was a time she thought she would.

A memory surfaces. She was tired of being that weird child, reading books under pines, playing with clubmosses. The other girls were going places. They'd be important, Consuls maybe. She wanted to be like them.

For a while, she almost was. She made a career, she got promoted. She married her husband. She had a son. Never mind that inside she felt dead.

She stops walking. She's about to turn back, but that's when she sees it—a light, red and gleaming, behind the farthest trees.

The Consul's stepping between trees, deeper and deeper into the forest. The red beacon isn't nearing. She's on the verge of being lost. There are bears in these woods, and worse things. She almost remembers.

She's about to give up when the air changes. Her nose is stuffy from crying, but when she breathes, it's undeniable—damp and rot, a whisper of fungus, and something else.

The scent gets stronger as she moves to the light. She trips on a log and almost tumbles. She sees it when she straightens—a clearing in the trees, a pile of logs in the centre, slick with moisture, and shining blue and orange with saprophytes. And under the logs, expanding in every direction, all the way to her own two feet, the earth is bursting with ghost pipe. It's too bright for her eyes, even under moonlight.

But it's what's sitting on the logs that takes her breath. The source of that gleam she's been tracking all night. She sucks in her breath.

The monster's ear flickers, and it starts to turn its head. Eyes fix on her, red flames. They were easier to look at through trees. Looking into them, her eyes sting. She drops her gaze as the monster pulls back its lips. Its incisors are longer than her arms.

The monster stretches its lips farther, and the Consul loses her breath. Her knees no longer support her. Behind the terror of those sharp, blood-dripping incisors, she sees what she lost all those years ago in the forest. She can barely make out the shape, but for once in her life, she's certain. There, behind fangs, is her bright red beating heart.

The memories rush back in a flood. The monster was smaller then, more of a pup than a beast, with sharp baby teeth. It's not so young now. There's grey around its muzzle, a fleck of white on its chest. Its fangs are brown and rotting.

A dragonfly lands on its snout, reflecting bright blue in the moonlight. The Consul watches it. She didn't know there were nighttime dragonflies. The monster shifts and the whole forest shudders. Her teeth rattle. She imagines her husband pausing his baking while the ground rumbles under him, and across the ocean, the petals of her nighttime roses vibrating.

When the monster focuses on her, her own heart jumps in its teeth. Her brain screams at her to run. But instead, she watches in horror, as her arm starts to extend, and her fingers reach out, grasping. The Consul wants to recoil, and to walk—no, run, back to the cabin. But her feet are stepping in the wrong direction. She's walking, arms forward, toward the monster, her body insisting on reunion with that lost piece of her.

She steps up on a log. Grabs a handhold and climbs higher. The saprophytes on the wood make her palms slip. She perseveres. Now she's only a few feet from the monster. Her whole body is trembling. The dragonfly spooks. The monster's breath is rotten. Her face is to its teeth.

She's so close now, she can feel the percussion in her spine. She inches closer, and her heart in its mouth beats faster. The sound's hypnotic. She's not used to it, but there's something about it. Hard to imagine now, how she existed all those years, oceans away... For a moment, she's back in her office in the Official Residence, toes in the rug, eyes straining. Chest dead silent. Some things are worse than monsters.

This time, she doesn't hesitate. She closes her eyes, and even though her hands won't stop shaking, she lets the intelligence of her body guide her fingers. There's the brush of bone, the tackiness of gums. Her fingers reach deeper. Then she feels it—something vital, electric. She doesn't breathe. It's thumping.

Her fingers can't quite reach around it. She squeezes her wrists through the space between its incisors. Then her elbows. She's in the monster to her armpits. She closes her fingers around her heart. It slows. She exhales.

When the monster's jaw loosens, the Consul isn't expecting the loss of resistance. Her legs slide, and before she can find her footing, she's sprayed in the face by a torrent of water. It knocks her to the ground. She hits her chin on a log and her knee on a rock, but the important thing—she's still holding her heart. Water streams into her boots. The ghost pipe's submerged.

The monster's weeping. It looks smaller without her heart. Now instead of fire in its eyes, there's only loss. Her eyes get wet. She knows what it's like to be in this world without a heart. She has a vision of the beast crying every full moon, drowning the forest in sorrow.

She starts back toward the cabin, but it's slow-going—the monster's tears are to her knees. She has to wade through water, and her soaked boots and pants weigh her down. Her heart thuds in her hand, warm and slimy. She tightens her fingers. She's only gone a few steps when the monster starts moaning. Sorrow cracks the night, and the Consul lets out a sob. She imagines her husband, crying into his brownie batter, and her son, wiping a tear from his book, blurring the print. The monster howls. The whole forest grieves in reply. The sound echoes in her chest and she remembers.

Last time, she stood facing the monster-pup as her child-heart fluttered in its teeth. The pup's eyes were sad. Her eyes filled up too, but she'd made her decision. She felt grown-up. Dragonflies flitted and she swatted them away.

She doesn't want the memory, but now she can't stop it. The monster didn't steal anything. She ripped her heart out by herself. She can still see the blood running between her fingers, the tears filling up her hollowed chest as she turned her back to the forest. She was still blinking, forcing back tears, when the moon came down and drowned them both with its brightness.

Now the water's so high, the Consul has to swim. She's out of shape and out of practice. The heart in her hand makes it harder. Every time the monster howls, the water surges. The world will be submerged by morning. The Consul struggles to keep her chin above water. She reaches out to a tree top and hugs it. Spits out salt water and tries not to go under.

An idea starts to form. There's no time to weigh her options or pull out that chart with the acronyms from the Ministry. Her title and helmet hair can't help her. She has only herself to decide if it's a fair compromise. She'll have to trust her diplomatic instincts, for once be a Consul.

She closes her eyes, and lifts her hand above water. Holding the tree top with her elbow, she opens her other palm wide. The forest goes silent.

The next instant, the monster's bounding to her, each step sloshing the woods. The Consul loses hold of the tree top and goes under in a wave. She swallows salt water and only barely keeps hold of her heart. She's swept left, then right, and upside down. Her lungs burn, there's no air, she can't find the way up. Panic rises, then overwhelming sleepiness. She's about to give in when her head bursts through the surface. By some miracle, she hasn't lost her heart.

She coughs and sputters, starved for air. Her eyes clear, and she's only inches from the monster. It smells of wet dog. The water's barely to its waist. It extends its arms and its claws reflect moonlight. The Consul's too spent to recoil, and she doesn't have any fear left in her. The monster reaches into her palm and takes her heart with cupped claws. When she looks again, her heart is beating, slow and constant, behind its blood-dripping teeth. The water's already receding.

The monster blinks, and fire returns to its eyes. It tilts its head, its eyes a question. The Consul considers. Can she live with the beast? She brings her hand to her chest. She can't fathom returning to post with that silence. The beast licks its lips and lets out a soft whine. She takes a breath. She's a diplomat, and it is, after all, a compromise.

She nods to the monster, and its arms and its legs bend inward. There's a scraping and a softening of bone, a pop. The monster squeezes its femurs through the narrow space between her ribs, followed by its scapulas and incisors. Once inside the empty space of her chest, it steps in circles to make a bed. The monster curls into a ball, warm and dry, and promptly falls asleep.

Her clothes are dry when she reaches the cabin, though her boots are likely unsalvageable. Her husband's left dinner in the fridge. There's even dessert, a homemade brownie with its own paper plate. He's set a place at the table, with a note that says, "Enjoy." She's surprised at her appetite.

Even though it's past midnight, her husband trades his fuzzy socks for shoes and her son leaves his book in the bedroom. They sit around a campfire, roast marshmallows, and listen for loons in the dark. Her husband sings a camp song and she and her son roll their eyes. They could almost be a family. She goes to bed smelling of salt, smoke, and animal. The moon's full, but she doesn't cry.

The next full moon, the Consul's in her Official Residence office, toes deep in a rug, a pile of documents on her desk. Her cheeks are dry. She's almost through the backlog—she's been catching up in the evenings, after her receptions and dinners.

She signs her name on the paper and writes 'approved'. She sits back in her chair, and something stirs in her chest. She puts her hand to where she used to be hollow and feels the monster inside, breathing. For a moment, she thinks it will leap out of her and show the world those teeth. Instead it sighs, and rolls from its haunches to its side. It gets cramped in there. The monster smacks its lips, then it's back to dreaming forests.

She still doesn't understand how it fits in her. Sometimes she worries that its teeth will slip if she jumps or loses her balance. But she likes when it tells her secrets. Now, when she goes to her dinners, she doesn't care whether her table companions talk to her.

There are complications, but that's to be expected with any compromise. The monster gets stiff when she spends all day at a desk. The Consul's started taking walks at lunch, before her afternoon meetings, so it can stretch. The monster likes birds. So does the Consul. The monster's urges are stronger. She's started to close the blinds in her office to avoid tempting it. The monster has an appetite. She's starting to suspect what it eats. She tries not to think how that sustains her. She tells herself her son was bound to lose his heart anyway, all that time in books. As for her husband... at least now she can bake.

One year later, she's back at the podium, looking down at an audience, at her very own national day. She's in her best helmet, three layers of foundation, and a technicolor blue power suit. She can't remember the last time she wore heels.

There's a hush in the audience. She has the notes her staff prepared, but she's feeling confident, so she keeps them in her pocket and gives her speech off-script. The audience, including the host country Foreign Minister listen, rapt. When she sees a little girl in the audience, she improvises, telling the crowd one day, that little girl will be a Consul. The audience claps, and the little girl beams. A bird, indigo and orange, flies over the stage. The Consul pauses her speech to admire it. No one notices how tightly she grips the podium. The audience waits. She puts a hand to her chest, to quiet the monster, then unrushed, continues to speak.

After the speech, she escapes to the washroom. Stands at the mirror and admires her helmet. She likes the way her foundation's cracked. She parts her lined lips, and her reflection does the same.

Since there's no one else in the washroom, she opens her mouth wider. Looks past her two golden molars and her titanium crown. In the back of her throat, two fire eyes gleam. She tilts her head farther. In the mirror, there's a flash of long teeth, then the percussion of a hundred beating hearts.

The rhythm takes her back to the forest. She breathes in evergreens, and faint fungal rot. The porcelain sink reflects moonlight. Pine trees and saprophytes sprout up in the toilet stalls. Ghost pipe bursts through the sink. The forest thrums with life, electric. The Consul and her beast smile at their reflection. Then, unrushed, they start to recite the secret name of trees.

See E.C. Dorgan's story "The Beast-Consul" online at Metaphorosis.
If you liked it, leave a comment. Authors love that!
Remember to subscribe to our e-mail updates so you'll know when new stories are posted.

About the story

I was walking in the woods with my dogs when this story first came to me. I was struck by the image of this character, a woman who cries and cries every full moon without knowing why. My hands were full, and I didn't have a pen or any way to capture it. When I got home, I jotted down what I could remember. I was in the middle of writing another story, and I already had an idea for my next story after that. I thought I could just write a few notes and save this story fragment for another day. The story had other ideas.

The next day when I was out walking, the image came to me again, this time more vivid. Over the following days, I'd be out in the woods and pieces of the story would come to me. The story started to weave together during my walks. I didn't have a pen, but it demanded to be written.

I tried bringing a pen and paper with me a few times, but I was worried about walking into a moose or more likely, a pick-up truck. I gave up, and starting cutting my walks short— rushing home and trying to remember and write down everything. It was early summer, and there were birds and dragonflies everywhere. And the trees were, as always, breathtaking...

Once I got the story down, I was able to walk in the woods in peace again.

A question for the author

Q: What is your favorite word?

A: Lately I've been loving the word 'skyward'. Now when I'm writing, I have to go back through my stories and make sure I'm not over-using it. By some wonder, it's not in "The Beast-Consul."

About the author

E.C. Dorgan writes dreamy dark fantasy and monster stories in Alberta, Canada. She spends too much time wandering in forests and watching birds.

Copyright

Title information

Metaphorosis 2023

ISBN: 978-1-64076-275-6 (e-book)
ISBN: 978-1-64076-277-0 (paperback)
ISBN: 978-1-64076-276-3 (hardcover)

Works of fiction

This book contains works of fiction. Characters, dialogue, places, organizations, incidents, and events portrayed in the works are fictional and are products of the author's imagination or used fictitiously. Any resemblance to actual persons, places, organizations, or events is coincidental.

All rights reserved

Moral rights asserted

Publisher

Metaphorosis
a magazine of speculative fiction

Metaphorosis Magazine is an imprint of
Metaphorosis Publishing
Neskowin, OR, USA

www.metaphorosis.com

"Metaphorosis" is a registered trademark.

Discounts available

Substantial discounts are available for educational institutions, including writing workshops. Discounts are also available for quantity purchases. For details, contact Metaphorosis at metaphorosis.com/about

Metaphorosis Publishing

Metaphorosis offers beautifully written science fiction and fantasy. Our imprints include:

Metaphorosis Magazine

Plant Based Press

Verdage

Vestige

Joyful Heave

You can also find us:
@metaphorosis.bsky.social
writing.exchange/@metaphorosis
www.facebook.com/metaphorosis

Help keep Metaphorosis running at
Patreon.com/metaphorosis

See more about some of our books on the following pages.

Metaphorosis

a magazine of speculative fiction

Metaphorosis is an online speculative fiction magazine dedicated to quality writing. We publish an original story every week, along with author bios, interviews, and notes on story origins.

We also publish monthly print and e-book issues, as well as yearly Best of and Complete anthologies.

Come and see us online at magazine.Metaphorosis.com.

Plant Based Press

Vegan-friendly science fiction and fantasy, including anthologies of the year's best SFF stories, from 2016-2020.

Verdage

Science fiction and fantasy books for writers – full of great stories, often with an additional focus on the craft of speculative fiction writing.

Reading 5X5 x3

Changes

How do stories move from 'maybe' to published?

Here are 15 case studies of stories published in *Metaphorosis* magazine.

Reading 5X5 x2

Duets

How do authors' voices change when they collaborate?

A round-robin of five talented science fiction and fantasy authors collaborating with each other and writing solo.

Including stories by Evan Marcroft, David Gallay, J. Tynan Burke, L'Erin Ogle, and Douglas Anstruther.

Score

an SFF symphony

An anthology with an emotional score from the heights of joy to the depths of despair – but always with a little hope shining through.

Reading 5X5

Five stories, five times

See how different writers take on the same material.

Reading 5X5

Writers' Edition

Two extra stories, the story seed, and authors' notes on writing.

Vestige

Novelettes, novellas, and novels by Metaphorosis authors.

The Nocturnals
Mariah Montoya

Night is Dangerous. Day is deadly.
Where day and night last thirty years, humans move constantly stay ahead of the night and cruel Nocturnals that call it home. But a boy is lost out there.

Science fiction and fantasy anthologies with innovative and unusual themes.

Museum Piece
an unusual collection

A gallery of the strange and outrageous

Step right up and enter a world of wonder and oddities! These museums are not your typical tourist traps. From the Museum of Lost Dreams to the Suicide Museum, each exhibit will take you on a journey you won't soon forget.